Watters • Leyh • Pietsch • Sotuyo • Laiho

LUMBERJANES™
TO THE MAX EDITION
VOLUME FOUR

BOOM! BOX™

BOOM! BOX™

LUMBERJANES TO THE MAX EDITION Volume Four, June 2018. Published by BOOM! Box, a division of Boom Entertainment, Inc. Lumberjanes is ™ & © 2018 Shannon Watters, Grace Ellis, Noelle Stevenson & Brooklyn Allen. Originally published in single magazine form as LUMBERJANES No. 25-32. ™ & © 2016 Shannon Watters, Grace Ellis, Noelle Stevenson & Brooklyn Allen. All rights reserved. BOOM! Box™ and the BOOM! Box logo are trademarks of Boom Entertainment, Inc., registered in various countries and categories. All characters, events, and institutions depicted herein are fictional. Any similarity between any of the names, characters, persons, events, and/or institutions in this publication to actual names, characters, and persons, whether living or dead, events, and/or institutions is unintended and purely coincidental. BOOM! Box does not read or accept unsolicited submissions of ideas, stories, or artwork.

BOOM! Studios, 5670 Wilshire Boulevard, Suite 400, Los Angeles, CA 90036-5679. Printed in China. First Printing.

ISBN: 978-1-68415-183-7, eISBN: 978-1-61398-998-2

THIS LUMBERJANES FIELD MANUAL BELONGS TO:

NAME:_____

TROOP:_____

DATE INVESTED:_____

FIELD MANUAL TABLE OF CONTENTS

LUMBERJANES FIELD MANUAL

For the Advanced Program

Tenth Edition • August 1984

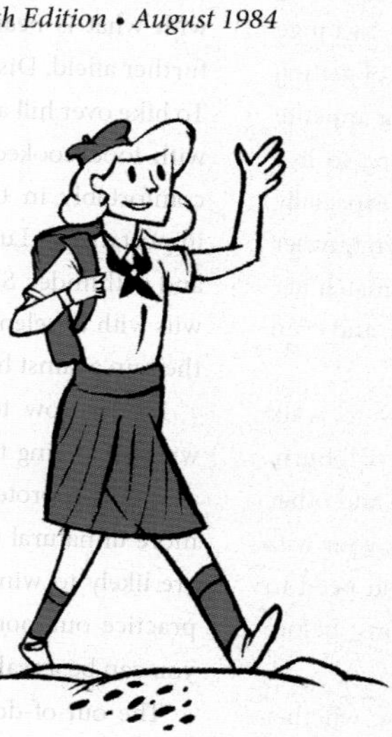

Prepared for the

Miss Qiunzella Thiskwin Penniquiqul Thistle Crumpet's

CAMP FOR [redacted] HARDCORE LADY-TYPES

"Friendship to the Max!"

WITHDRAWN

A MESSAGE FROM THE LUMBERJANES HIGH COUNCIL

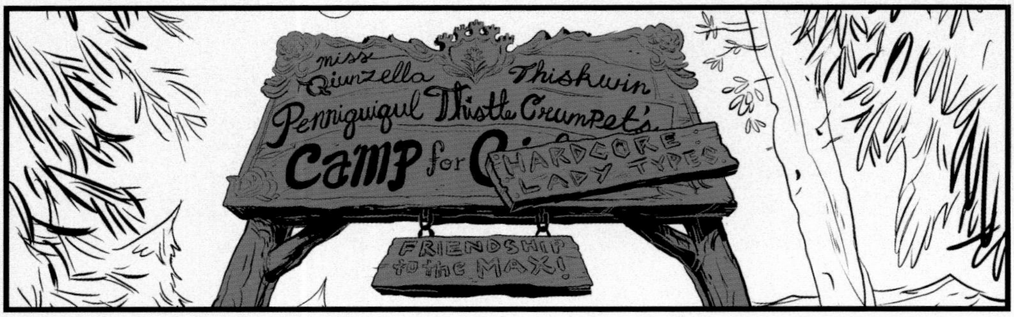
miss Quinzella Thiskwin
Penniquiqul Thistle Crumpet's
Camp for
HARDCORE LADY TYPES
FRIENDSHIP to the MAX!

When you look out at the horizon, what do you see? Is it a gleaming, glorious future laid out before you, or do you look out into the distance and see only the forests and enormous rock formations that stand between you and it, and think of traversing that long and difficult way, through briars and bogs, twisted ankles and uncertainty? In many cases, it is best to temper both our optimism and our pessimism with realism.

After all, things are not as bad as they might seem when a problem first presents itself, or as they feel when you're tired and discouraged. You may worry that a mistake will be unfixable, but this is not true! It may take time and distance, or a fresh pair of eyes and a mug of warm tea, but with the help of your friends and family repairs can be made, and in the cool light of day, all will be brighter and better! If you ever feel that everything is going wrong, it is good to remember the grand scheme of things. So many things over the course of your life have gone well, and more will follow, despite this hiccup. Perhaps even because of it. You will learn to better foresee the things that can cause problems, and deal with them as they come.

Equally, but oppositely, when you first begin a project you might feel a burst of enthusiasm and excitement for the work you're about to depart on. Maybe you're starting work toward earning your next Lumberjanes Badge, or you're going to help your family paint several rooms in their house, or you'd like to start a small business! Boundless enthusiasm and inspiration are so wonderful when they come to us. However, just like it is often wise to remember the bigger picture when you are inclined to think the worst of a situation, when you are inclined toward optimism, it is a good idea to consider the small details that may go wrong. That way, you are prepared for all eventualities, just in case and if anything does trip you up, you will be ready to pick yourself up, brush yourself off and continue flying toward your goal.

THE LUMBERJANES PLEDGE

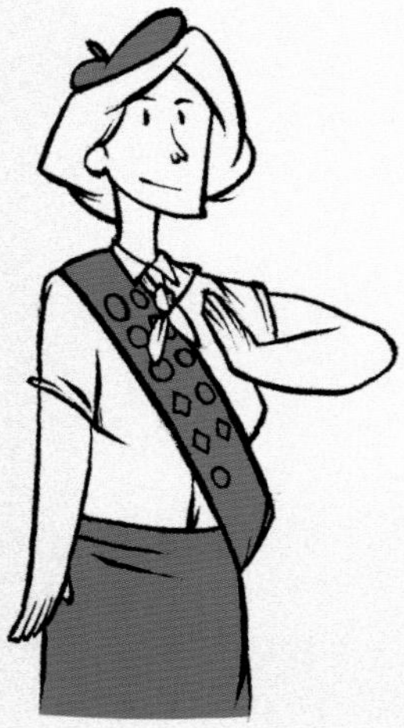

I solemnly swear to do my best
Every day, and in all that I do,
To be brave and strong,
To be truthful and compassionate,
To be interesting and interested,
To pay attention and question
The world around me,
To think of others first,
To always help and protect my friends,
[redacted]
And to make the world a better place
For Lumberjane scouts
And for everyone else.

THEN THERE'S A LINE ABOUT GOD, OR WHATEVER

LUMBERJANES™
TO THE MAX EDITION

Created by **Shannon Watters, Grace Ellis, Noelle Stevenson & Brooklyn Allen**

Written by
Shannon Watters & Kat Leyh

Illustrated by
Carey Pietsch
(Chapters Twenty-Five, Twenty-Nine through Thirty-Two)
Ayme Sotuyo
(Chapters Twenty-Six through Twenty-Eight)

Colors by
Maarta Laiho

Letters by
Aubrey Aiese

"And Your Bird Can Sing"

Written by
Chynna Clugston Flores

Illustrated by
Laura Lewis & Mad Rupert

Colors by
Maarta Laiho

Letters by
Warren Montgomery

Designer
Kara Leopard

Badge Designs by
Kelsey Dieterich

Assistant Editor
Sophie Philips-Roberts

Editor
Dafna Pleban

Special thanks to **Kelsey Pate** *for giving the Lumberjanes their name.*

LUMBERJANES FIELD MANUAL

CHAPTER TWENTY-FIVE

Lumberjanes "Heart to Heart" Program Field

SPARROW A MOMENT BADGE

"Don't miss out on life's mysteries"

At camp, as in life, there is always much to do: games to be played, crafts to be crafted, badges to be earned. Barreling through your days at breakneck speed can be great fun, but it is important to take time and care, too. When a friend is struggling, you can make a world of difference just by taking the time to be by their side, or by offering a helping hand.

It can be difficult to put yourself in someone else's shoes, or to ever fully understand what the difficulties of someone else's life might be. Sometimes, all you can offer is a listening ear. But other times there maybe more that you can do, whether it's writing a kind letter, or helping to carry heavy boxes. Little things can add up to a lot!

The Sparrow a Moment badge is a badge that focuses on helping others, and taking the time out of your day to improve someone else's. Being considerate of others is a skill that we are all constantly learning, from the age that we first realize that playing with blocks or dolls

becomes more fun when we can share with our friends.

When you were very small, something as simple as sharing a snack or a toy may have seemed impossible (And if you don't remember, perhaps you've noticed this stubborn trait in your own younger siblings or cousins!). But now that you're older, you understand that making someone else happy will actually mean more fun for both of you, even if it means giving up something you care about for a brief time. As you get older, your ability to empathize broadens and deepens. Now that you're older, you can understand so many different ways to brighten someone's day and to offer help and love where it is needed, and to those who need it.

Try looking around your camp or cabin, and see if you can spy anyone who might benefit from a small surprise, or an offer of help. Listen when they tell you what will help them, since it will be different for every person, and try to focus on offering what they might need. Some might want a shoulder to cry on

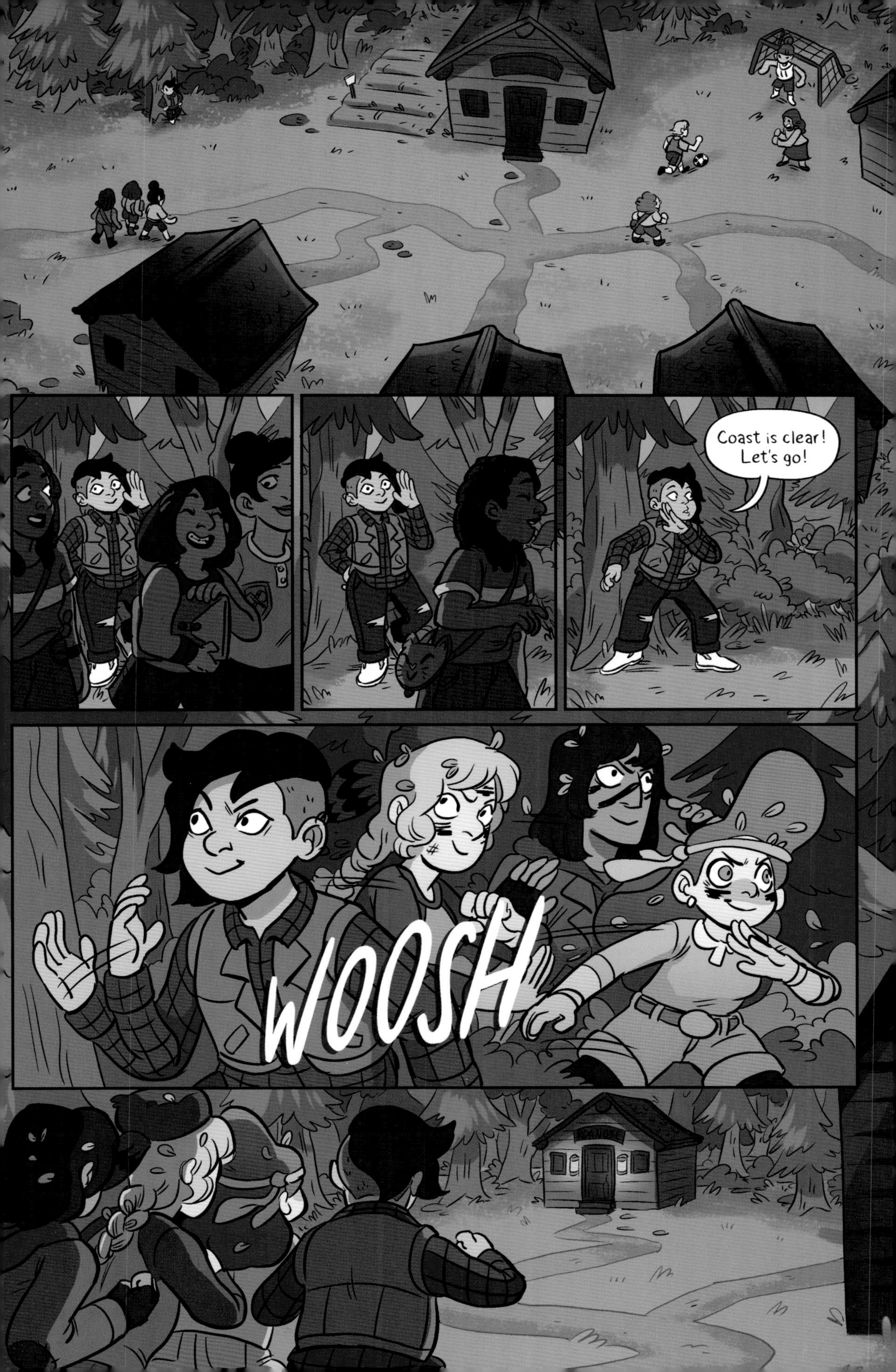
Coast is clear! Let's go!
WOOSH

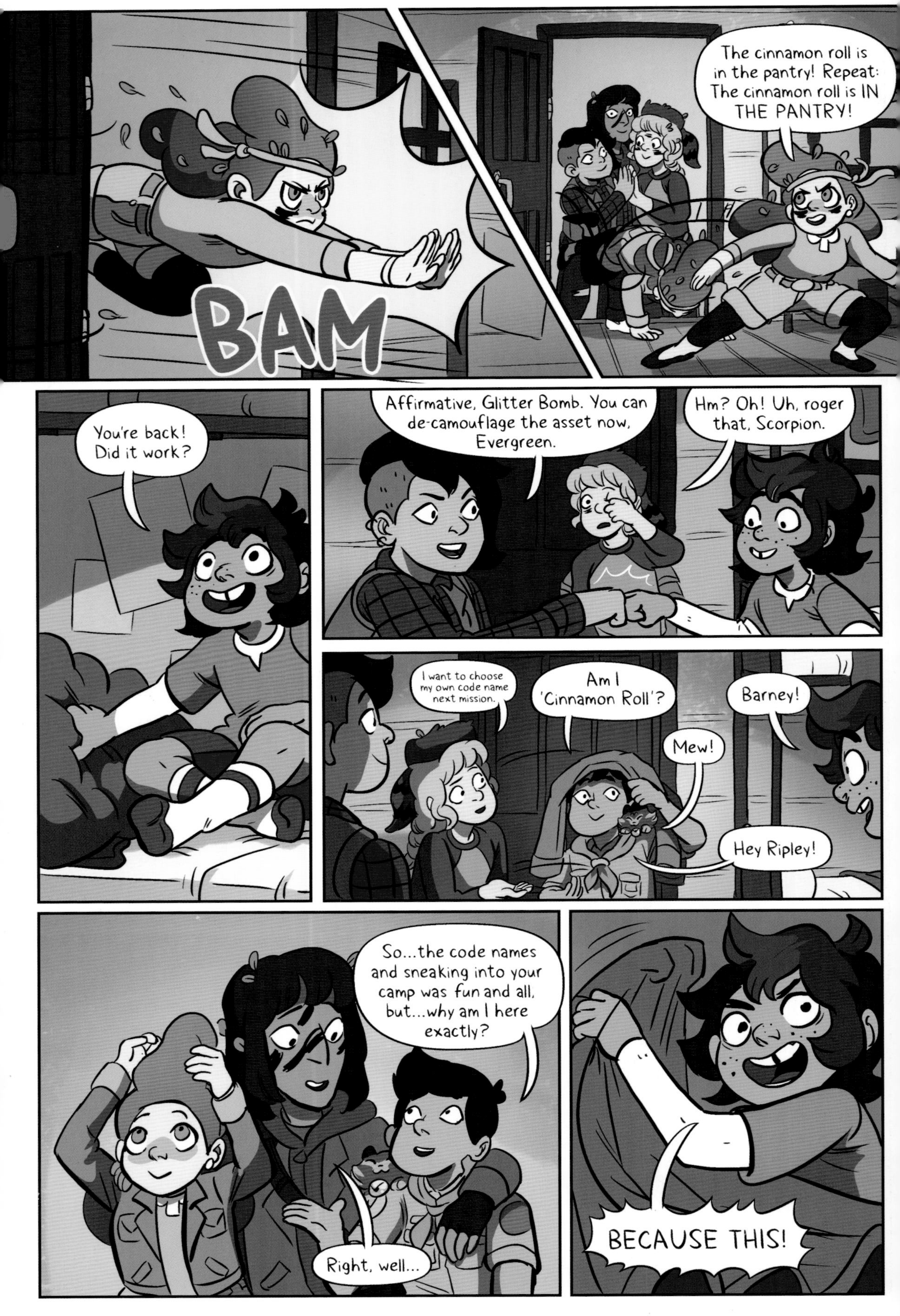
BAM
The cinnamon roll is in the pantry! Repeat: The cinnamon roll is IN THE PANTRY!
You're back! Did it work?
Affirmative, Glitter Bomb. You can de-camouflage the asset now, Evergreen.
Hm? Oh! Uh, roger that, Scorpion.
I want to choose my own code name next mission.
Am I 'Cinnamon Roll'?
Barney!
Mew!
Hey Ripley!
So...the code names and sneaking into your camp was fun and all, but...why am I here exactly?
Right, well...
BECAUSE THIS!

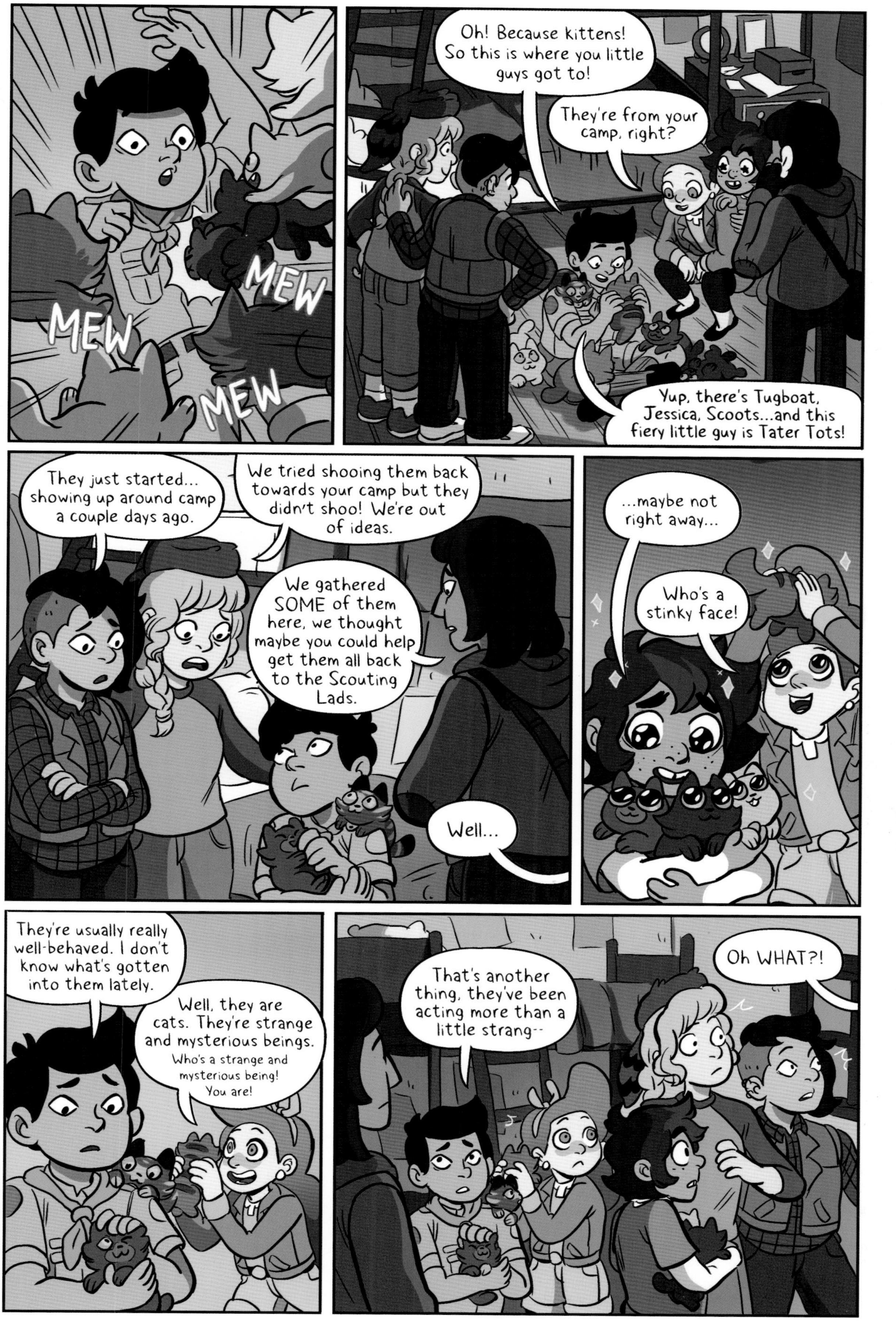
MEW
MEW
MEW
Oh! Because kittens! So this is where you little guys got to!
They're from your camp, right?
Yup, there's Tugboat, Jessica, Scoots...and this fiery little guy is Tater Tots!
They just started... showing up around camp a couple days ago.
We tried shooing them back towards your camp but they didn't shoo! We're out of ideas.
We gathered SOME of them here, we thought maybe you could help get them all back to the Scouting Lads.
Well...
...maybe not right away...
Who's a stinky face!
They're usually really well-behaved. I don't know what's gotten into them lately.
Well, they are cats. They're strange and mysterious beings.
Who's a strange and mysterious being! You are!
That's another thing, they've been acting more than a little strang--
Oh WHAT?!

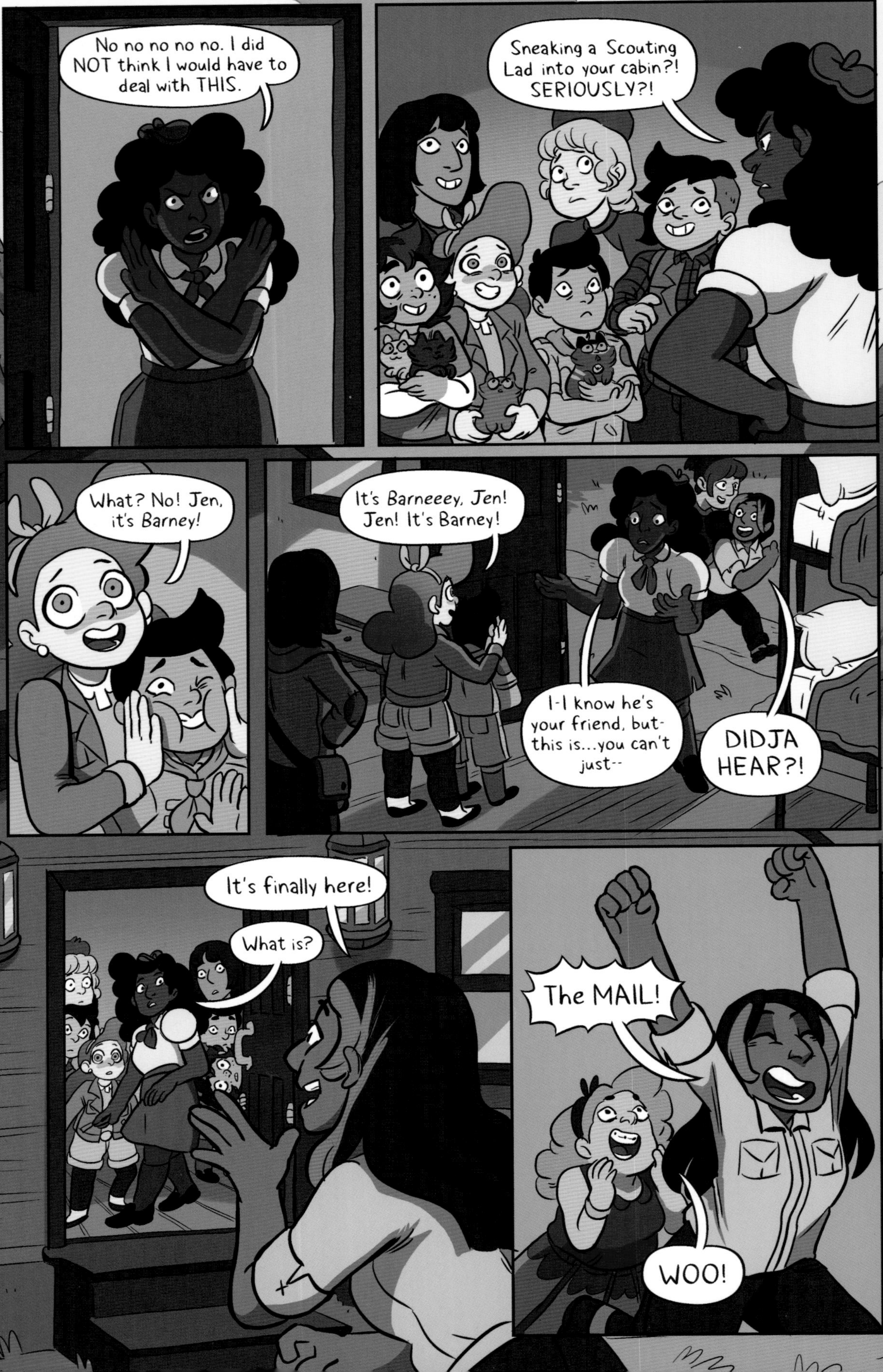

No no no no no. I did NOT think I would have to deal with THIS.
Sneaking a Scouting Lad into your cabin?! SERIOUSLY?!
What? No! Jen, it's Barney!
It's *Barneeey*, Jen! Jen! It's Barney!
I-I know he's your friend, but- this is...you can't just--
DIDJA HEAR?!
It's finally here!
What is?
The MAIL!
WOO!

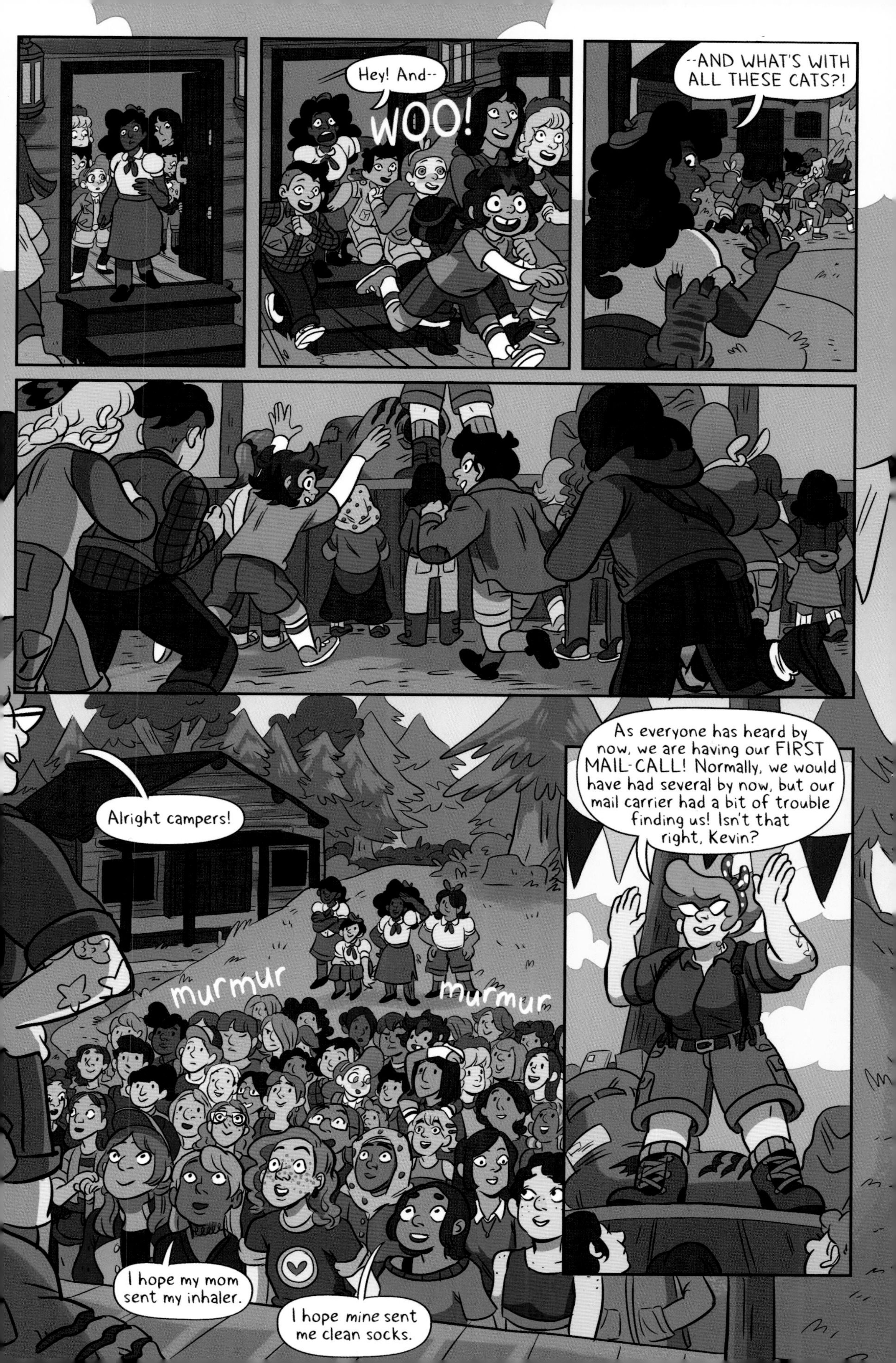
Hey! And--
WOO!
--AND WHAT'S WITH ALL THESE CATS?!
Alright campers!
murmur
murmur
As everyone has heard by now, we are having our FIRST MAIL-CALL! Normally, we would have had several by now, but our mail carrier had a bit of trouble finding us! Isn't that right, Kevin?
I hope my mom sent my inhaler.
I hope mine sent me clean socks.

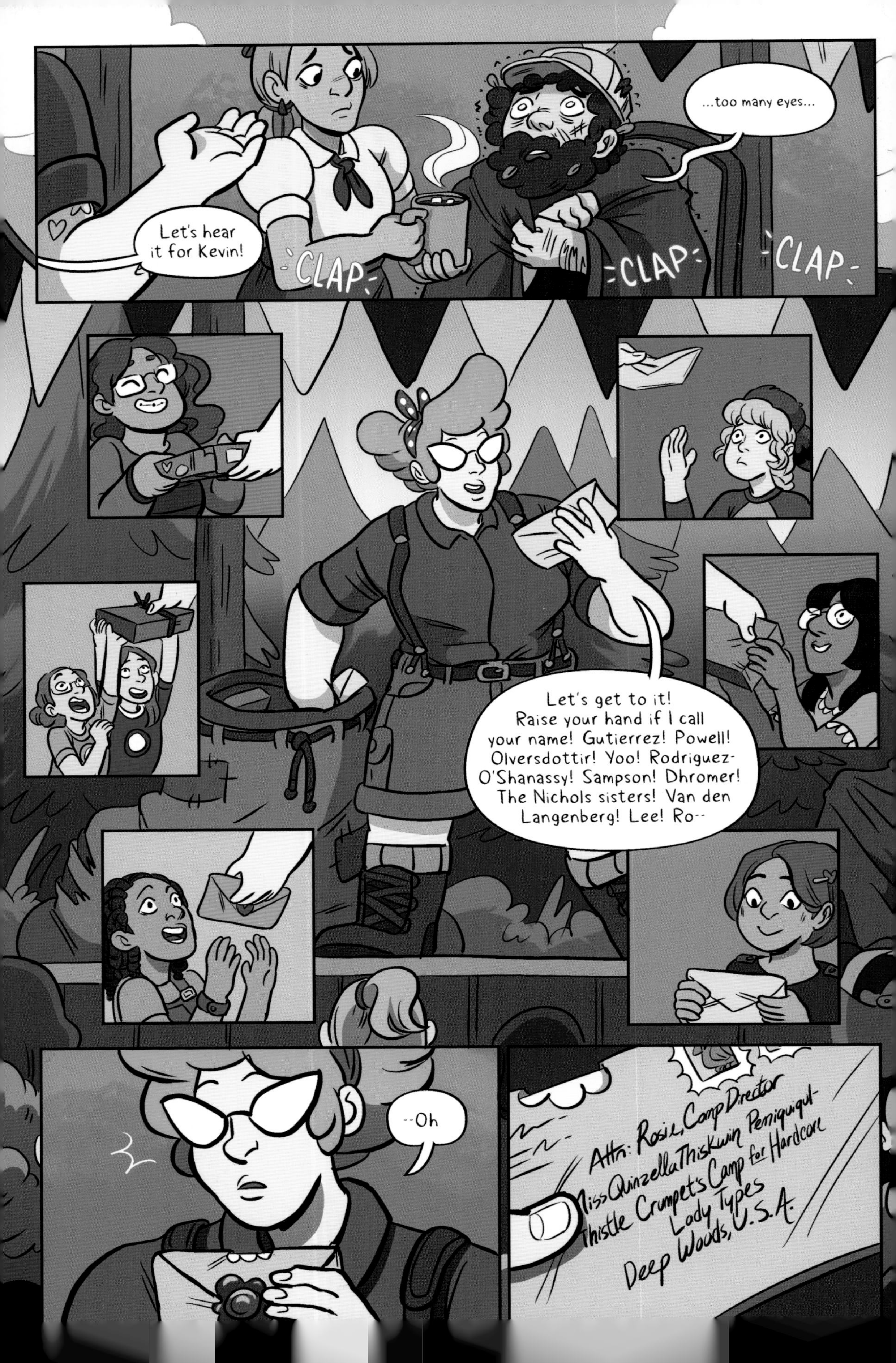

...too many eyes...
Let's hear it for Kevin!
CLAP
CLAP
CLAP
Let's get to it! Raise your hand if I call your name! Gutierrez! Powell! Olversdottir! Yoo! Rodriguez-O'Shanassy! Sampson! Dhromer! The Nichols sisters! Van den Langenberg! Lee! Ro--
--Oh
Attn: Rosie, Camp Director
Miss Quinzella Thiskwin Penniquiqul-Thistle Crumpet's Camp for Hardcore Lady Types
Deep Woods, U.S.A.

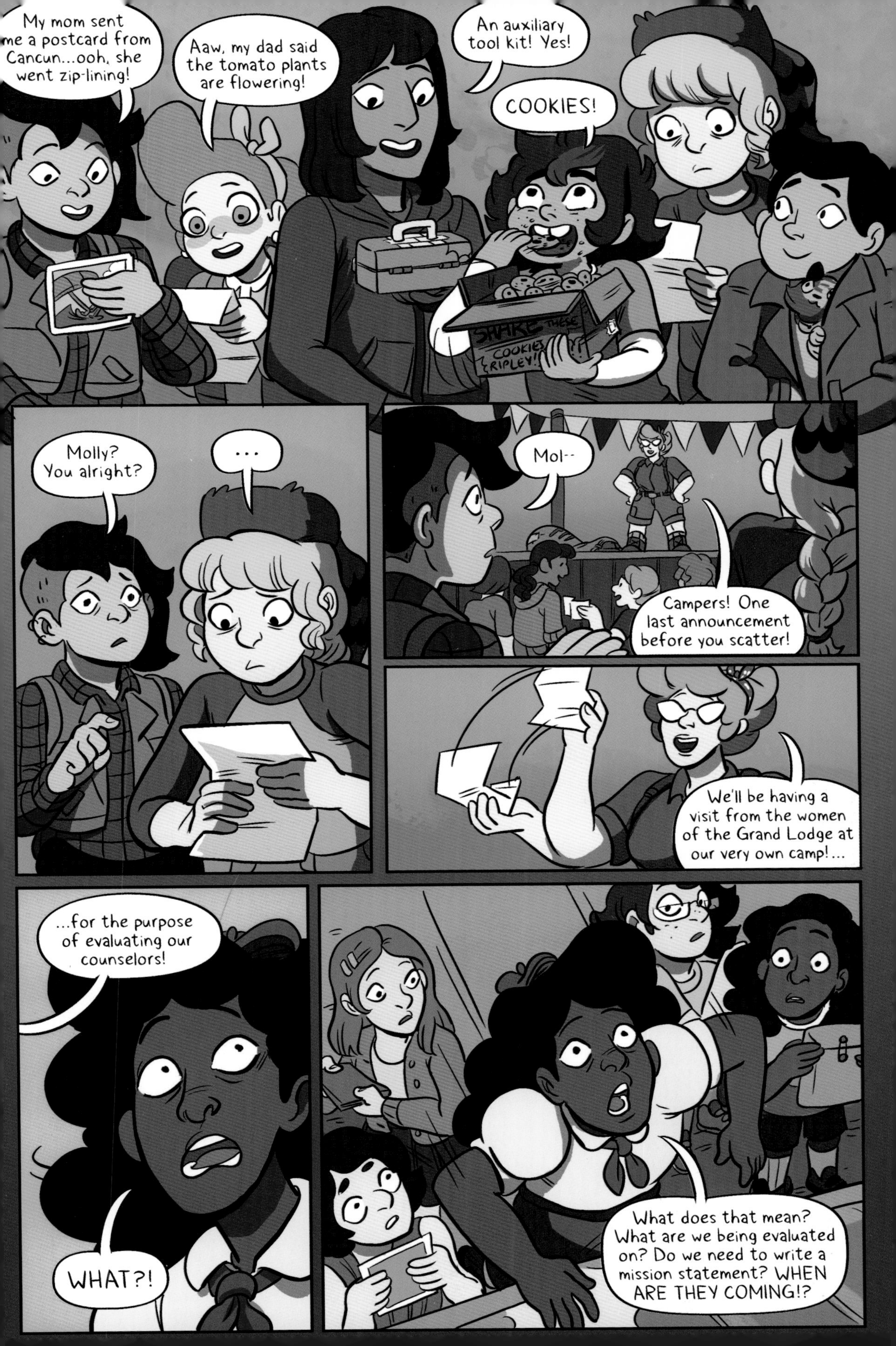
My mom sent me a postcard from Cancun...ooh, she went zip-lining!
Aaw, my dad said the tomato plants are flowering!
An auxiliary tool kit! Yes!
COOKIES!
SHARE THESE COOKIES RIPLEY!
Molly? You alright?
...
Mol--
Campers! One last announcement before you scatter!
We'll be having a visit from the women of the Grand Lodge at our very own camp!...
...for the purpose of evaluating our counselors!
WHAT?!
What does that mean? What are we being evaluated on? Do we need to write a mission statement? WHEN ARE THEY COMING!?

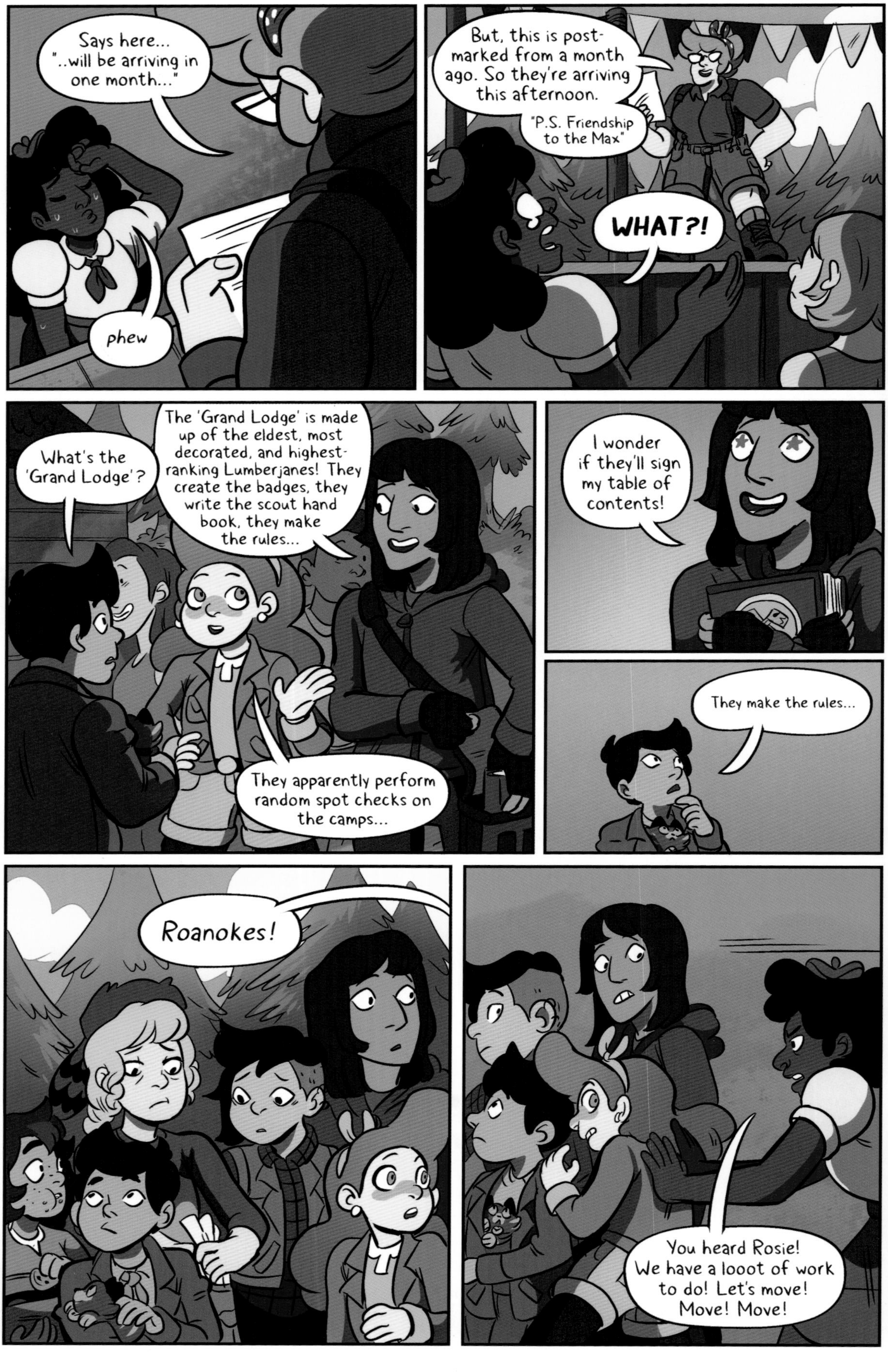
Says here... "..will be arriving in one month..."
phew
But, this is post-marked from a month ago. So they're arriving this afternoon.
"P.S. Friendship to the Max"
WHAT?!
What's the 'Grand Lodge'?
The 'Grand Lodge' is made up of the eldest, most decorated, and highest-ranking Lumberjanes! They create the badges, they write the scout hand book, they make the rules...
They apparently perform random spot checks on the camps...
I wonder if they'll sign my table of contents!
They make the rules...
Roanokes!
You heard Rosie! We have a looot of work to do! Let's move! Move! Move!

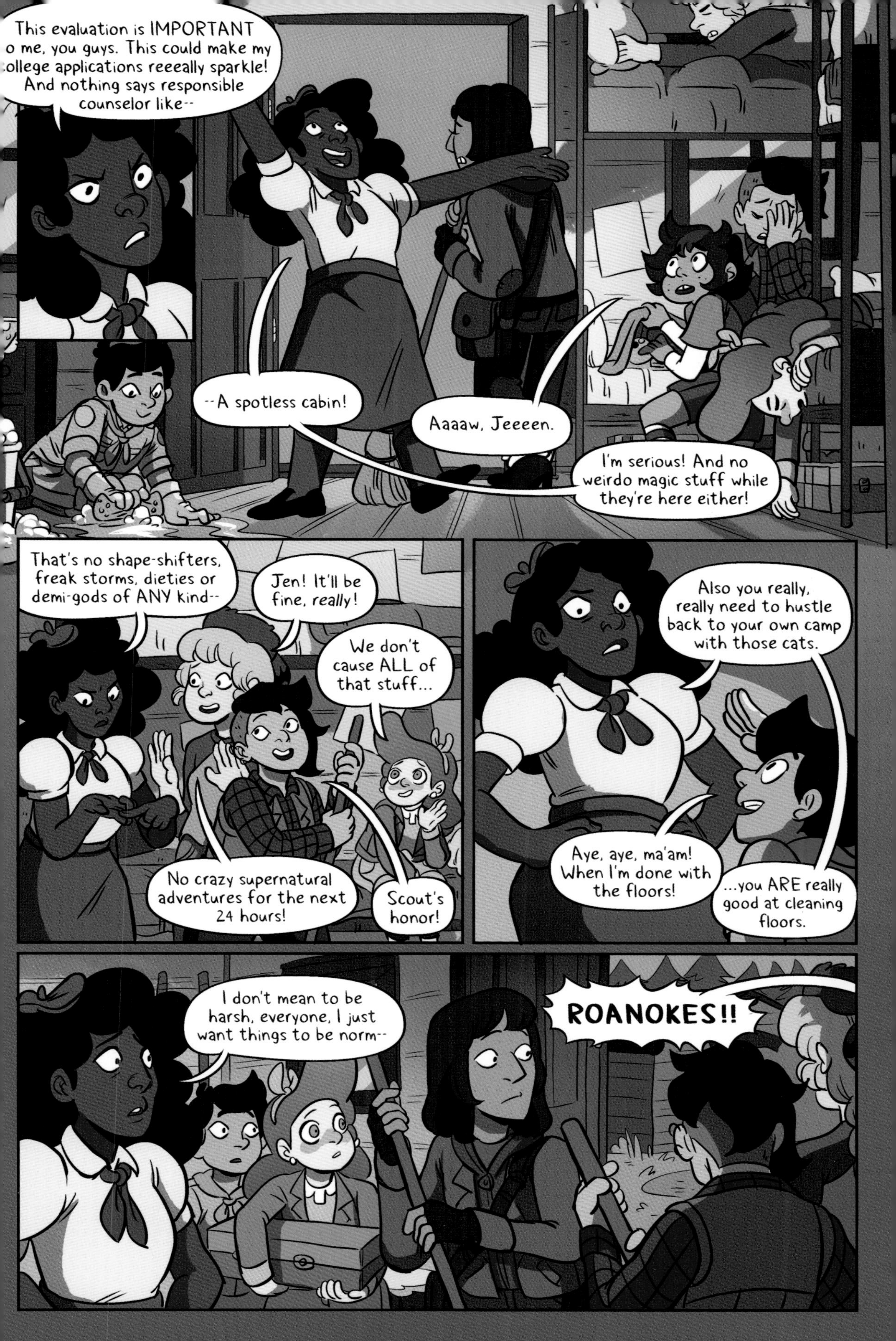
This evaluation is IMPORTANT to me, you guys. This could make my college applications reeeally sparkle! And nothing says responsible counselor like--
--A spotless cabin!
Aaaaw, Jeeeen.
I'm serious! And no weirdo magic stuff while they're here either!
That's no shape-shifters, freak storms, dieties or demi-gods of ANY kind--
Jen! It'll be fine, really!
We don't cause ALL of that stuff...
No crazy supernatural adventures for the next 24 hours!
Scout's honor!
Also you really, really need to hustle back to your own camp with those cats.
Aye, aye, ma'am! When I'm done with the floors!
...you ARE really good at cleaning floors.
I don't mean to be harsh, everyone, I just want things to be norm--
ROANOKES!!

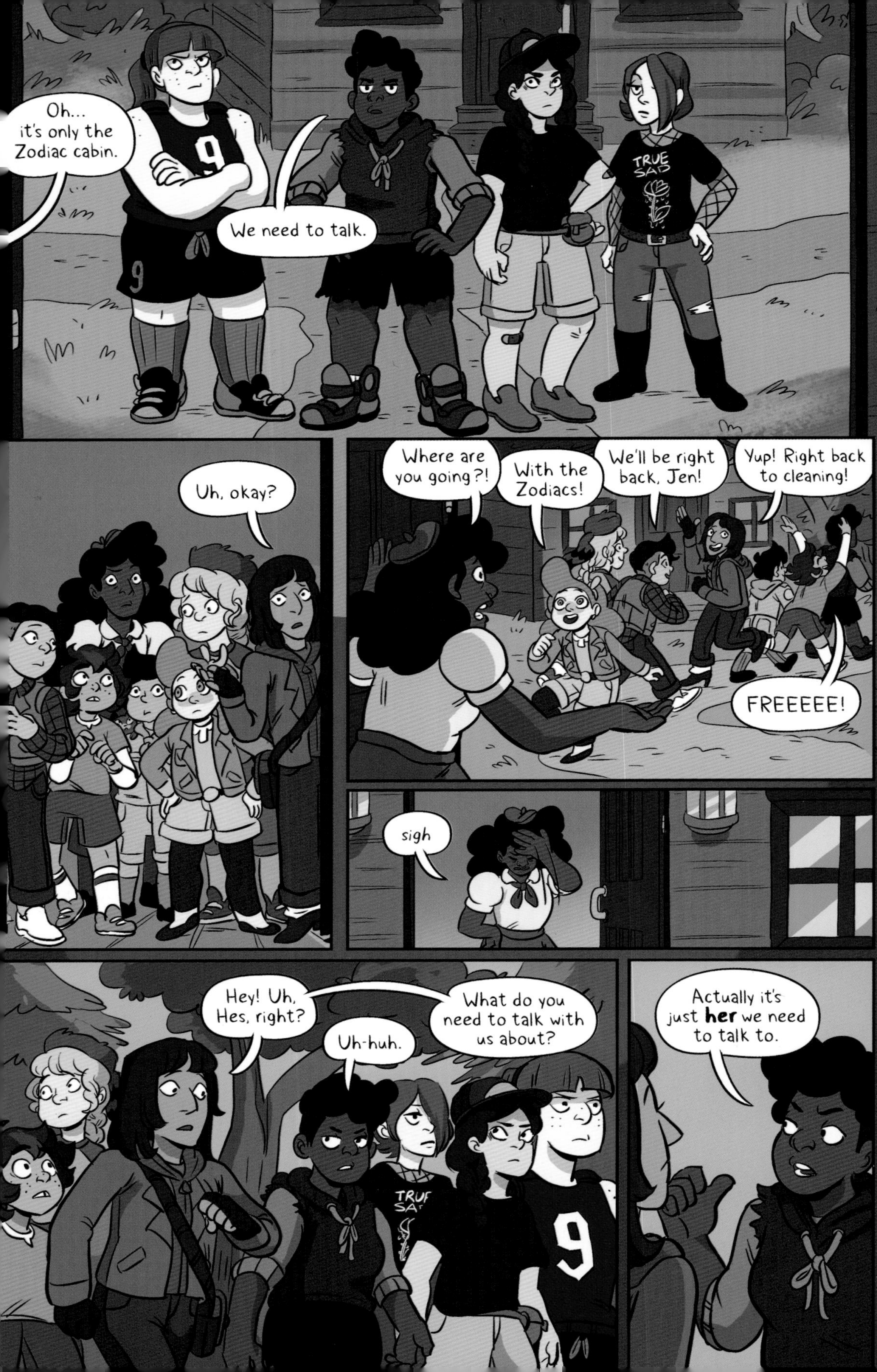
Oh... it's only the Zodiac cabin.
We need to talk.
Uh, okay?
Where are you going?!
With the Zodiacs!
We'll be right back, Jen!
Yup! Right back to cleaning!
FREEEEE!
sigh
Hey! Uh, Hes, right?
Uh-huh.
What do you need to talk with us about?
Actually it's just her we need to talk to.

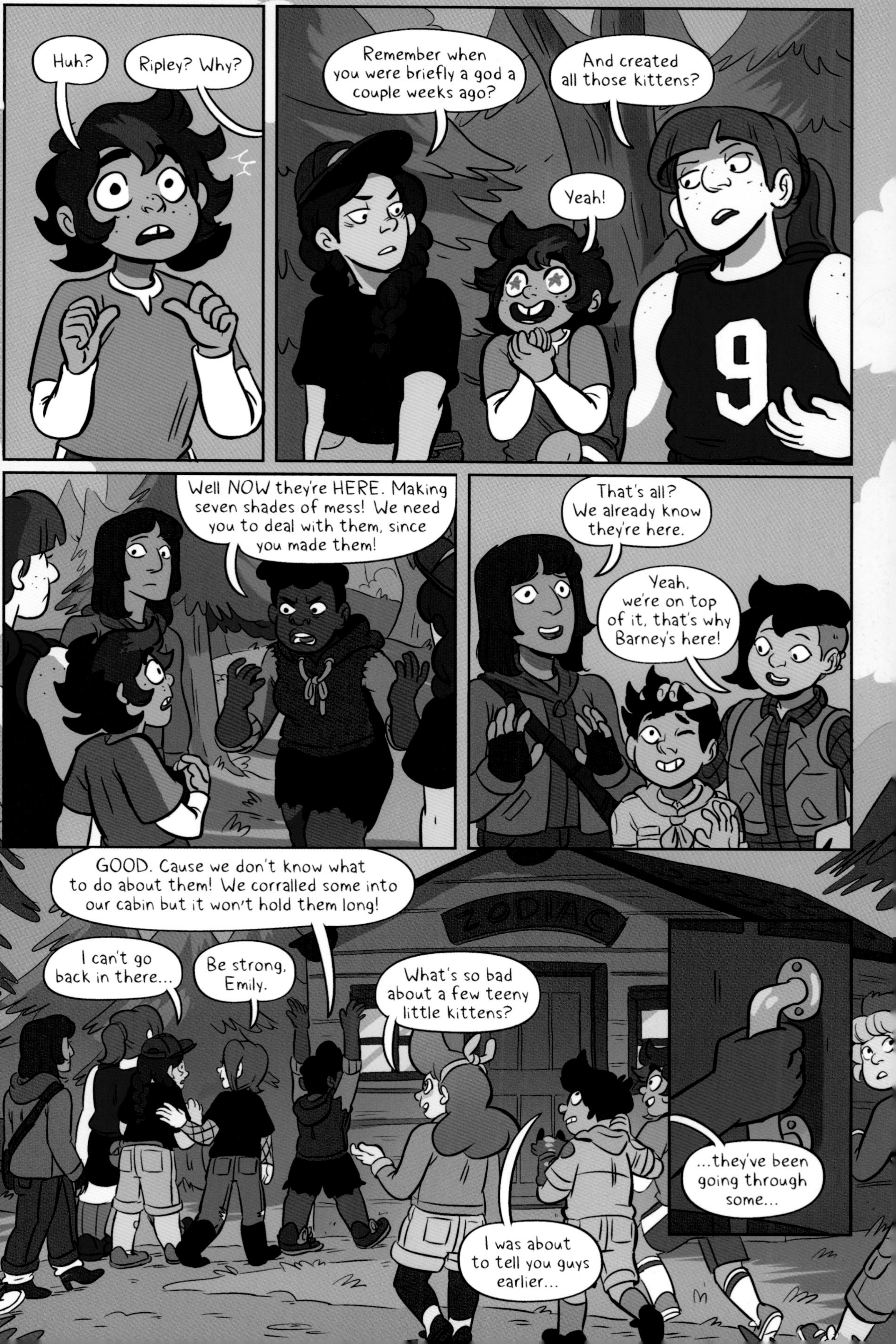
Huh?
Ripley? Why?
Remember when you were briefly a god a couple weeks ago?
And created all those kittens?
Yeah!
Well NOW they're HERE. Making seven shades of mess! We need you to deal with them, since you made them!
That's all? We already know they're here.
Yeah, we're on top of it, that's why Barney's here!
GOOD. Cause we don't know what to do about them! We corralled some into our cabin but it won't hold them long!
ZODIAC
I can't go back in there...
Be strong, Emily.
What's so bad about a few teeny little kittens?
I was about to tell you guys earlier...
...they've been going through some...

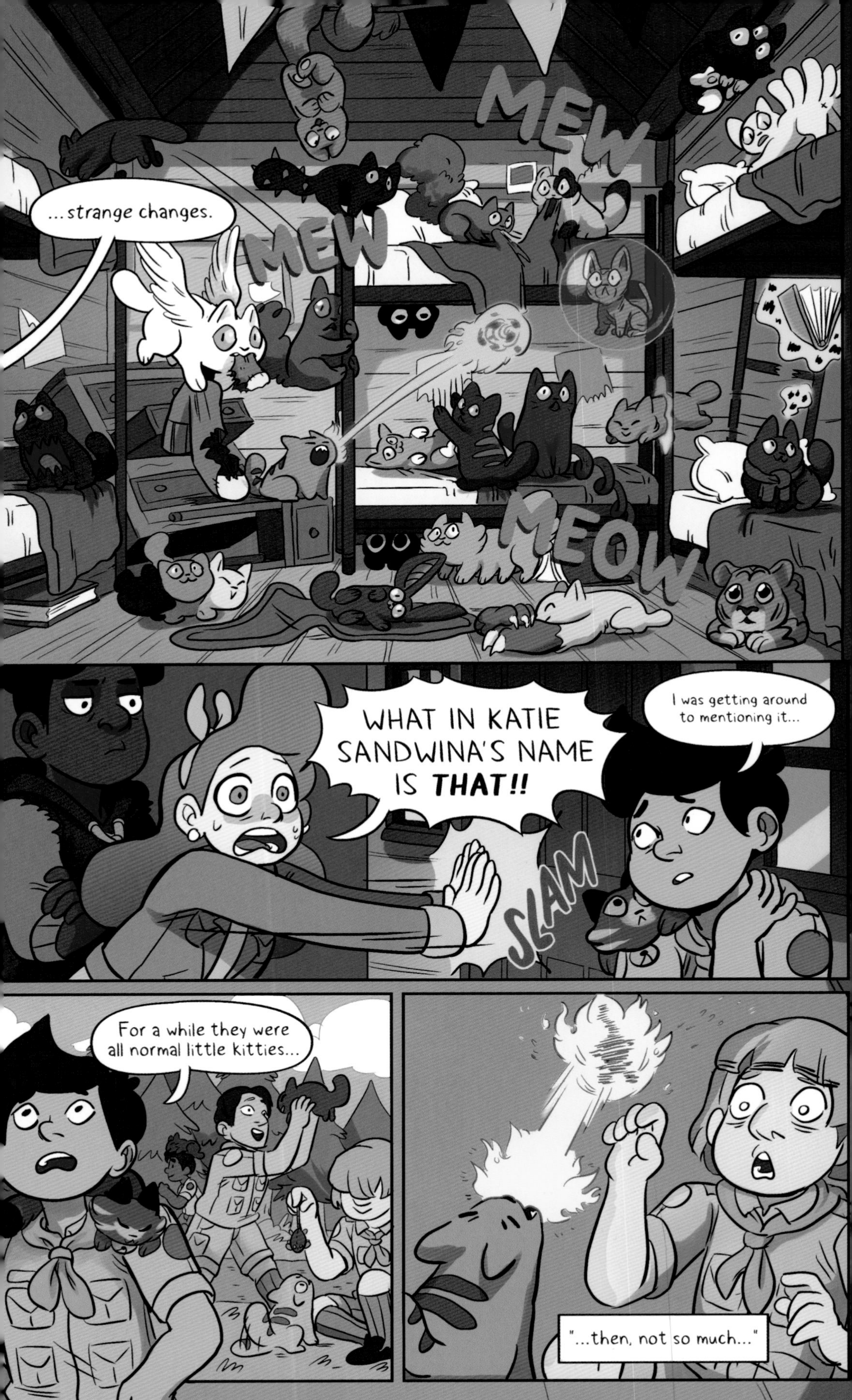
MEW
...strange changes.
MEW
MEOW
WHAT IN KATIE SANDWINA'S NAME IS **THAT!!**
I was getting around to mentioning it...
SLAM
For a while they were all normal little kitties...
"...then, not so much..."

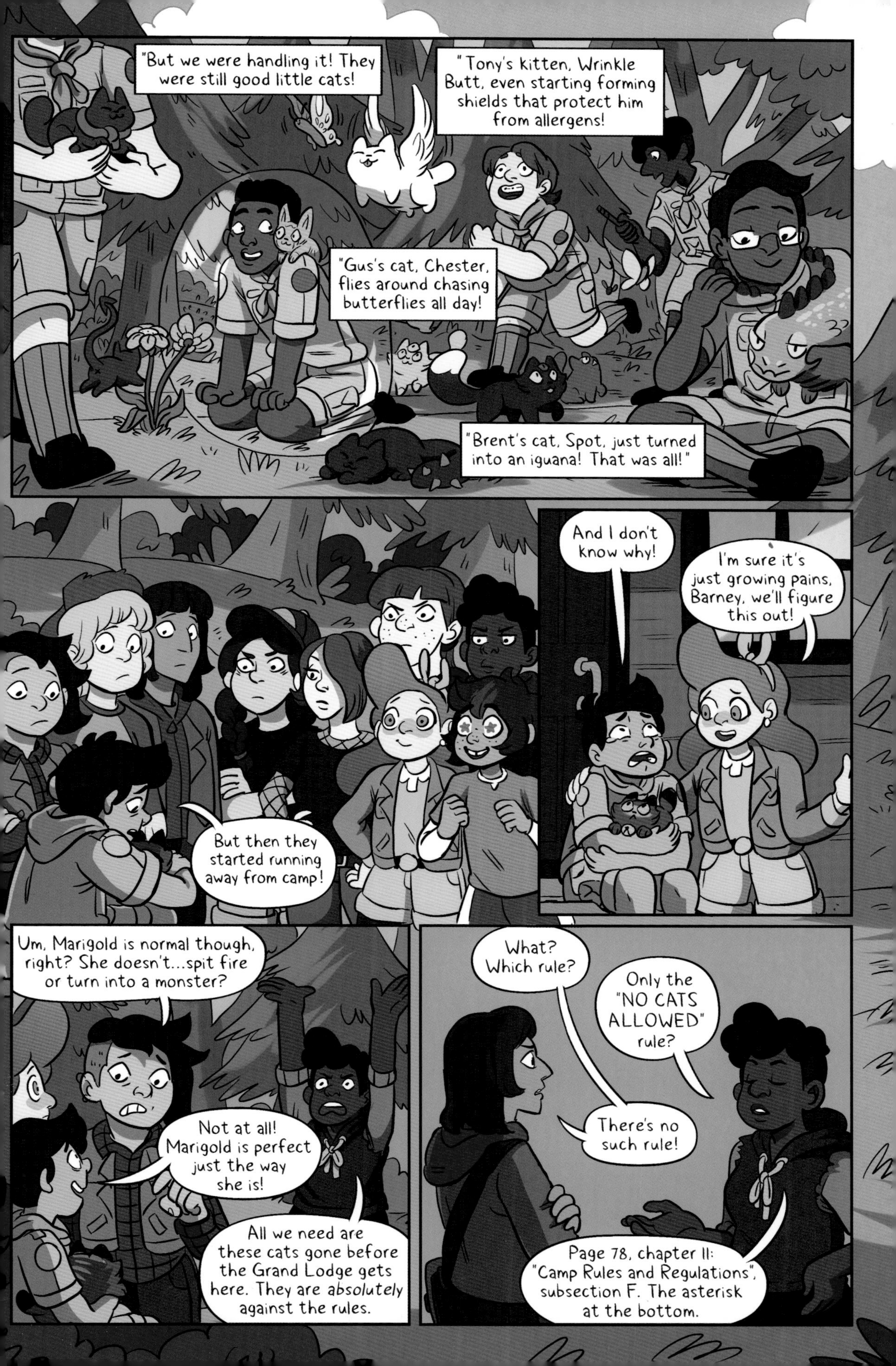
"But we were handling it! They were still good little cats!
"Tony's kitten, Wrinkle Butt, even starting forming shields that protect him from allergens!
"Gus's cat, Chester, flies around chasing butterflies all day!
"Brent's cat, Spot, just turned into an iguana! That was all!"
But then they started running away from camp!
And I don't know why!
I'm sure it's just growing pains, Barney, we'll figure this out!
Um, Marigold is normal though, right? She doesn't...spit fire or turn into a monster?
Not at all! Marigold is perfect just the way she is!
All we need are these cats gone before the Grand Lodge gets here. They are *absolutely* against the rules.
What? Which rule?
Only the "NO CATS ALLOWED" rule?
There's no such rule!
Page 78, chapter 11: "Camp Rules and Regulations", subsection F. The asterisk at the bottom.

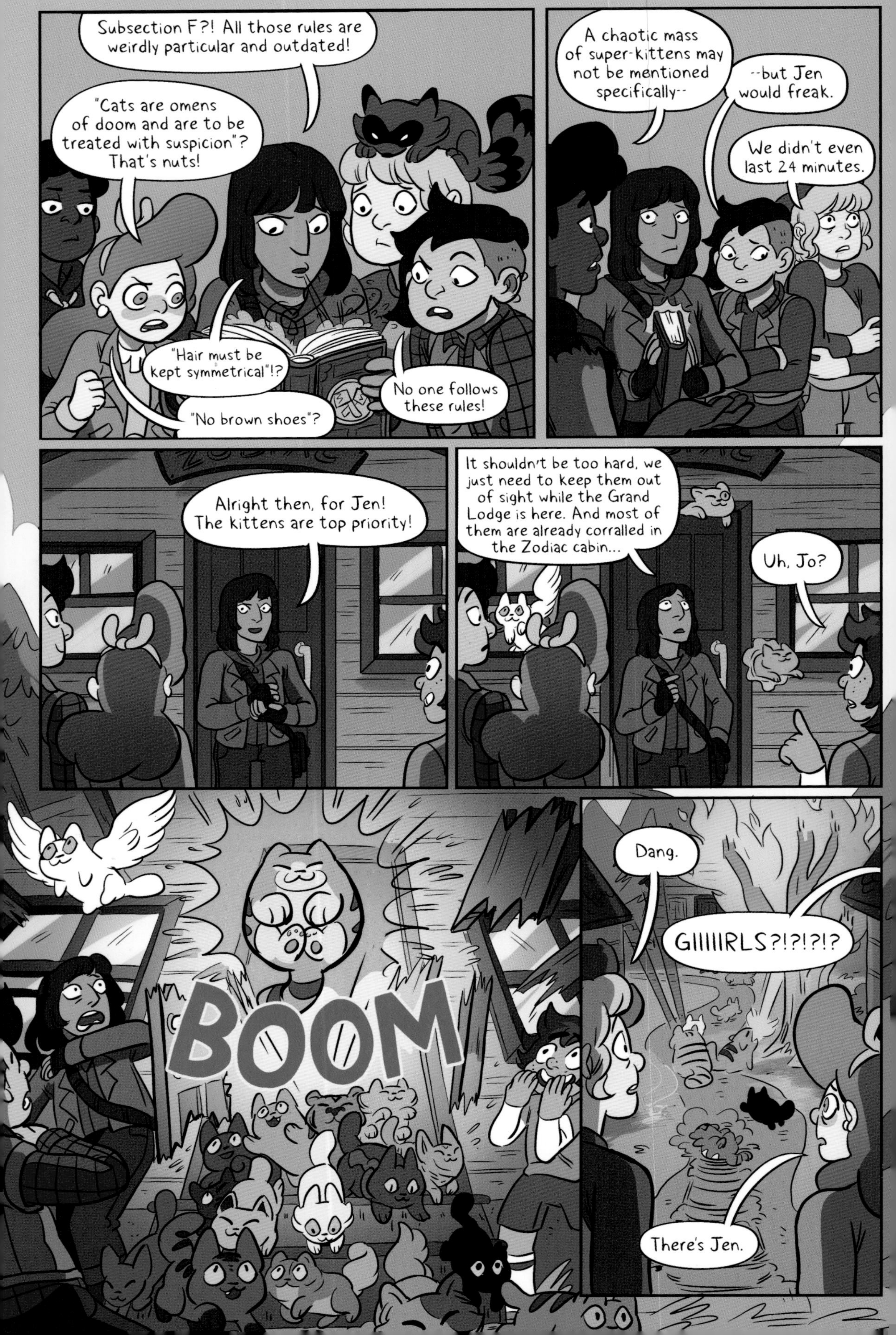
Subsection F?! All those rules are weirdly particular and outdated!
"Cats are omens of doom and are to be treated with suspicion"? That's nuts!
"Hair must be kept symmetrical"!?
"No brown shoes"?
No one follows these rules!
A chaotic mass of super-kittens may not be mentioned specifically--
--but Jen would freak.
We didn't even last 24 minutes.
Alright then, for Jen! The kittens are top priority!
It shouldn't be too hard, we just need to keep them out of sight while the Grand Lodge is here. And most of them are already corralled in the Zodiac cabin...
Uh, Jo?
BOOM
Dang.
GIIIIIRLS?!?!?!?
There's Jen.

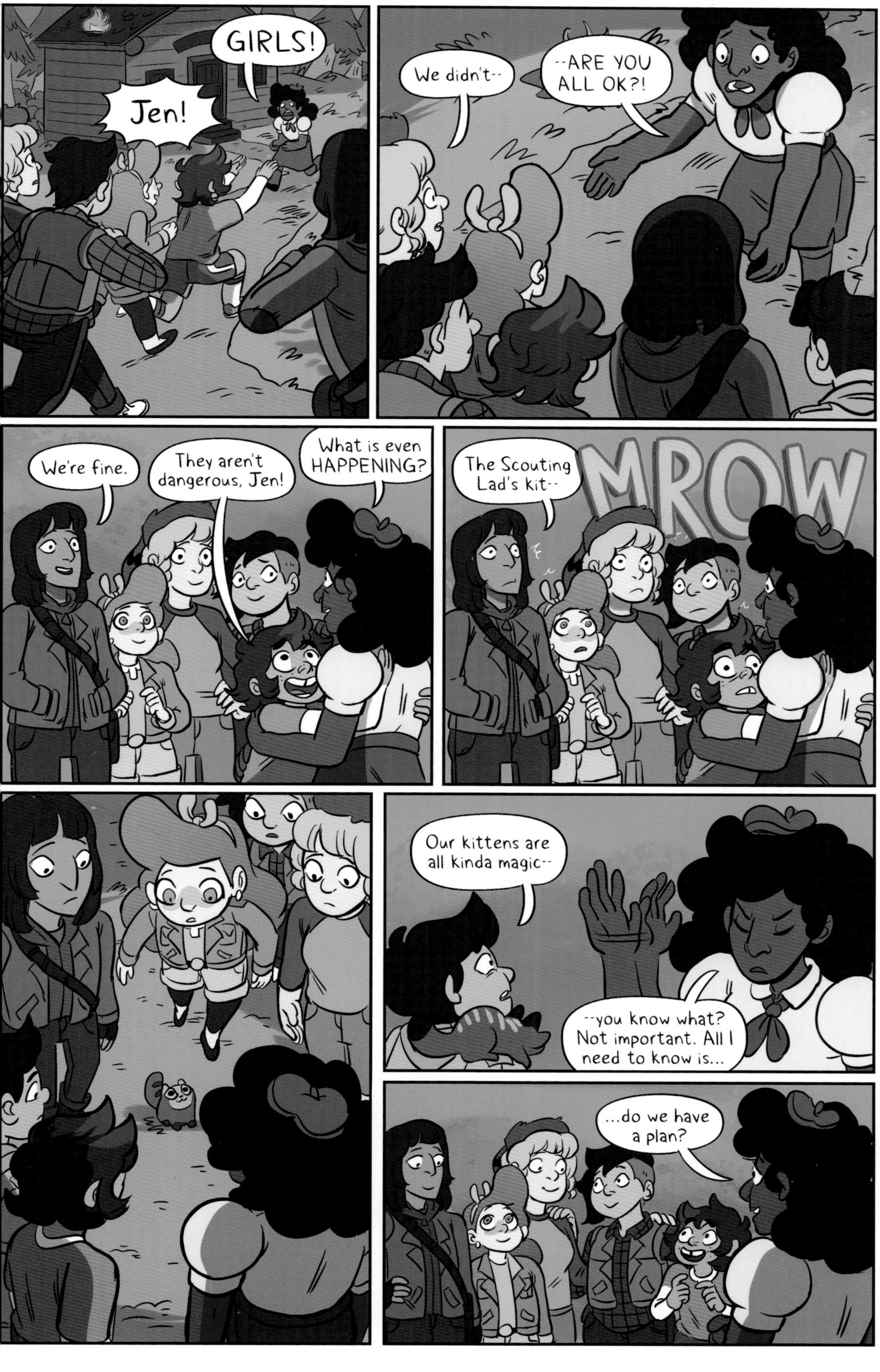
GIRLS!
Jen!
We didn't--
--ARE YOU ALL OK?!
We're fine.
They aren't dangerous, Jen!
What is even HAPPENING?
The Scouting Lad's kit--
MROW
Our kittens are all kinda magic--
--you know what? Not important. All I need to know is...
...do we have a plan?

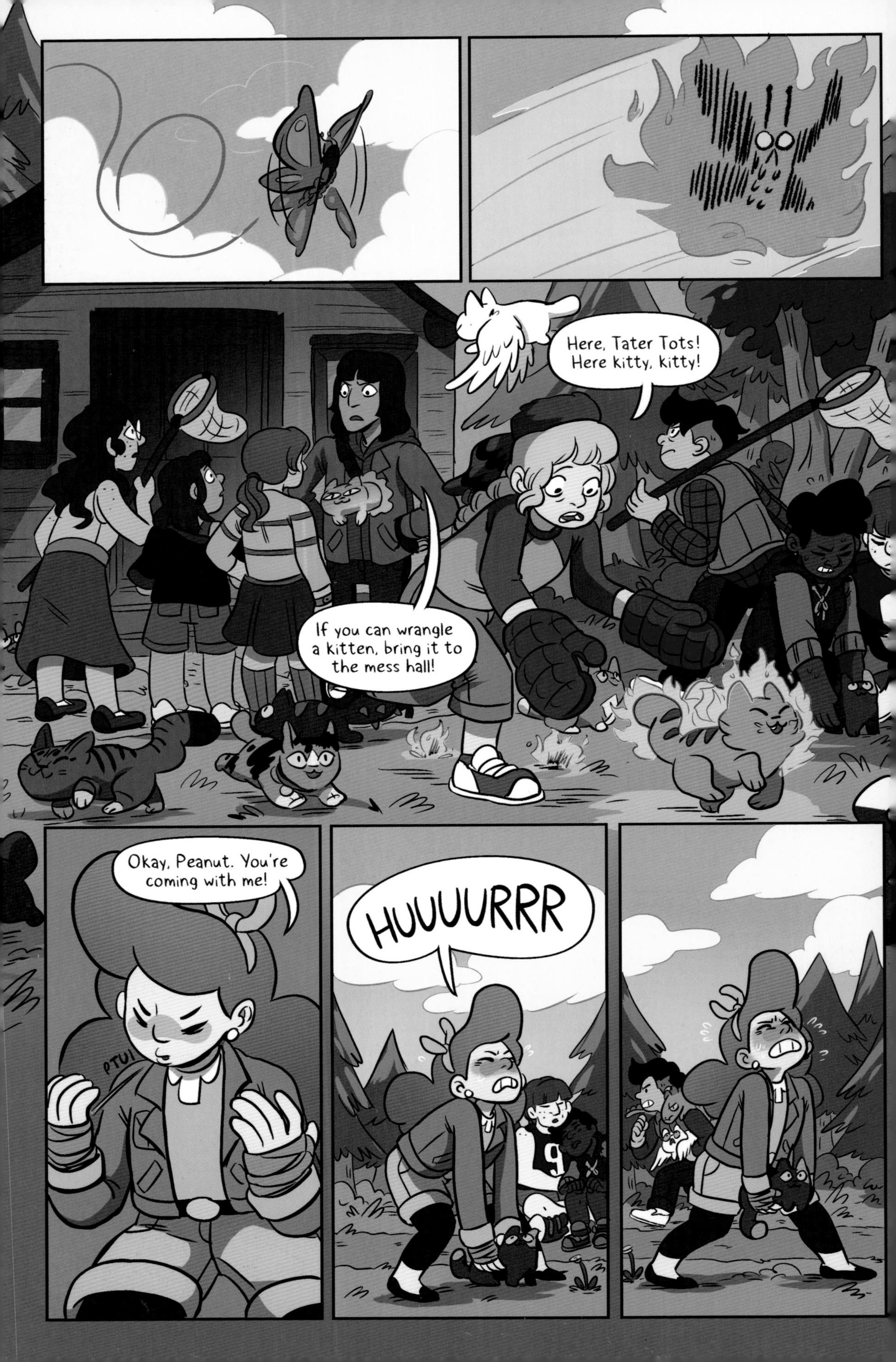
Here, Tater Tots!
Here kitty, kitty!
If you can wrangle a kitten, bring it to the mess hall!
Okay, Peanut. You're coming with me!
PTU!
HUUUURRR

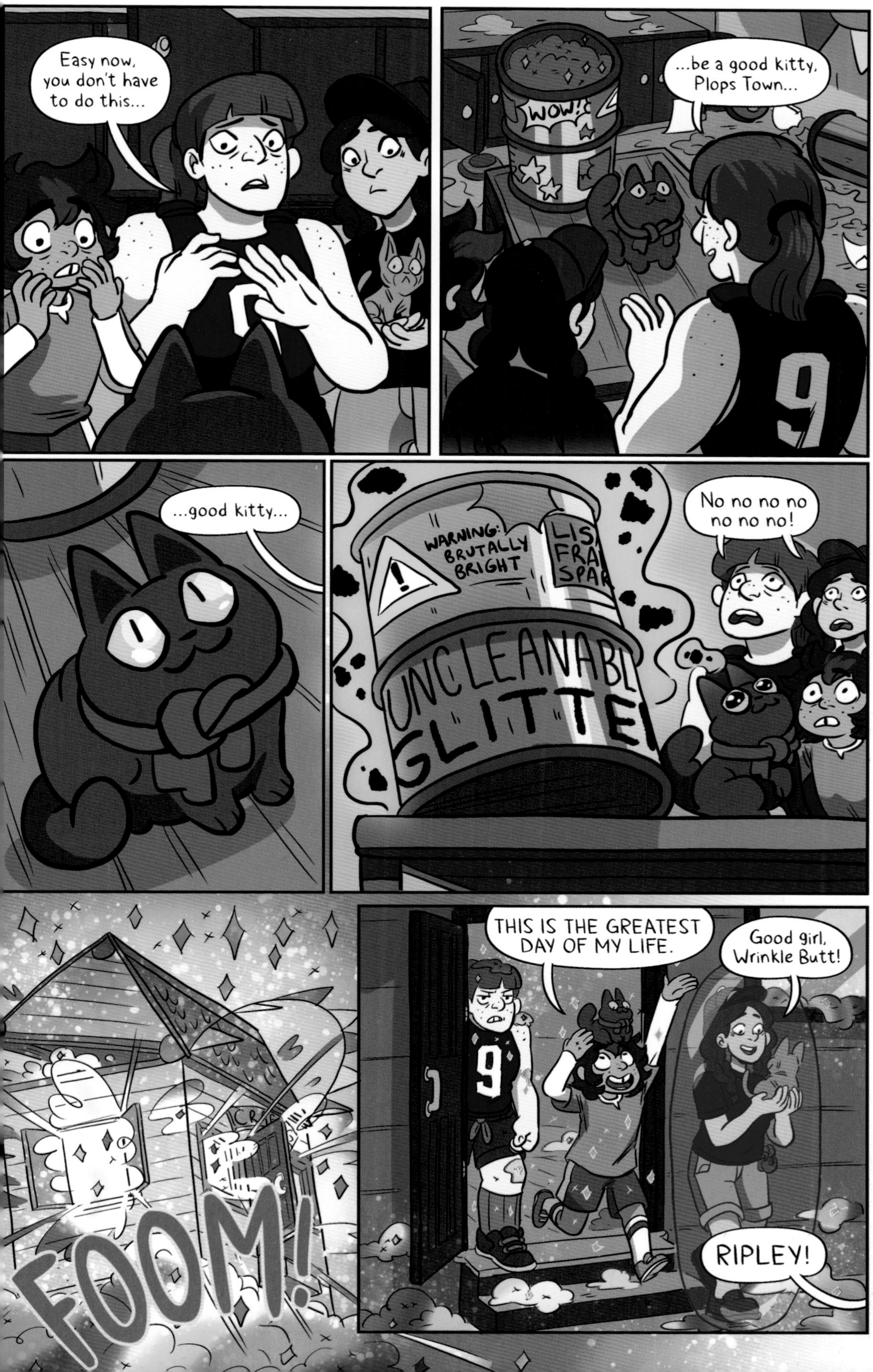

Easy now, you don't have to do this...
...be a good kitty, Plops Town...
WOW!
...good kitty...
WARNING: BRUTALLY BRIGHT
UNCLEANABL GLITTE
No no no no no no no!
FOOM!
THIS IS THE GREATEST DAY OF MY LIFE.
Good girl, Wrinkle Butt!
RIPLEY!

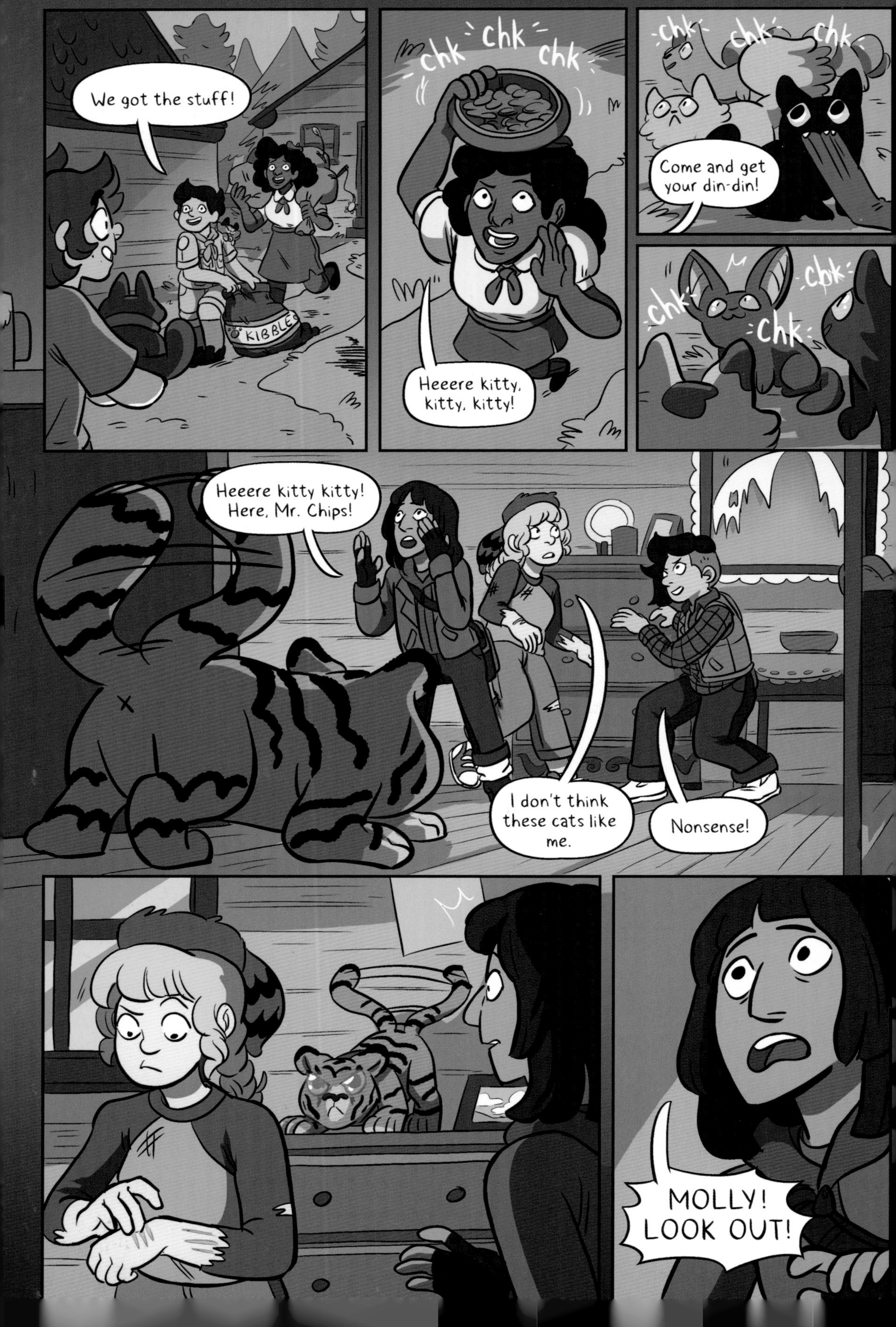
We got the stuff!
KIBBLE
chk
chk
chk
Heeere kitty, kitty, kitty!
chk
chk
chk
Come and get your din-din!
chk
chk
chk
Heeere kitty kitty! Here, Mr. Chips!
I don't think these cats like me.
Nonsense!
MOLLY! LOOK OUT!

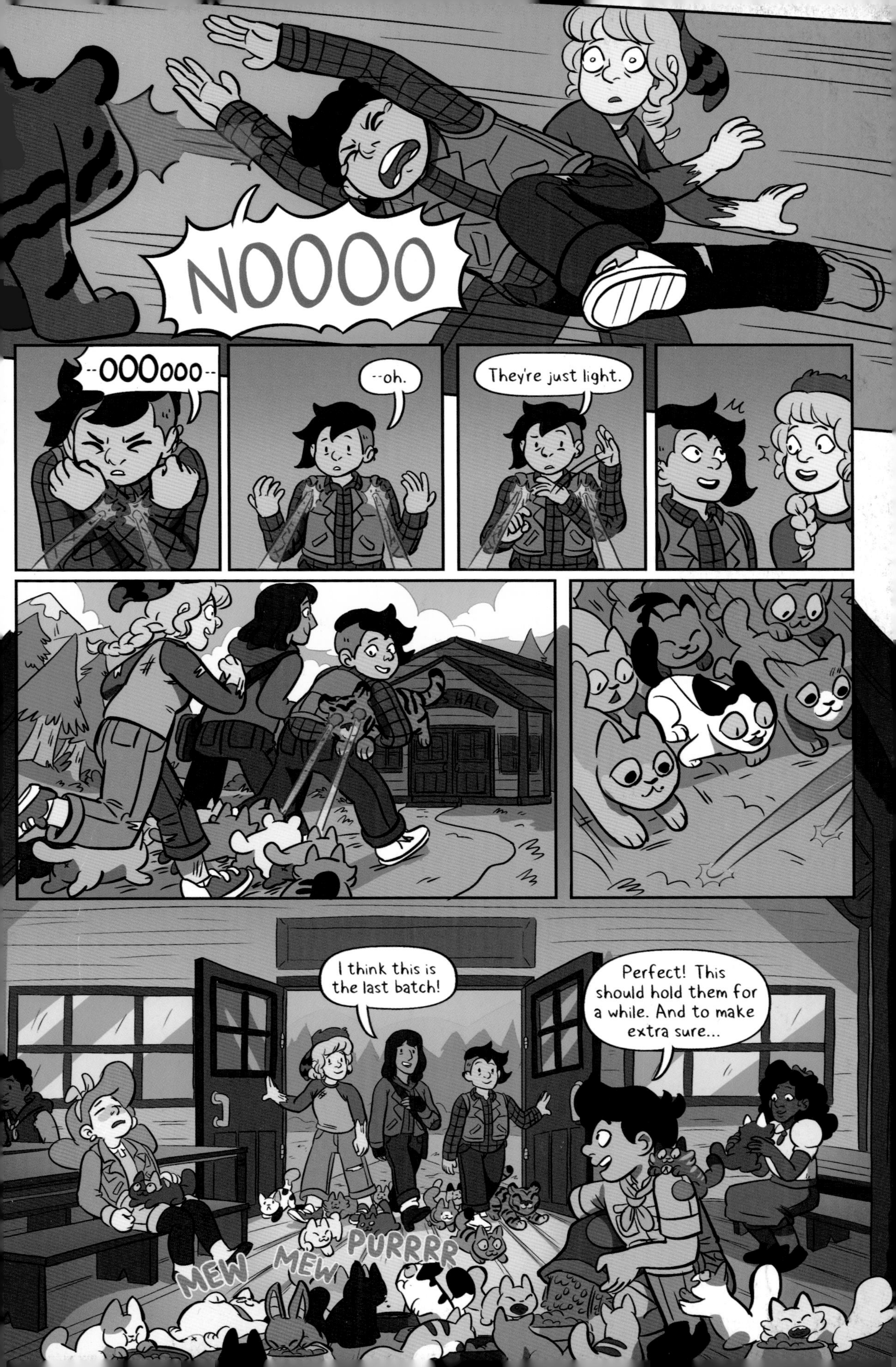
NOOOO
--OOOooo--
--oh.
They're just light.
I think this is the last batch!
Perfect! This should hold them for a while. And to make extra sure...
MEW
MEW
PURRRR

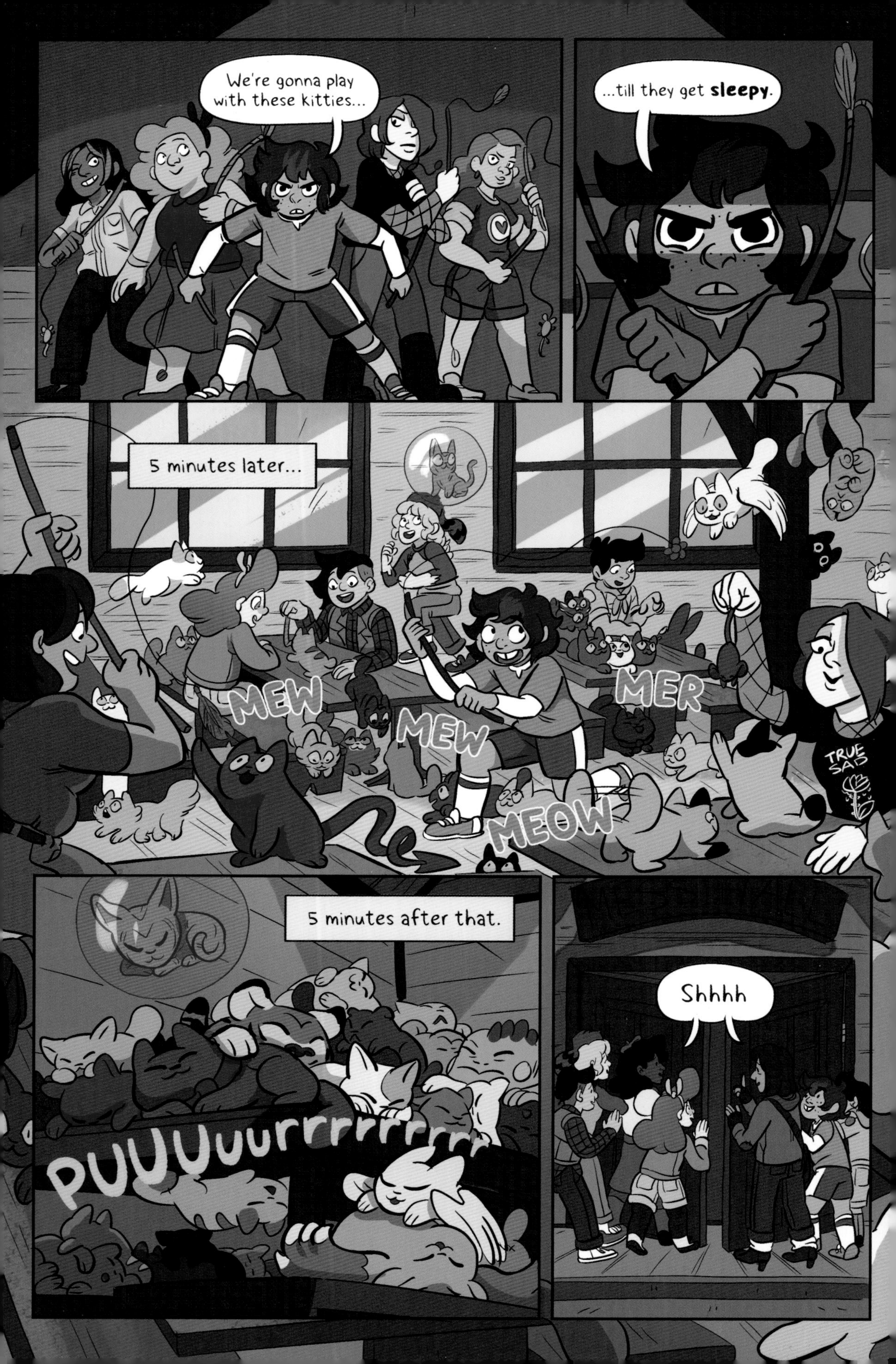
We're gonna play with these kitties...
...till they get **sleepy**.
5 minutes later...
MEW
MEW
MER
MEOW
TRUE SAID
5 minutes after that.
PUUUuurrrrrrrr
Shhhh

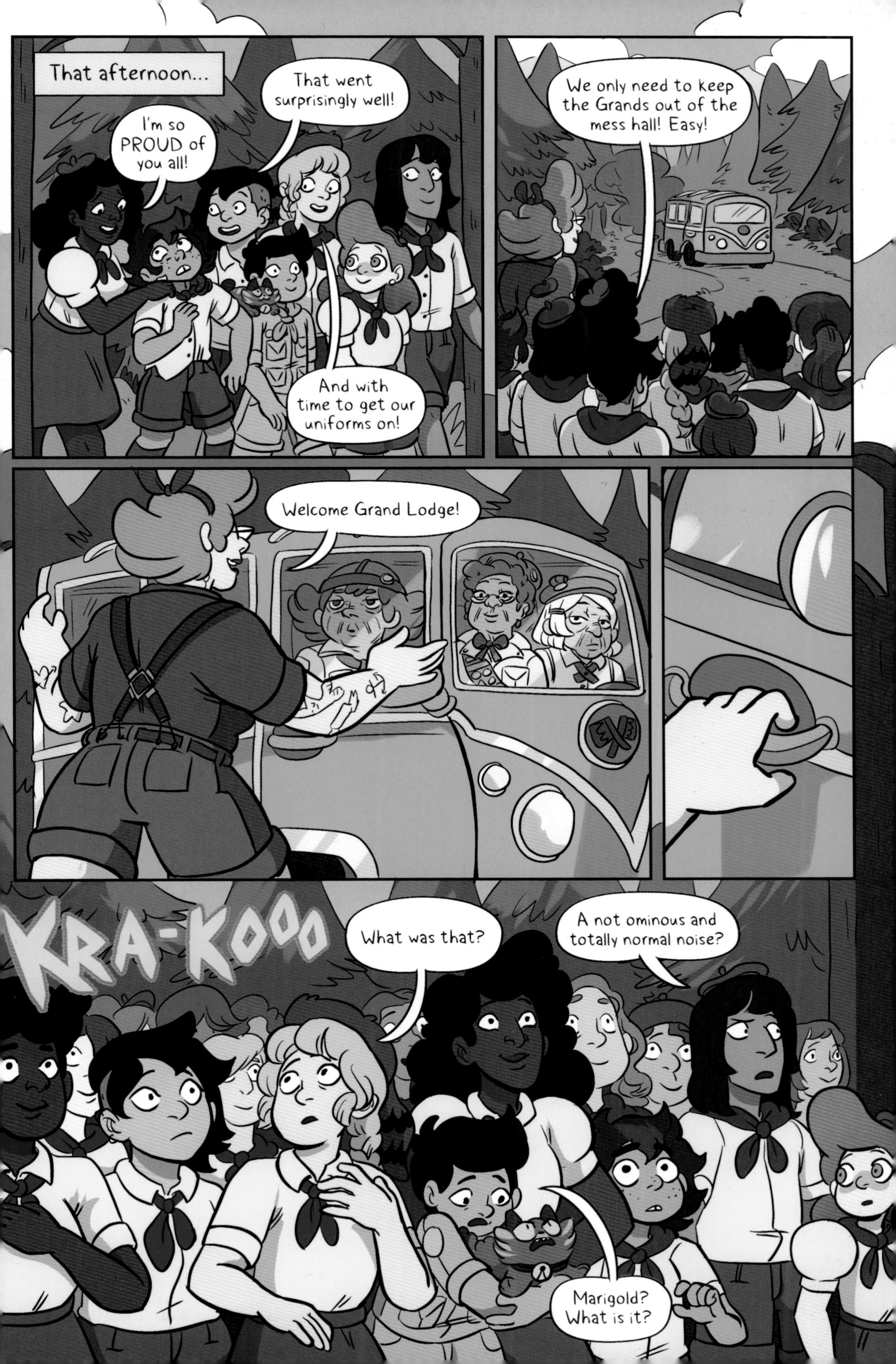
That afternoon...
I'm so PROUD of you all!
That went surprisingly well!
And with time to get our uniforms on!
We only need to keep the Grands out of the mess hall! Easy!
Welcome Grand Lodge!
KRA-KOOO
What was that?
A not ominous and totally normal noise?
Marigold? What is it?

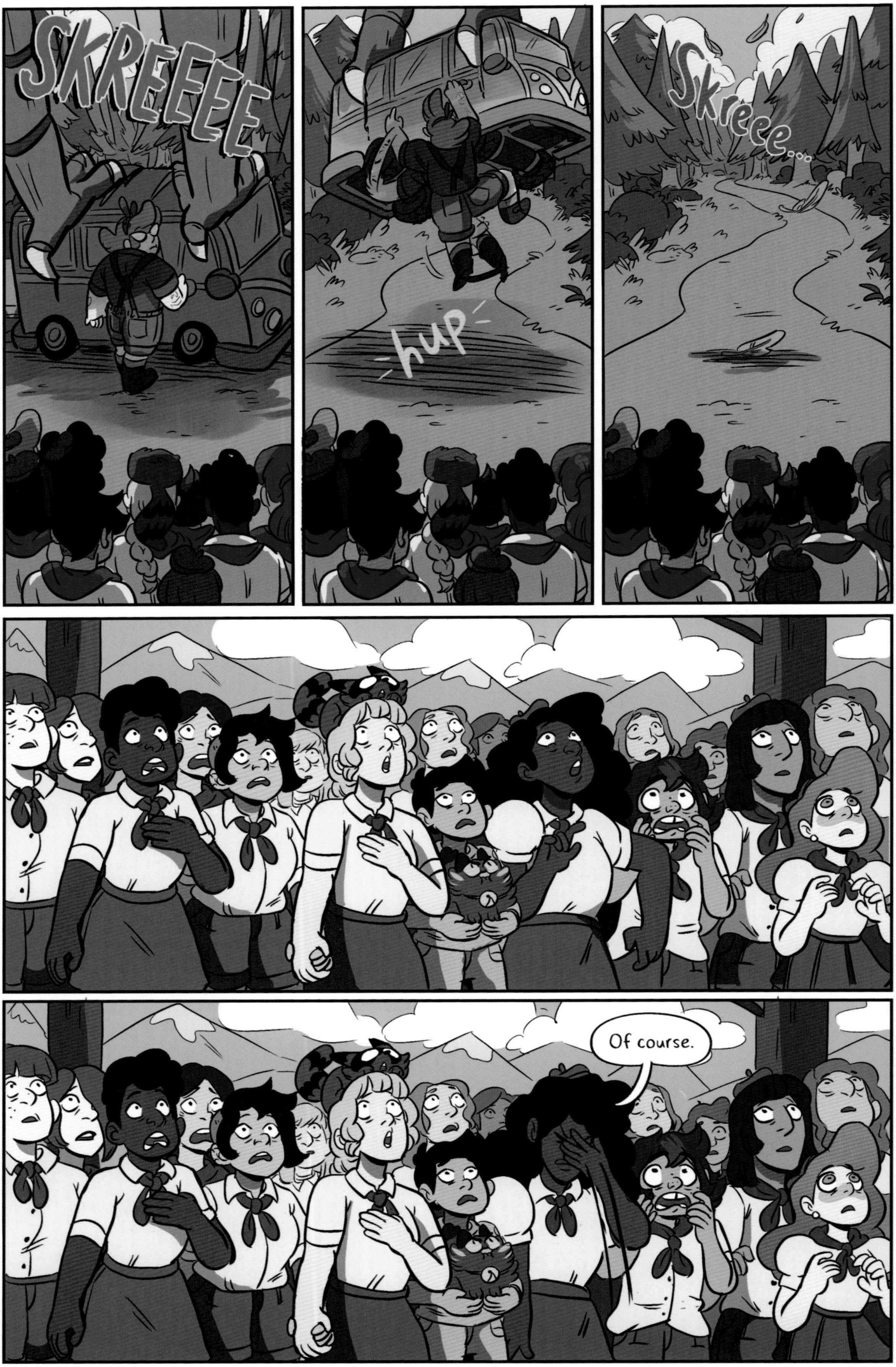
SKREEEEE
hup
Skreeee...
Of course.

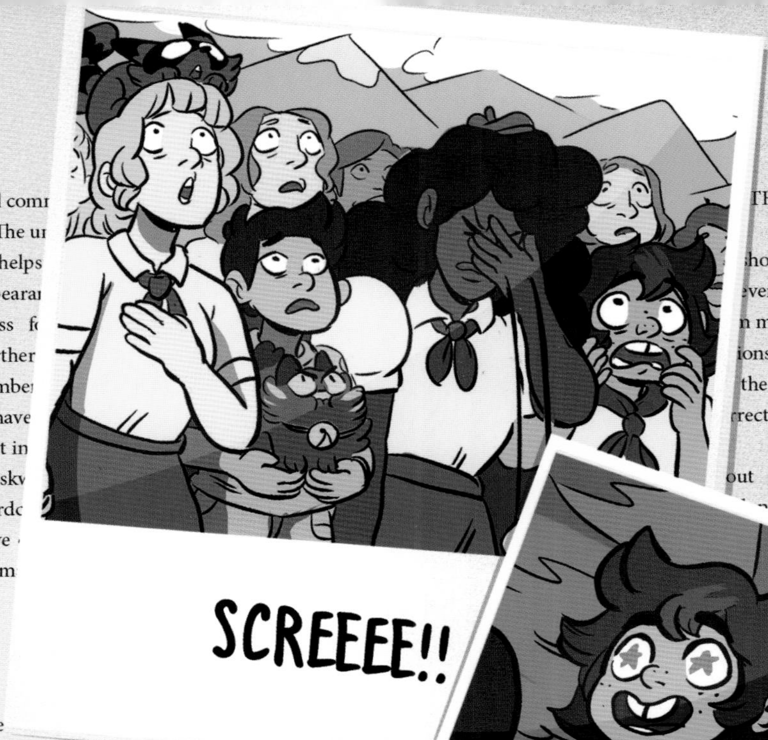
SCREEEE!!

will comm

The ur
It helps
appearan
dress fo
Further
Lumbe
to have
part in
Thiskv
Hardc
have
them

THE UNIFORM

should be worn at camp
events when Lumberjanes
n may also be worn at other
ions. It should be worn as a
the uniform dress with
rrect shoes, and stocking or

out grows her uniform or
ng to anoter Lumberjane.
insignia she has
her
her

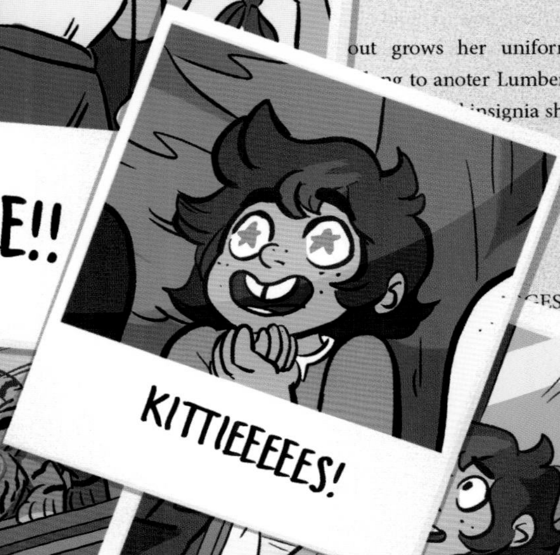
KITTIEEEEES!

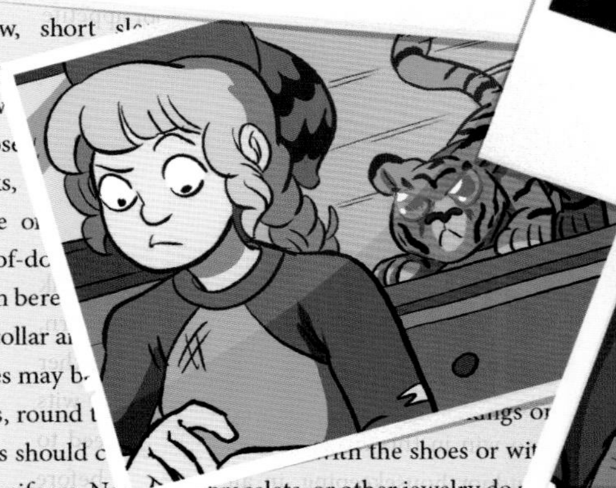

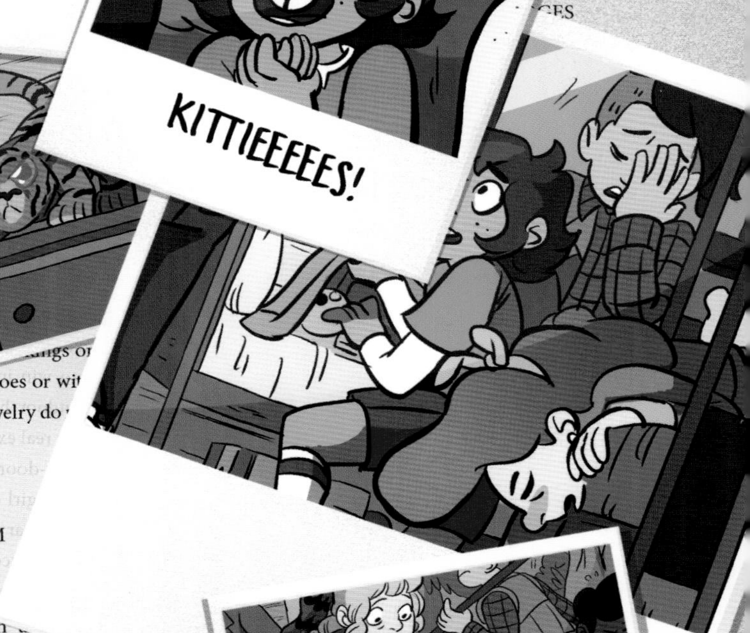

The
yellow, short sl
emb
the w
choose
slacks,
made o
out-of-do
green bere
the collar a
Shoes may b
heels, round t … ings or
socks should c … ith the shoes or wi
the uniform. Ne … es, bracelets, or other jewelry do
belong with a Lumberjane uniform.

HOW TO WEAR THE UNIFORM

To look well in a uniform demands first of … uniform be kept in good condition—clean … pressed. See that the skirt is the right length for your own height and build, that the belt is adjusted to your waist, that your shoes and stockings are in keeping with the uniform, that you watch your posture and carry yourself with dignity and grace. If the beret is removed indoors, be sure that your hair is neat and kept in place with an insonspicuous clip or ribbon. When you wear a Lumberjane uniform you are identified as a member of this organization and you should be doubly careful to conduct yourself in a way that will show everyone that courtesy and thoughtfullness are part of being a Lumberjane. People are likely to judge a whole nation by the selfishness of a few individuals, to criticize a whole family because of the misconduct of one member, and to feel unkindly toward and organization because of the

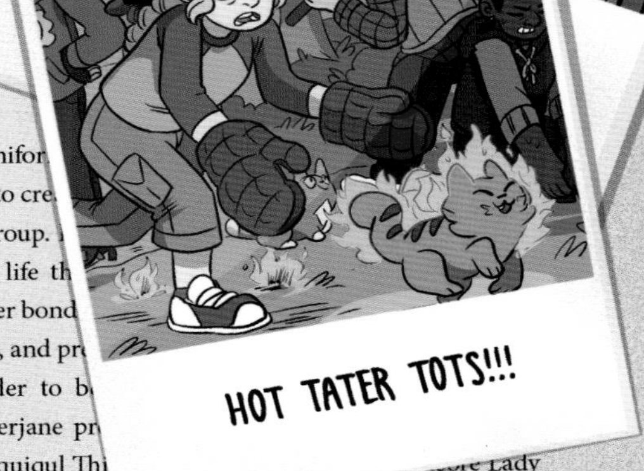
HOT TATER TOTS!!!

The unifor
helps to cre
in a group.
active life th
another bond
future, and pr
in order to b
Lumberjane pr
Penniquiqul Thi … ore Lady
Types, but most … will wish to have one. They
can either buy the uniform, or make it themselves from
materials available at the trading post.

LUMBERJANES FIELD MANUAL

CHAPTER TWENTY-SIX

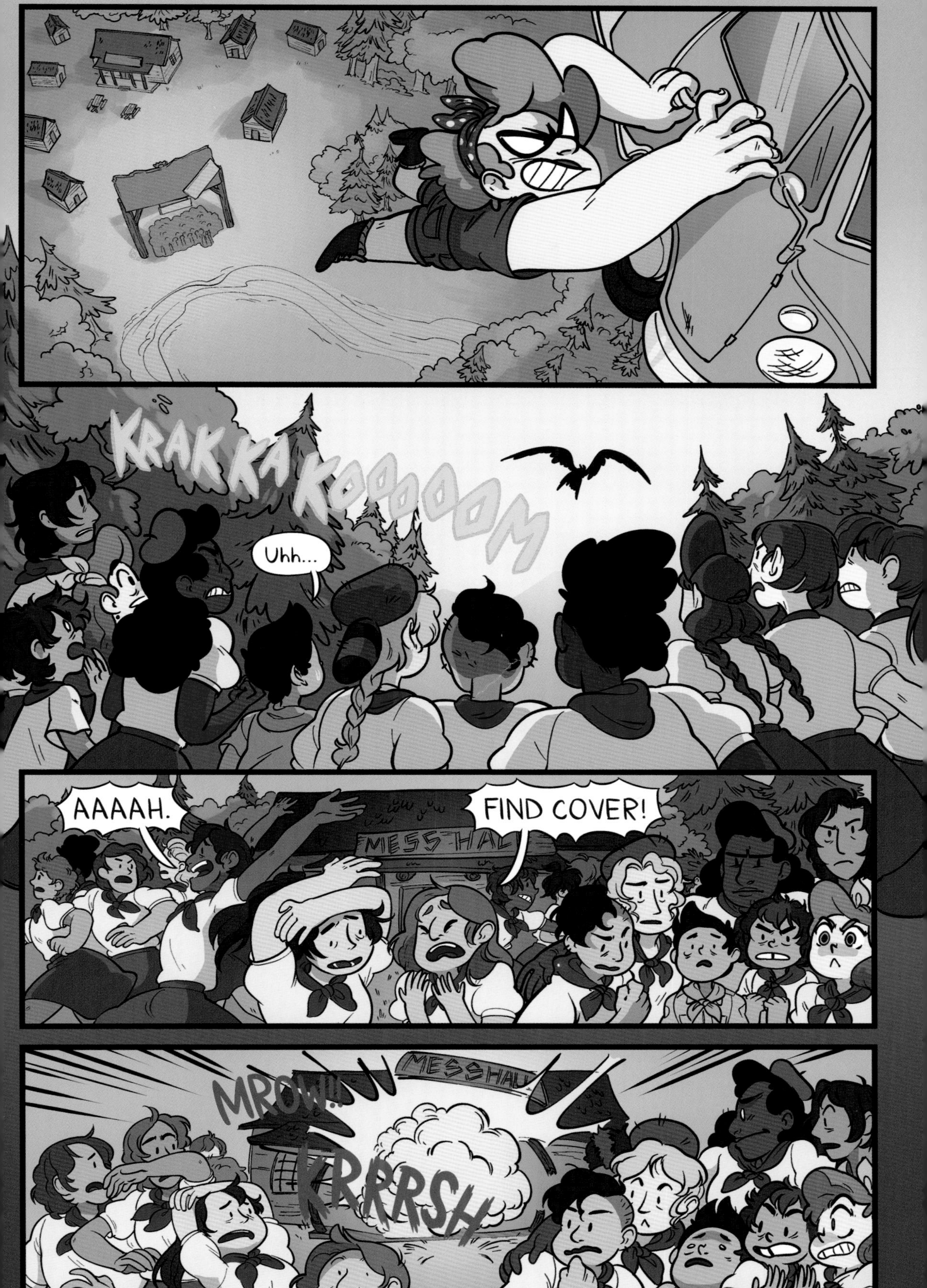
KRAK KA KOOOOOOM
Uhh...
AAAAH.
FIND COVER!
MESS HALL
MESS HALL
MROW!!
KRRRSH

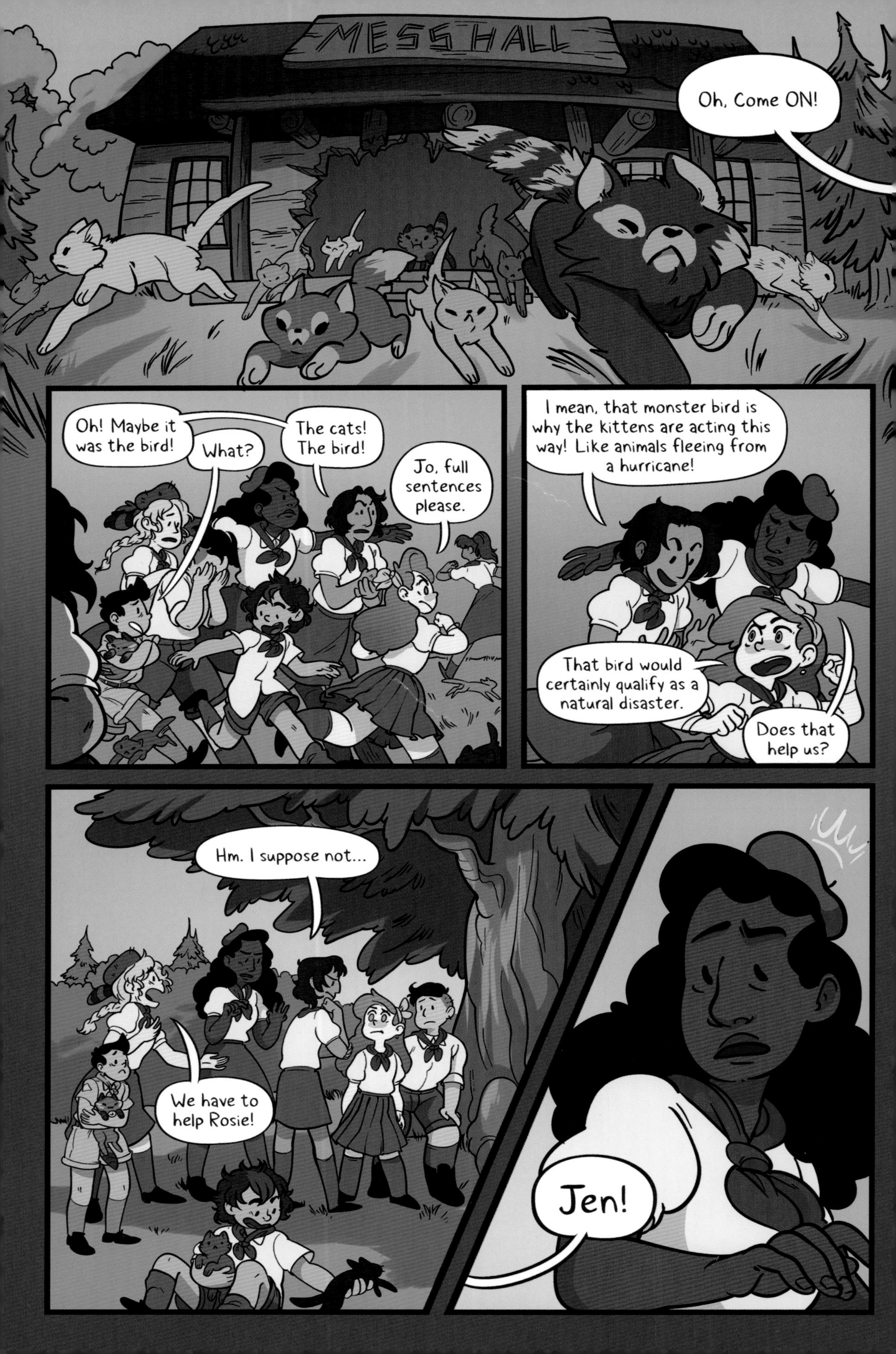
MESS HALL
Oh, Come ON!
Oh! Maybe it was the bird!
The cats! The bird!
What?
Jo, full sentences please.
I mean, that monster bird is why the kittens are acting this way! Like animals fleeing from a hurricane!
That bird would certainly qualify as a natural disaster.
Does that help us?
Hm. I suppose not...
We have to help Rosie!
Jen!

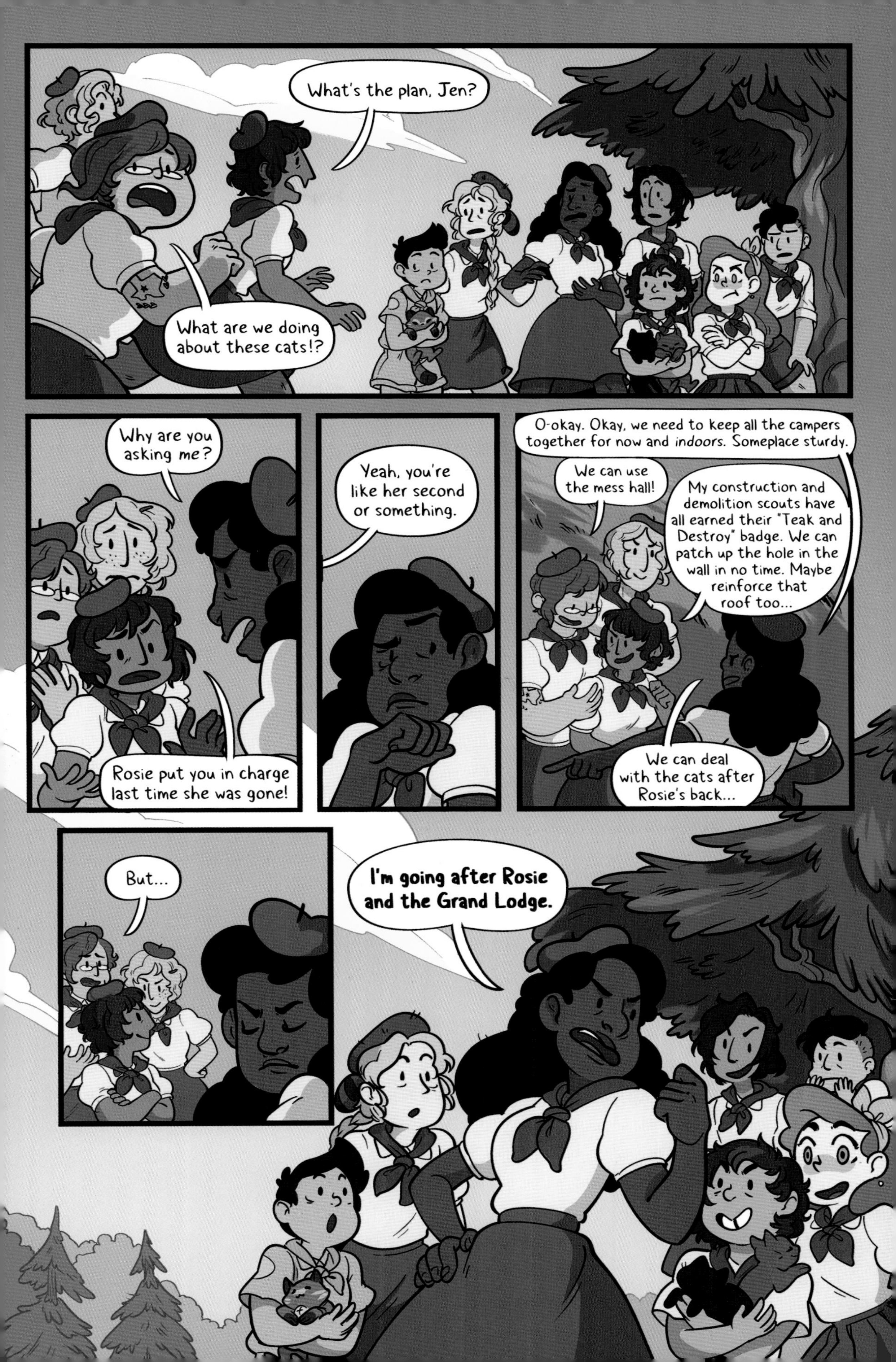
What's the plan, Jen?
What are we doing about these cats!?
Why are you asking me?
Rosie put you in charge last time she was gone!
Yeah, you're like her second or something.
O-okay. Okay, we need to keep all the campers together for now and *indoors*. Someplace sturdy.
We can use the mess hall!
My construction and demolition scouts have all earned their "Teak and Destroy" badge. We can patch up the hole in the wall in no time. Maybe reinforce that roof too...
We can deal with the cats after Rosie's back...
But...
I'm going after Rosie and the Grand Lodge.

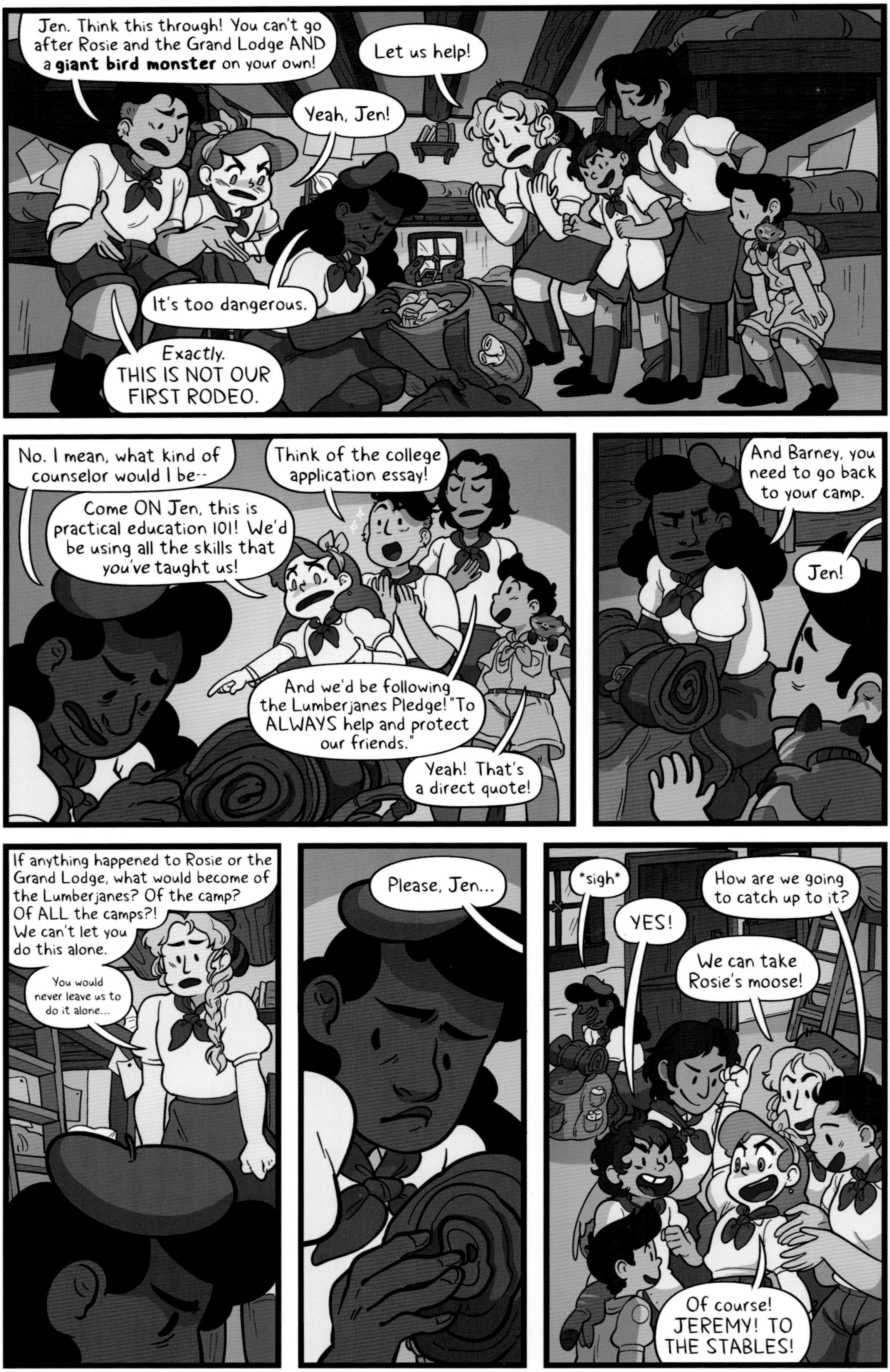
Jen. Think this through! You can't go after Rosie and the Grand Lodge AND a **giant bird monster** on your own!
Let us help!
Yeah, Jen!
It's too dangerous.
Exactly. THIS IS NOT OUR FIRST RODEO.
No. I mean, what kind of counselor would I be--
Think of the college application essay!
Come ON Jen, this is practical education 101! We'd be using all the skills that *you've* taught us!
And we'd be following the Lumberjanes Pledge! "To ALWAYS help and protect our friends."
Yeah! That's a direct quote!
And Barney, you need to go back to your camp.
Jen!
If anything happened to Rosie or the Grand Lodge, what would become of the Lumberjanes? Of the camp? Of ALL the camps?! We can't let you do this alone.
You would never leave us to do it alone...
Please, Jen...
sigh
YES!
How are we going to catch up to it?
We can take Rosie's moose!
Of course! JEREMY! TO THE STABLES!

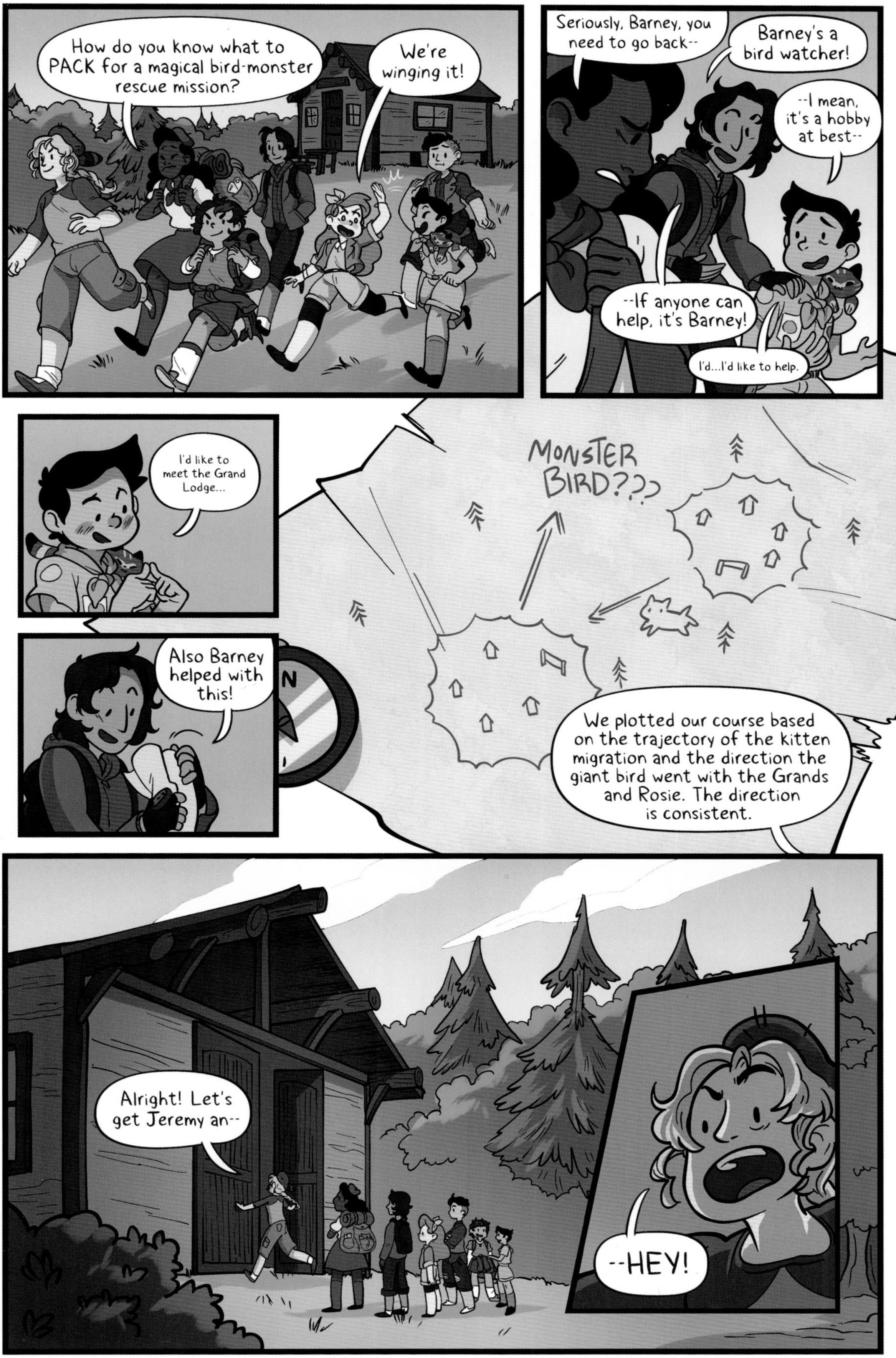
How do you know what to PACK for a magical bird-monster rescue mission?
We're winging it!
Seriously, Barney, you need to go back--
Barney's a bird watcher!
--I mean, it's a hobby at best--
--If anyone can help, it's Barney!
I'd...I'd like to help.
I'd like to meet the Grand Lodge...
MONSTER BIRD???
N
Also Barney helped with this!
We plotted our course based on the trajectory of the kitten migration and the direction the giant bird went with the Grands and Rosie. The direction is consistent.
Alright! Let's get Jeremy an--
--HEY!

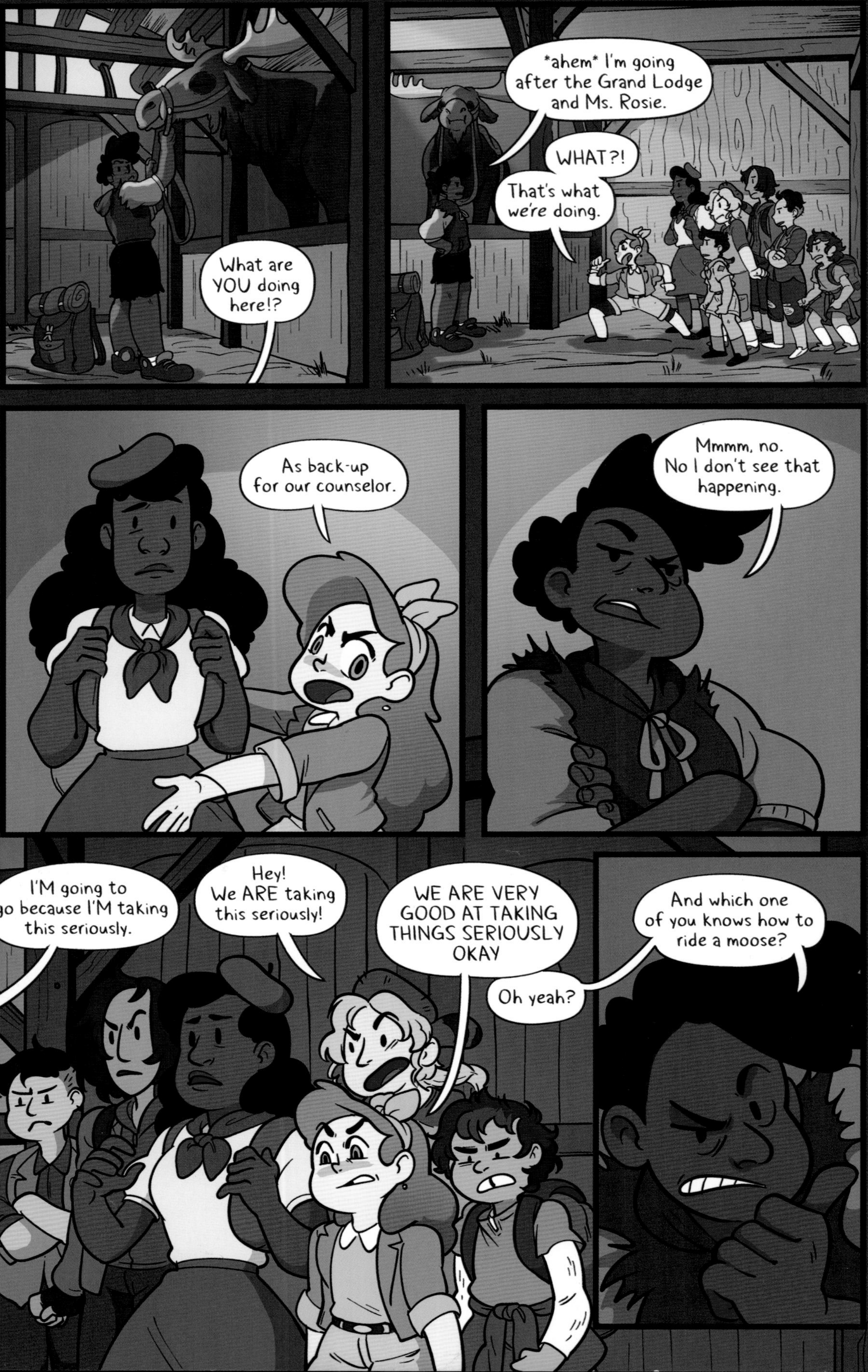
What are YOU doing here!?
ahem I'm going after the Grand Lodge and Ms. Rosie.
WHAT?!
That's what we're doing.
As back-up for our counselor.
Mmmm, no. No I don't see that happening.
I'M going to go because I'M taking this seriously.
Hey! We ARE taking this seriously!
WE ARE VERY GOOD AT TAKING THINGS SERIOUSLY OKAY
Oh yeah?
And which one of you knows how to ride a moose?

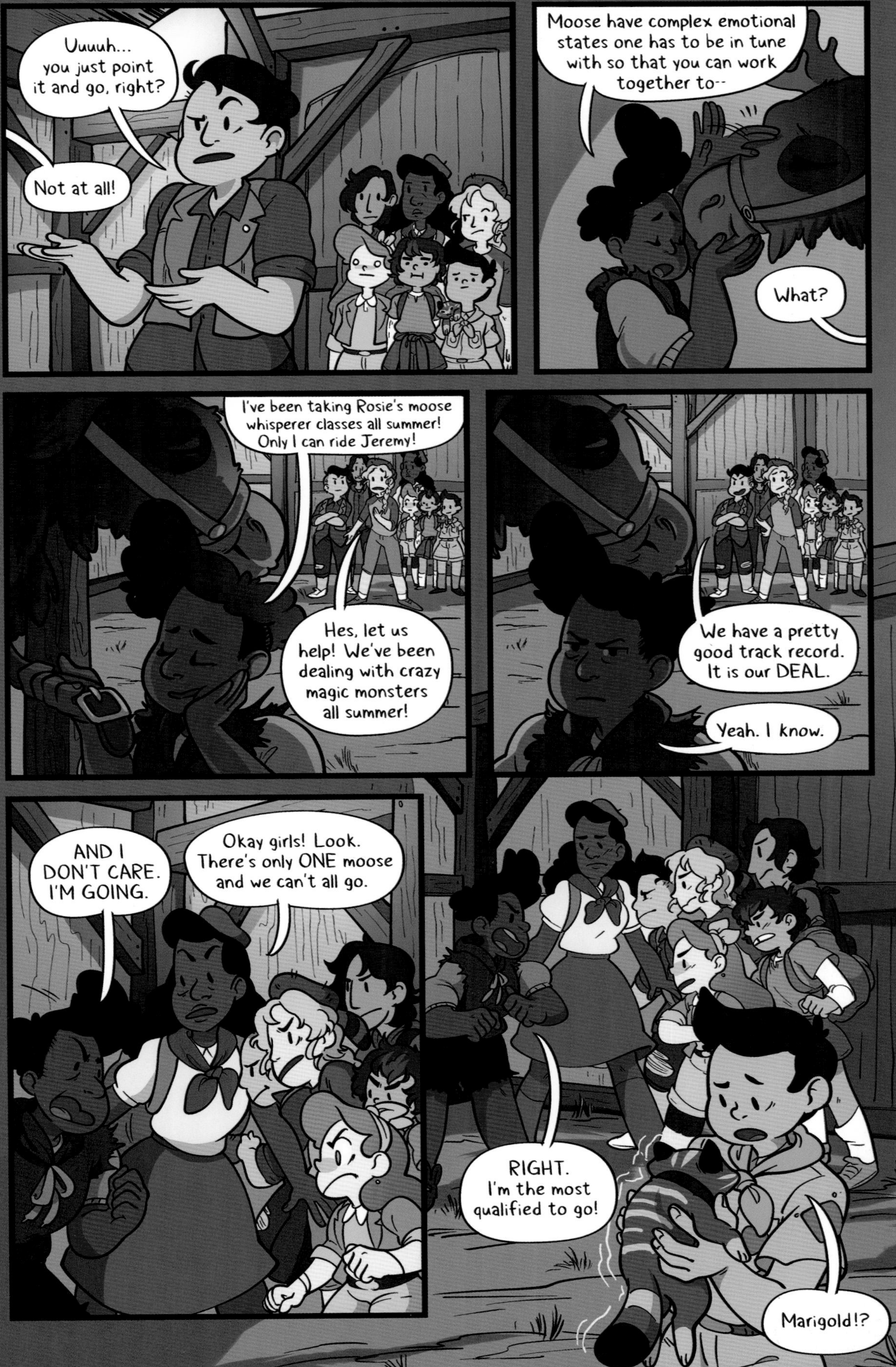
Uuuuh... you just point it and go, right?
Not at all!
Moose have complex emotional states one has to be in tune with so that you can work together to--
What?
I've been taking Rosie's moose whisperer classes all summer! Only I can ride Jeremy!
Hes, let us help! We've been dealing with crazy magic monsters all summer!
We have a pretty good track record. It is our DEAL.
Yeah. I know.
AND I DON'T CARE. I'M GOING.
Okay girls! Look. There's only ONE moose and we can't all go.
RIGHT. I'm the most qualified to go!
Marigold!?

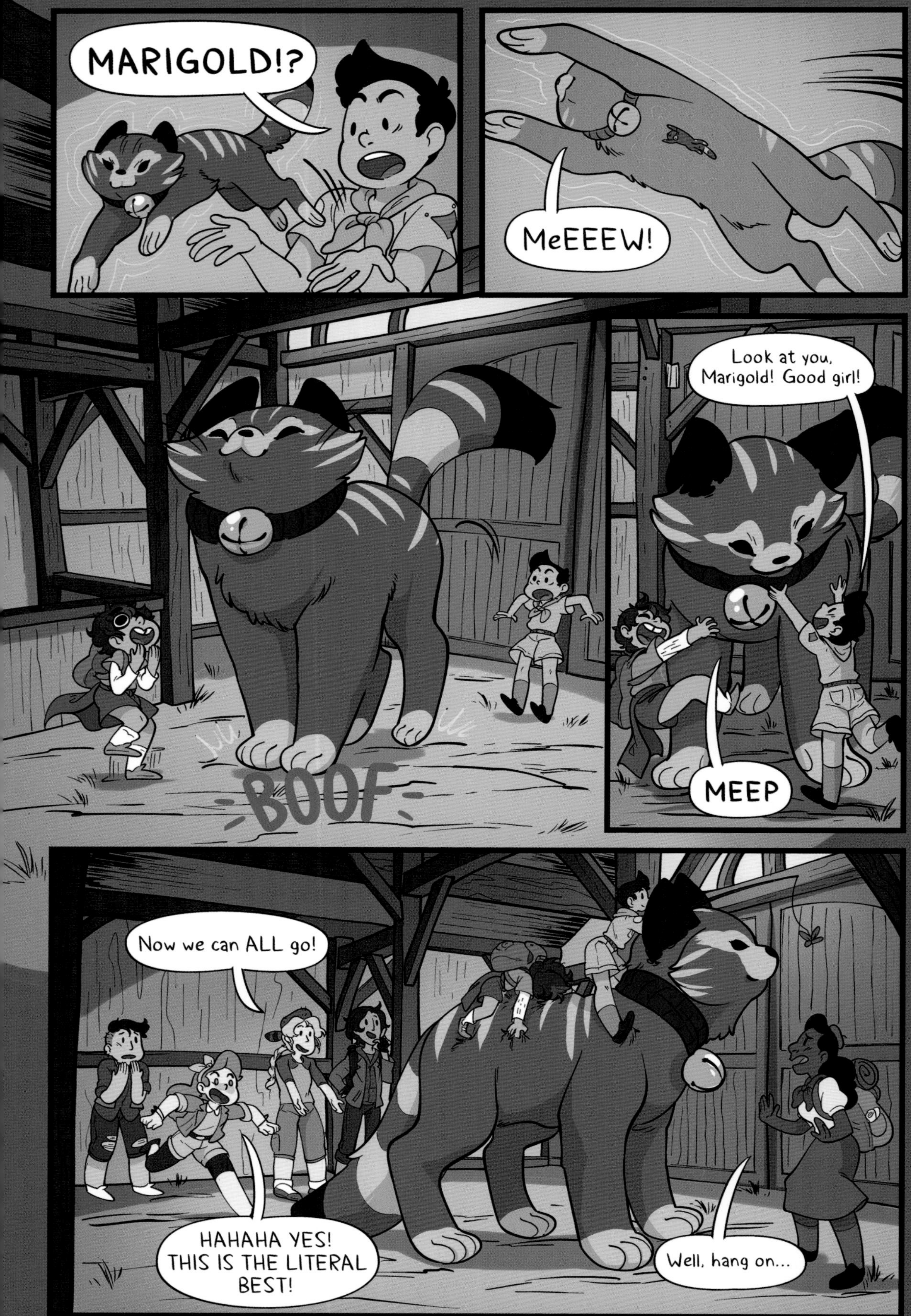
MARIGOLD!?
MeEEEW!
BOOF
Look at you, Marigold! Good girl!
MEEP
Now we can ALL go!
HAHAHA YES! THIS IS THE LITERAL BEST!
Well, hang on...

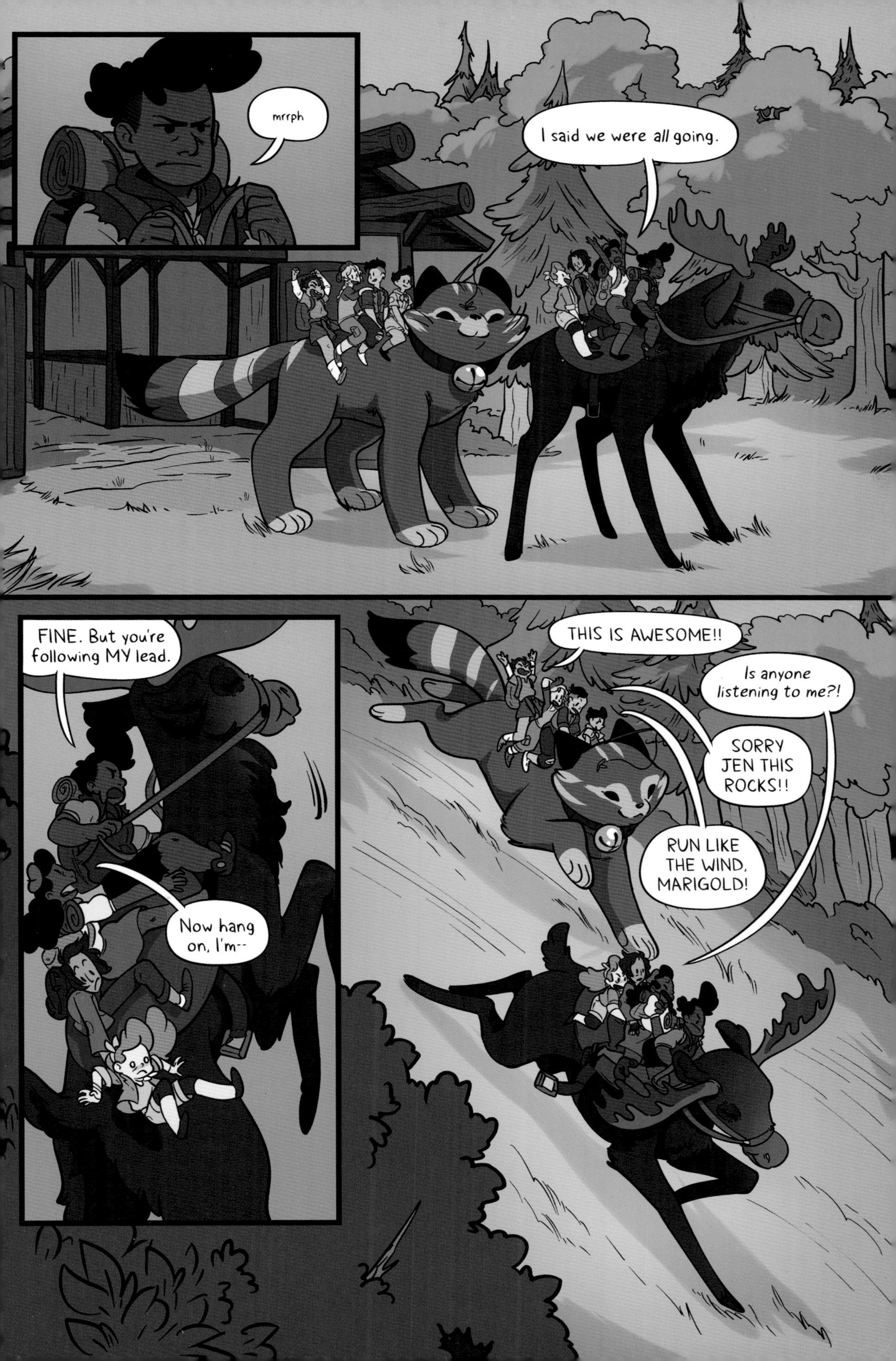
mrrph
I said we were all going.
FINE. But you're following MY lead.
Now hang on, I'm--
THIS IS AWESOME!!
Is anyone listening to me?!
SORRY JEN THIS ROCKS!!
RUN LIKE THE WIND, MARIGOLD!

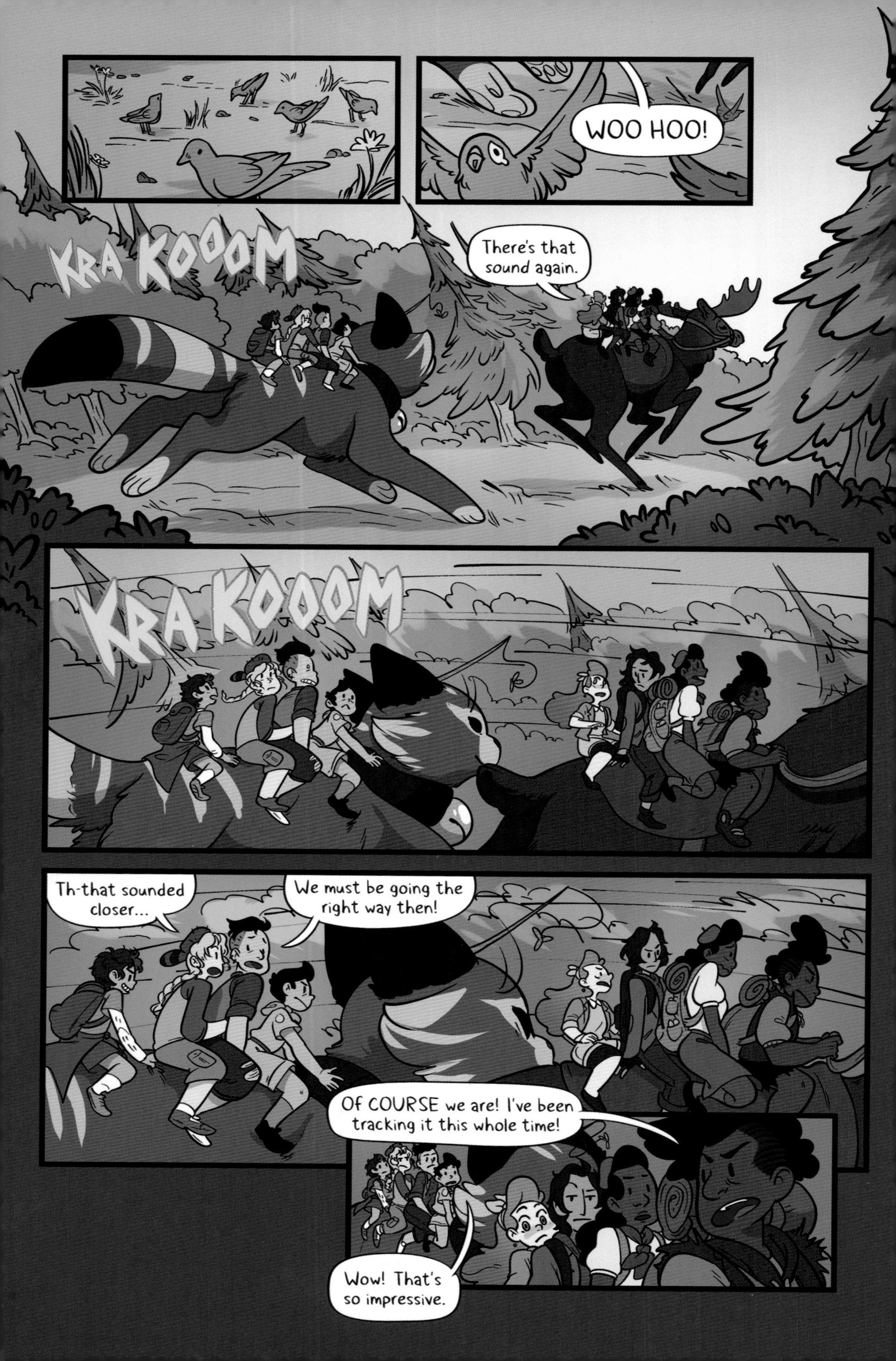
WOO HOO!
KRA KOOOM
There's that sound again.
KRA KOOOM
Th-that sounded closer...
We must be going the right way then!
Of COURSE we are! I've been tracking it this whole time!
Wow! That's so impressive.

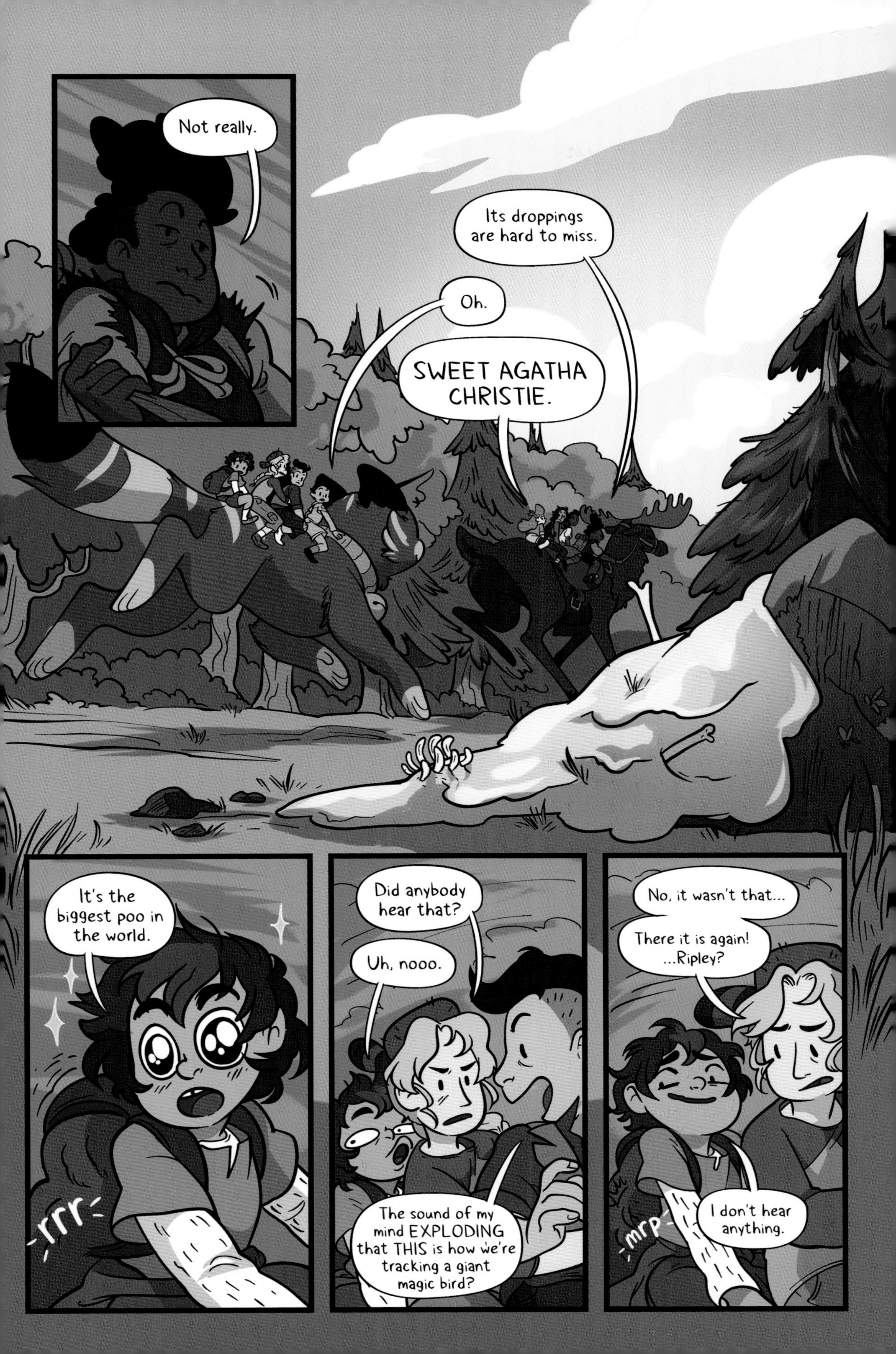
Not really.
Its droppings are hard to miss.
Oh.
SWEET AGATHA CHRISTIE.
It's the biggest poo in the world.
rrr
Did anybody hear that?
Uh, nooo.
The sound of my mind EXPLODING that THIS is how we're tracking a giant magic bird?
No, it wasn't that...
There it is again! ...Ripley?
mrp
I don't hear anything.

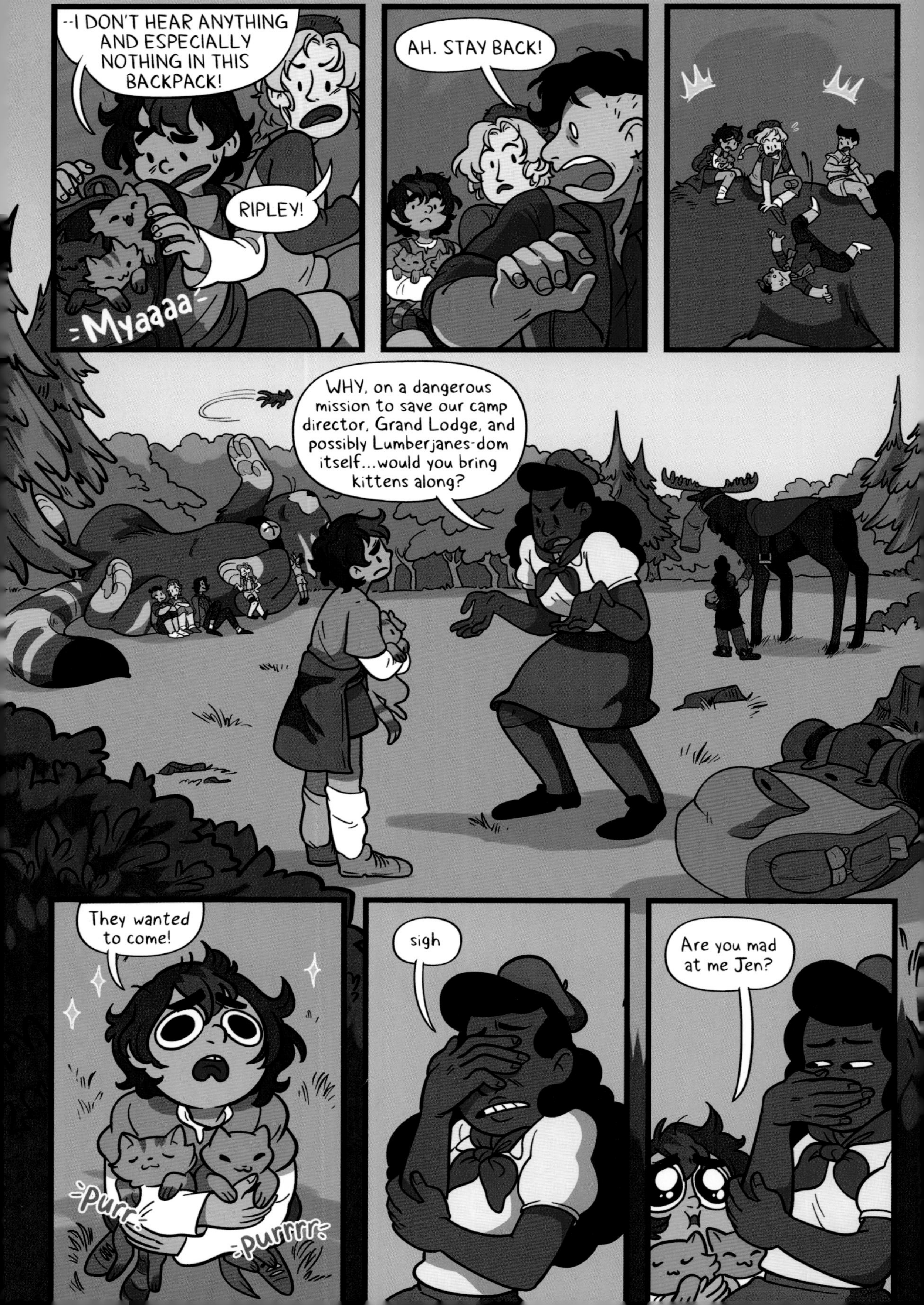
--I DON'T HEAR ANYTHING AND ESPECIALLY NOTHING IN THIS BACKPACK!
RIPLEY!
Myaaaa
AH. STAY BACK!
WHY, on a dangerous mission to save our camp director, Grand Lodge, and possibly Lumberjanes-dom itself...would you bring kittens along?
They wanted to come!
Purr
Purrrr
sigh
Are you mad at me Jen?

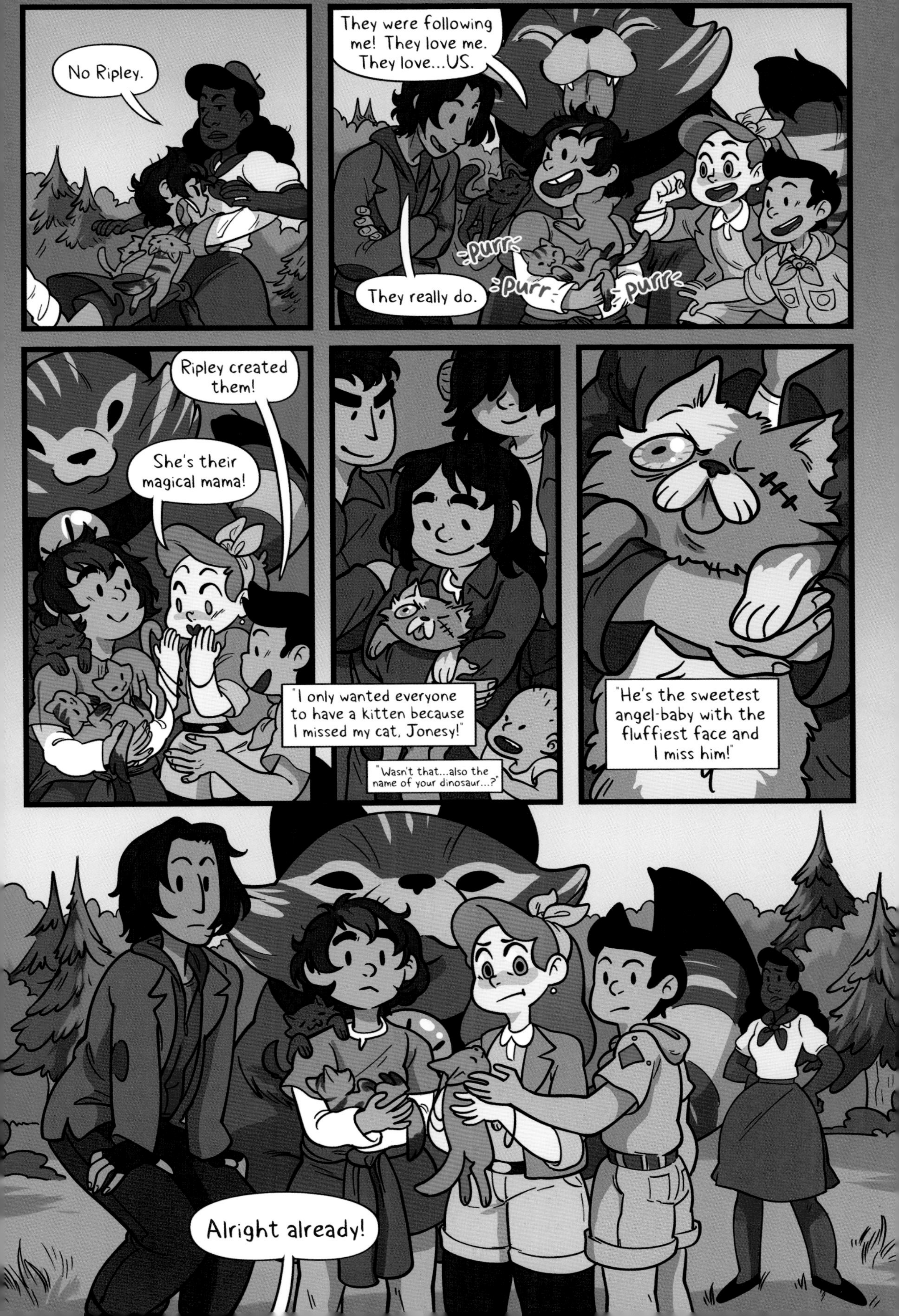
No Ripley.
They were following me! They love me. They love...US.
They really do.
-purr-
-purr-
-purr-
Ripley created them!
She's their magical mama!
"I only wanted everyone to have a kitten because I missed my cat, Jonesy!"
"Wasn't that...also the name of your dinosaur...?"
"He's the sweetest angel-baby with the fluffiest face and I miss him!"
Alright already!

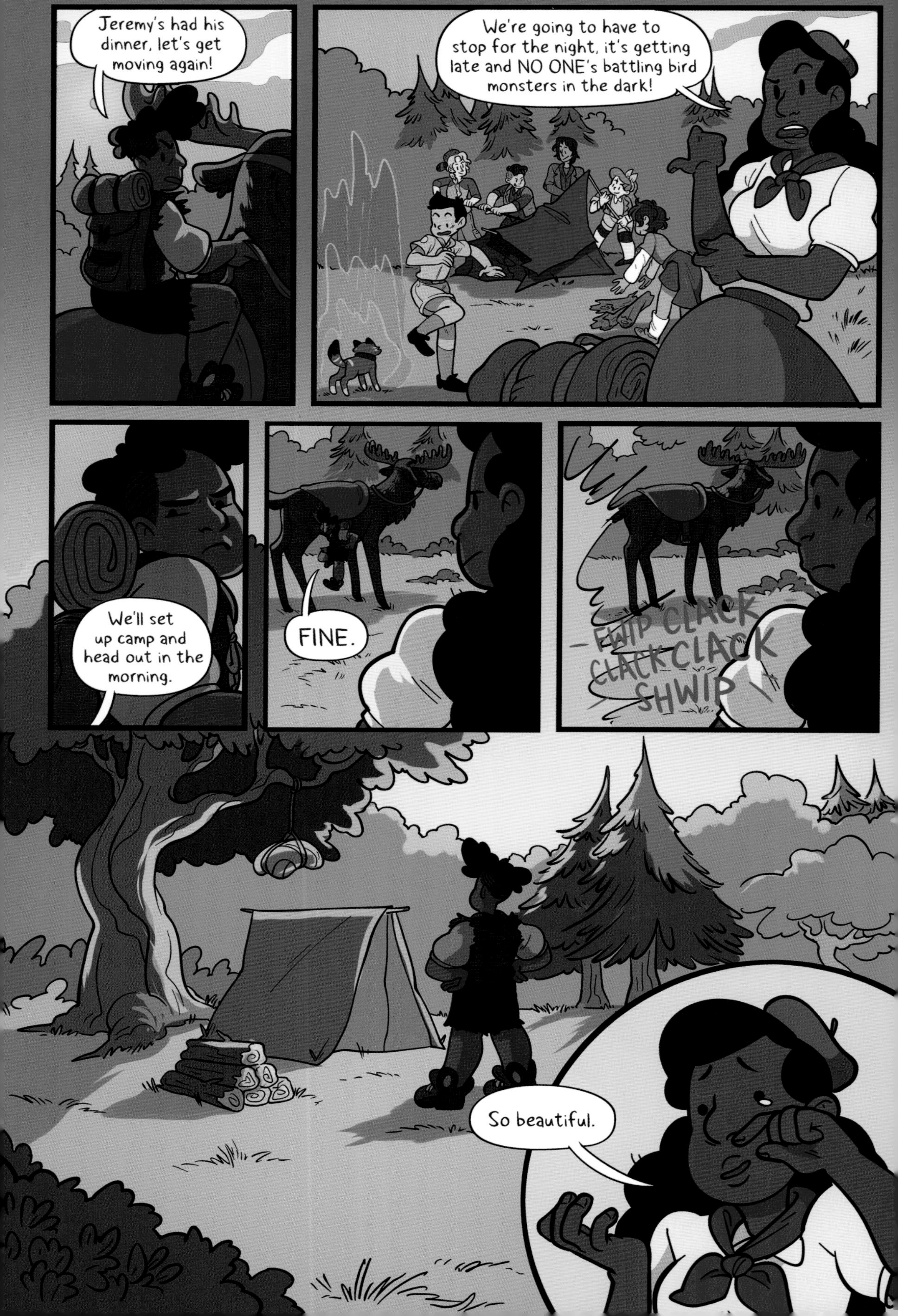
Jeremy's had his dinner, let's get moving again!
We're going to have to stop for the night, it's getting late and NO ONE's battling bird monsters in the dark!
We'll set up camp and head out in the morning.
FINE.
FWIP CLACK
CLACK CLACK
SHWIP
So beautiful.

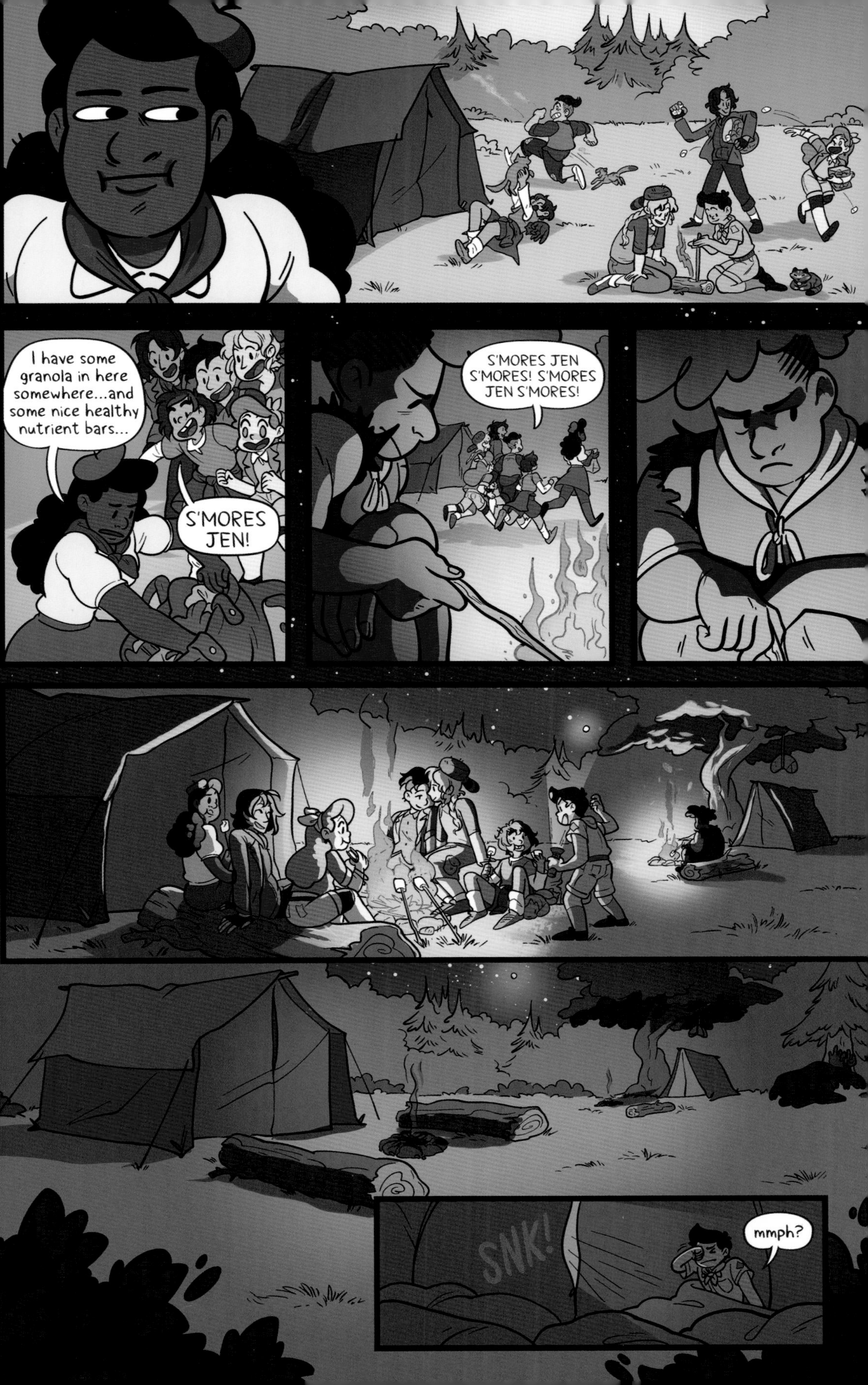
I have some granola in here somewhere...and some nice healthy nutrient bars...
S'MORES JEN!
S'MORES JEN S'MORES! S'MORES JEN S'MORES!
SNK!
mmph?

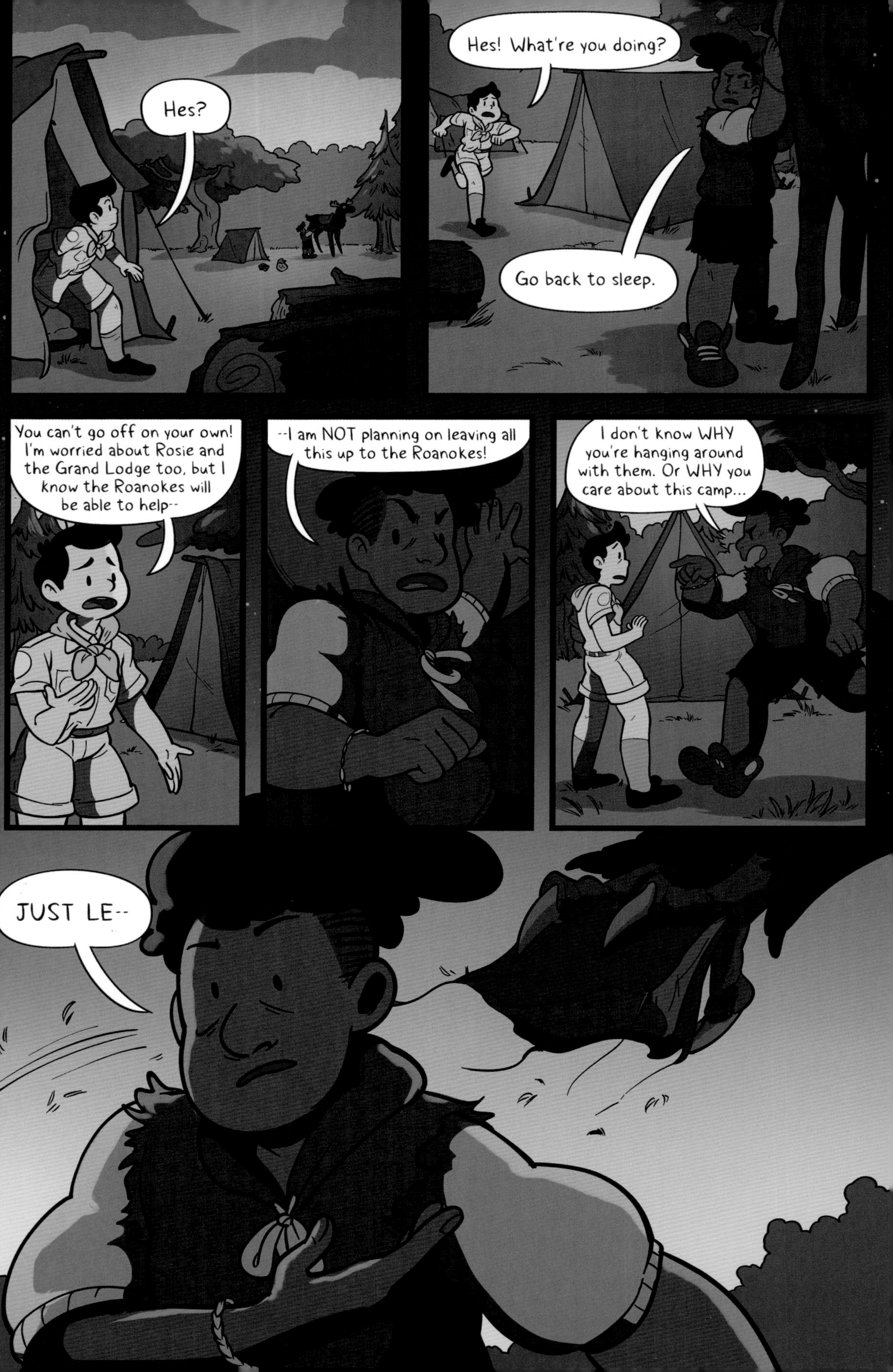
Hes?
Hes! What're you doing?
Go back to sleep.
You can't go off on your own! I'm worried about Rosie and the Grand Lodge too, but I know the Roanokes will be able to help--
--I am NOT planning on leaving all this up to the Roanokes!
I don't know WHY you're hanging around with them. Or WHY you care about this camp...
JUST LE--

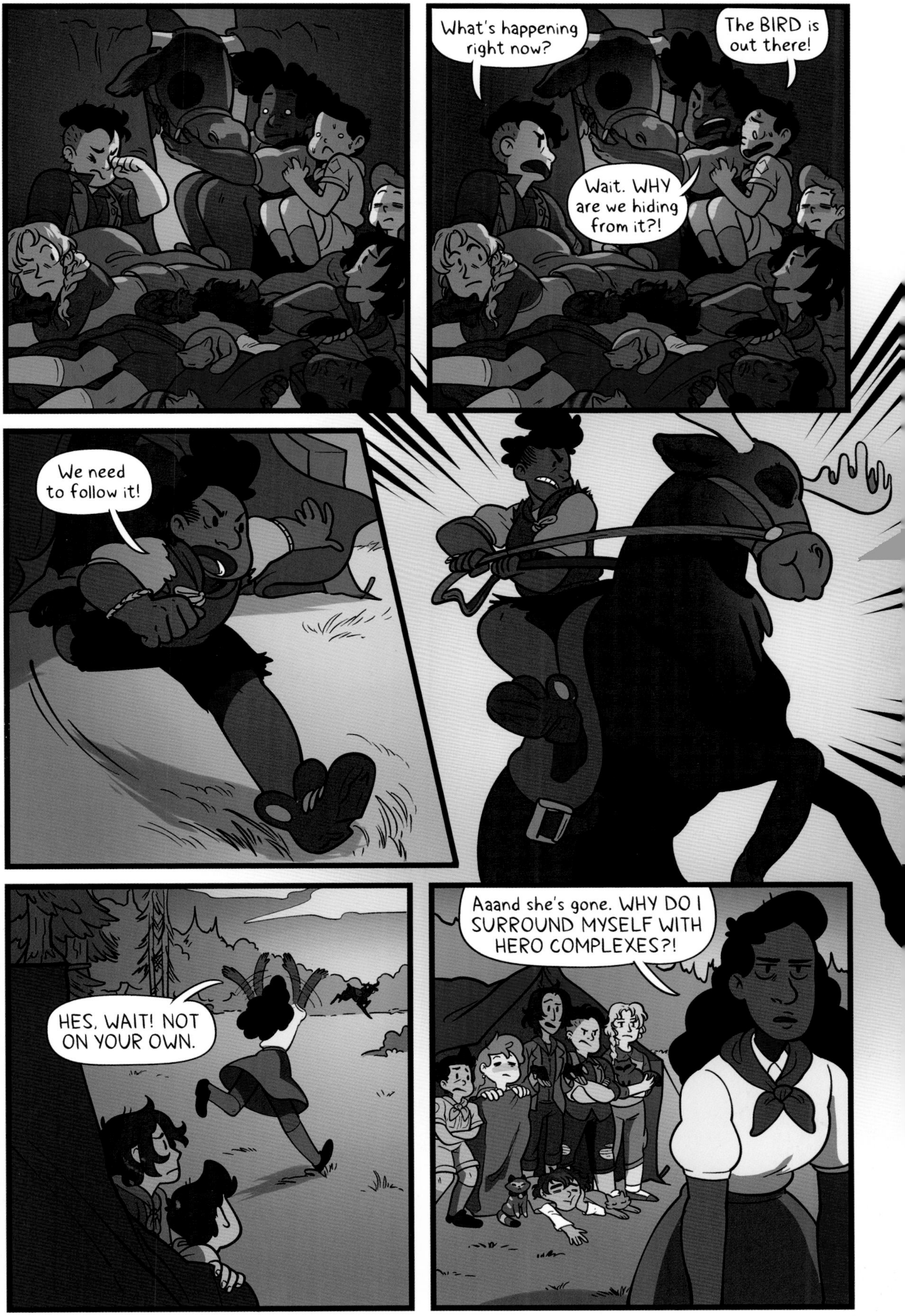
What's happening right now?
The BIRD is out there!
Wait. WHY are we hiding from it?!
We need to follow it!
HES, WAIT! NOT ON YOUR OWN.
Aaand she's gone. WHY DO I SURROUND MYSELF WITH HERO COMPLEXES?!

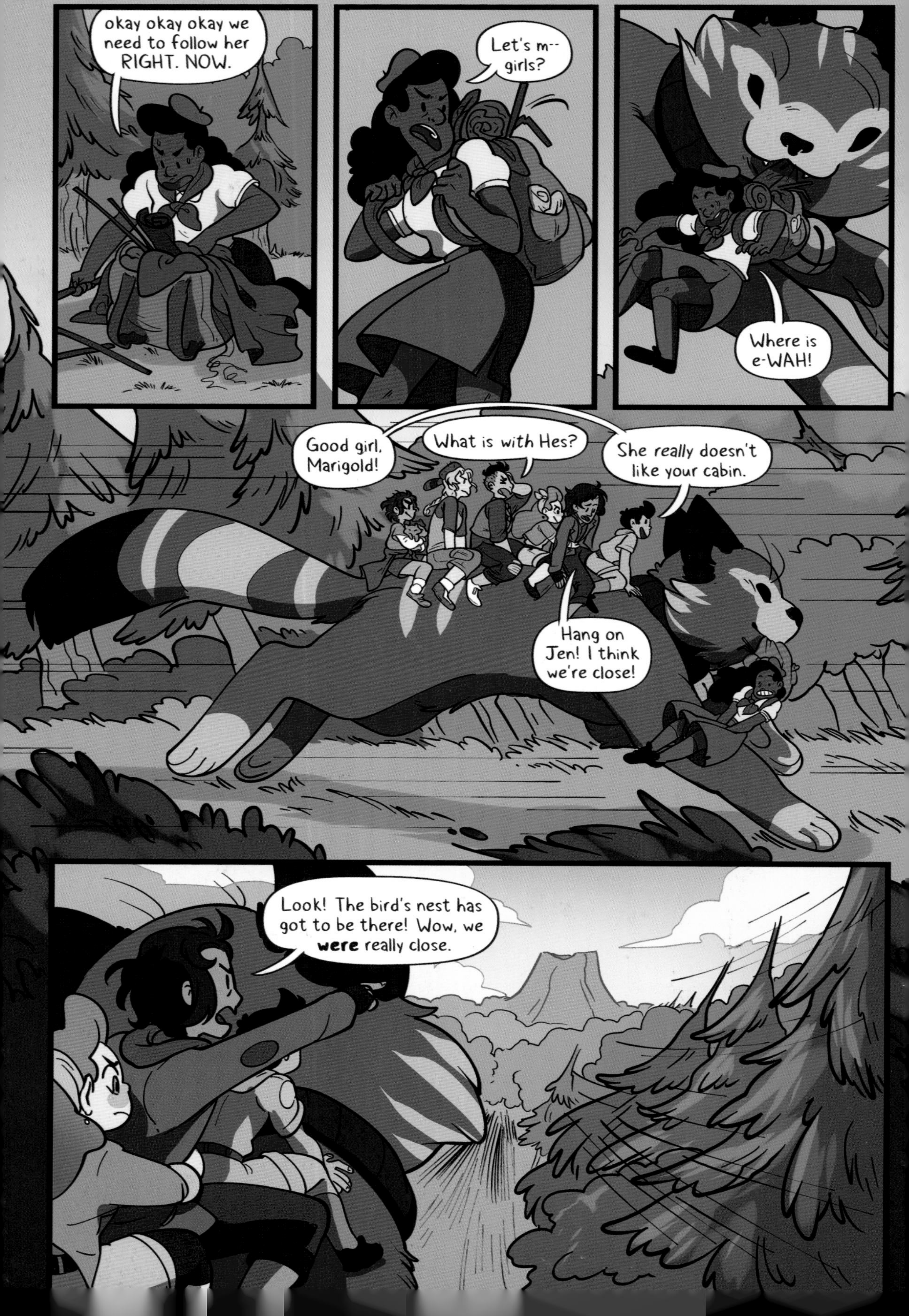
okay okay okay we need to follow her RIGHT. NOW.
Let's m-- girls?
Where is e-WAH!
Good girl, Marigold!
What is with Hes?
She really doesn't like your cabin.
Hang on Jen! I think we're close!
Look! The bird's nest has got to be there! Wow, we **were** really close.

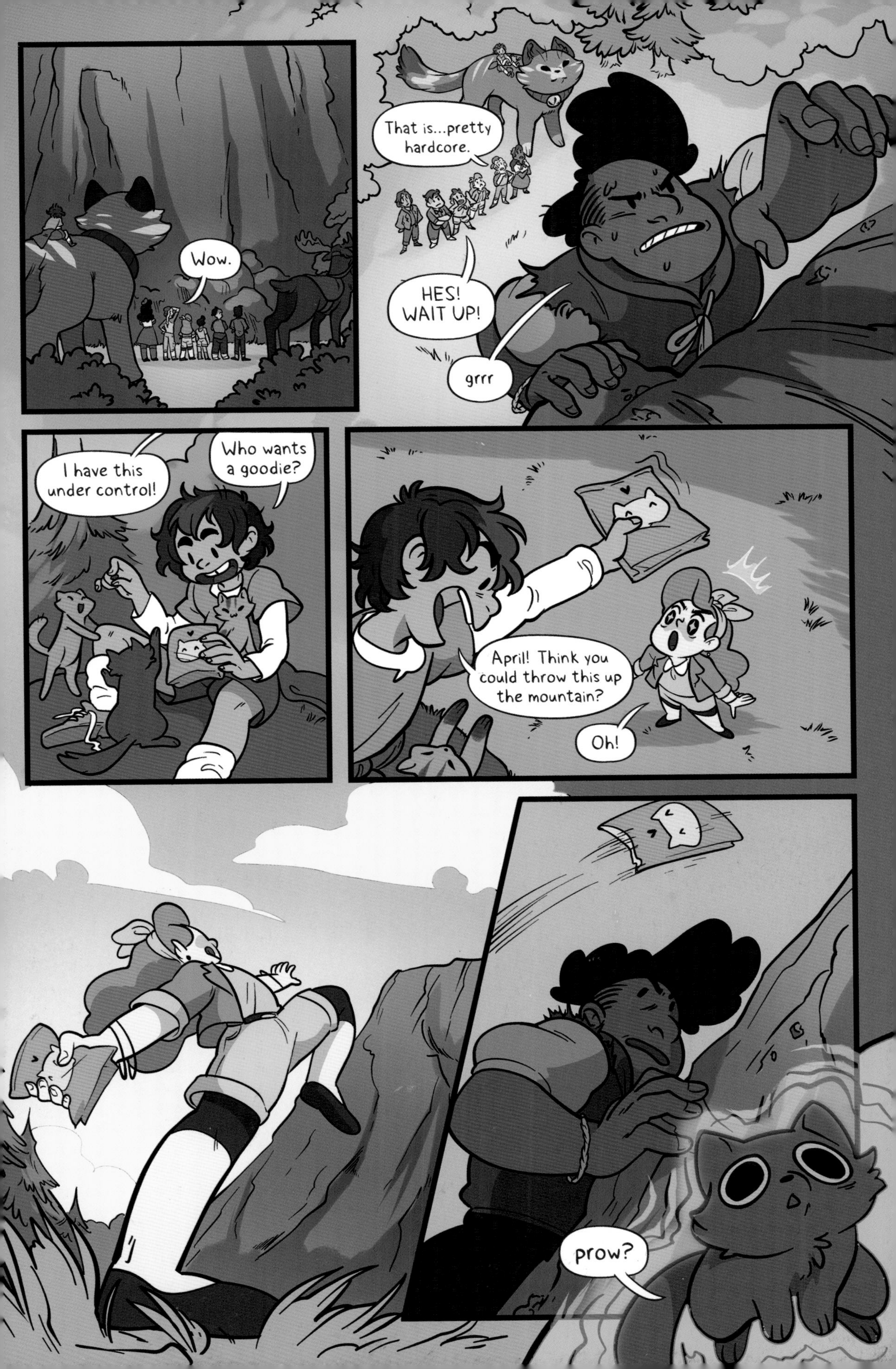
Wow.
That is...pretty hardcore.
HES! WAIT UP!
grrr
I have this under control!
Who wants a goodie?
April! Think you could throw this up the mountain?
Oh!
prow?

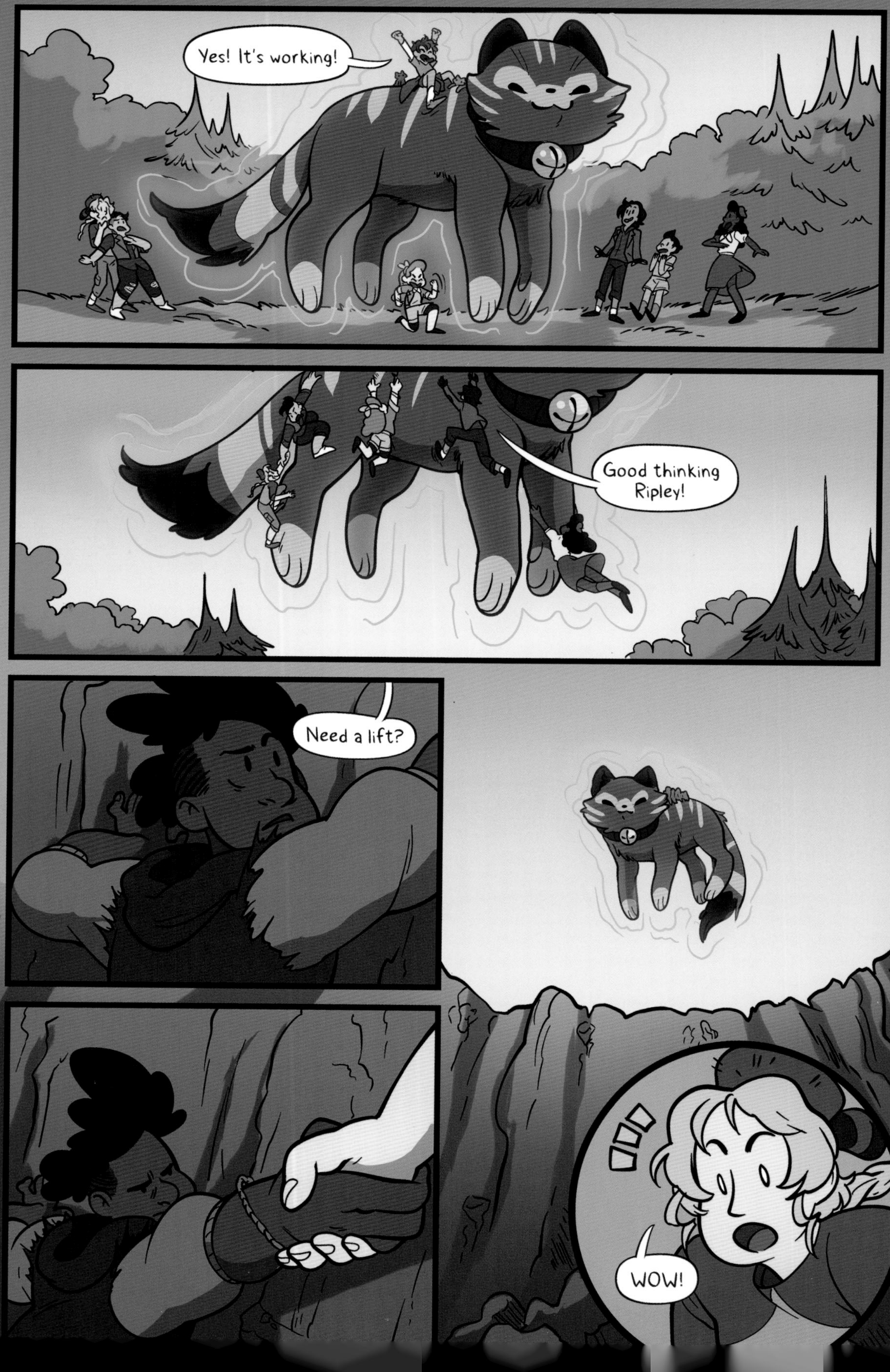
Yes! It's working!
Good thinking Ripley!
Need a lift?
WOW!

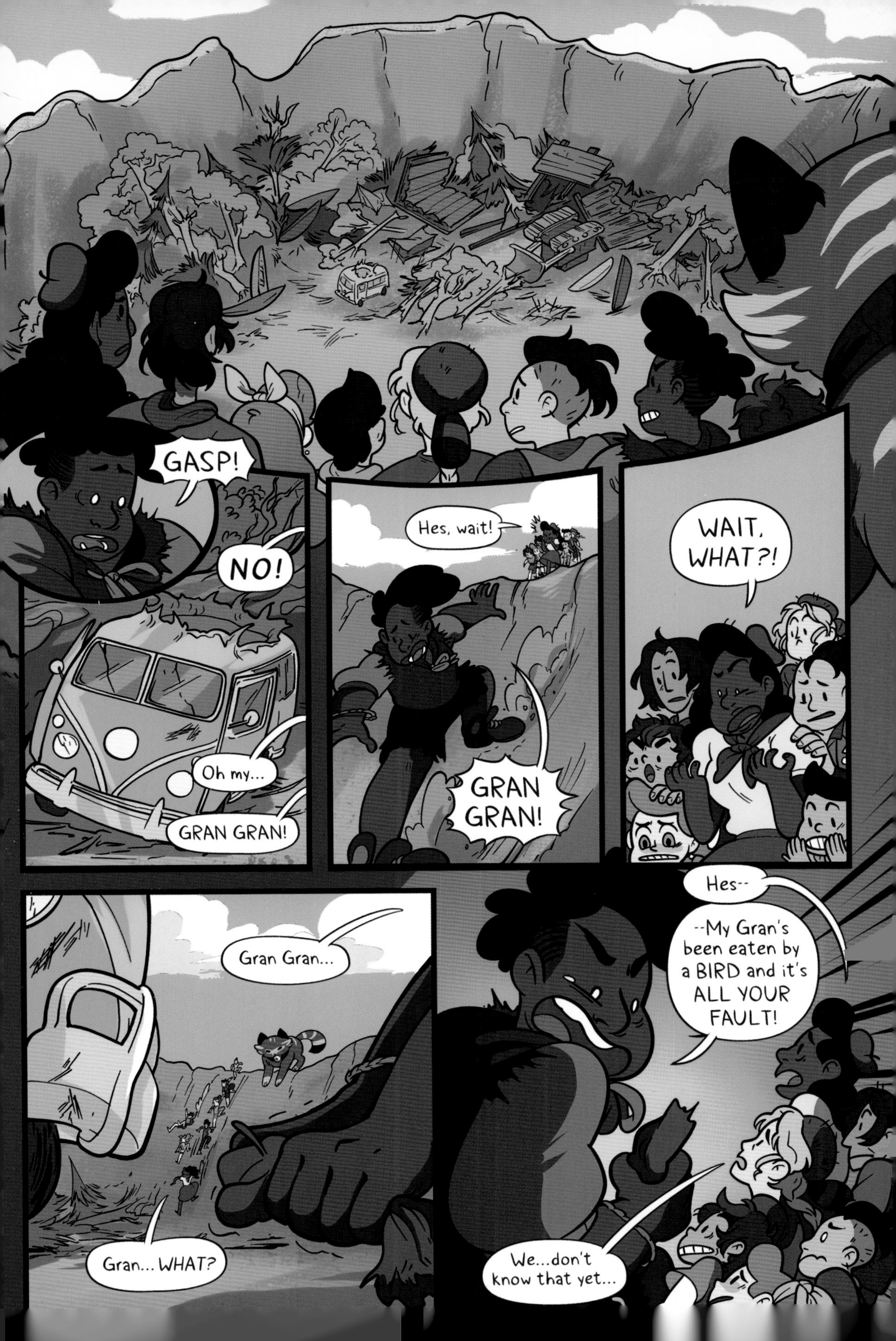
GASP!
NO!
Oh my...
GRAN GRAN!
Hes, wait!
GRAN GRAN!
WAIT, WHAT?!
Gran Gran...
Gran... WHAT?
Hes--
--My Gran's been eaten by a BIRD and it's ALL YOUR FAULT!
We...don't know that yet...

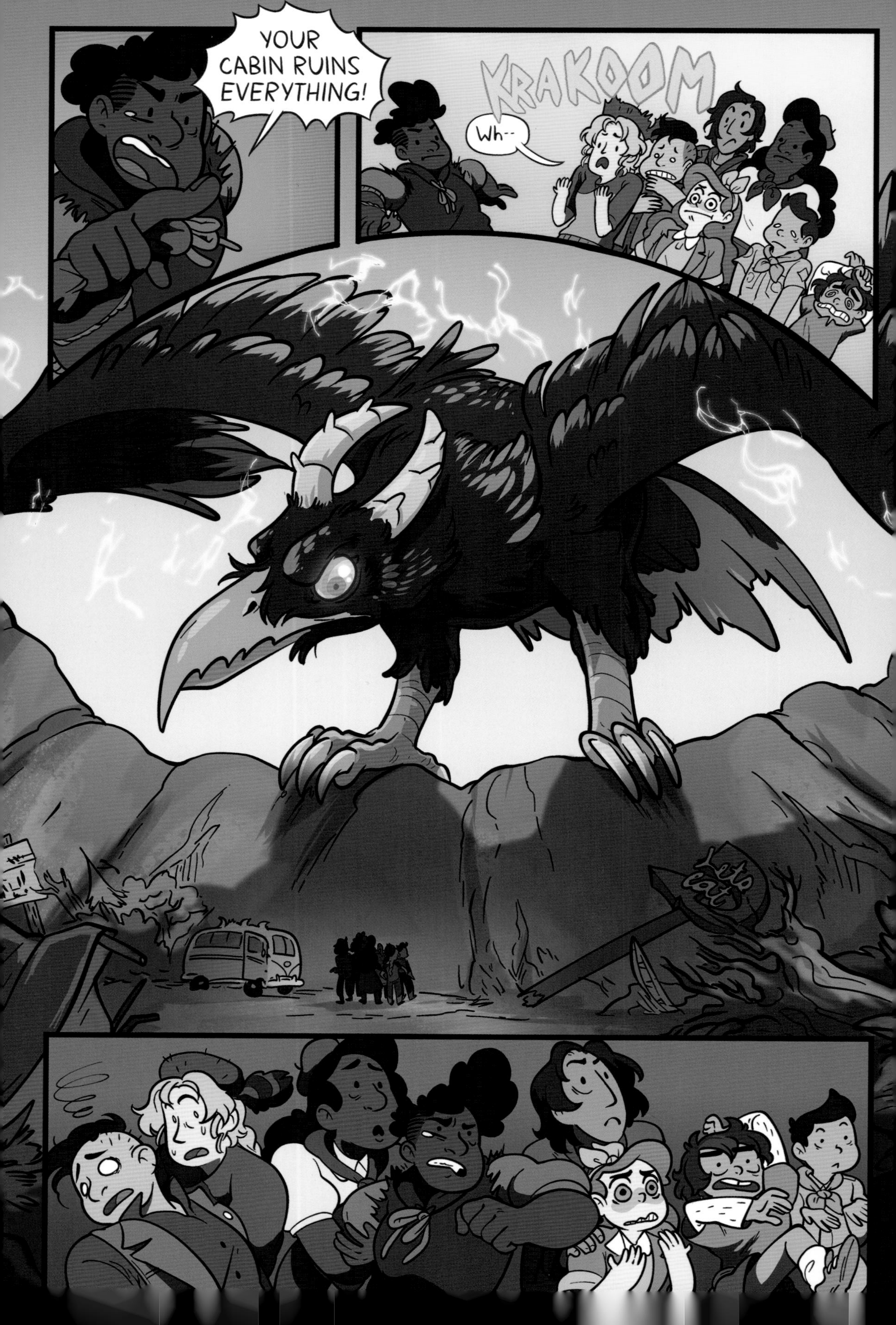

YOUR CABIN RUINS EVERYTHING!
KRAKOOM
Wh--
Lets eat

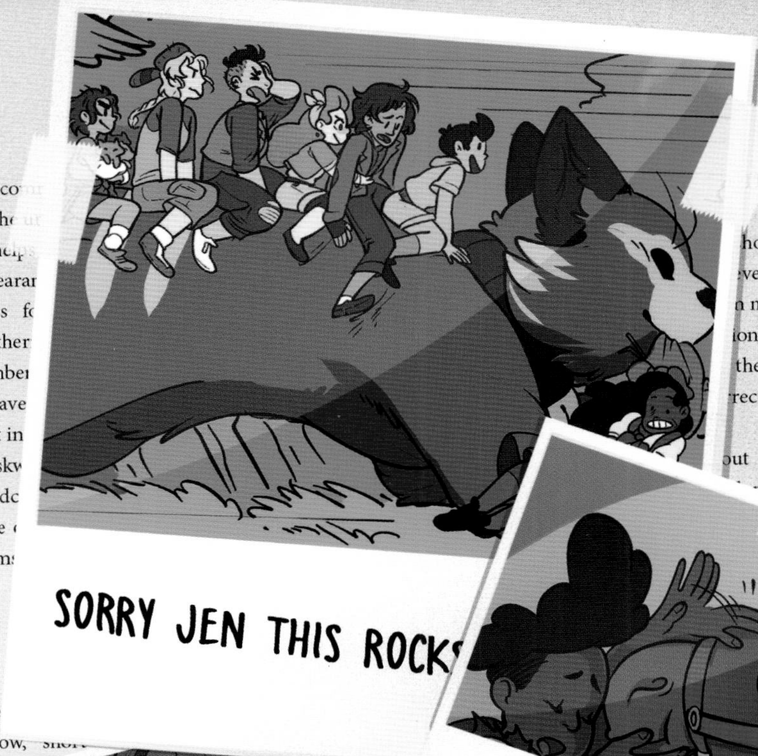
SORRY JEN THIS ROCKS

will com

The

It help

appearar

dress fo

Further

Lumber

to have

part in

Thiskw

Hardc

have

thems

HE UNIFORM

hould be worn at camp events when Lumberjanes n may also be worn at other ions. It should be worn as a the uniform dress with rrect shoes, and stocking or

out grows her uniform or ter Lumberjane. a she has her her

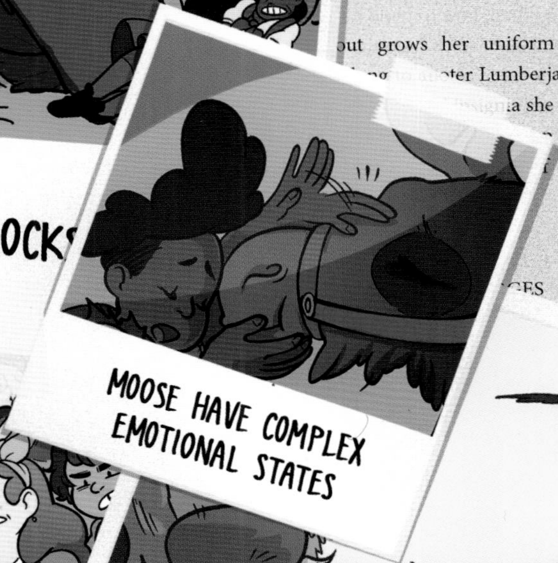
MOOSE HAVE COMPLEX
EMOTIONAL STATES

The yellow, emb the w choose slacks, made o out-of-do green bere the colla Shoes ma heels, rou ings or socks shou ith the shoes or wi the uniform. Ne bracelets, or other jewelry do belong with a Lumberjane uniform.

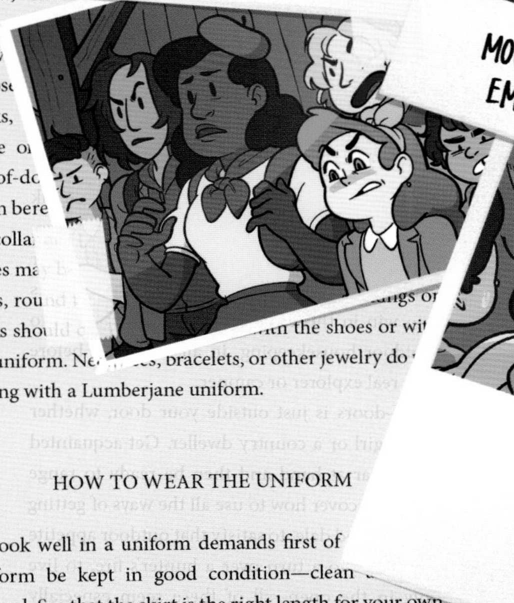

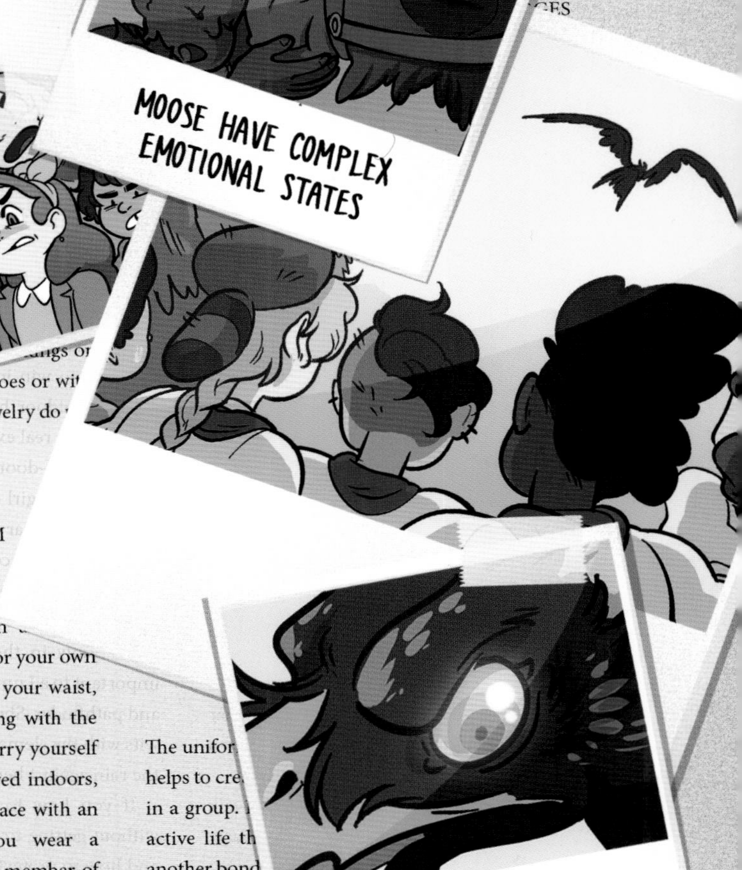

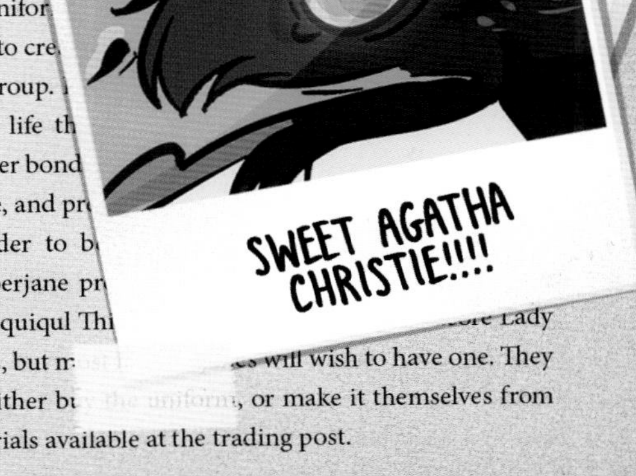
SWEET AGATHA
CHRISTIE!!!!

HOW TO WEAR THE UNIFORM

To look well in a uniform demands first of uniform be kept in good condition—clean a pressed. See that the skirt is the right length for your own height and build, that the belt is adjusted to your waist, that your shoes and stockings are in keeping with the uniform, that you watch your posture and carry yourself with dignity and grace. If the beret is removed indoors, be sure that your hair is neat and kept in place with an insonspicuous clip or ribbon. When you wear a Lumberjane uniform you are identified as a member of this organization and you should be doubly careful to conduct yourself in a way that will show everyone that courtesy and thoughtfullness are part of being a Lumberjane. People are likely to judge a whole nation by the selfishness of a few individuals, to criticize a whole family because of the misconduct of one member, and to feel unkindly toward and organization because of the

The unifor helps to cre in a group. active life th another bond future, and pr in order to b Lumberjane pr Penniquiqul Thi ore Lady Types, but m will wish to have one. They can either bu uniform, or make it themselves from materials available at the trading post.

LUMBERJANES FIELD MANUAL

CHAPTER TWENTY-SEVEN

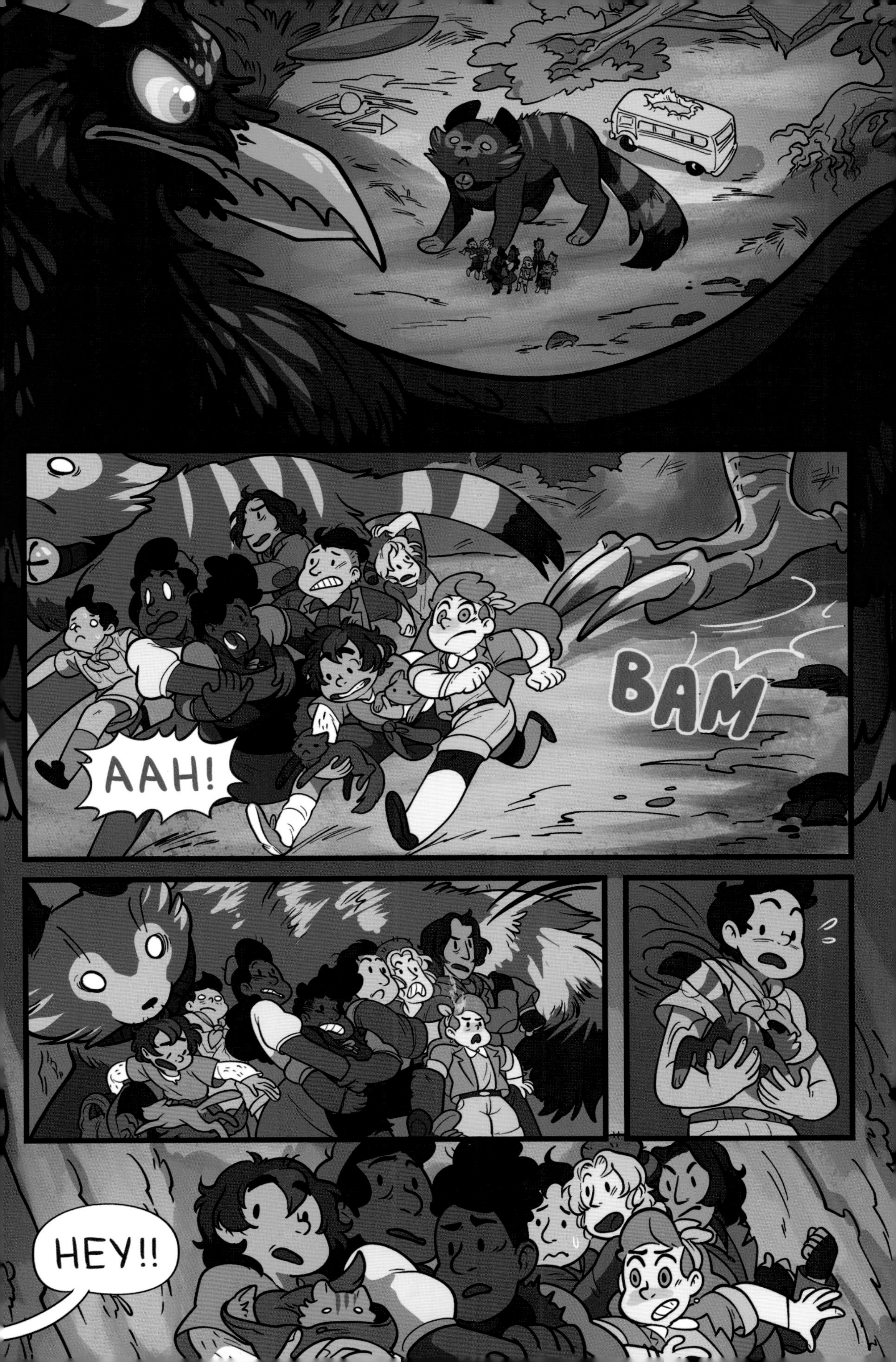

BAM
AAH!
HEY!!

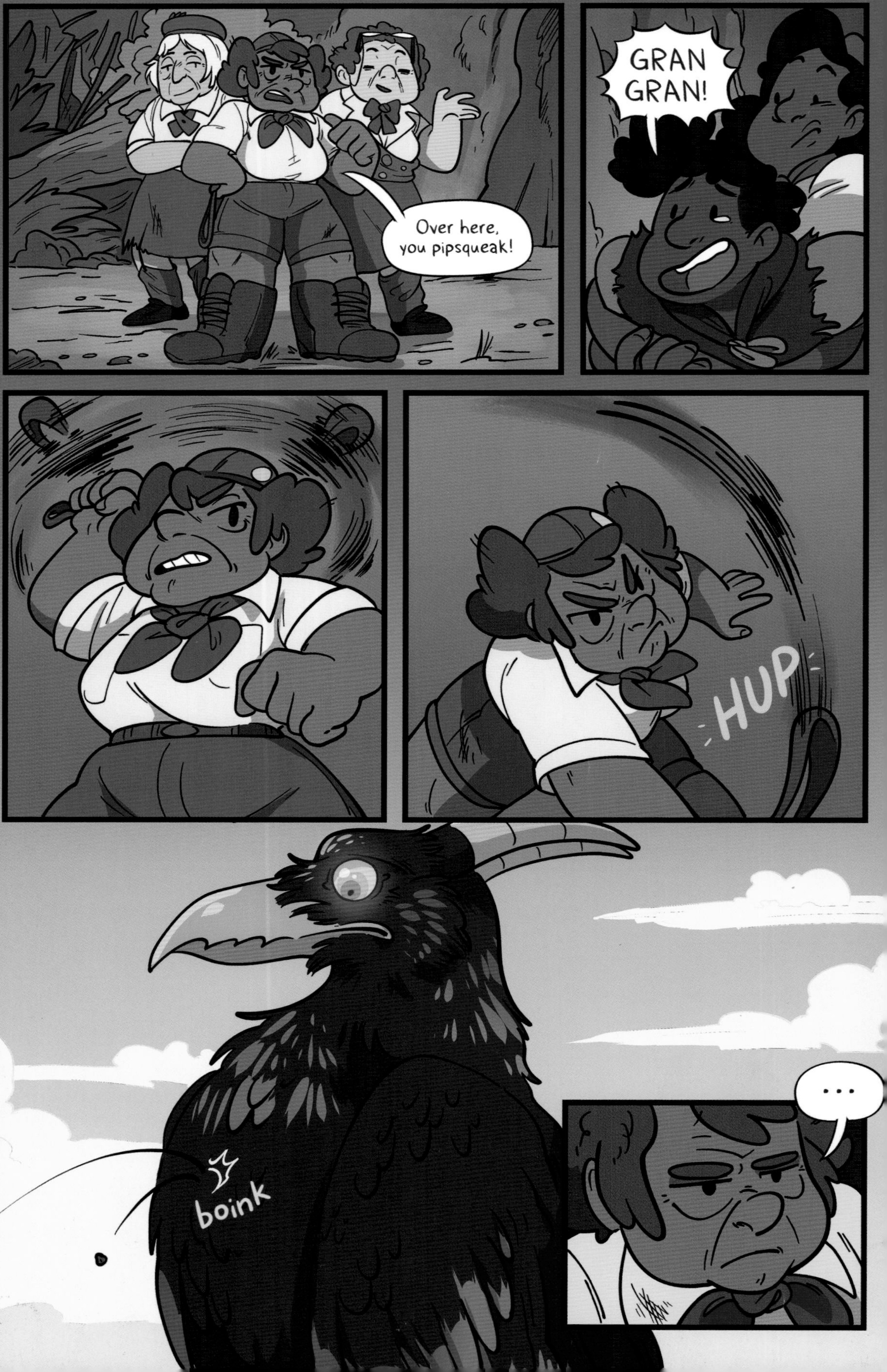
Over here,
you pipsqueak!
GRAN
GRAN!
HUP
boink
...

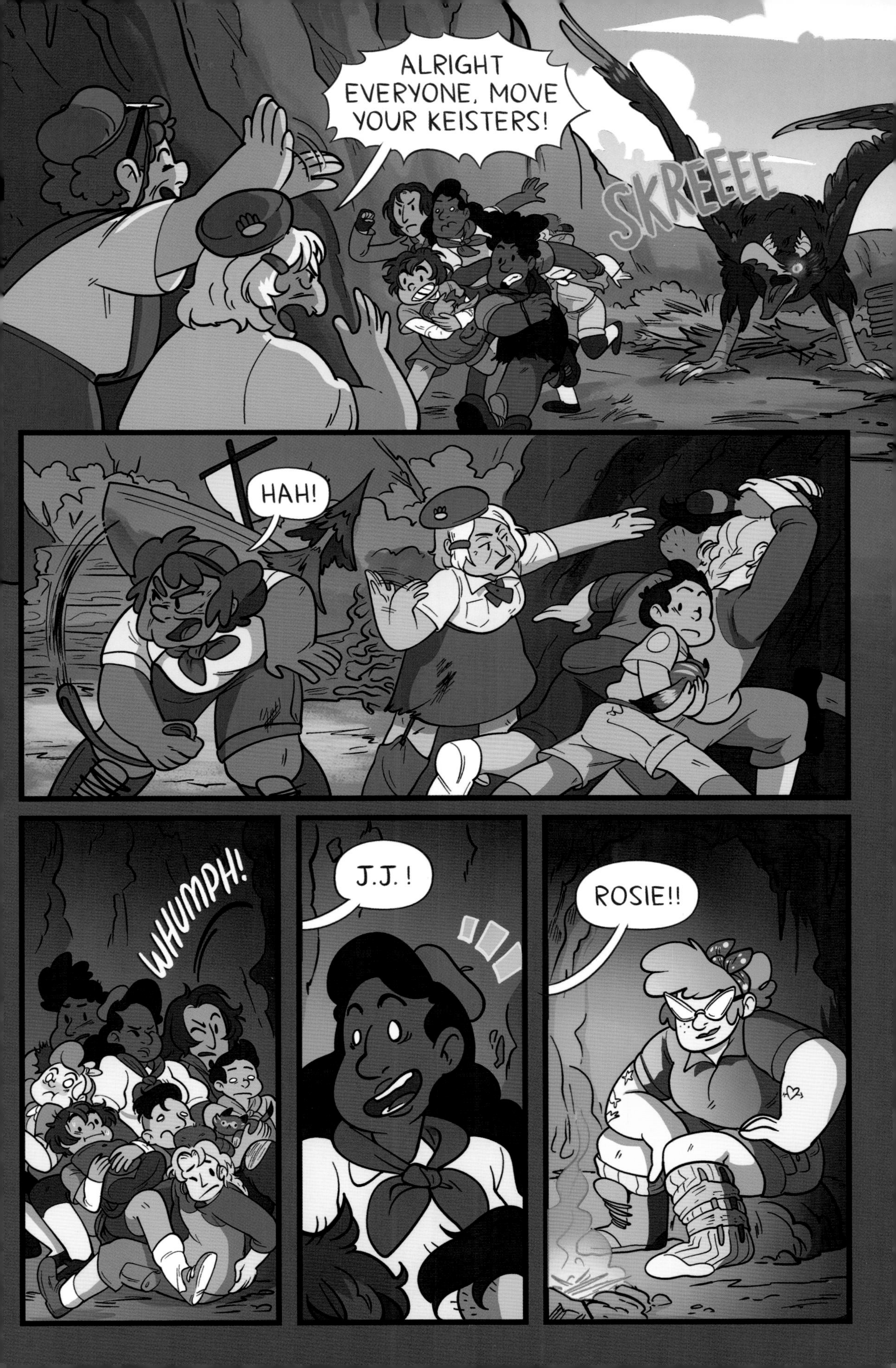
ALRIGHT EVERYONE, MOVE YOUR KEISTERS!
SKREEEE
HAH!
WHUMPH!
J.J.!
ROSIE!!

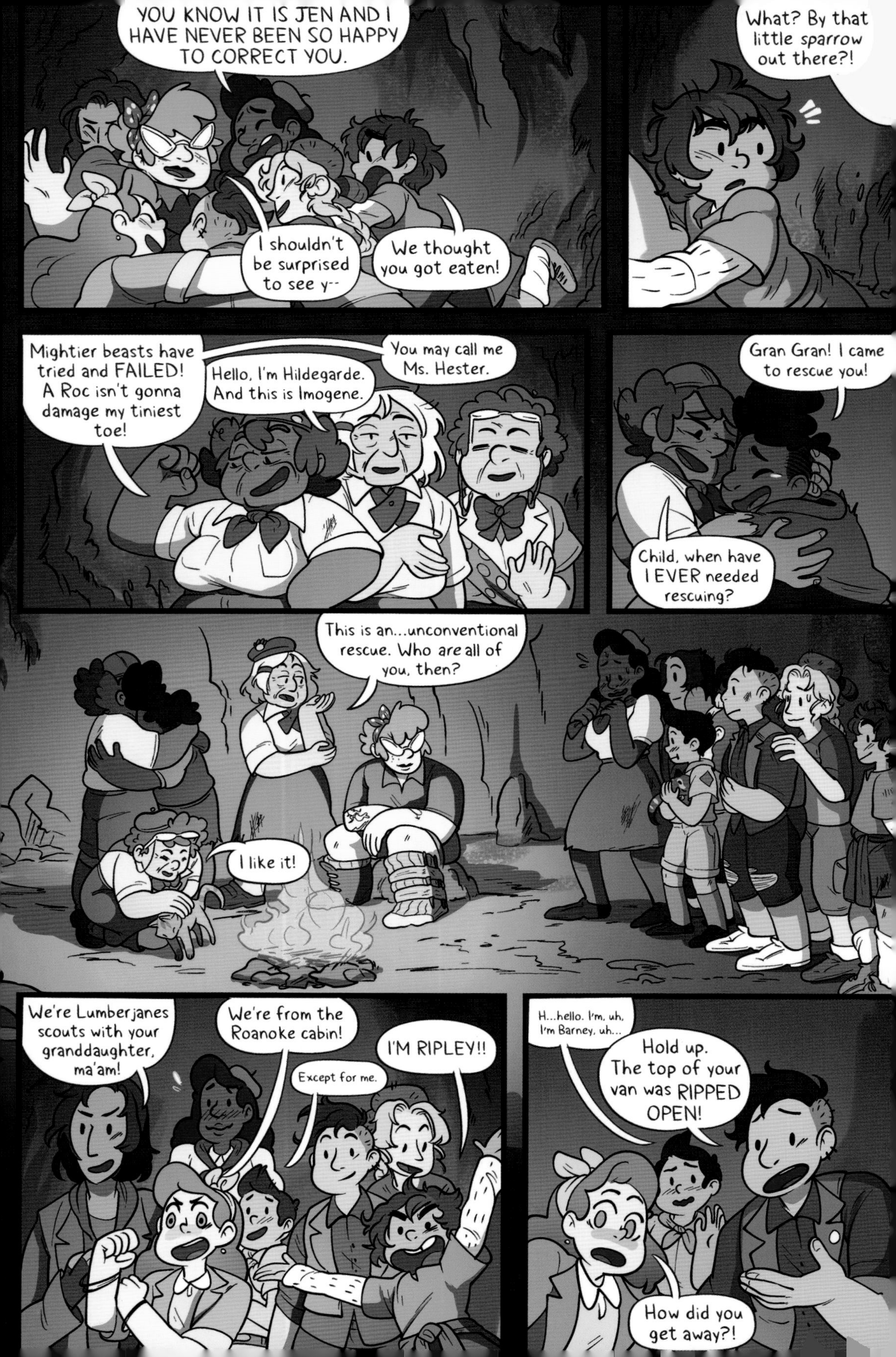
YOU KNOW IT IS JEN AND I HAVE NEVER BEEN SO HAPPY TO CORRECT YOU.
I shouldn't be surprised to see y--
We thought you got eaten!
What? By that little sparrow out there?!
Mightier beasts have tried and FAILED! A Roc isn't gonna damage my tiniest toe!
Hello, I'm Hildegarde. And this is Imogene.
You may call me Ms. Hester.
Gran Gran! I came to rescue you!
Child, when have I EVER needed rescuing?
This is an...unconventional rescue. Who are all of you, then?
I like it!
We're Lumberjanes scouts with your granddaughter, ma'am!
We're from the Roanoke cabin!
Except for me.
I'M RIPLEY!!
H...hello. I'm, uh, I'm Barney, uh...
Hold up. The top of your van was RIPPED OPEN!
How did you get away?!

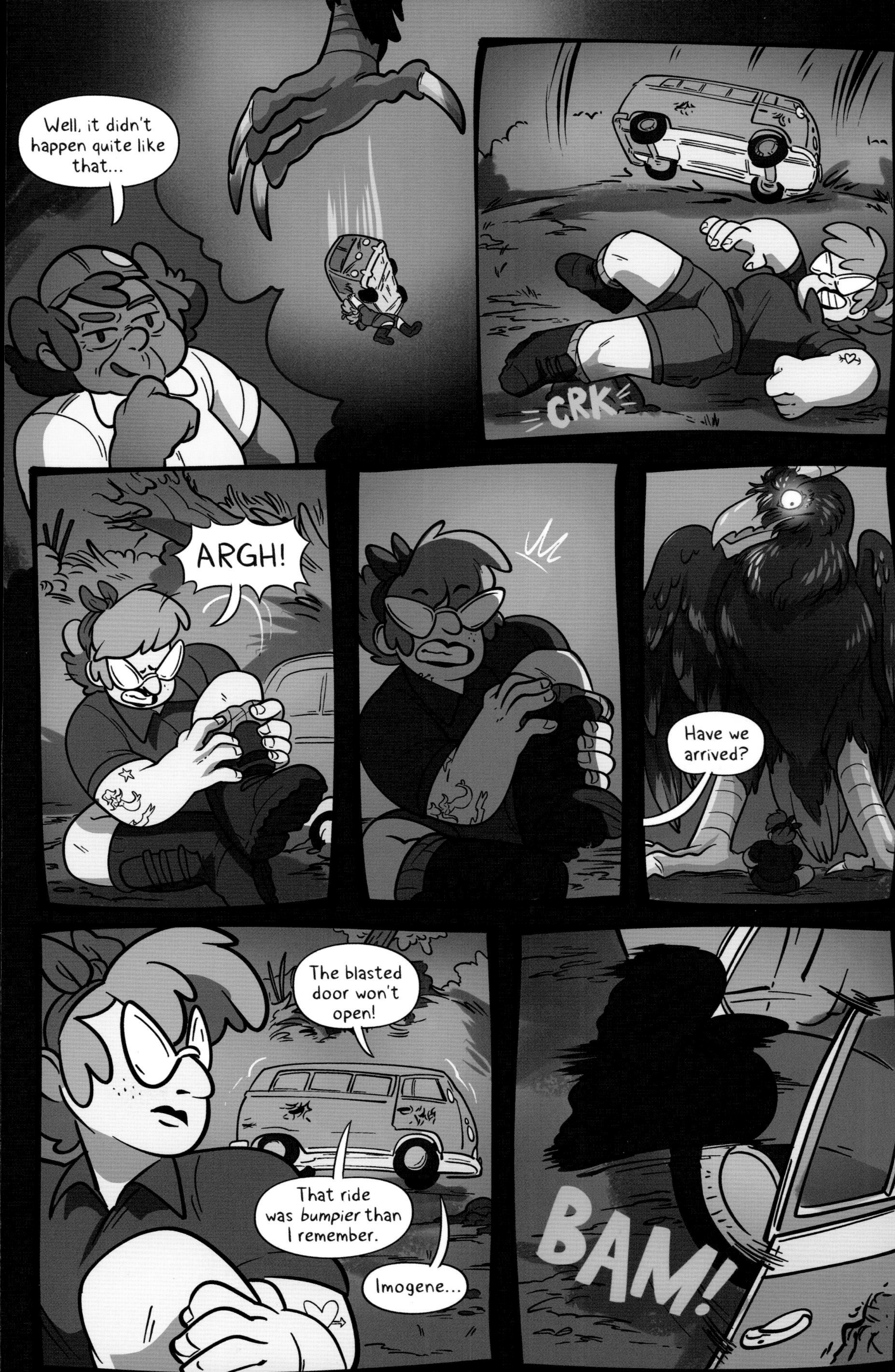
Well, it didn't happen quite like that...
CRK
ARGH!
Have we arrived?
The blasted door won't open!
That ride was *bumpier* than I remember.
Imogene...
BAM!

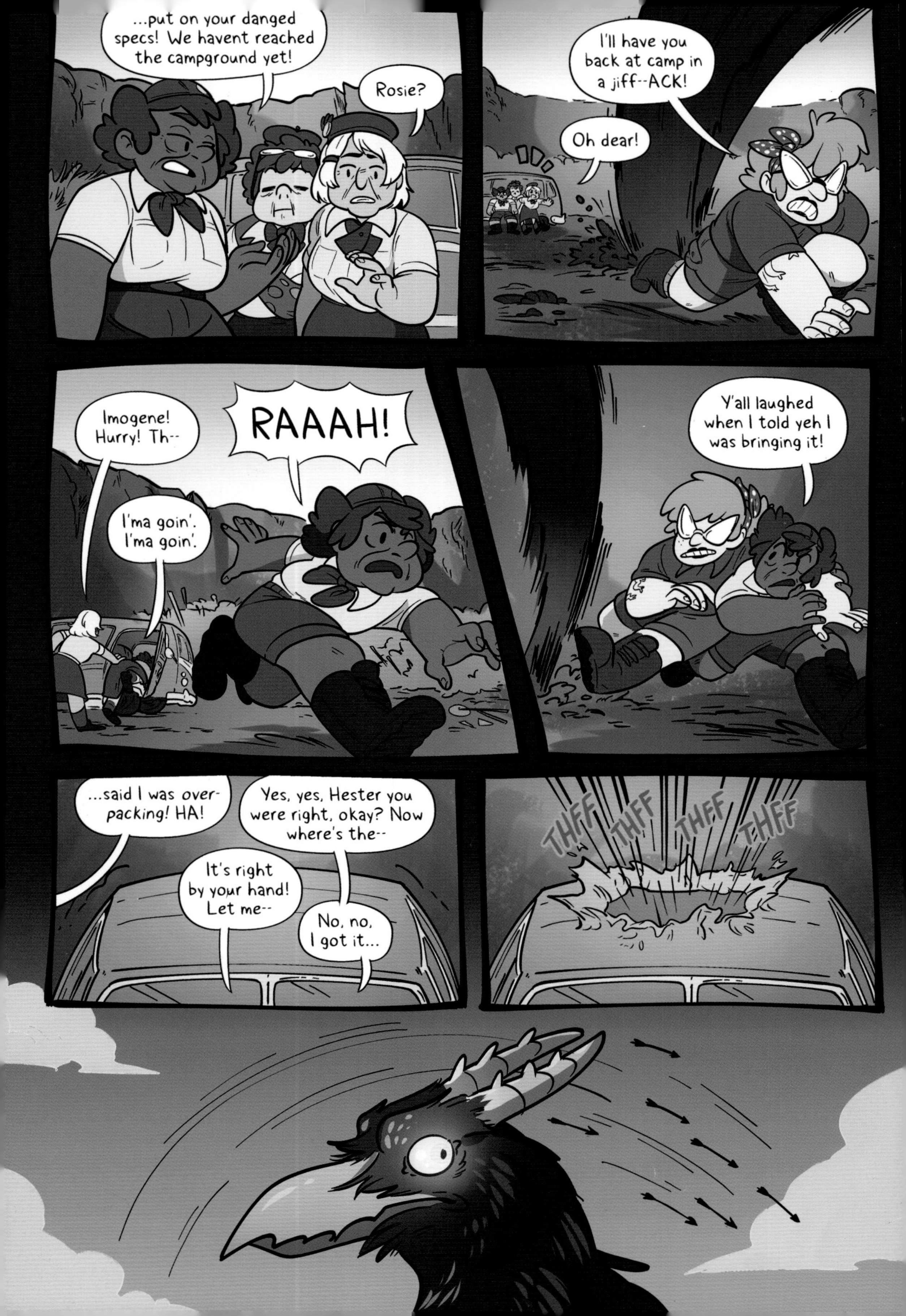
...put on your danged specs! We havent reached the campground yet!
Rosie?
I'll have you back at camp in a jiff--ACK!
Oh dear!
Imogene! Hurry! Th--
RAAAH!
I'ma goin'. I'ma goin'.
Y'all laughed when I told yeh I was bringing it!
...said I was over-packing! HA!
Yes, yes, Hester you were right, okay? Now where's the--
It's right by your hand! Let me--
No, no, I got it...
THFF THFF THFF THFF

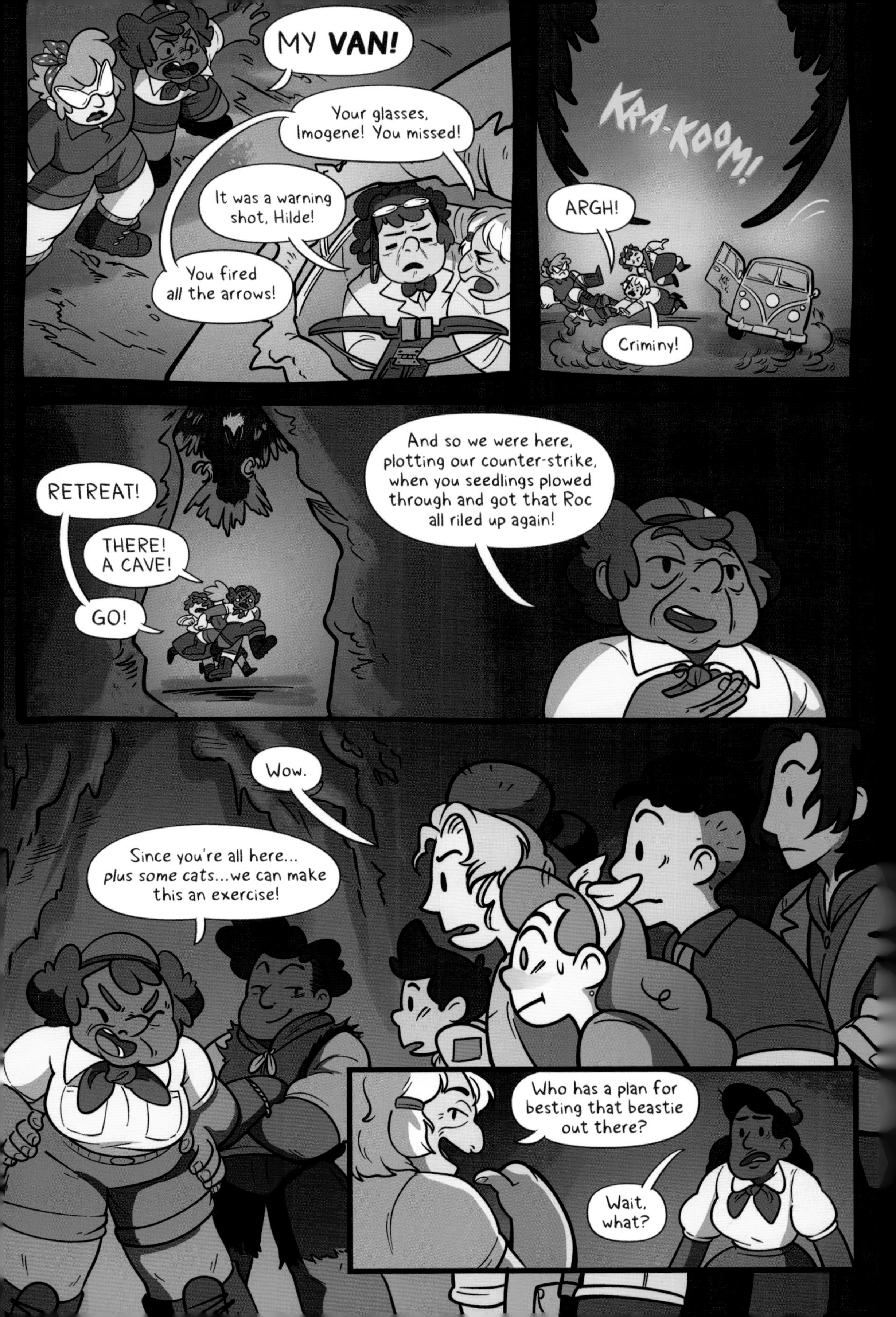

MY VAN!
Your glasses, Imogene! You missed!
It was a warning shot, Hilde!
You fired all the arrows!
KRA-KOOM!
ARGH!
Criminy!
RETREAT!
THERE! A CAVE!
GO!
And so we were here, plotting our counter-strike, when you seedlings plowed through and got that Roc all riled up again!
Wow.
Since you're all here... plus some cats...we can make this an exercise!
Who has a plan for besting that beastie out there?
Wait, what?

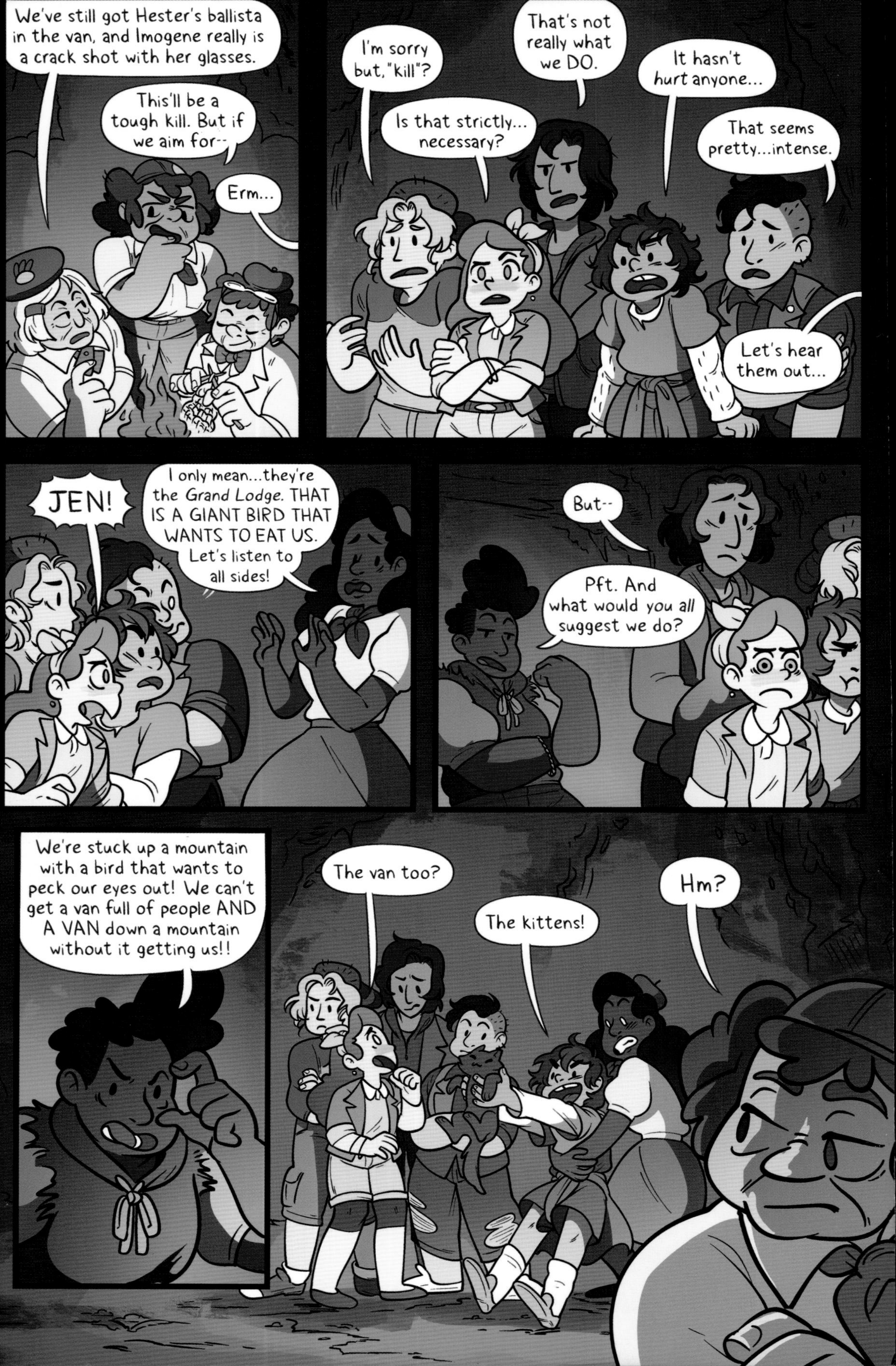
We've still got Hester's ballista in the van, and Imogene really is a crack shot with her glasses.
This'll be a tough kill. But if we aim for--
Erm...
I'm sorry but, "kill"?
Is that strictly... necessary?
That's not really what we DO.
It hasn't *hurt* anyone...
That seems pretty...intense.
Let's hear them out...
JEN!
I only mean...they're the *Grand Lodge*. THAT IS A GIANT BIRD THAT WANTS TO EAT US. Let's listen to all sides!
But--
Pft. And what would *you all* suggest we do?
We're stuck up a mountain with a bird that wants to peck our eyes out! We can't get a van full of people AND A VAN down a mountain without it getting us!!
The van too?
The kittens!
Hm?

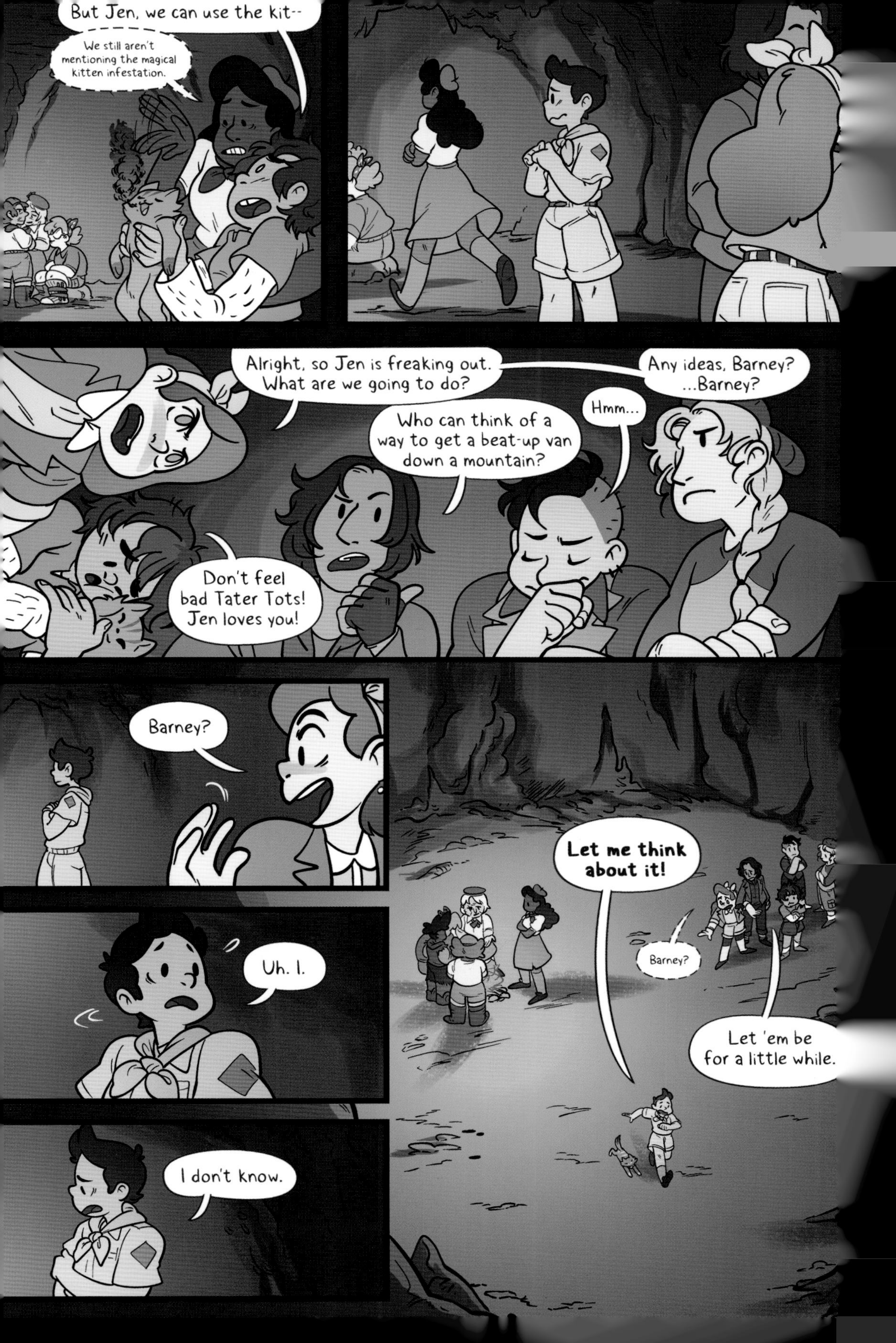
But Jen, we can use the kit--
We still aren't mentioning the magical kitten infestation.
Alright, so Jen is freaking out. What are we going to do?
Any ideas, Barney? ...Barney?
Who can think of a way to get a beat-up van down a mountain?
Hmm...
Don't feel bad Tater Tots! Jen loves you!
Barney?
Uh. I.
I don't know.
Let me think about it!
Barney?
Let 'em be for a little while.

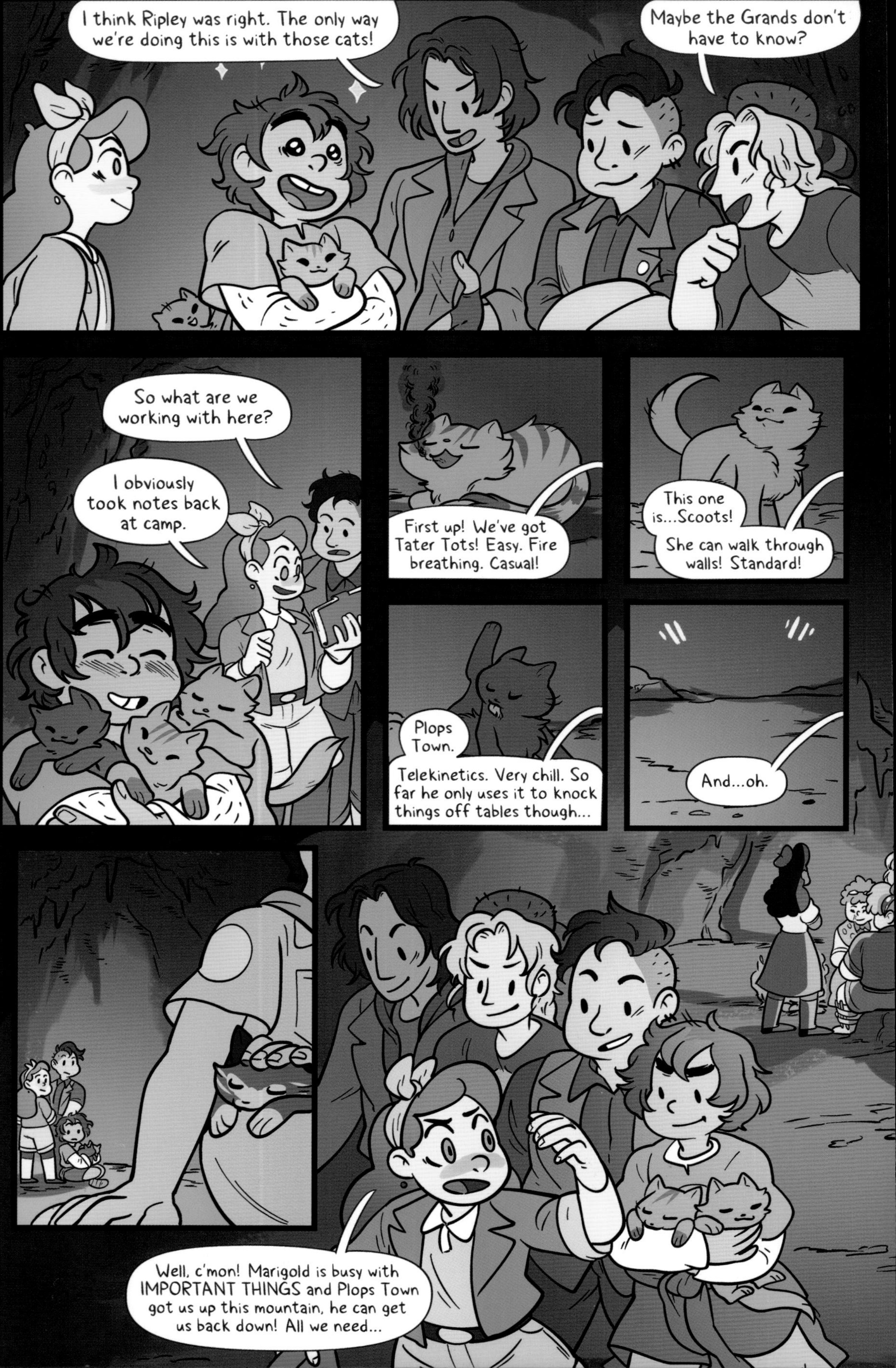
I think Ripley was right. The only way we're doing this is with those cats!
Maybe the Grands don't have to know?
So what are we working with here?
I obviously took notes back at camp.
First up! We've got Tater Tots! Easy. Fire breathing. Casual!
This one is...Scoots!
She can walk through walls! Standard!
Plops Town.
Telekinetics. Very chill. So far he only uses it to knock things off tables though...
And...oh.
Well, c'mon! Marigold is busy with IMPORTANT THINGS and Plops Town got us up this mountain, he can get us back down! All we need...

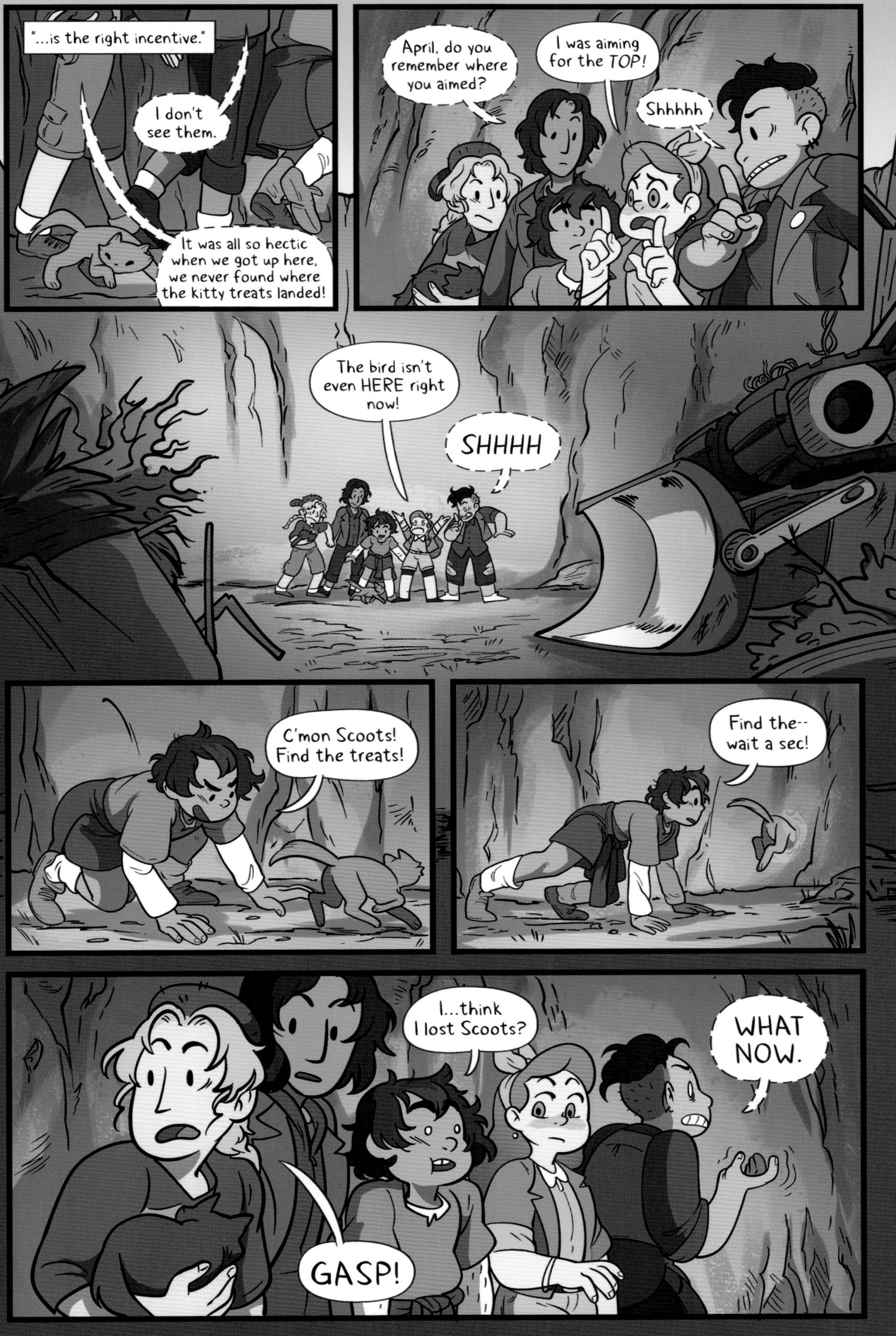
"...is the right incentive."
I don't see them.
It was all so hectic when we got up here, we never found where the kitty treats landed!
April, do you remember where you aimed?
I was aiming for the TOP!
Shhhhh
The bird isn't even HERE right now!
SHHHH
C'mon Scoots! Find the treats!
Find the-- wait a sec!
I...think I lost Scoots?
WHAT NOW.
GASP!

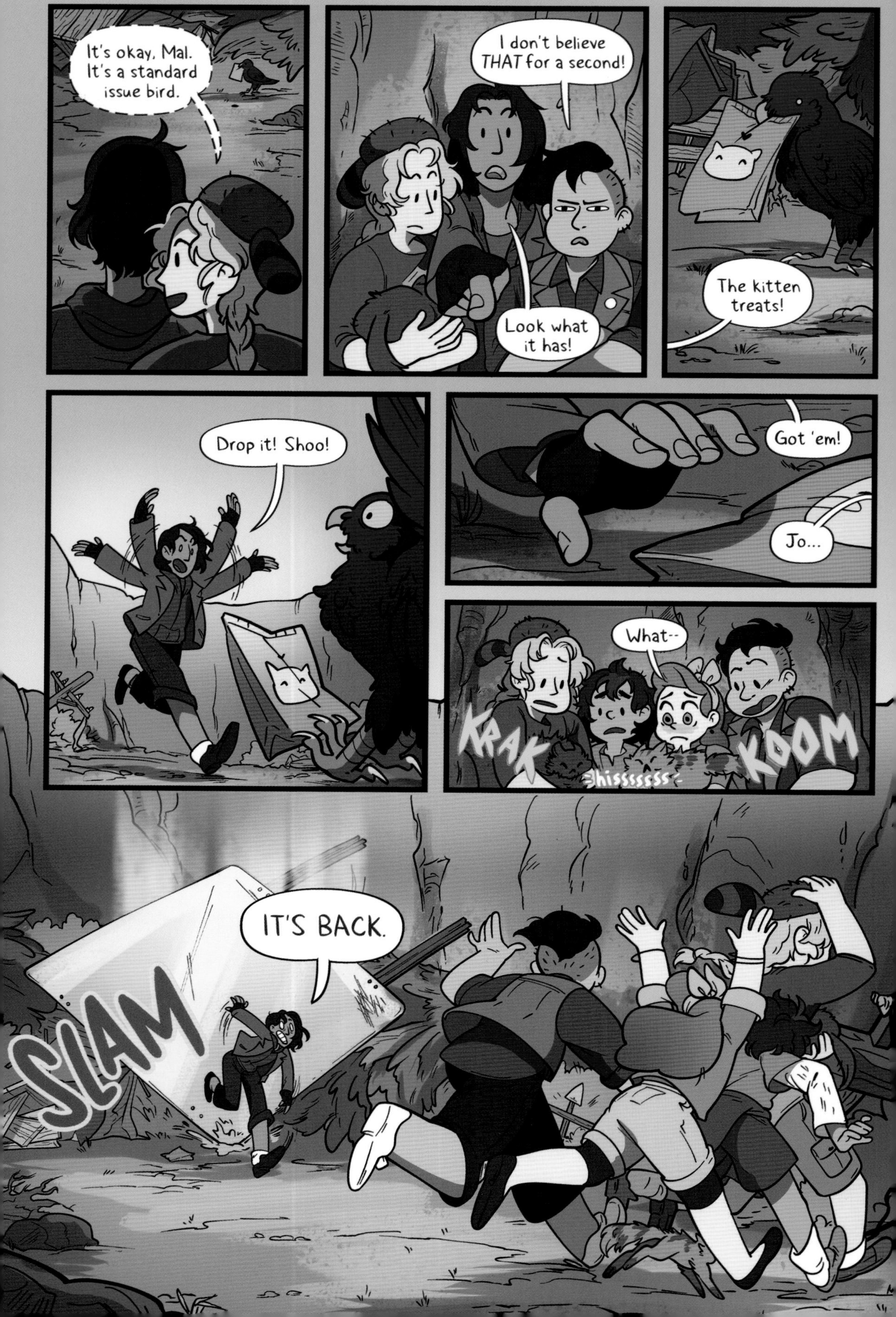
It's okay, Mal. It's a standard issue bird.
I don't believe THAT for a second!
Look what it has!
The kitten treats!
Drop it! Shoo!
Got 'em!
Jo...
What--
KRAK
KOOM
hissssssss
IT'S BACK.
SLAM

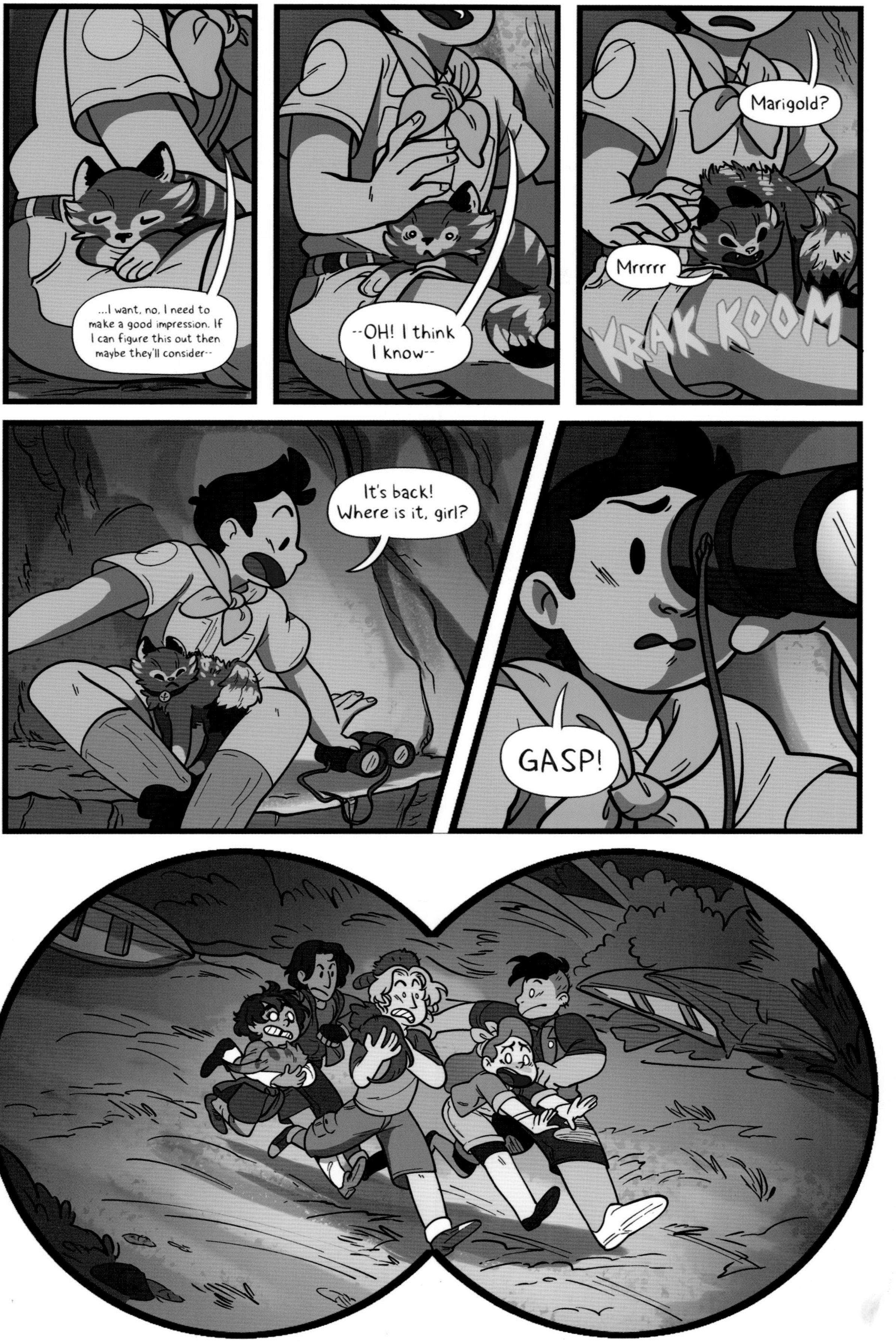
...I want, no, I need to make a good impression. If I can figure this out then maybe they'll consider--
--OH! I think I know--
Marigold?
Mrrrrr
KRAK KOOM
It's back! Where is it, girl?
GASP!

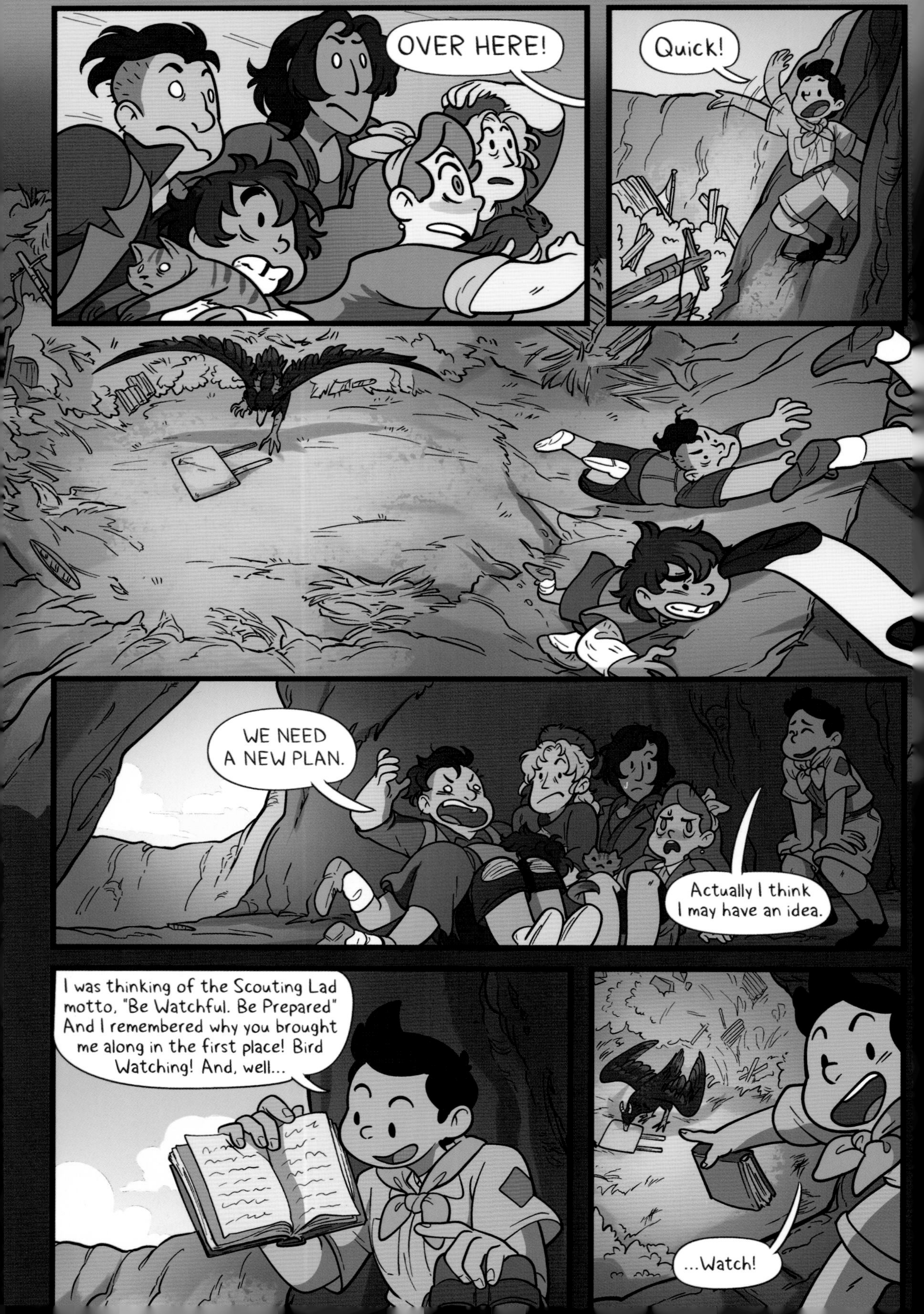
OVER HERE!
Quick!
WE NEED A NEW PLAN.
Actually I think I may have an idea.
I was thinking of the Scouting Lad motto, "Be Watchful. Be Prepared" And I remembered why you brought me along in the first place! Bird Watching! And, well...
...Watch!

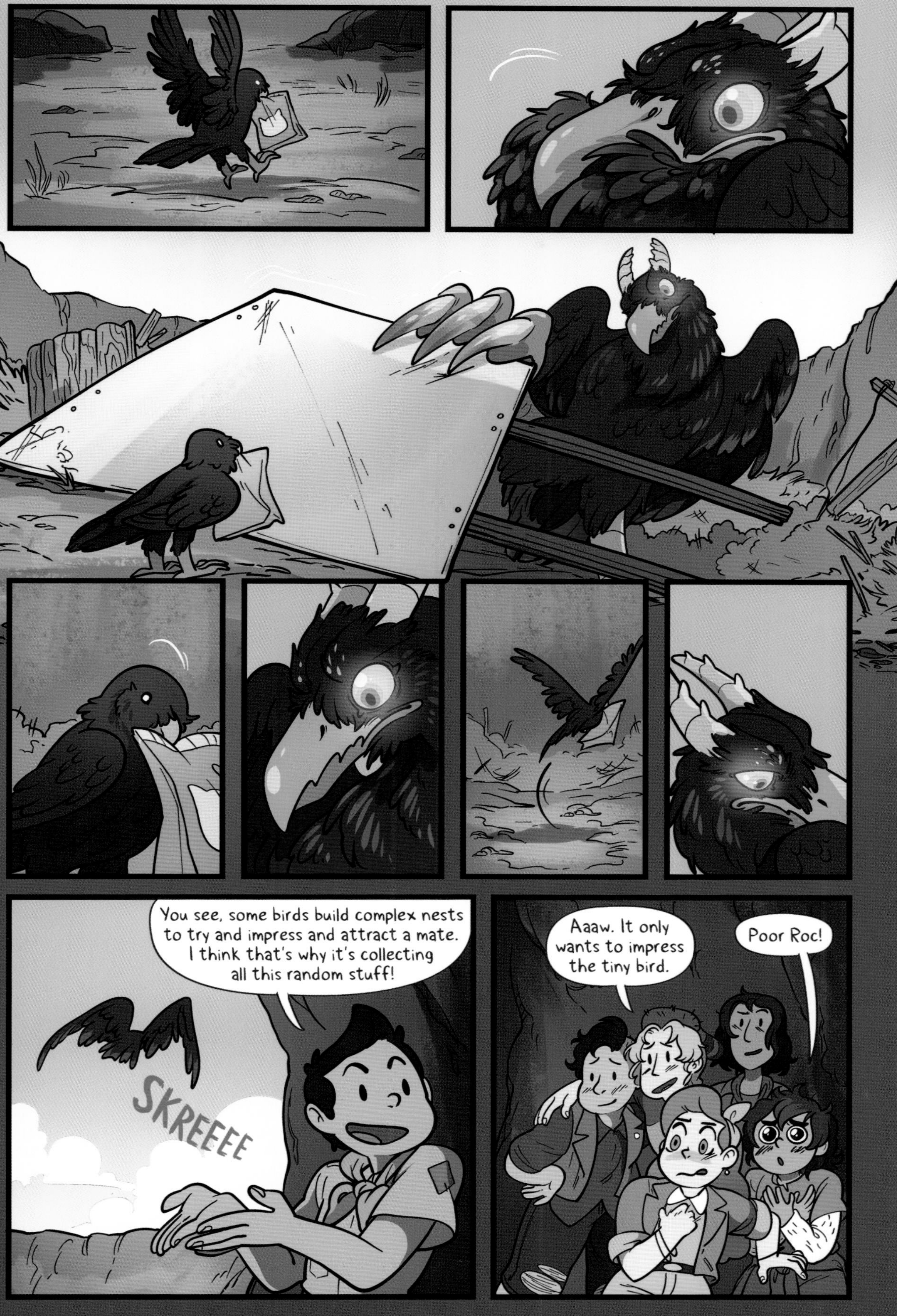
You see, some birds build complex nests to try and impress and attract a mate. I think that's why it's collecting all this random stuff!
SKREEEE
Aaaw. It only wants to impress the tiny bird.
Poor Roc!

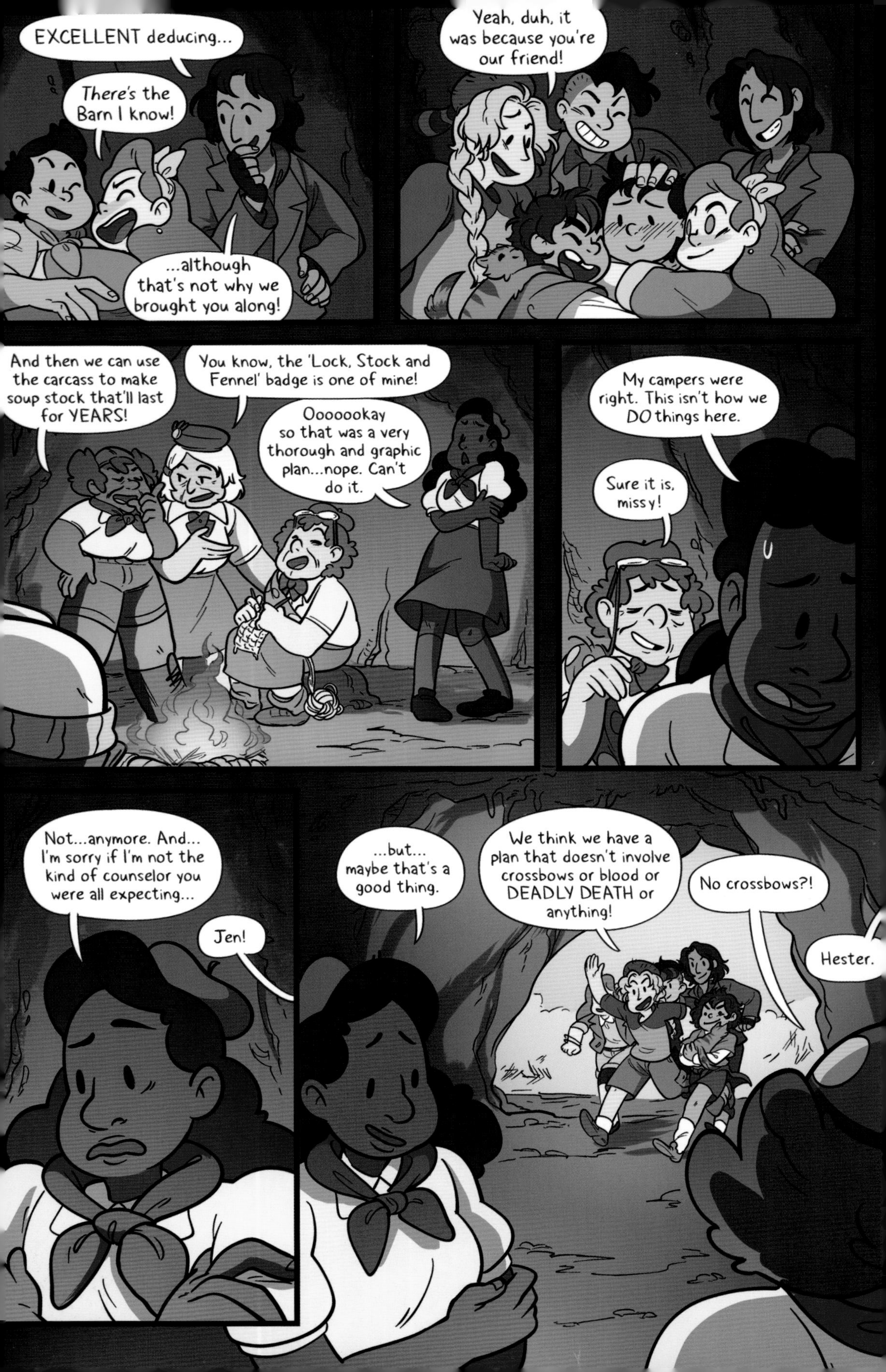
EXCELLENT deducing...
There's the Barn I know!
...although that's not why we brought you along!
Yeah, duh, it was because you're our friend!
And then we can use the carcass to make soup stock that'll last for YEARS!
You know, the 'Lock, Stock and Fennel' badge is one of mine!
Oooooookay so that was a very thorough and graphic plan...nope. Can't do it.
My campers were right. This isn't how we DO things here.
Sure it is, missy!
Not...anymore. And... I'm sorry if I'm not the kind of counselor you were all expecting...
Jen!
...but... maybe that's a good thing.
We think we have a plan that doesn't involve crossbows or blood or DEADLY DEATH or anything!
No crossbows?!
Hester.

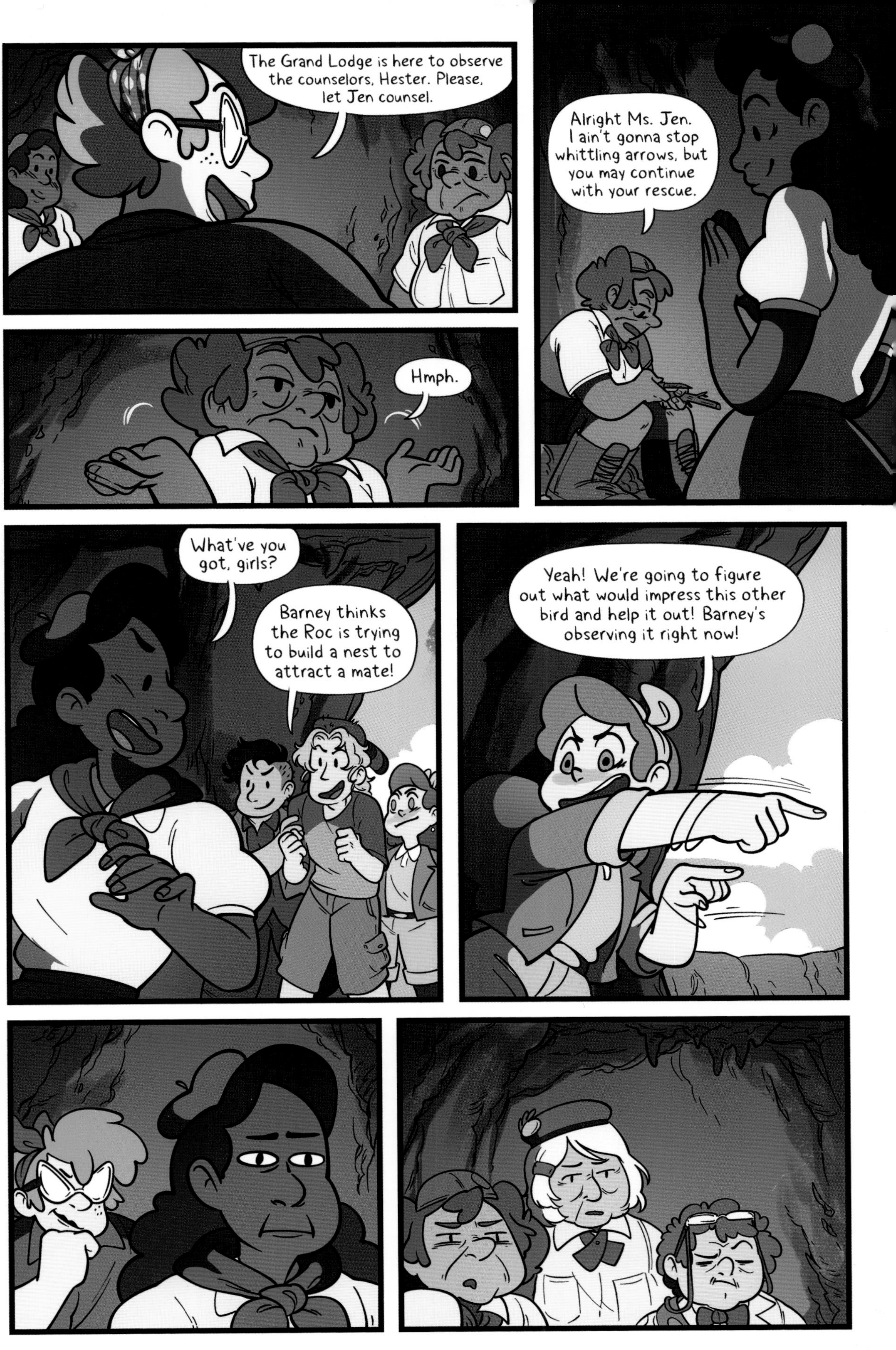
The Grand Lodge is here to observe the counselors, Hester. Please, let Jen counsel.
Hmph.
Alright Ms. Jen. I ain't gonna stop whittling arrows, but you may continue with your rescue.
What've you got, girls?
Barney thinks the Roc is trying to build a nest to attract a mate!
Yeah! We're going to figure out what would impress this other bird and help it out! Barney's observing it right now!

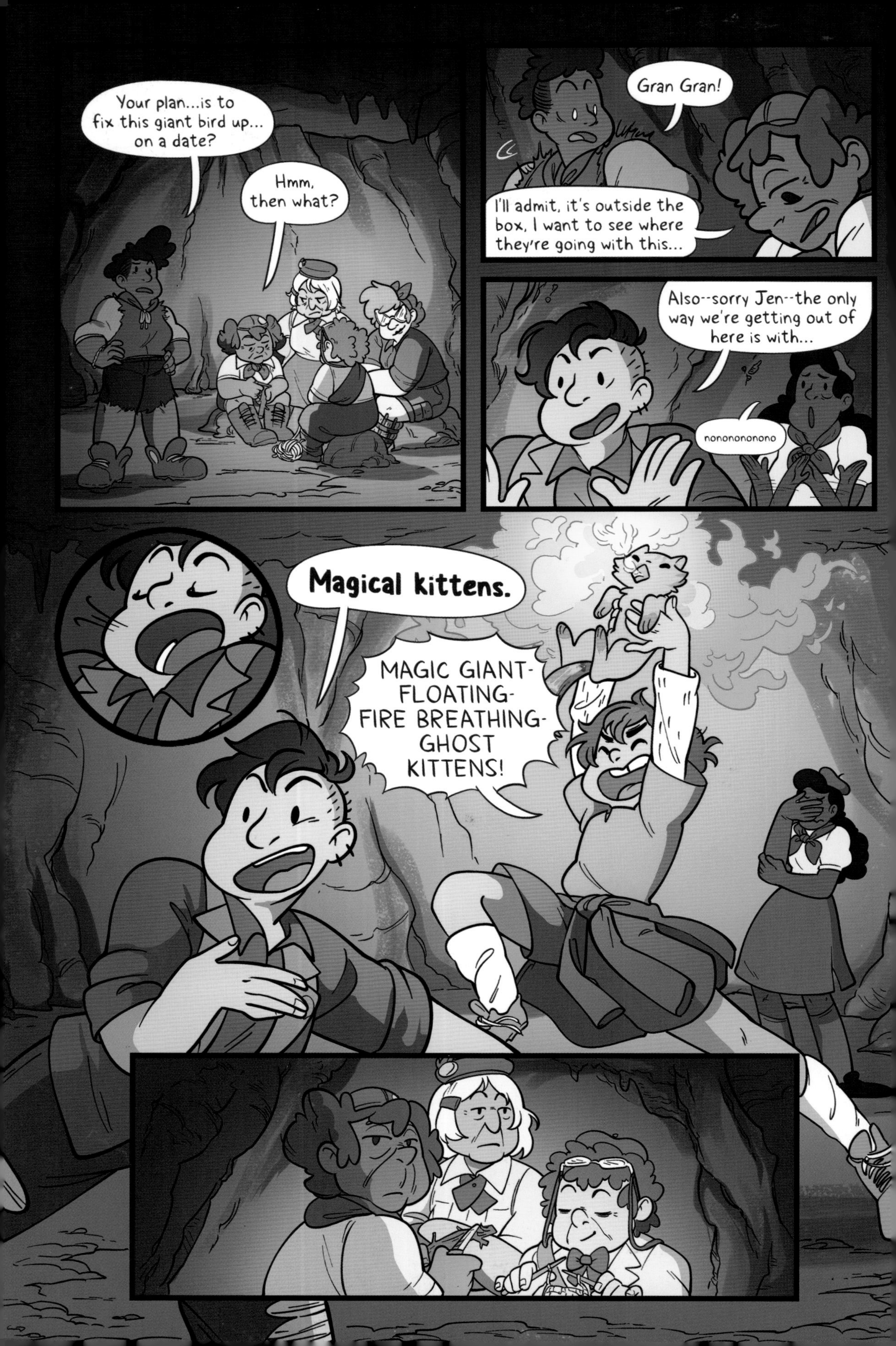
Your plan...is to fix this giant bird up... on a date?
Hmm, then what?
Gran Gran!
I'll admit, it's outside the box, I want to see where they're going with this...
Also--sorry Jen--the only way we're getting out of here is with...
nononononono
Magical kittens.
MAGIC GIANT-FLOATING-FIRE BREATHING-GHOST KITTENS!

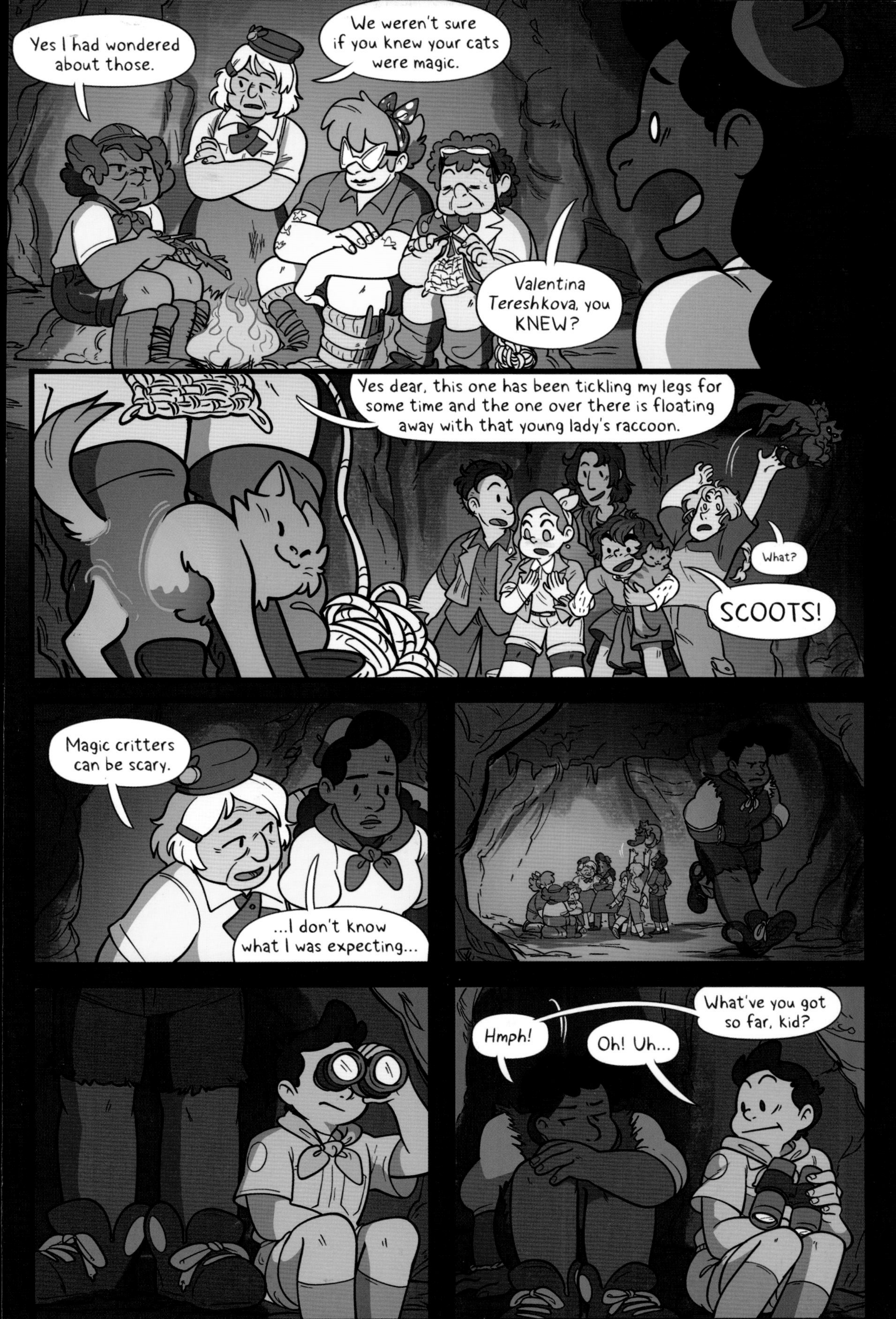
Yes I had wondered about those.
We weren't sure if you knew your cats were magic.
Valentina Tereshkova, you KNEW?
Yes dear, this one has been tickling my legs for some time and the one over there is floating away with that young lady's raccoon.
What?
SCOOTS!
Magic critters can be scary.
...I don't know what I was expecting...
Hmph!
What've you got so far, kid?
Oh! Uh...

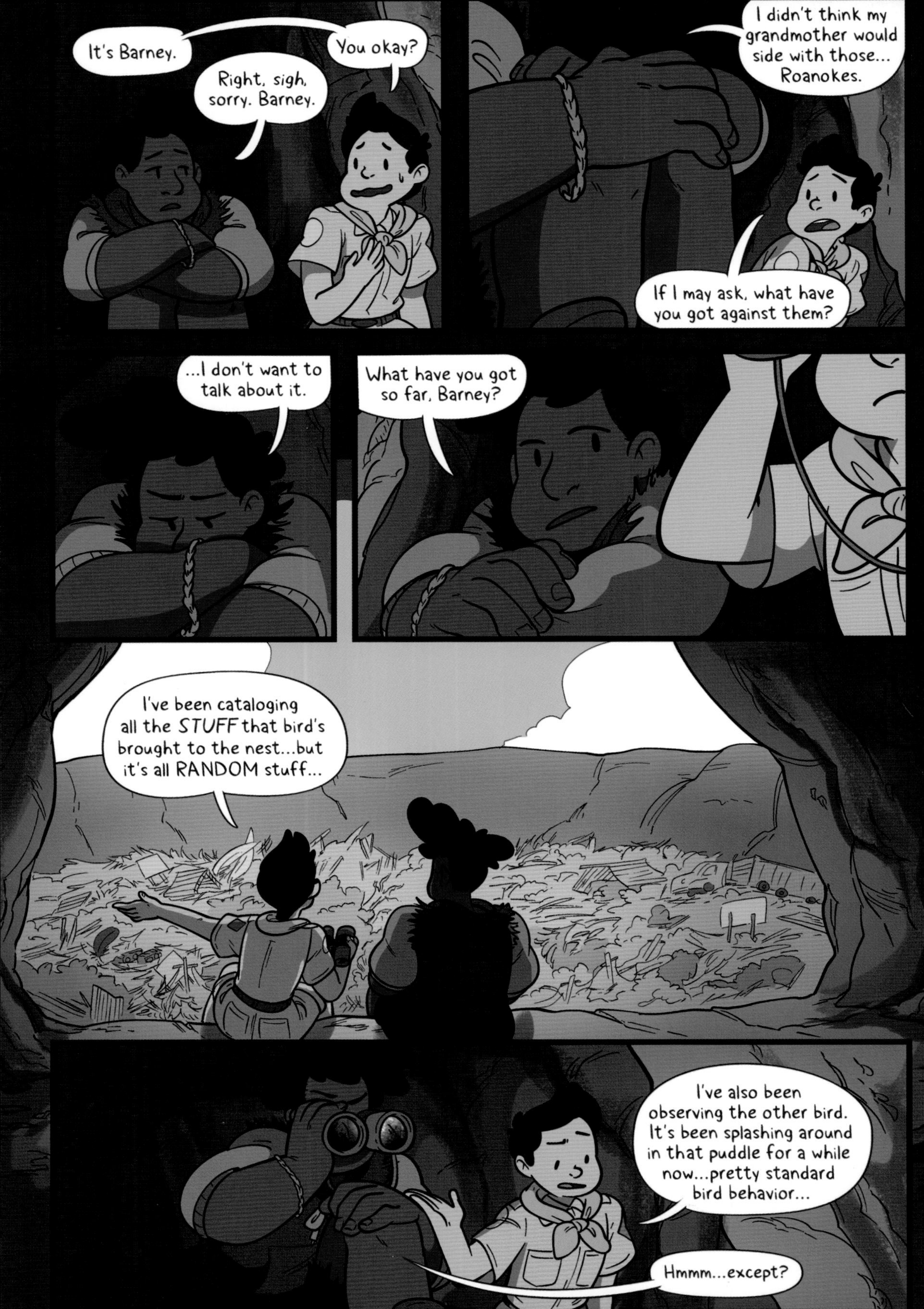
It's Barney.
You okay?
Right, sigh, sorry. Barney.
I didn't think my grandmother would side with those... Roanokes.
If I may ask, what have you got against them?
...I don't want to talk about it.
What have you got so far, Barney?
I've been cataloging all the STUFF that bird's brought to the nest...but it's all RANDOM stuff...
I've also been observing the other bird. It's been splashing around in that puddle for a while now...pretty standard bird behavior...
Hmmm...except?

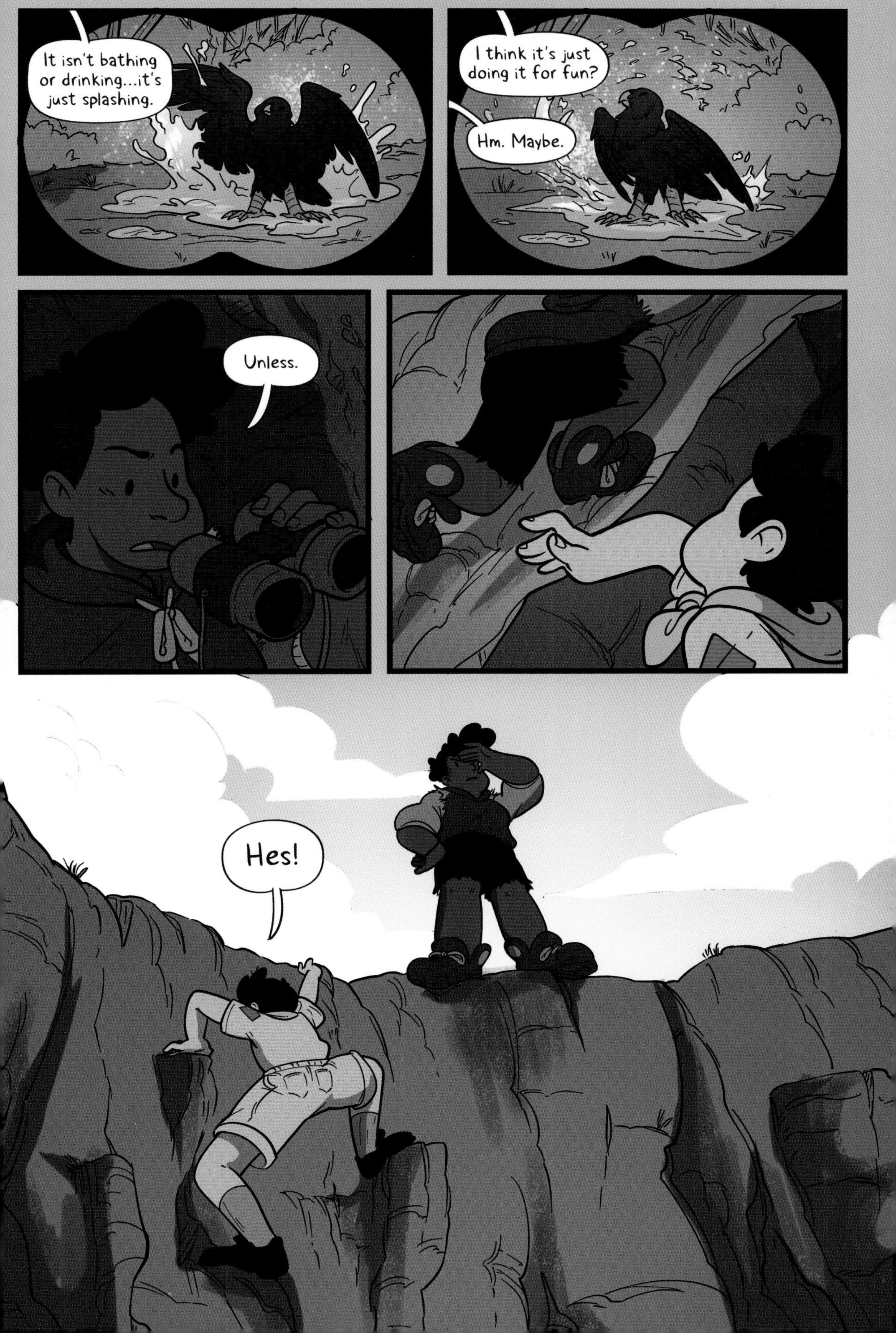
It isn't bathing or drinking...it's just splashing.
I think it's just doing it for fun?
Hm. Maybe.
Unless.
Hes!

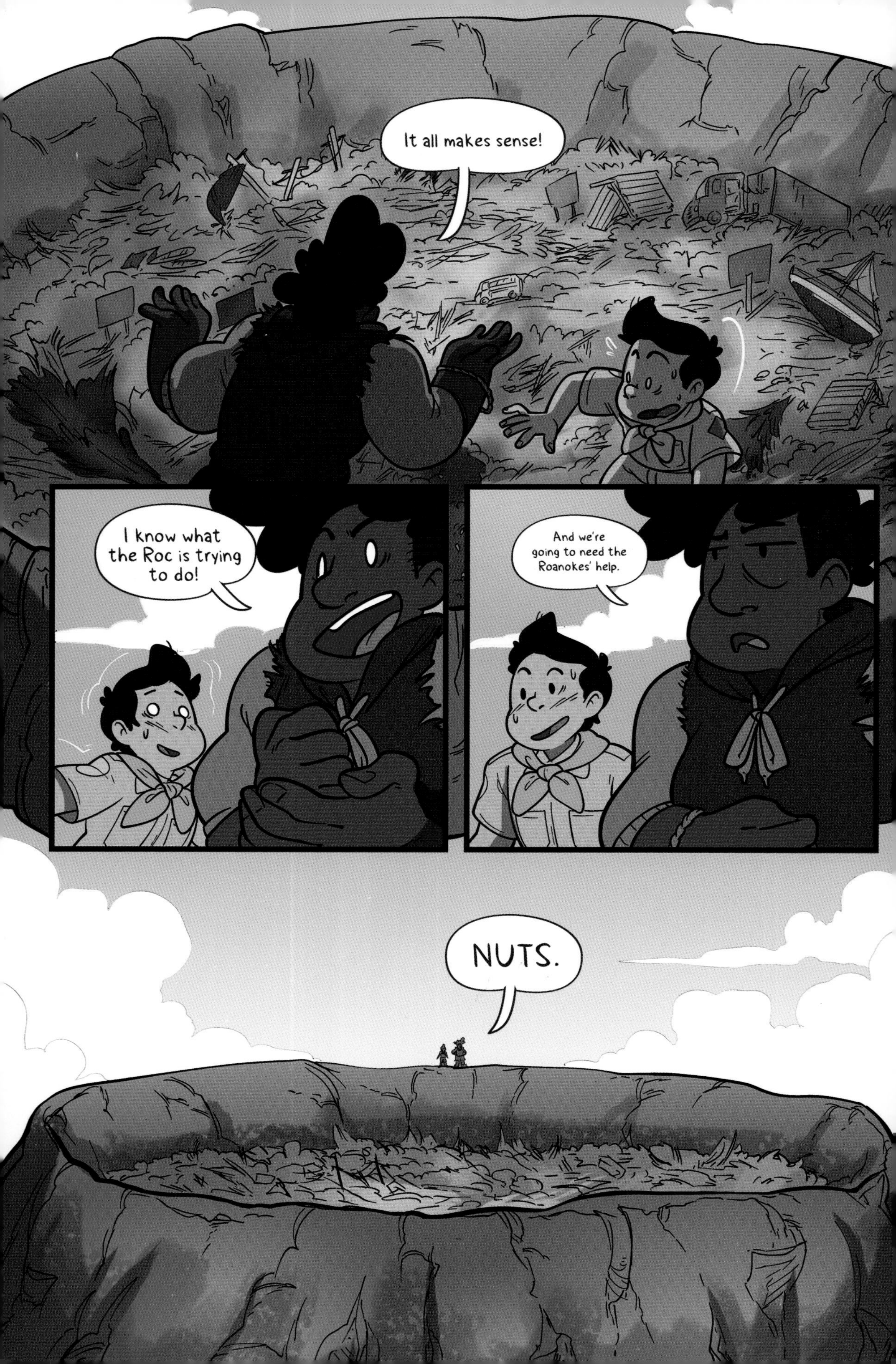
It all makes sense!
I know what the Roc is trying to do!
And we're going to need the Roanokes' help.
NUTS.

will co

The u

It he

appeara

dress f

Further

Lumbe

to have

part in

Thiskv

Hardc

have

them

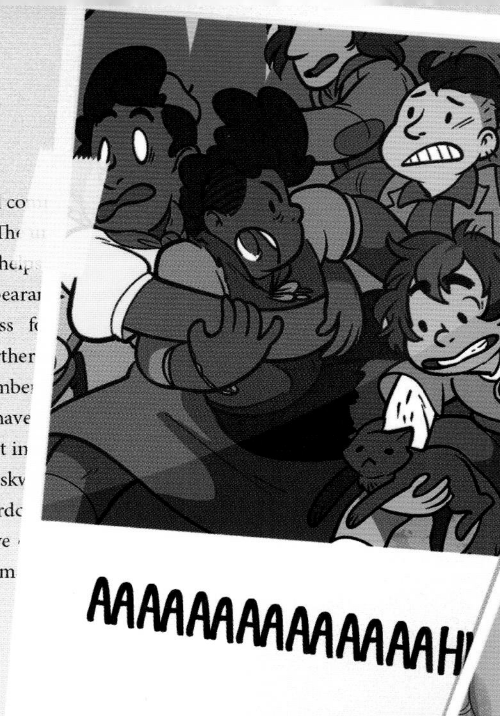
AAAAAAAAAAAAAAAH!

HE UNIFORM

should be worn at camp events when Lumberjanes n may also be worn at other ions. It should be worn as a the uniform dress with rrect shoes, and stocking or

out grows her uniform or ter Lumberjane. a she has her her

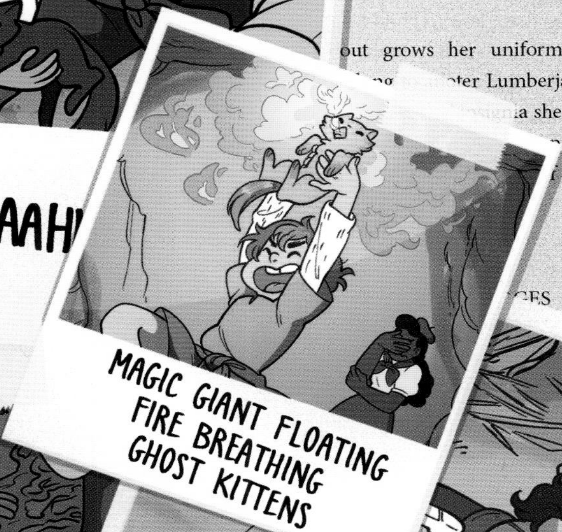
MAGIC GIANT FLOATING
FIRE BREATHING
GHOST KITTENS

GES

The yellow, short sl emb the w choose slacks, made o out-of-do green bere the colla Shoes ma heels, rou ings or socks shou with the shoes or wit the uniform. Ne es, bracelets, or other jewelry do belong with a Lumberjane uniform.

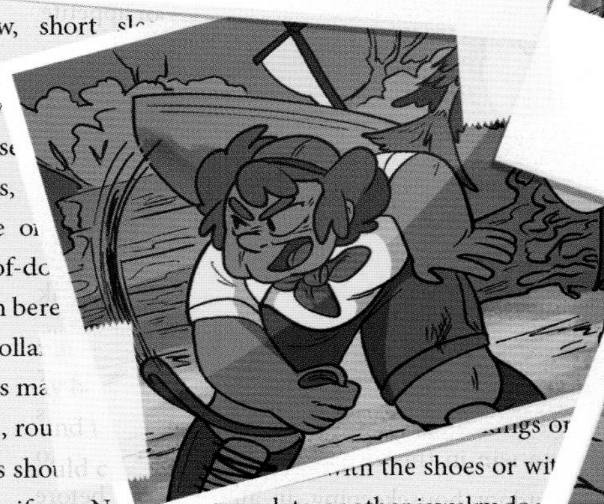

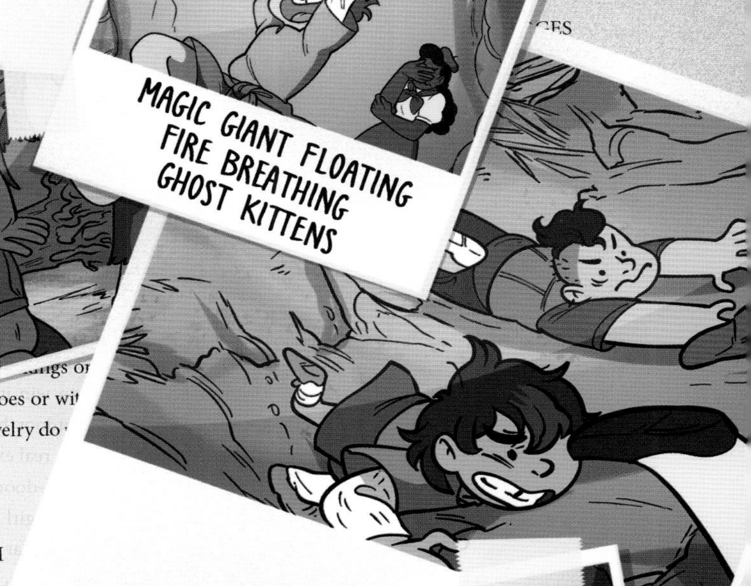

HOW TO WEAR THE UNIFORM

To look well in a uniform demands first of uniform be kept in good condition—clean pressed. See that the skirt is the right length for your own height and build, that the belt is adjusted to your waist, that your shoes and stockings are in keeping with the uniform, that you watch your posture and carry yourself with dignity and grace. If the beret is removed indoors, be sure that your hair is neat and kept in place with an insonspicuous clip or ribbon. When you wear a Lumberjane uniform you are identified as a member of this organization and you should be doubly careful to conduct yourself in a way that will show everyone that courtesy and thoughtfullness are part of being a Lumberjane. People are likely to judge a whole nation by the selfishness of a few individuals, to criticize a whole family because of the misconduct of one member, and to feel unkindly toward and organization because of the

The unifor helps to cre in a group. active life th another bond future, and pr in order to b Lumberjane pr Penniquiqul Thi ore Lady Types, but m will wish to have one. They can either bu uniform, or make it themselves from materials available at the trading post.

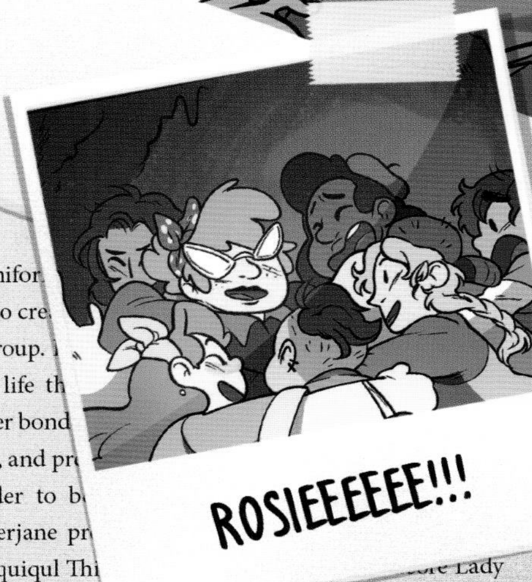
ROSIEEEEEE!!!

LUMBERJANES FIELD MANUAL

CHAPTER TWENTY-EIGHT

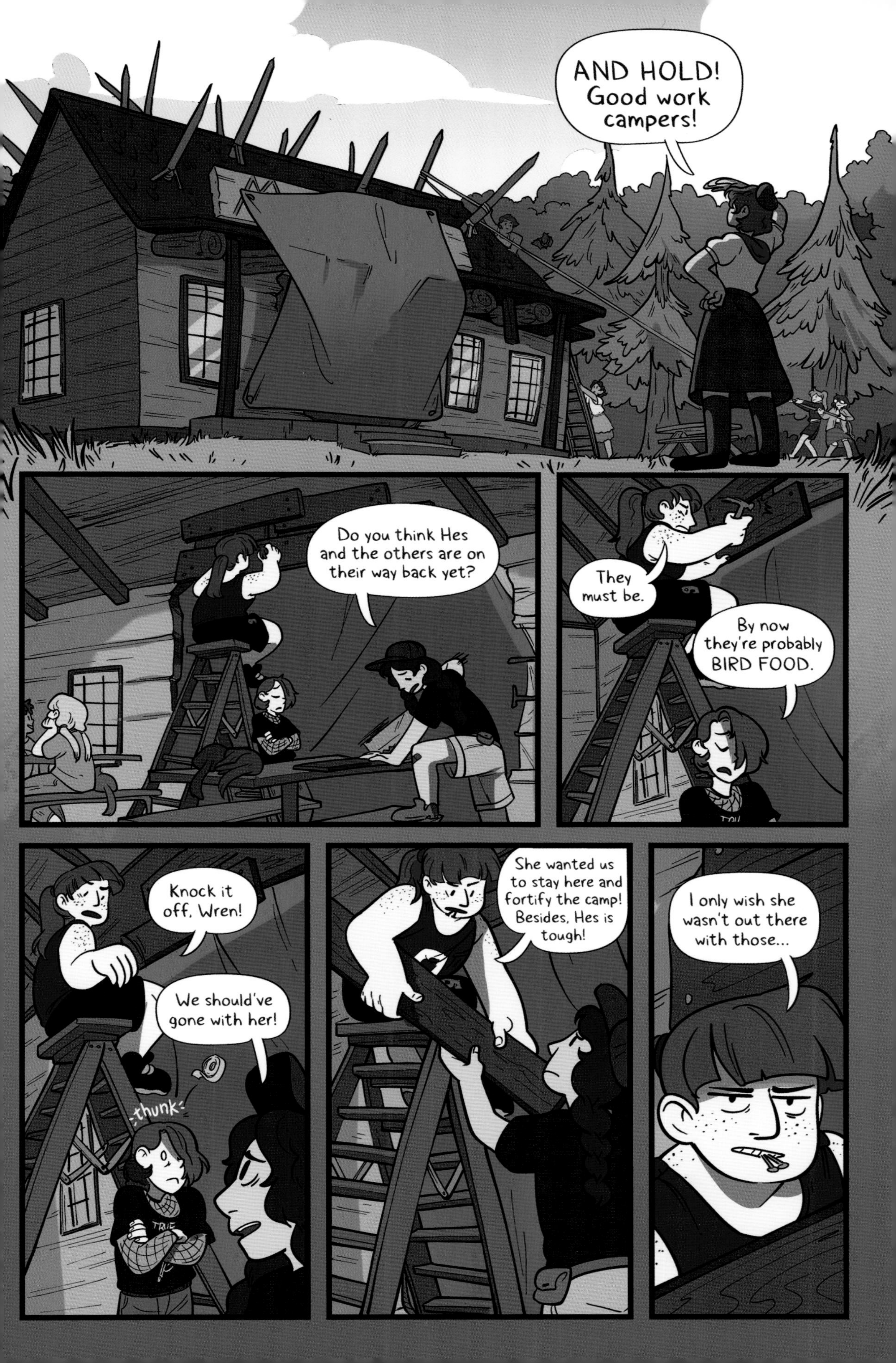
AND HOLD! Good work campers!
Do you think Hes and the others are on their way back yet?
They must be.
By now they're probably BIRD FOOD.
Knock it off, Wren!
We should've gone with her!
thunk
She wanted us to stay here and fortify the camp! Besides, Hes is tough!
I only wish she wasn't out there with those...

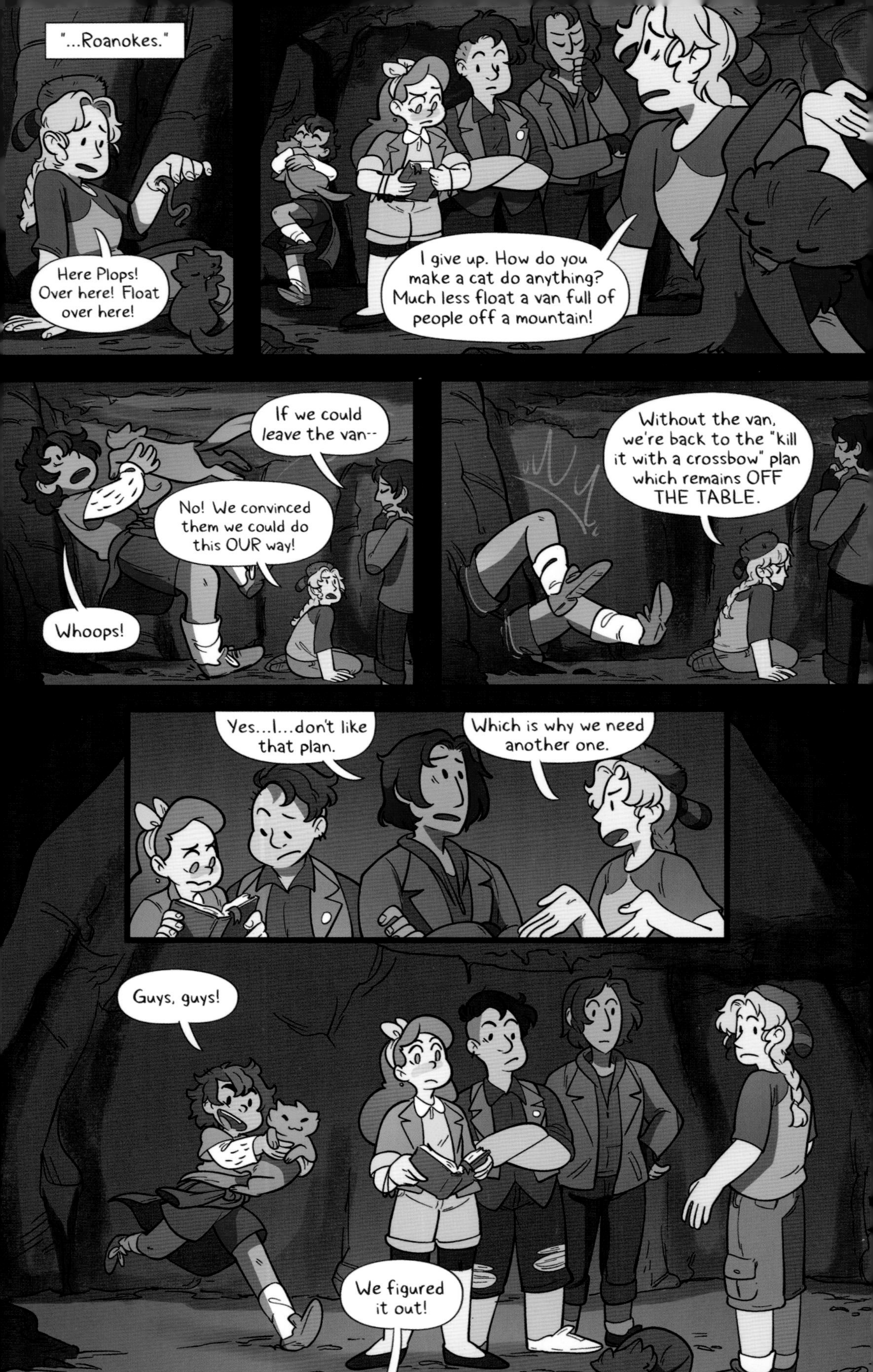
"...Roanokes."
Here Plops! Over here! Float over here!
I give up. How do you make a cat do anything? Much less float a van full of people off a mountain!
If we could leave the van--
No! We convinced them we could do this OUR way!
Whoops!
Without the van, we're back to the "kill it with a crossbow" plan which remains OFF THE TABLE.
Yes...I...don't like that plan.
Which is why we need another one.
Guys, guys!
We figured it out!

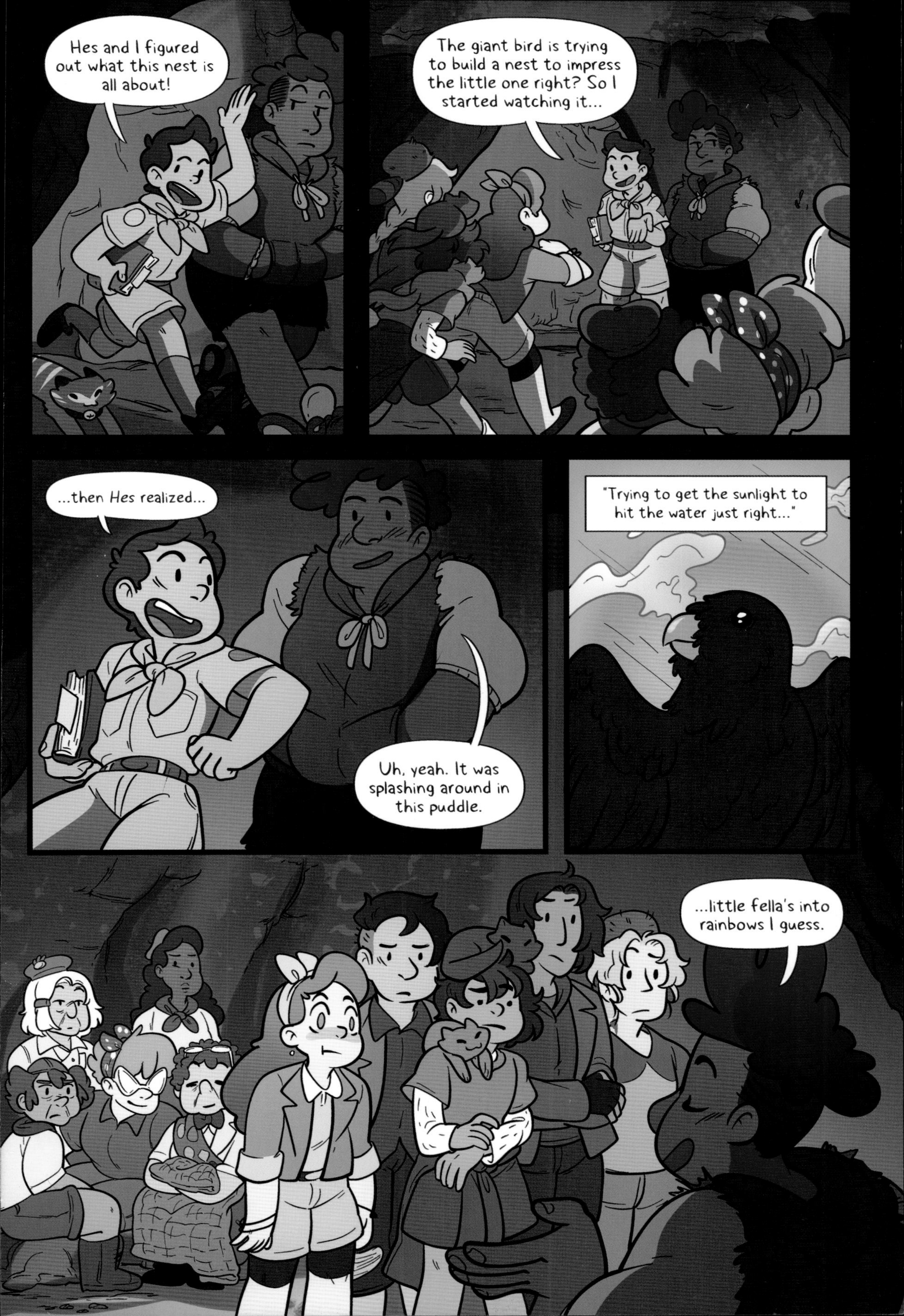
Hes and I figured out what this nest is all about!
The giant bird is trying to build a nest to impress the little one right? So I started watching it...
...then Hes realized...
"Trying to get the sunlight to hit the water just right..."
Uh, yeah. It was splashing around in this puddle.
...little fella's into rainbows I guess.

A rainbow! We thought all that STUFF out there was random--but it's arranged by color! The order's just wrong if it's trying to match the actual color spectrum.

THAT WAS AWESOME! All right Barney!

Way to go!

Okay, so we rearrange the nest a bit, and we help that nightmare creature win over that tiny bird!

And how do you plan on doing that?

Plops Town of course! Once we figure out how--

And if you can't? You're making up this entire plan as you go, based on something you don't even know is POSSIBLE OR NOT and based off of our supposition!

Girls...

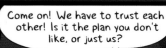

Come on! We have to trust each other! Is it the plan you don't like, or just us?

Yeah, Hes, you've had a bee in your bonnet about us from the beginning of all this! The Grand Lodge doesn't care about those old rules at all!

Forget it! I don't--

ENOUGH.

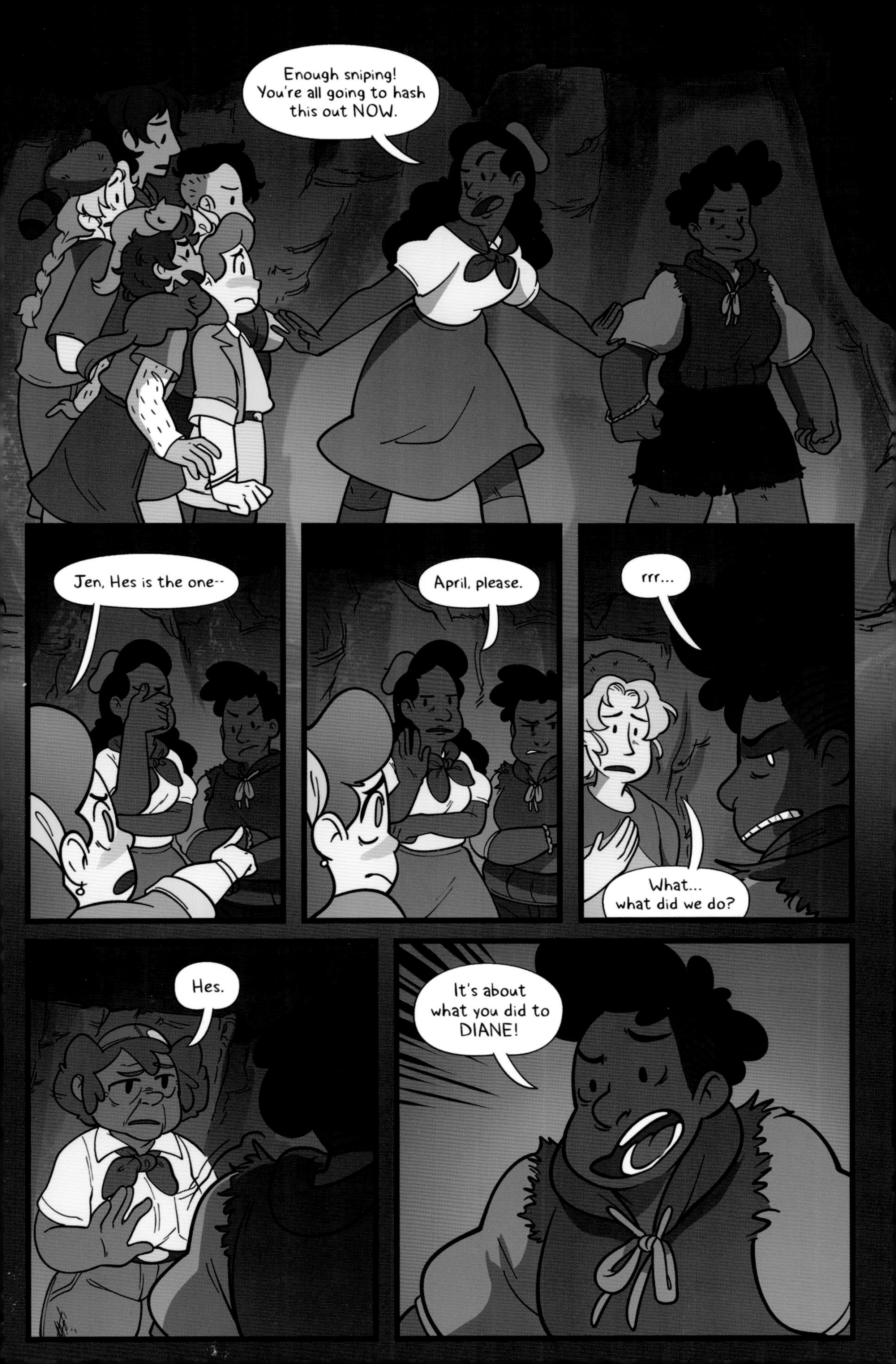
Enough sniping! You're all going to hash this out NOW.
Jen, Hes is the one--
April, please.
rrr...
What... what did we do?
Hes.
It's about what you did to DIANE!

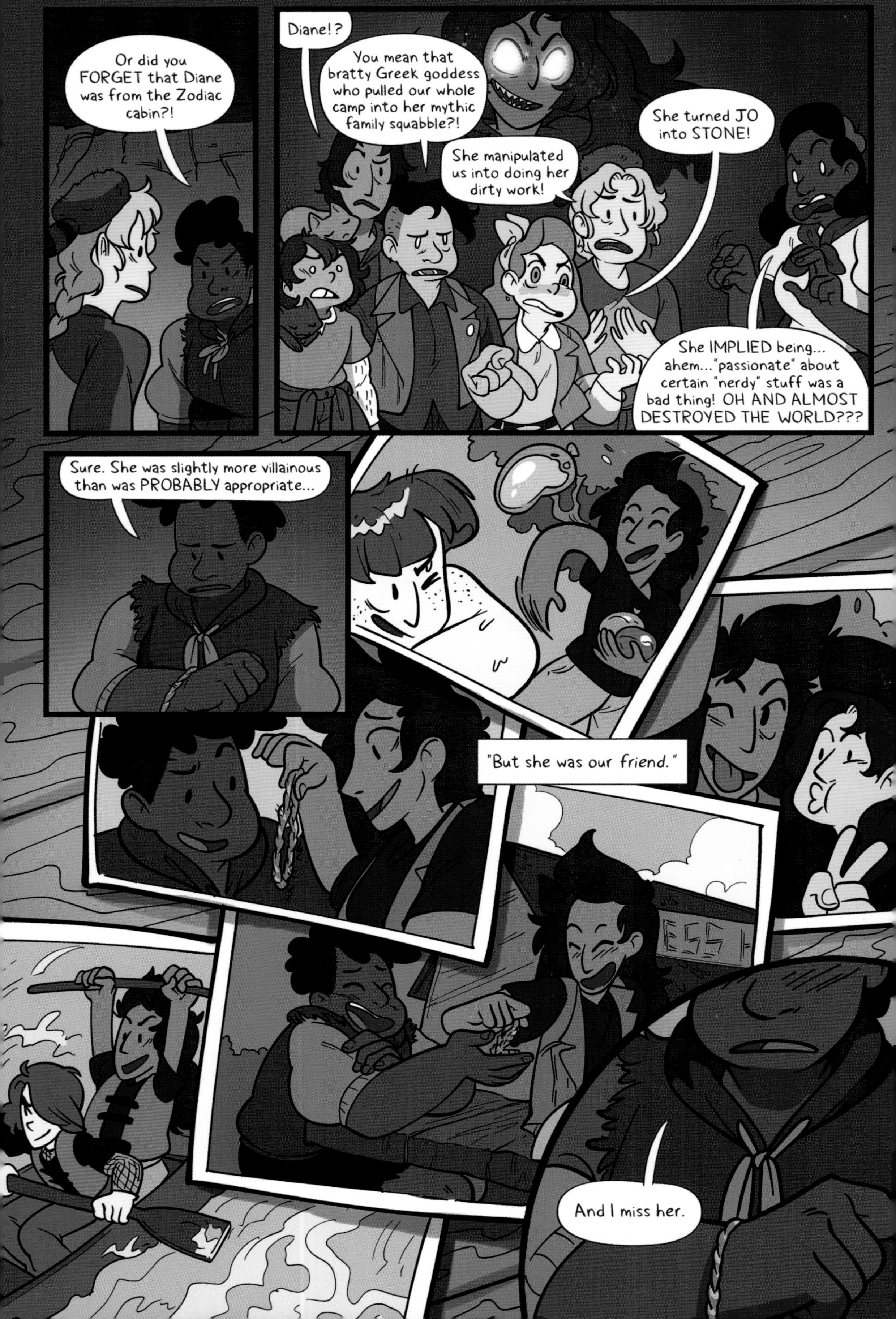
Or did you FORGET that Diane was from the Zodiac cabin?!
Diane!?
You mean that bratty Greek goddess who pulled our whole camp into her mythic family squabble?!
She manipulated us into doing her dirty work!
She turned JO into STONE!
She IMPLIED being... ahem..."passionate" about certain "nerdy" stuff was a bad thing! OH AND ALMOST DESTROYED THE WORLD???
Sure. She was slightly more villainous than was PROBABLY appropriate...
"But she was our friend."
And I miss her.

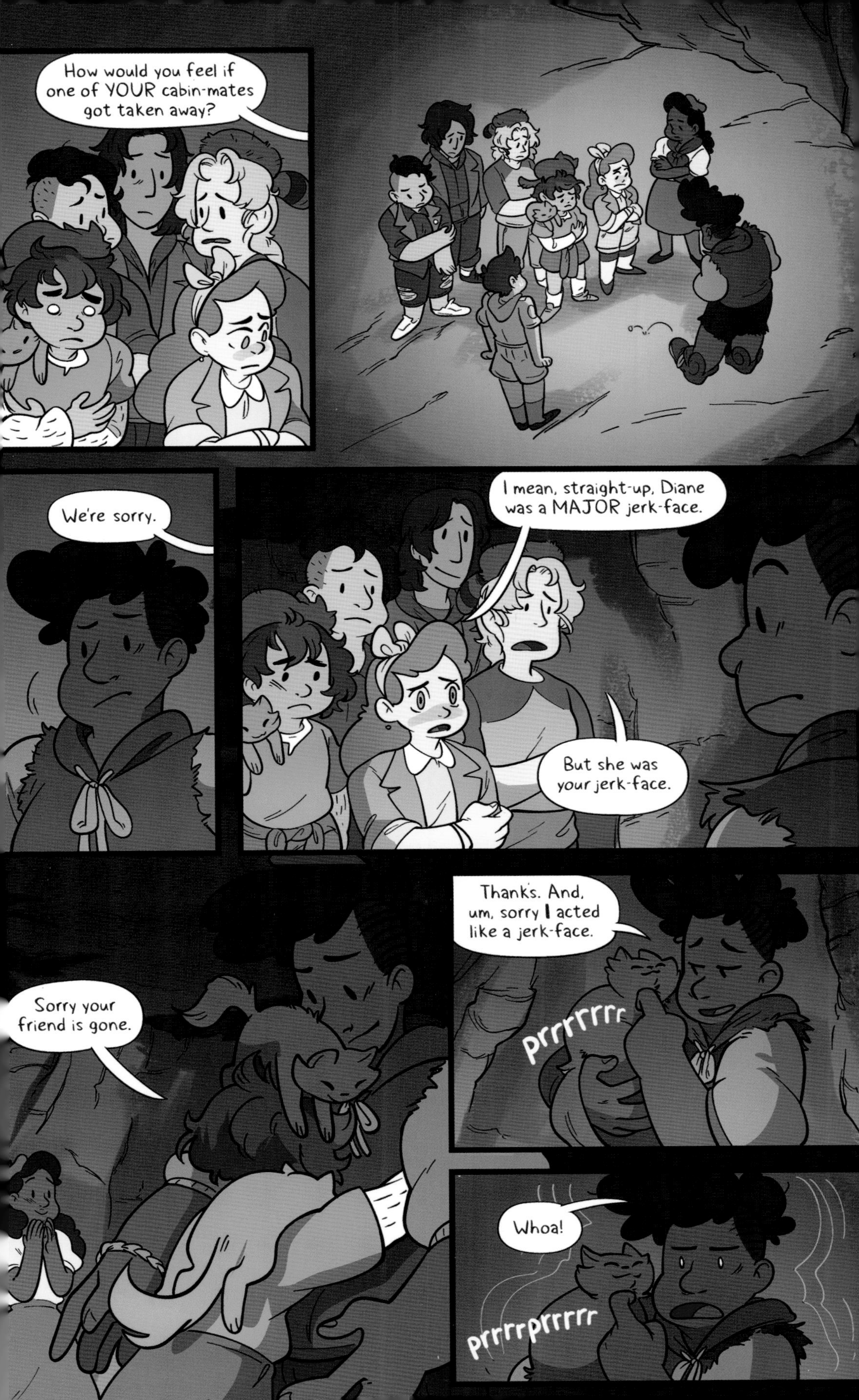
How would you feel if one of YOUR cabin-mates got taken away?
We're sorry.
I mean, straight-up, Diane was a MAJOR jerk-face.
But she was your jerk-face.
Sorry your friend is gone.
Thanks. And, um, sorry I acted like a jerk-face.
prrrrrrr
Whoa!
prrrrprrrrr

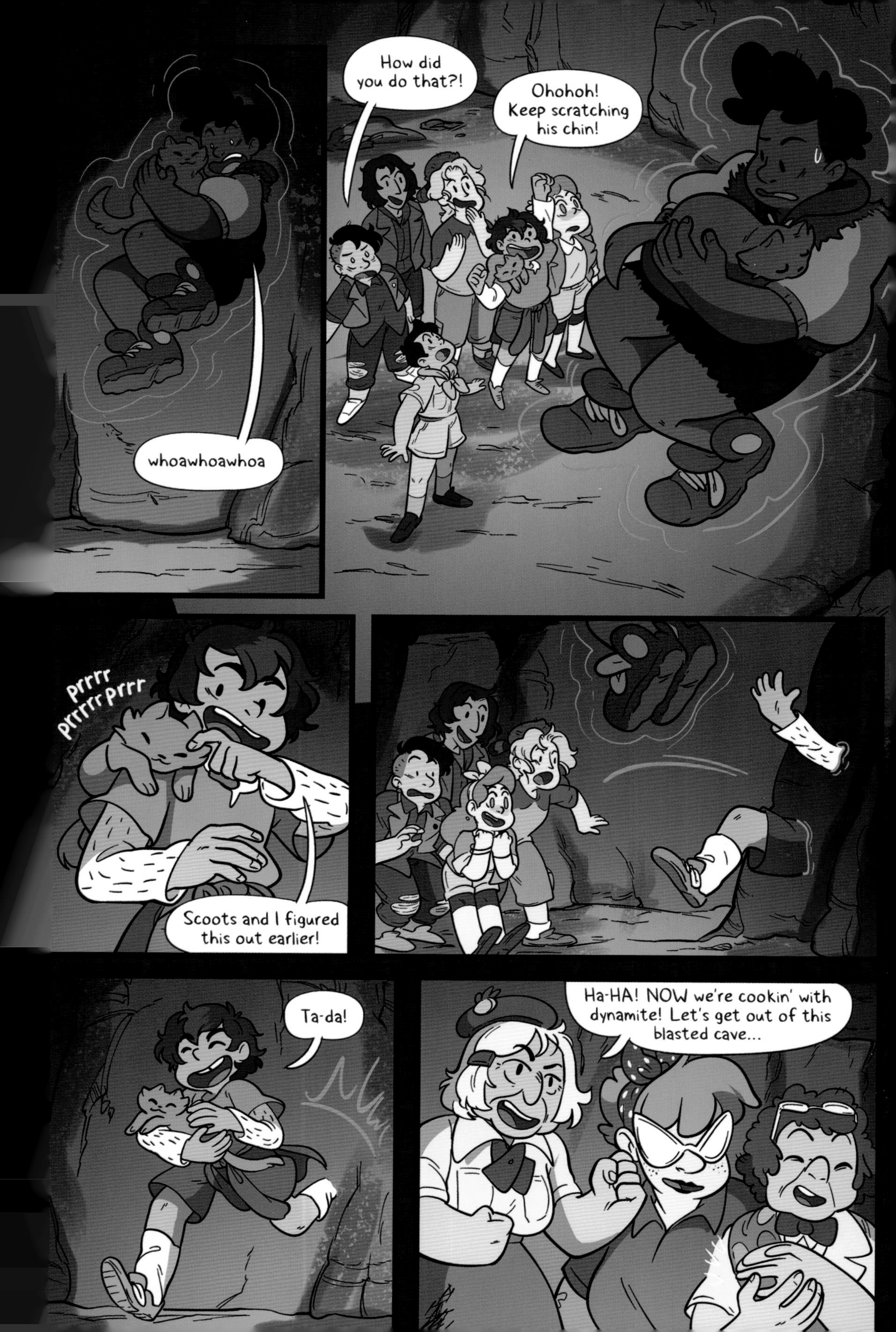
whoawhoawhoa
How did you do that?!
Ohohoh! Keep scratching his chin!
prrrr prrrrr prrr
Scoots and I figured this out earlier!
Ta-da!
Ha-HA! NOW we're cookin' with dynamite! Let's get out of this blasted cave...

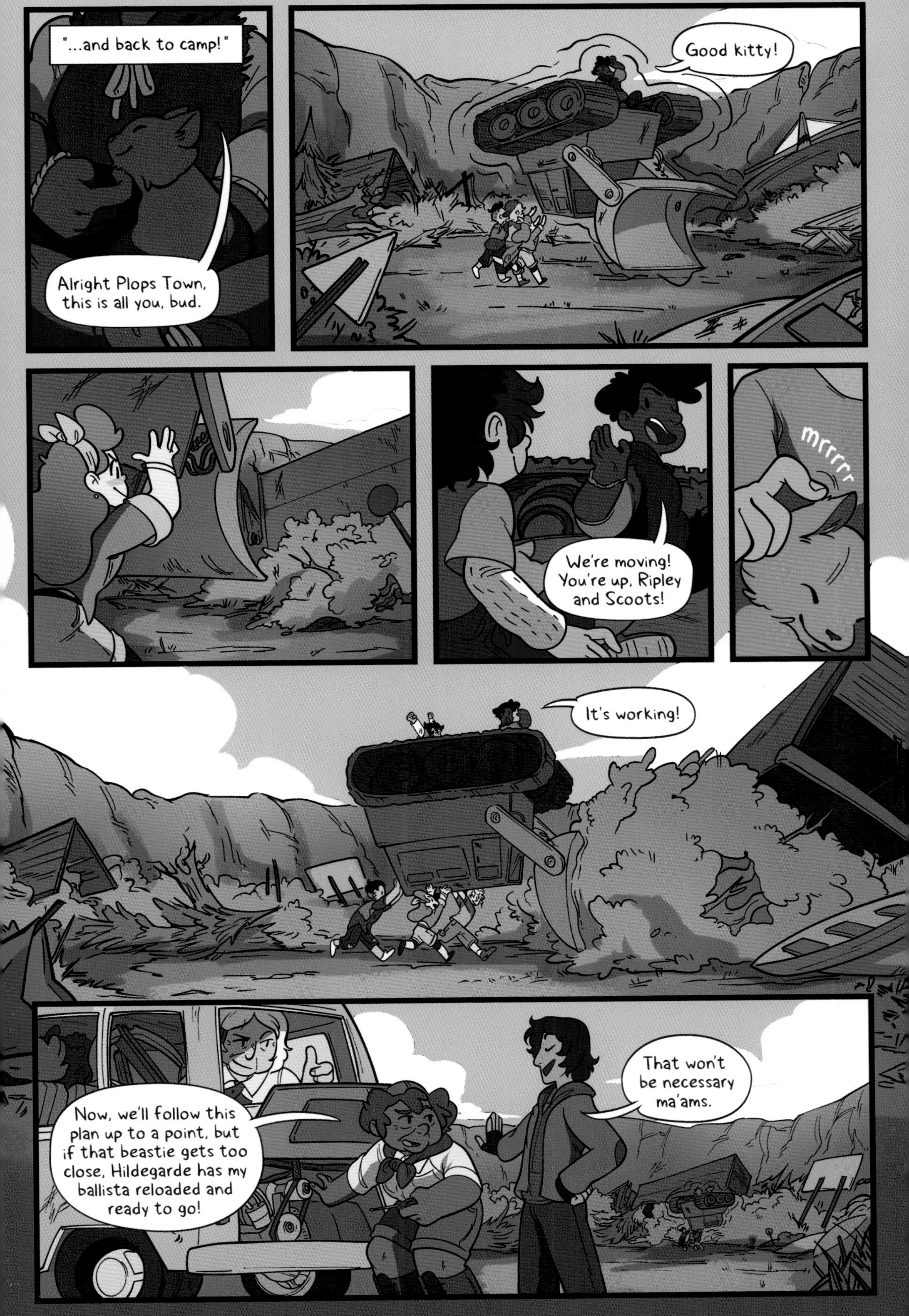
"...and back to camp!"
Alright Plops Town, this is all you, bud.
Good kitty!
We're moving! You're up, Ripley and Scoots!
mrrrrr
It's working!
Now, we'll follow this plan up to a point, but if that beastie gets too close, Hildegarde has my ballista reloaded and ready to go!
That won't be necessary ma'ams.

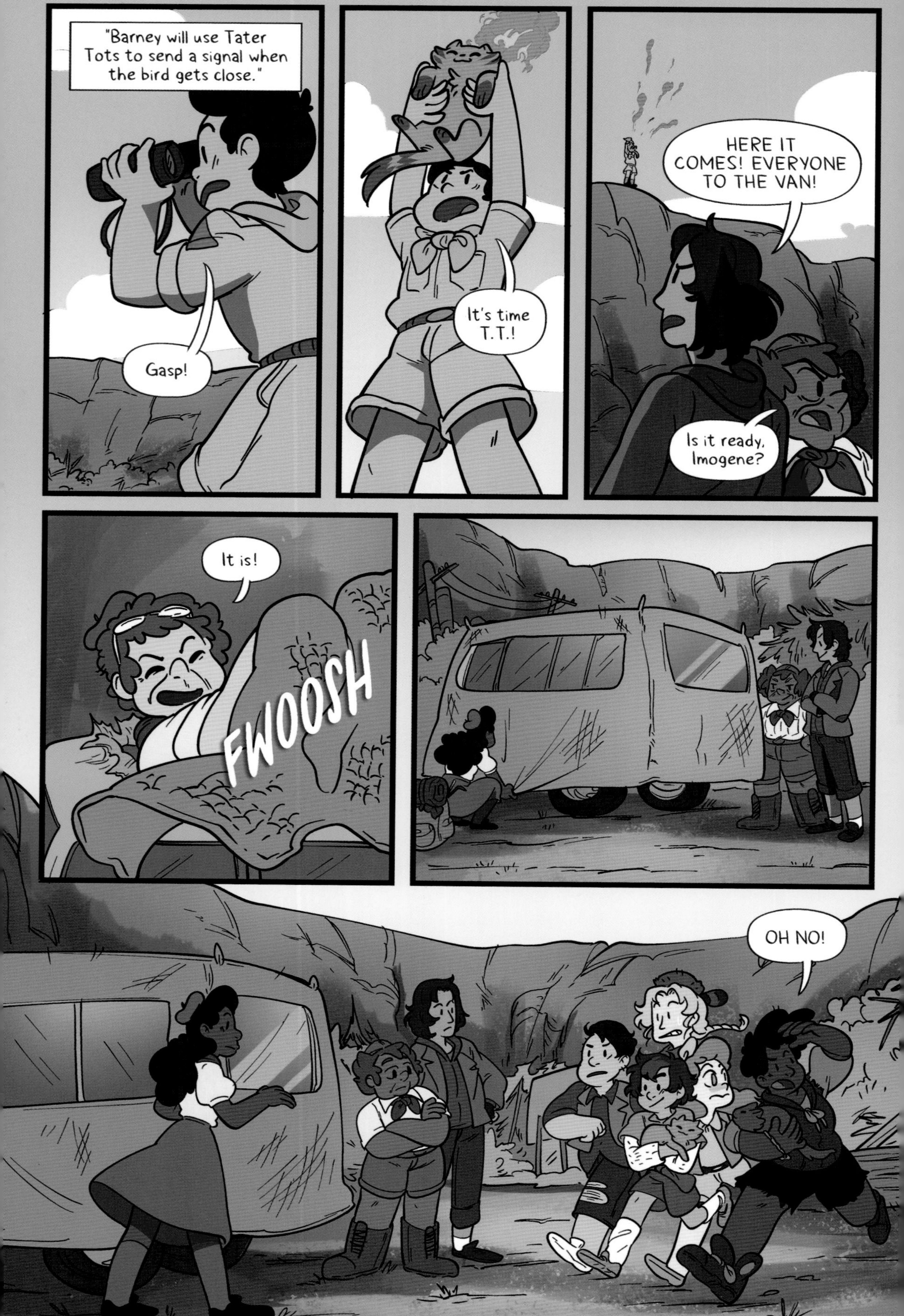
"Barney will use Tater Tots to send a signal when the bird gets close."
Gasp!
It's time T.T.!
HERE IT COMES! EVERYONE TO THE VAN!
Is it ready, Imogene?
It is!
FWOOSH
OH NO!

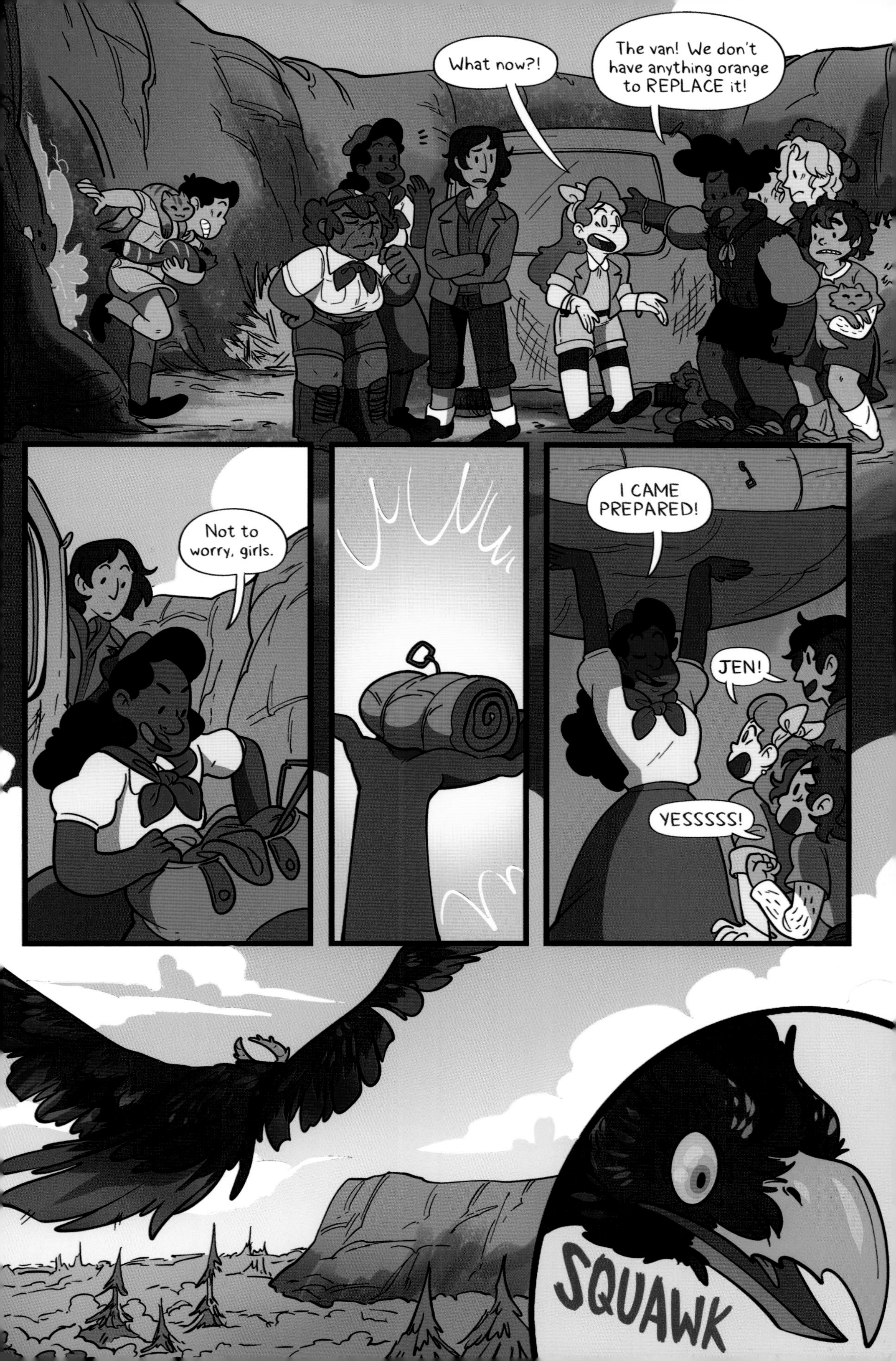
What now?!
The van! We don't have anything orange to REPLACE it!
Not to worry, girls.
I CAME PREPARED!
JEN!
YESSSSS!
SQUAWK

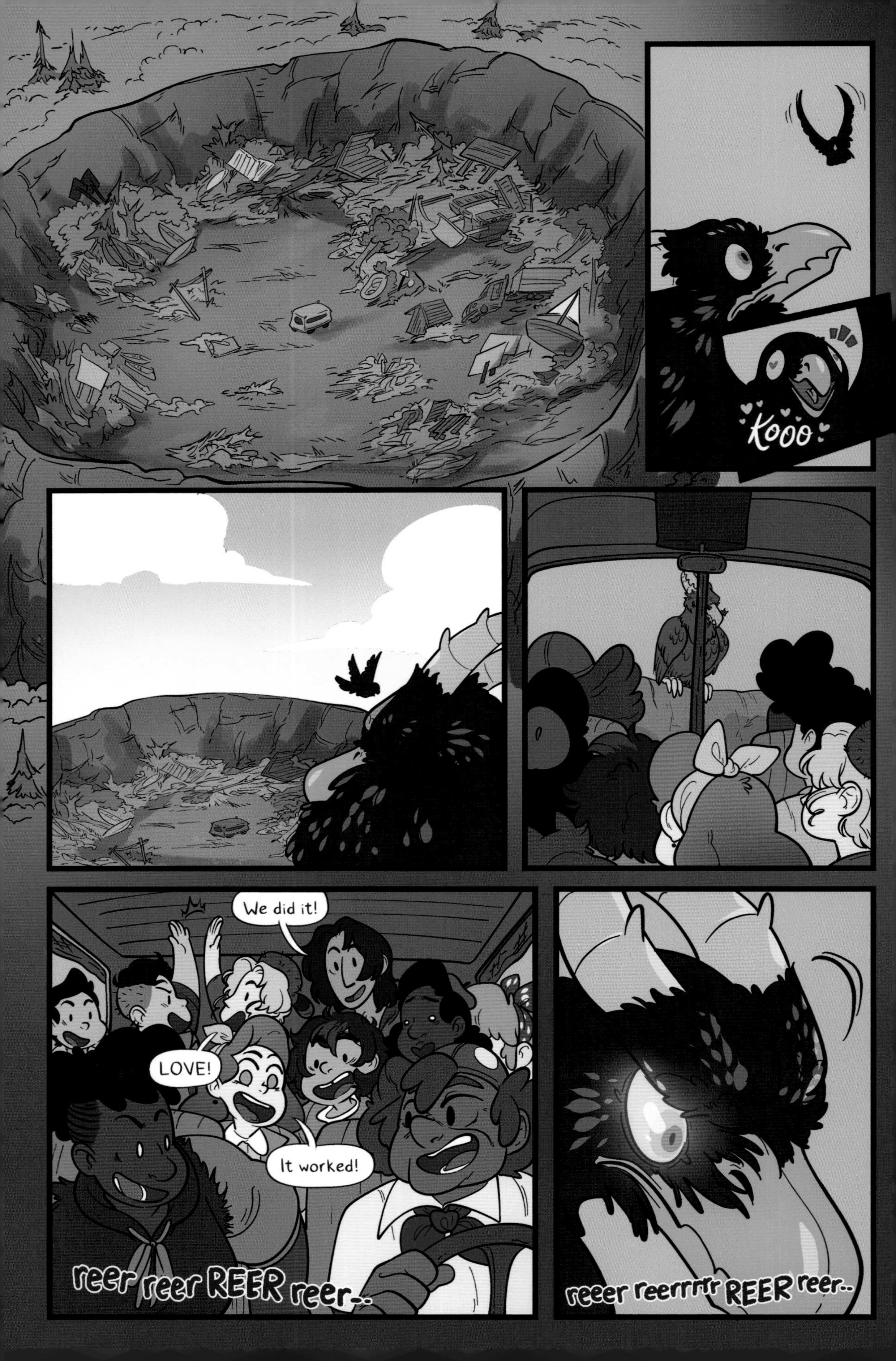
KOOO
We did it!
LOVE!
It worked!
reer reer REER reer..
reeer reerrrrr REER reer..

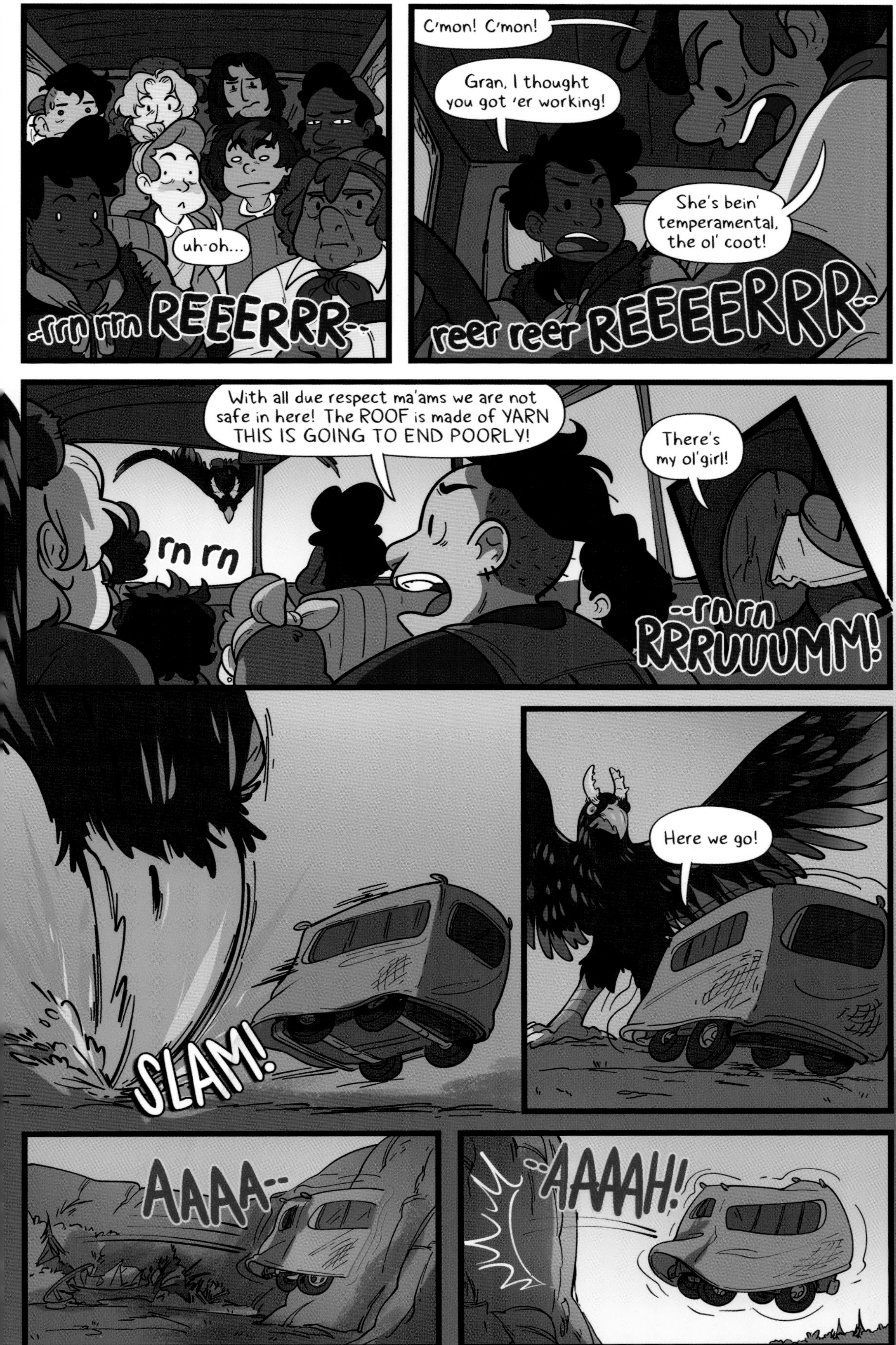
uh-oh...
-rrn rrn REEERRR-
C'mon! C'mon!
Gran, I thought you got 'er working!
She's bein' temperamental, the ol' coot!
reer reer REEEERRR-
With all due respect ma'ams we are not safe in here! The ROOF is made of YARN THIS IS GOING TO END POORLY!
rn rn
There's my ol'girl!
--rn rn RRRUUUMM!
SLAM!
Here we go!
AAAA--
--AAAAH!

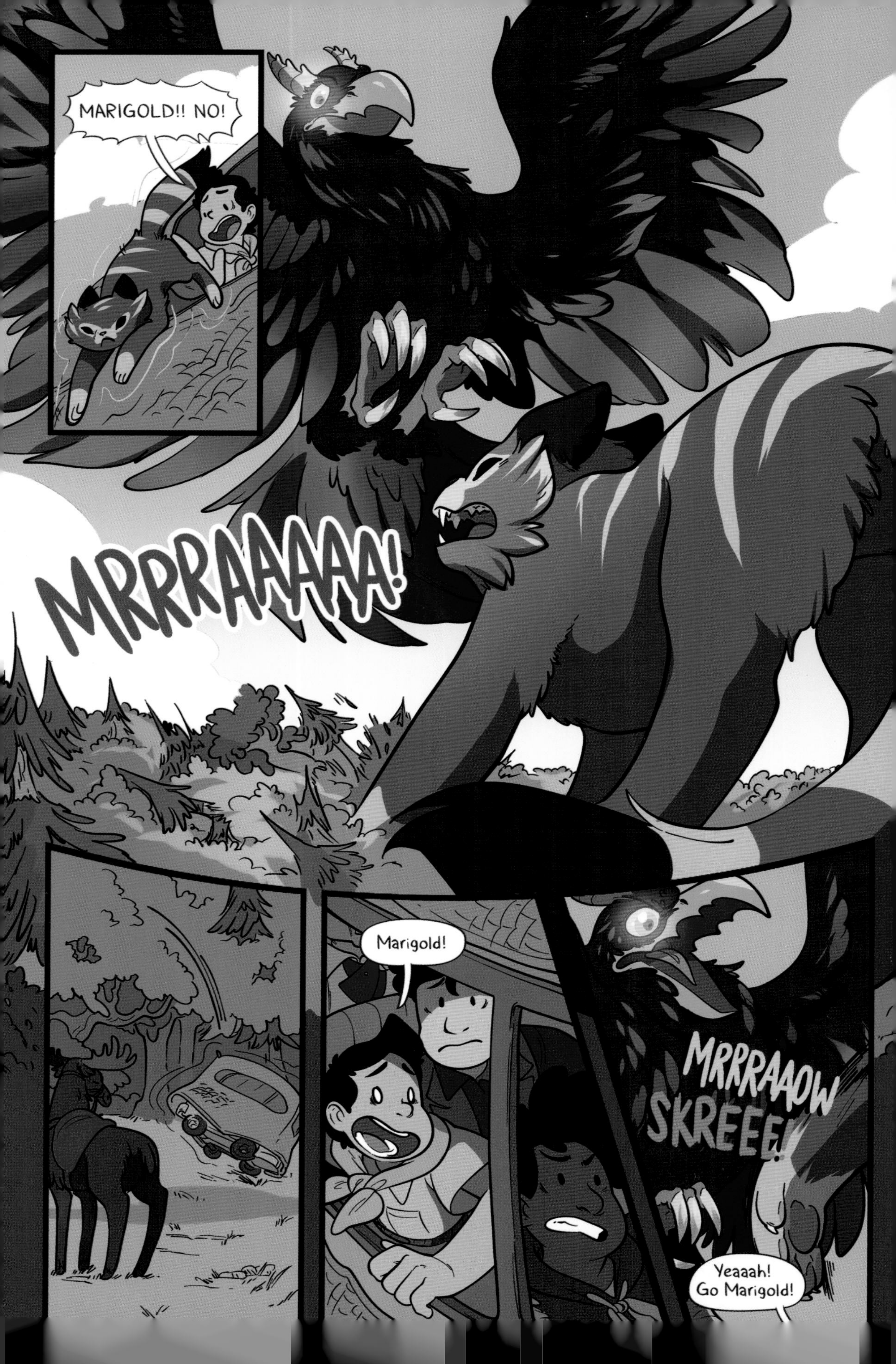
MARIGOLD!! NO!
MRRRAAAAA!
Marigold!
MRRRAAOW
SKREEE!
Yeaaah!
Go Marigold!

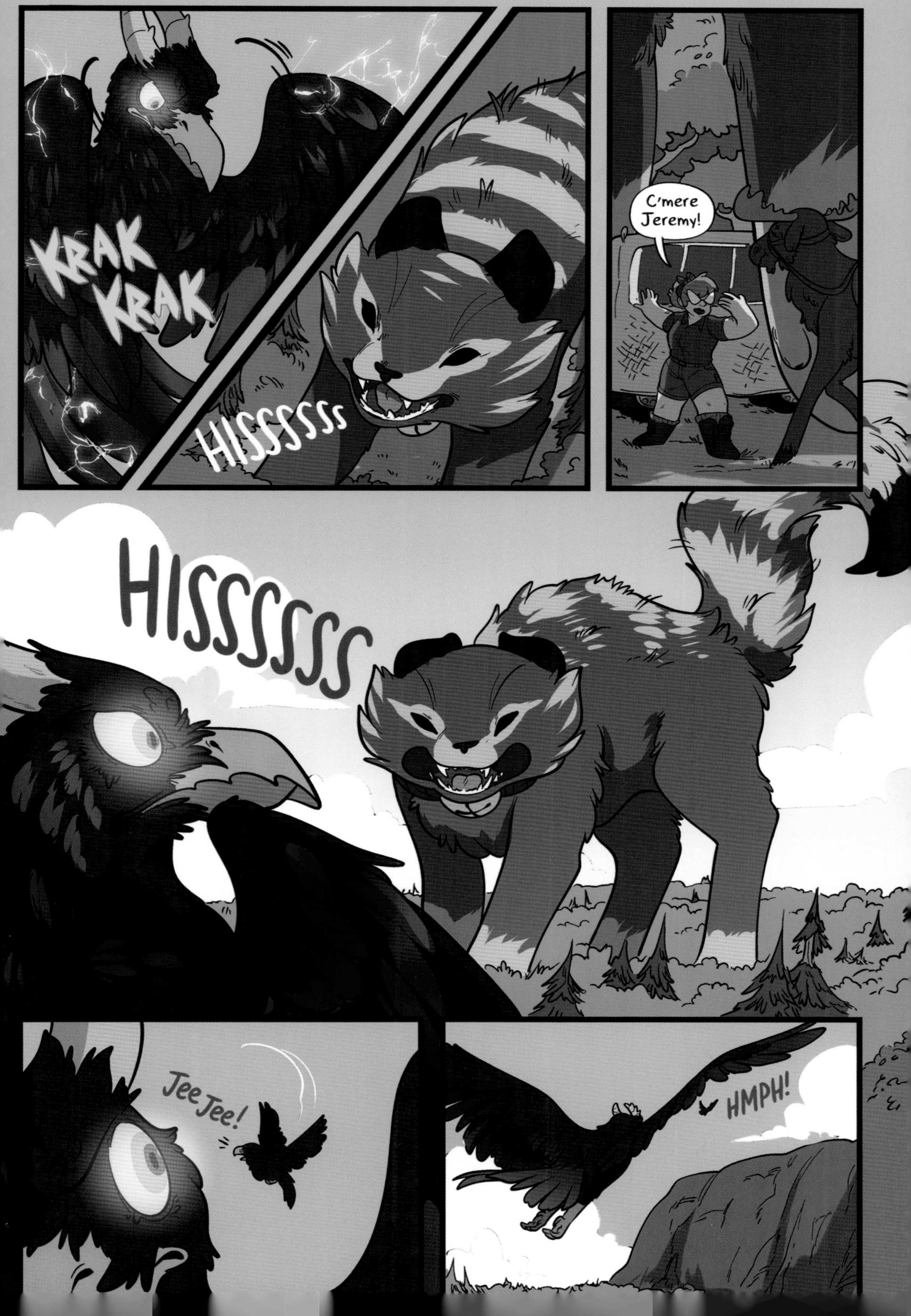
KRAK KRAK
HISSSSSs
C'mere Jeremy!
HISSSSSS
Jee Jee!
HMPH!

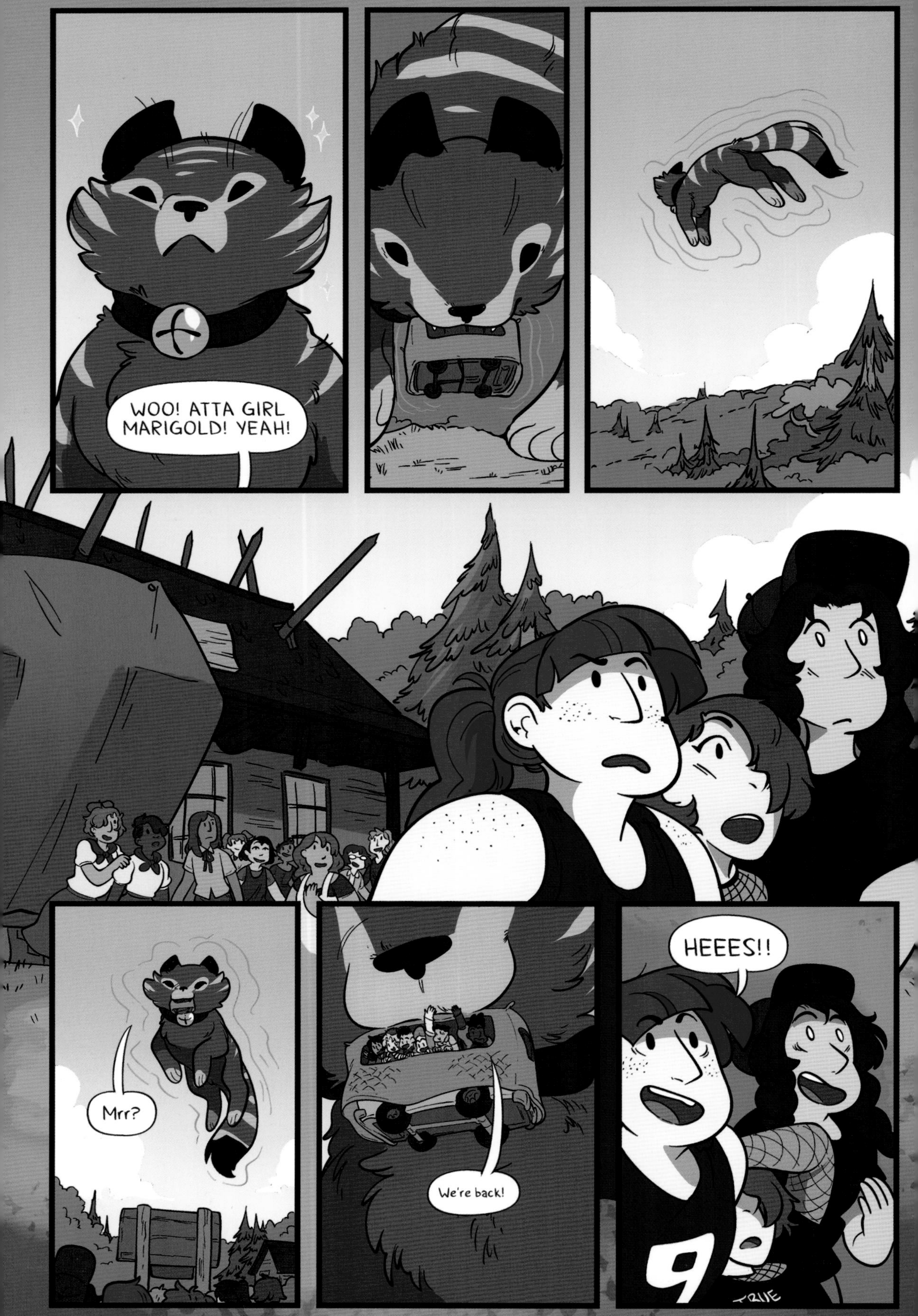
WOO! ATTA GIRL MARIGOLD! YEAH!
Mrr?
We're back!
HEEES!!

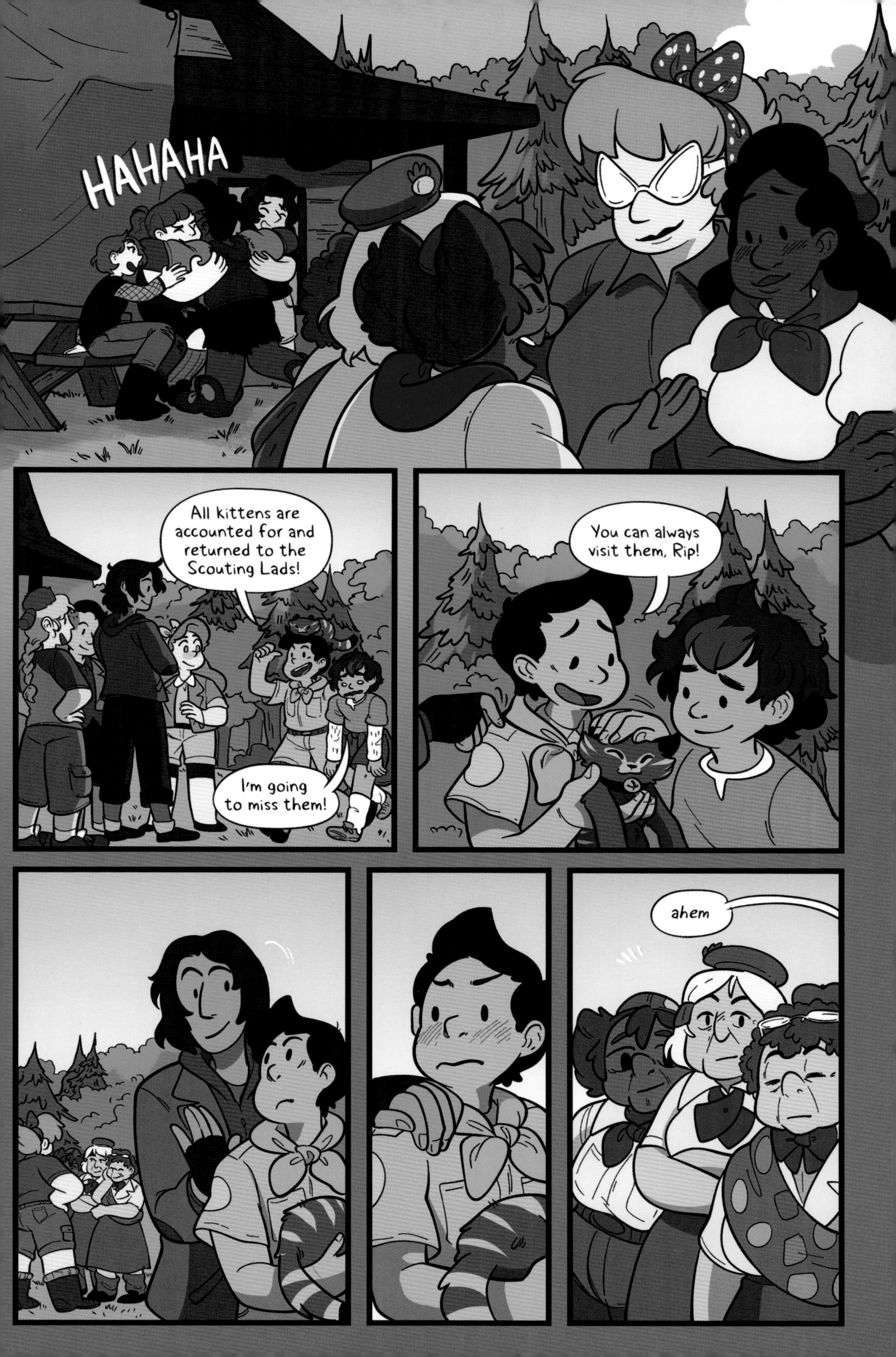
HAHAHA
All kittens are accounted for and returned to the Scouting Lads!
I'm going to miss them!
You can always visit them, Rip!
ahem

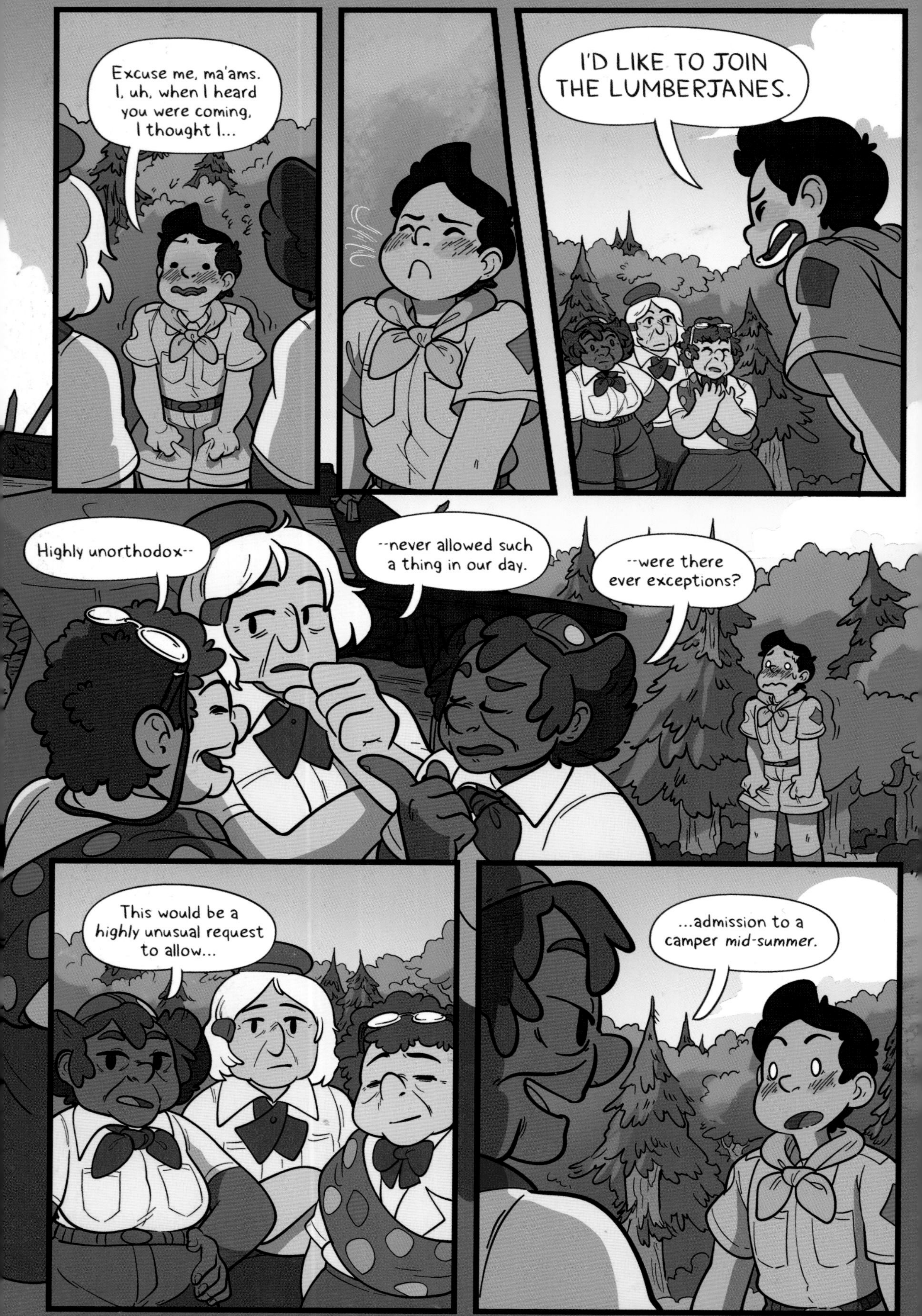

Excuse me, ma'ams. I, uh, when I heard you were coming, I thought I...
I'D LIKE TO JOIN THE LUMBERJANES.
Highly unorthodox--
--never allowed such a thing in our day.
--were there ever exceptions?
This would be a *highly* unusual request to allow...
...admission to a camper mid-summer.

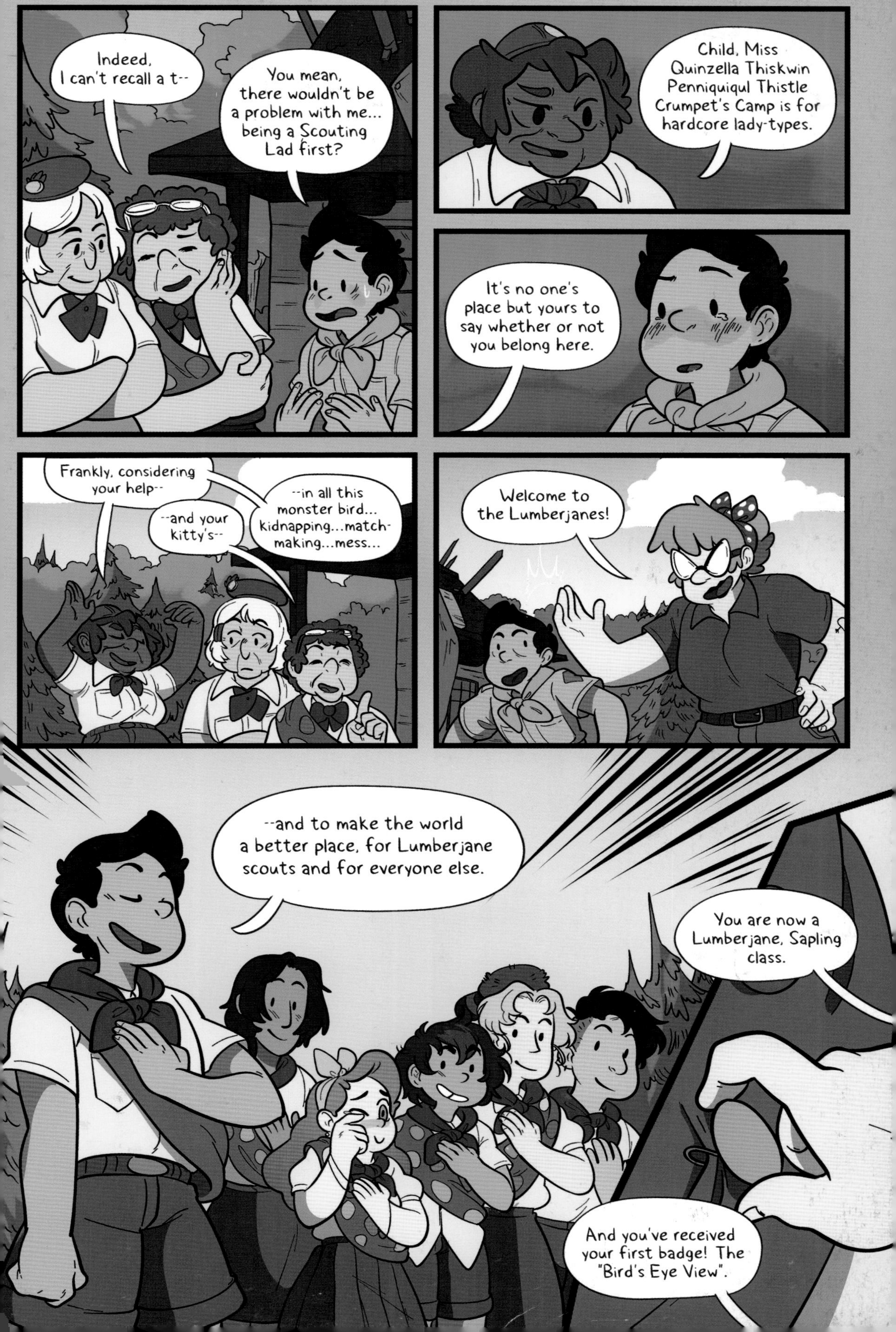
Indeed, I can't recall a t--
You mean, there wouldn't be a problem with me... being a Scouting Lad first?
Child, Miss Quinzella Thiskwin Penniquiqul Thistle Crumpet's Camp is for hardcore lady-types.
It's no one's place but yours to say whether or not you belong here.
Frankly, considering your help--
--and your kitty's--
--in all this monster bird... kidnapping...match-making...mess...
Welcome to the Lumberjanes!
--and to make the world a better place, for Lumberjane scouts and for everyone else.
You are now a Lumberjane, Sapling class.
And you've received your first badge! The "Bird's Eye View".

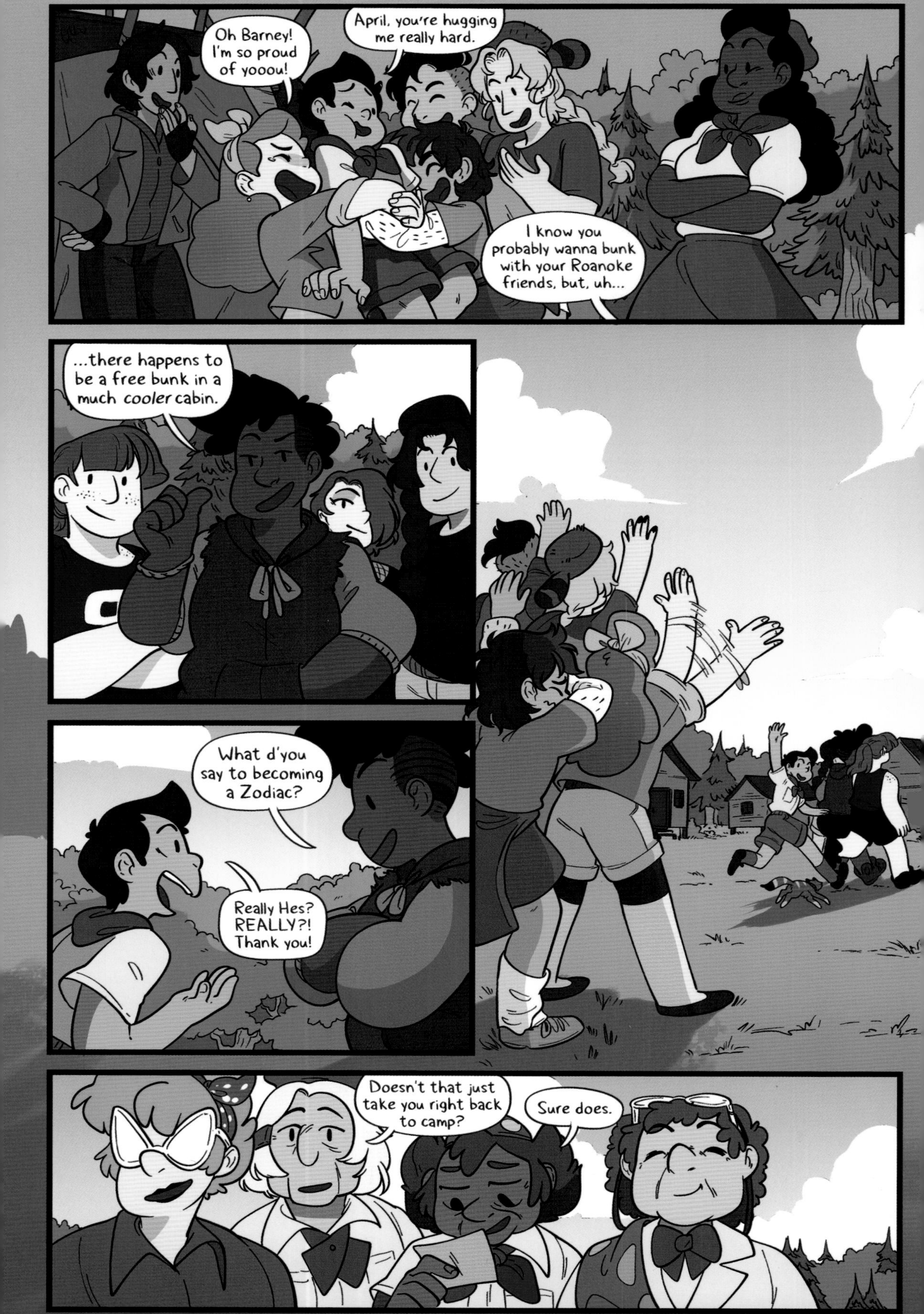

Oh Barney! I'm so proud of yooou!
April, you're hugging me really hard.
I know you probably wanna bunk with your Roanoke friends, but, uh...
...there happens to be a free bunk in a much *cooler* cabin.
What d'you say to becoming a Zodiac?
Really Hes? REALLY?! Thank you!
Doesn't that just take you right back to camp?
Sure does.

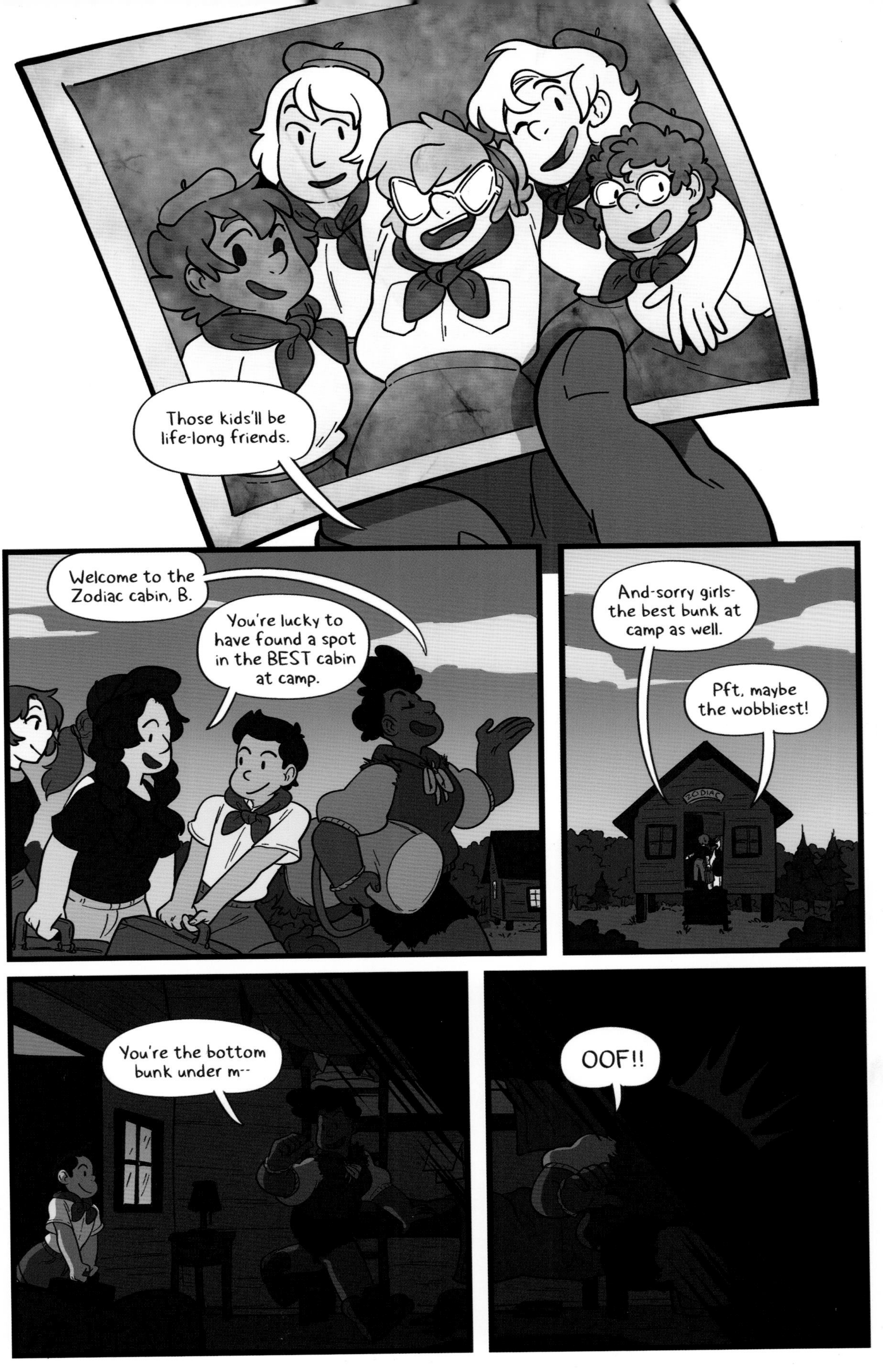
Those kids'll be life-long friends.
Welcome to the Zodiac cabin, B.
You're lucky to have found a spot in the BEST cabin at camp.
And-sorry girls- the best bunk at camp as well.
Pft, maybe the wobbliest!
ZODIAC
You're the bottom bunk under m--
OOF!!

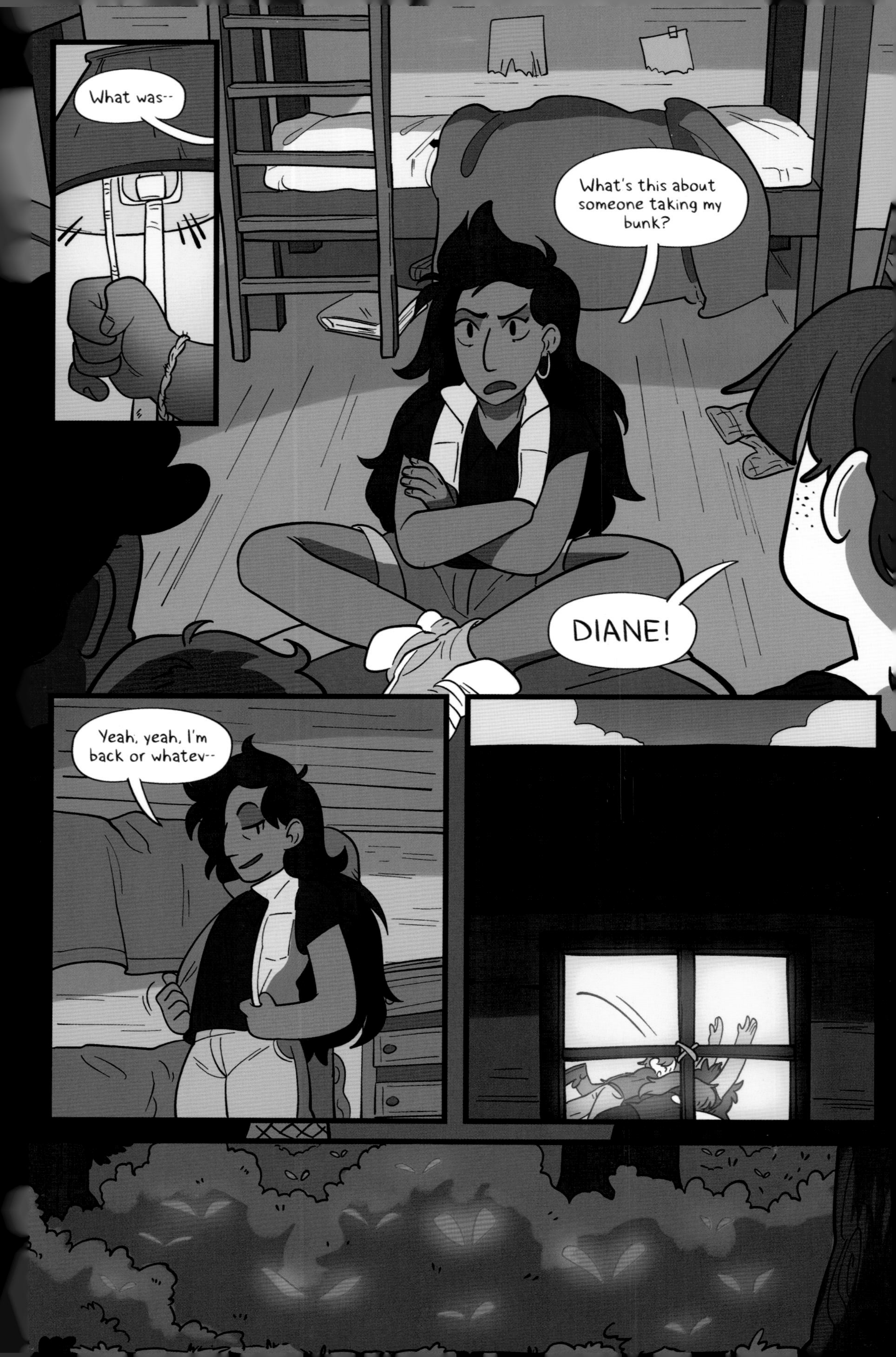
What was--
What's this about someone taking my bunk?
DIANE!
Yeah, yeah, I'm back or whatev--

will co...

The u... ...IE UNIFORM

It helps ...should be worn at camp

appearan... ...events when Lumberjanes

dress fo... ...n may also be worn at other

Further ... ...ions. It should be worn as a

Lumber... the uniform dress with

to have... ...rect shoes, and stocking or

part in...

Thiskv... ...out grows her uniform or

Hardc... ...ter Lumberjane.

have ... ...a she has

them ... ...her

BARNEY'S FIRST BADGE

ATTA GIRL, MARIGOLD!

WE'RE BACK

The ...

yellow, short sl...

emb...

the w...

choose...

slacks,

made o...

out-of-do...

green bere...

the colla...

Shoes m...

heels, roun...

socks should...

the uniform. Ne... ...bracelets, or other jewelry do...

belong with a Lumberjane uniform.

HOW TO WEAR THE UNIFORM

To look well in a uniform demands first of...
uniform be kept in good condition—clean a...
pressed. See that the skirt is the right length for your own
height and build, that the belt is adjusted to your waist,
that your shoes and stockings are in keeping with the
uniform, that you watch your posture and carry yourself
with dignity and grace. If the beret is removed indoors,
be sure that your hair is neat and kept in place with an
insconspicuous clip or ribbon. When you wear a
Lumberjane uniform you are identified as a member of
this organization and you should be doubly careful to
conduct yourself in a way that will show everyone that
courtesy and thoughtfullness are part of being a
Lumberjane. People are likely to judge a whole nation by
the selfishness of a few individuals, to criticize a whole
family because of the misconduct of one member, and to
feel unkindly toward and organization because of the

The unifor... ...
helps to cre...
in a group. ...
active life th...
another bond...
future, and pr...
in order to b...
Lumberjane pr...
Penniquiqul Thi... ...re Lady
Types, but m... ...es will wish to have one. They
can either bu... ...e uniform, or make it themselves from
materials available at the trading post.

LUMBERJANES FIELD MANUAL
CHAPTER TWENTY-NINE

Lumberjanes "Heart to Heart" Program Field

CUT LOOSE BADGE

"It's just one of the hair necessities"

The styling and coiffure of one's hair is something that we all must grapple with-- whether with combs and gel, or clips and elastics, or even bodkins and curlers. Whether it's long and strong, or short and pert, your hair can speak volumes about you. Hair can reflect one's culture as well as one's personality, and while you are away at camp, you have the freedom to do with and to your hair as you like.

Perhaps when you were a little child, your parents would insist on helping you with your hair-- teasing out tangles, fixing it up in braids and pigtails for school, telling the stylist what cut they thought would look most becoming on you-- but you are coming into the years of young adulthood now, and your hair will start to become more and more your own responsibility.

While you are here at camp, your hair can truly be yours, maybe for the first time in your young life. When to wash it, how to brush it, even how to cut it... these questions are yours to answer, and yours alone.

While most hair stylists recommend against cutting one's own hair, and while perhaps in your older years you'll look back on these days and shake your more conservatively-styled head at your youthful enthusiasm and bold choices, we encourage you to use your hair as a tool of reinvention and self-discovery while you are here at camp, as part of earning the Cut Loose Badge. There is no better time or place to try new things.

So, grow your hair as long as you like. Practice three, and five, and seven stranded braids. Cut the back short and keep the front long and flowing, or go in the opposite direction and wear a mullet with pride. Meet a sister you never knew you had and cut your hair to match hers, or shave your head down to only a quarter inch of stubble, and fall asleep each night running your hands over the peach fuzz of your skull.

Encourage your curls to grow outward and upward, and ever more and more beautifully voluminous, or tuck them safely into intricate cornrows. Tie your hair up into a scarf, or wear it long and tumbling and brightly colored, or trim it as short as can be, and never look at a comb again all summer. Here, you have the freedom to do what you will with your hair. After all, it does grow back.

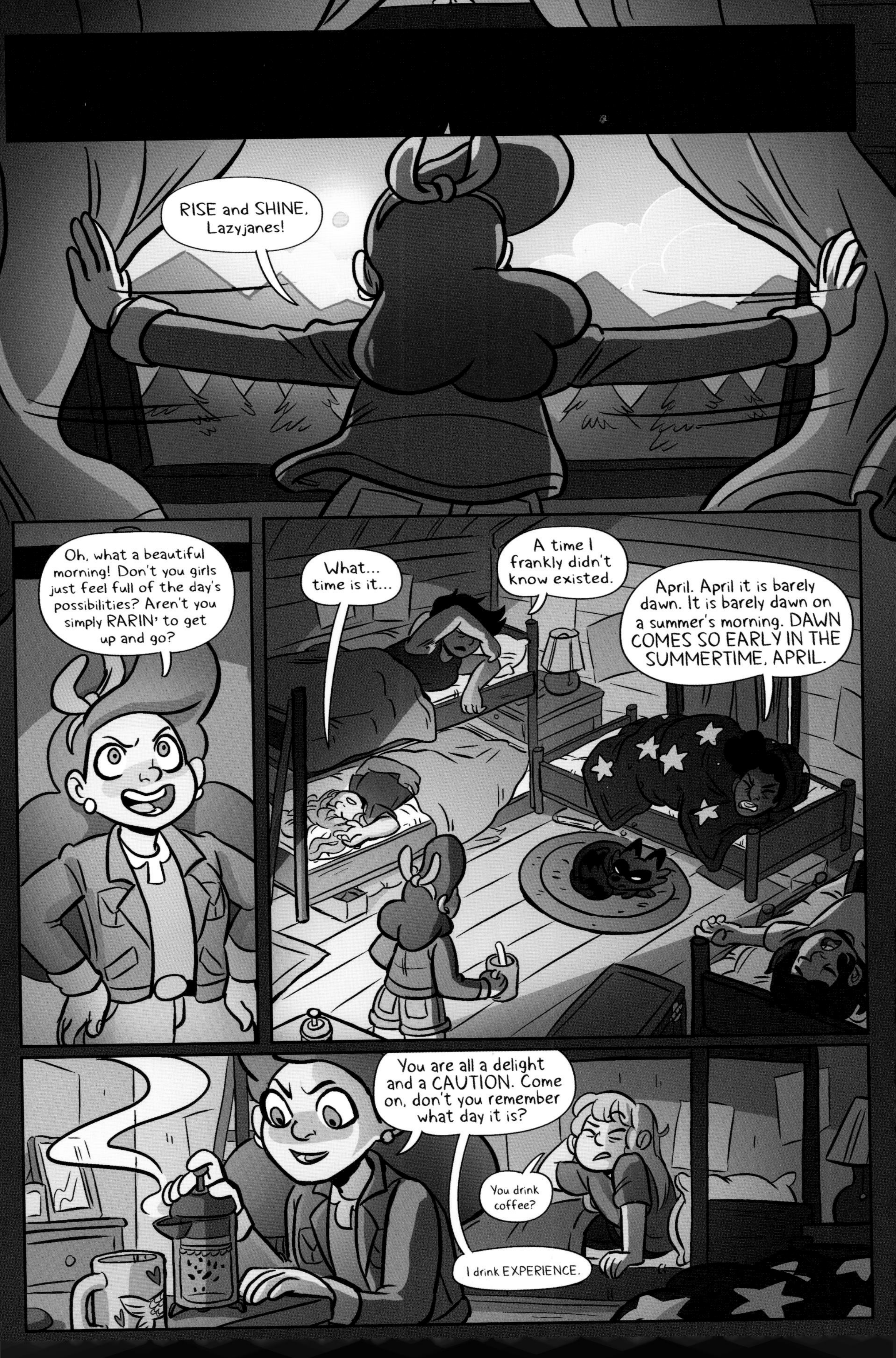
[redacted]
RISE and SHINE, Lazyjanes!
Oh, what a beautiful morning! Don't you girls just feel full of the day's possibilities? Aren't you simply RARIN' to get up and go?
What... time is it...
A time I frankly didn't know existed.
April. April it is barely dawn. It is barely dawn on a summer's morning. DAWN COMES SO EARLY IN THE SUMMERTIME, APRIL.
You are all a delight and a CAUTION. Come on, don't you remember what day it is?
You drink coffee?
I drink EXPERIENCE.

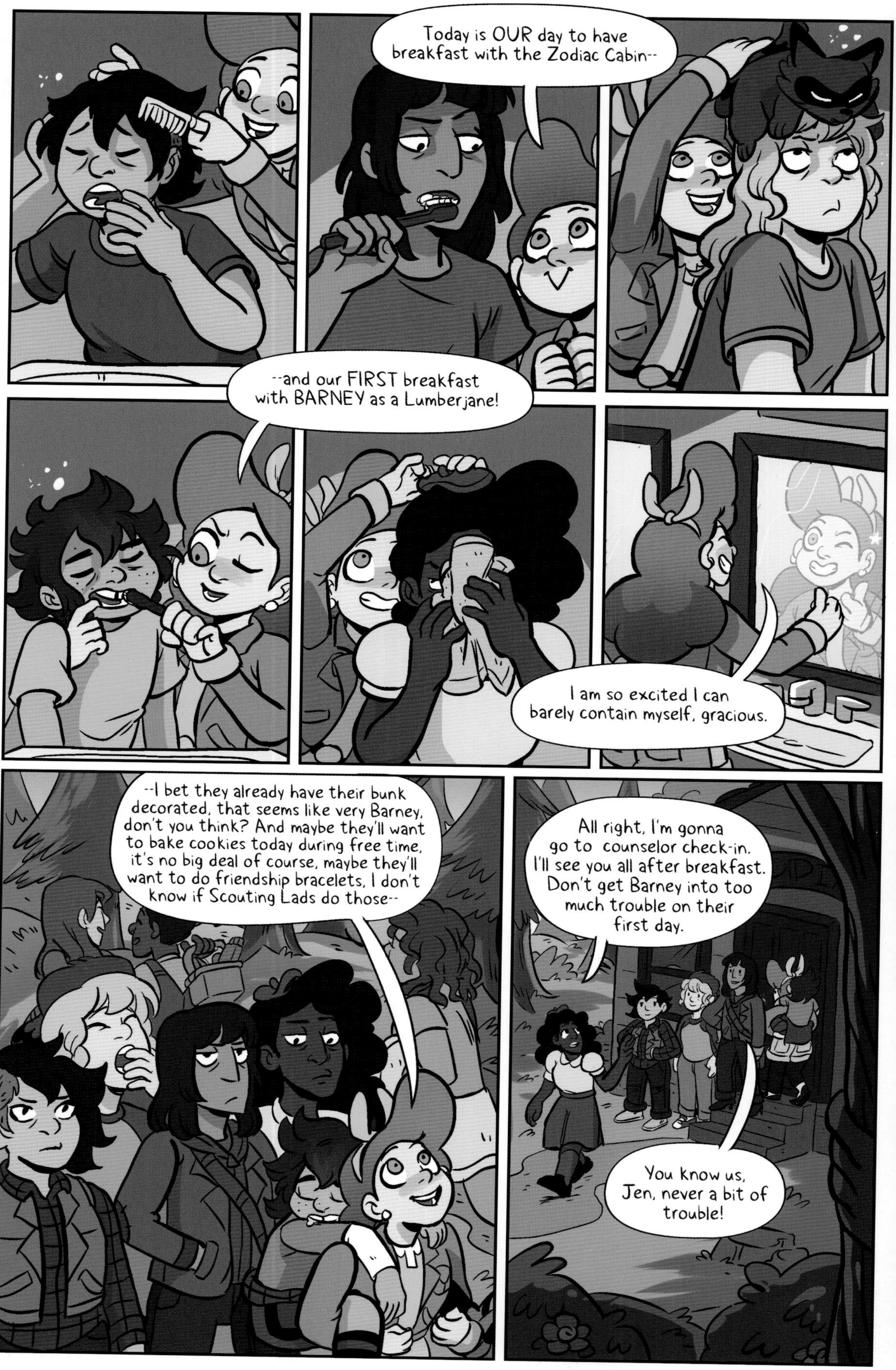

Today is OUR day to have breakfast with the Zodiac Cabin--
--and our FIRST breakfast with BARNEY as a Lumberjane!
I am so excited I can barely contain myself, gracious.
--I bet they already have their bunk decorated, that seems like very Barney, don't you think? And maybe they'll want to bake cookies today during free time, it's no big deal of course, maybe they'll want to do friendship bracelets, I don't know if Scouting Lads do those--
All right, I'm gonna go to counselor check-in. I'll see you all after breakfast. Don't get Barney into too much trouble on their first day.
You know us, Jen, never a bit of trouble!

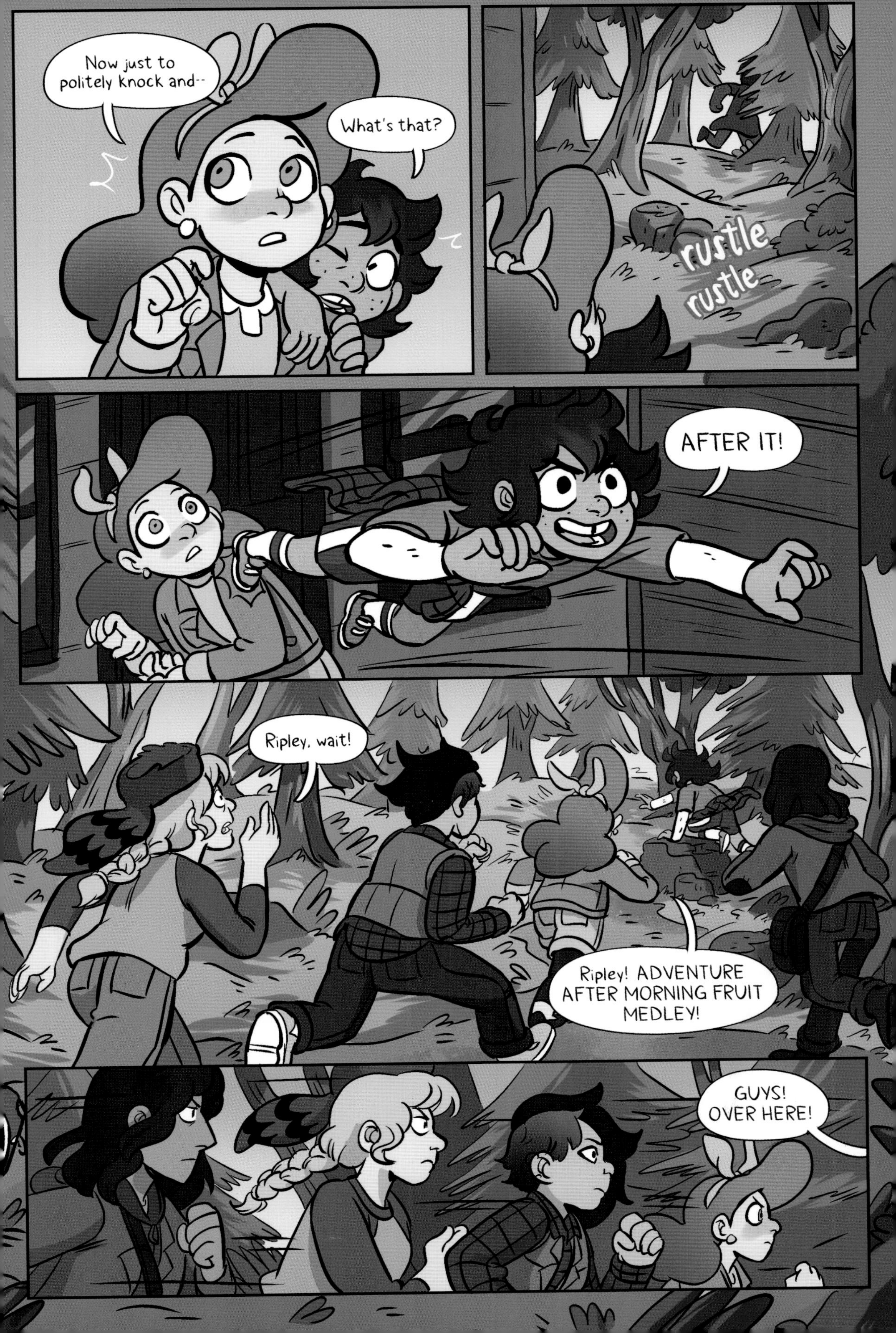
Now just to politely knock and--
What's that?
rustle
rustle
AFTER IT!
Ripley, wait!
Ripley! ADVENTURE AFTER MORNING FRUIT MEDLEY!
GUYS! OVER HERE!

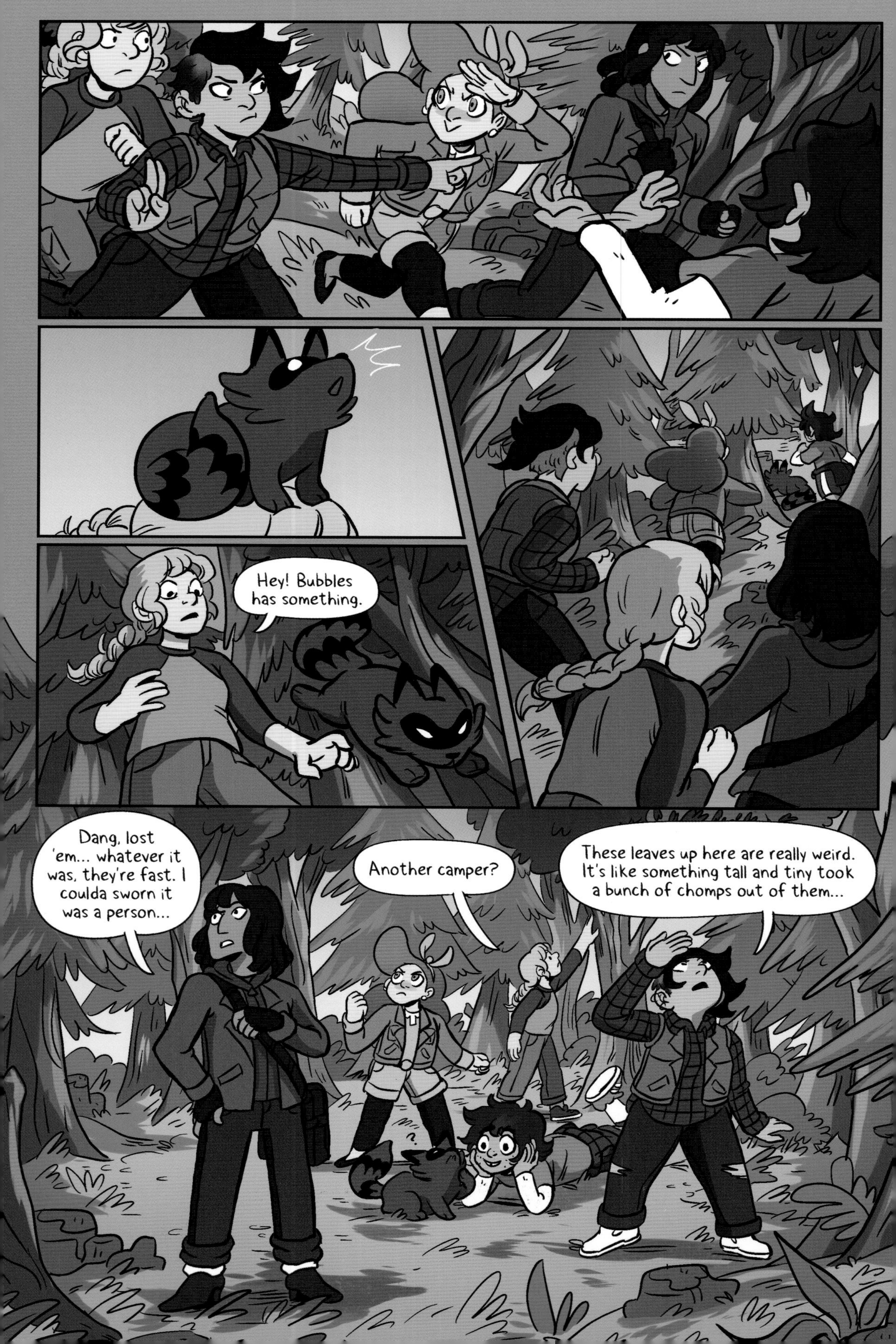
Hey! Bubbles has something.
Dang, lost 'em... whatever it was, they're fast. I coulda sworn it was a person...
Another camper?
These leaves up here are really weird. It's like something tall and tiny took a bunch of chomps out of them...

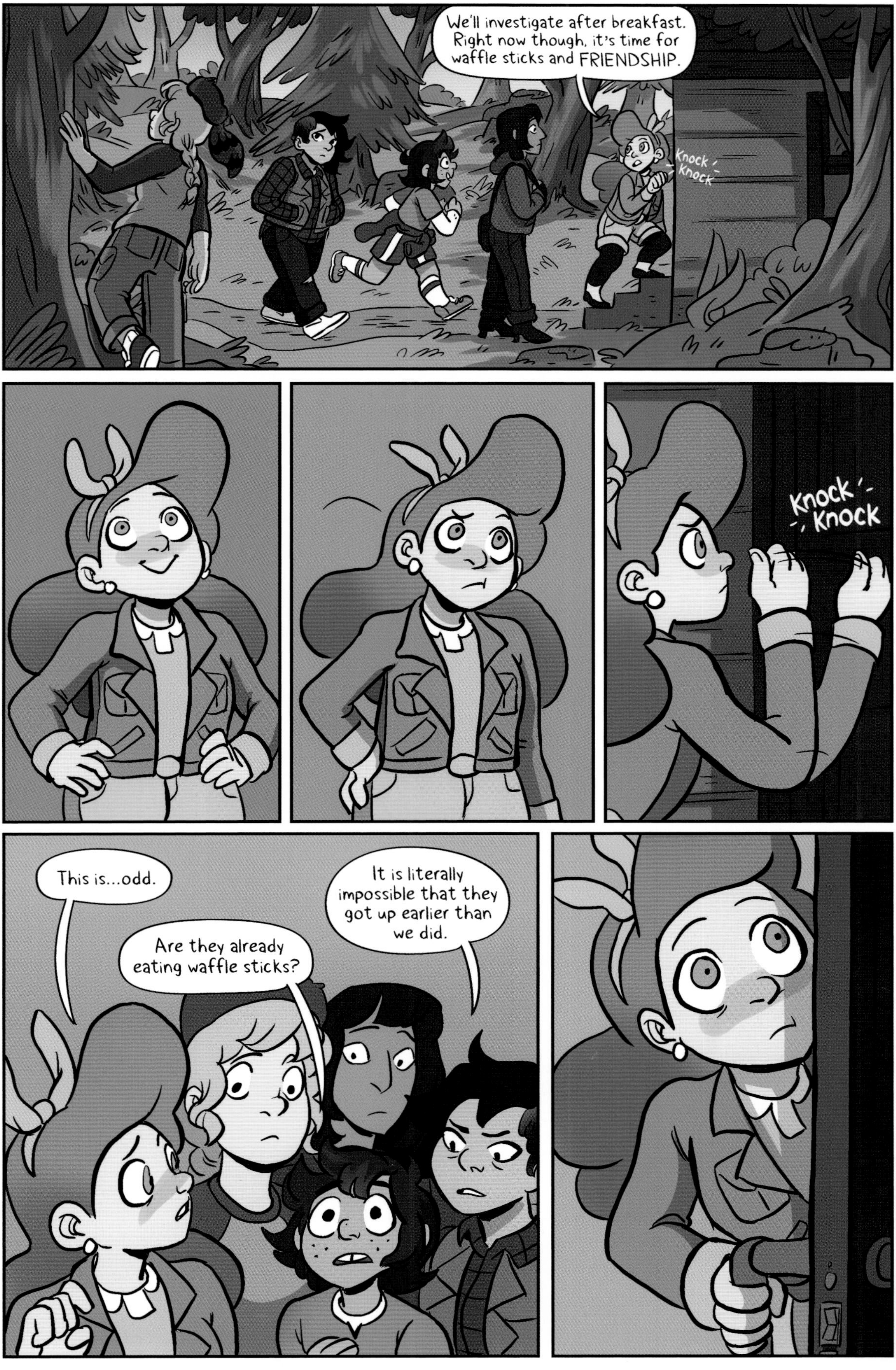
We'll investigate after breakfast. Right now though, it's time for waffle sticks and FRIENDSHIP.
Knock Knock
Knock Knock
This is...odd.
Are they already eating waffle sticks?
It is literally impossible that they got up earlier than we did.

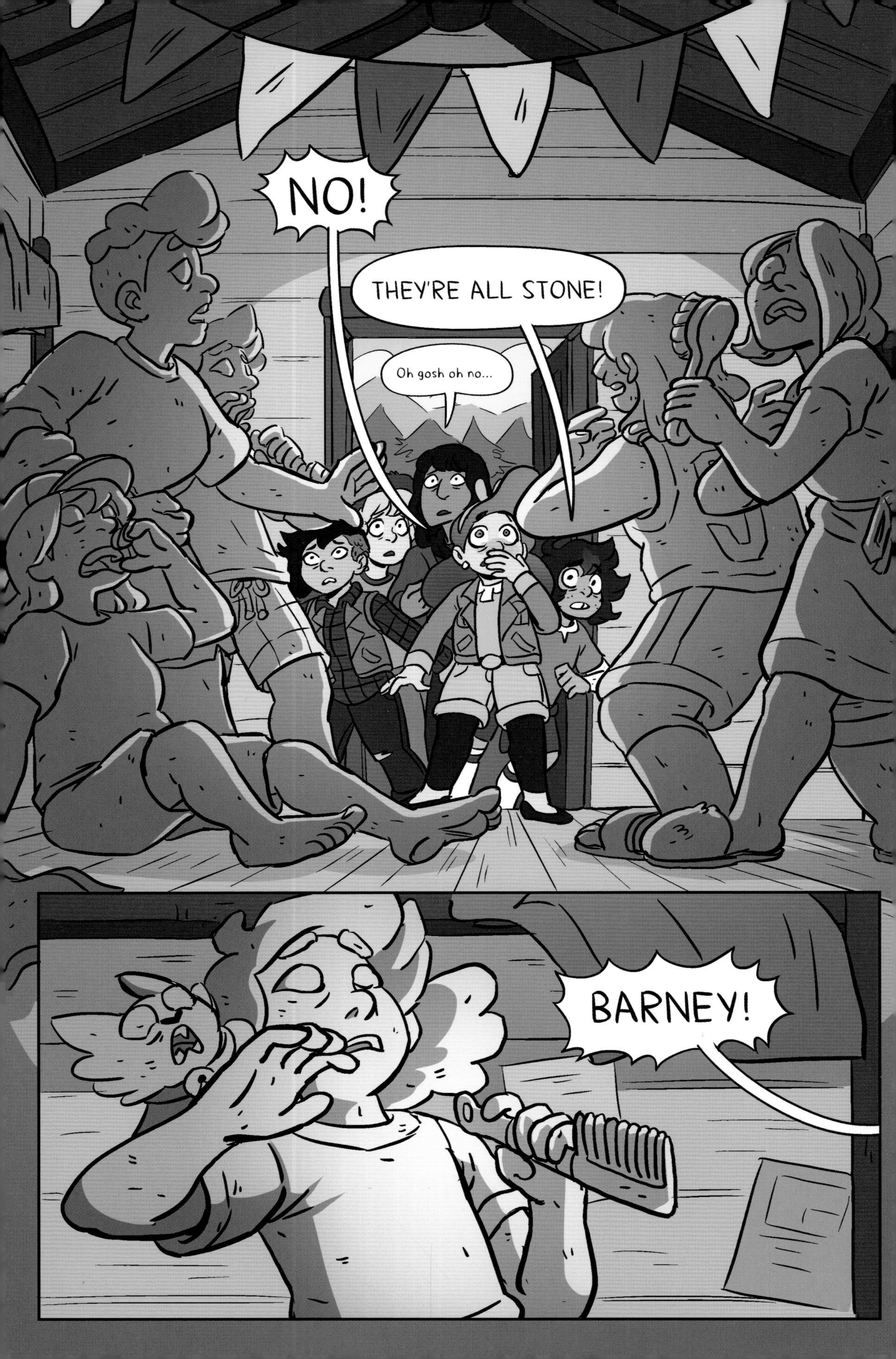
NO!
THEY'RE ALL STONE!
Oh gosh oh no...
BARNEY!

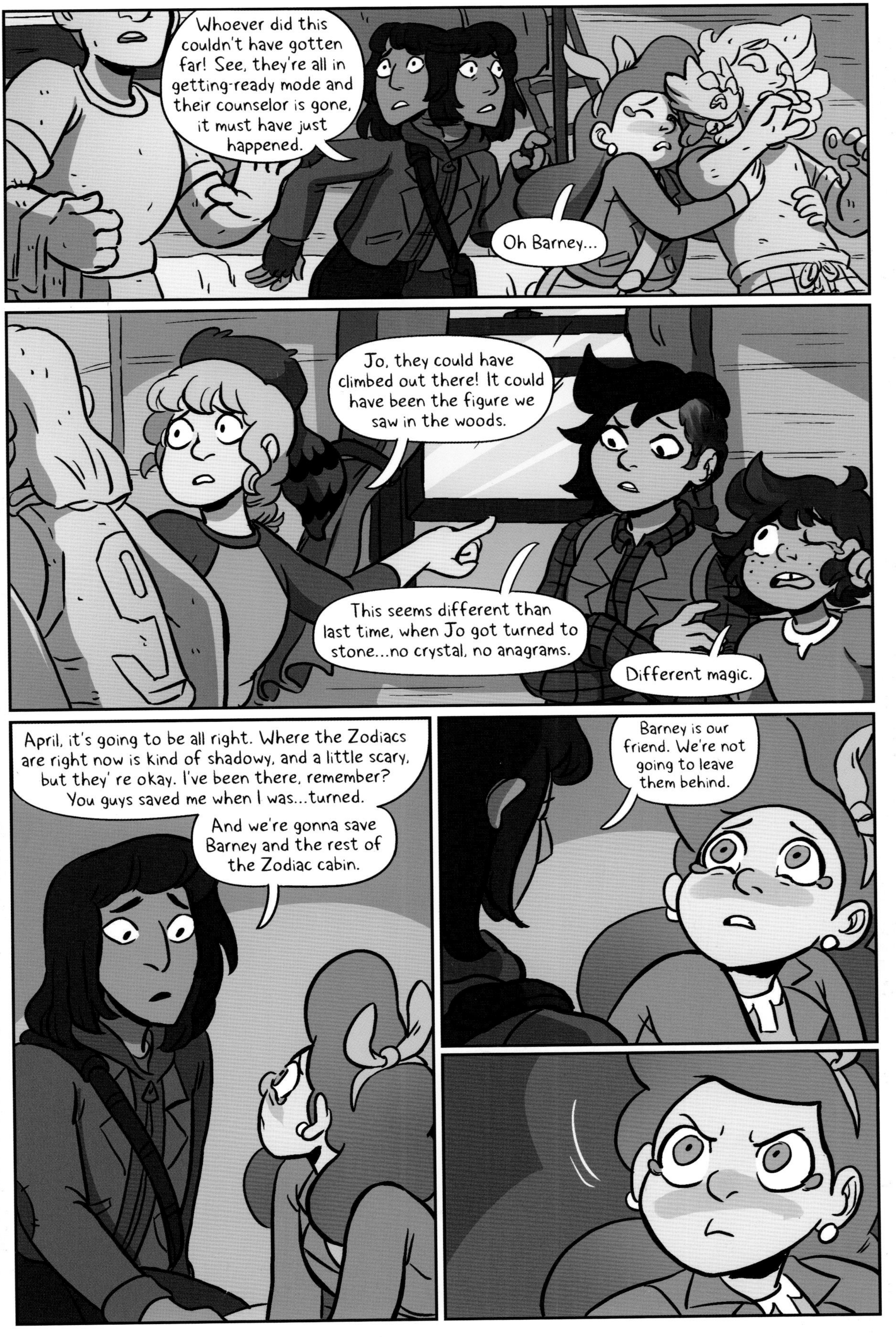
Whoever did this couldn't have gotten far! See, they're all in getting-ready mode and their counselor is gone, it must have just happened.
Oh Barney...
Jo, they could have climbed out there! It could have been the figure we saw in the woods.
This seems different than last time, when Jo got turned to stone...no crystal, no anagrams.
Different magic.
April, it's going to be all right. Where the Zodiacs are right now is kind of shadowy, and a little scary, but they're okay. I've been there, remember? You guys saved me when I was...turned.
And we're gonna save Barney and the rest of the Zodiac cabin.
Barney is our friend. We're not going to leave them behind.

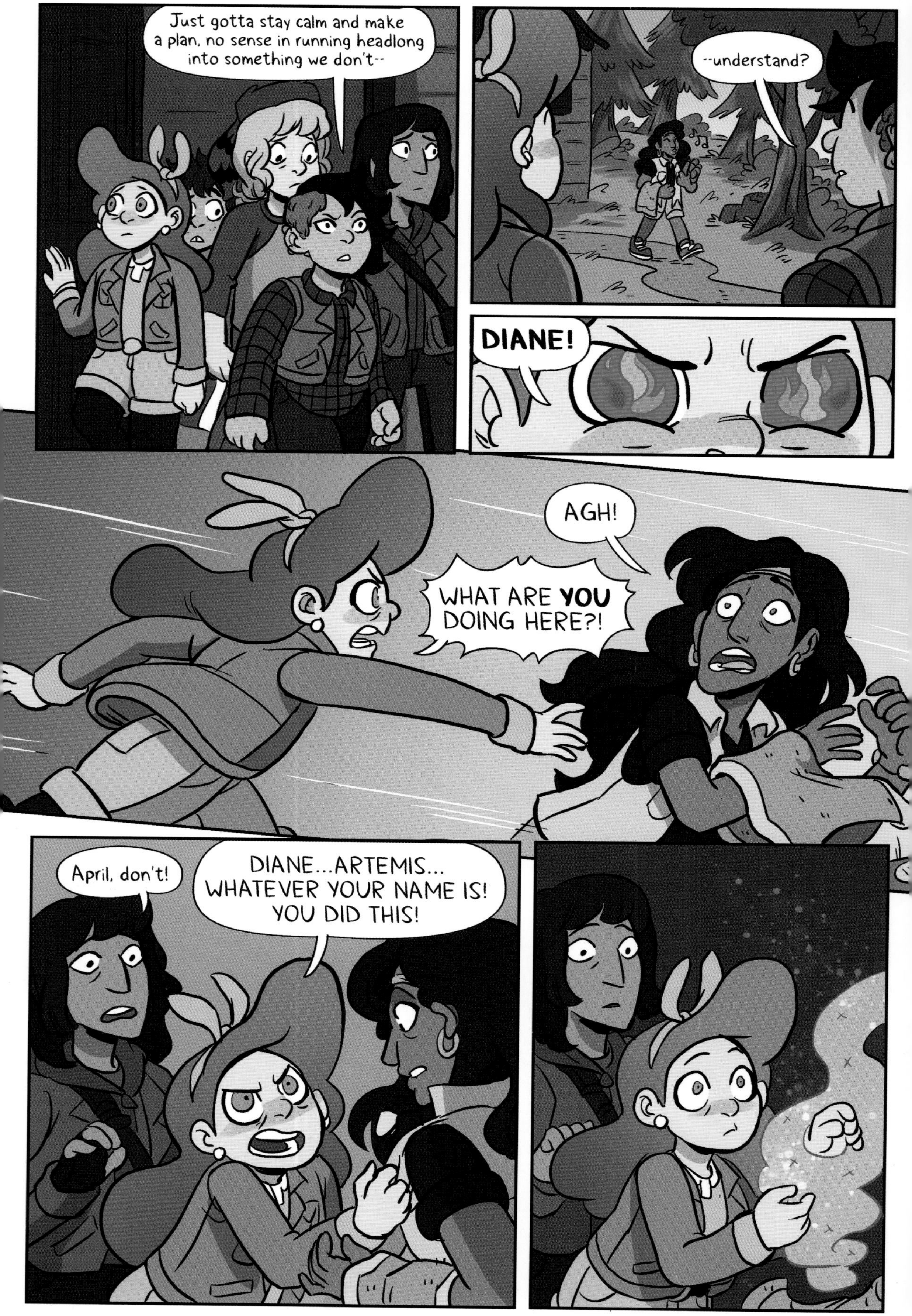
Just gotta stay calm and make a plan, no sense in running headlong into something we don't--
--understand?
DIANE!
AGH!
WHAT ARE **YOU** DOING HERE?!
April, don't!
DIANE...ARTEMIS... WHATEVER YOUR NAME IS! YOU DID THIS!

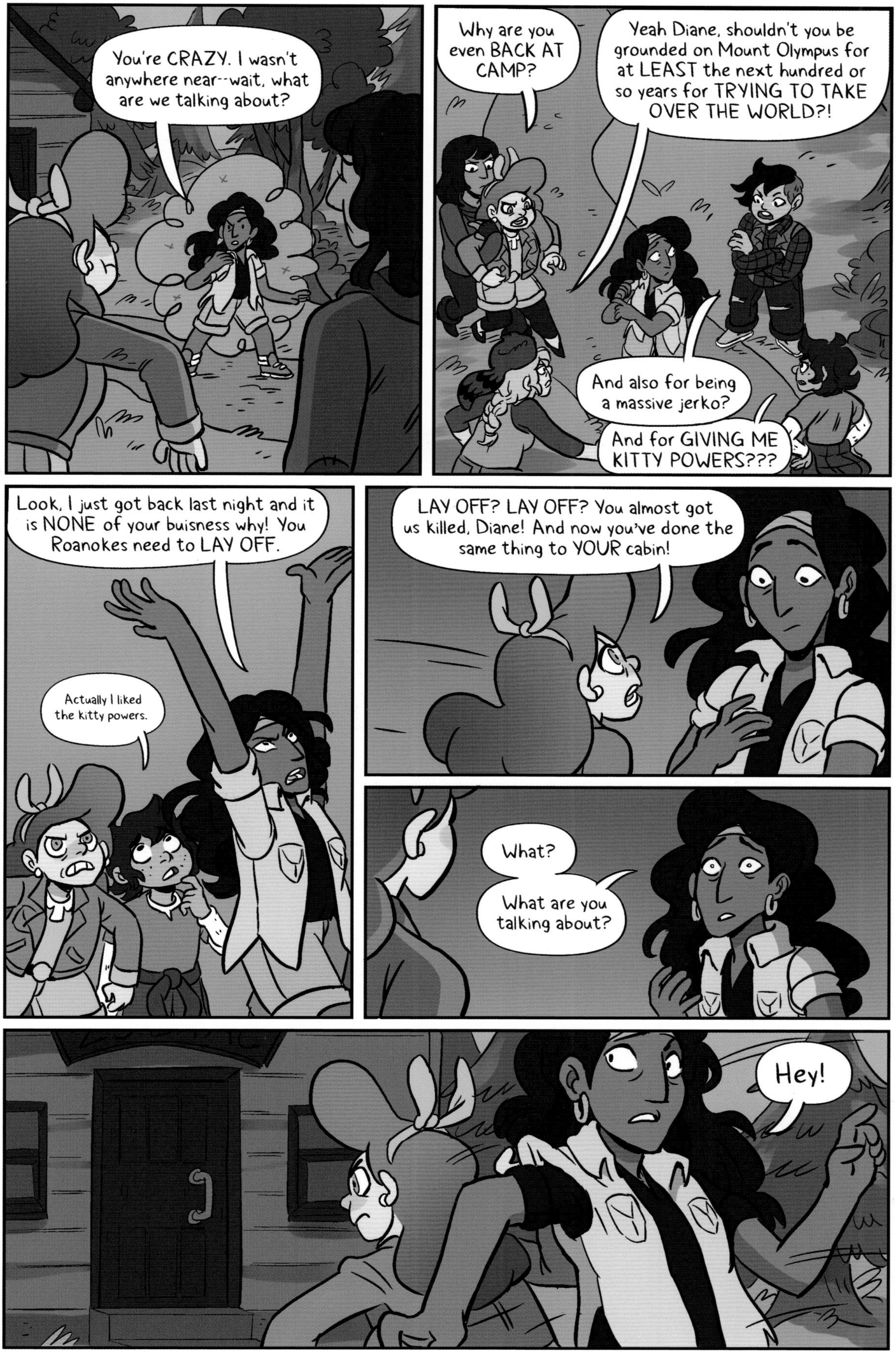
You're CRAZY. I wasn't anywhere near--wait, what are we talking about?
Why are you even BACK AT CAMP?
Yeah Diane, shouldn't you be grounded on Mount Olympus for at LEAST the next hundred or so years for TRYING TO TAKE OVER THE WORLD?!
And also for being a massive jerko?
And for GIVING ME KITTY POWERS???
Look, I just got back last night and it is NONE of your buisness why! You Roanokes need to LAY OFF.
Actually I liked the kitty powers.
LAY OFF? LAY OFF? You almost got us killed, Diane! And now you've done the same thing to YOUR cabin!
What?
What are you talking about?
Hey!

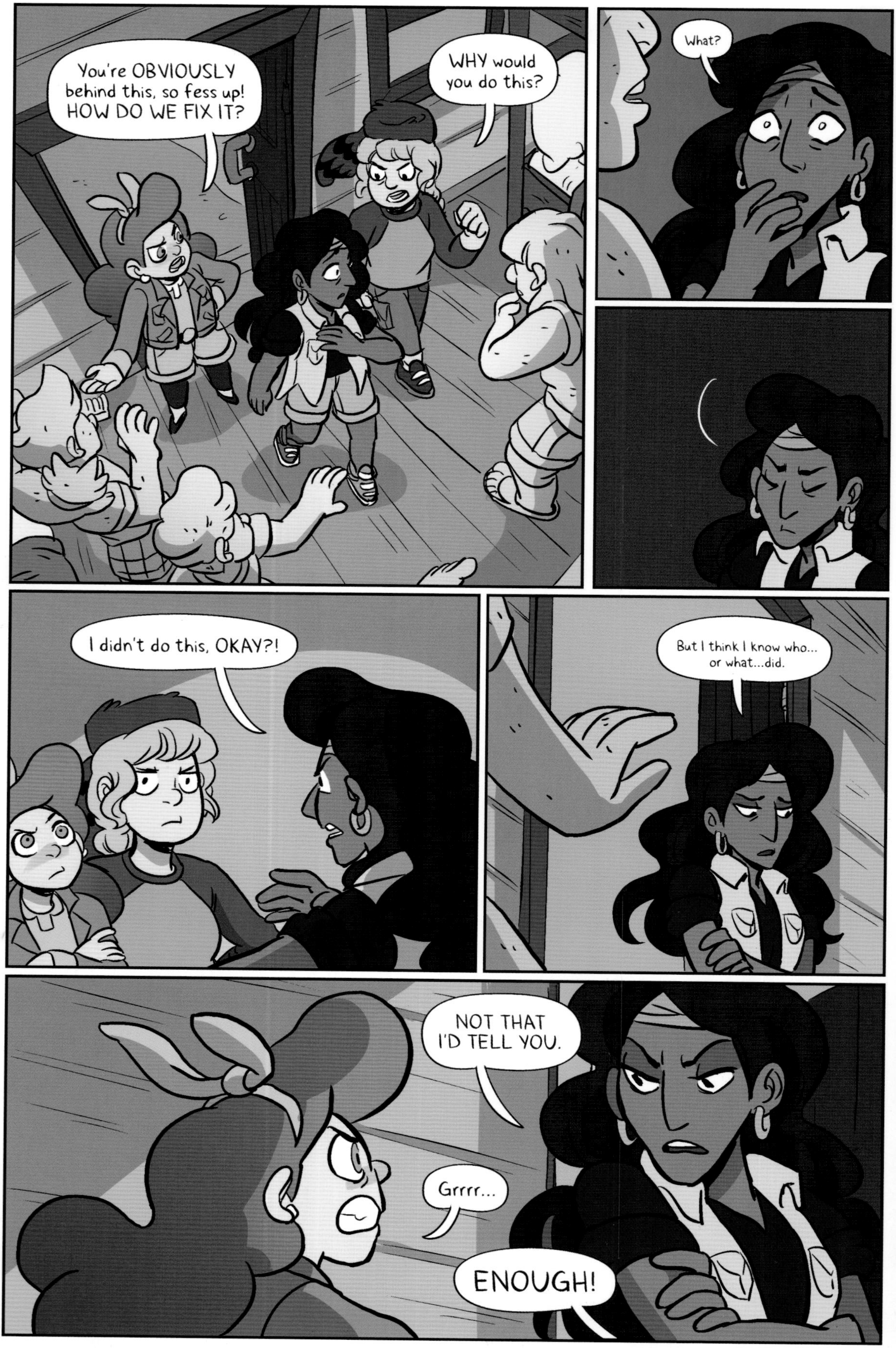
You're OBVIOUSLY behind this, so fess up! HOW DO WE FIX IT?
WHY would you do this?
What?
I didn't do this, OKAY?!
But I think I know who... or what...did.
NOT THAT I'D TELL YOU.
Grrrr...
ENOUGH!

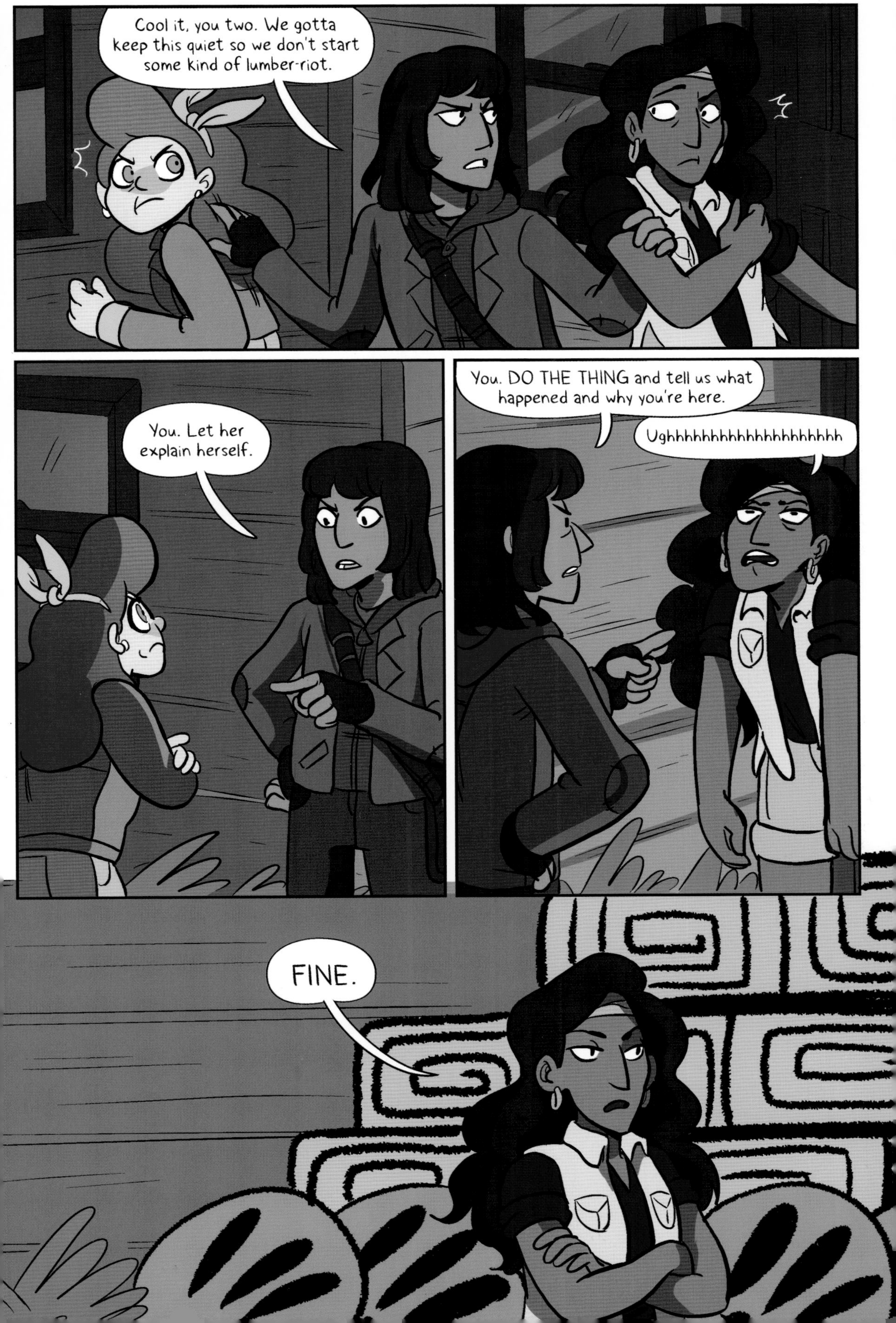
Cool it, you two. We gotta keep this quiet so we don't start some kind of lumber-riot.
You. Let her explain herself.
You. DO THE THING and tell us what happened and why you're here.
Ughhhhhhhhhhhhhhhhhhhh
FINE.

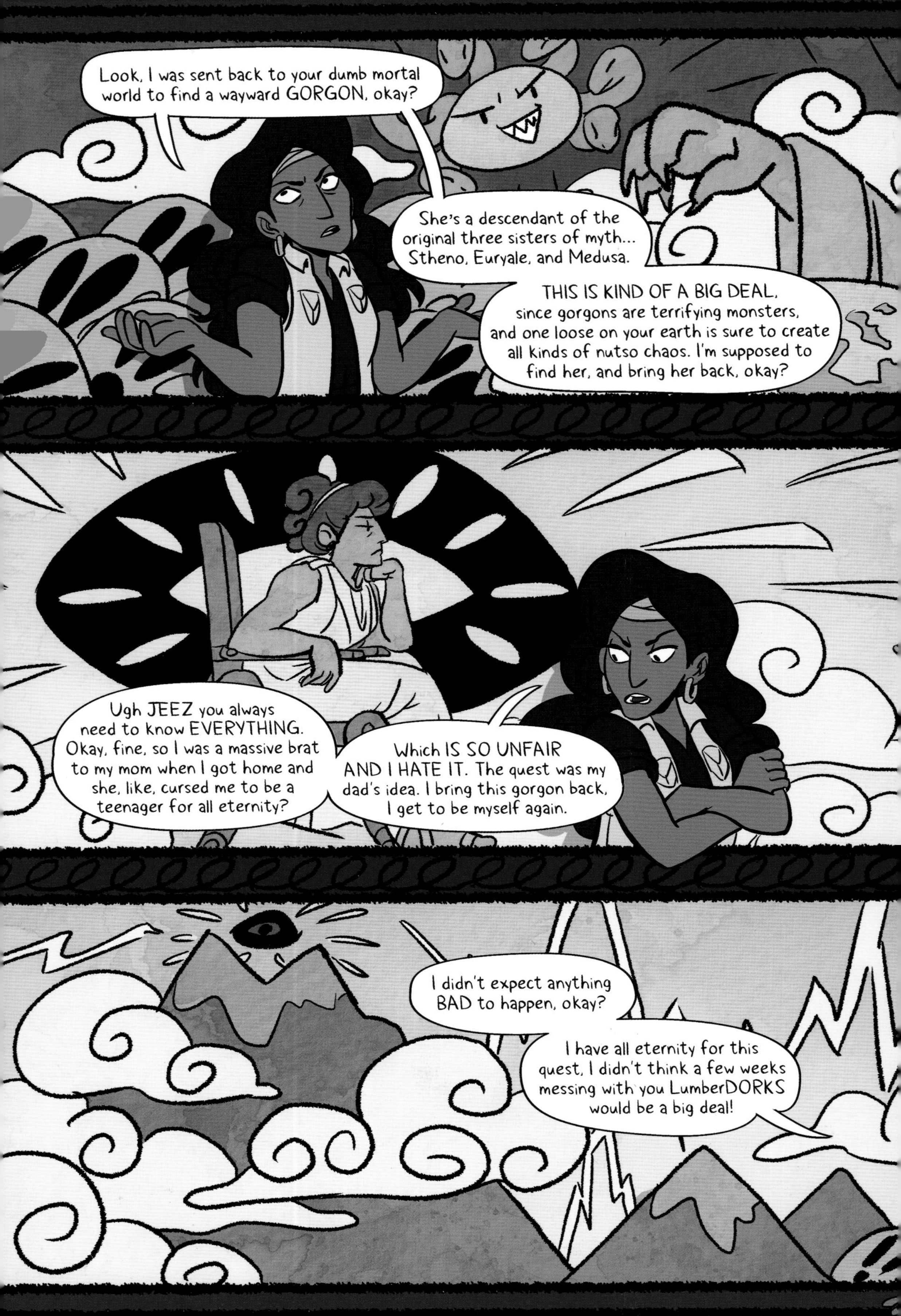

Look, I was sent back to your dumb mortal world to find a wayward GORGON, okay?
She's a descendant of the original three sisters of myth... Stheno, Euryale, and Medusa.
THIS IS KIND OF A BIG DEAL, since gorgons are terrifying monsters, and one loose on your earth is sure to create all kinds of nutso chaos. I'm supposed to find her, and bring her back, okay?
Ugh JEEZ you always need to know EVERYTHING. Okay, fine, so I was a massive brat to my mom when I got home and she, like, cursed me to be a teenager for all eternity?
Which IS SO UNFAIR AND I HATE IT. The quest was my dad's idea. I bring this gorgon back, I get to be myself again.
I didn't expect anything BAD to happen, okay?
I have all eternity for this quest, I didn't think a few weeks messing with you LumberDORKS would be a big deal!

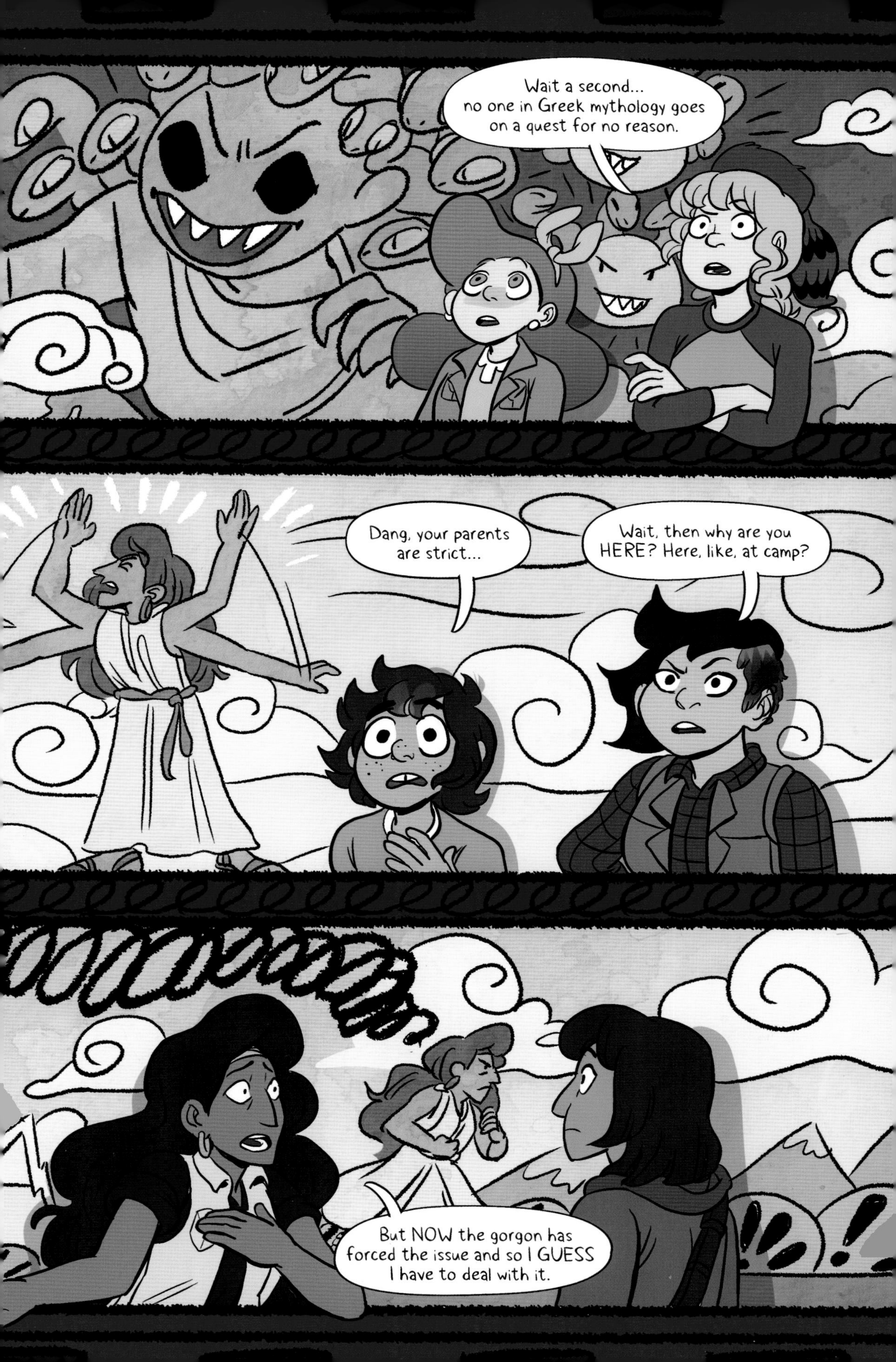
Wait a second... no one in Greek mythology goes on a quest for no reason.
Dang, your parents are strict...
Wait, then why are you HERE? Here, like, at camp?
But NOW the gorgon has forced the issue and so I GUESS I have to deal with it.

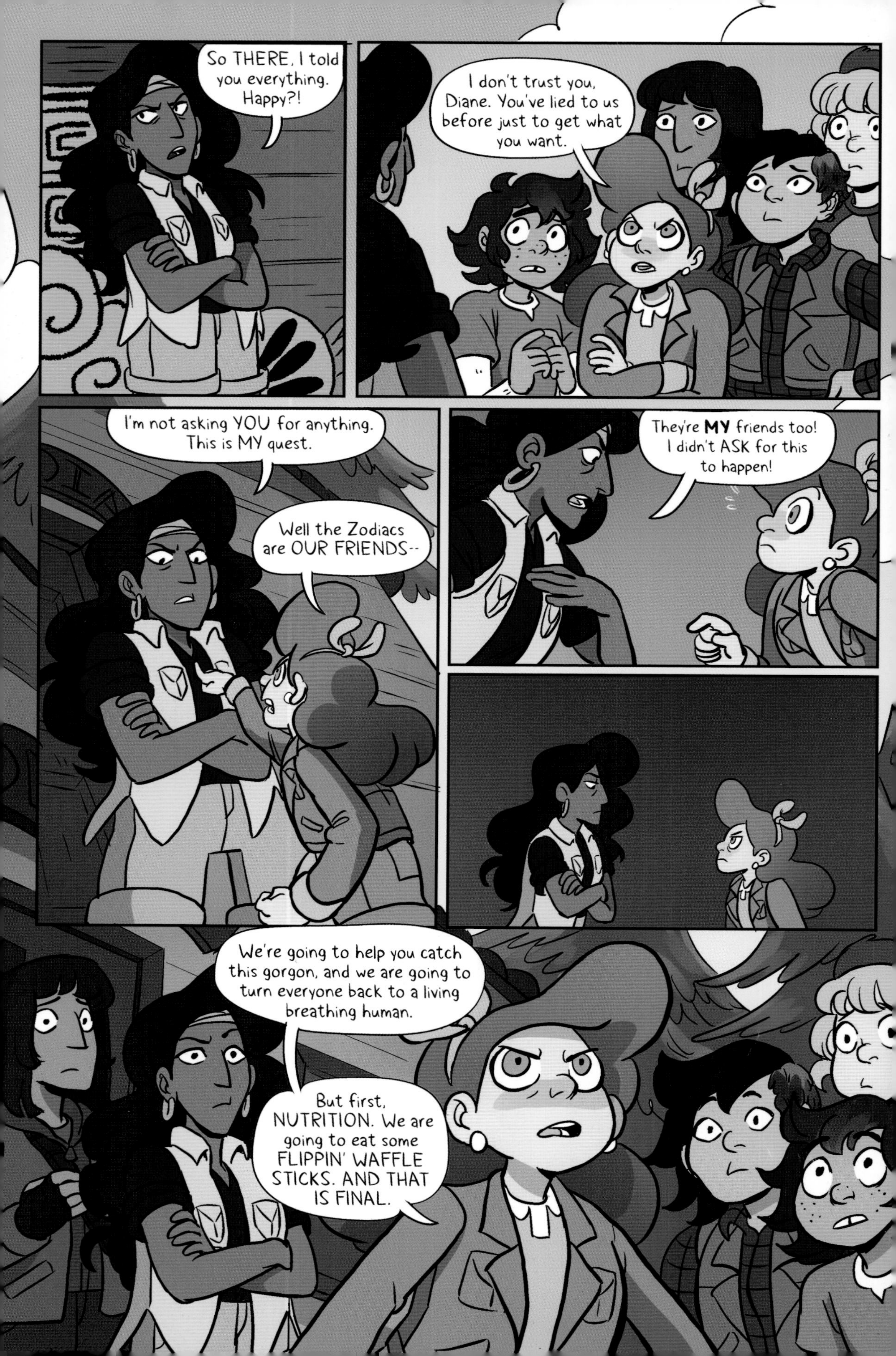
So THERE, I told you everything. Happy?!
I don't trust you, Diane. You've lied to us before just to get what you want.
I'm not asking YOU for anything. This is MY quest.
Well the Zodiacs are OUR FRIENDS--
They're **MY** friends too! I didn't ASK for this to happen!
We're going to help you catch this gorgon, and we are going to turn everyone back to a living breathing human.
But first, NUTRITION. We are going to eat some FLIPPIN' WAFFLE STICKS. AND THAT IS FINAL.

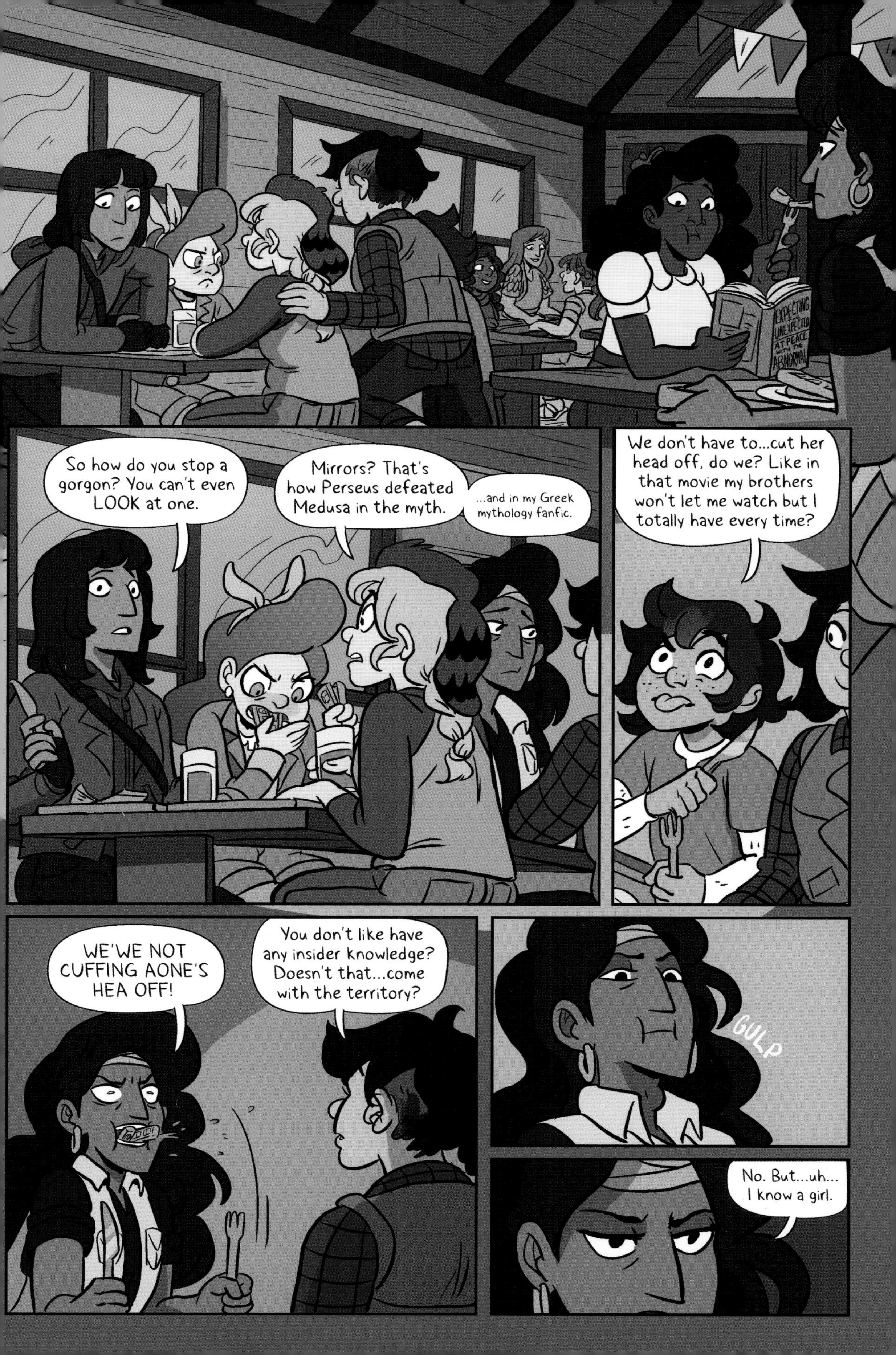
EXPECTING THE UNEXPECTED AT PEACE WITH THE ABNORMAL
So how do you stop a gorgon? You can't even LOOK at one.
Mirrors? That's how Perseus defeated Medusa in the myth.
...and in my Greek mythology fanfic.
We don't have to...cut her head off, do we? Like in that movie my brothers won't let me watch but I totally have every time?
WE'WE NOT CUFFING AONE'S HEA OFF!
You don't like have any insider knowledge? Doesn't that...come with the territory?
GULP
No. But...uh... I know a girl.

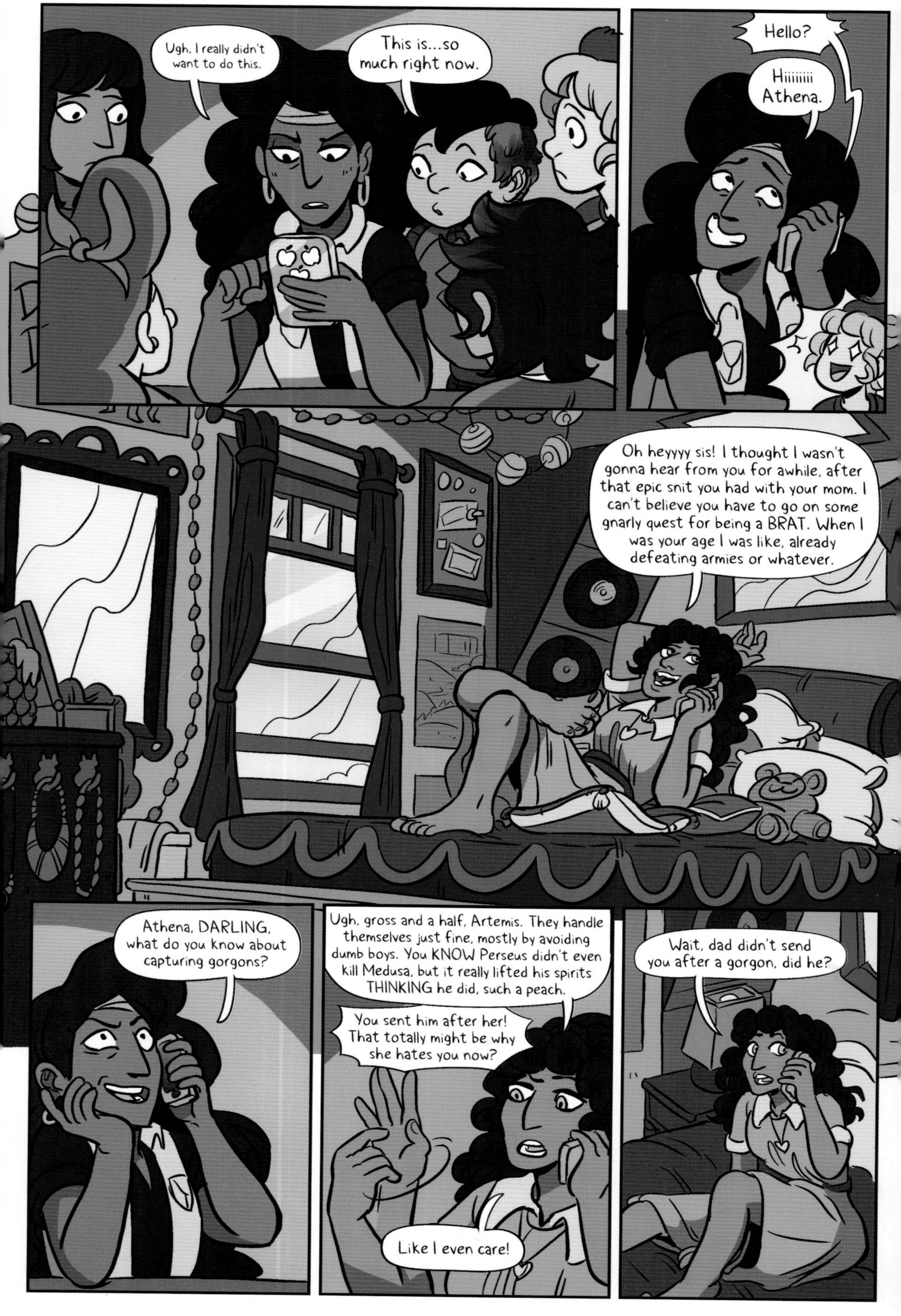

Ugh, I really didn't want to do this.
This is...so much right now.
Hello?
Hiiiiiiii Athena.
Oh heyyyy sis! I thought I wasn't gonna hear from you for awhile, after that epic snit you had with your mom. I can't believe you have to go on some gnarly quest for being a BRAT. When I was your age I was like, already defeating armies or whatever.
Athena, DARLING, what do you know about capturing gorgons?
Ugh, gross and a half, Artemis. They handle themselves just fine, mostly by avoiding dumb boys. You KNOW Perseus didn't even kill Medusa, but it really lifted his spirits THINKING he did, such a peach.
You sent him after her! That totally might be why she hates you now?
Like I even care!
Wait, dad didn't send you after a gorgon, did he?

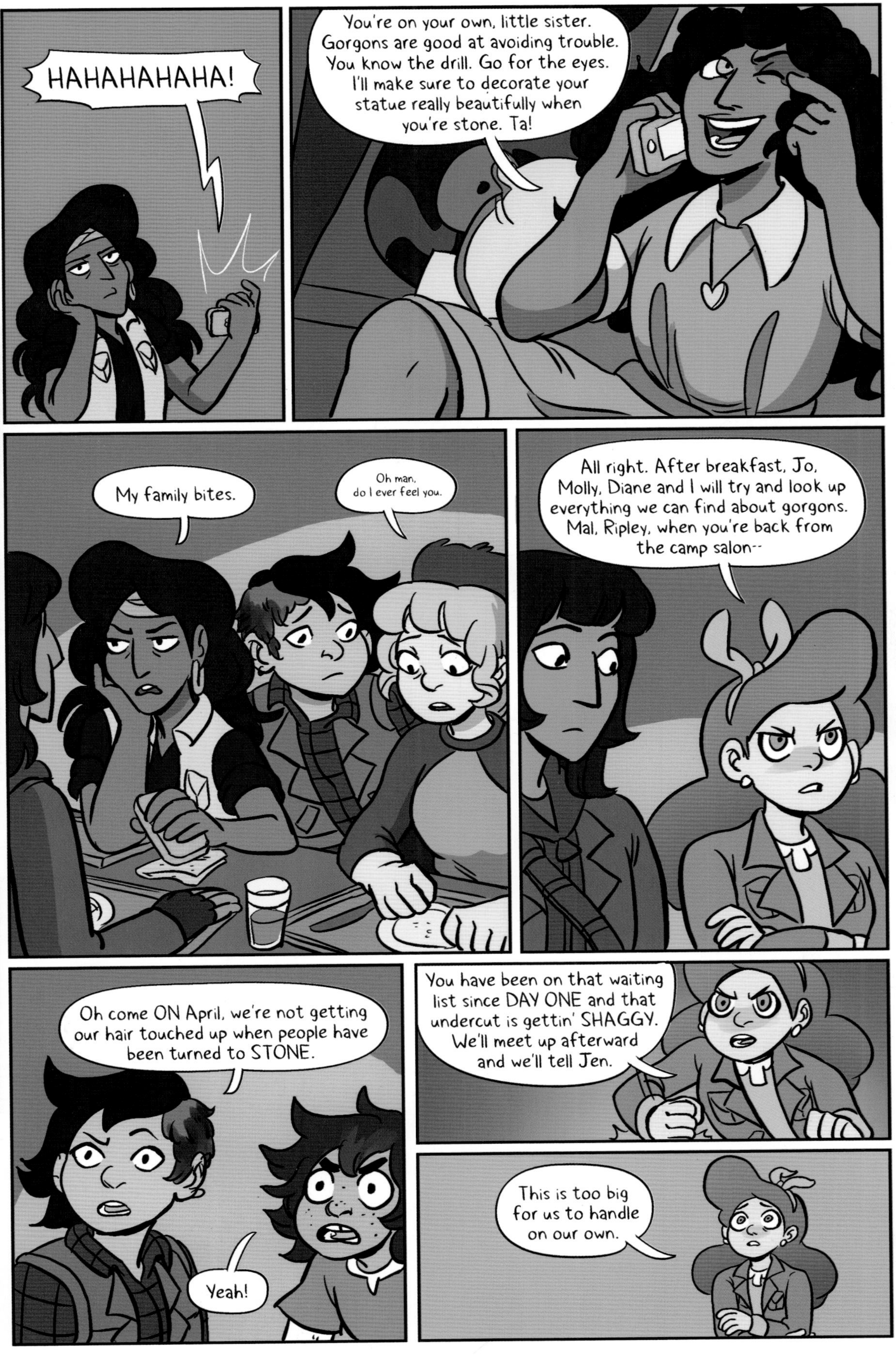
HAHAHAHAHA!
You're on your own, little sister. Gorgons are good at avoiding trouble. You know the drill. Go for the eyes. I'll make sure to decorate your statue really beautifully when you're stone. Ta!
My family bites.
Oh man, do I ever feel you.
All right. After breakfast, Jo, Molly, Diane and I will try and look up everything we can find about gorgons. Mal, Ripley, when you're back from the camp salon--
Oh come ON April, we're not getting our hair touched up when people have been turned to STONE.
Yeah!
You have been on that waiting list since DAY ONE and that undercut is gettin' SHAGGY. We'll meet up afterward and we'll tell Jen.
This is too big for us to handle on our own.

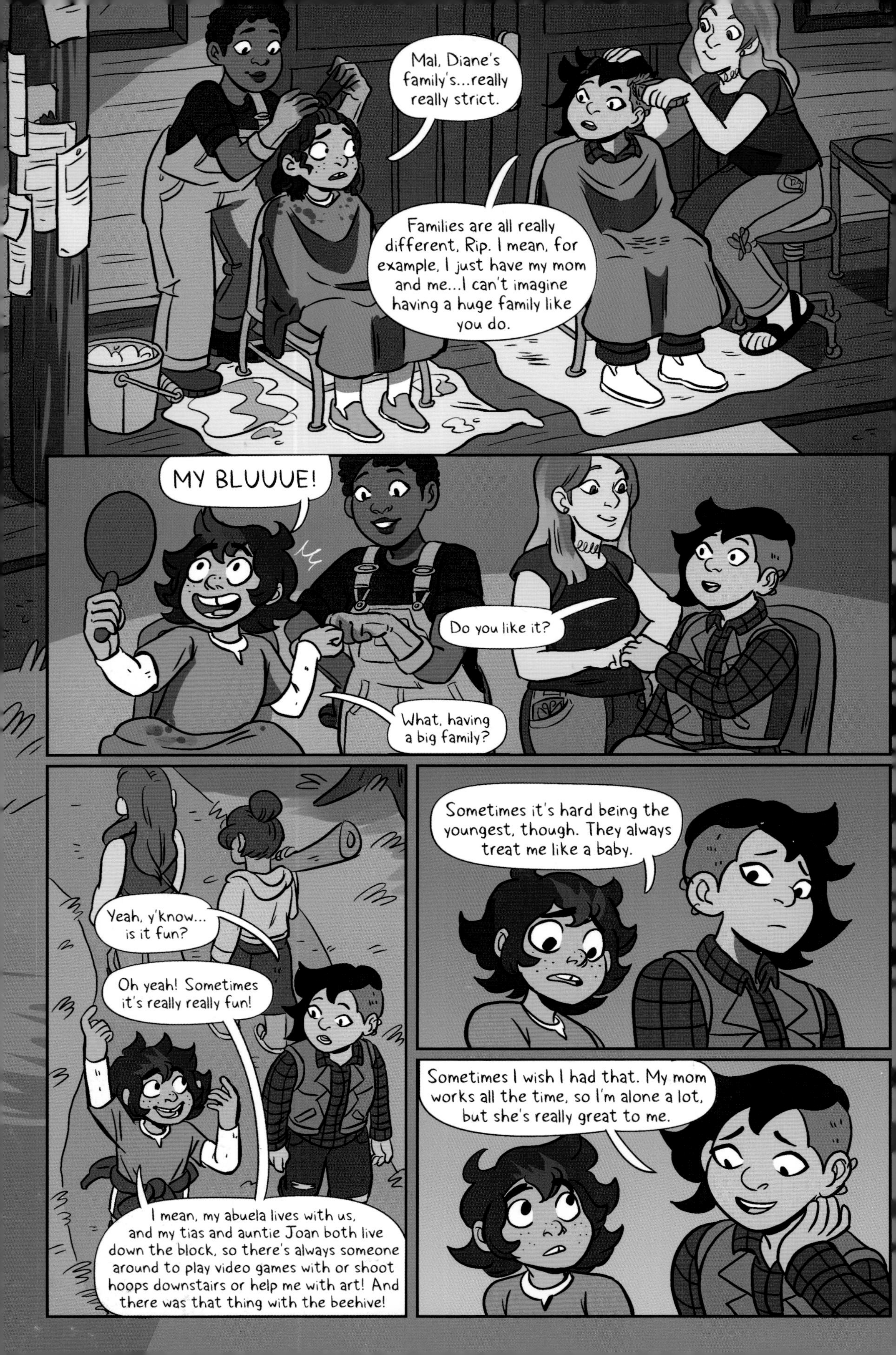
Mal, Diane's family's...really really strict.
Families are all really different, Rip. I mean, for example, I just have my mom and me...I can't imagine having a huge family like you do.
MY BLUUUE!
Do you like it?
What, having a big family?
Yeah, y'know... is it fun?
Oh yeah! Sometimes it's really really fun!
I mean, my abuela lives with us, and my tias and auntie Joan both live down the block, so there's always someone around to play video games with or shoot hoops downstairs or help me with art! And there was that thing with the beehive!
Sometimes it's hard being the youngest, though. They always treat me like a baby.
Sometimes I wish I had that. My mom works all the time, so I'm alone a lot, but she's really great to me.

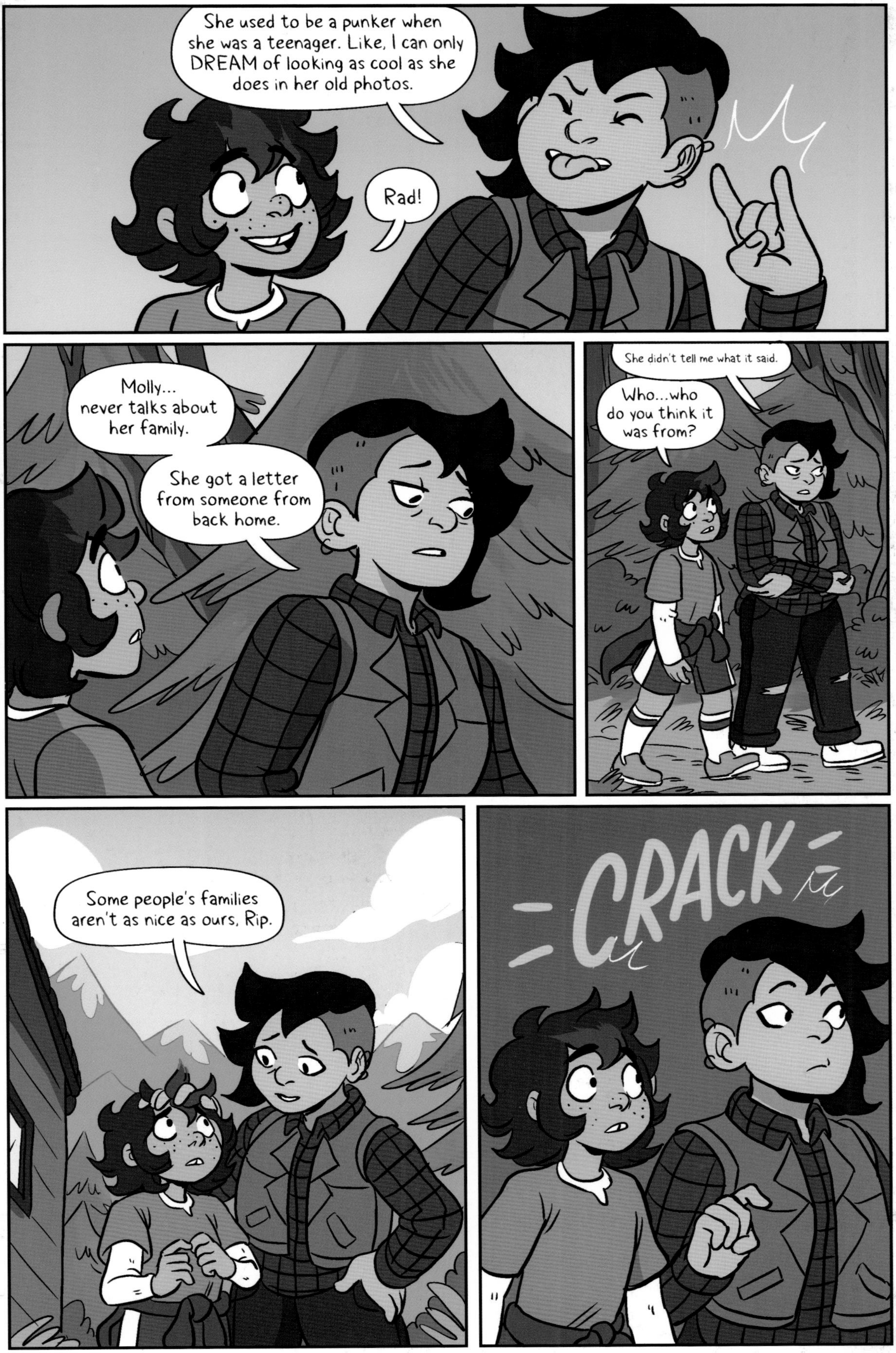
She used to be a punker when she was a teenager. Like, I can only DREAM of looking as cool as she does in her old photos.
Rad!
Molly... never talks about her family.
She got a letter from someone from back home.
She didn't tell me what it said.
Who...who do you think it was from?
Some people's families aren't as nice as ours, Rip.
CRACK

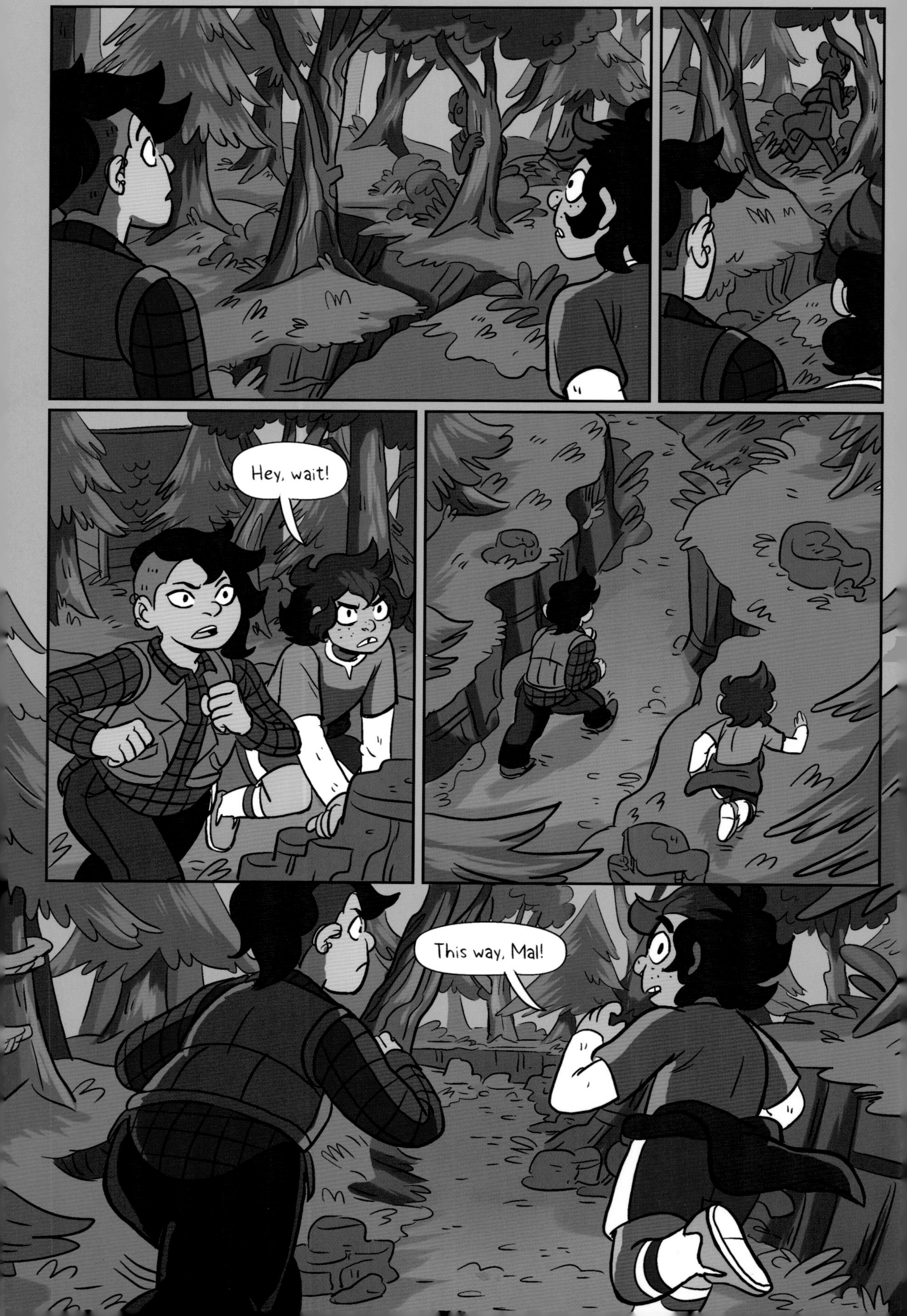

Hey, wait!
This way, Mal!

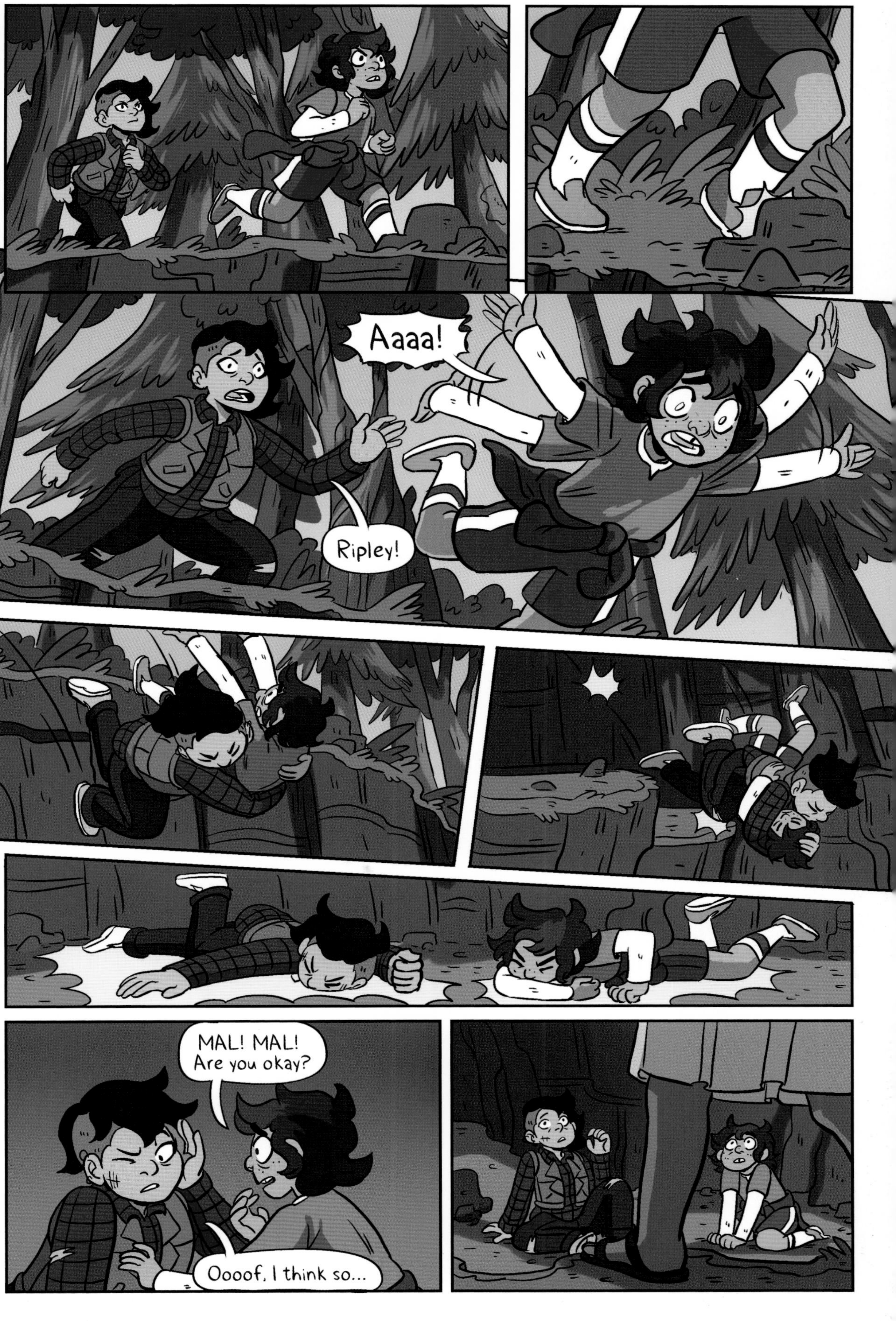
Aaaa!
Ripley!
MAL! MAL!
Are you okay?
Oooof, I think so...

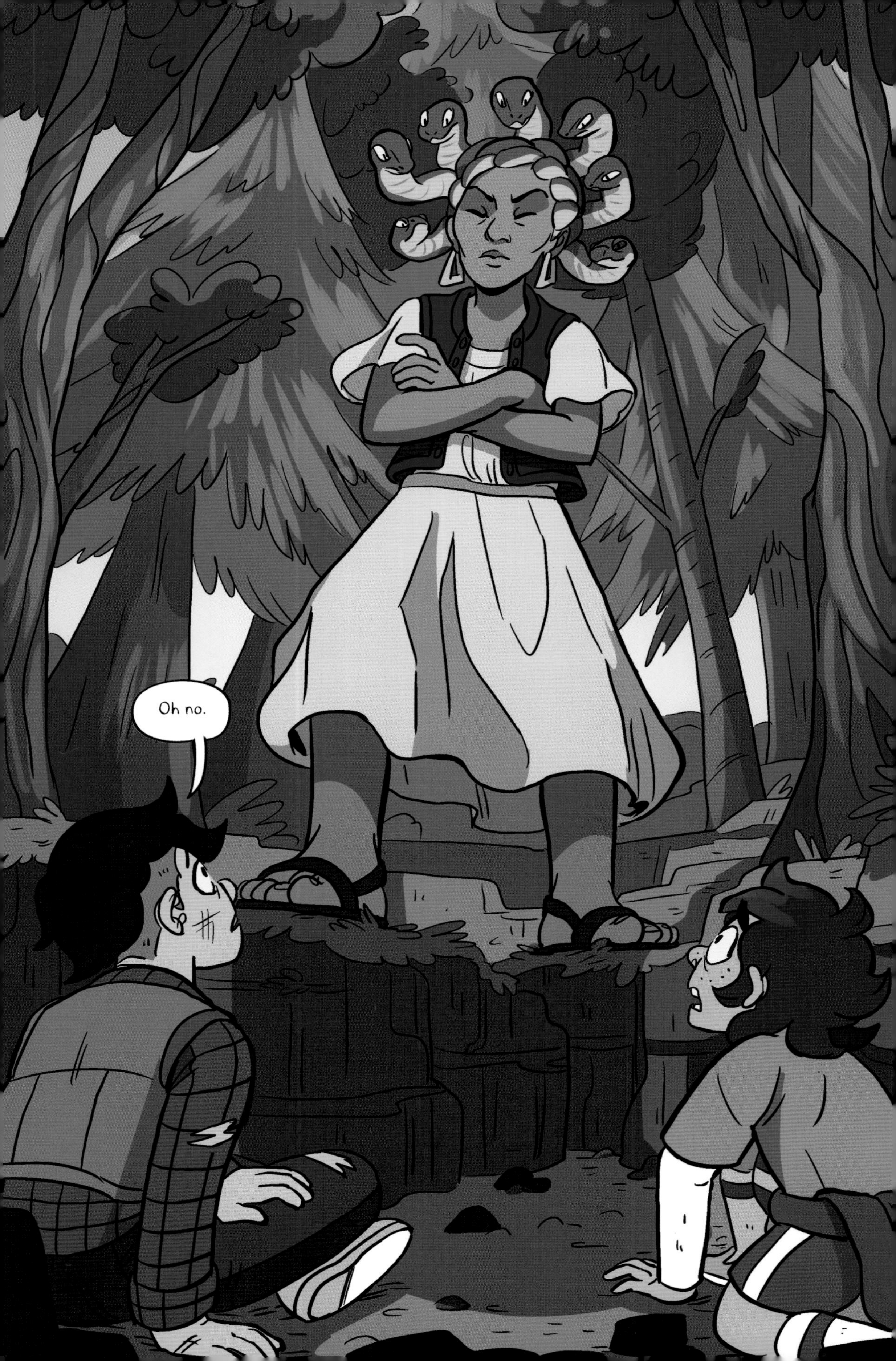
Oh no.

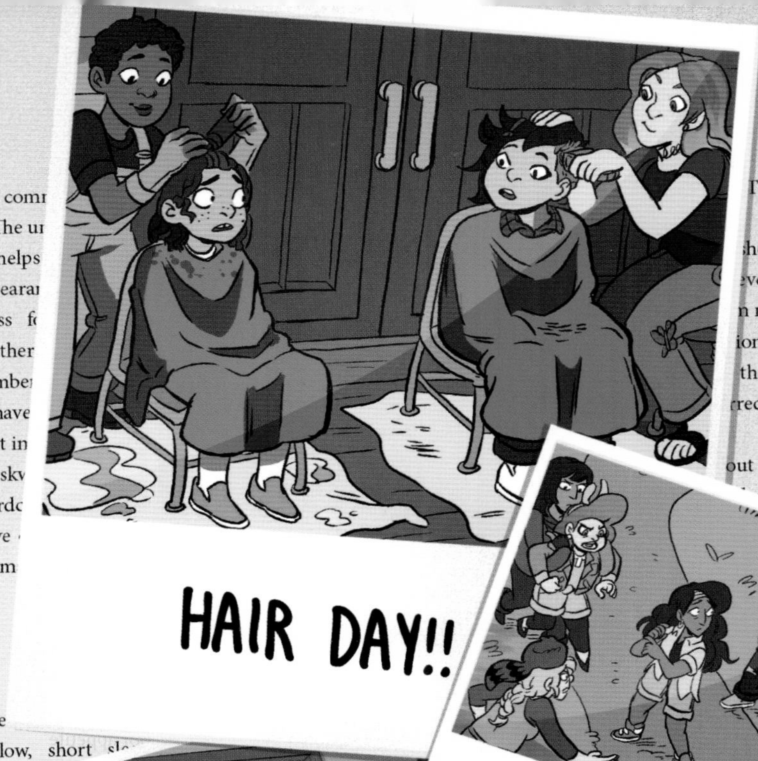
HAIR DAY!!

will comm

The u
It helps
appeara
dress f
Further
Lumbe
to have
part in
Thiskw
Hardc
have
them

THE UNIFORM

should be worn at camp
events when Lumberjanes
n may also be worn at other
ions. It should be worn as a
the uniform dress with
rrect shoes, and stocking or

out grows her uniform or
ng to anoter Lumberjane.
insignia she has
her
her

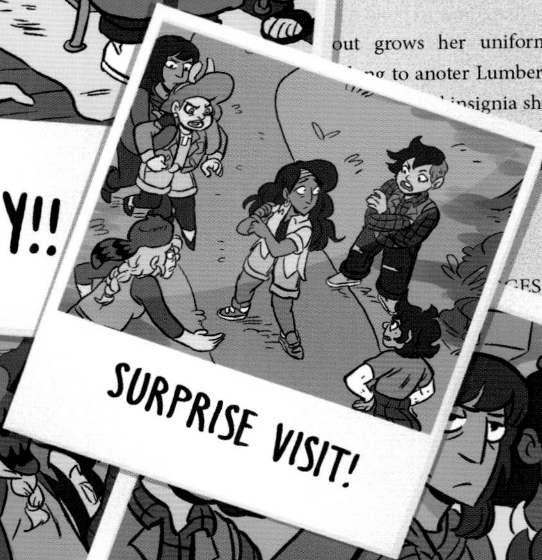
SURPRISE VISIT!

CES

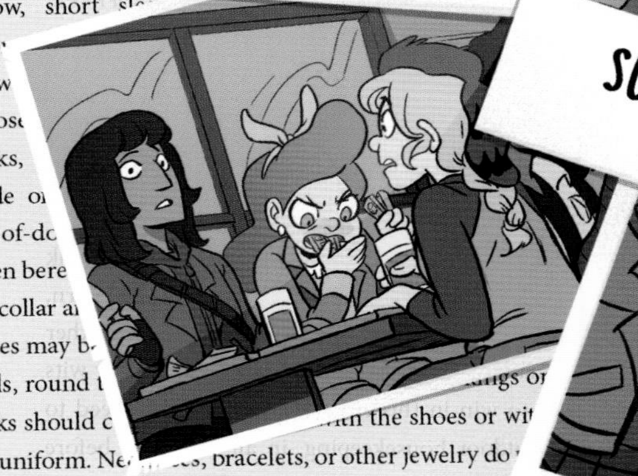

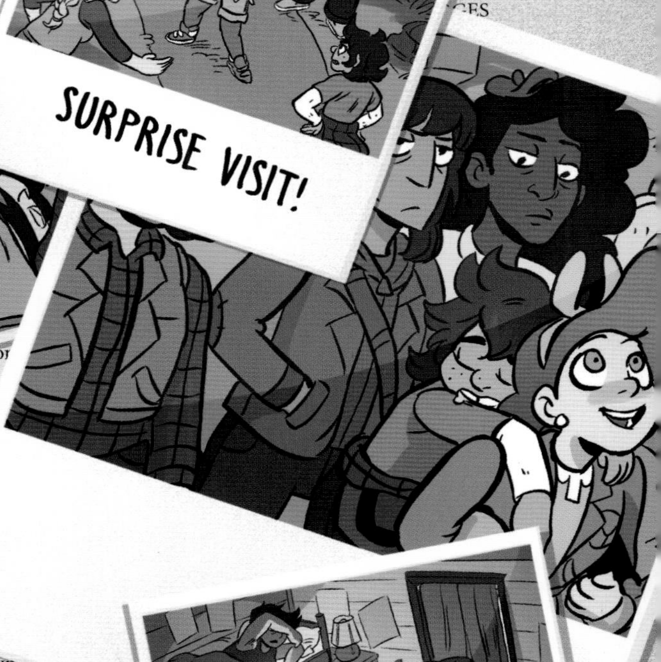

The
yellow, short sl
emb
the w
choos
slacks,
made o
out-of-do
green bere
the collar a
Shoes may b
heels, round t ings or
socks should c th the shoes or wi
the uniform. Ne es, bracelets, or other jewelry do
belong with a Lumberjane uniform.

HOW TO WEAR THE UNIFORM

To look well in a uniform demands first of uniform be kept in good condition—clean pressed. See that the skirt is the right length for your own height and build, that the belt is adjusted to your waist, that your shoes and stockings are in keeping with the uniform, that you watch your posture and carry yourself with dignity and grace. If the beret is removed indoors, be sure that your hair is neat and kept in place with an insonspicuous clip or ribbon. When you wear a Lumberjane uniform you are identified as a member of this organization and you should be doubly careful to conduct yourself in a way that will show everyone that courtesy and thoughtfullness are part of being a Lumberjane. People are likely to judge a whole nation by the selfishness of a few individuals, to criticize a whole family because of the misconduct of one member, and to feel unkindly toward and organization because of the

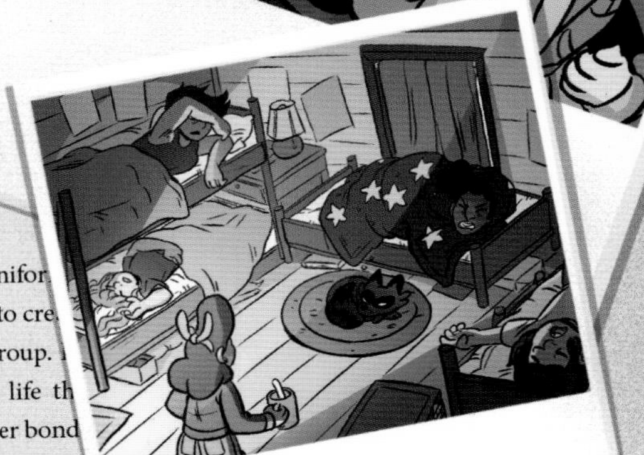
MORNING PERSON VS ...

The unifor
helps to cre
in a group.
active life th
another bond
future, and pr
in order to b
Lumberjane pr
Penniquiqul Thi ore Lady
Types, but most anes will wish to have one. They
can either buy the uniform, or make it themselves from
materials available at the trading post.

LUMBERJANES FIELD MANUAL

CHAPTER
THIRTY

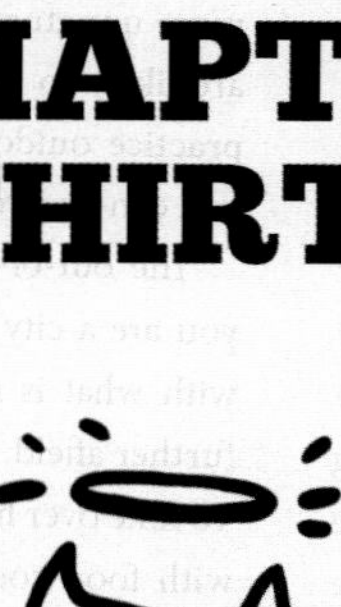

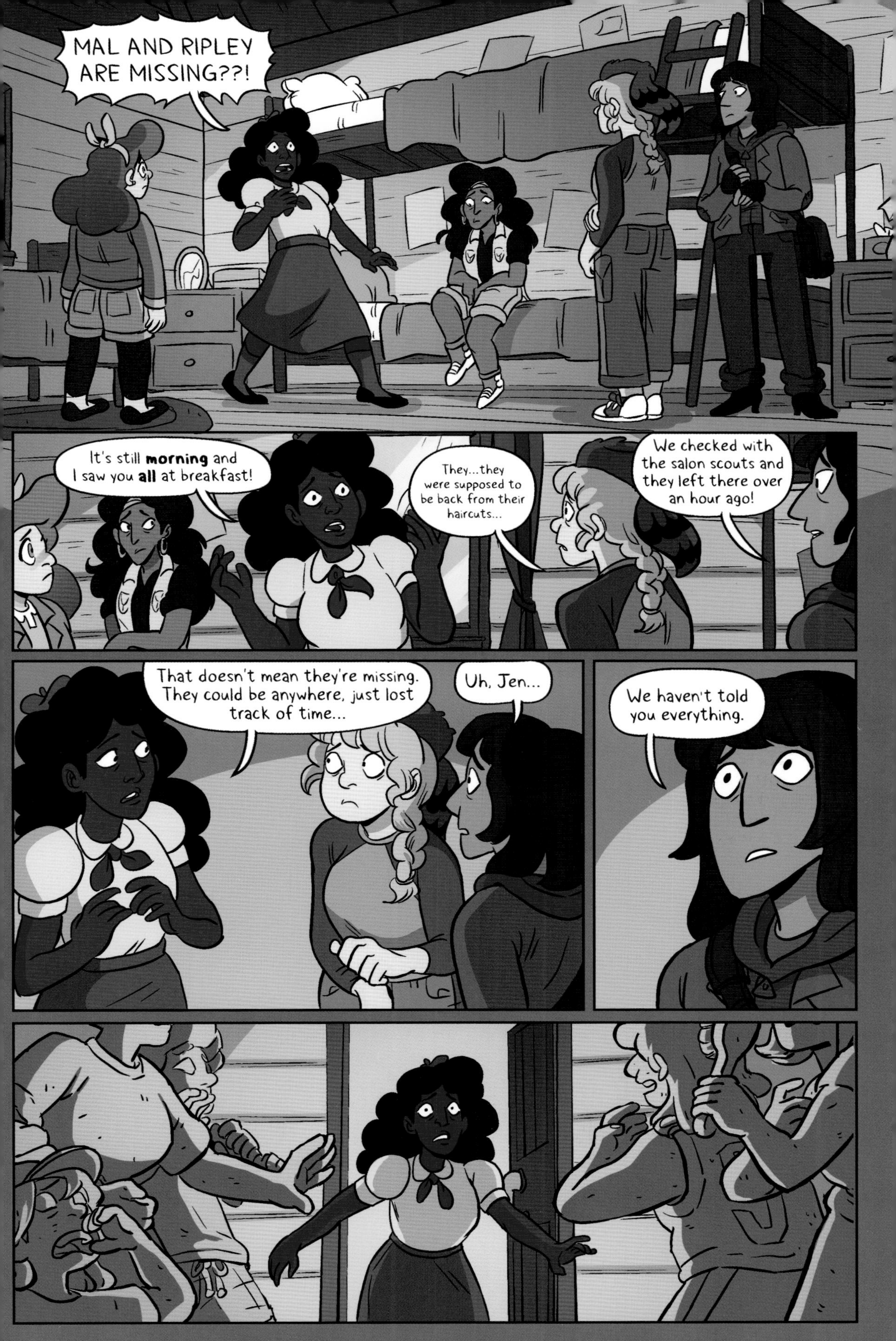
MAL AND RIPLEY ARE MISSING??!
It's still morning and I saw you all at breakfast!
They...they were supposed to be back from their haircuts...
We checked with the salon scouts and they left there over an hour ago!
That doesn't mean they're missing. They could be anywhere, just lost track of time...
Uh, Jen...
We haven't told you everything.

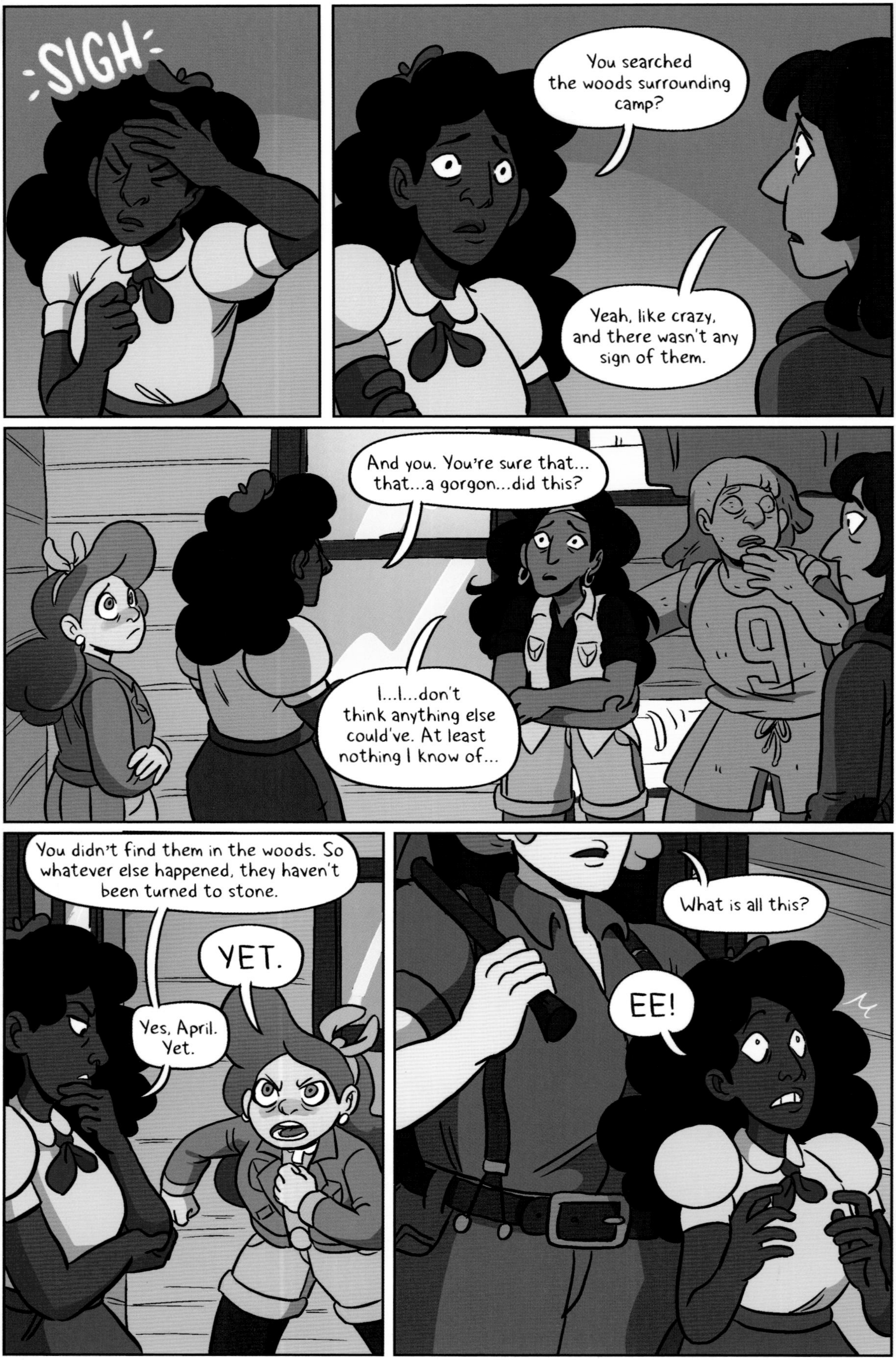
SIGH
You searched the woods surrounding camp?
Yeah, like crazy, and there wasn't any sign of them.
And you. You're sure that... that...a gorgon...did this?
I...I...don't think anything else could've. At least nothing I know of...
You didn't find them in the woods. So whatever else happened, they haven't been turned to stone.
YET.
Yes, April. Yet.
What is all this?
EE!

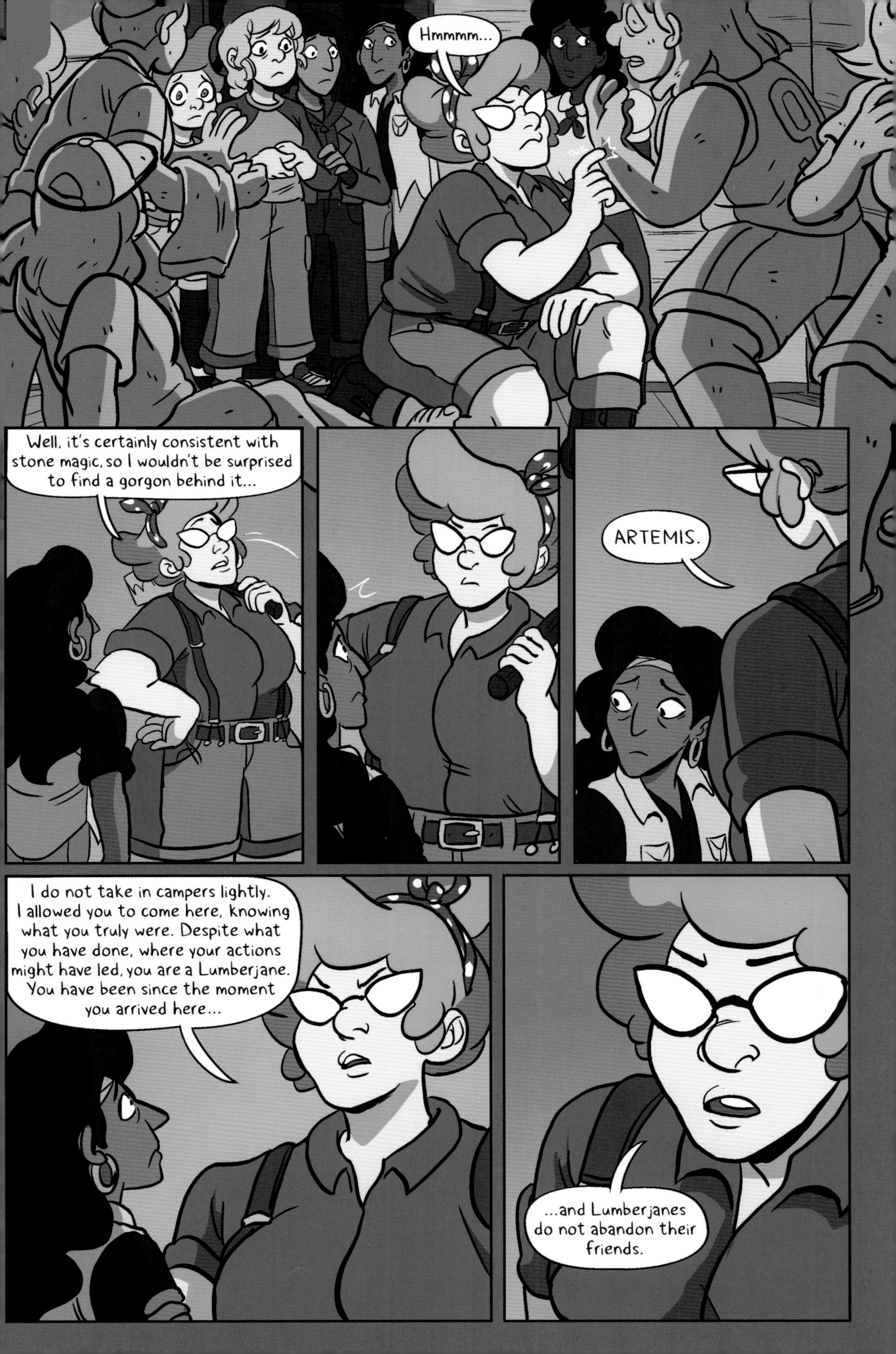
Hmmmm...
TNK
Well, it's certainly consistent with stone magic, so I wouldn't be surprised to find a gorgon behind it...
ARTEMIS.
I do not take in campers lightly. I allowed you to come here, knowing what you truly were. Despite what you have done, where your actions might have led, you are a Lumberjane. You have been since the moment you arrived here...
...and Lumberjanes do not abandon their friends.

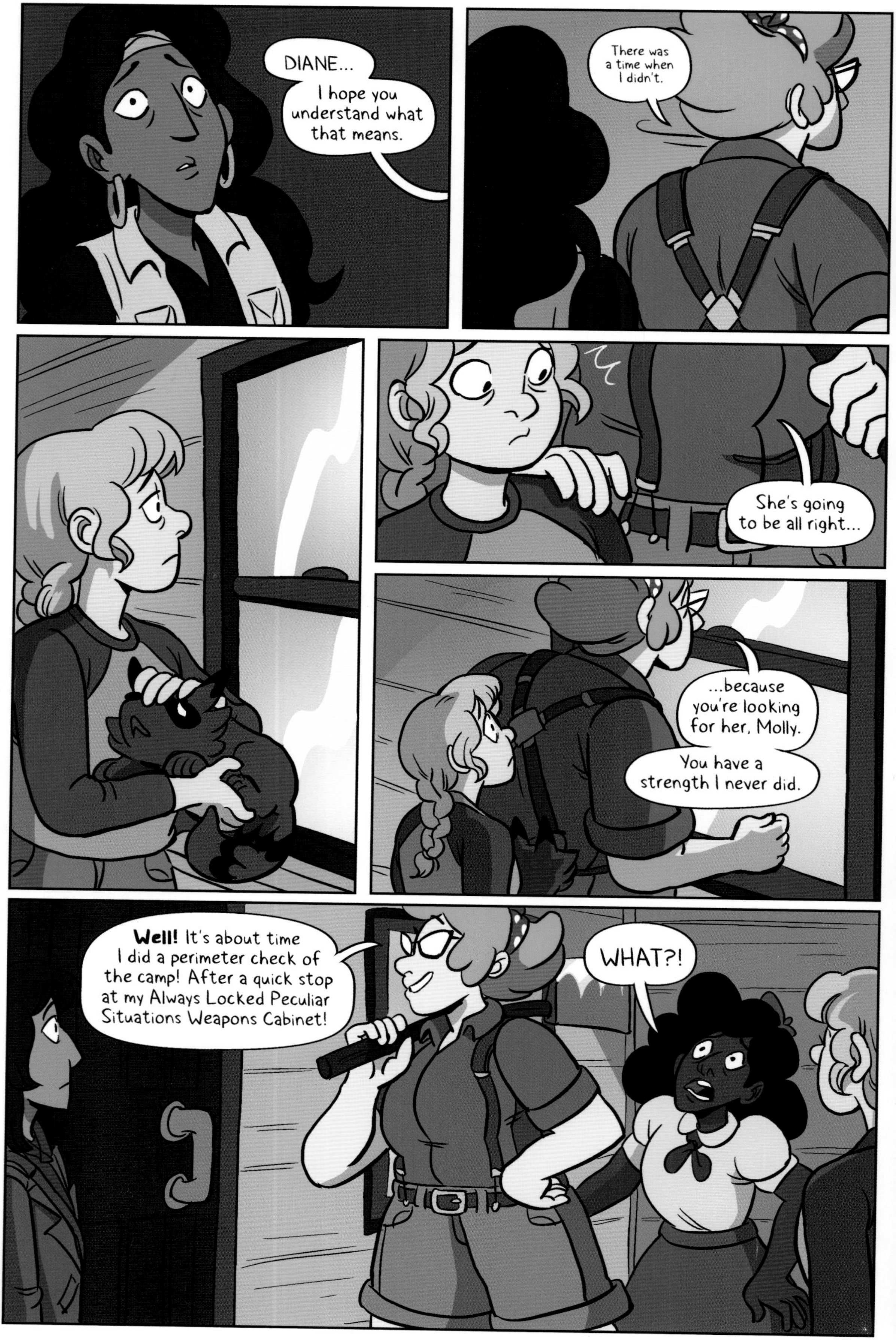
DIANE...
I hope you understand what that means.
There was a time when I didn't.
She's going to be all right...
...because you're looking for her, Molly.
You have a strength I never did.
Well! It's about time I did a perimeter check of the camp! After a quick stop at my Always Locked Peculiar Situations Weapons Cabinet!
WHAT?!

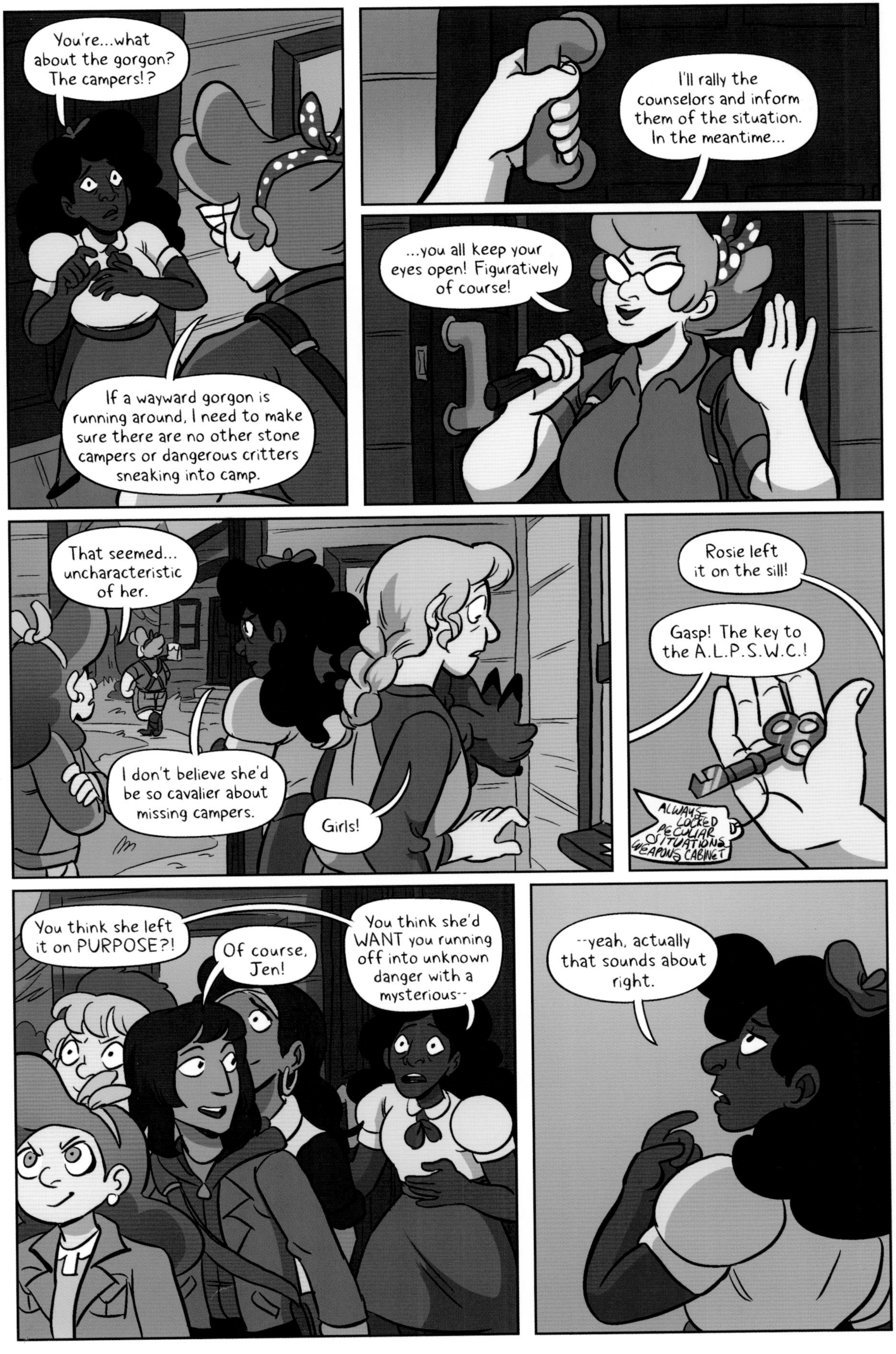
You're...what about the gorgon? The campers!?
If a wayward gorgon is running around, I need to make sure there are no other stone campers or dangerous critters sneaking into camp.
I'll rally the counselors and inform them of the situation. In the meantime...
...you all keep your eyes open! Figuratively of course!
That seemed... uncharacteristic of her.
I don't believe she'd be so cavalier about missing campers.
Girls!
Rosie left it on the sill!
Gasp! The key to the A.L.P.S.W.C.!
ALWAYS LOCKED PECULIAR SITUATIONS WEAPONS CABINET
You think she left it on PURPOSE?!
Of course, Jen!
You think she'd WANT you running off into unknown danger with a mysterious--
--yeah, actually that sounds about right.

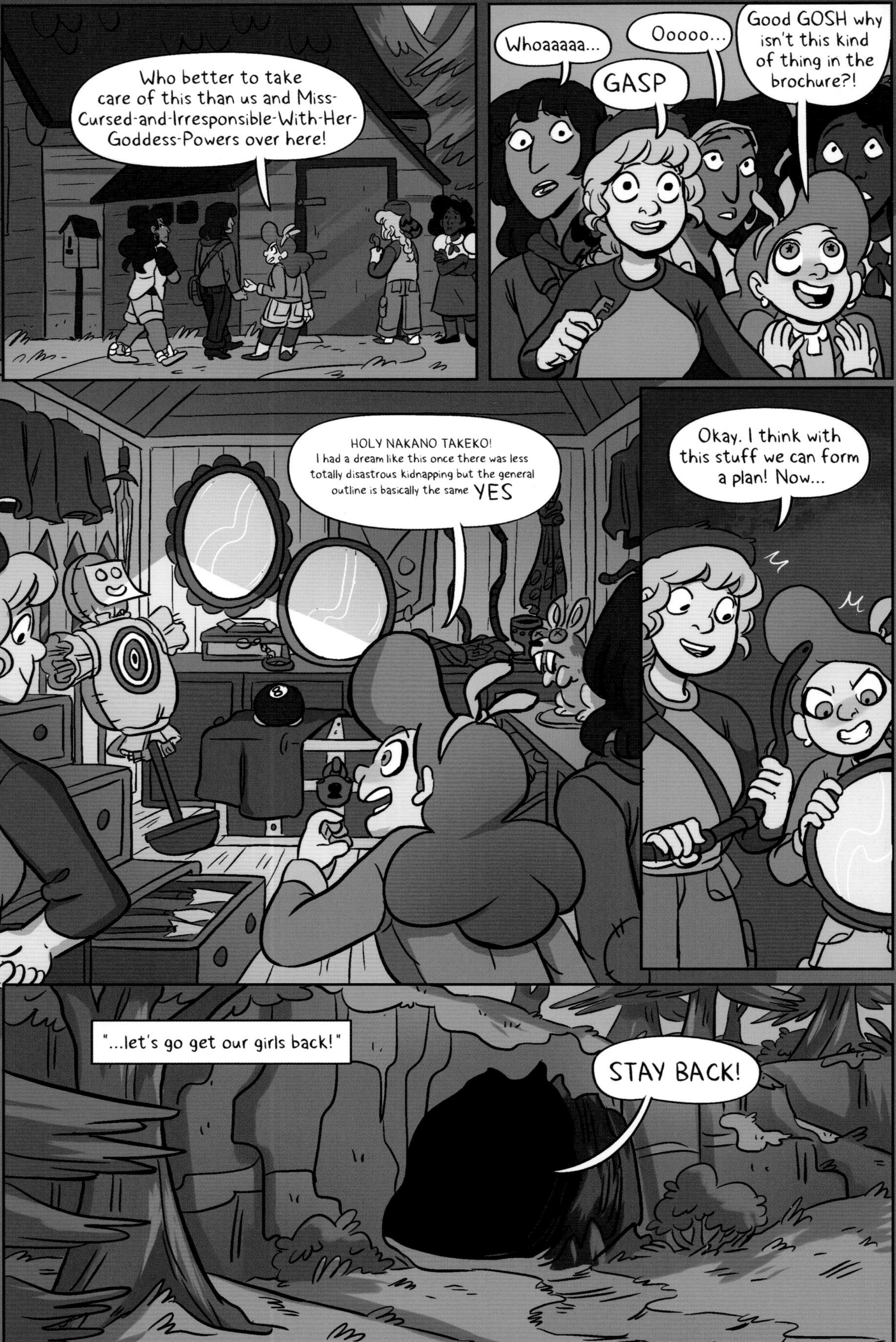
Who better to take care of this than us and Miss-Cursed-and-Irresponsible-With-Her-Goddess-Powers over here!
Whoaaaaa...
GASP
Ooooo...
Good GOSH why isn't this kind of thing in the brochure?!
HOLY NAKANO TAKEKO! I had a dream like this once there was less totally disastrous kidnapping but the general outline is basically the same YES
Okay. I think with this stuff we can form a plan! Now...
"...let's go get our girls back!"
STAY BACK!

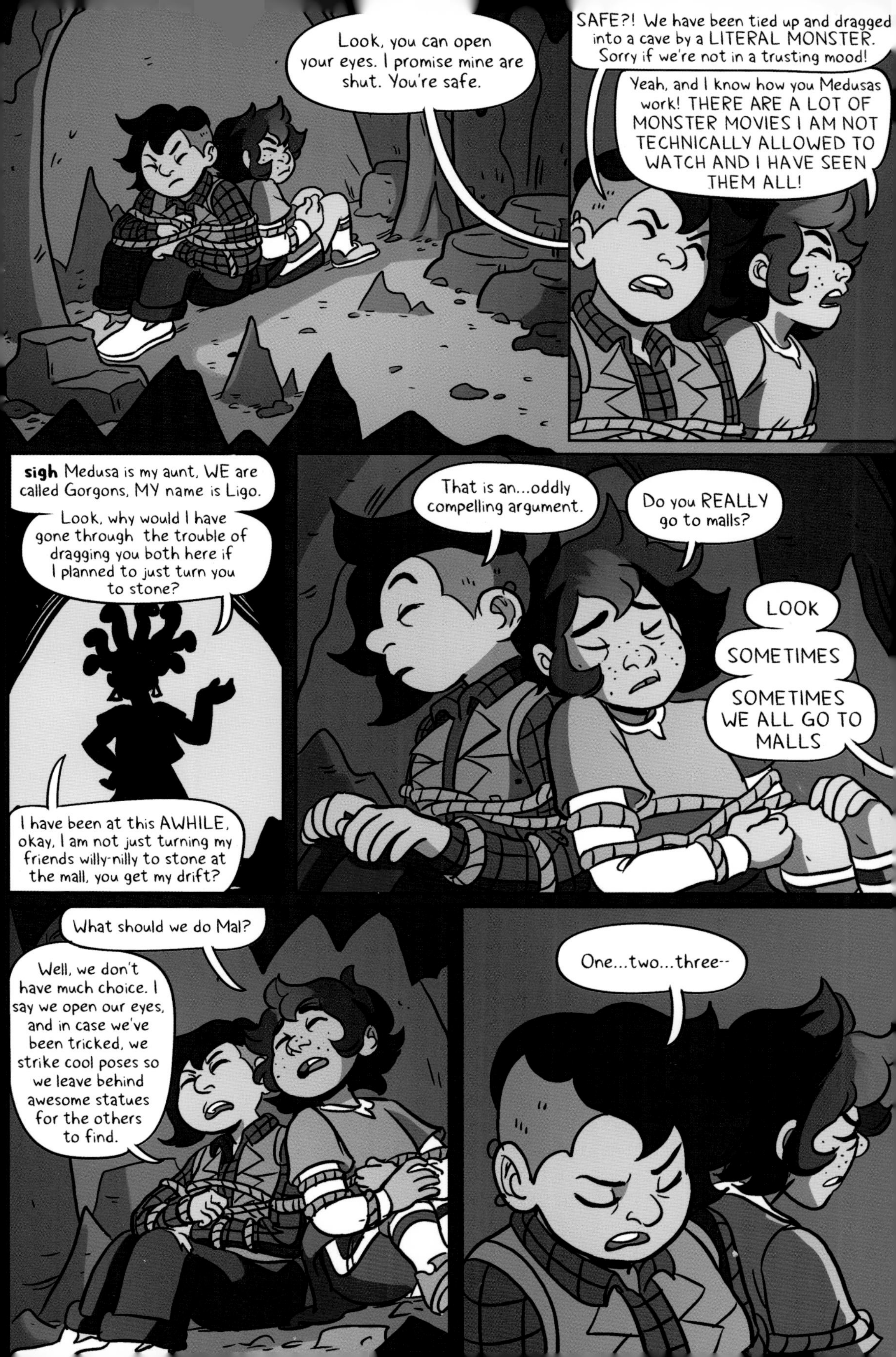

Look, you can open your eyes. I promise mine are shut. You're safe.
SAFE?! We have been tied up and dragged into a cave by a LITERAL MONSTER. Sorry if we're not in a trusting mood!
Yeah, and I know how you Medusas work! THERE ARE A LOT OF MONSTER MOVIES I AM NOT TECHNICALLY ALLOWED TO WATCH AND I HAVE SEEN THEM ALL!
sigh Medusa is my aunt, WE are called Gorgons, MY name is Ligo.
Look, why would I have gone through the trouble of dragging you both here if I planned to just turn you to stone?
I have been at this AWHILE, okay, I am not just turning my friends willy-nilly to stone at the mall, you get my drift?
That is an...oddly compelling argument.
Do you REALLY go to malls?
LOOK
SOMETIMES
SOMETIMES WE ALL GO TO MALLS
What should we do Mal?
Well, we don't have much choice. I say we open our eyes, and in case we've been tricked, we strike cool poses so we leave behind awesome statues for the others to find.
One...two...three--

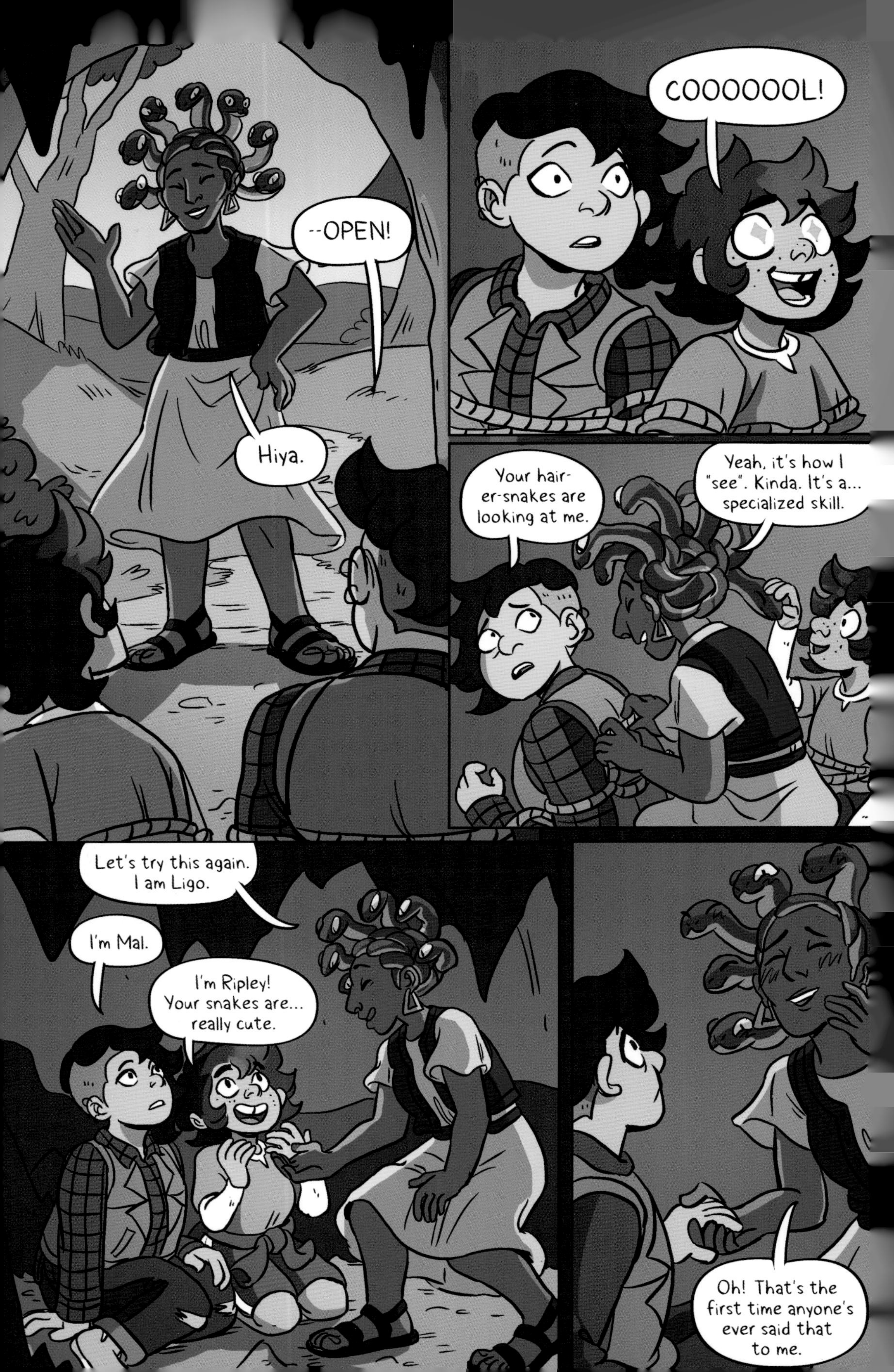
--OPEN!
Hiya.
COOOOOOL!
Your hair-er-snakes are looking at me.
Yeah, it's how I "see". Kinda. It's a... specialized skill.
Let's try this again. I am Ligo.
I'm Mal.
I'm Ripley! Your snakes are... really cute.
Oh! That's the first time anyone's ever said that to me.

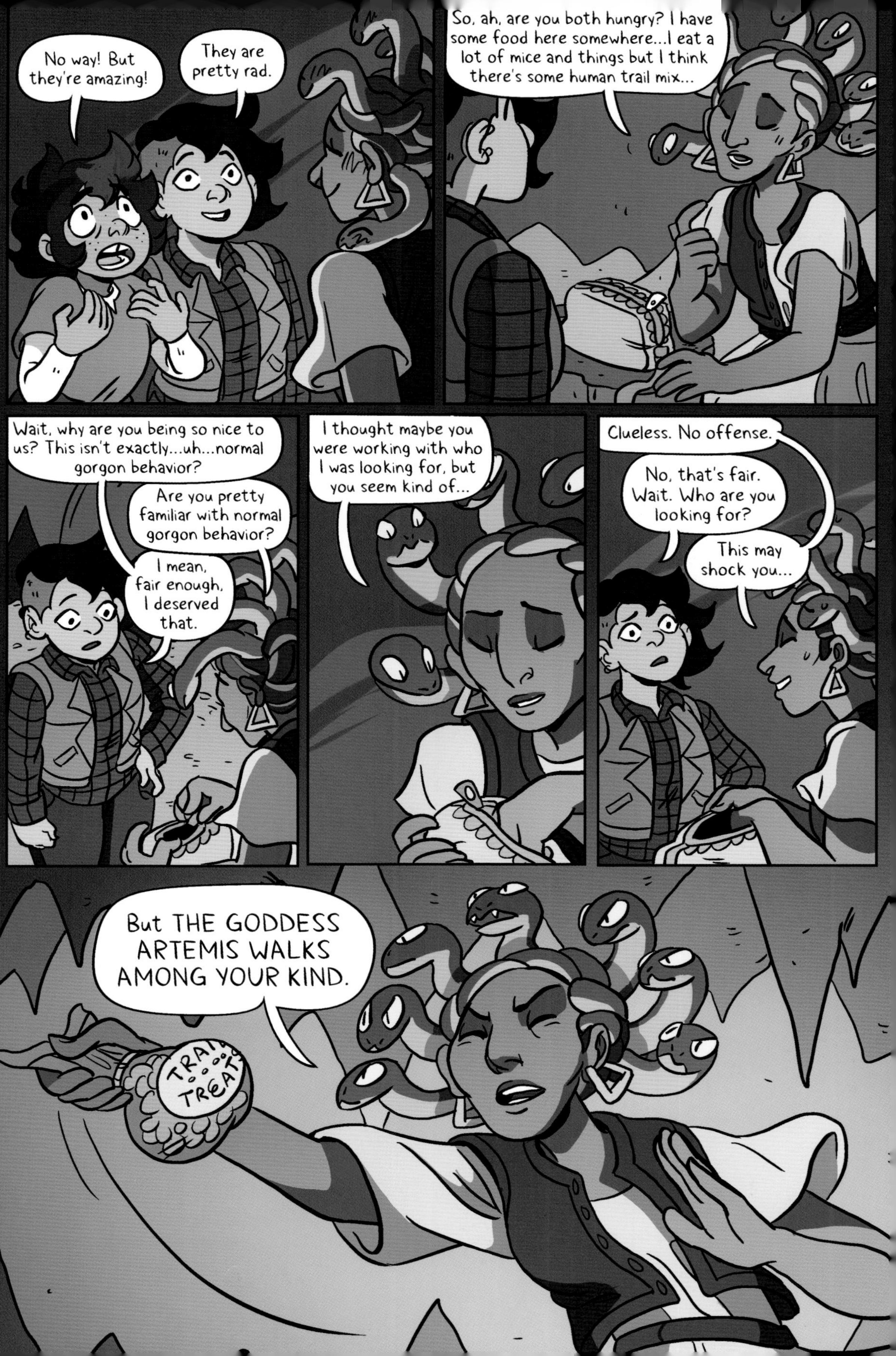
No way! But they're amazing!
They are pretty rad.
So, ah, are you both hungry? I have some food here somewhere...I eat a lot of mice and things but I think there's some human trail mix...
Wait, why are you being so nice to us? This isn't exactly...uh...normal gorgon behavior?
Are you pretty familiar with normal gorgon behavior?
I mean, fair enough, I deserved that.
I thought maybe you were working with who I was looking for, but you seem kind of...
Clueless. No offense.
No, that's fair. Wait. Who are you looking for?
This may shock you...
But THE GODDESS ARTEMIS WALKS AMONG YOUR KIND.

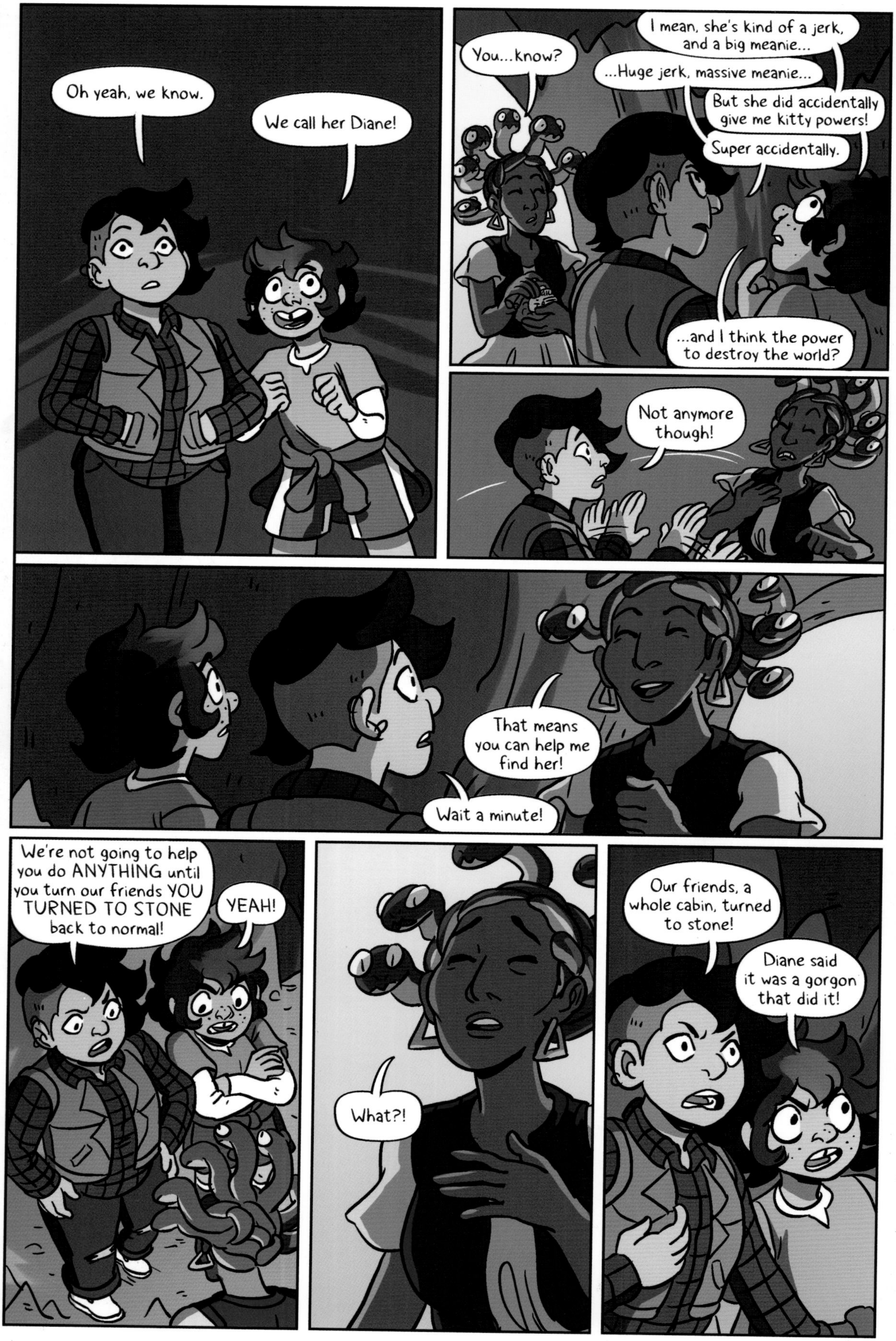
Oh yeah, we know.
We call her Diane!
You...know?
I mean, she's kind of a jerk, and a big meanie...
...Huge jerk, massive meanie...
But she did accidentally give me kitty powers!
Super accidentally.
...and I think the power to destroy the world?
Not anymore though!
That means you can help me find her!
Wait a minute!
We're not going to help you do ANYTHING until you turn our friends YOU TURNED TO STONE back to normal!
YEAH!
What?!
Our friends, a whole cabin, turned to stone!
Diane said it was a gorgon that did it!

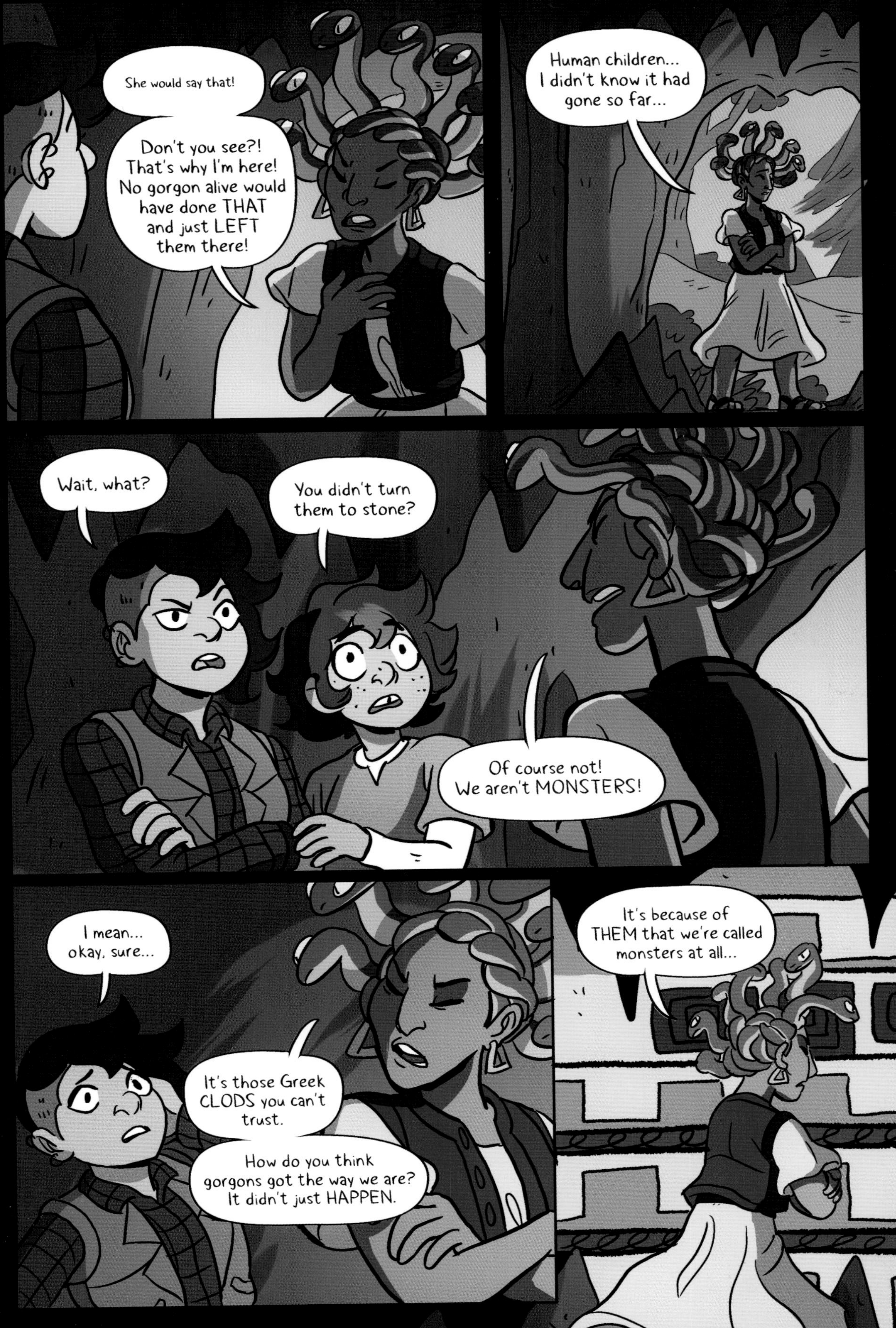
She would say that!
Don't you see?! That's why I'm here! No gorgon alive would have done THAT and just LEFT them there!
Human children... I didn't know it had gone so far...
Wait, what?
You didn't turn them to stone?
Of course not! We aren't MONSTERS!
I mean... okay, sure...
It's those Greek CLODS you can't trust.
How do you think gorgons got the way we are? It didn't just HAPPEN.
It's because of THEM that we're called monsters at all...

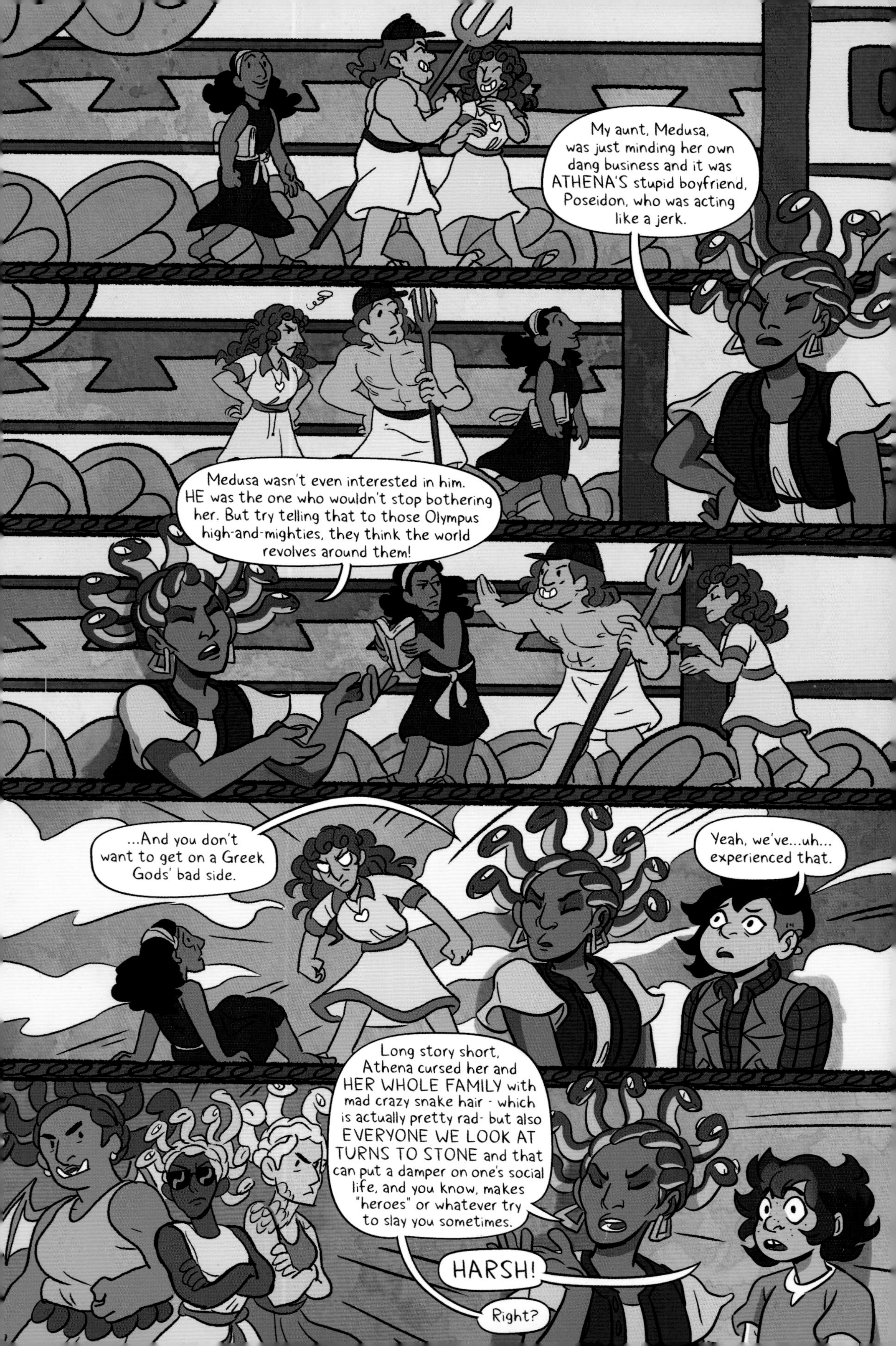
My aunt, Medusa, was just minding her own dang business and it was ATHENA'S stupid boyfriend, Poseidon, who was acting like a jerk.
Medusa wasn't even interested in him. HE was the one who wouldn't stop bothering her. But try telling that to those Olympus high-and-mighties, they think the world revolves around them!
...And you don't want to get on a Greek Gods' bad side.
Yeah, we've...uh... experienced that.
Long story short, Athena cursed her and HER WHOLE FAMILY with mad crazy snake hair - which is actually pretty rad- but also EVERYONE WE LOOK AT TURNS TO STONE and that can put a damper on one's social life, and you know, makes "heroes" or whatever try to slay you sometimes.
HARSH!
Right?

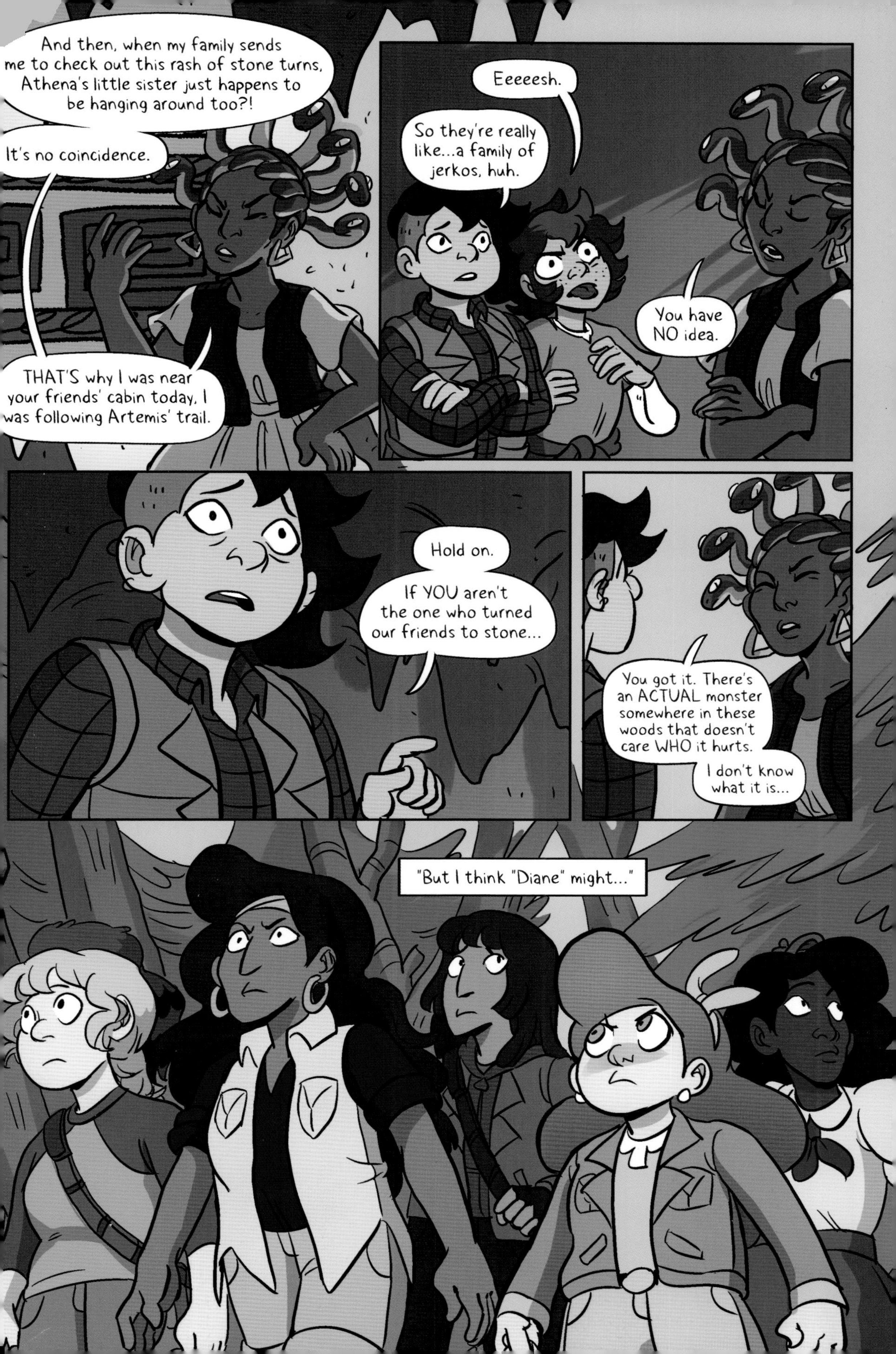
And then, when my family sends me to check out this rash of stone turns, Athena's little sister just happens to be hanging around too?!
It's no coincidence.
THAT'S why I was near your friends' cabin today. I was following Artemis' trail.
Eeeeesh.
So they're really like...a family of jerkos, huh.
You have NO idea.
Hold on.
If YOU aren't the one who turned our friends to stone...
You got it. There's an ACTUAL monster somewhere in these woods that doesn't care WHO it hurts.
I don't know what it is...
"But I think "Diane" might..."

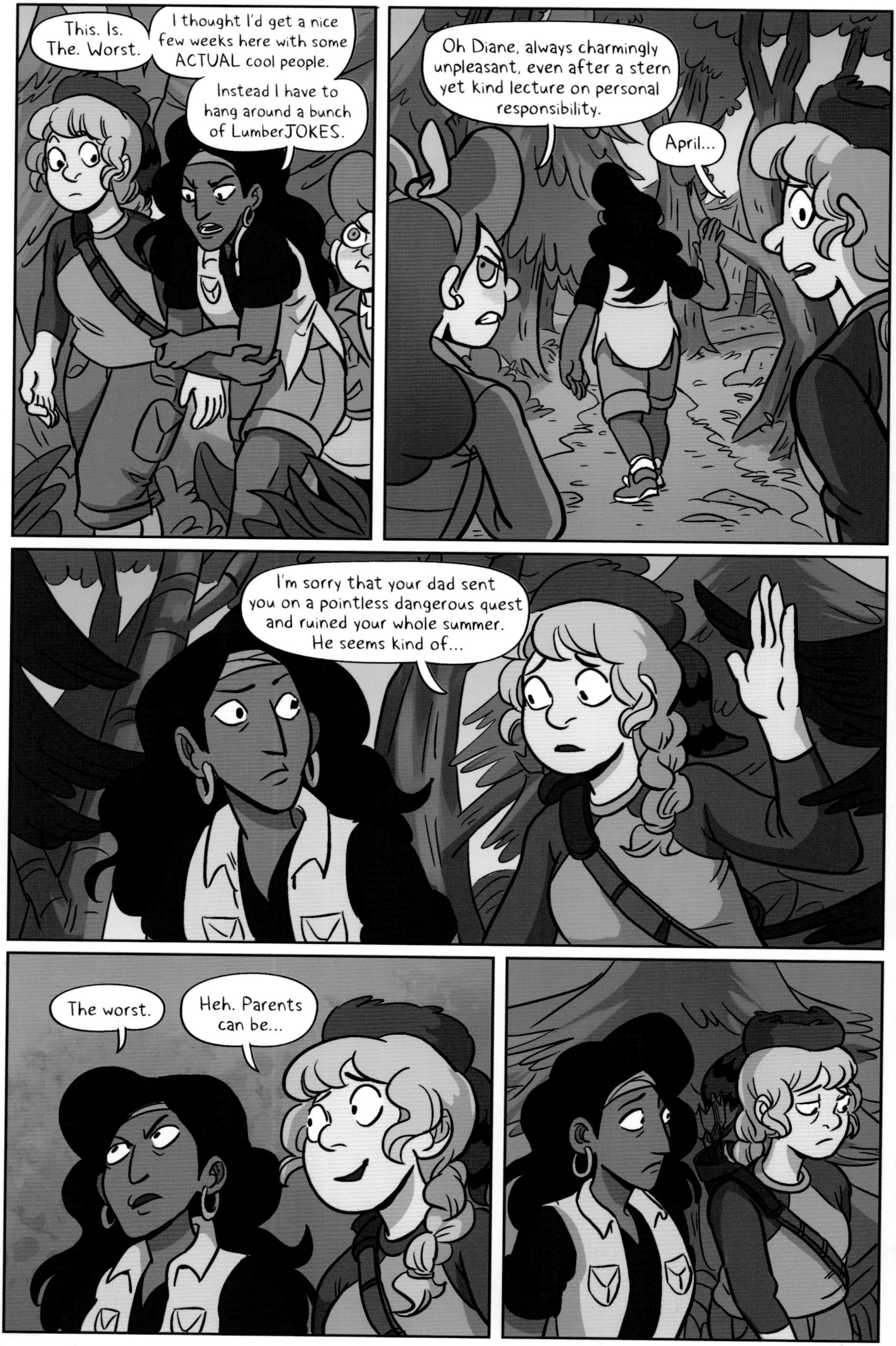
This. Is. The. Worst.
I thought I'd get a nice few weeks here with some ACTUAL cool people.
Instead I have to hang around a bunch of LumberJOKES.
Oh Diane, always charmingly unpleasant, even after a stern yet kind lecture on personal responsibility.
April...
I'm sorry that your dad sent you on a pointless dangerous quest and ruined your whole summer. He seems kind of...
The worst.
Heh. Parents can be...

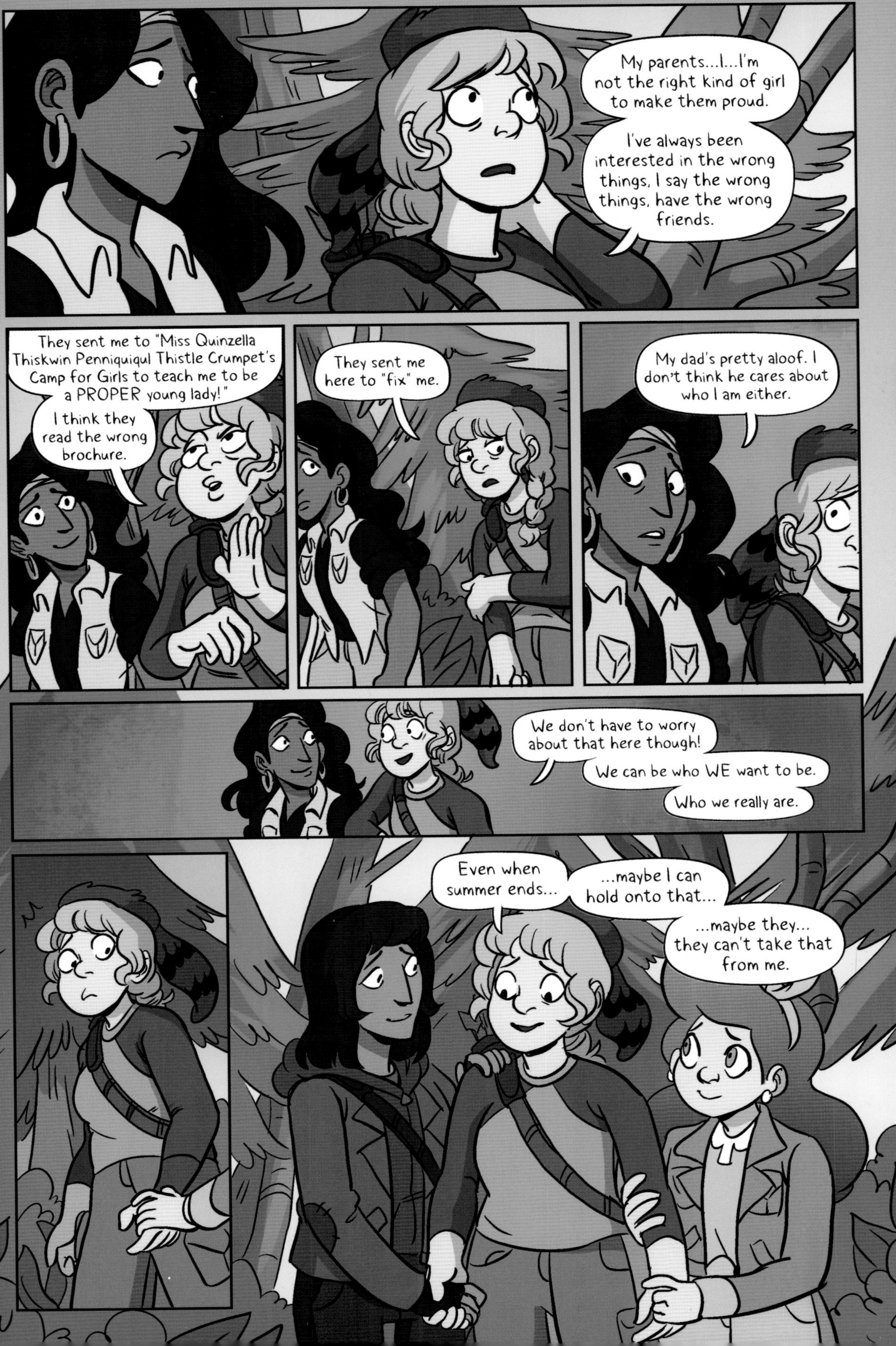
My parents...I...I'm not the right kind of girl to make them proud.
I've always been interested in the wrong things, I say the wrong things, have the wrong friends.
They sent me to "Miss Quinzella Thiskwin Penniquiqul Thistle Crumpet's Camp for Girls to teach me to be a PROPER young lady!"
I think they read the wrong brochure.
They sent me here to "fix" me.
My dad's pretty aloof. I don't think he cares about who I am either.
We don't have to worry about that here though!
We can be who WE want to be.
Who we really are.
Even when summer ends...
...maybe I can hold onto that...
...maybe they... they can't take that from me.

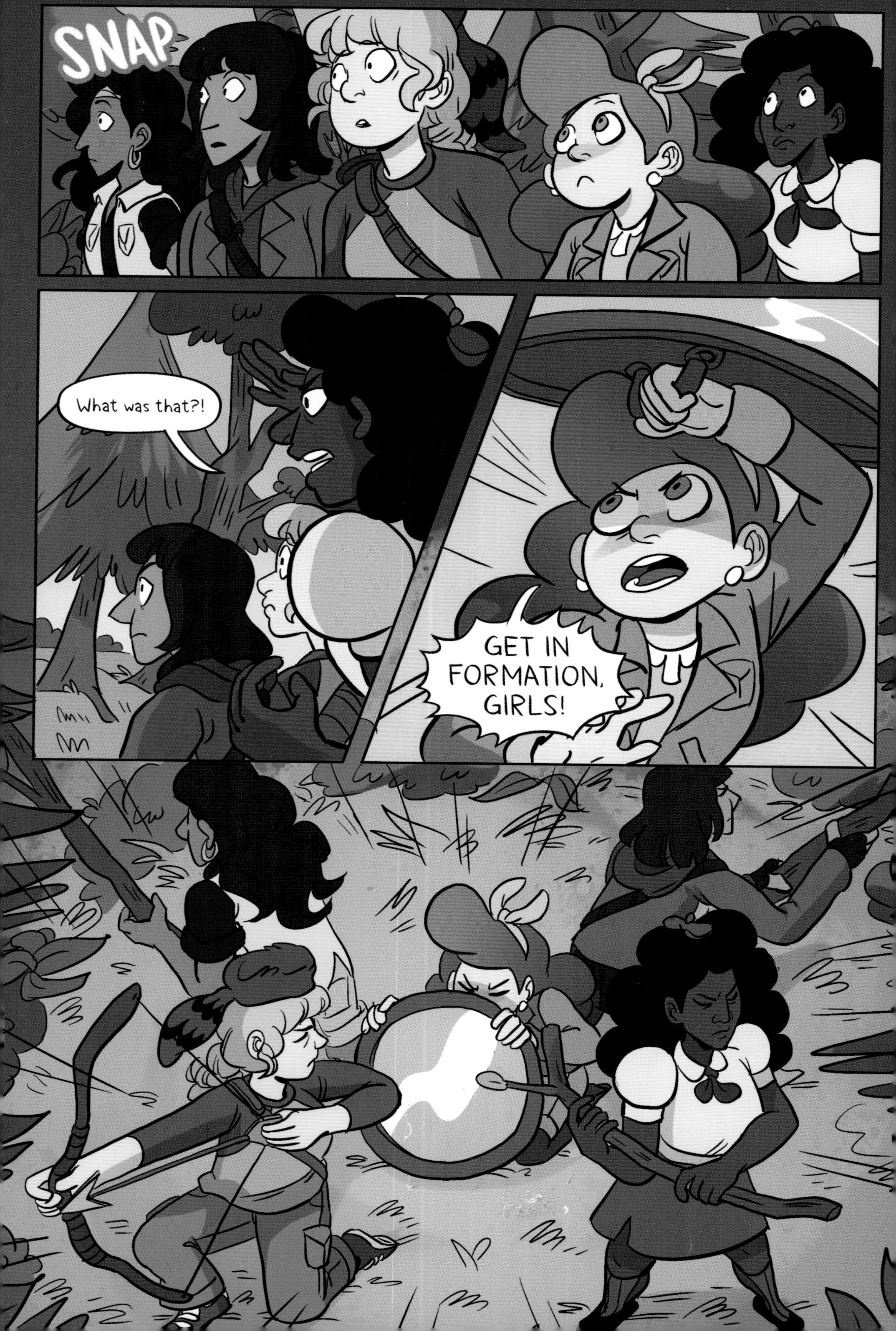
SNAP
What was that?!
GET IN FORMATION, GIRLS!

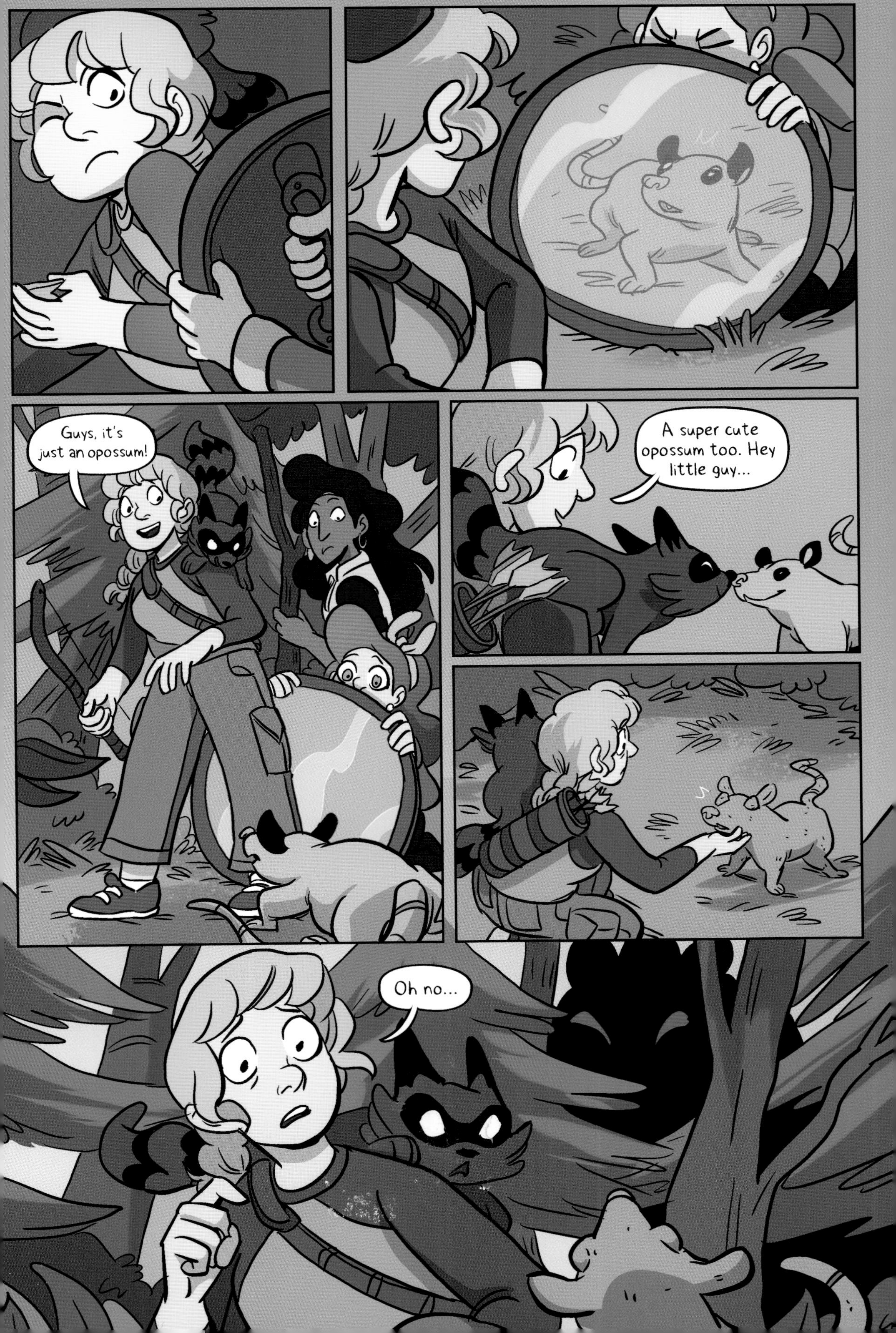

Guys, it's just an opossum!
A super cute opossum too. Hey little guy...
Oh no...

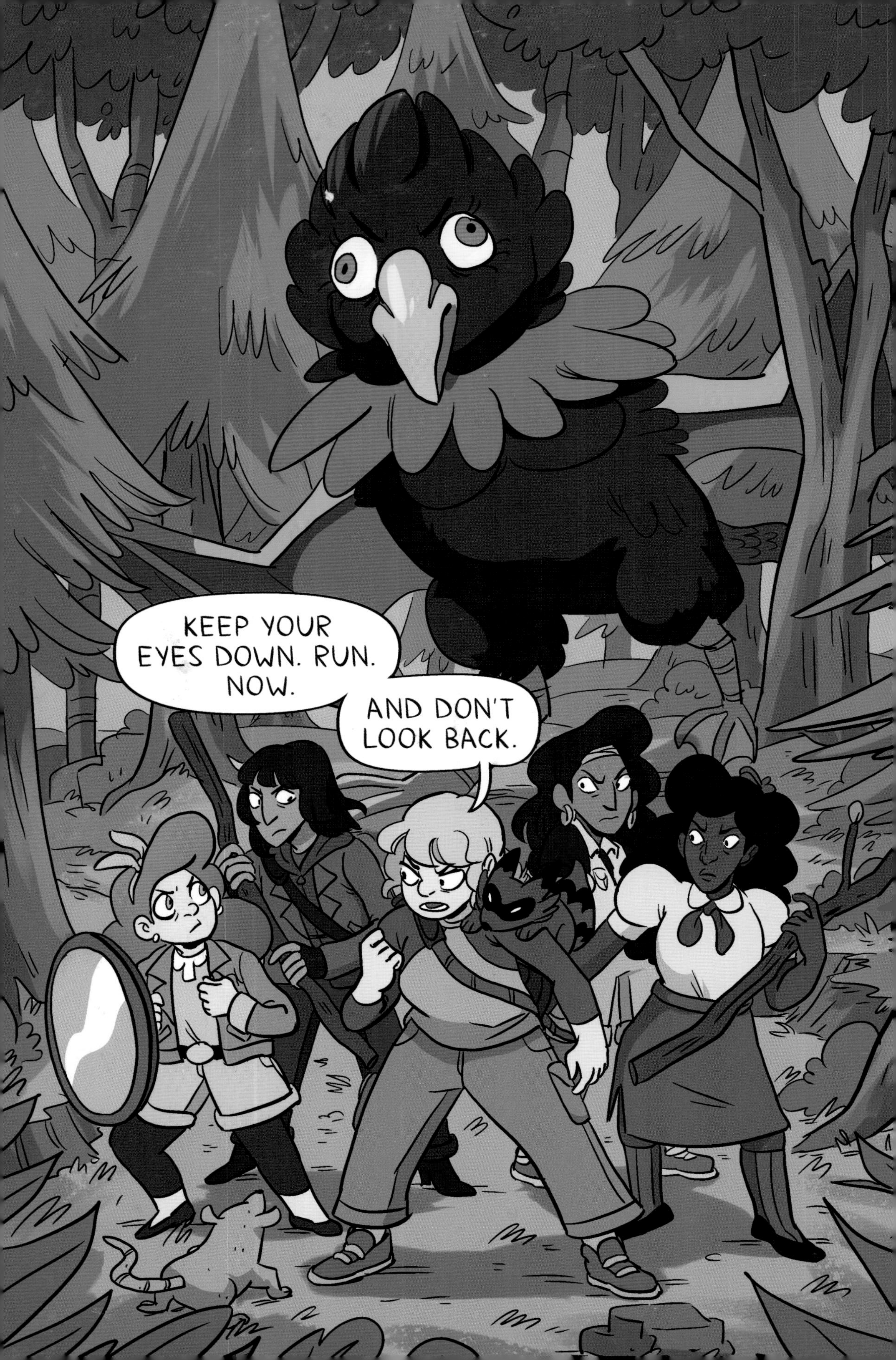
KEEP YOUR EYES DOWN. RUN. NOW.
AND DON'T LOOK BACK.

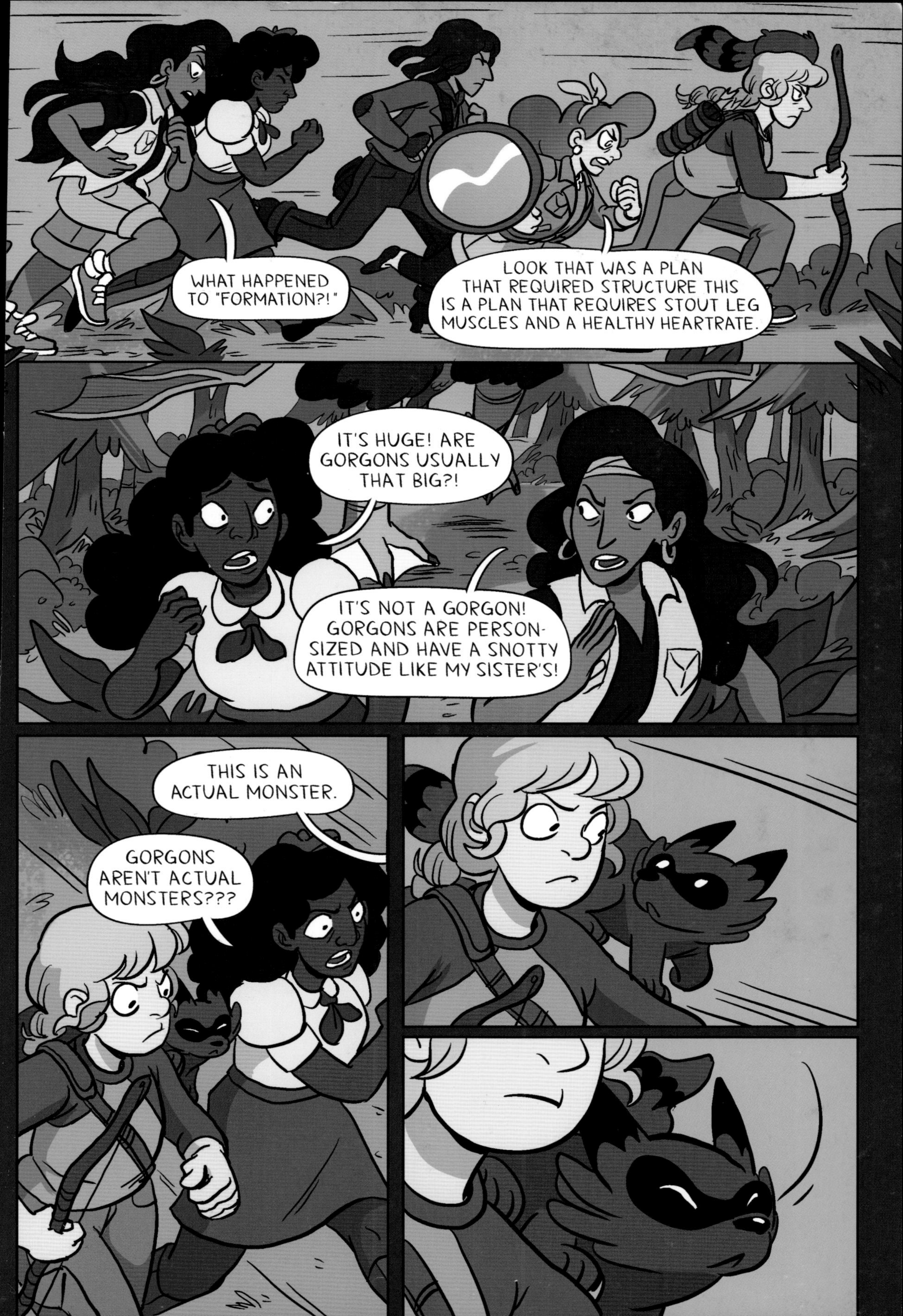
WHAT HAPPENED TO "FORMATION?!"
LOOK THAT WAS A PLAN THAT REQUIRED STRUCTURE THIS IS A PLAN THAT REQUIRES STOUT LEG MUSCLES AND A HEALTHY HEARTRATE.
IT'S HUGE! ARE GORGONS USUALLY THAT BIG?!
IT'S NOT A GORGON! GORGONS ARE PERSON-SIZED AND HAVE A SNOTTY ATTITUDE LIKE MY SISTER'S!
THIS IS AN ACTUAL MONSTER.
GORGONS AREN'T ACTUAL MONSTERS???

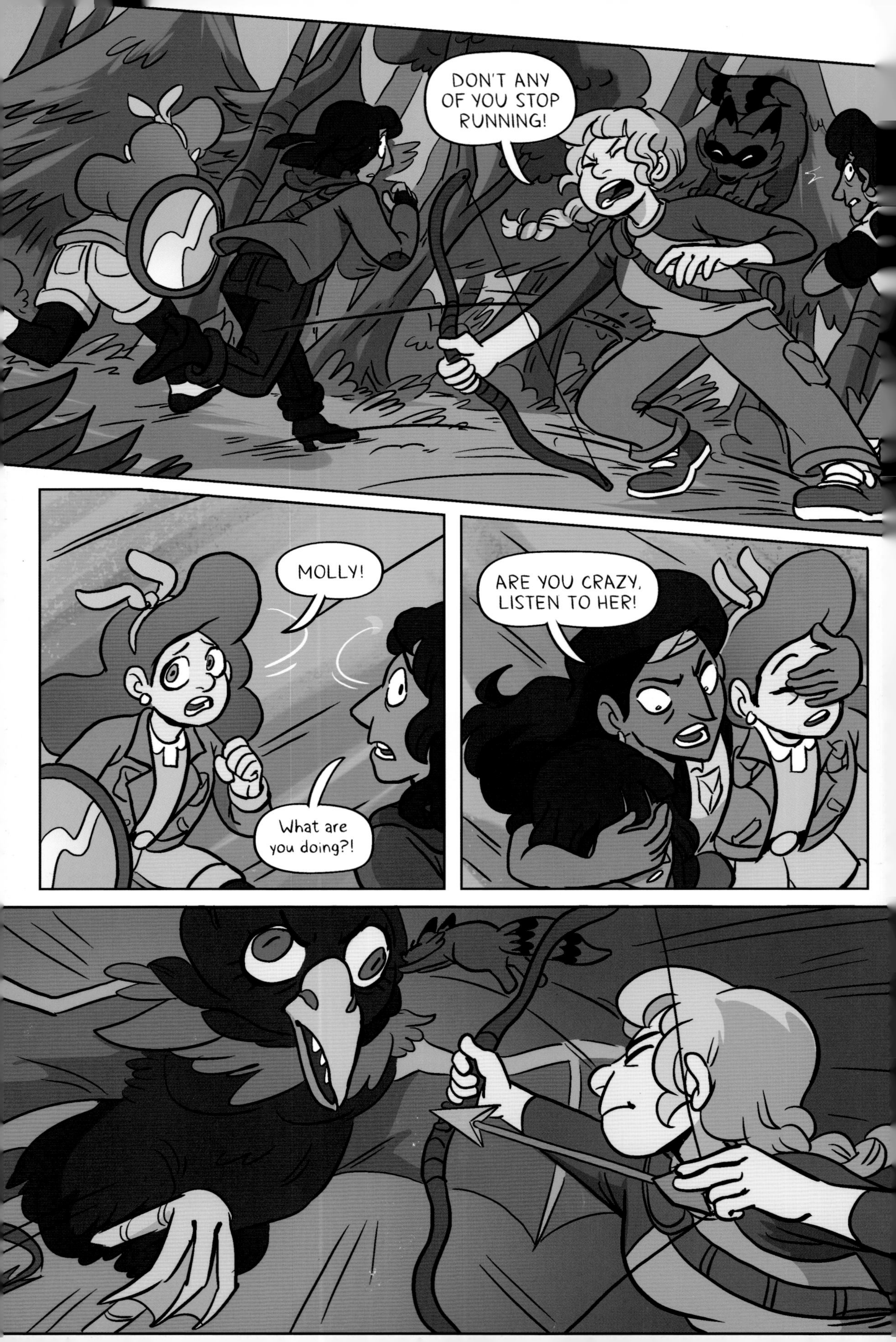
DON'T ANY OF YOU STOP RUNNING!
MOLLY!
What are you doing?!
ARE YOU CRAZY, LISTEN TO HER!

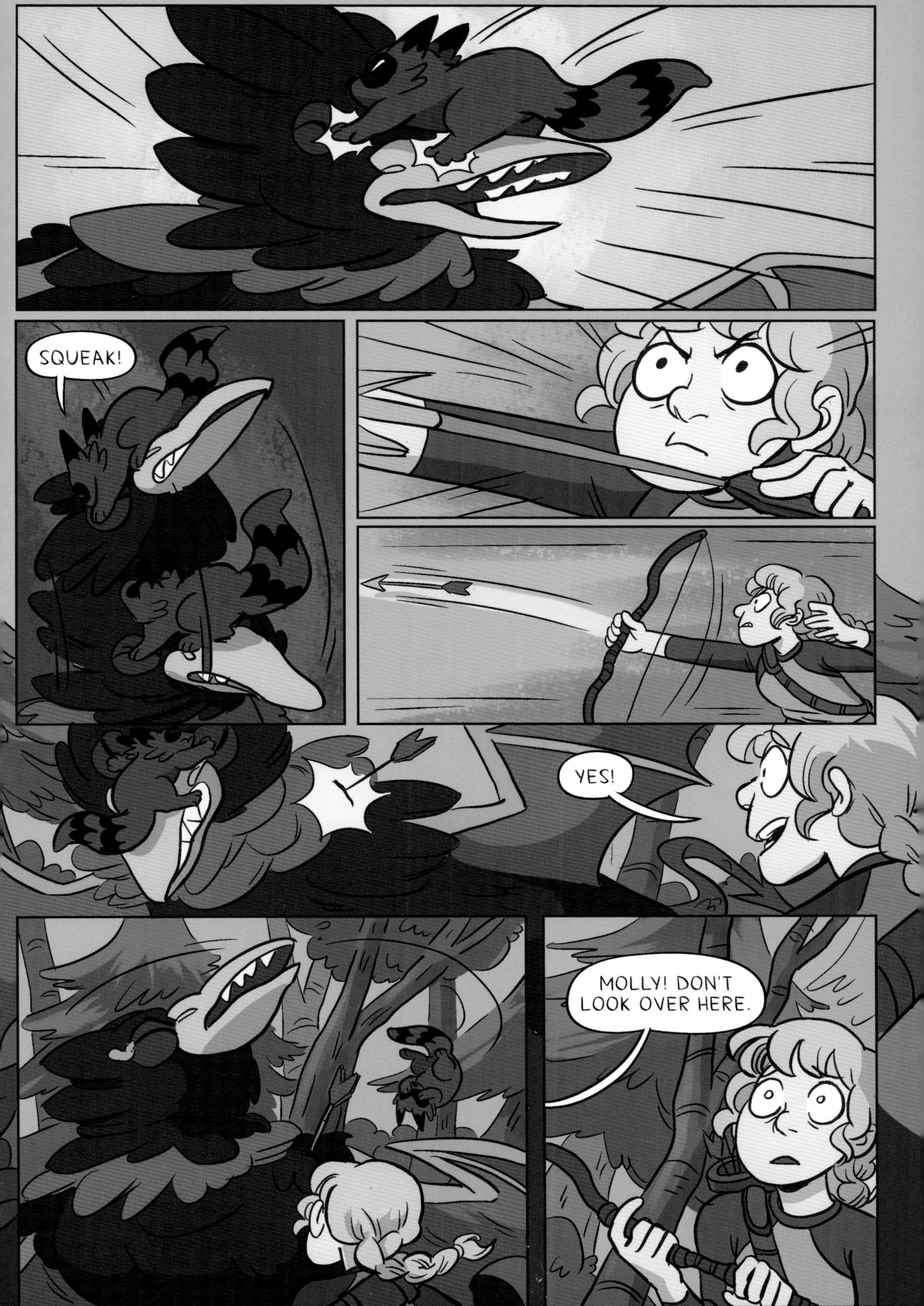
SQUEAK!
YES!
MOLLY! DON'T LOOK OVER HERE.

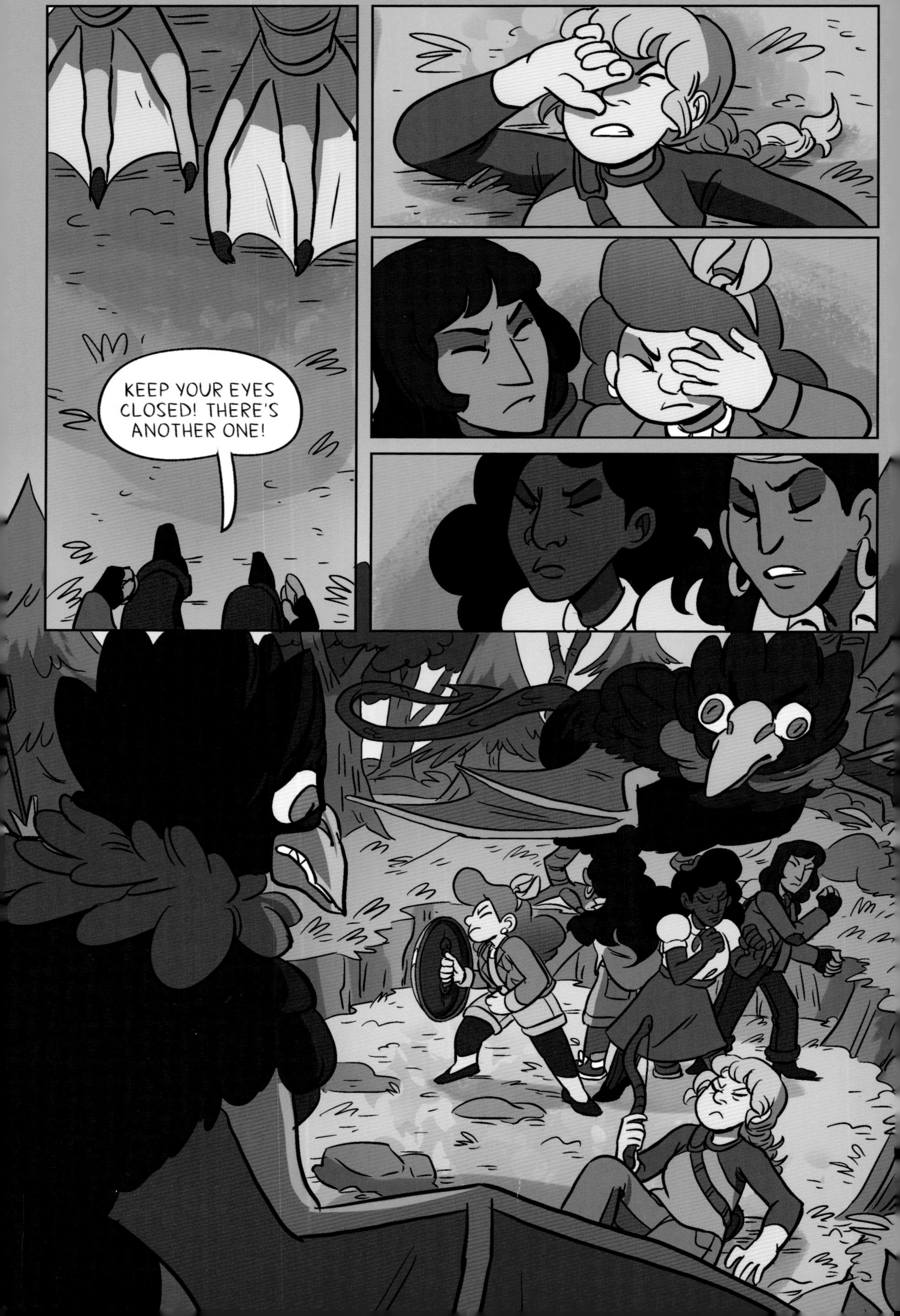
KEEP YOUR EYES CLOSED! THERE'S ANOTHER ONE!

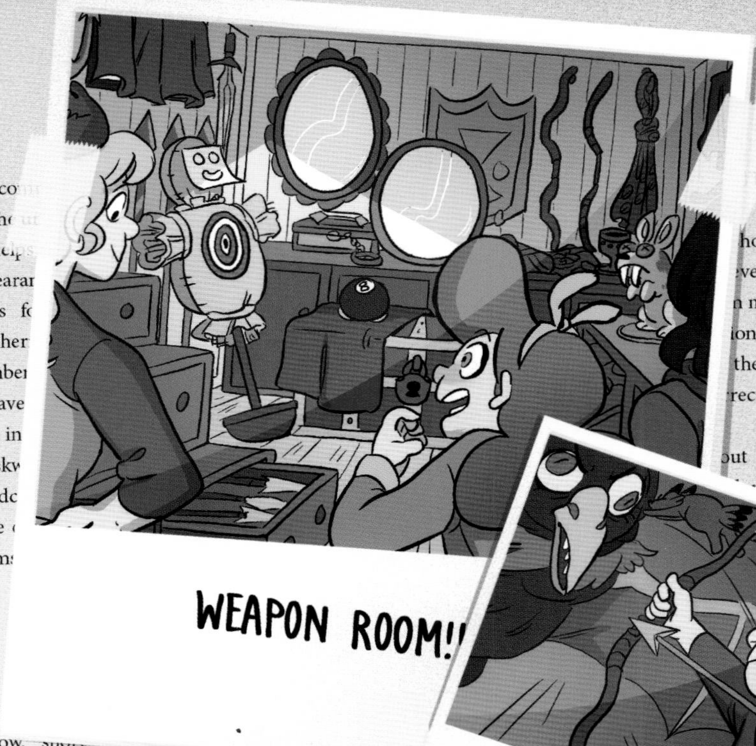
WEAPON ROOM!!

will co…

The… It helps… appearar… dress fo… Further… Lumber… to have… part in… Thiskw… Hardc… have… thems…

…HE UNIFORM

…hould be worn at camp …vents when Lumberjanes …n may also be worn at other …ions. It should be worn as a … the uniform dress with …rrect shoes, and stocking or

…out grows her uniform or …ng to another Lumberjane. …insignia she has … her … her

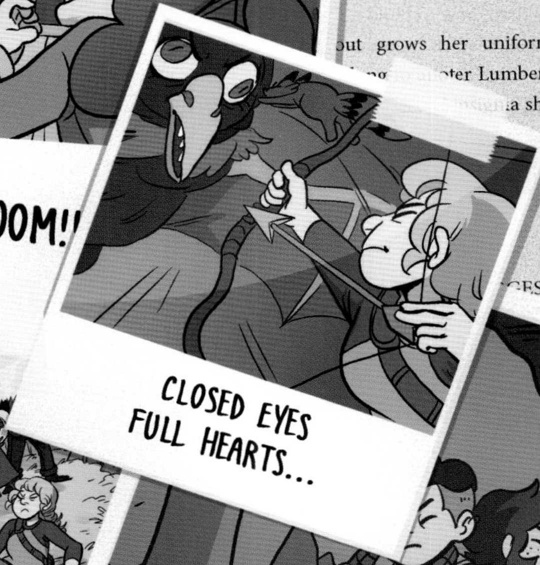
CLOSED EYES
FULL HEARTS...

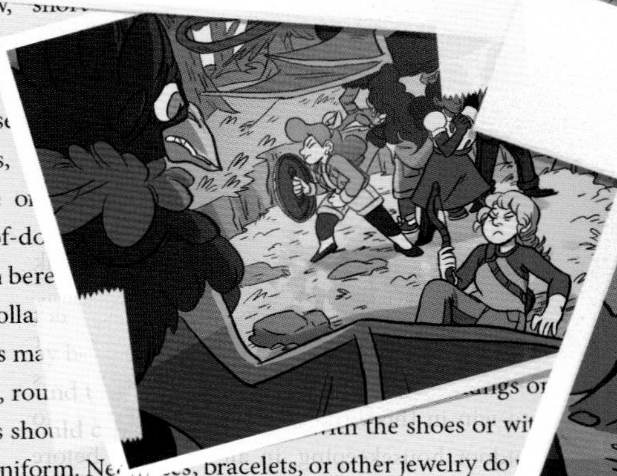

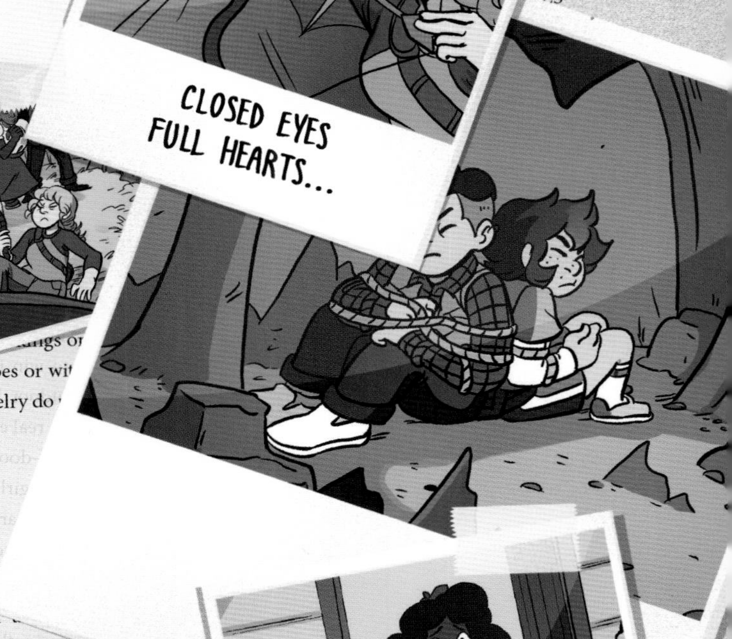

The… yellow, shor… emb… the w… choose… slacks,… made o… out-of-do… green bere… the colla… Shoes ma… heels, rou… …ings or socks shou… …with the shoes or wit… the uniform. Ne…es, bracelets, or other jewelry do… belong with a Lumberjane uniform.

HOW TO WEAR THE UNIFORM

To look well in a uniform demands first of … uniform be kept in good condition—clean … pressed. See that the skirt is the right length for your own height and build, that the belt is adjusted to your waist, that your shoes and stockings are in keeping with the uniform, that you watch your posture and carry yourself with dignity and grace. If the beret is removed indoors, be sure that your hair is neat and kept in place with an insonspicuous clip or ribbon. When you wear a Lumberjane uniform you are identified as a member of this organization and you should be doubly careful to conduct yourself in a way that will show everyone that courtesy and thoughtfullness are part of being a Lumberjane. People are likely to judge a whole nation by the selfishness of a few individuals, to criticize a whole family because of the misconduct of one member, and to feel unkindly toward and organization because of the

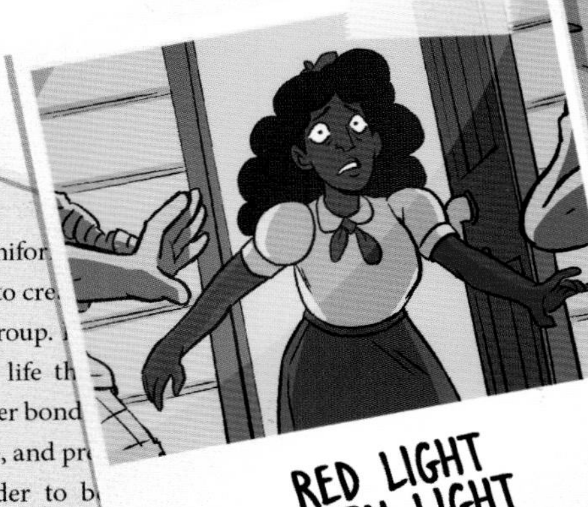
RED LIGHT
GREEN LIGHT

The unifor… helps to cre… in a group. … active life th… another bond… future, and pr… in order to b… Lumberjane pr… Penniquiqul Thi… …ore Lady Types, but m… …es will wish to have one. They can either bu… …the uniform, or make it themselves from materials available at the trading post.

LUMBERJANES FIELD MANUAL
CHAPTER
THIRTY-ONE

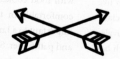

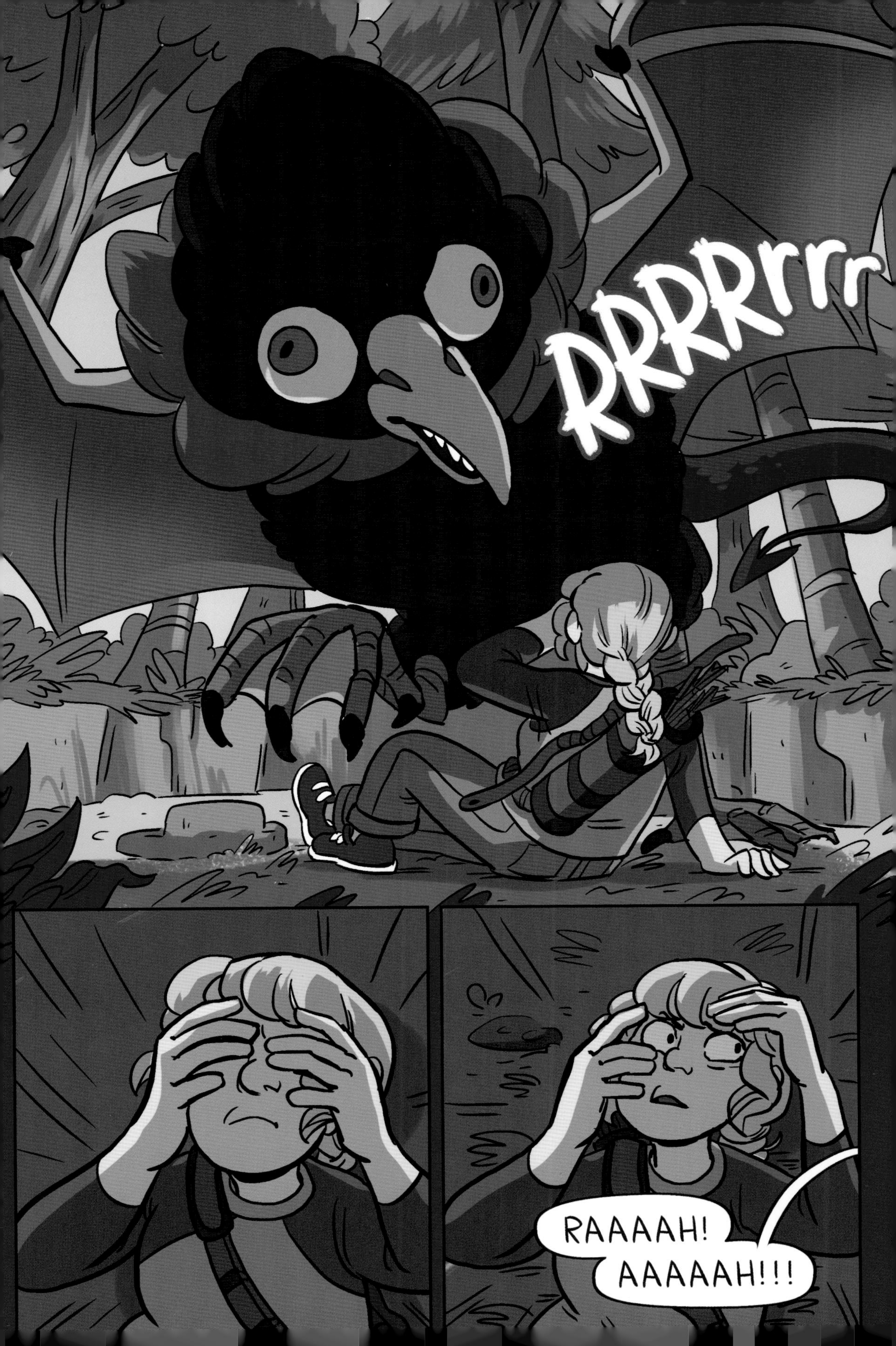
RRRRrrr
RAAAAH! AAAAAH!!!

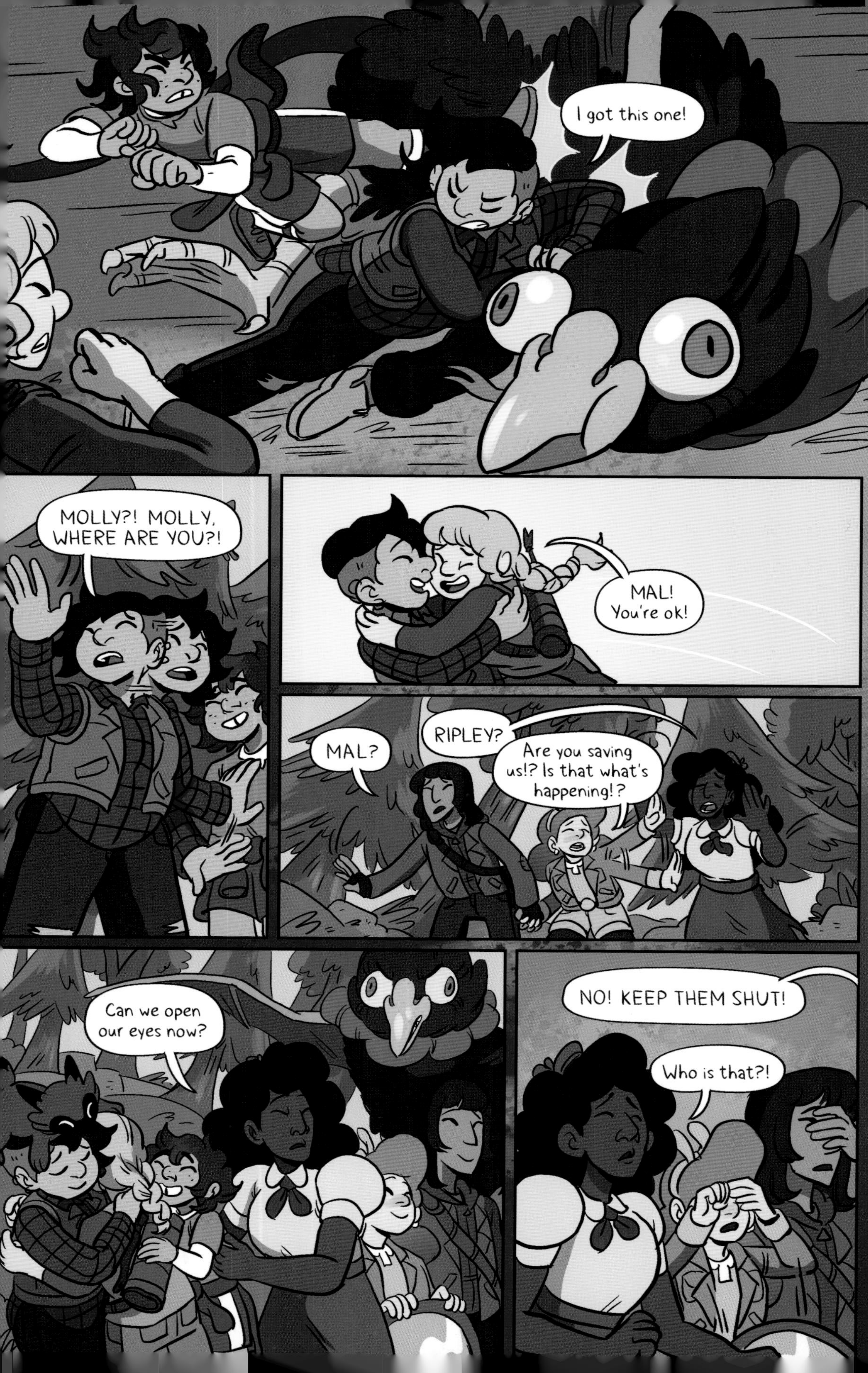

I got this one!
MOLLY?! MOLLY, WHERE ARE YOU?!
MAL! You're ok!
MAL?
RIPLEY?
Are you saving us!? Is that what's happening!?
Can we open our eyes now?
NO! KEEP THEM SHUT!
Who is that?!

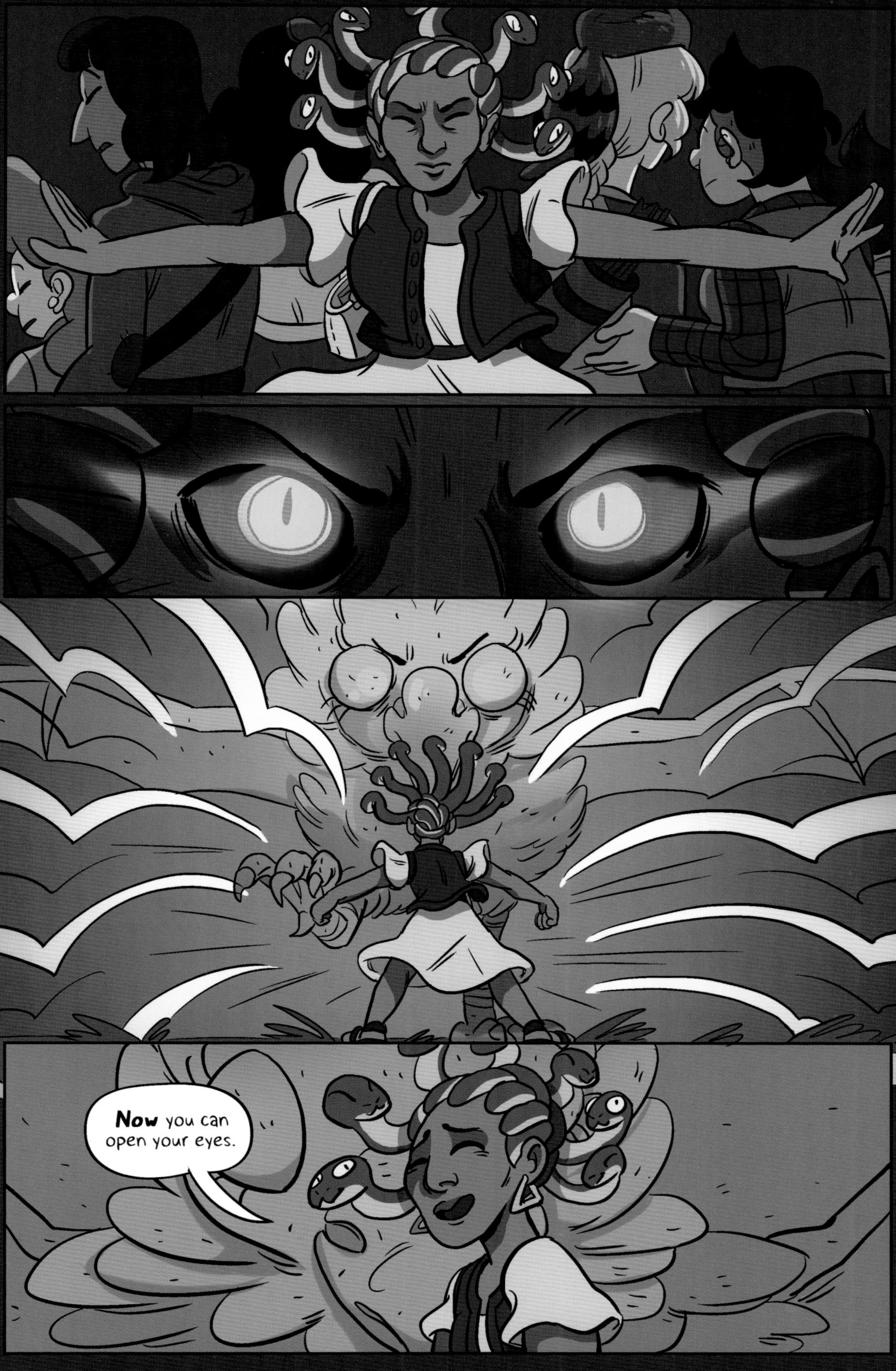
Now you can open your eyes.

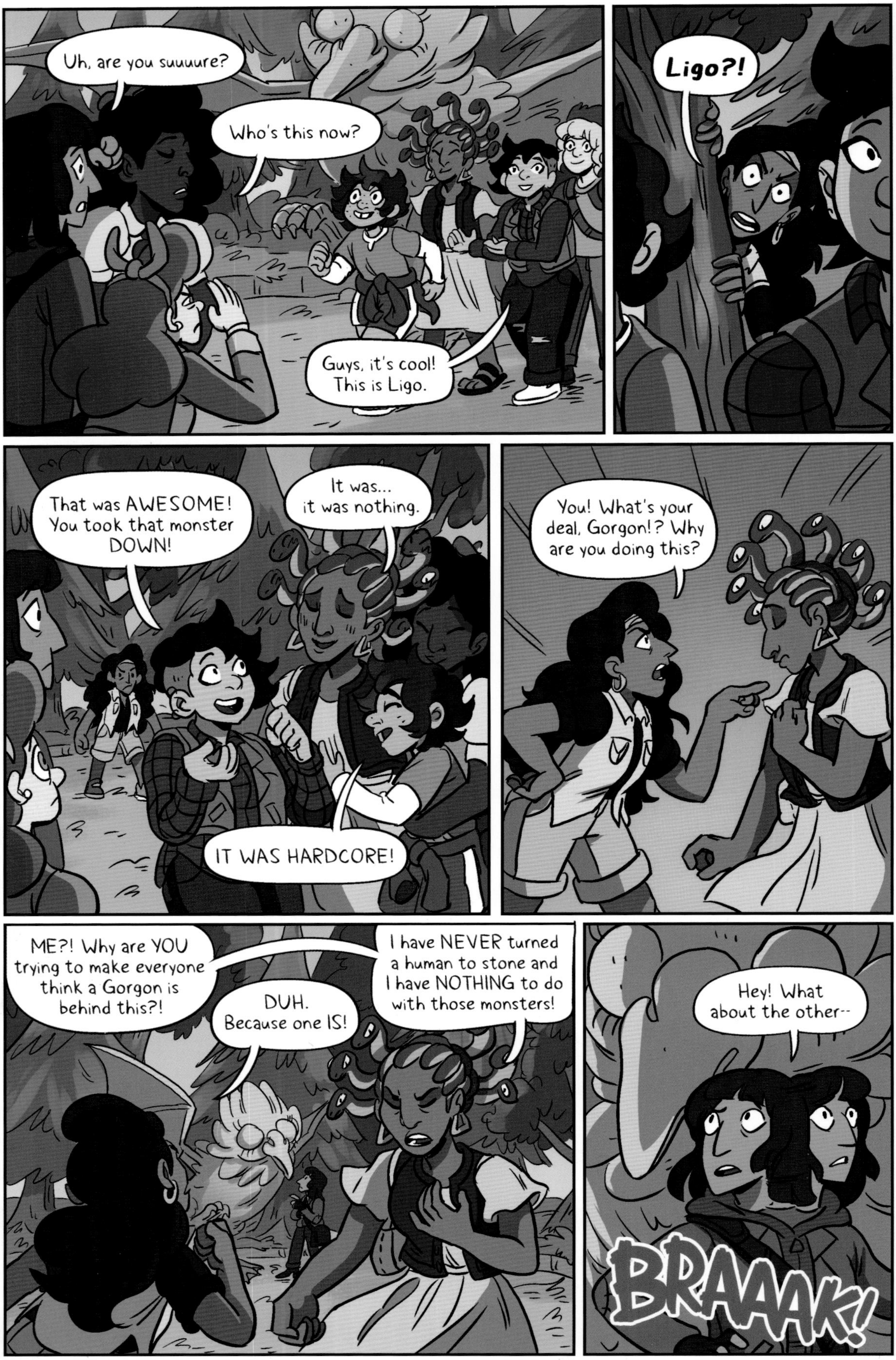
Uh, are you suuuure?
Who's this now?
Guys, it's cool! This is Ligo.
Ligo?!
That was AWESOME! You took that monster DOWN!
It was... it was nothing.
IT WAS HARDCORE!
You! What's your deal, Gorgon!? Why are you doing this?
ME?! Why are YOU trying to make everyone think a Gorgon is behind this?!
DUH. Because one IS!
I have NEVER turned a human to stone and I have NOTHING to do with those monsters!
Hey! What about the other--
BRAAAK!

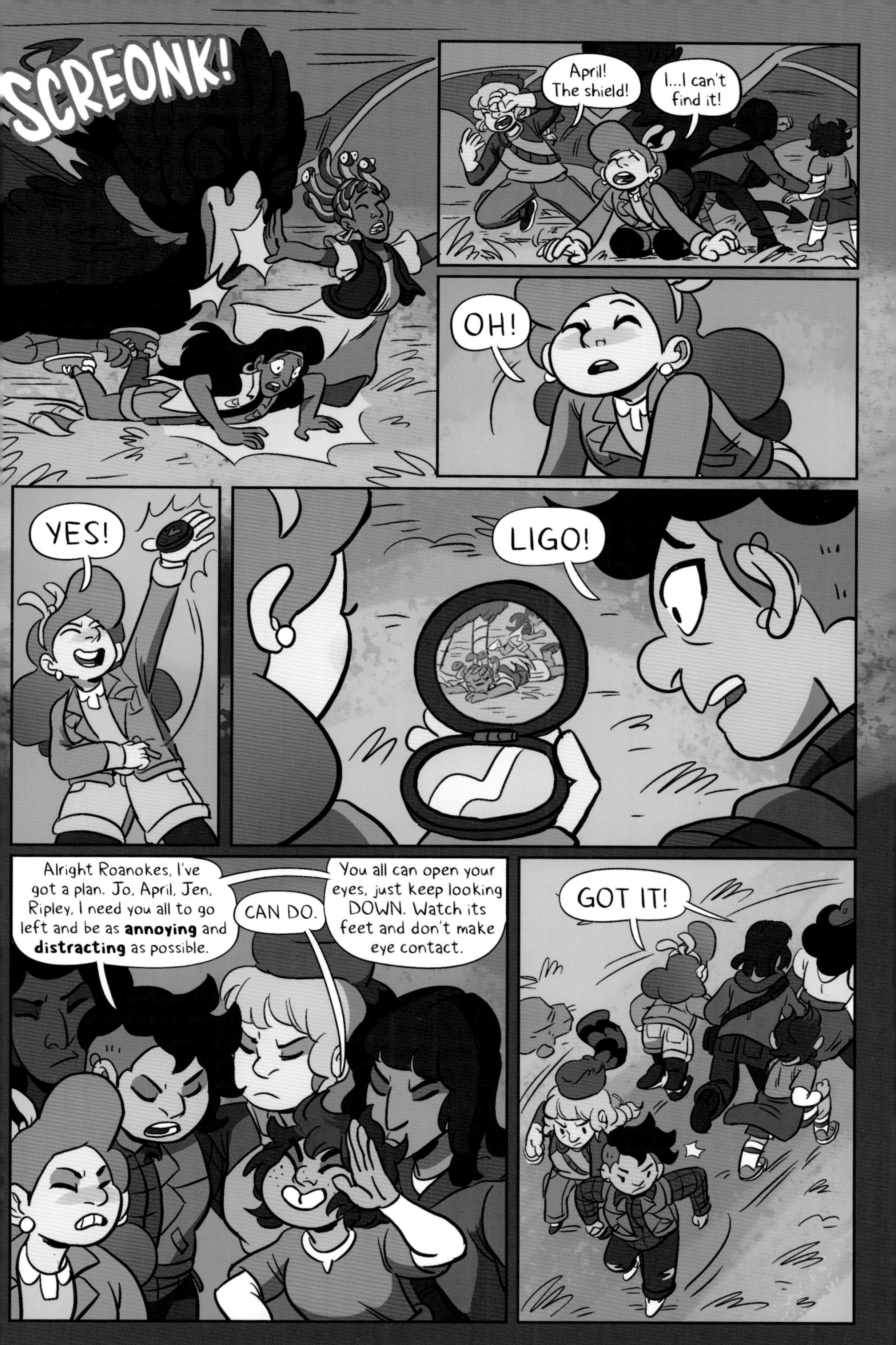
SCREONK!
April! The shield!
I...I can't find it!
OH!
YES!
LIGO!
Alright Roanokes, I've got a plan. Jo, April, Jen, Ripley, I need you all to go left and be as **annoying** and **distracting** as possible.
CAN DO.
You all can open your eyes, just keep looking DOWN. Watch its feet and don't make eye contact.
GOT IT!

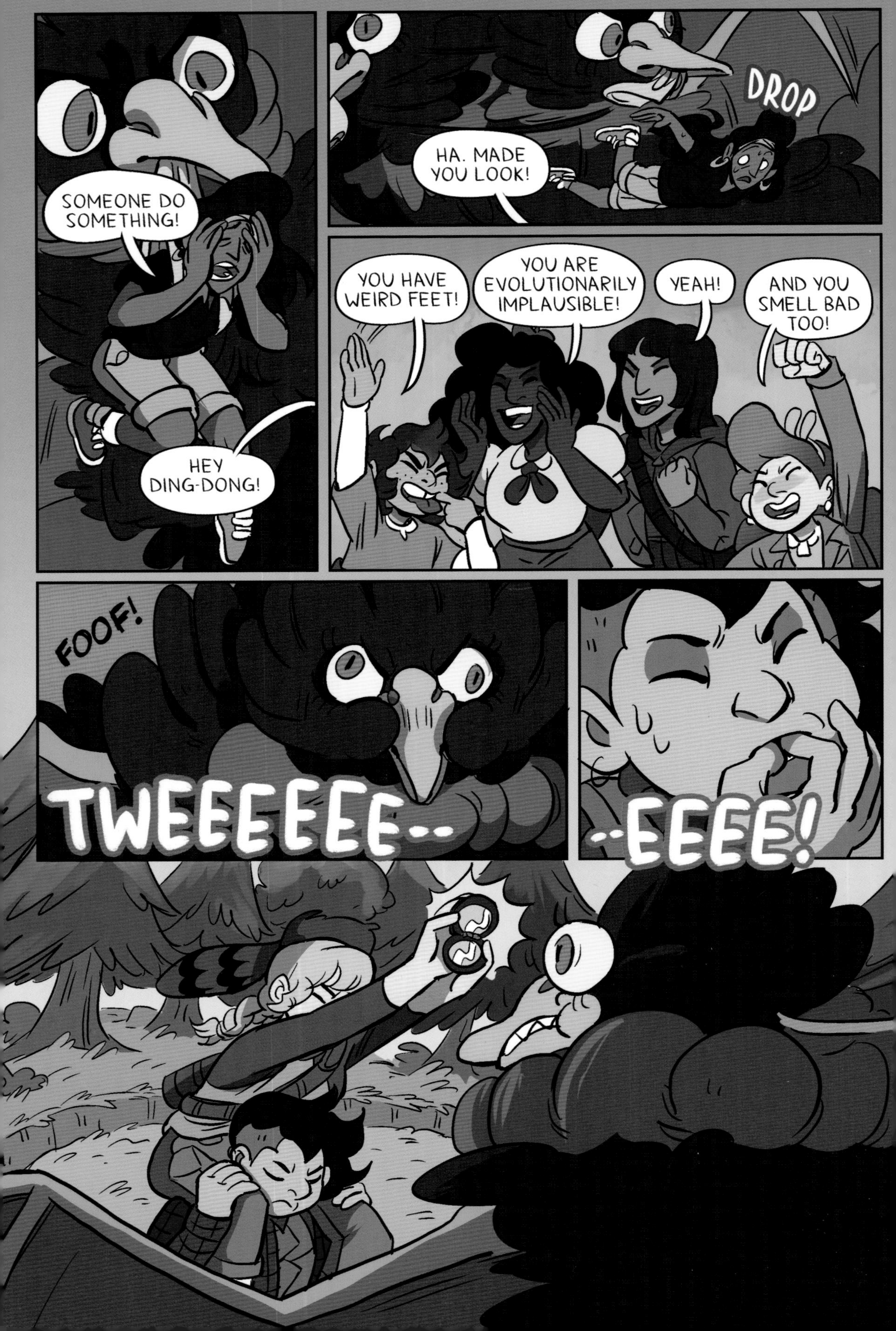
SOMEONE DO SOMETHING!
HEY DING-DONG!
HA. MADE YOU LOOK!
DROP
YOU HAVE WEIRD FEET!
YOU ARE EVOLUTIONARILY IMPLAUSIBLE!
YEAH!
AND YOU SMELL BAD TOO!
FOOF!
TWEEEEEE--
--EEEE!

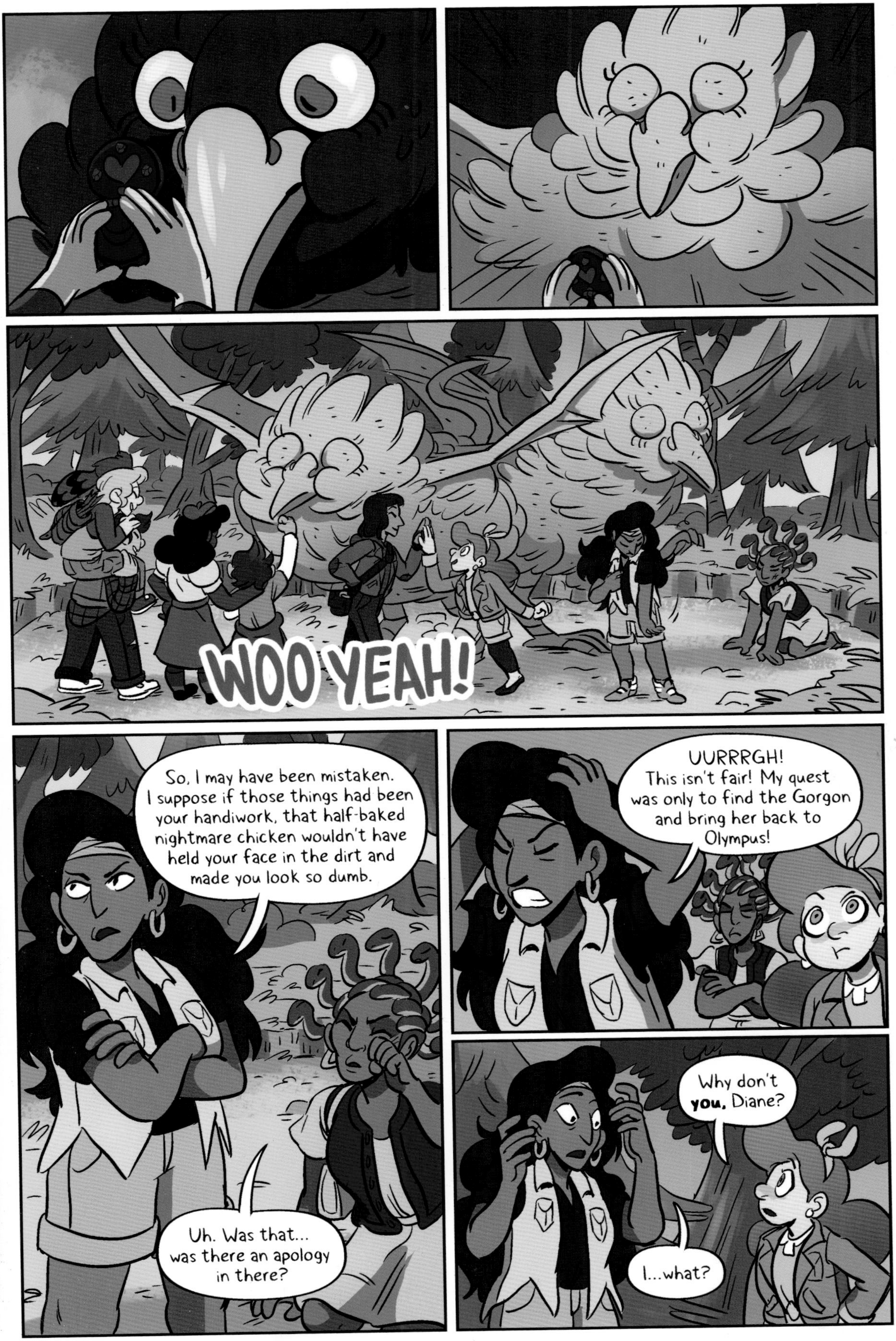
WOO YEAH!
So, I may have been mistaken. I suppose if those things had been your handiwork, that half-baked nightmare chicken wouldn't have held your face in the dirt and made you look so dumb.
Uh. Was that... was there an apology in there?
UURRRGH! This isn't fair! My quest was only to find the Gorgon and bring her back to Olympus!
Why don't **you**, Diane?
I...what?

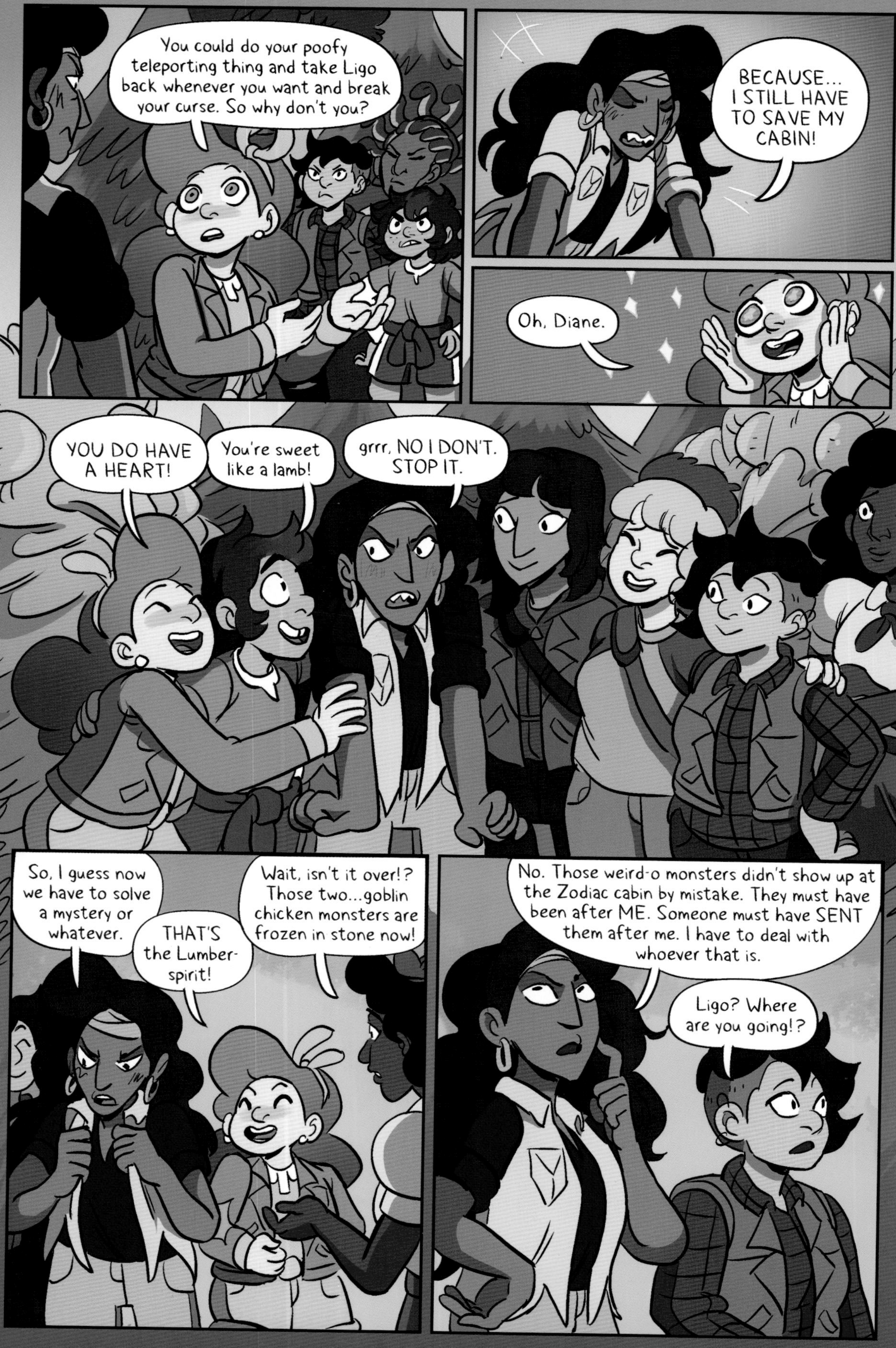
You could do your poofy teleporting thing and take Ligo back whenever you want and break your curse. So why don't you?
BECAUSE... I STILL HAVE TO SAVE MY CABIN!
Oh, Diane.
YOU DO HAVE A HEART!
You're sweet like a lamb!
grrr, NO I DON'T. STOP IT.
So, I guess now we have to solve a mystery or whatever.
THAT'S the Lumber-spirit!
Wait, isn't it over!? Those two...goblin chicken monsters are frozen in stone now!
No. Those weird-o monsters didn't show up at the Zodiac cabin by mistake. They must have been after ME. Someone must have SENT them after me. I have to deal with whoever that is.
Ligo? Where are you going!?

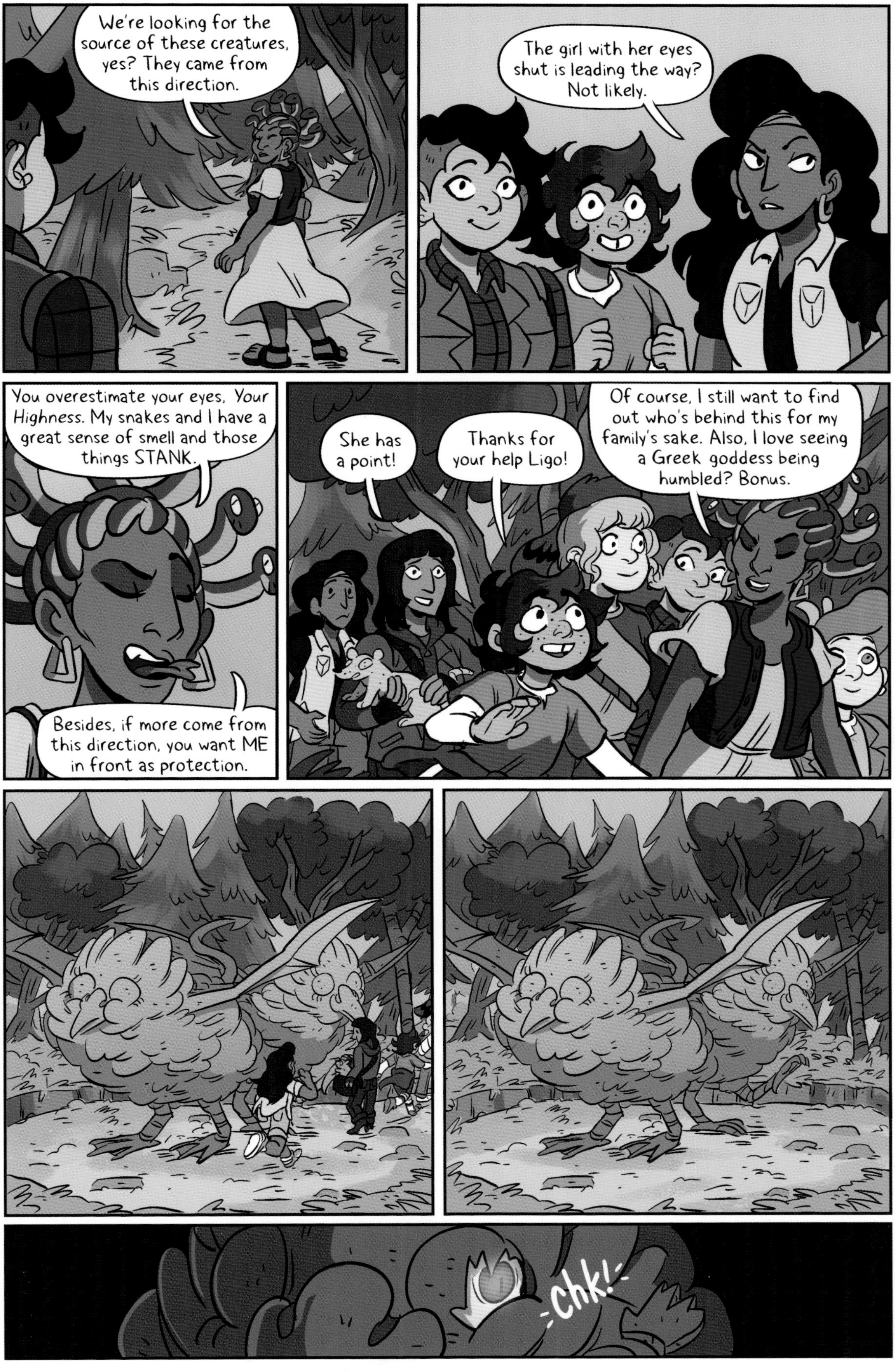

We're looking for the source of these creatures, yes? They came from this direction.
The girl with her eyes shut is leading the way? Not likely.
You overestimate your eyes, *Your Highness*. My snakes and I have a great sense of smell and those things STANK.
Besides, if more come from this direction, you want ME in front as protection.
She has a point!
Thanks for your help Ligo!
Of course, I still want to find out who's behind this for my family's sake. Also, I love seeing a Greek goddess being humbled? Bonus.
Chk!

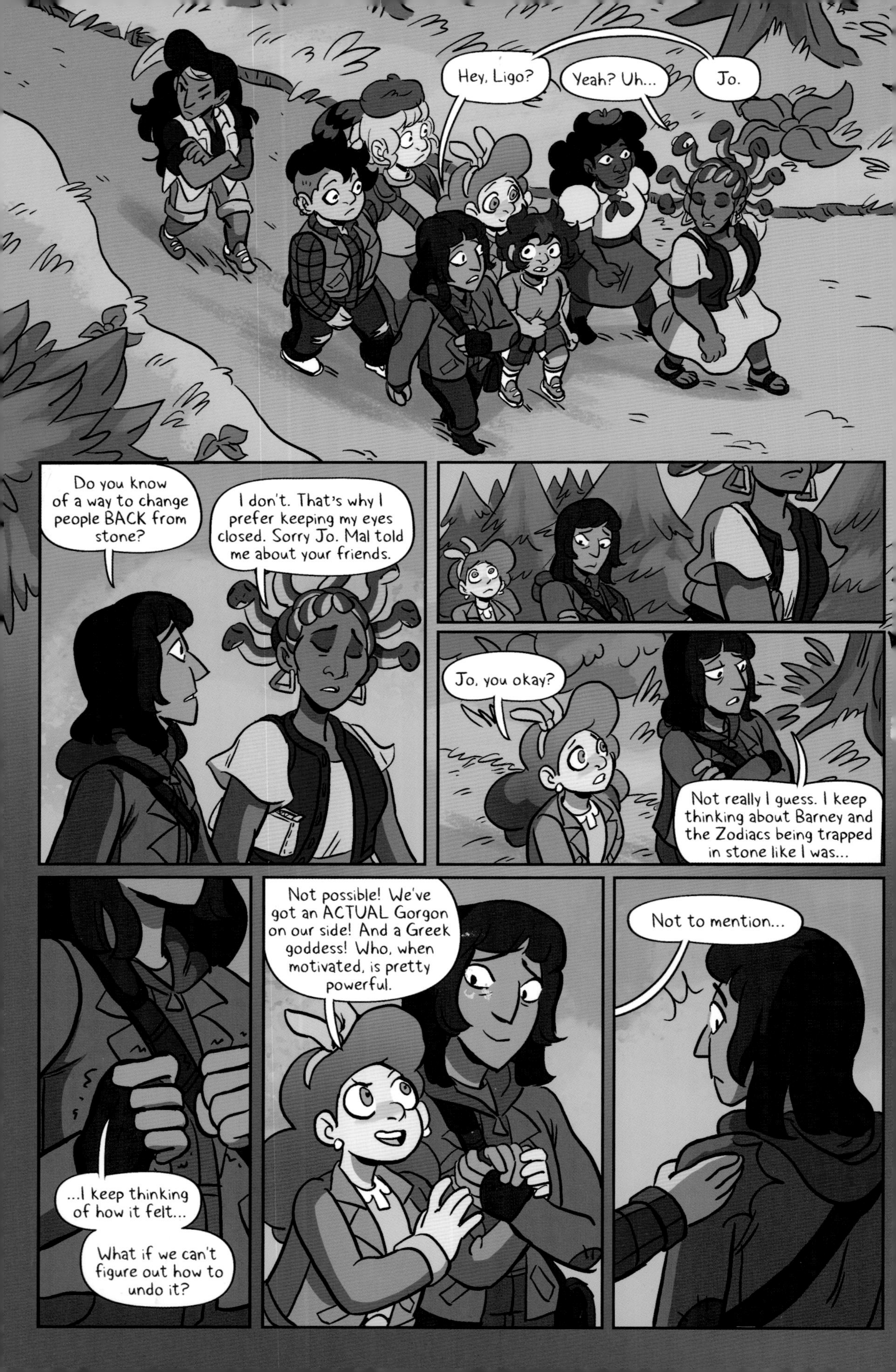
Hey, Ligo?
Yeah? Uh...
Jo.
Do you know of a way to change people BACK from stone?
I don't. That's why I prefer keeping my eyes closed. Sorry Jo. Mal told me about your friends.
Jo, you okay?
Not really I guess. I keep thinking about Barney and the Zodiacs being trapped in stone like I was...
...I keep thinking of how it felt...
What if we can't figure out how to undo it?
Not possible! We've got an ACTUAL Gorgon on our side! And a Greek goddess! Who, when motivated, is pretty powerful.
Not to mention...

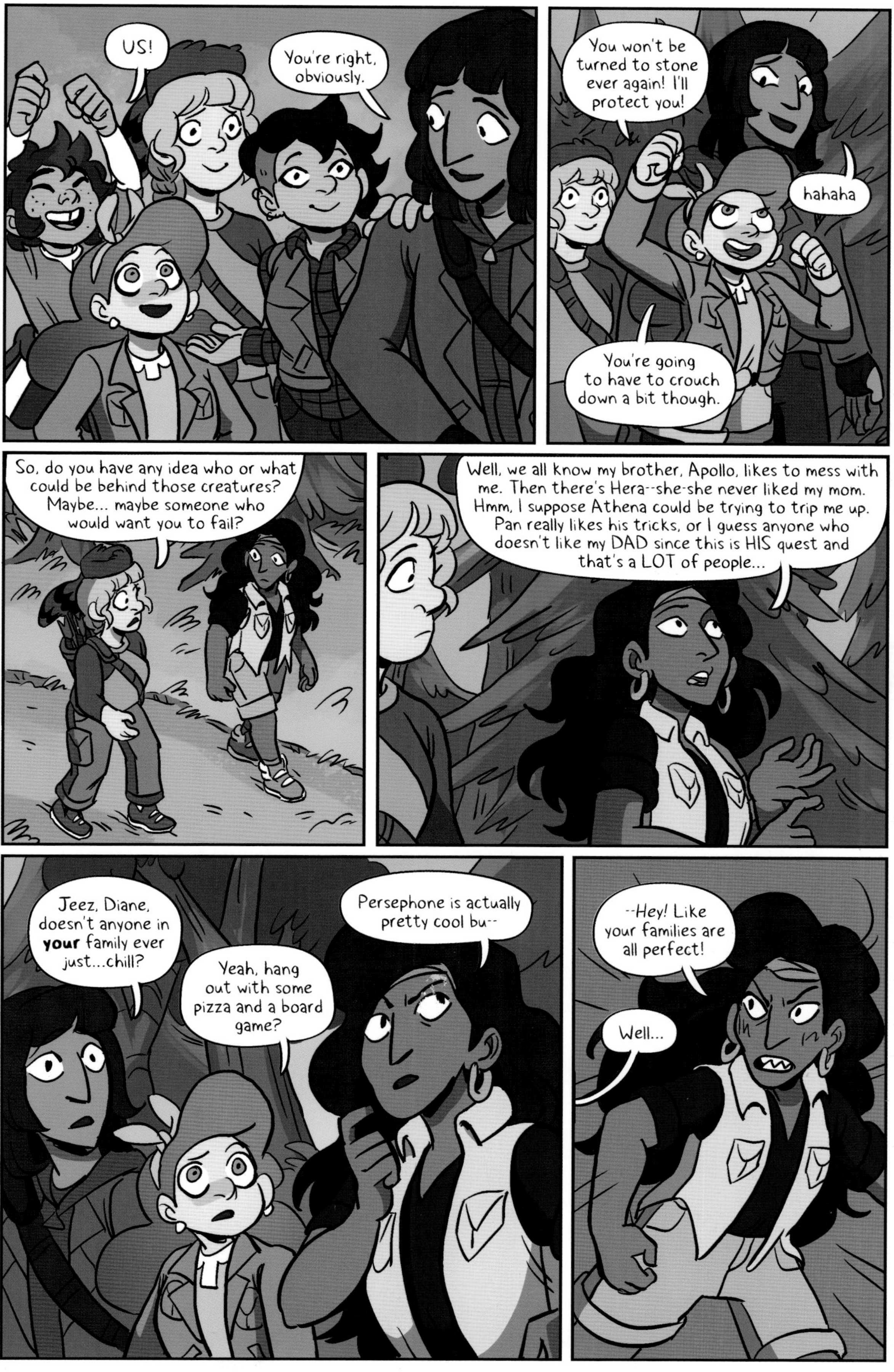
US!
You're right, obviously.
You won't be turned to stone ever again! I'll protect you!
hahaha
You're going to have to crouch down a bit though.
So, do you have any idea who or what could be behind those creatures? Maybe... maybe someone who would want you to fail?
Well, we all know my brother, Apollo, likes to mess with me. Then there's Hera--she-she never liked my mom. Hmm, I suppose Athena could be trying to trip me up. Pan really likes his tricks, or I guess anyone who doesn't like my DAD since this is HIS quest and that's a LOT of people...
Jeez, Diane, doesn't anyone in **your** family ever just...chill?
Yeah, hang out with some pizza and a board game?
Persephone is actually pretty cool bu--
--Hey! Like your families are all perfect!
Well...

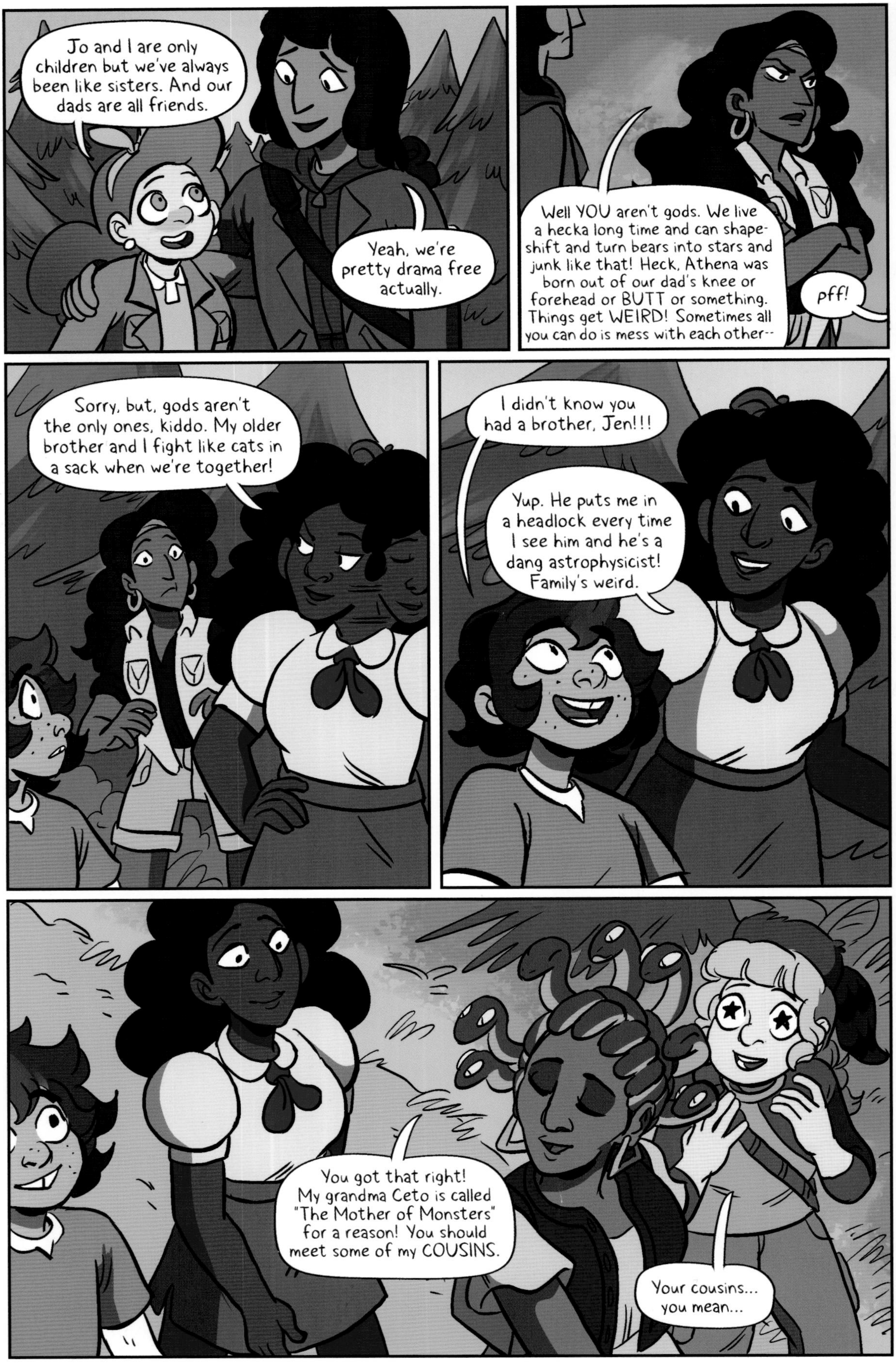
Jo and I are only children but we've always been like sisters. And our dads are all friends.
Yeah, we're pretty drama free actually.
Well YOU aren't gods. We live a hecka long time and can shape-shift and turn bears into stars and junk like that! Heck, Athena was born out of our dad's knee or forehead or BUTT or something. Things get WEIRD! Sometimes all you can do is mess with each other--
pff!
Sorry, but, gods aren't the only ones, kiddo. My older brother and I fight like cats in a sack when we're together!
I didn't know you had a brother, Jen!!!
Yup. He puts me in a headlock every time I see him and he's a dang astrophysicist! Family's weird.
You got that right! My grandma Ceto is called "The Mother of Monsters" for a reason! You should meet some of my COUSINS.
Your cousins... you mean...

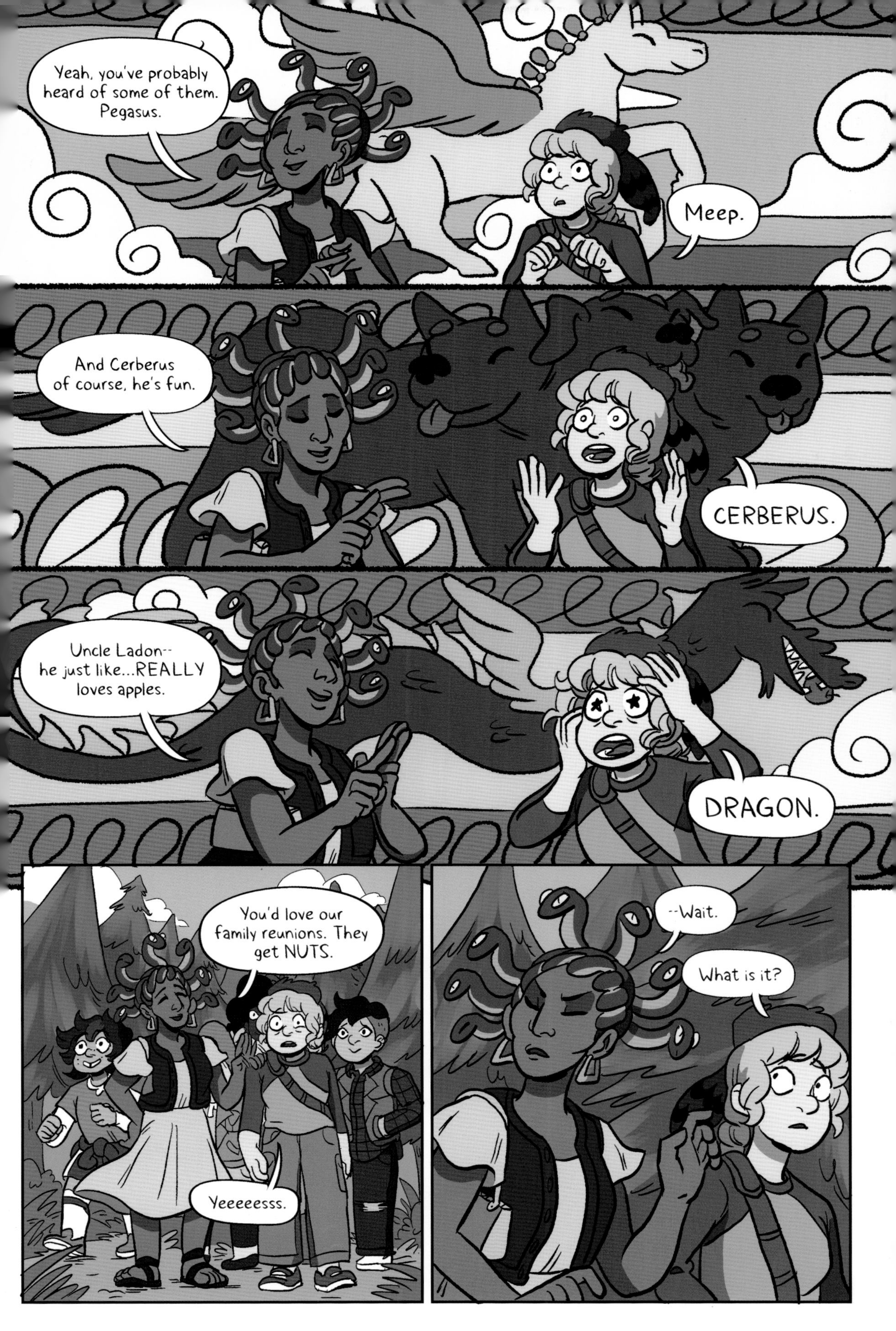
Yeah, you've probably heard of some of them. Pegasus.
Meep.
And Cerberus of course, he's fun.
CERBERUS.
Uncle Ladon-- he just like...REALLY loves apples.
DRAGON.
You'd love our family reunions. They get NUTS.
Yeeeeesss.
--Wait.
What is it?

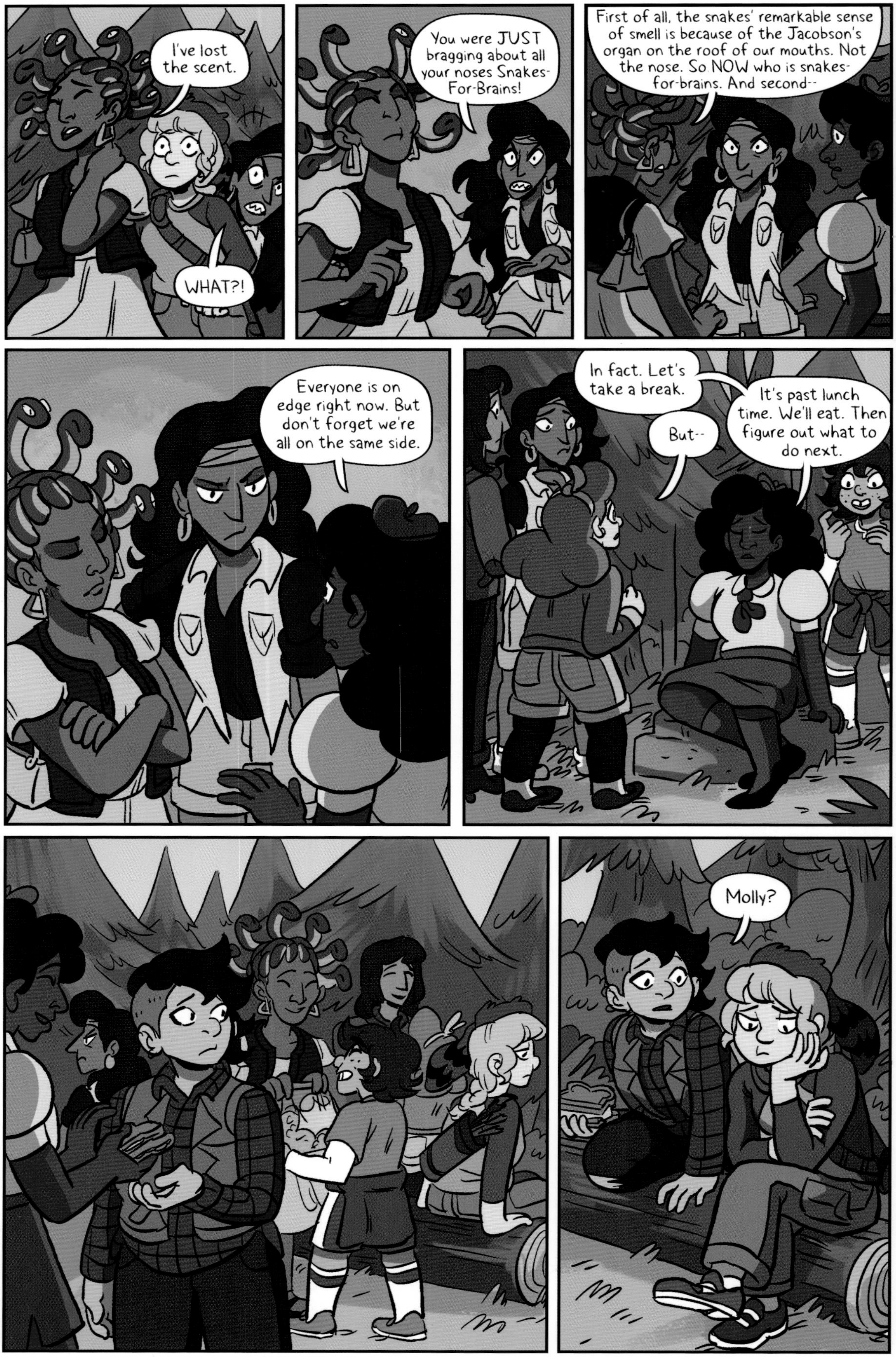
I've lost the scent.
WHAT?!
You were JUST bragging about all your noses Snakes-For-Brains!
First of all, the snakes' remarkable sense of smell is because of the Jacobson's organ on the roof of our mouths. Not the nose. So NOW who is snakes-for-brains. And second--
Everyone is on edge right now. But don't forget we're all on the same side.
In fact. Let's take a break.
But--
It's past lunch time. We'll eat. Then figure out what to do next.
Molly?

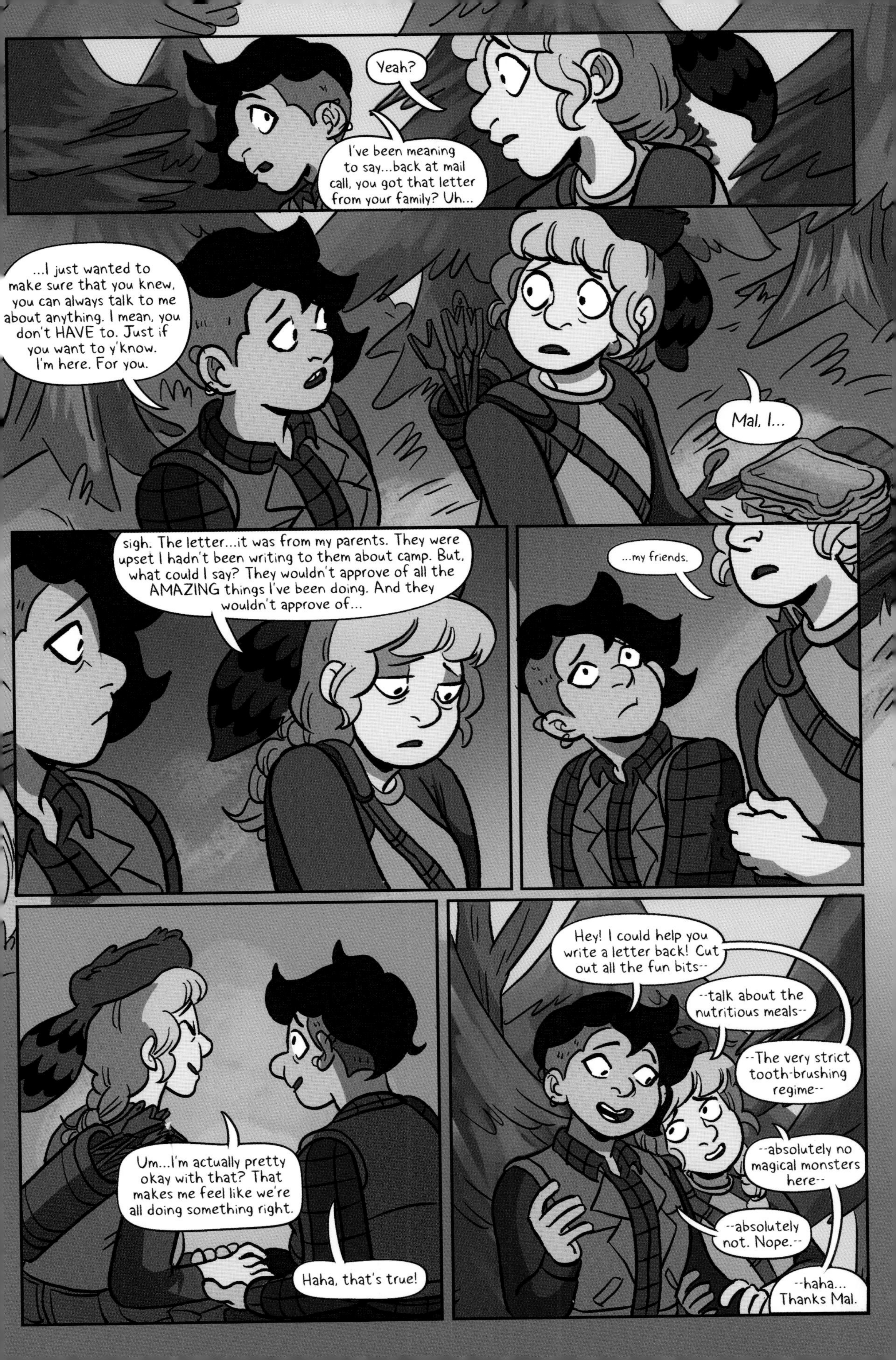
Yeah?
I've been meaning to say...back at mail call, you got that letter from your family? Uh...
...I just wanted to make sure that you knew, you can always talk to me about anything. I mean, you don't HAVE to. Just if you want to y'know. I'm here. For you.
Mal, I...
sigh. The letter...it was from my parents. They were upset I hadn't been writing to them about camp. But, what could I say? They wouldn't approve of all the AMAZING things I've been doing. And they wouldn't approve of...
...my friends.
Um...I'm actually pretty okay with that? That makes me feel like we're all doing something right.
Haha, that's true!
Hey! I could help you write a letter back! Cut out all the fun bits--
--talk about the nutritious meals--
--The very strict tooth-brushing regime--
--absolutely no magical monsters here--
--absolutely not. Nope.--
--haha... Thanks Mal.

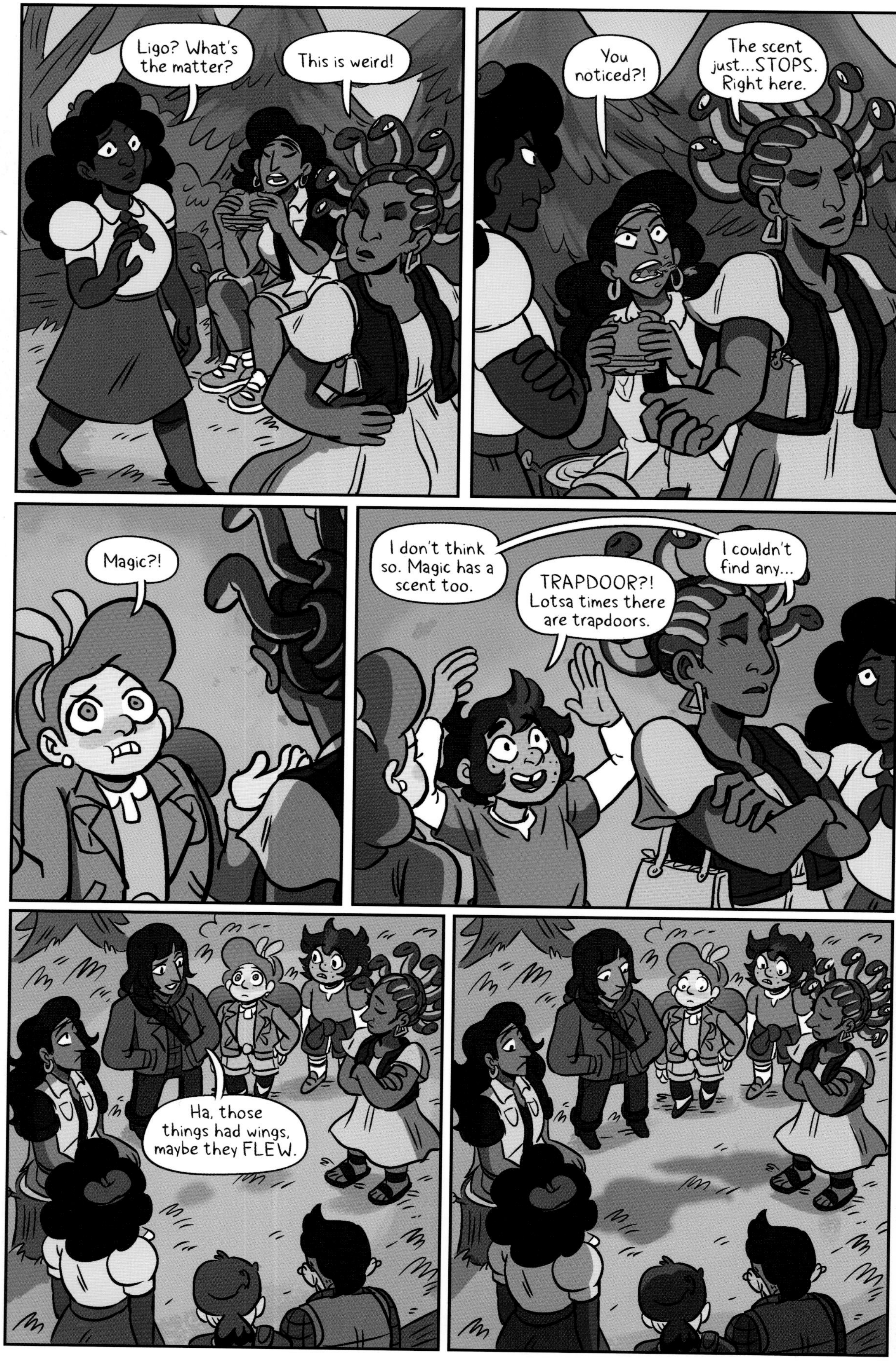
Ligo? What's the matter?
This is weird!
You noticed?!
The scent just...STOPS. Right here.
Magic?!
I don't think so. Magic has a scent too.
I couldn't find any...
TRAPDOOR?! Lotsa times there are trapdoors.
Ha, those things had wings, maybe they FLEW.

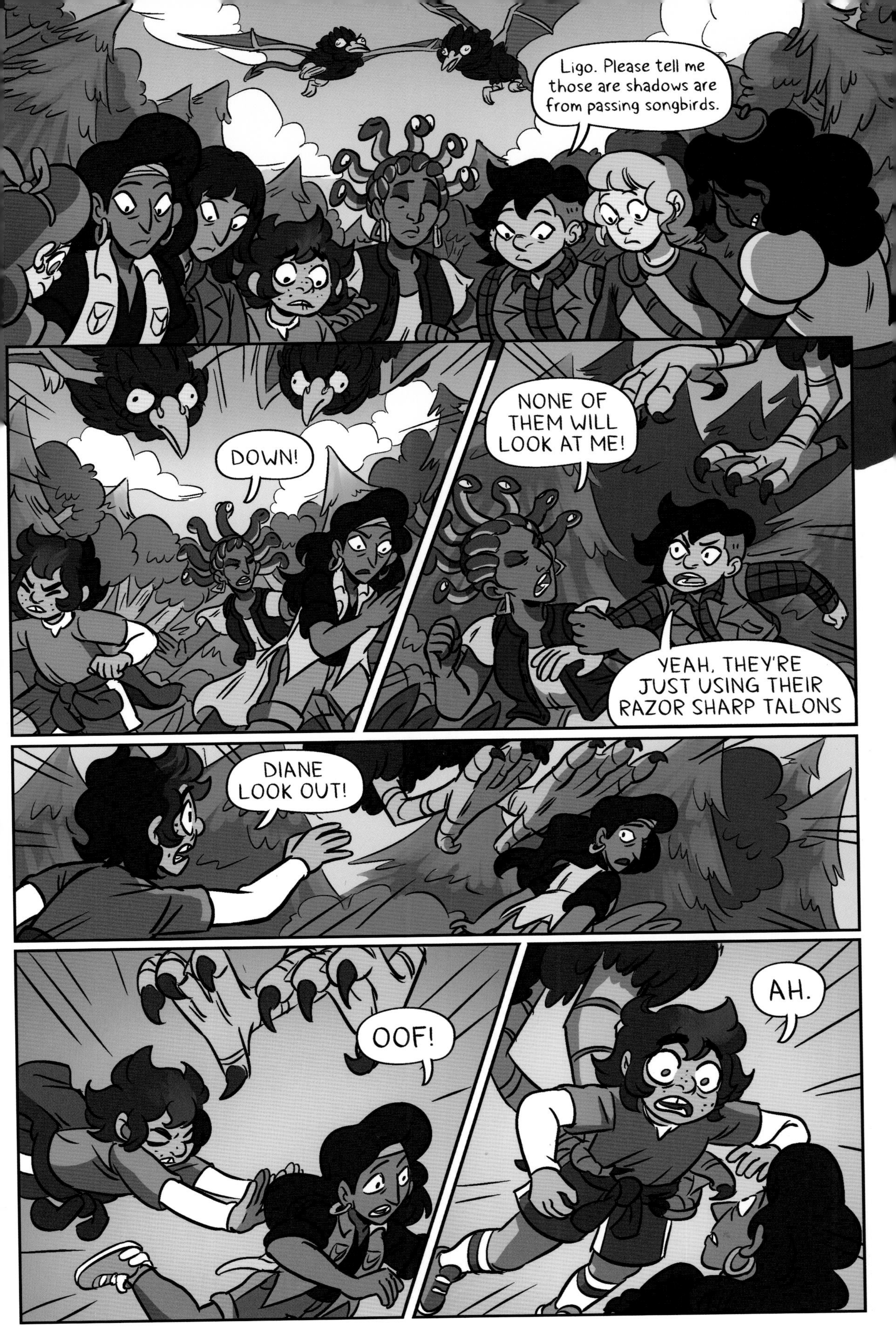
Ligo. Please tell me those are shadows are from passing songbirds.
DOWN!
NONE OF THEM WILL LOOK AT ME!
YEAH, THEY'RE JUST USING THEIR RAZOR SHARP TALONS
DIANE LOOK OUT!
OOF!
AH.

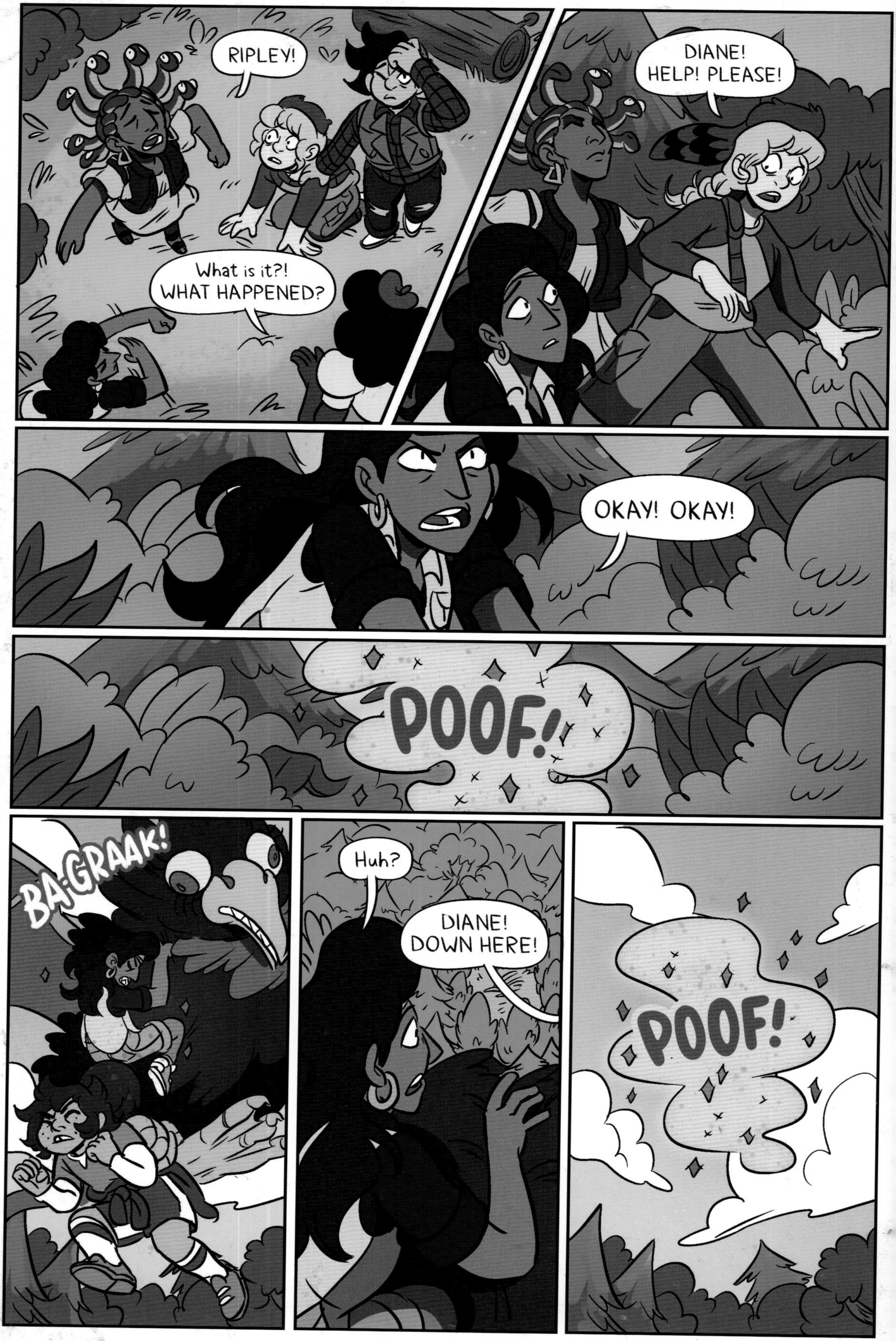
RIPLEY!
What is it?! WHAT HAPPENED?
DIANE! HELP! PLEASE!
OKAY! OKAY!
POOF!
BA-GRAAK!
Huh?
DIANE! DOWN HERE!
POOF!

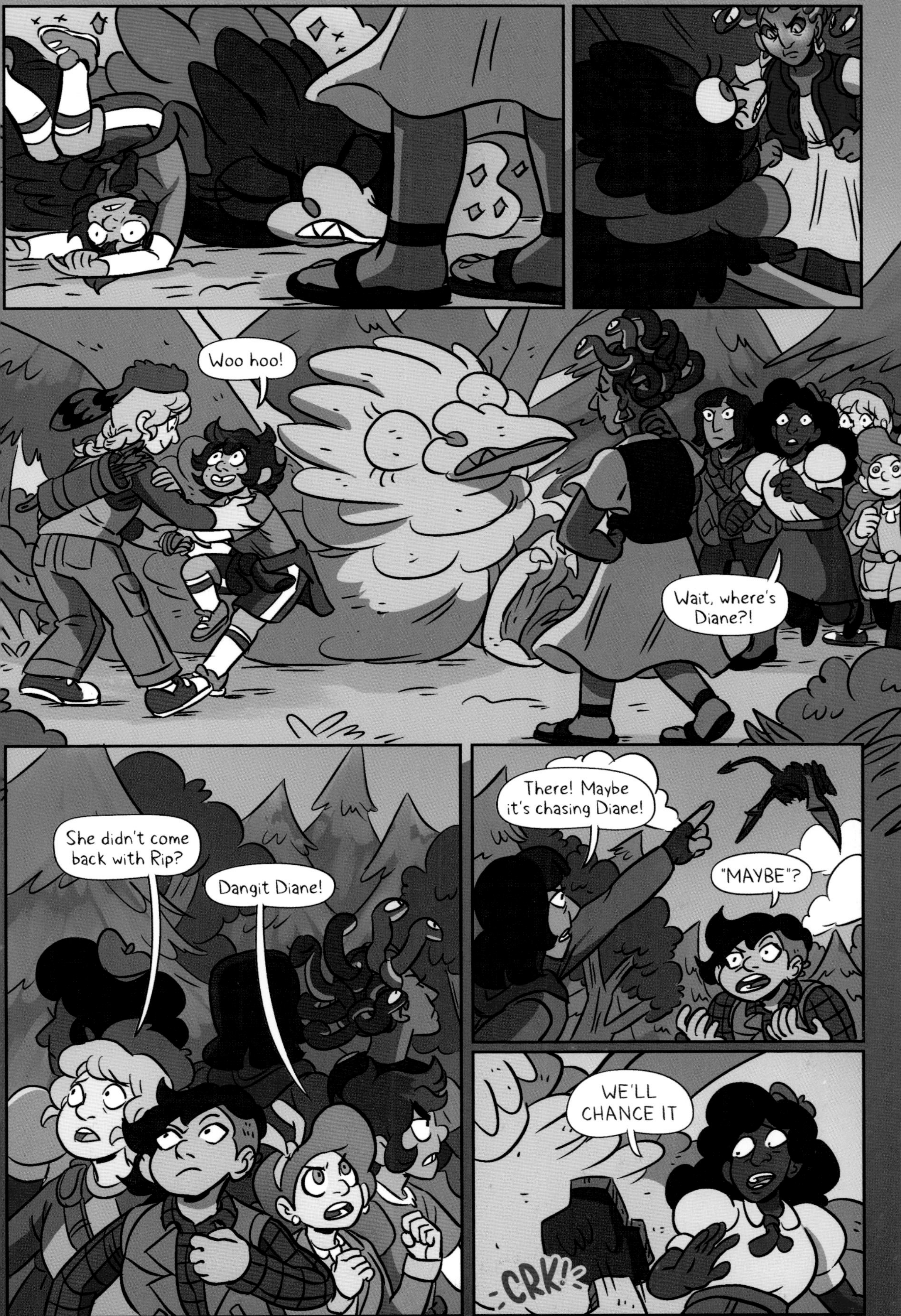

Woo hoo!
Wait, where's Diane?!
She didn't come back with Rip?
Dangit Diane!
There! Maybe it's chasing Diane!
"MAYBE"?
WE'LL CHANCE IT
CRK!

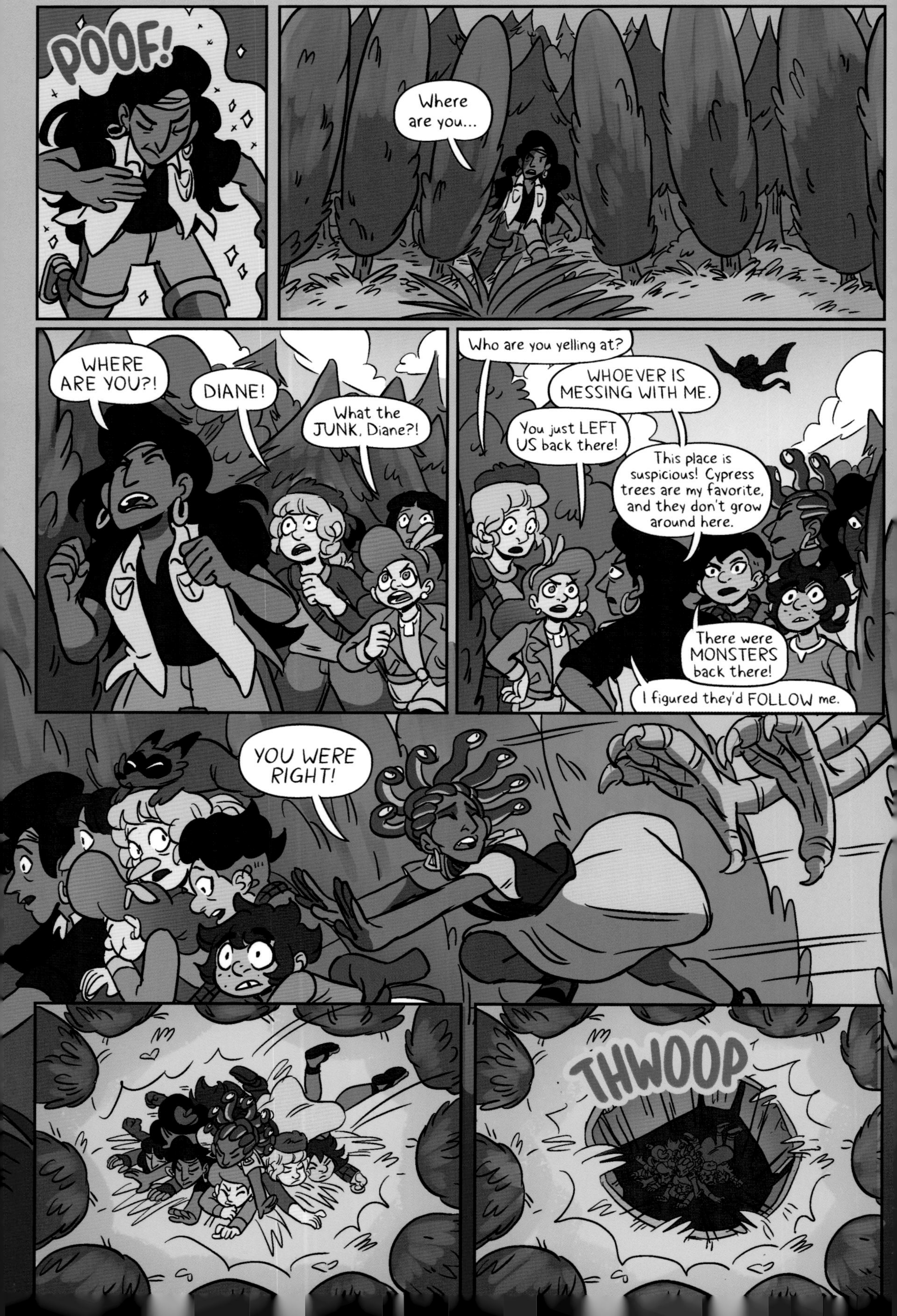
POOF!
Where are you...
WHERE ARE YOU?!
DIANE!
What the JUNK, Diane?!
Who are you yelling at?
WHOEVER IS MESSING WITH ME.
You just LEFT US back there!
This place is suspicious! Cypress trees are my favorite, and they don't grow around here.
There were MONSTERS back there!
I figured they'd FOLLOW me.
YOU WERE RIGHT!
THWOOP

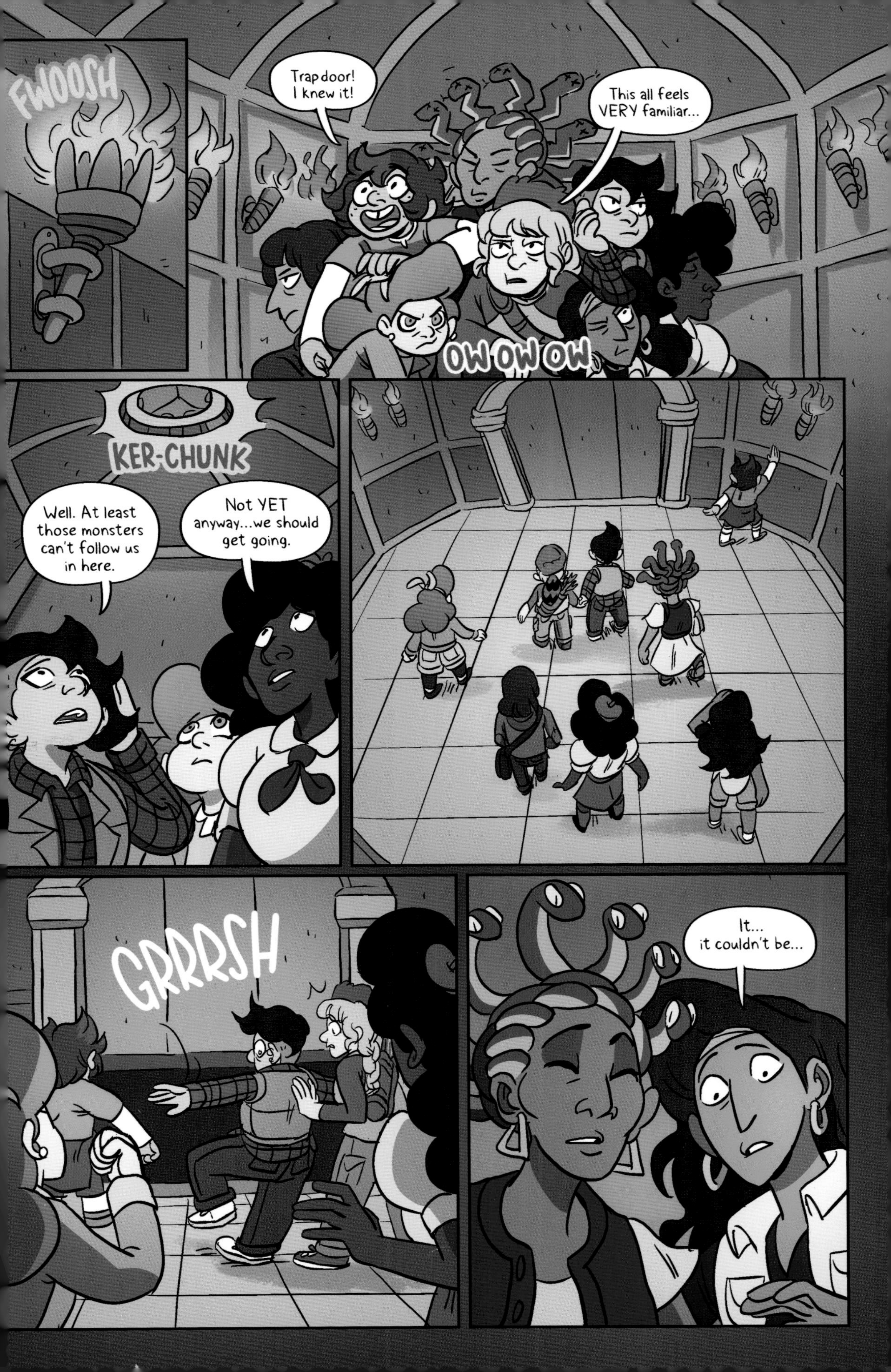
FWOOSH
Trap door! I knew it!
This all feels VERY familiar...
OW OW OW
KER-CHUNK
Well. At least those monsters can't follow us in here.
Not YET anyway...we should get going.
GRRRSH
It... it couldn't be...

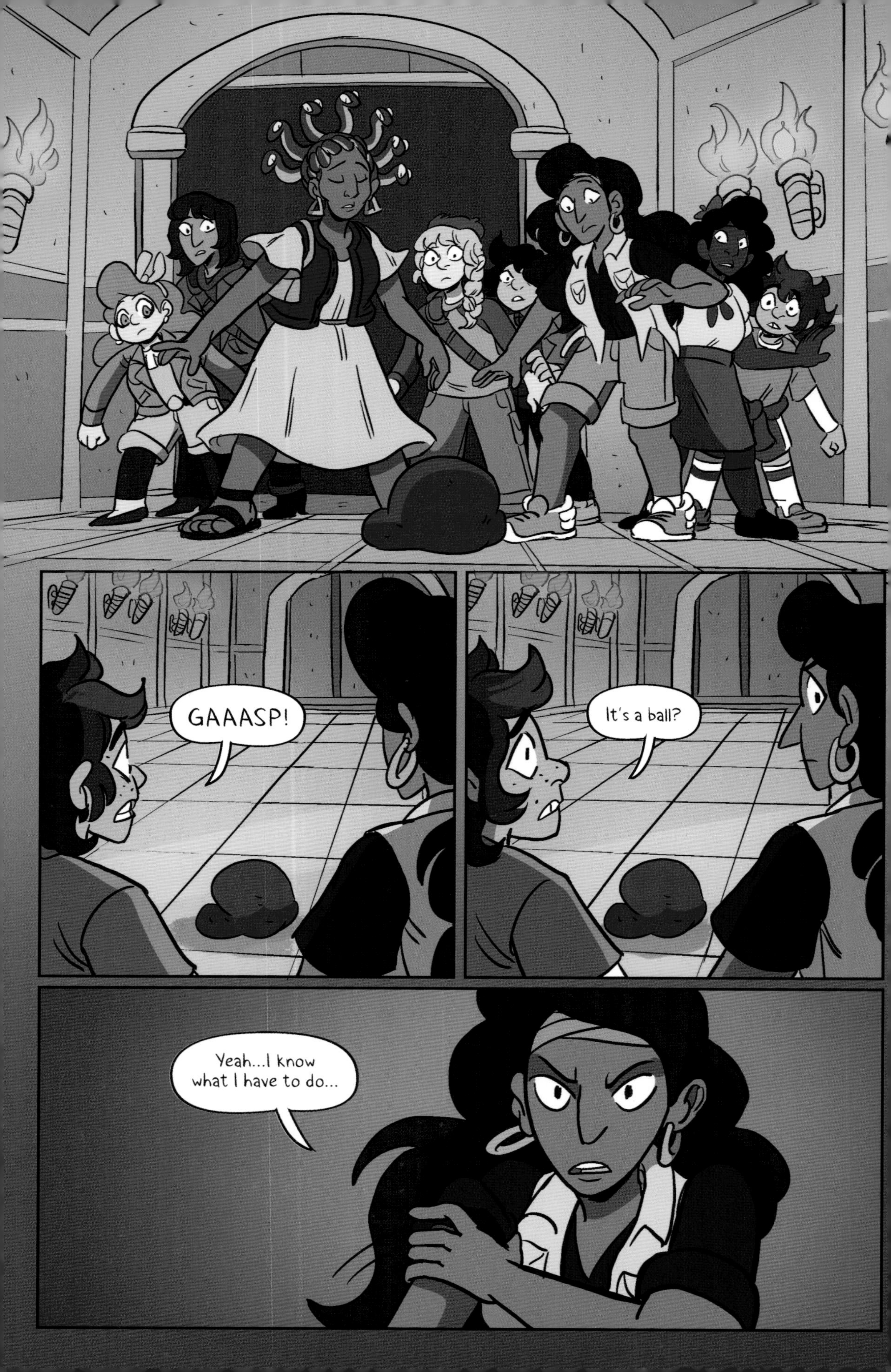
GAAASP!
It's a ball?
Yeah...I know what I have to do...

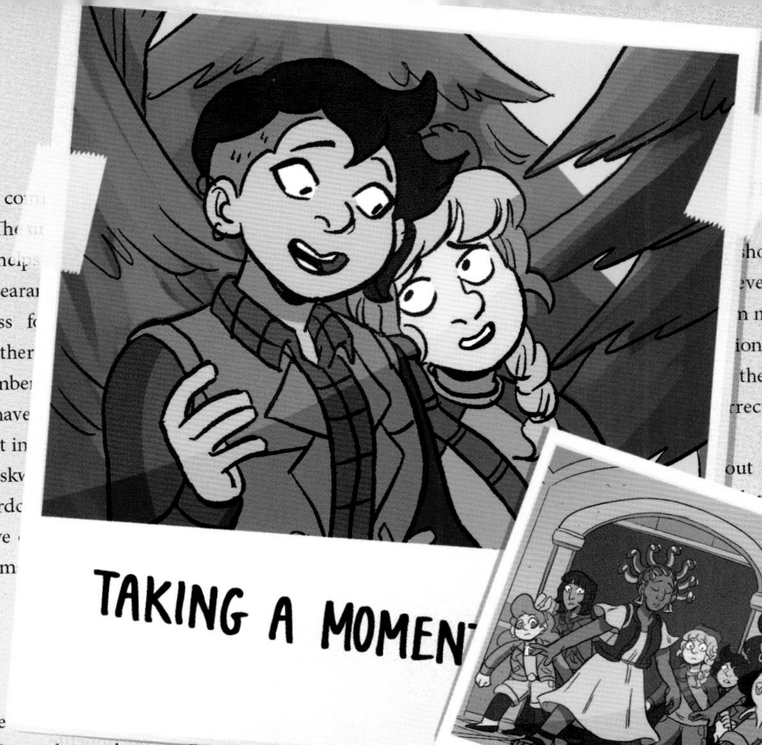
TAKING A MOMENT

will co

The

It helps

appeara

dress fo

Further

Lumbe

to have

part in

Thiskw

Hardc

have

them

HE UNIFORM

should be worn at camp events when Lumberjanes n may also be worn at other ions. It should be worn as a the uniform dress with rrect shoes, and stocking or

out grows her uniform or ... another Lumberjane. ... insignia she has ... her ... her

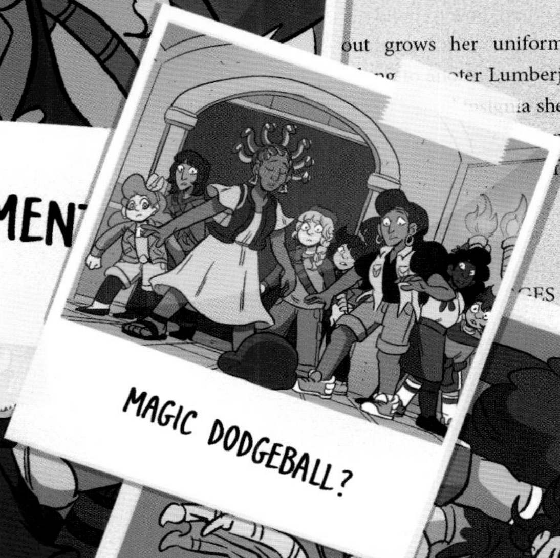
MAGIC DODGEBALL?

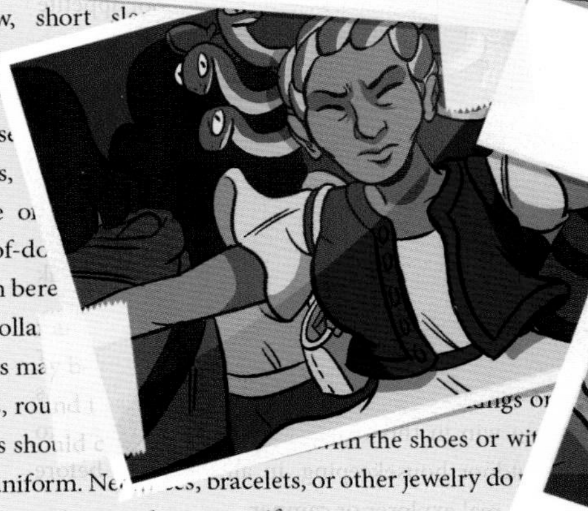

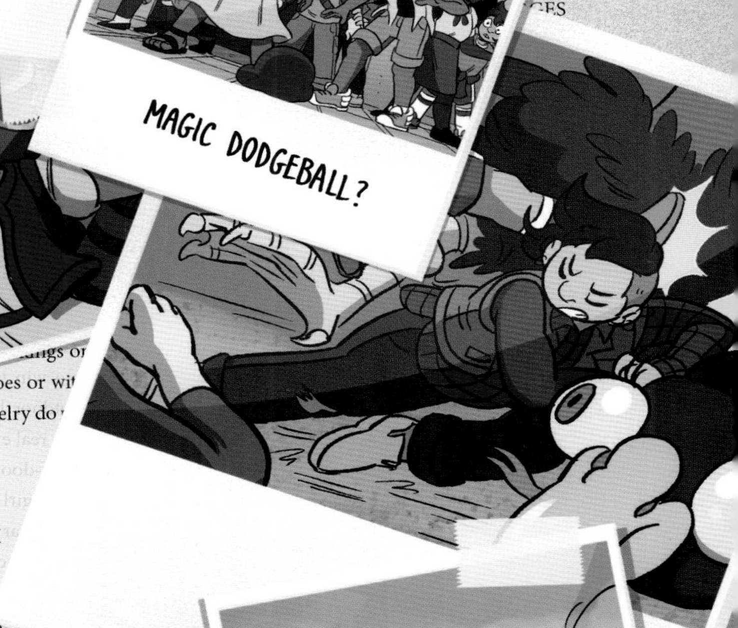

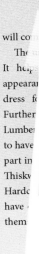

The

yellow, short sl

emb

the w

choose

slacks,

made o

out-of-do

green bere

the colla

Shoes may b

heels, round ... ings or

socks should ... with the shoes or wi

the uniform. Ne... ces, bracelets, or other jewelry do

belong with a Lumberjane uniform.

GES

HOW TO WEAR THE UNIFORM

To look well in a uniform demands first of ... uniform be kept in good condition—clean ... pressed. See that the skirt is the right length for your own height and build, that the belt is adjusted to your waist, that your shoes and stockings are in keeping with the uniform, that you watch your posture and carry yourself with dignity and grace. If the beret is removed indoors, be sure that your hair is neat and kept in place with an insonspicuous clip or ribbon. When you wear a Lumberjane uniform you are identified as a member of this organization and you should be doubly careful to conduct yourself in a way that will show everyone that courtesy and thoughtfullness are part of being a Lumberjane. People are likely to judge a whole nation by the selfishness of a few individuals, to criticize a whole family because of the misconduct of one member, and to feel unkindly toward and organization because of the

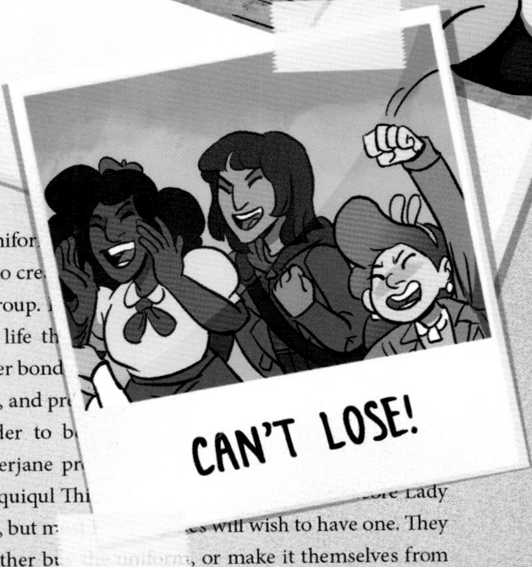
CAN'T LOSE!

The unifor

helps to cre

in a group.

active life th

another bond

future, and pr

in order to b

Lumberjane pr

Penniquiqul Thi ... Lady

Types, but m ... will wish to have one. They can either bu ... uniform, or make it themselves from materials available at the trading post.

LUMBERJANES FIELD MANUAL

CHAPTER
THIRTY-TWO

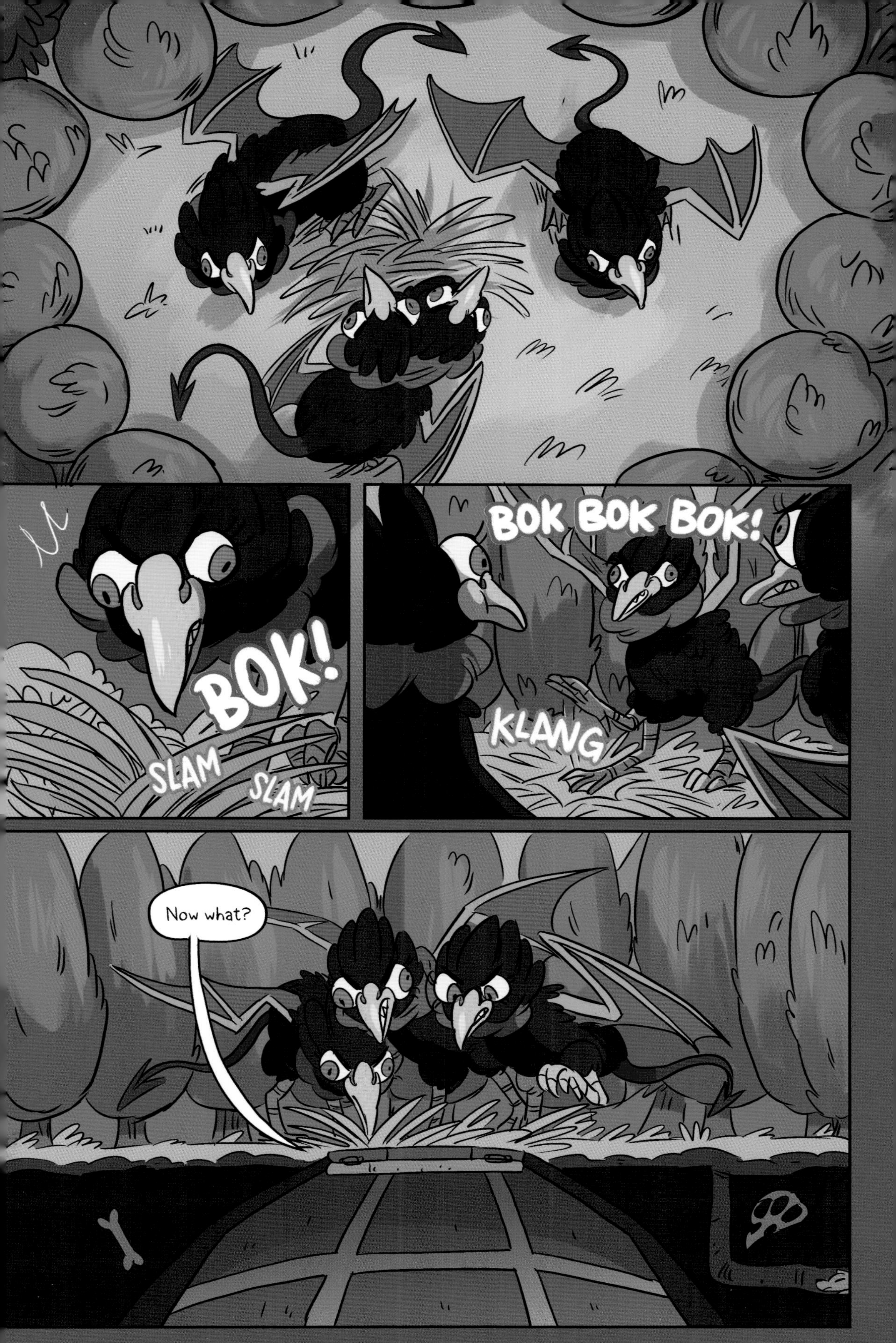
BOK!
SLAM
SLAM
BOK BOK BOK!
KLANG
Now what?

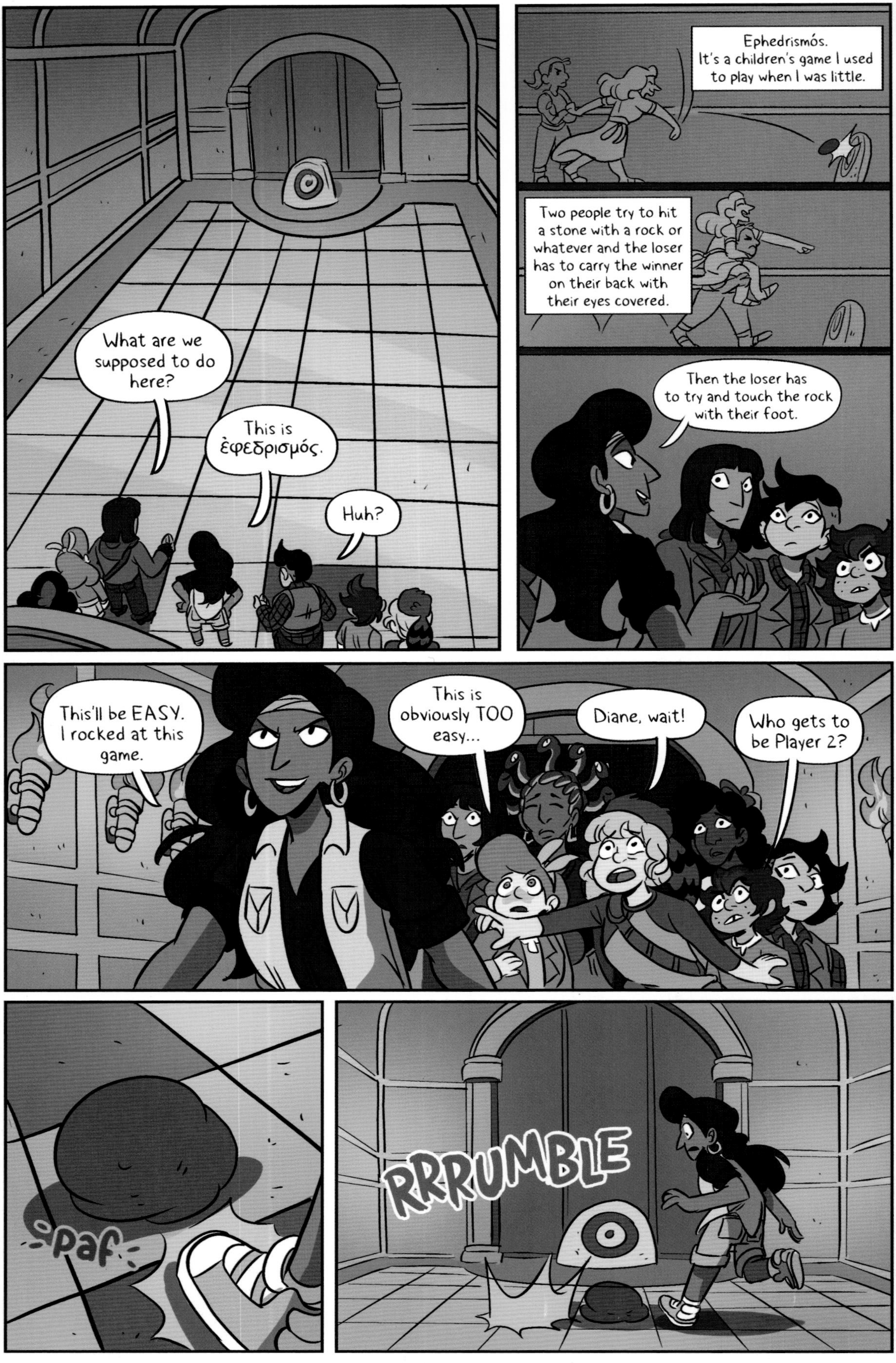
What are we supposed to do here?
This is ἐφεδρισμός.
Huh?
Ephedrismós. It's a children's game I used to play when I was little.
Two people try to hit a stone with a rock or whatever and the loser has to carry the winner on their back with their eyes covered.
Then the loser has to try and touch the rock with their foot.
This'll be EASY. I rocked at this game.
This is obviously TOO easy...
Diane, wait!
Who gets to be Player 2?
paf
RRRUMBLE

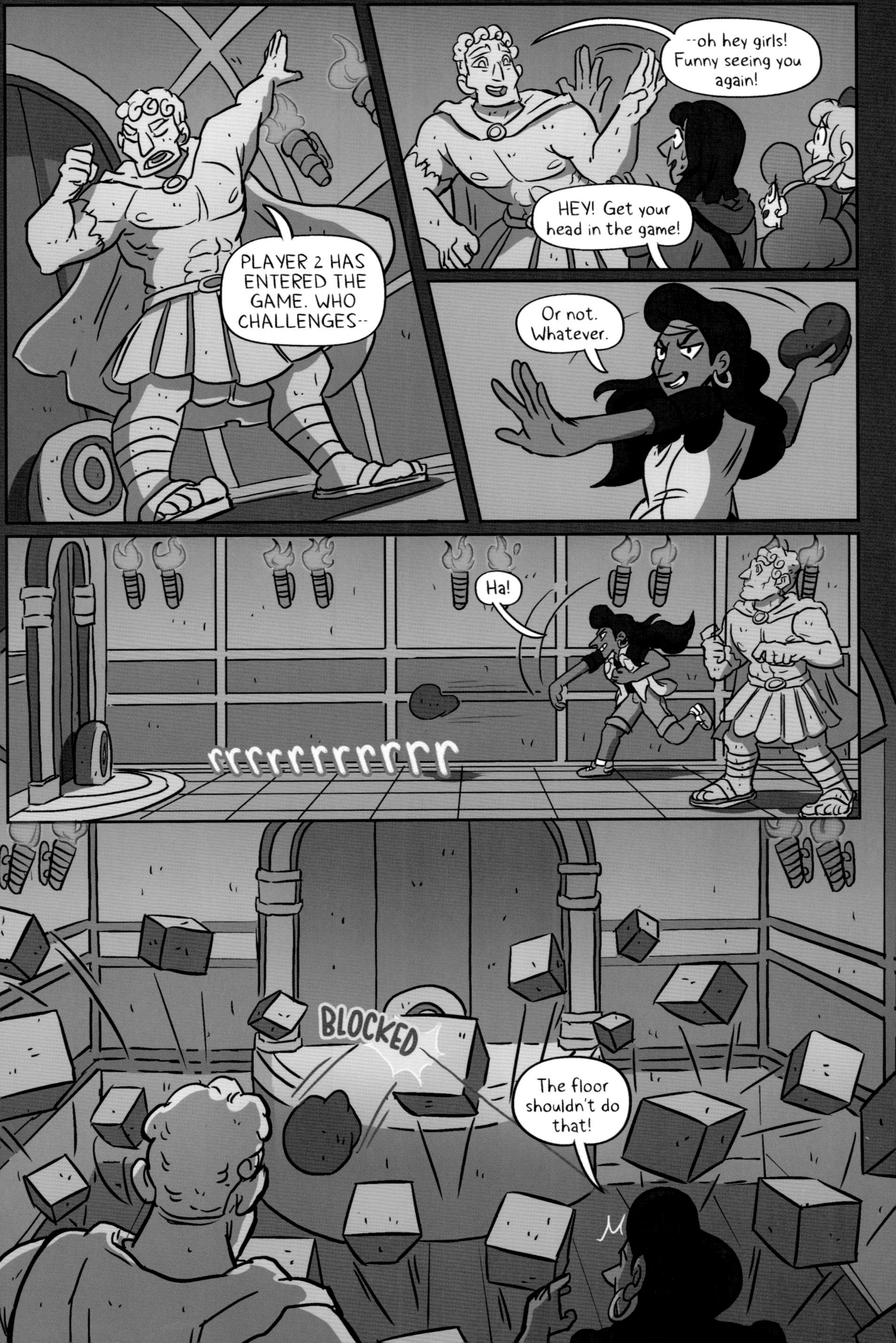
PLAYER 2 HAS ENTERED THE GAME. WHO CHALLENGES--
--oh hey girls! Funny seeing you again!
HEY! Get your head in the game!
Or not. Whatever.
Ha!
rrrrrrrrrr
BLOCKED
The floor shouldn't do that!

You were a
little hasty there.

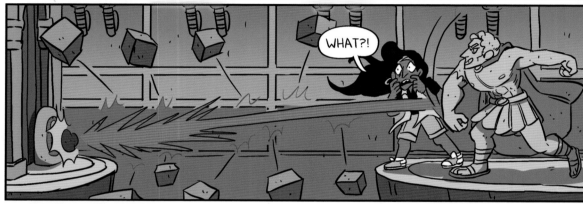
WHAT?!

ARGH! What
do you want!?
I'm not the flippin'
Goddess of Biceps!

After everything,
are you STILL not
getting the power of
teamwork, Diane?

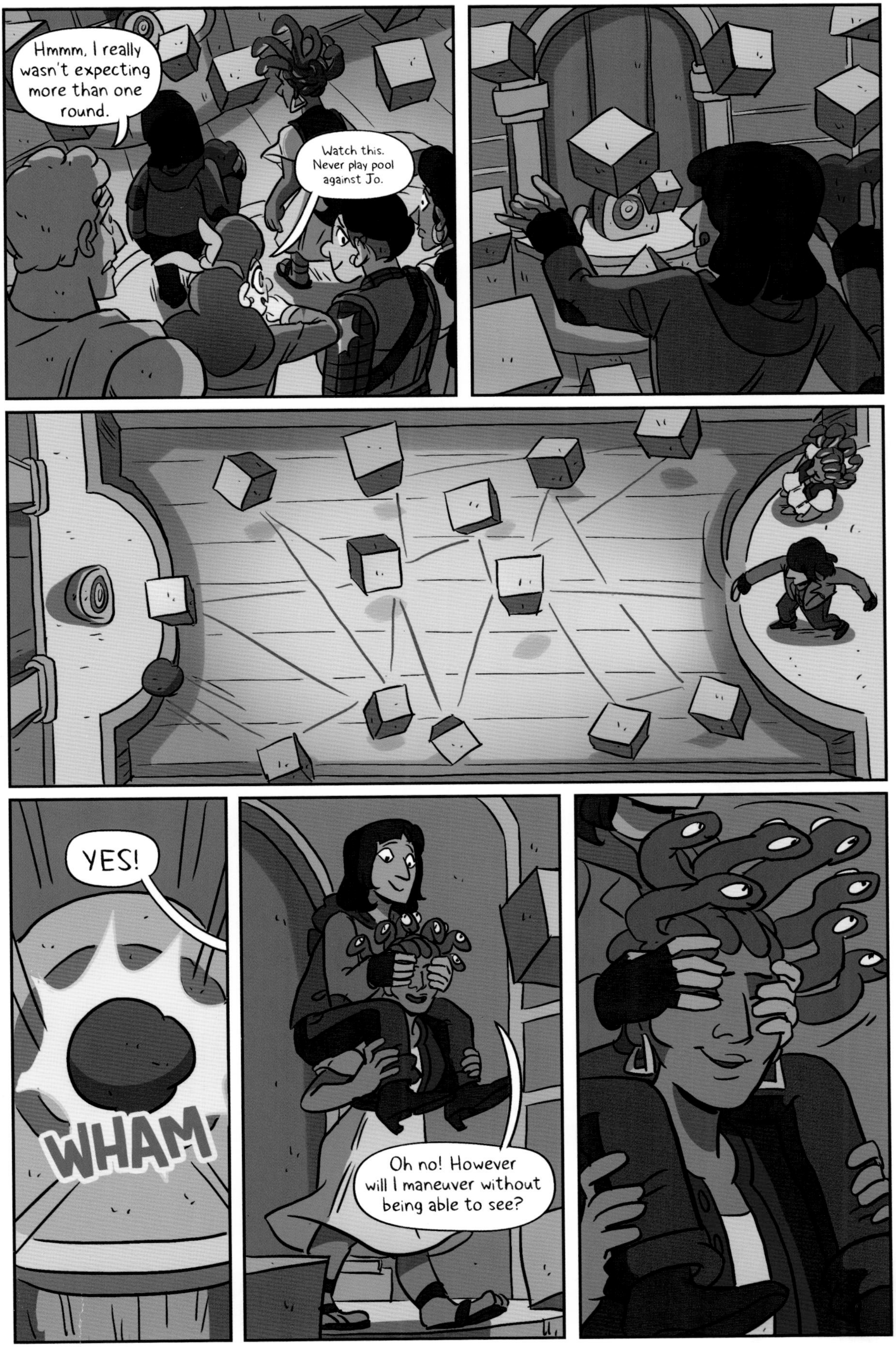
Hmmm, I really wasn't expecting more than one round.
Watch this. Never play pool against Jo.
YES!
WHAM
Oh no! However will I maneuver without being able to see?

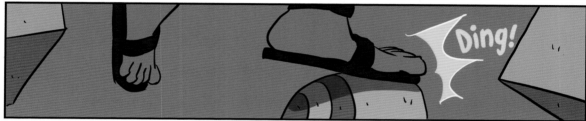

Ding!

WOO! YEAH! GO JO! GO LIGO!

Hey. Uh. Good job. And thanks for the help or whatever.

No problem. I played that game when I was a kid too.

Oh! Oh! Is this another game?! I want to play!

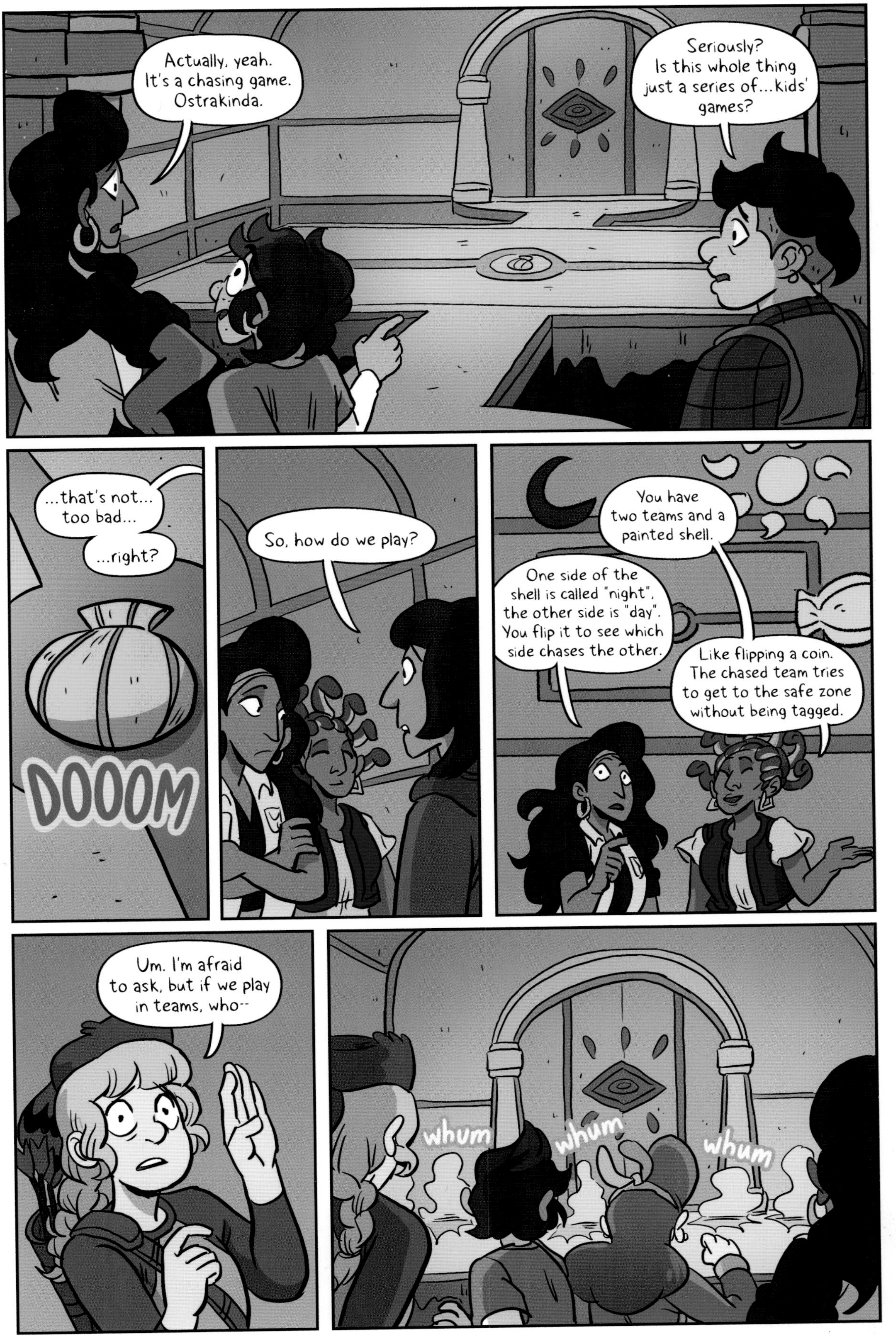
Actually, yeah. It's a chasing game. Ostrakinda.
Seriously? Is this whole thing just a series of...kids' games?
...that's not... too bad...
...right?
DOOOM
So, how do we play?
You have two teams and a painted shell.
One side of the shell is called "night", the other side is "day". You flip it to see which side chases the other.
Like flipping a coin. The chased team tries to get to the safe zone without being tagged.
Um. I'm afraid to ask, but if we play in teams, who--
whum
whum
whum

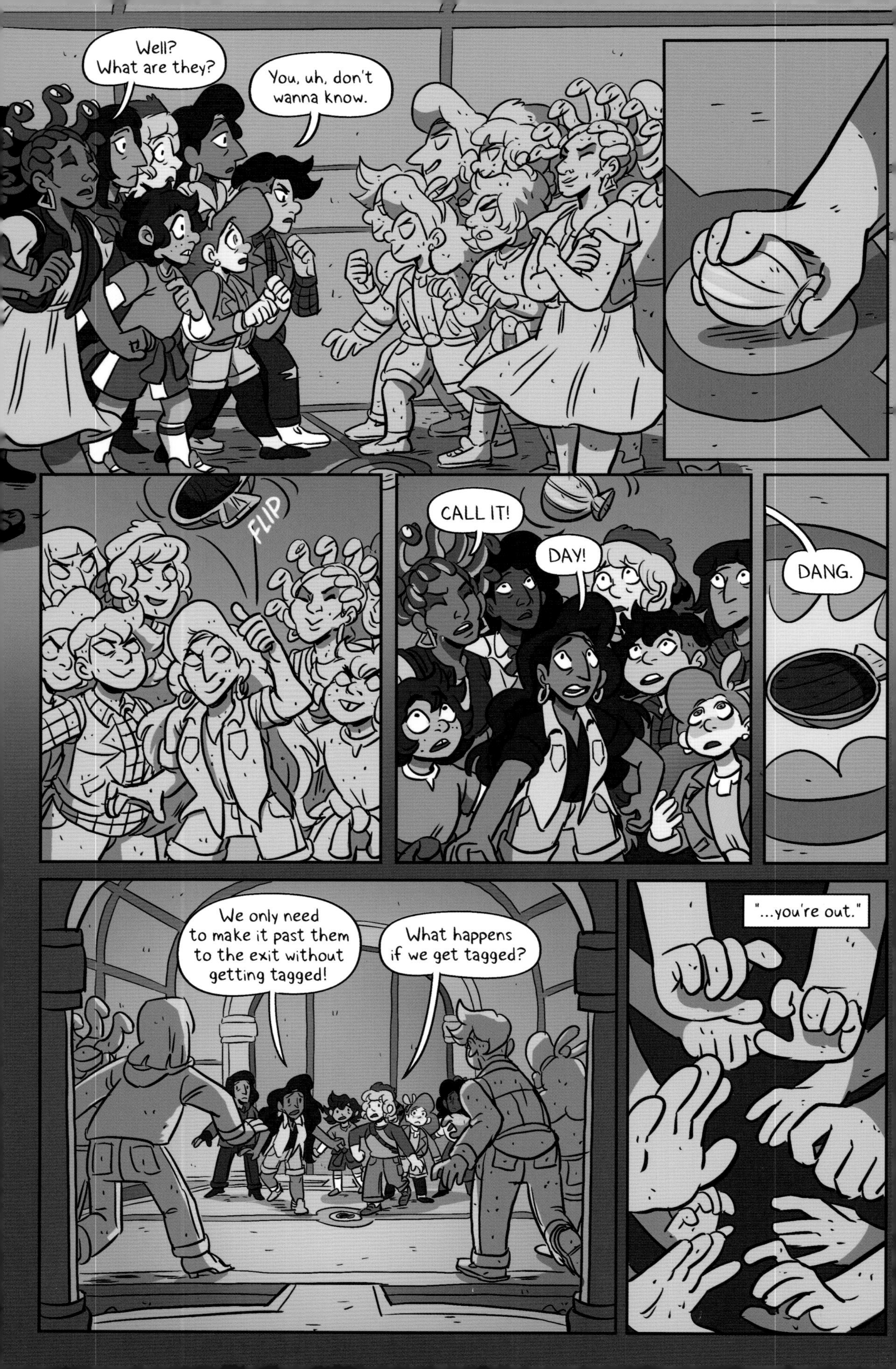
Well? What are they?
You, uh, don't wanna know.
FLIP
CALL IT!
DAY!
DANG.
We only need to make it past them to the exit without getting tagged!
What happens if we get tagged?
"...you're out."

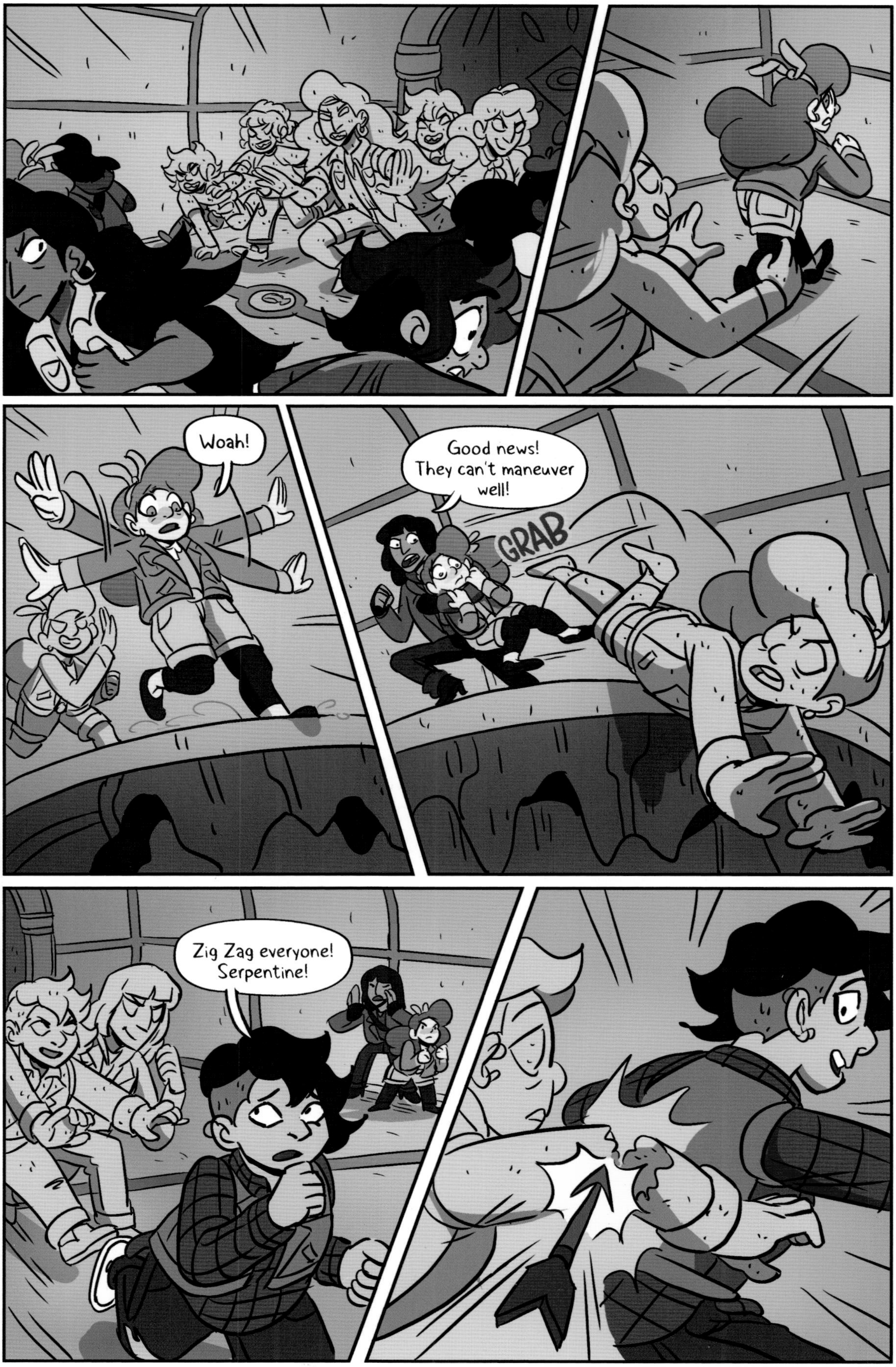
Woah!
Good news! They can't maneuver well!
GRAB
Zig Zag everyone! Serpentine!

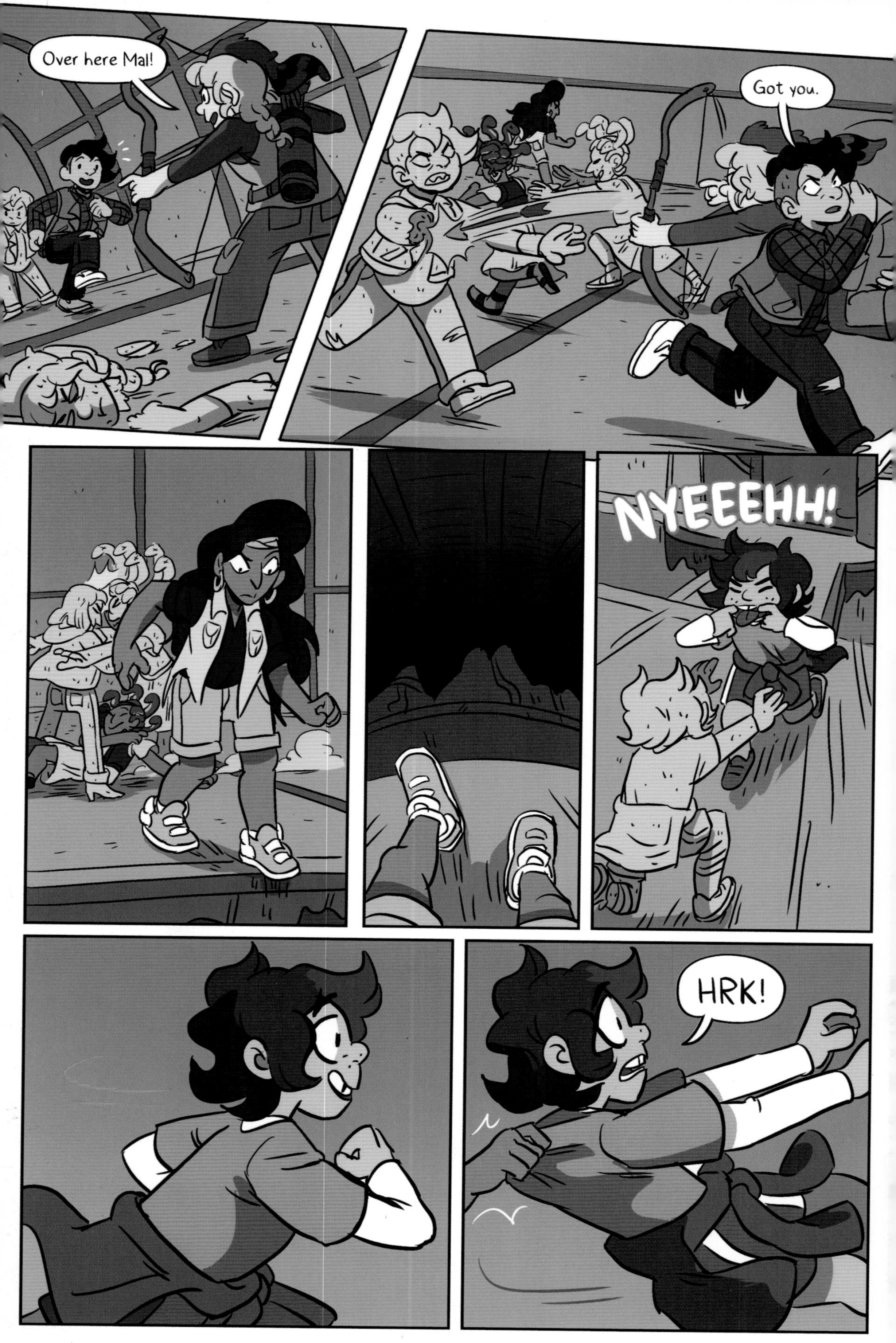
Over here Mal!
Got you.
NYEEEHH!
HRK!

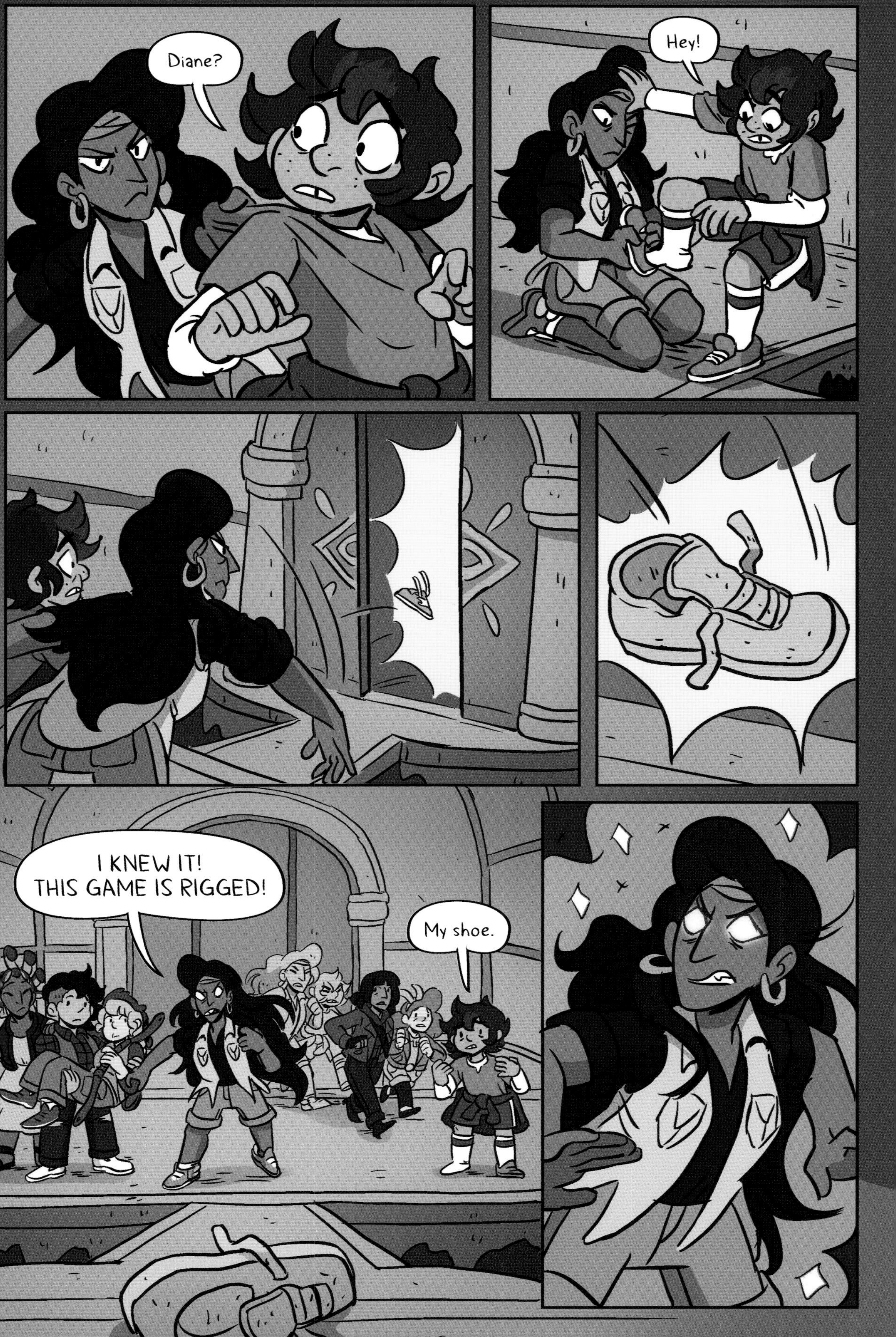

Diane?
Hey!
I KNEW IT!
THIS GAME IS RIGGED!
My shoe.

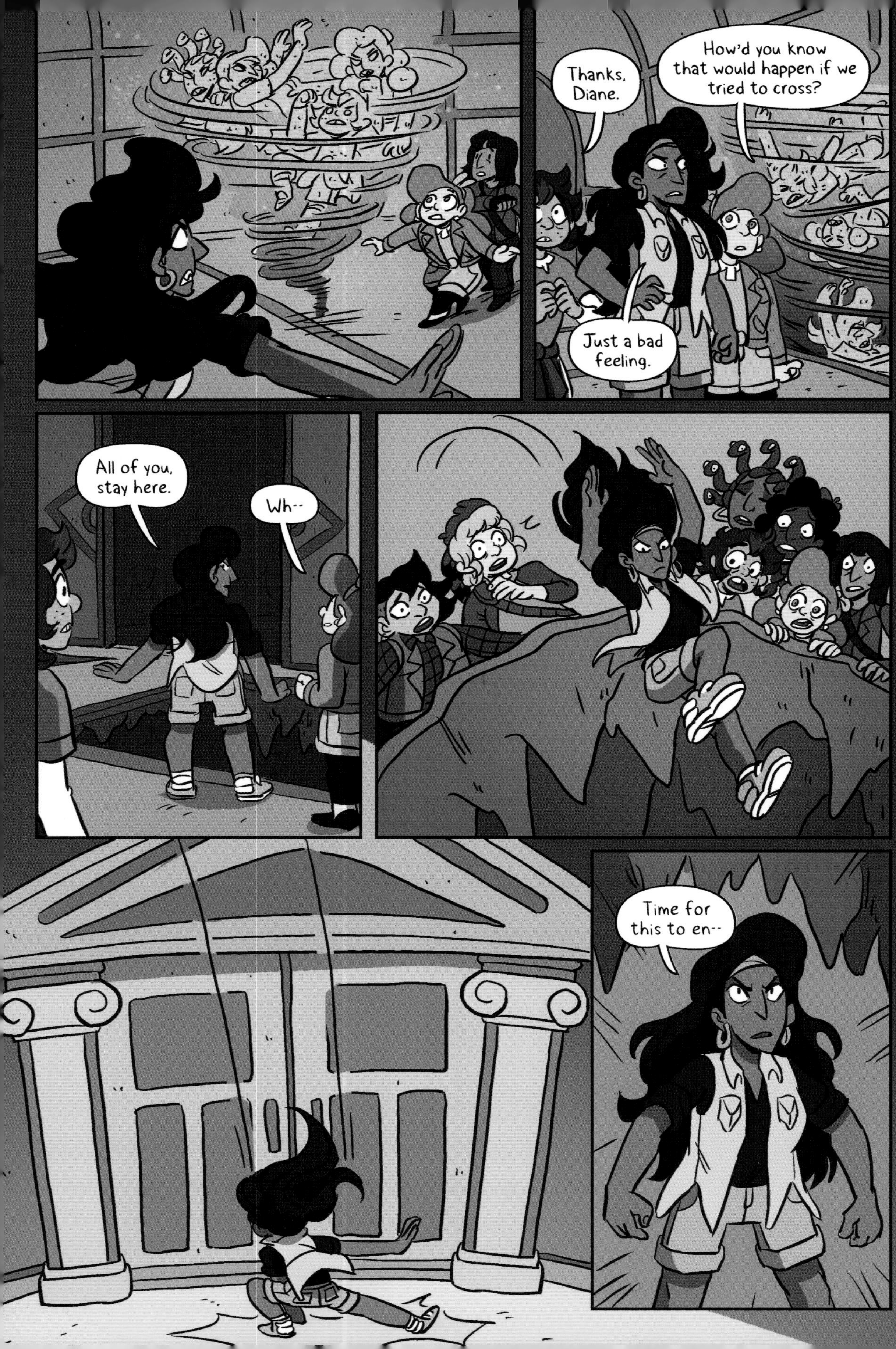
Thanks, Diane.
How'd you know that would happen if we tried to cross?
Just a bad feeling.
All of you, stay here.
Wh--
Time for this to en--

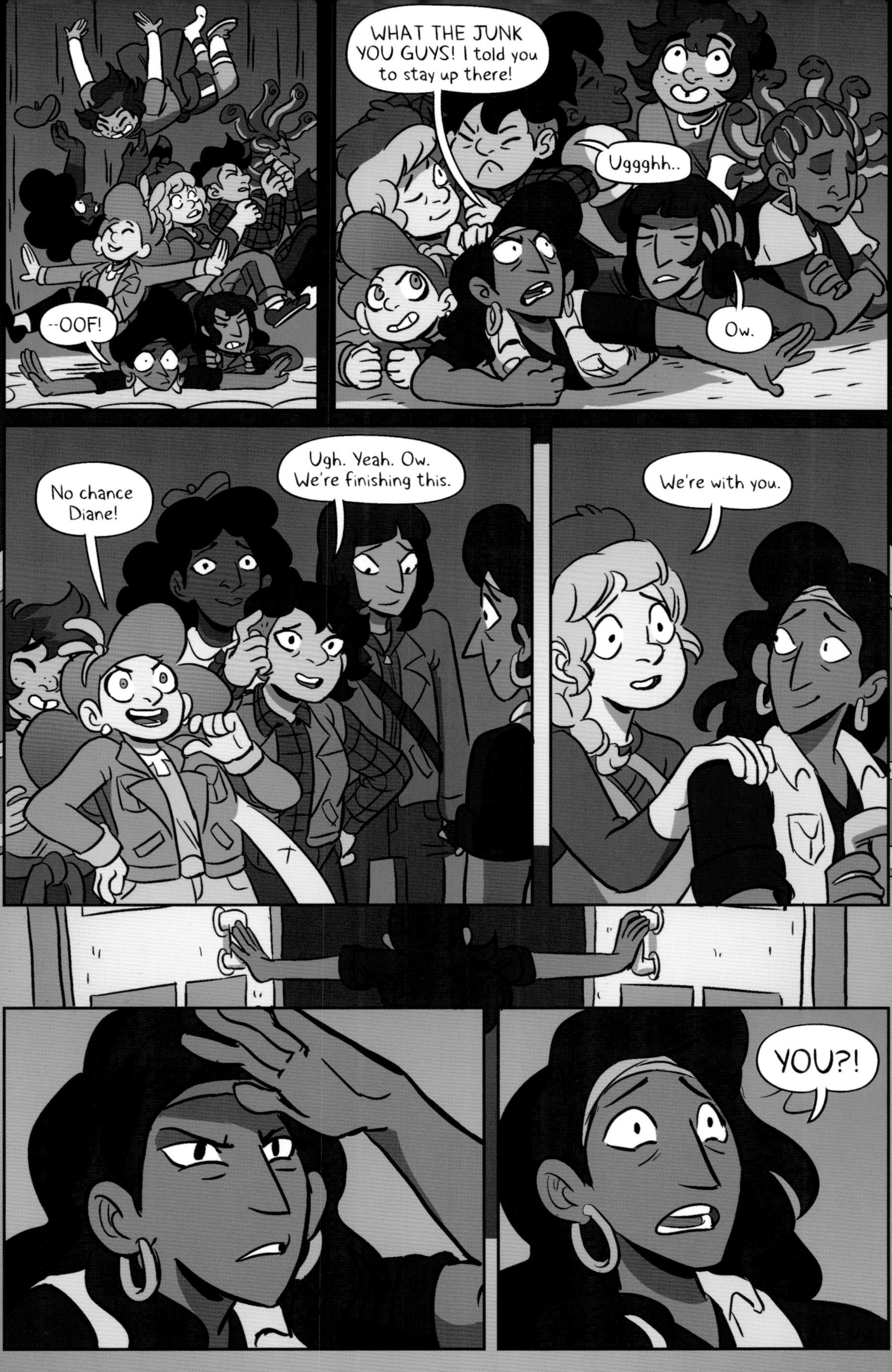
--OOF!
WHAT THE JUNK YOU GUYS! I told you to stay up there!
Uggghh..
Ow.
No chance Diane!
Ugh. Yeah. Ow. We're finishing this.
We're with you.
YOU?!

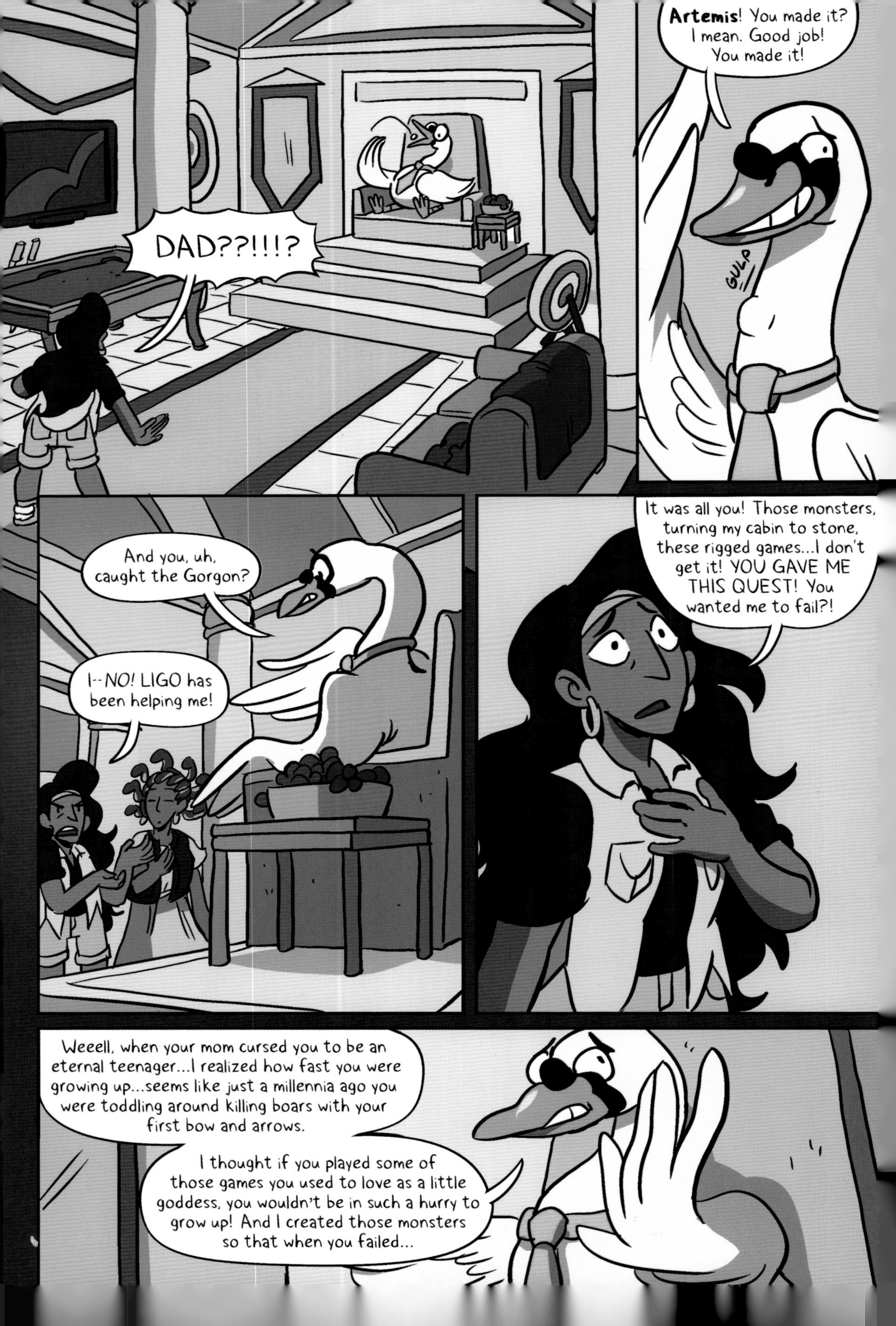
DAD??!!!?
Artemis! You made it? I mean. Good job! You made it!
GULP
And you, uh, caught the Gorgon?
I--NO! LIGO has been helping me!
It was all you! Those monsters, turning my cabin to stone, these rigged games...I don't get it! YOU GAVE ME THIS QUEST! You wanted me to fail?!
Weeell, when your mom cursed you to be an eternal teenager...I realized how fast you were growing up...seems like just a millennia ago you were toddling around killing boars with your first bow and arrows.
I thought if you played some of those games you used to love as a little goddess, you wouldn't be in such a hurry to grow up! And I created those monsters so that when you failed...

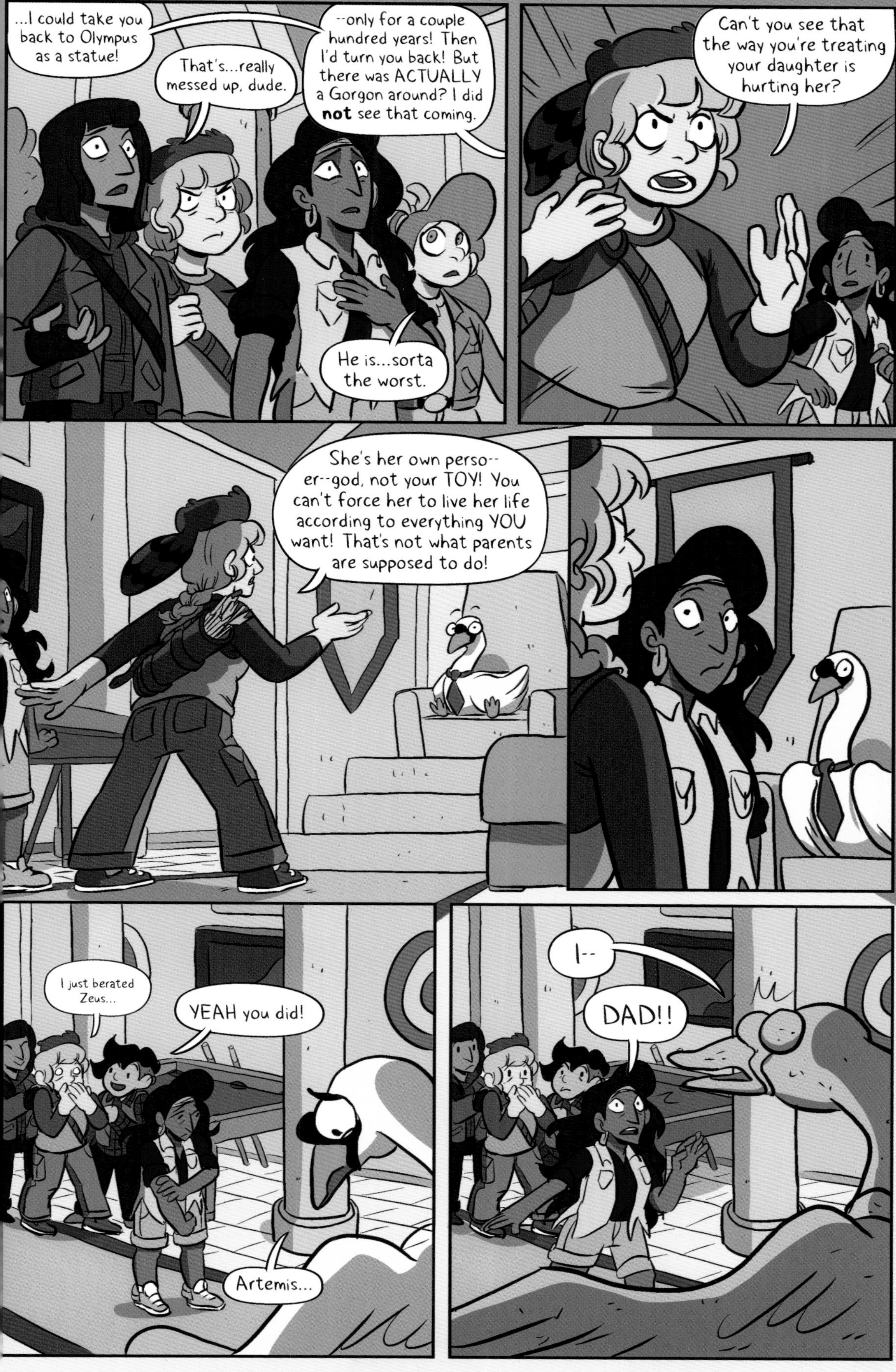

...I could take you back to Olympus as a statue!
--only for a couple hundred years! Then I'd turn you back! But there was ACTUALLY a Gorgon around? I did **not** see that coming.
That's...really messed up, dude.
He is...sorta the worst.
Can't you see that the way you're treating your daughter is hurting her?
She's her own perso-- er--god, not your TOY! You can't force her to live her life according to everything YOU want! That's not what parents are supposed to do!
I just berated Zeus...
YEAH you did!
Artemis...
I--
DAD!!

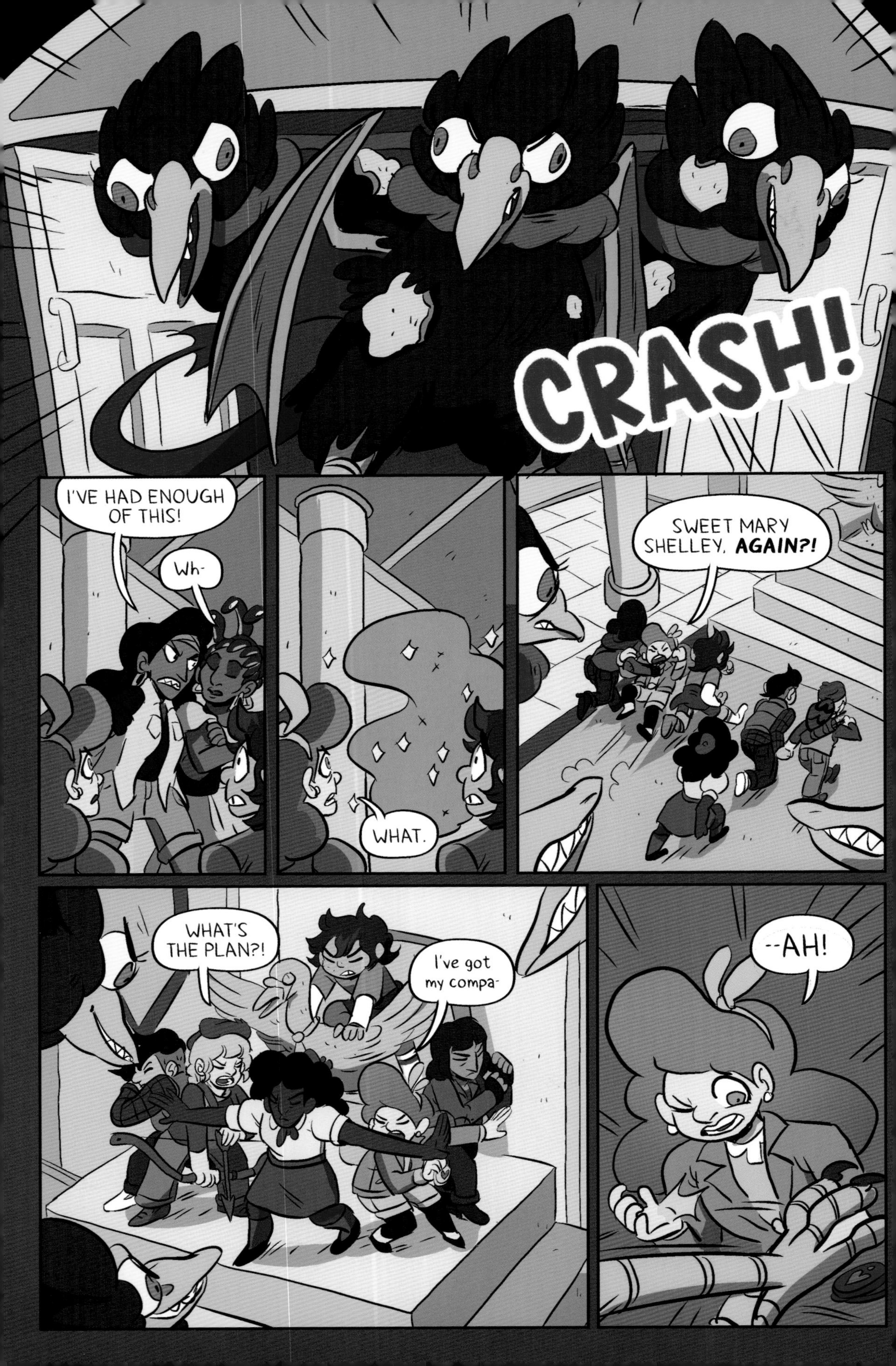
CRASH!
I'VE HAD ENOUGH OF THIS!
Wh-
WHAT.
SWEET MARY SHELLEY, **AGAIN?!**
WHAT'S THE PLAN?!
I've got my compa-
--AH!

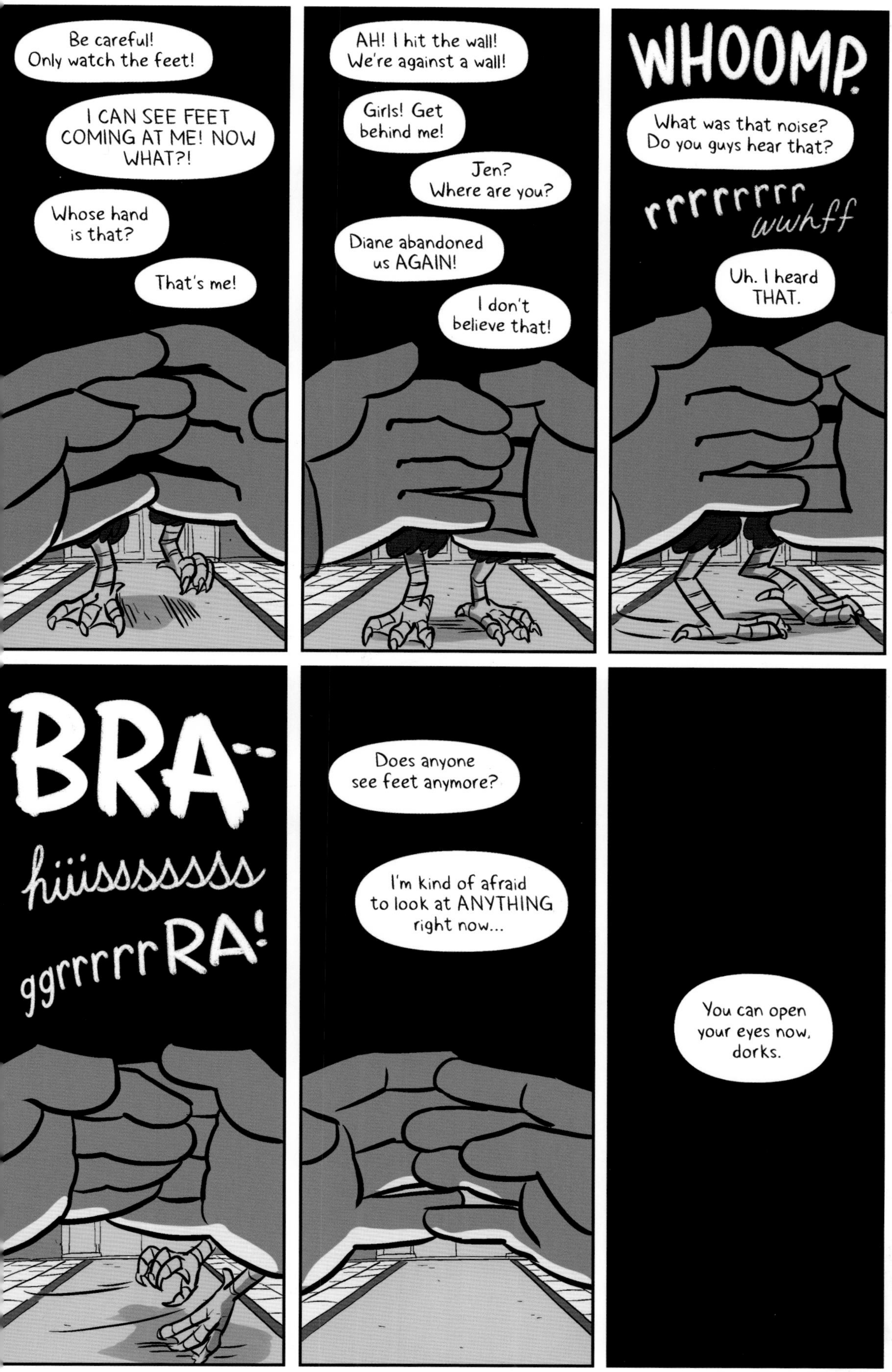
Be careful!
Only watch the feet!
I CAN SEE FEET COMING AT ME! NOW WHAT?!
Whose hand is that?
That's me!
AH! I hit the wall! We're against a wall!
Girls! Get behind me!
Jen? Where are you?
Diane abandoned us AGAIN!
I don't believe that!
WHOOMP.
What was that noise? Do you guys hear that?
rrrrrrrr
wwhff
Uh. I heard THAT.
BRA--
hiiissssss
ggrrrrrRA!
Does anyone see feet anymore?
I'm kind of afraid to look at ANYTHING right now...
You can open your eyes now, dorks.

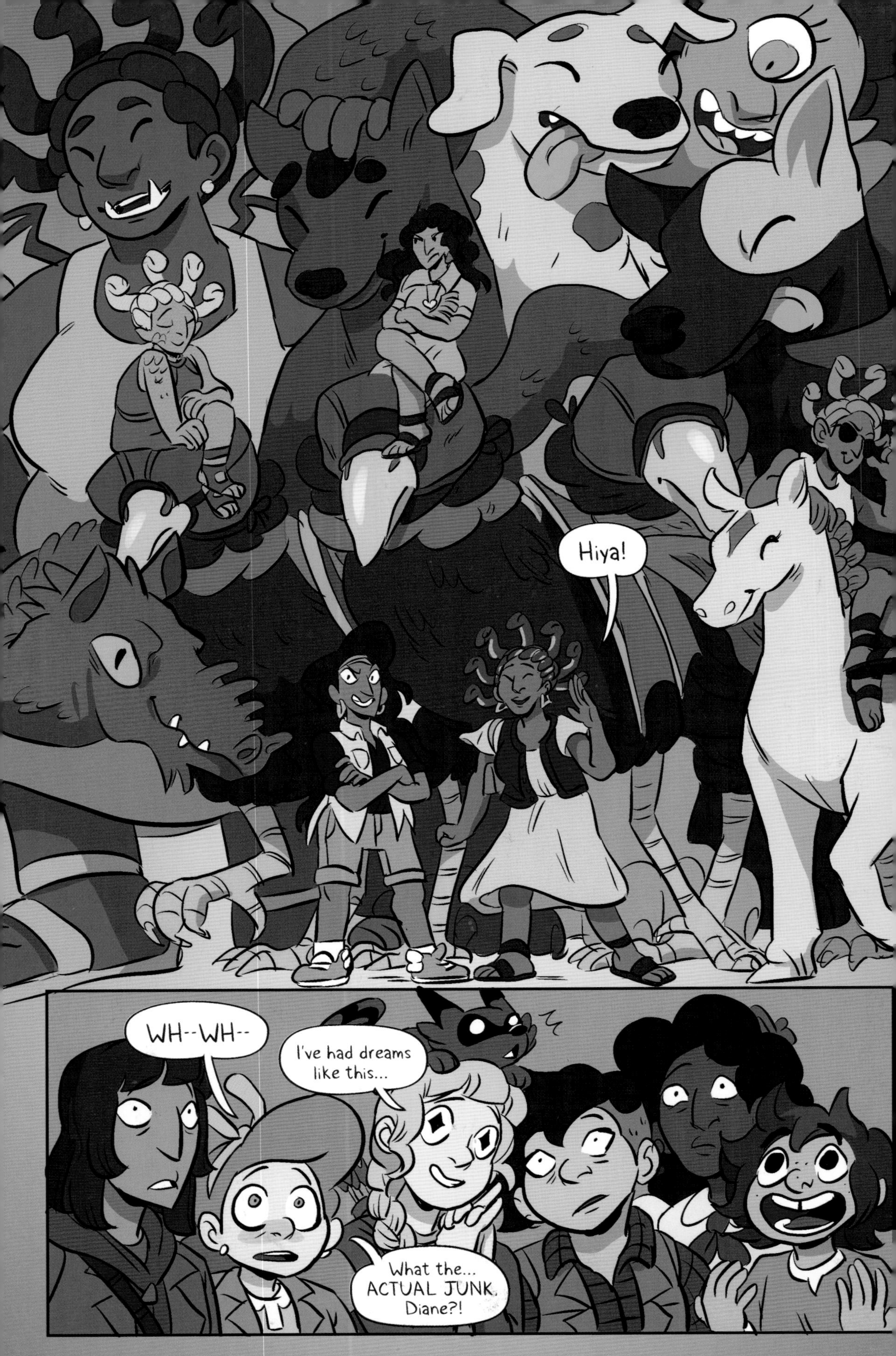
Hiya!
WH--WH--
I've had dreams like this...
What the... ACTUAL JUNK, Diane?!

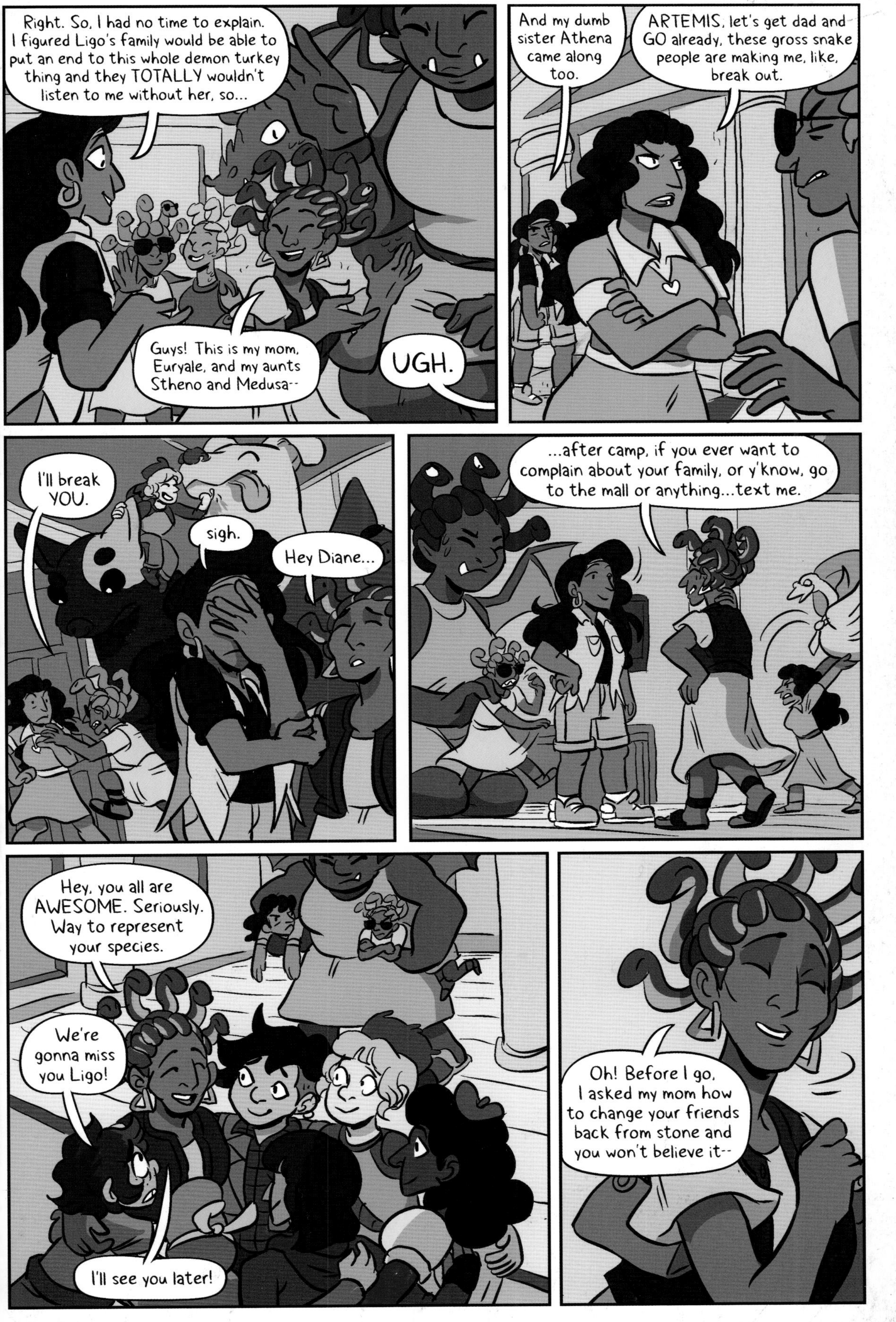
Right. So, I had no time to explain. I figured Ligo's family would be able to put an end to this whole demon turkey thing and they TOTALLY wouldn't listen to me without her, so...
Guys! This is my mom, Euryale, and my aunts Stheno and Medusa--
UGH.
And my dumb sister Athena came along too.
ARTEMIS, let's get dad and GO already, these gross snake people are making me, like, break out.
I'll break YOU.
sigh.
Hey Diane...
...after camp, if you ever want to complain about your family, or y'know, go to the mall or anything...text me.
Hey, you all are AWESOME. Seriously. Way to represent your species.
We're gonna miss you Ligo!
I'll see you later!
Oh! Before I go, I asked my mom how to change your friends back from stone and you won't believe it--

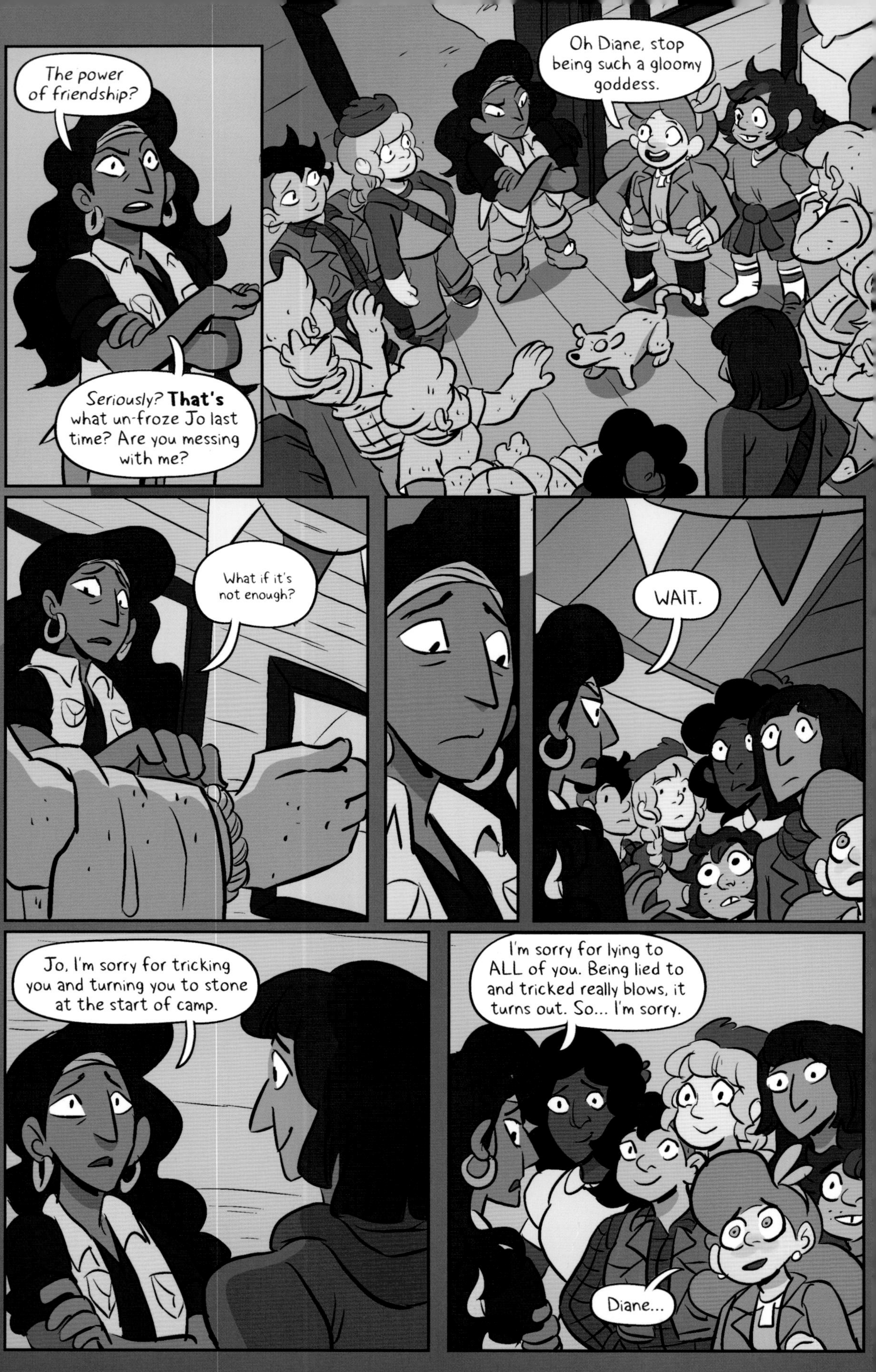
The power of friendship?
Oh Diane, stop being such a gloomy goddess.
Seriously? **That's** what un-froze Jo last time? Are you messing with me?
What if it's not enough?
WAIT.
Jo, I'm sorry for tricking you and turning you to stone at the start of camp.
I'm sorry for lying to ALL of you. Being lied to and tricked really blows, it turns out. So... I'm sorry.
Diane...

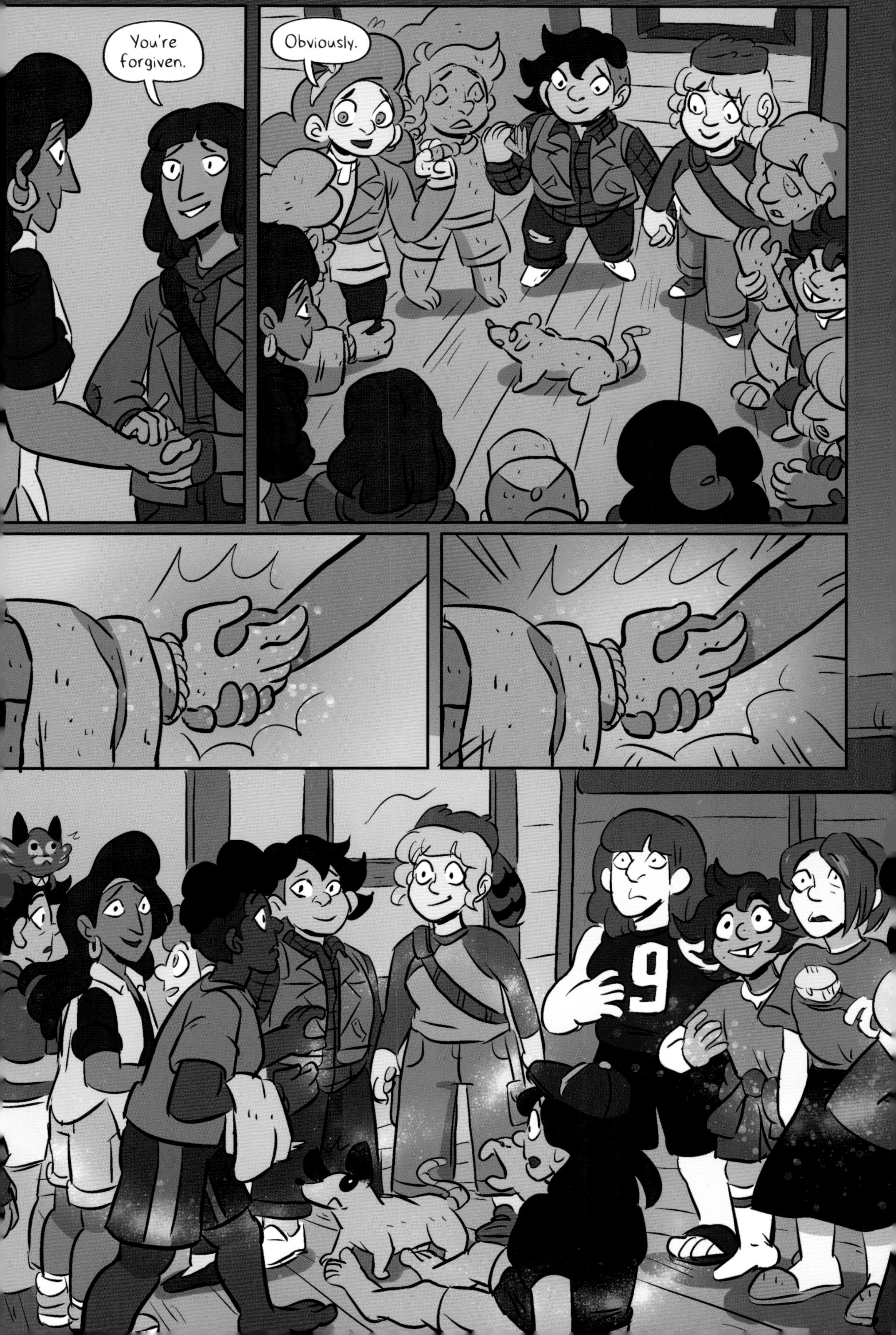
You're forgiven.
Obviously.
9

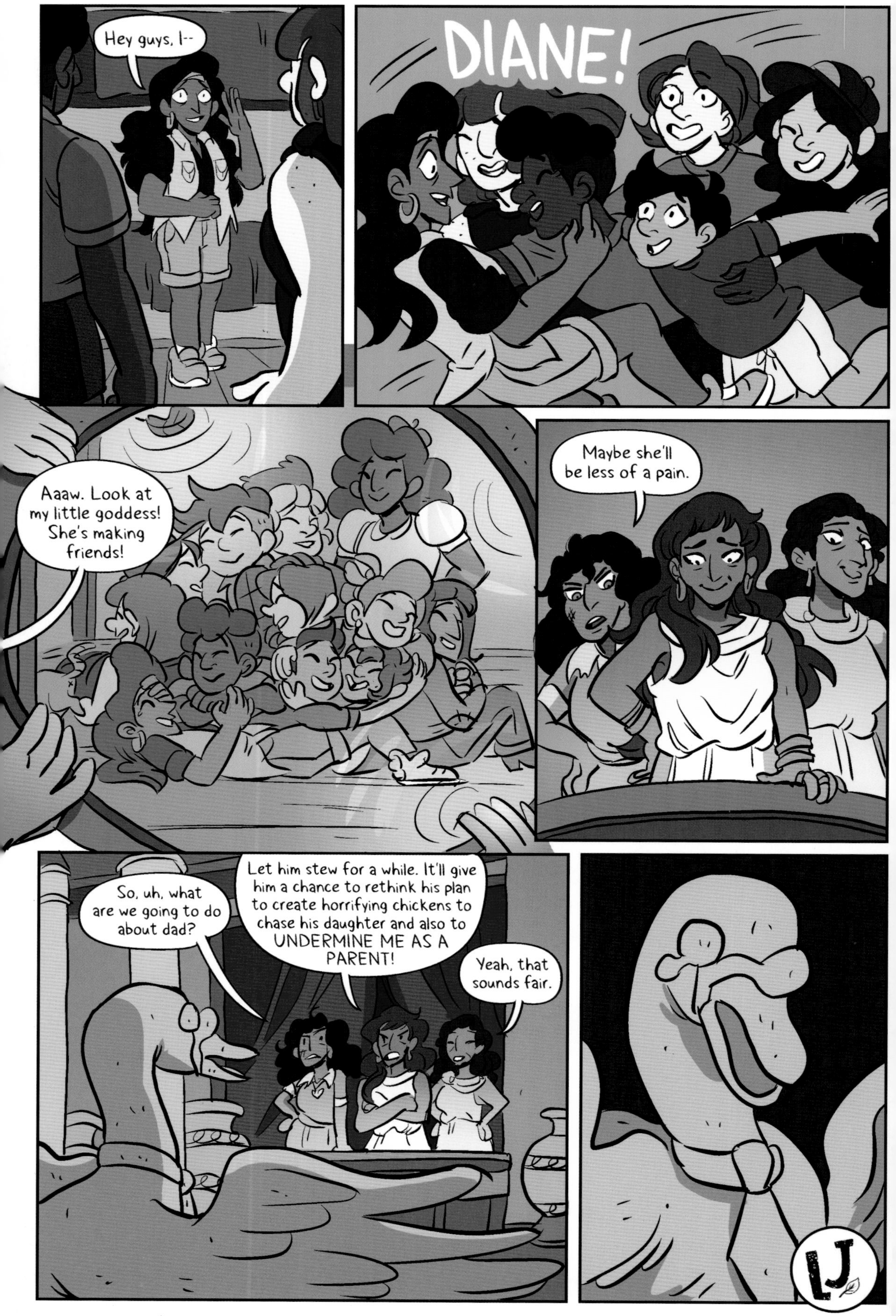
Hey guys, I--
DIANE!
Aaaw. Look at my little goddess! She's making friends!
Maybe she'll be less of a pain.
So, uh, what are we going to do about dad?
Let him stew for a while. It'll give him a chance to rethink his plan to create horrifying chickens to chase his daughter and also to UNDERMINE ME AS A PARENT!
Yeah, that sounds fair.

hould be worn at camp events when Lumberjanes may also be worn at other ions. It should be worn as a the uniform dress with rect shoes, and stocking or out grows her uniform or ter Lumberjane. a she has her her

HOW TO WEAR THE UNIFORM

To look well in a uniform demands first of uniform be kept in good condition—clean pressed. See that the skirt is the right length for your own height and build, that the belt is adjusted to your waist, that your shoes and stockings are in keeping with the uniform, that you watch your posture and carry yourself with dignity and grace. If the beret is removed indoors, be sure that your hair is neat and kept in place with an insconspicuous clip or ribbon. When you wear a Lumberjane uniform you are identified as a member of this organization and you should be doubly careful to conduct yourself in a way that will show everyone that courtesy and thoughtfullness are part of being a Lumberjane. People are likely to judge a whole nation by the selfishness of a few individuals, to criticize a whole family because of the misconduct of one member, and to feel unkindly toward and organization because of the

The unifor helps to cre in a group. active life th another bond future, and pr in order to b Lumberjane pr Penniquiqul Thi ore Lady Types, but m es will wish to have one. They can either b uniform, or make it themselves from materials available at the trading post.

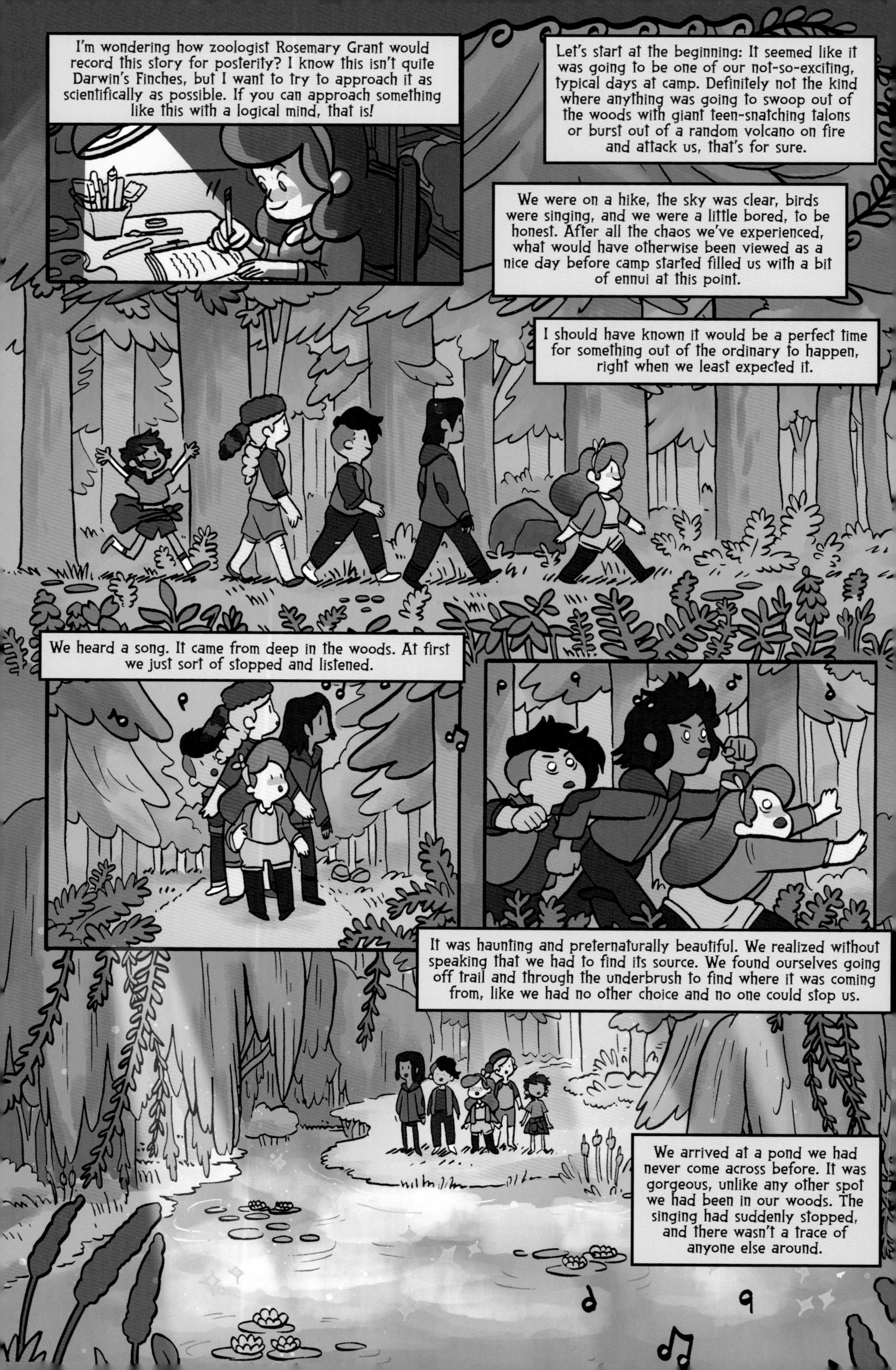
I'm wondering how zoologist Rosemary Grant would record this story for posterity? I know this isn't quite Darwin's Finches, but I want to try to approach it as scientifically as possible. If you can approach something like this with a logical mind, that is!
Let's start at the beginning: It seemed like it was going to be one of our not-so-exciting, typical days at camp. Definitely not the kind where anything was going to swoop out of the woods with giant teen-snatching talons or burst out of a random volcano on fire and attack us, that's for sure.
We were on a hike, the sky was clear, birds were singing, and we were a little bored, to be honest. After all the chaos we've experienced, what would have otherwise been viewed as a nice day before camp started filled us with a bit of ennui at this point.
I should have known it would be a perfect time for something out of the ordinary to happen, right when we least expected it.
We heard a song. It came from deep in the woods. At first we just sort of stopped and listened.
It was haunting and preternaturally beautiful. We realized without speaking that we had to find its source. We found ourselves going off trail and through the underbrush to find where it was coming from, like we had no other choice and no one could stop us.
We arrived at a pond we had never come across before. It was gorgeous, unlike any other spot we had been in our woods. The singing had suddenly stopped, and there wasn't a trace of anyone else around.

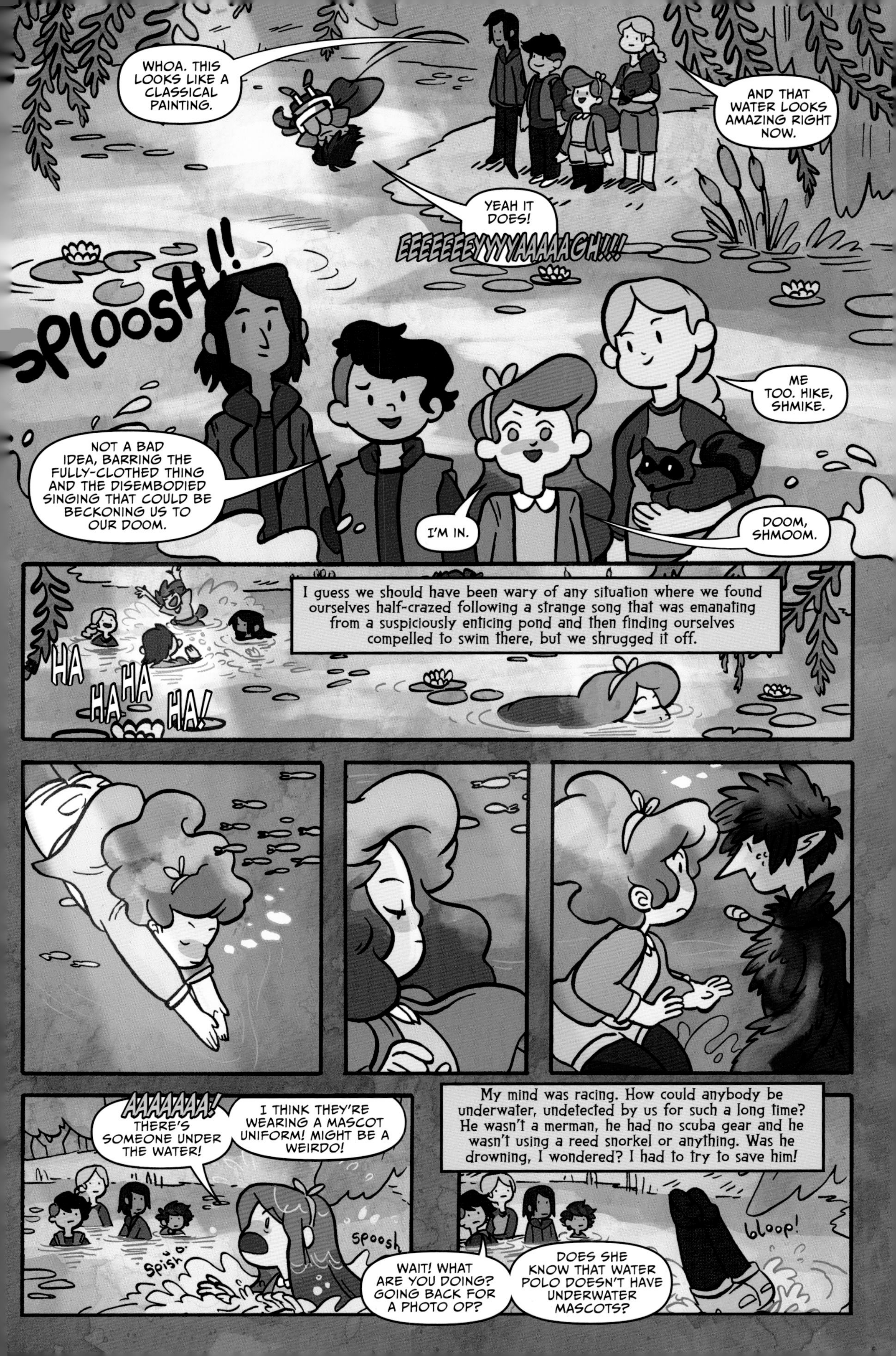

WHOA. THIS LOOKS LIKE A CLASSICAL PAINTING.
AND THAT WATER LOOKS AMAZING RIGHT NOW.
YEAH IT DOES!
EEEEEEEYYYYAAAAACH!!!
SPLOOSH!!
ME TOO. HIKE, SHMIKE.
NOT A BAD IDEA, BARRING THE FULLY-CLOTHED THING AND THE DISEMBODIED SINGING THAT COULD BE BECKONING US TO OUR DOOM.
I'M IN.
DOOM, SHMOOM.
I guess we should have been wary of any situation where we found ourselves half-crazed following a strange song that was emanating from a suspiciously enticing pond and then finding ourselves compelled to swim there, but we shrugged it off.
HA HA HA HA!
AAAAAAA! THERE'S SOMEONE UNDER THE WATER!
I THINK THEY'RE WEARING A MASCOT UNIFORM! MIGHT BE A WEIRDO!
spish
sploosh
My mind was racing. How could anybody be underwater, undetected by us for such a long time? He wasn't a merman, he had no scuba gear and he wasn't using a reed snorkel or anything. Was he drowning, I wondered? I had to try to save him!
bloop!
WAIT! WHAT ARE YOU DOING? GOING BACK FOR A PHOTO OP?
DOES SHE KNOW THAT WATER POLO DOESN'T HAVE UNDERWATER MASCOTS?

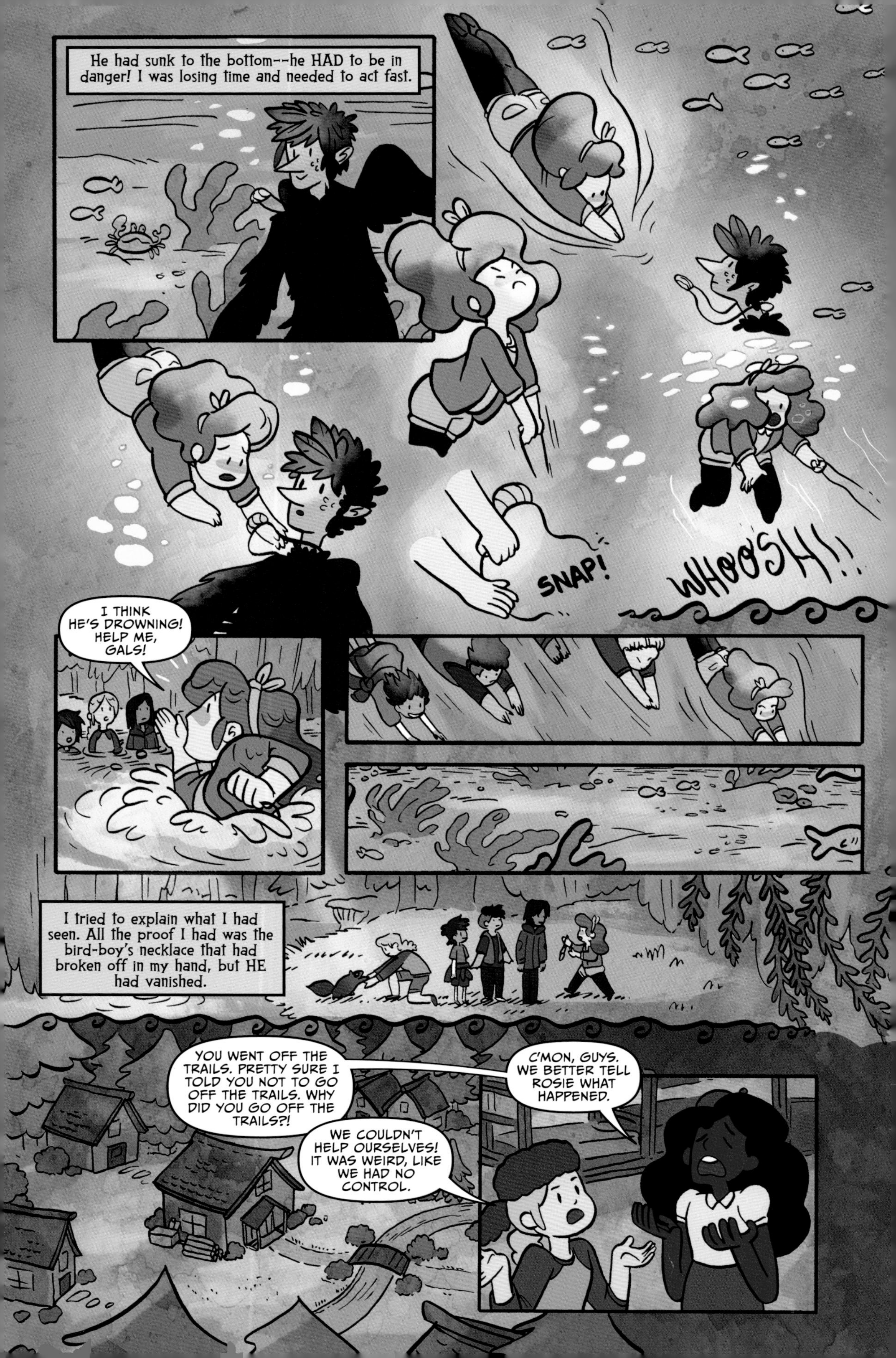
He had sunk to the bottom--he HAD to be in danger! I was losing time and needed to act fast.
SNAP!
WHOOSH!!
I THINK HE'S DROWNING! HELP ME, GALS!
I tried to explain what I had seen. All the proof I had was the bird-boy's necklace that had broken off in my hand, but HE had vanished.
YOU WENT OFF THE TRAILS. PRETTY SURE I TOLD YOU NOT TO GO OFF THE TRAILS. WHY DID YOU GO OFF THE TRAILS?!
WE COULDN'T HELP OURSELVES! IT WAS WEIRD, LIKE WE HAD NO CONTROL.
C'MON, GUYS. WE BETTER TELL ROSIE WHAT HAPPENED.

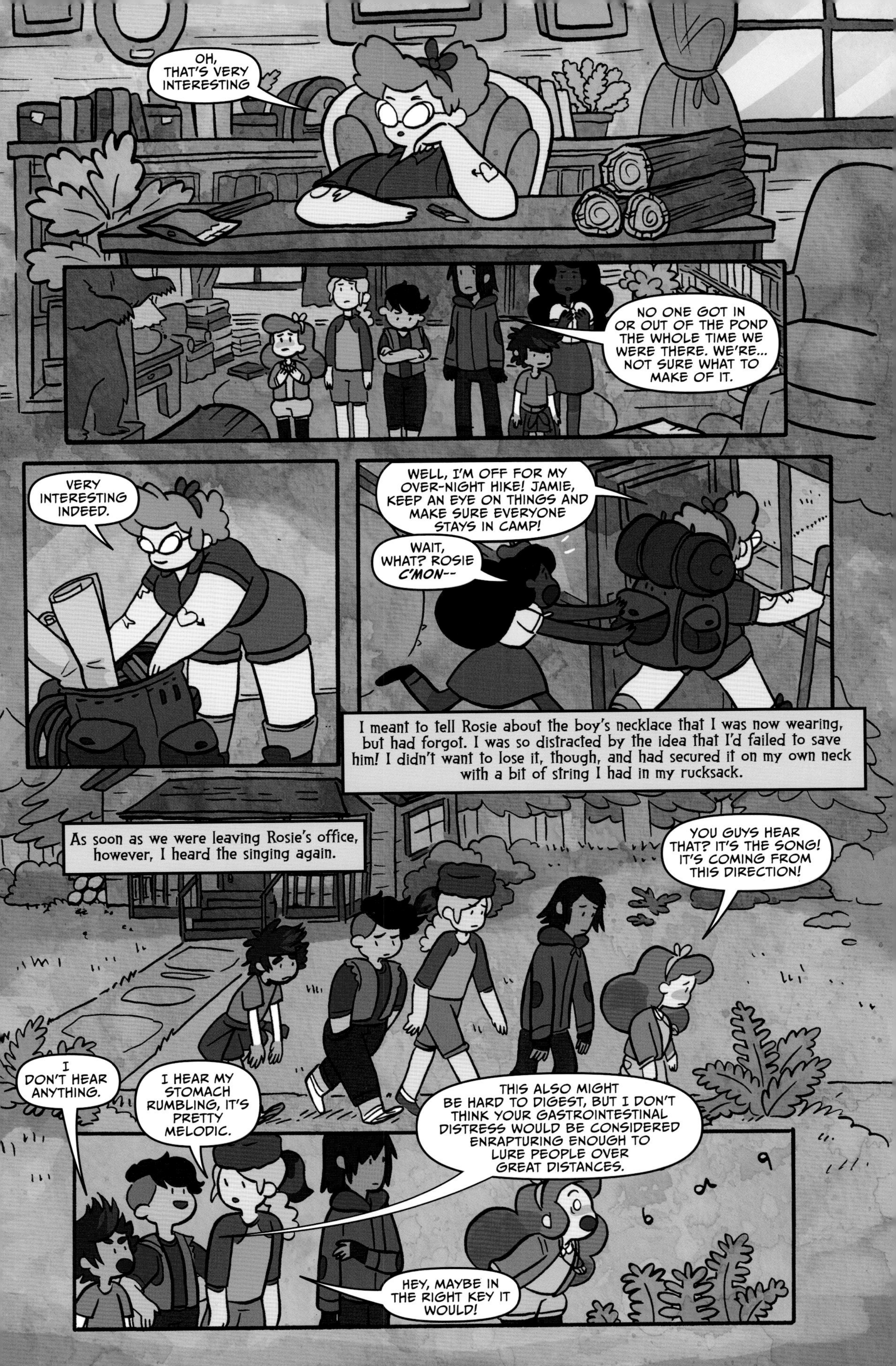
OH, THAT'S VERY INTERESTING
NO ONE GOT IN OR OUT OF THE POND THE WHOLE TIME WE WERE THERE. WE'RE... NOT SURE WHAT TO MAKE OF IT.
VERY INTERESTING INDEED.
WELL, I'M OFF FOR MY OVER-NIGHT HIKE! JAMIE, KEEP AN EYE ON THINGS AND MAKE SURE EVERYONE STAYS IN CAMP!
WAIT, WHAT? ROSIE *C'MON--*
I meant to tell Rosie about the boy's necklace that I was now wearing, but had forgot. I was so distracted by the idea that I'd failed to save him! I didn't want to lose it, though, and had secured it on my own neck with a bit of string I had in my rucksack.
As soon as we were leaving Rosie's office, however, I heard the singing again.
YOU GUYS HEAR THAT? IT'S THE SONG! IT'S COMING FROM THIS DIRECTION!
I DON'T HEAR ANYTHING.
I HEAR MY STOMACH RUMBLING, IT'S PRETTY MELODIC.
THIS ALSO MIGHT BE HARD TO DIGEST, BUT I DON'T THINK YOUR GASTROINTESTINAL DISTRESS WOULD BE CONSIDERED ENRAPTURING ENOUGH TO LURE PEOPLE OVER GREAT DISTANCES.
HEY, MAYBE IN THE RIGHT KEY IT WOULD!

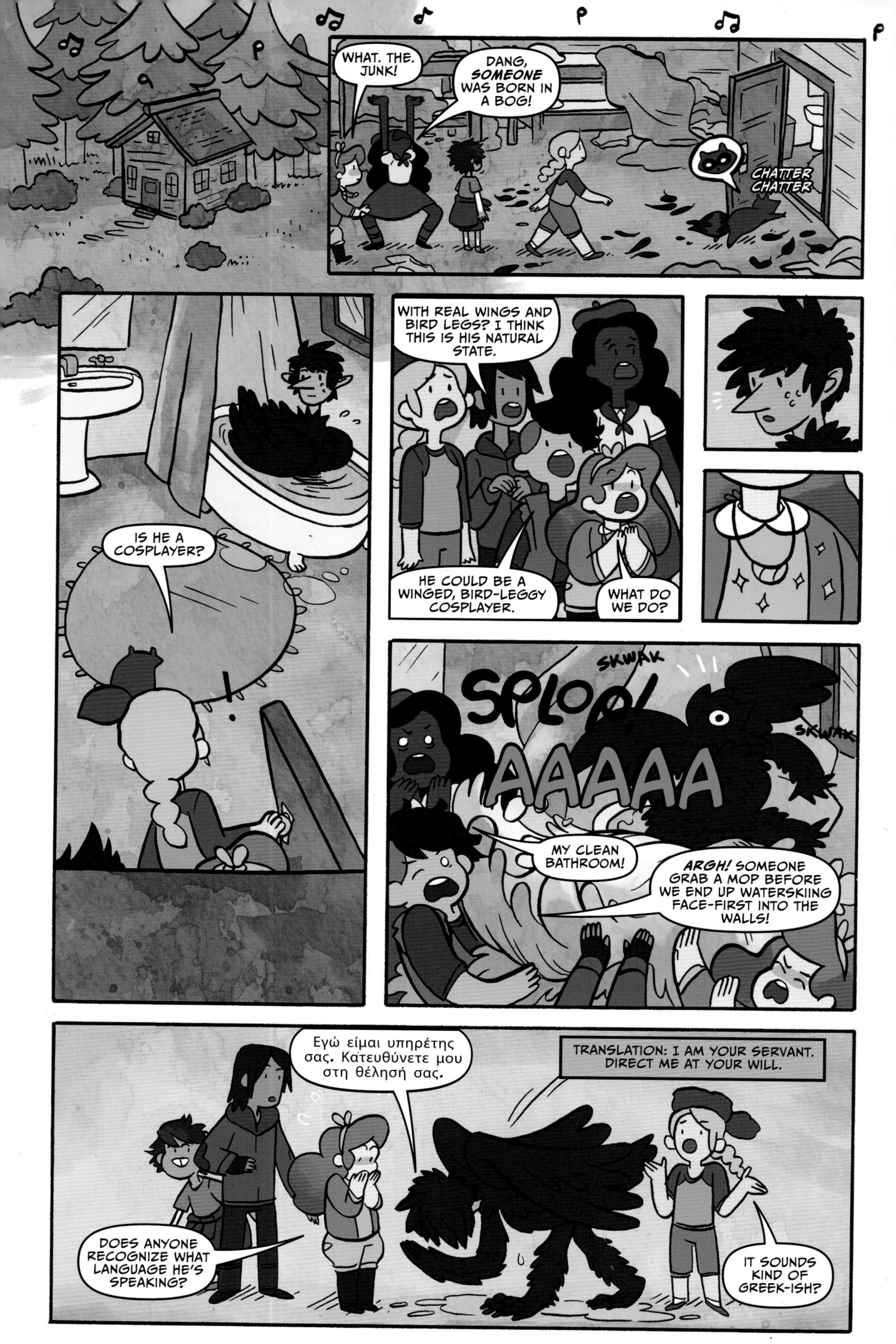
WHAT. THE. JUNK!
DANG, SOMEONE WAS BORN IN A BOG!
CHATTER CHATTER
IS HE A COSPLAYER?
WITH REAL WINGS AND BIRD LEGS? I THINK THIS IS HIS NATURAL STATE.
HE COULD BE A WINGED, BIRD-LEGGY COSPLAYER.
WHAT DO WE DO?
SKWAK
SPLOP!
SKWAK
AAAAA
MY CLEAN BATHROOM!
ARGH! SOMEONE GRAB A MOP BEFORE WE END UP WATERSKIING FACE-FIRST INTO THE WALLS!
Εγώ είμαι υπηρέτης σας. Κατευθύνετε μου στη θέλησή σας.
TRANSLATION: I AM YOUR SERVANT. DIRECT ME AT YOUR WILL.
DOES ANYONE RECOGNIZE WHAT LANGUAGE HE'S SPEAKING?
IT SOUNDS KIND OF GREEK-ISH?

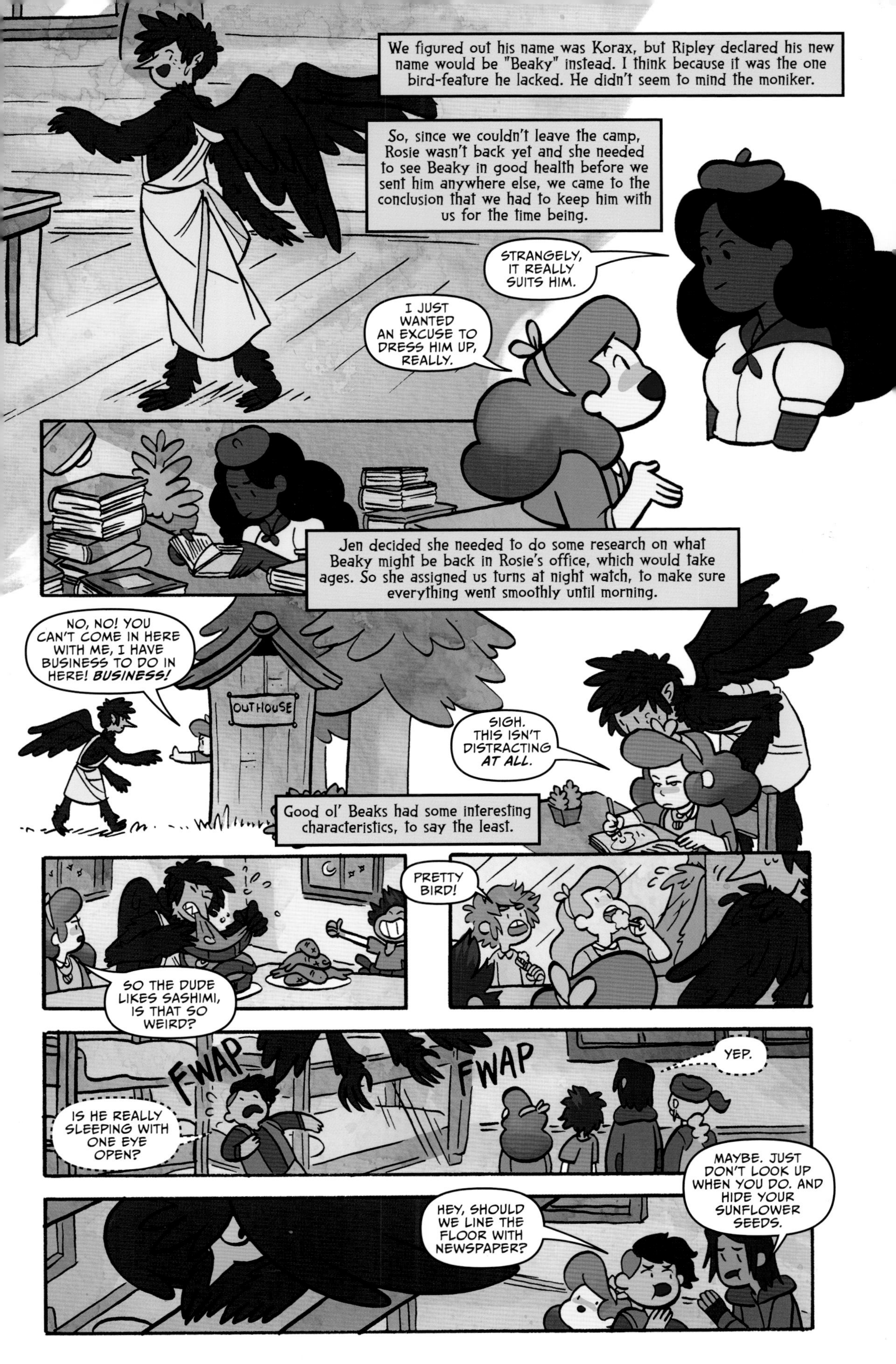

We figured out his name was Korax, but Ripley declared his new name would be "Beaky" instead. I think because it was the one bird-feature he lacked. He didn't seem to mind the moniker.
So, since we couldn't leave the camp, Rosie wasn't back yet and she needed to see Beaky in good health before we sent him anywhere else, we came to the conclusion that we had to keep him with us for the time being.
STRANGELY, IT REALLY SUITS HIM.
I JUST WANTED AN EXCUSE TO DRESS HIM UP, REALLY.
Jen decided she needed to do some research on what Beaky might be back in Rosie's office, which would take ages. So she assigned us turns at night watch, to make sure everything went smoothly until morning.
NO, NO! YOU CAN'T COME IN HERE WITH ME, I HAVE BUSINESS TO DO IN HERE! BUSINESS!
OUTHOUSE
SIGH. THIS ISN'T DISTRACTING AT ALL.
Good ol' Beaks had some interesting characteristics, to say the least.
SO THE DUDE LIKES SASHIMI, IS THAT SO WEIRD?
PRETTY BIRD!
FWAP
FWAP
IS HE REALLY SLEEPING WITH ONE EYE OPEN?
YEP.
HEY, SHOULD WE LINE THE FLOOR WITH NEWSPAPER?
MAYBE. JUST DON'T LOOK UP WHEN YOU DO. AND HIDE YOUR SUNFLOWER SEEDS.

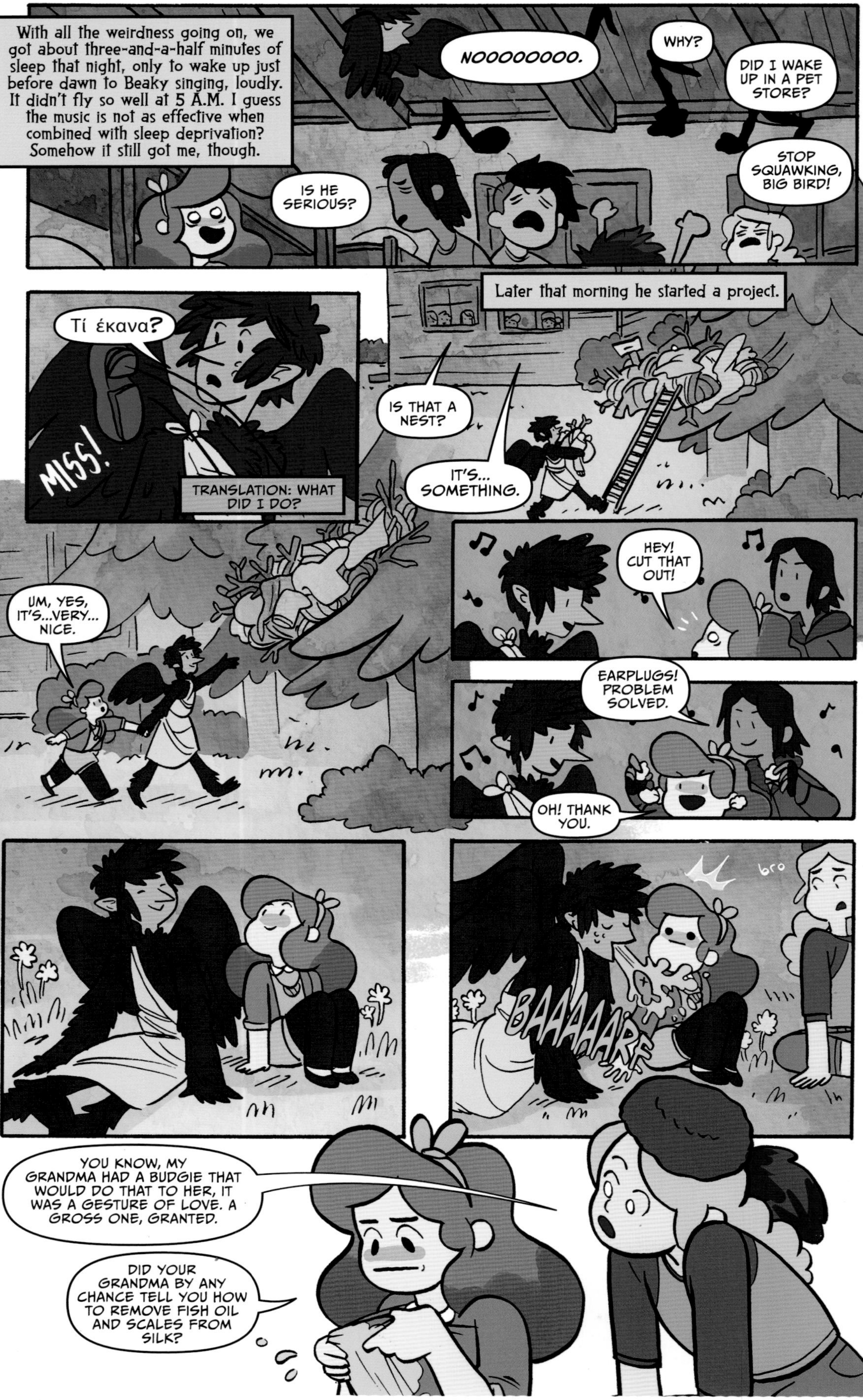

With all the weirdness going on, we got about three-and-a-half minutes of sleep that night, only to wake up just before dawn to Beaky singing, loudly. It didn't fly so well at 5 A.M. I guess the music is not as effective when combined with sleep deprivation? Somehow it still got me, though.
NOOOOOOOO.
WHY?
DID I WAKE UP IN A PET STORE?
IS HE SERIOUS?
STOP SQUAWKING, BIG BIRD!
Τί έκανα?
MISS!
TRANSLATION: WHAT DID I DO?
Later that morning he started a project.
IS THAT A NEST?
IT'S... SOMETHING.
UM, YES, IT'S...VERY... NICE.
HEY! CUT THAT OUT!
EARPLUGS! PROBLEM SOLVED.
OH! THANK YOU.
bro
BAAAAARF
YOU KNOW, MY GRANDMA HAD A BUDGIE THAT WOULD DO THAT TO HER, IT WAS A GESTURE OF LOVE. A GROSS ONE, GRANTED.
DID YOUR GRANDMA BY ANY CHANCE TELL YOU HOW TO REMOVE FISH OIL AND SCALES FROM SILK?

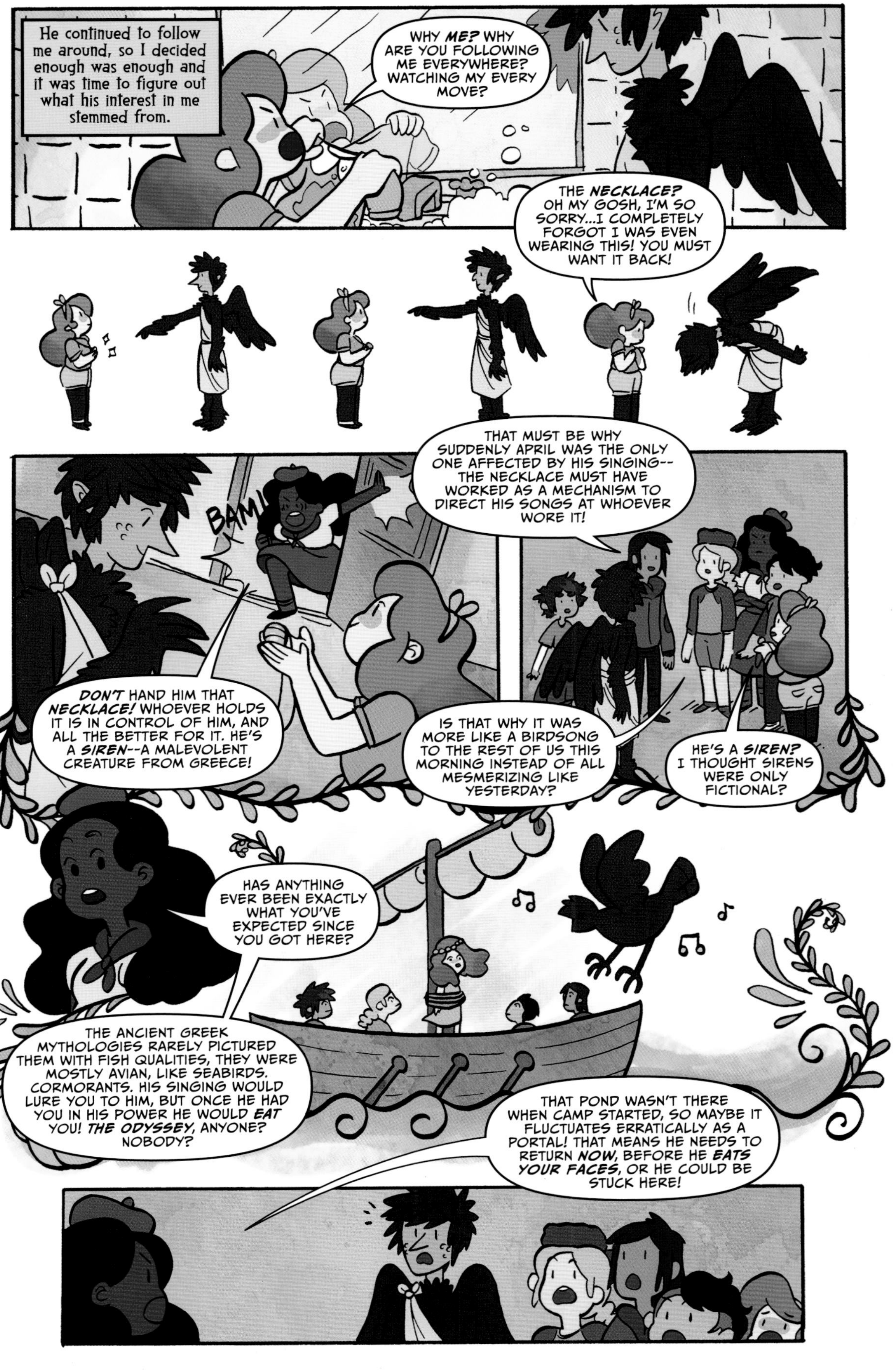
He continued to follow me around, so I decided enough was enough and it was time to figure out what his interest in me stemmed from.
WHY *ME?* WHY ARE YOU FOLLOWING ME EVERYWHERE? WATCHING MY EVERY MOVE?
THE *NECKLACE?* OH MY GOSH, I'M SO SORRY...I COMPLETELY FORGOT I WAS EVEN WEARING THIS! YOU MUST WANT IT BACK!
THAT MUST BE WHY SUDDENLY APRIL WAS THE ONLY ONE AFFECTED BY HIS SINGING-- THE NECKLACE MUST HAVE WORKED AS A MECHANISM TO DIRECT HIS SONGS AT WHOEVER WORE IT!
BAM!
DON'T HAND HIM THAT *NECKLACE!* WHOEVER HOLDS IT IS IN CONTROL OF HIM, AND ALL THE BETTER FOR IT. HE'S A *SIREN*--A MALEVOLENT CREATURE FROM GREECE!
IS THAT WHY IT WAS MORE LIKE A BIRDSONG TO THE REST OF US THIS MORNING INSTEAD OF ALL MESMERIZING LIKE YESTERDAY?
HE'S A *SIREN?* I THOUGHT SIRENS WERE ONLY FICTIONAL?
HAS ANYTHING EVER BEEN EXACTLY WHAT YOU'VE EXPECTED SINCE YOU GOT HERE?
THE ANCIENT GREEK MYTHOLOGIES RARELY PICTURED THEM WITH FISH QUALITIES, THEY WERE MOSTLY AVIAN, LIKE SEABIRDS. CORMORANTS. HIS SINGING WOULD LURE YOU TO HIM, BUT ONCE HE HAD YOU IN HIS POWER HE WOULD *EAT* YOU! *THE ODYSSEY*, ANYONE? NOBODY?
THAT POND WASN'T THERE WHEN CAMP STARTED, SO MAYBE IT FLUCTUATES ERRATICALLY AS A PORTAL! THAT MEANS HE NEEDS TO RETURN *NOW*, BEFORE HE *EATS YOUR FACES*, OR HE COULD BE STUCK HERE!

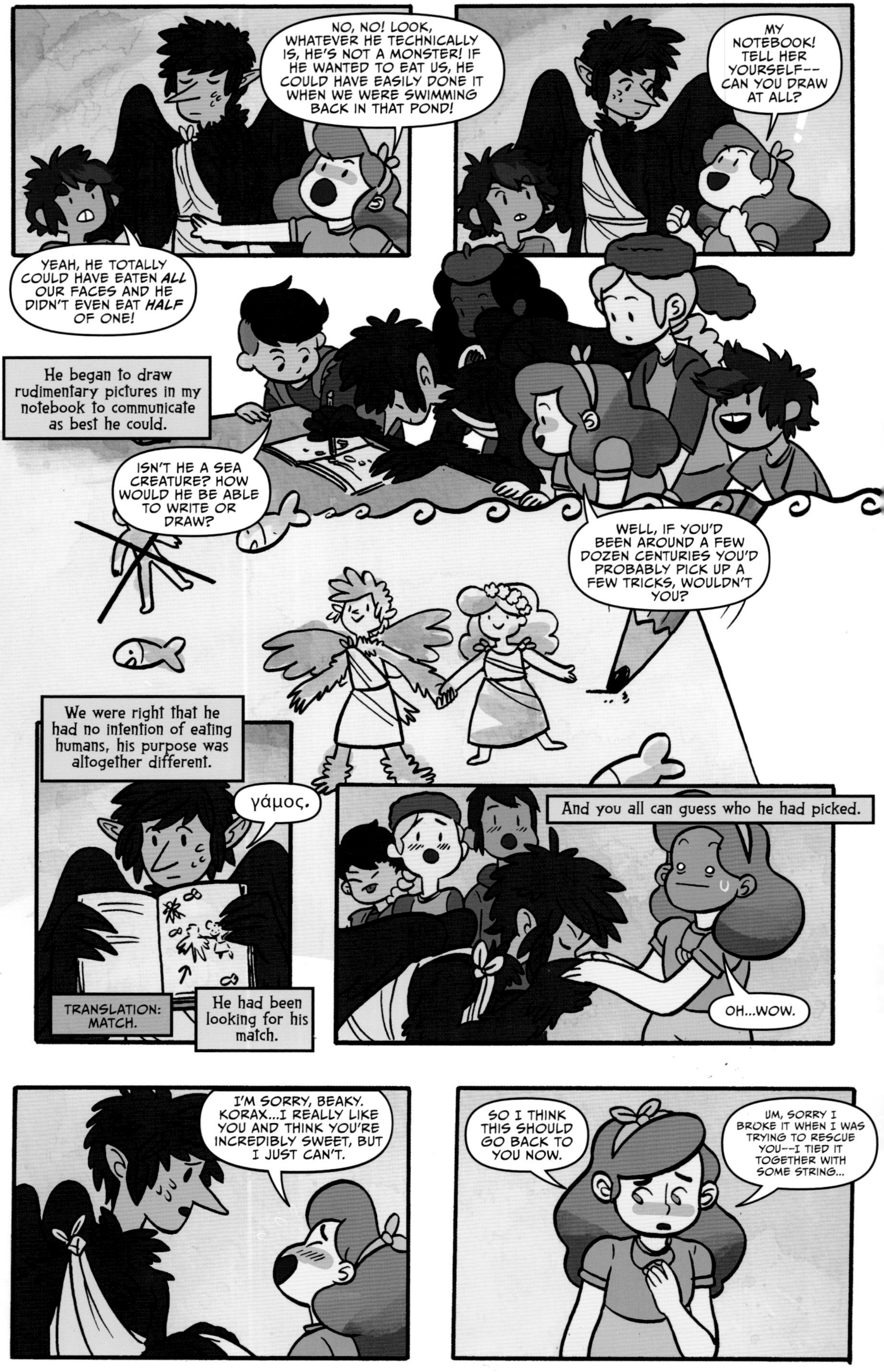
NO, NO! LOOK, WHATEVER HE TECHNICALLY IS, HE'S NOT A MONSTER! IF HE WANTED TO EAT US, HE COULD HAVE EASILY DONE IT WHEN WE WERE SWIMMING BACK IN THAT POND!
YEAH, HE TOTALLY COULD HAVE EATEN ALL OUR FACES AND HE DIDN'T EVEN EAT HALF OF ONE!
MY NOTEBOOK! TELL HER YOURSELF--CAN YOU DRAW AT ALL?
He began to draw rudimentary pictures in my notebook to communicate as best he could.
ISN'T HE A SEA CREATURE? HOW WOULD HE BE ABLE TO WRITE OR DRAW?
WELL, IF YOU'D BEEN AROUND A FEW DOZEN CENTURIES YOU'D PROBABLY PICK UP A FEW TRICKS, WOULDN'T YOU?
We were right that he had no intention of eating humans, his purpose was altogether different.
γάμος.
TRANSLATION: MATCH.
He had been looking for his match.
And you all can guess who he had picked.
OH...WOW.
I'M SORRY, BEAKY. KORAX...I REALLY LIKE YOU AND THINK YOU'RE INCREDIBLY SWEET, BUT I JUST CAN'T.
SO I THINK THIS SHOULD GO BACK TO YOU NOW.
UM, SORRY I BROKE IT WHEN I WAS TRYING TO RESCUE YOU--I TIED IT TOGETHER WITH SOME STRING...

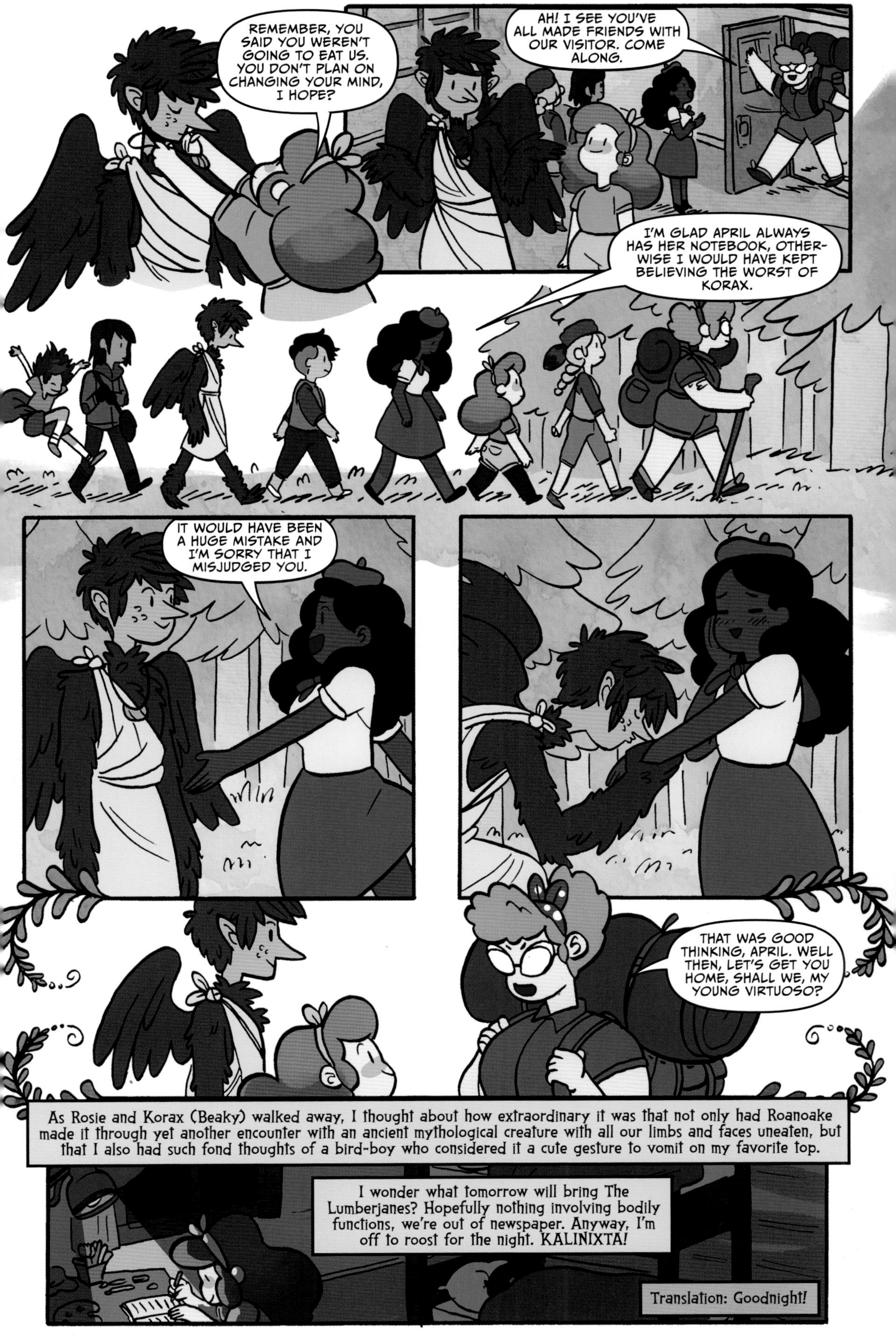
REMEMBER, YOU SAID YOU WEREN'T GOING TO EAT US. YOU DON'T PLAN ON CHANGING YOUR MIND, I HOPE?
AH! I SEE YOU'VE ALL MADE FRIENDS WITH OUR VISITOR. COME ALONG.
I'M GLAD APRIL ALWAYS HAS HER NOTEBOOK, OTHER-WISE I WOULD HAVE KEPT BELIEVING THE WORST OF KORAX.
IT WOULD HAVE BEEN A HUGE MISTAKE AND I'M SORRY THAT I MISJUDGED YOU.
THAT WAS GOOD THINKING, APRIL. WELL THEN, LET'S GET YOU HOME, SHALL WE, MY YOUNG VIRTUOSO?
As Rosie and Korax (Beaky) walked away, I thought about how extraordinary it was that not only had Roanoake made it through yet another encounter with an ancient mythological creature with all our limbs and faces uneaten, but that I also had such fond thoughts of a bird-boy who considered it a cute gesture to vomit on my favorite top.
I wonder what tomorrow will bring The Lumberjanes? Hopefully nothing involving bodily functions, we're out of newspaper. Anyway, I'm off to roost for the night. KALINIXTA!
Translation: Goodnight!

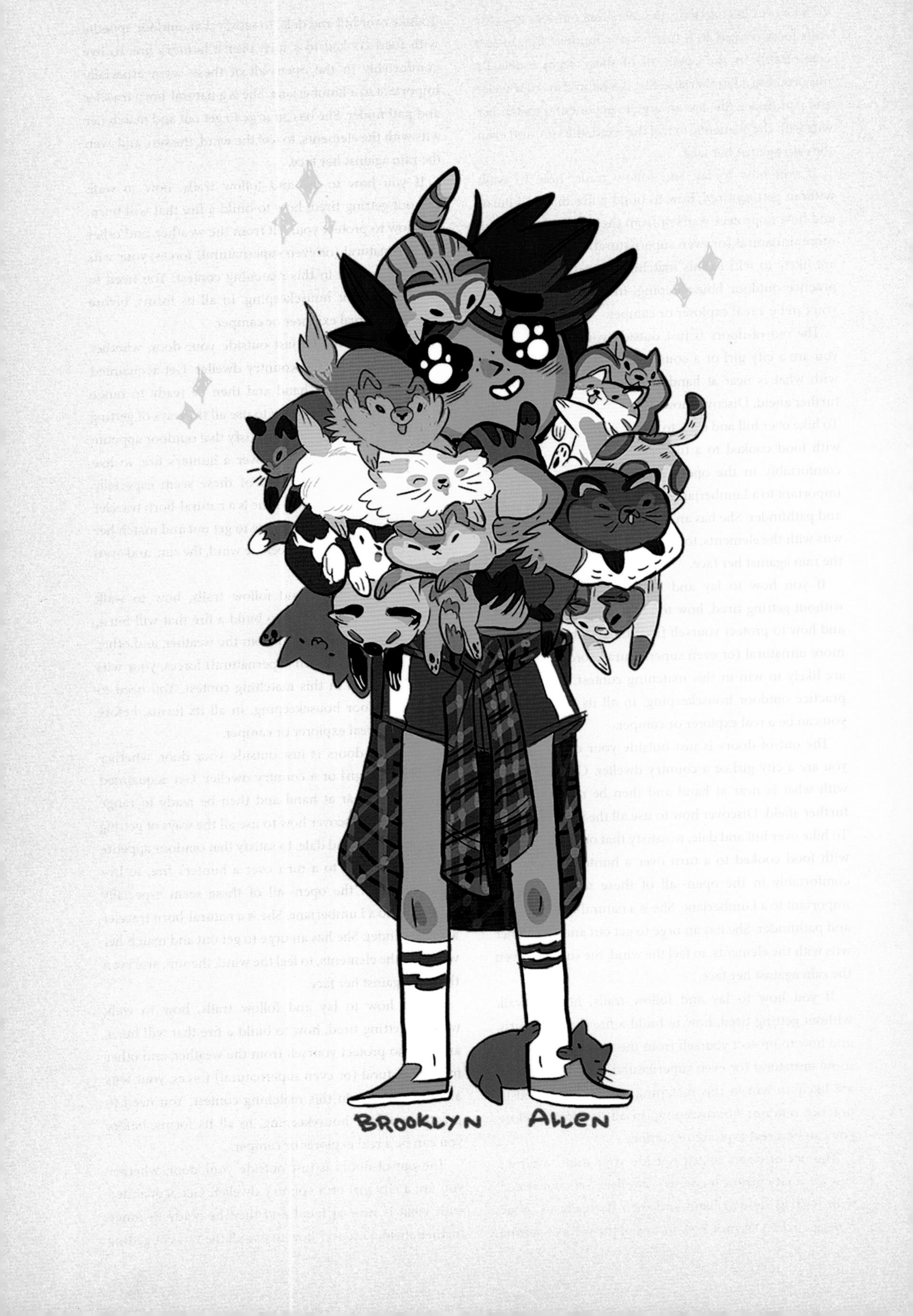
BROOKLYN ALLEN

will co
The
It help
appearar
dress fo
Further
Lumber
to have
part in
Thiskw
Hardc
have
them

.E UNIFORM

hould be worn at camp
vents when Lumberjanes
a may also be worn at other
ons. It should be worn as a
the uniform dress with
rect shoes, and stocking or
ut grows her uniform or
ter Lumberjane.
a she has
her
her

IT'S BEAUTIFUL!!!

SO ARE YOU!

The
yellow, short sl
emb
the w
choose
slacks,
made o
out-of-do
green bere
the colla
Shoes ma
heels, rou
socks shou
the uniform. Ne
belong with a Lumberjane uniform.

ings or
the shoes or wi
, pracelets, or other jewelry do

SKWAK

WE'RE ON A BOAT

HOW TO WEAR THE UNIFORM

To look well in a uniform demands first of
uniform be kept in good condition—clean
pressed. See that the skirt is the right length for your own
height and build, that the belt is adjusted to your waist,
that your shoes and stockings are in keeping with the
uniform, that you watch your posture and carry yourself
with dignity and grace. If the beret is removed indoors,
be sure that your hair is neat and kept in place with an
insonspicuous clip or ribbon. When you wear a
Lumberjane uniform you are identified as a member of
this organization and you should be doubly careful to
conduct yourself in a way that will show everyone that
courtesy and thoughtfullness are part of being a
Lumberjane. People are likely to judge a whole nation by
the selfishness of a few individuals, to criticize a whole
family because of the misconduct of one member, and to
feel unkindly toward and organization because of the

The unifor
helps to cre
in a group.
active life th
another bond
future, and pre
in order to b
Lumberjane pr
Penniquiqul Thi
Types, but m
can either b
materials available at the trading post.

Lady
s will wish to have one. They
e uniform, or make it themselves from

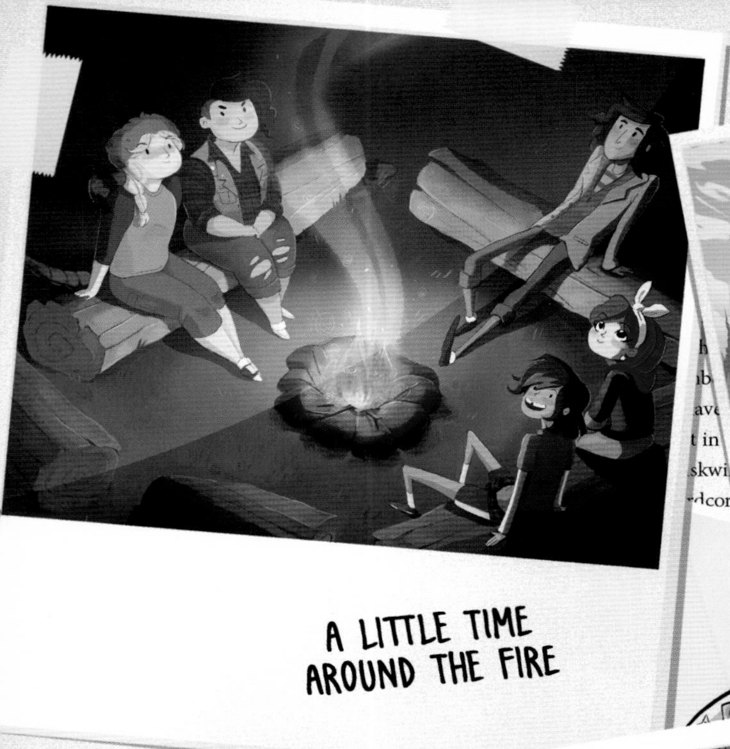
A LITTLE TIME
AROUND THE FIRE

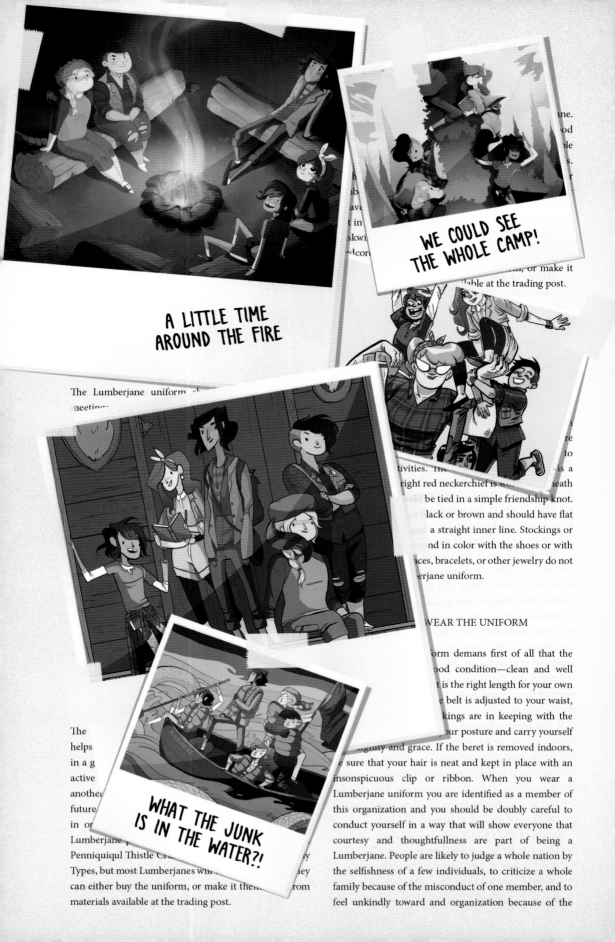

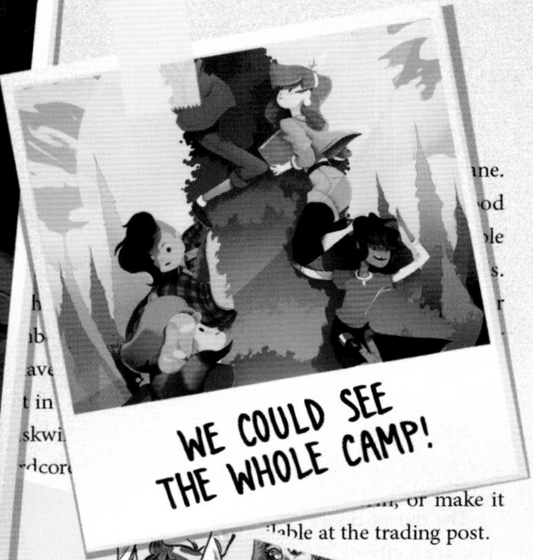
WE COULD SEE
THE WHOLE CAMP!

...m, or make it
...ilable at the trading post.

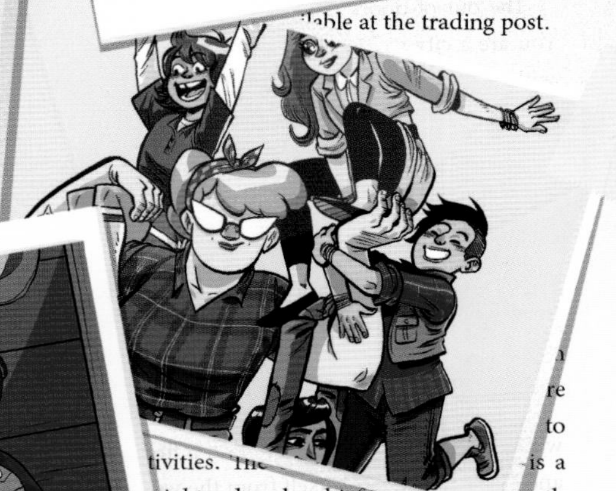

The Lumberjane uniform sh...
meeting...

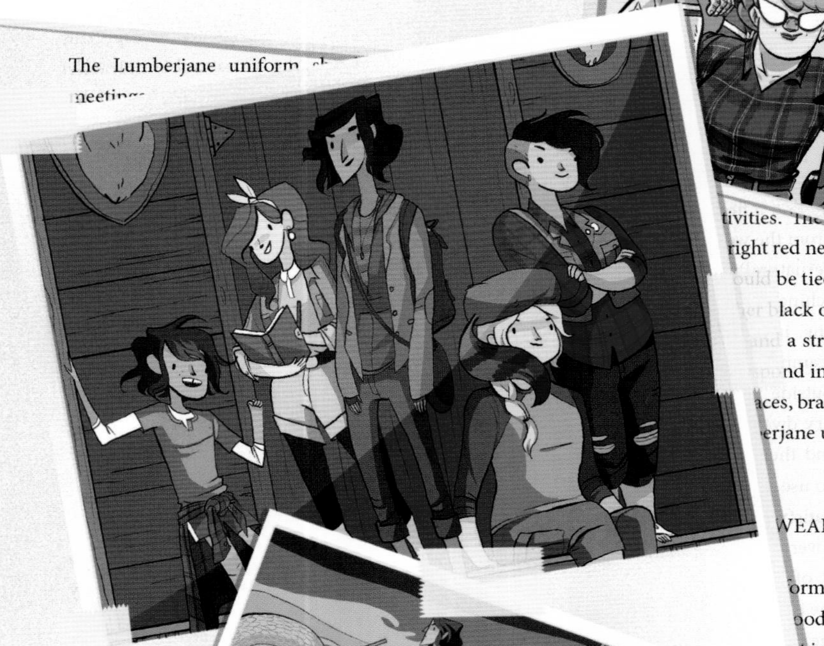

...tivities. The ... is a
...right red neckerchief is wo... neath
...ould be tied in a simple friendship knot.
...lack or brown and should have flat
...a straight inner line. Stockings or
...nd in color with the shoes or with
...aces, bracelets, or other jewelry do not
...erjane uniform.

...WEAR THE UNIFORM

...orm demans first of all that the
...ood condition—clean and well
...t is the right length for your own
...e belt is adjusted to your waist,
...kings are in keeping with the
...our posture and carry yourself
...dignity and grace. If the beret is removed indoors, be sure that your hair is neat and kept in place with an insonspicuous clip or ribbon. When you wear a Lumberjane uniform you are identified as a member of this organization and you should be doubly careful to conduct yourself in a way that will show everyone that courtesy and thoughtfullness are part of being a Lumberjane. People are likely to judge a whole nation by the selfishness of a few individuals, to criticize a whole family because of the misconduct of one member, and to feel unkindly toward and organization because of the

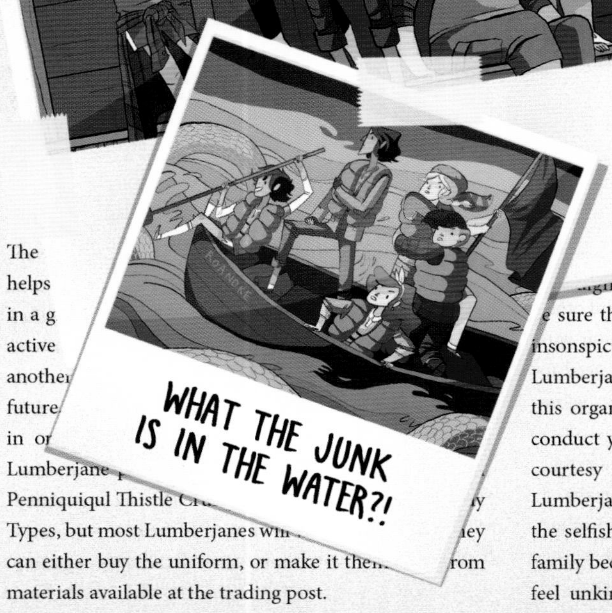
ROANOKE
WHAT THE JUNK
IS IN THE WATER?!

The ...
helps ...
in a g...
active ...
another ...
future. ...
in or...
Lumberjane p...
Penniquiqul Thistle Cru... ...ly
Types, but most Lumberjanes wi... ...ney
can either buy the uniform, or make it them... ...rom
materials available at the trading post.

COVER GALLERY

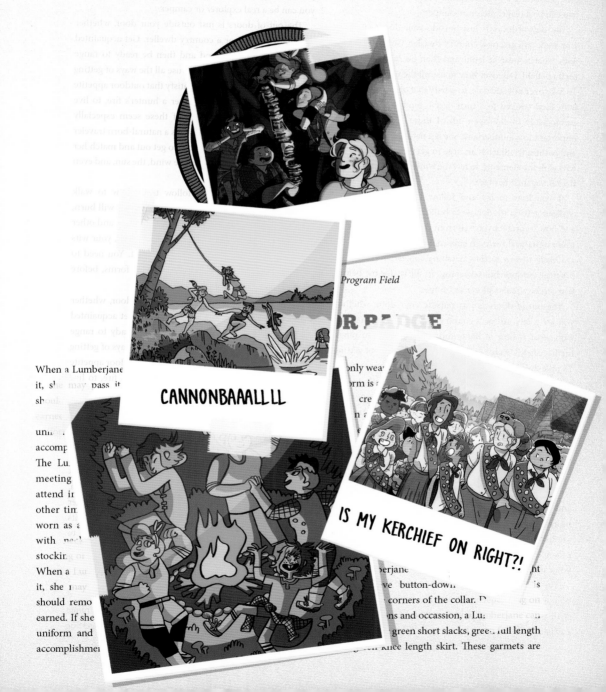

CANNONBAAALLLL

IS MY KERCHIEF ON RIGHT?!

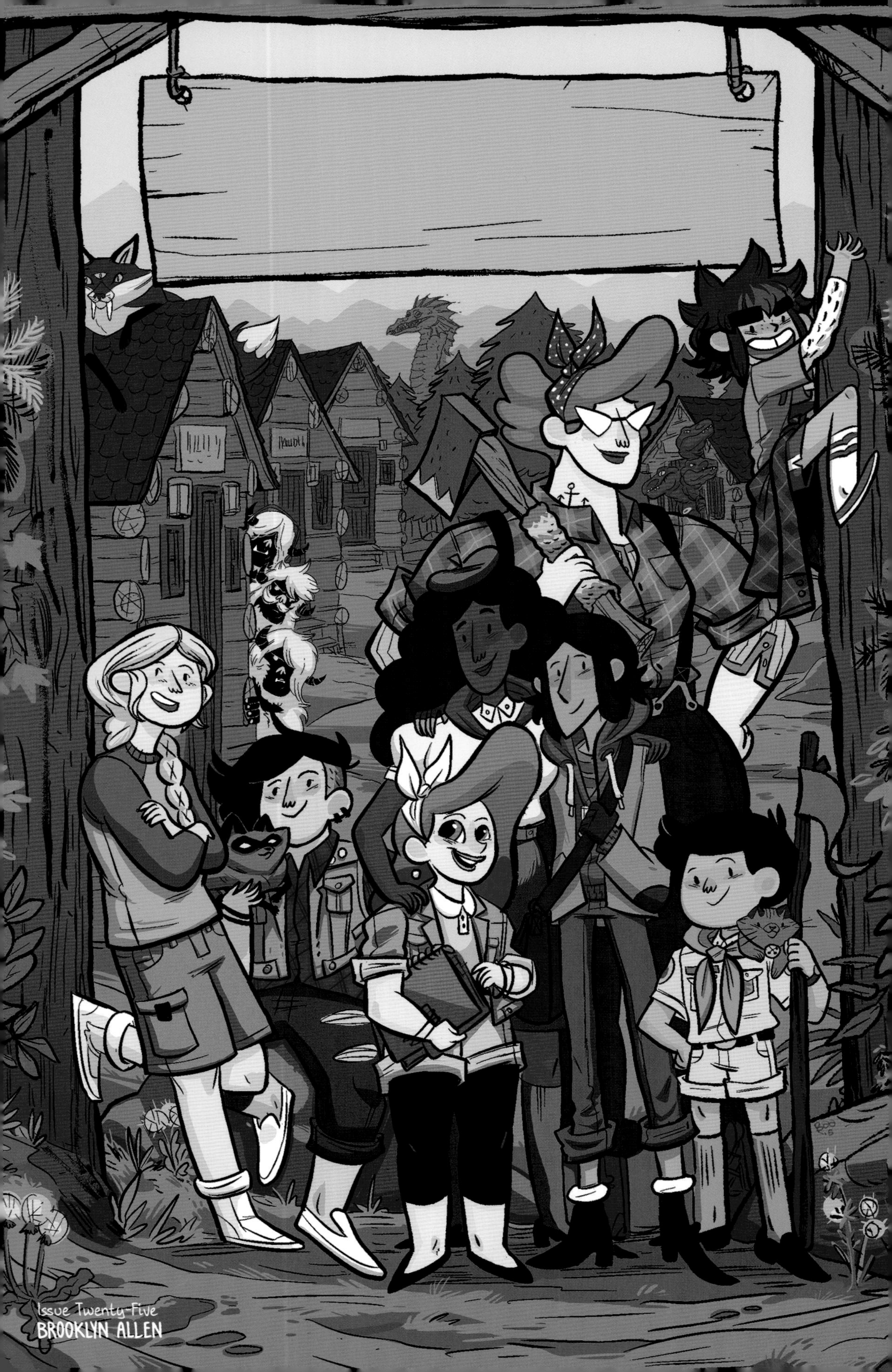
Issue Twenty-Five
BROOKLYN ALLEN

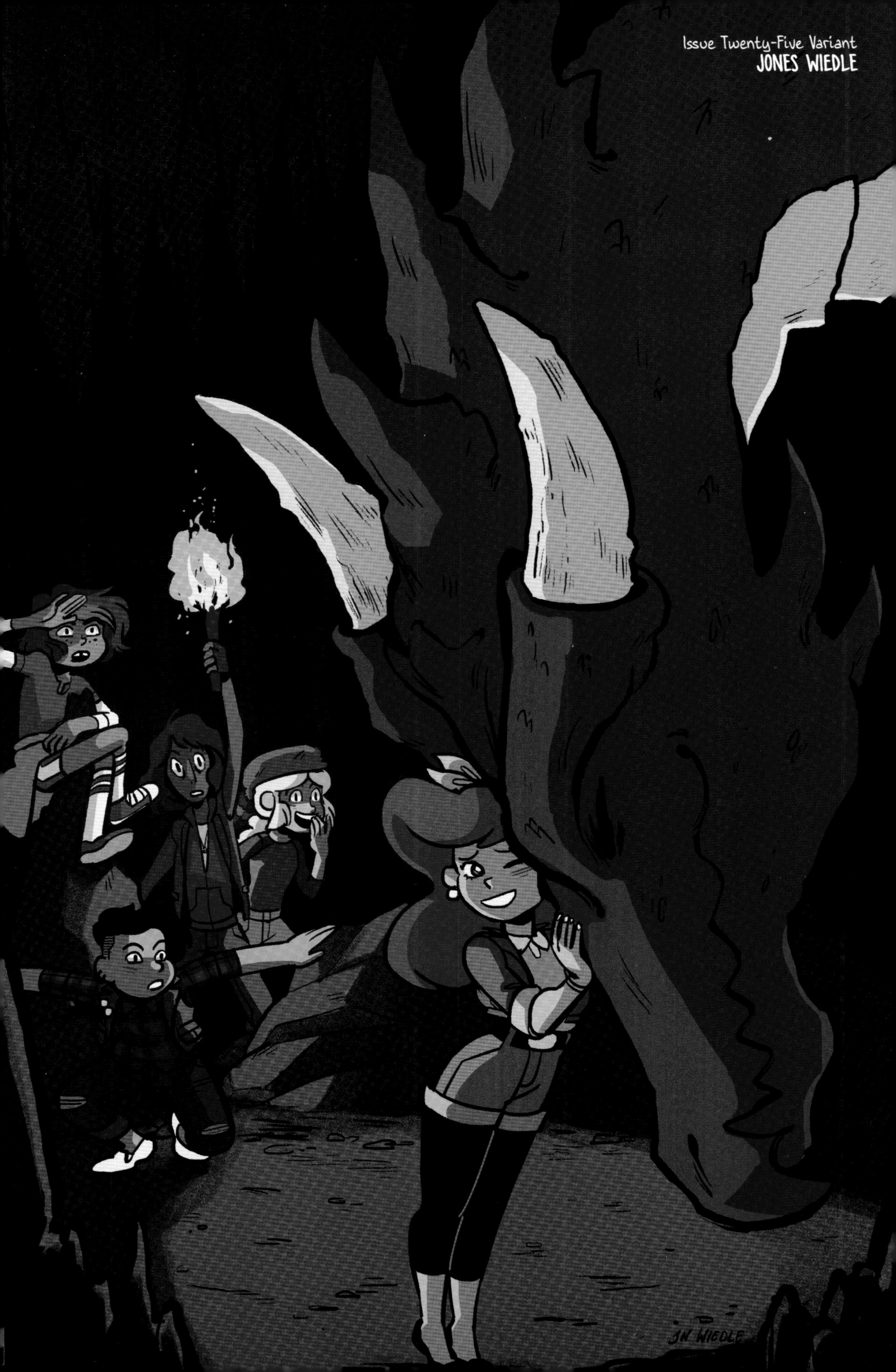
Issue Twenty-Five Variant
JONES WIEDLE
JN WIEDLE

Issue Twenty-Five FanMail
KAT LEYH

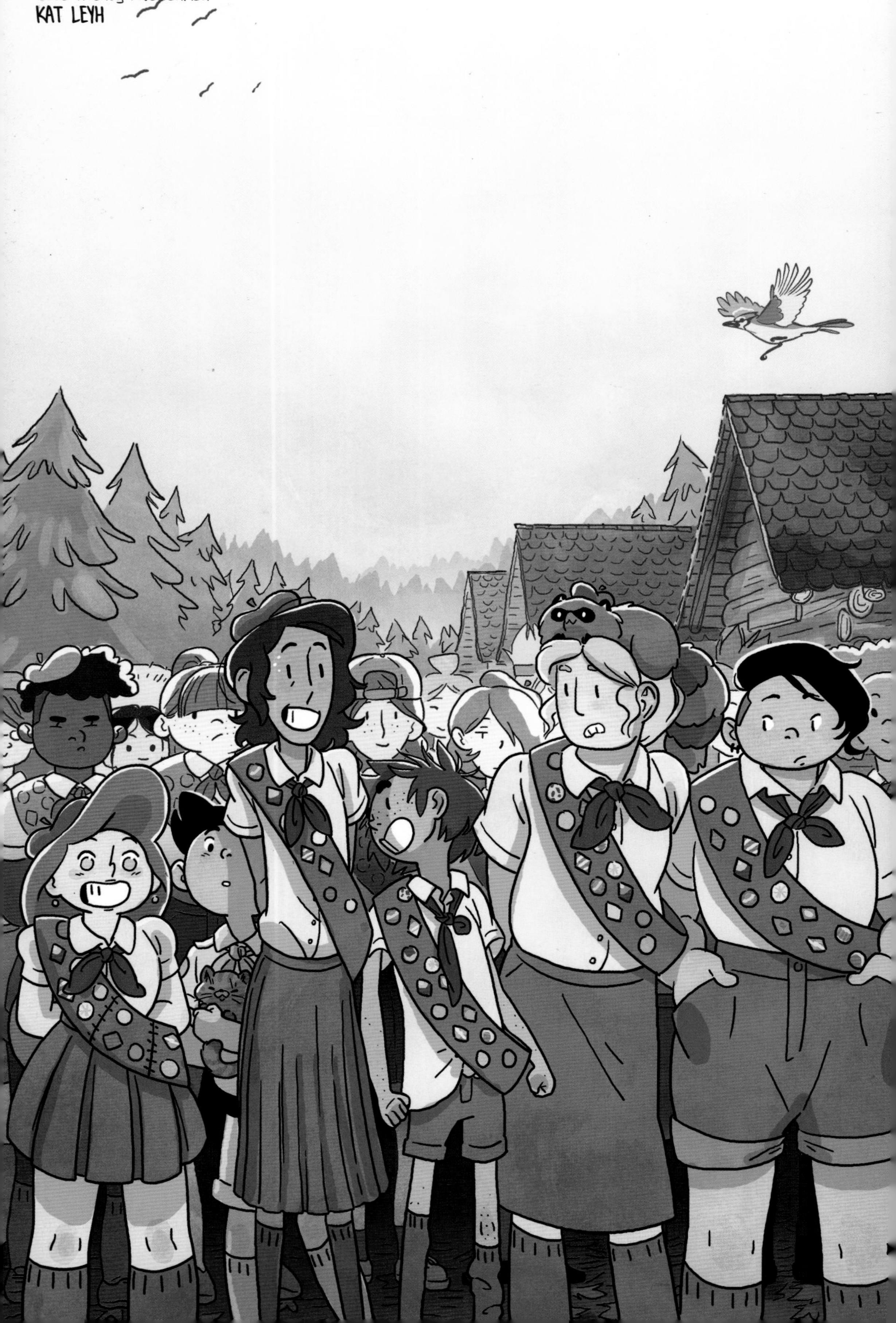

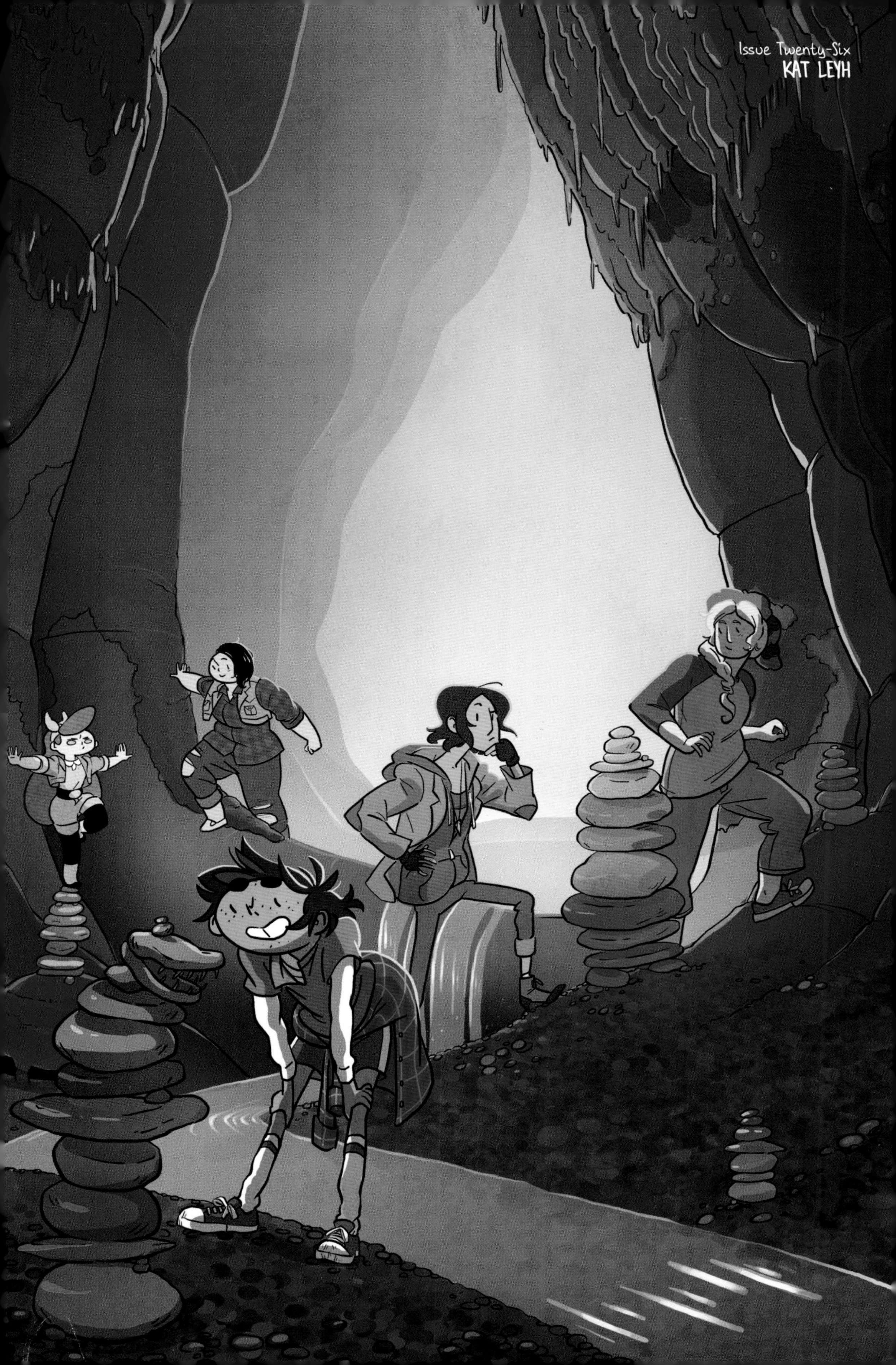
Issue Twenty-Six
KAT LEYH

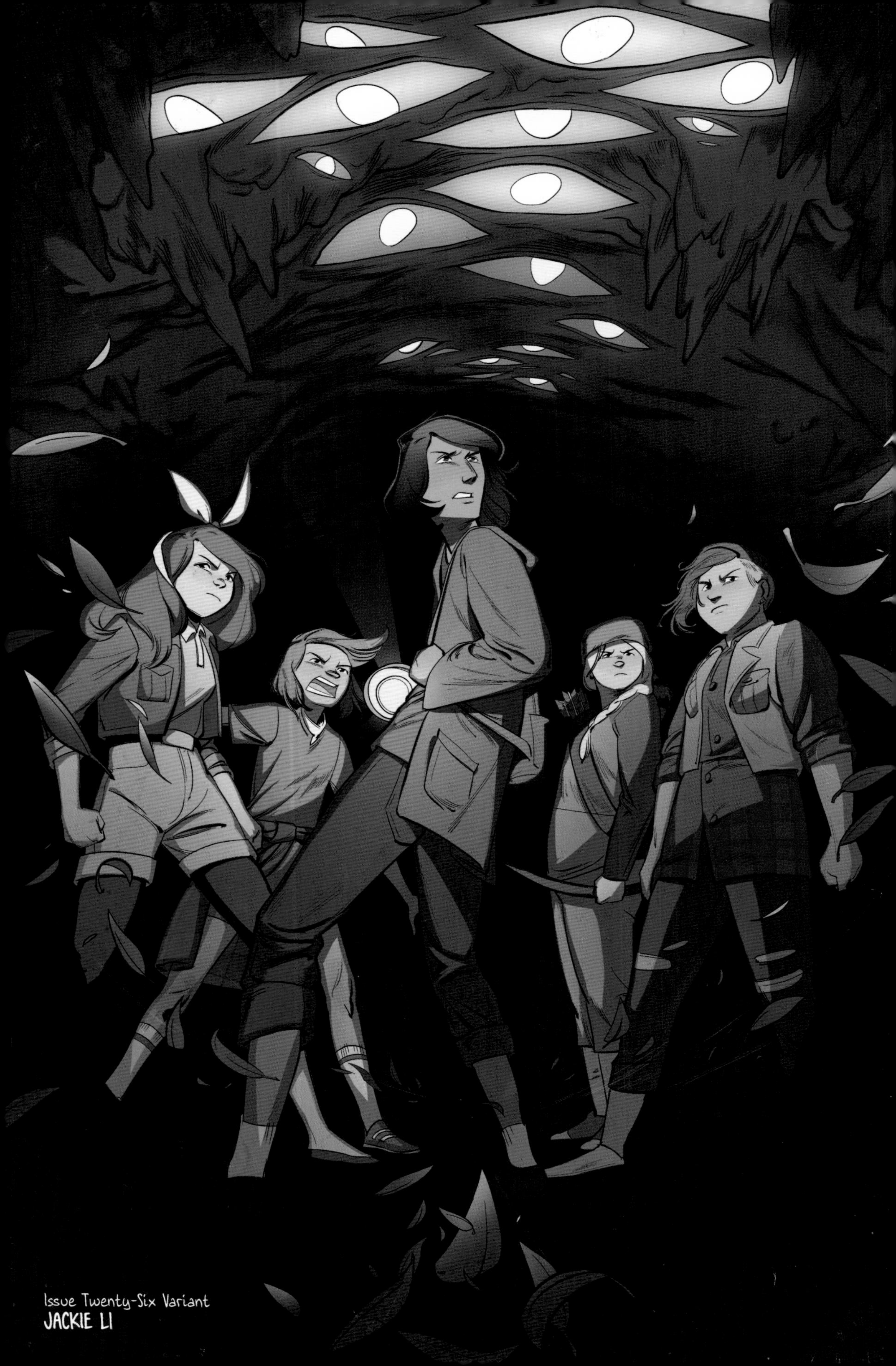

Issue Twenty-Six Variant
JACKIE LI

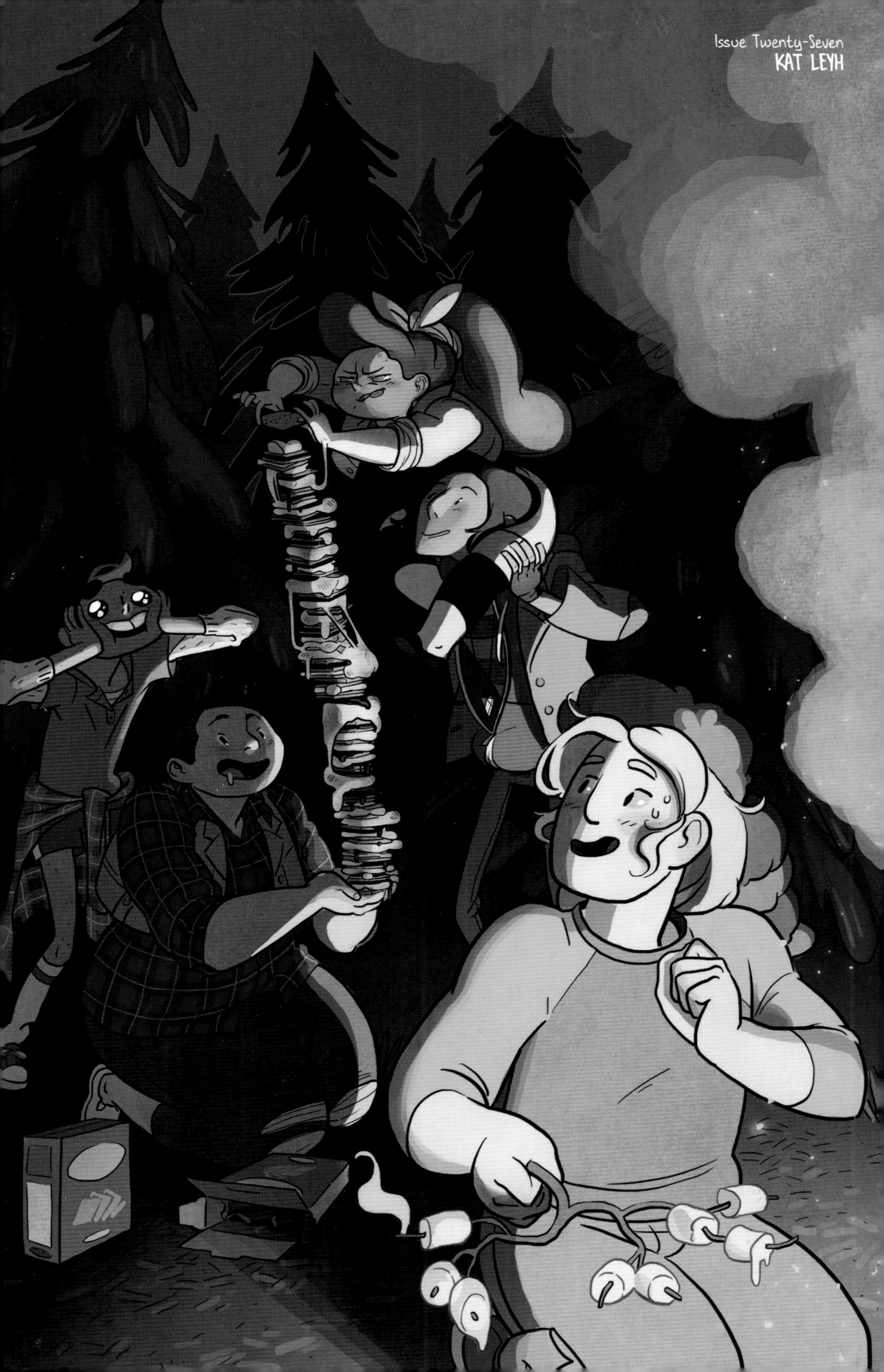
Issue Twenty-Seven
KAT LEYH

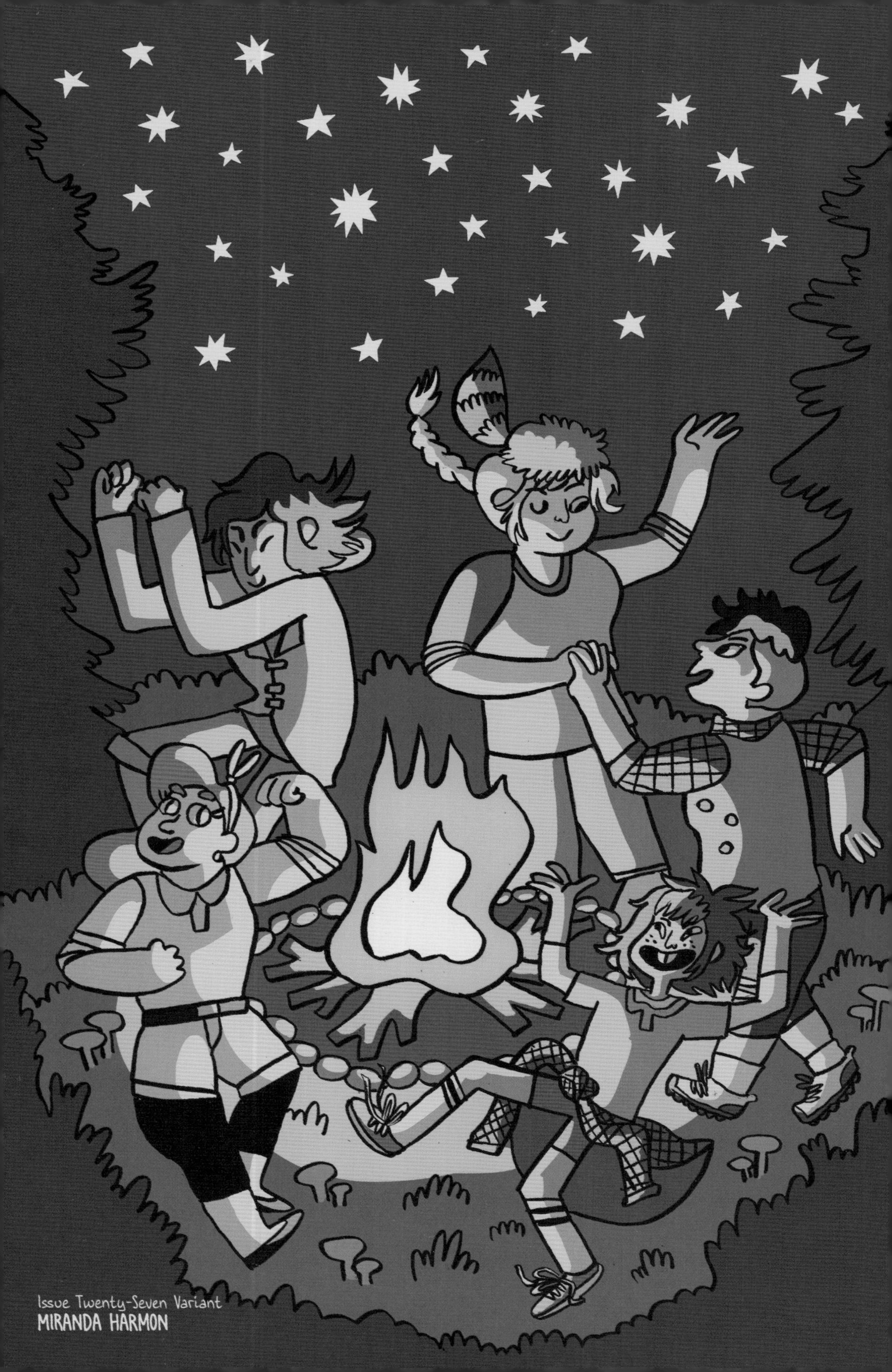

Issue Twenty-Seven Variant
MIRANDA HARMON

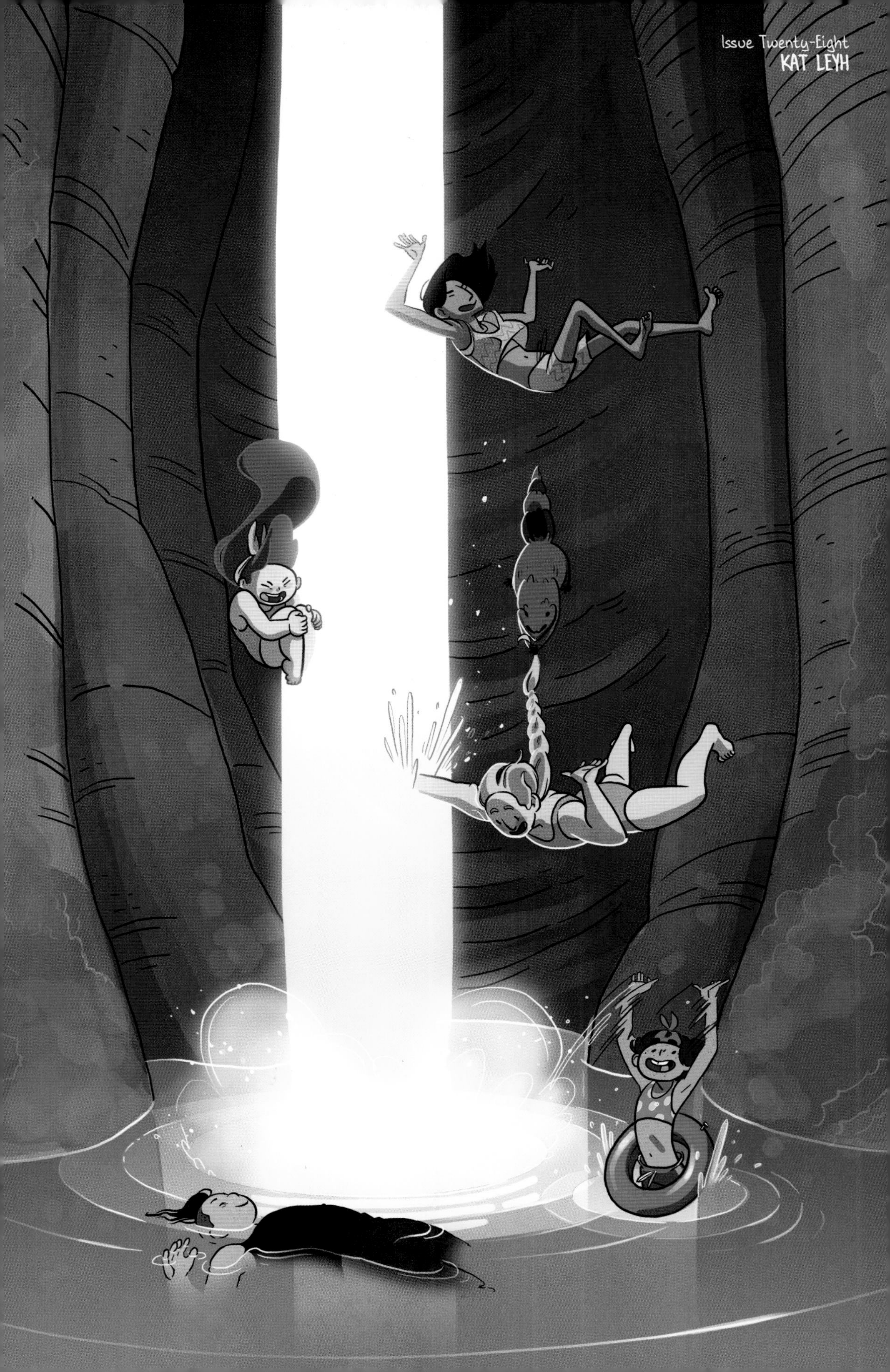
Issue Twenty-Eight
KAT LEYH

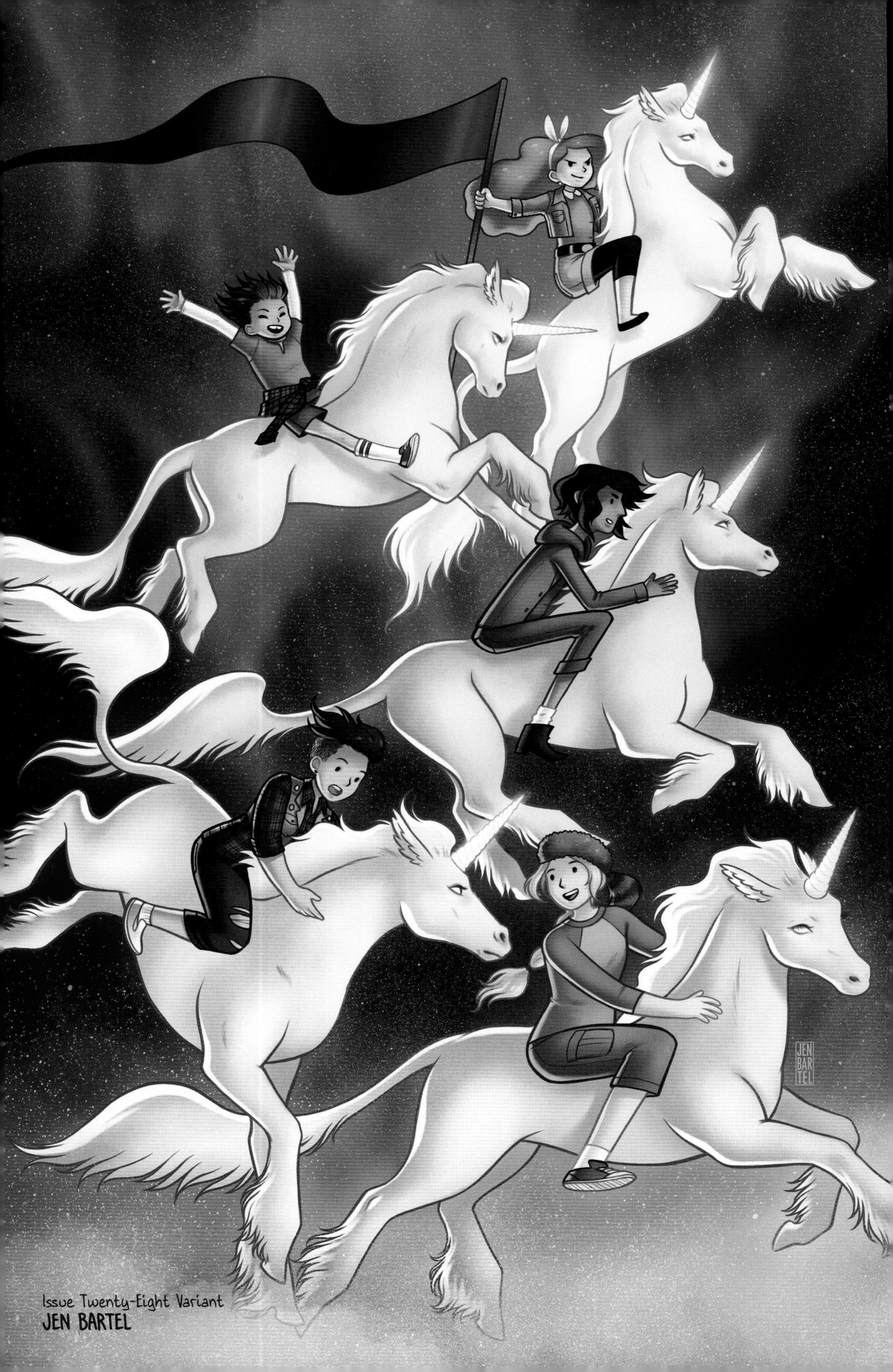
JEN
BAR
TEL

Issue Twenty-Eight Variant
JEN BARTEL

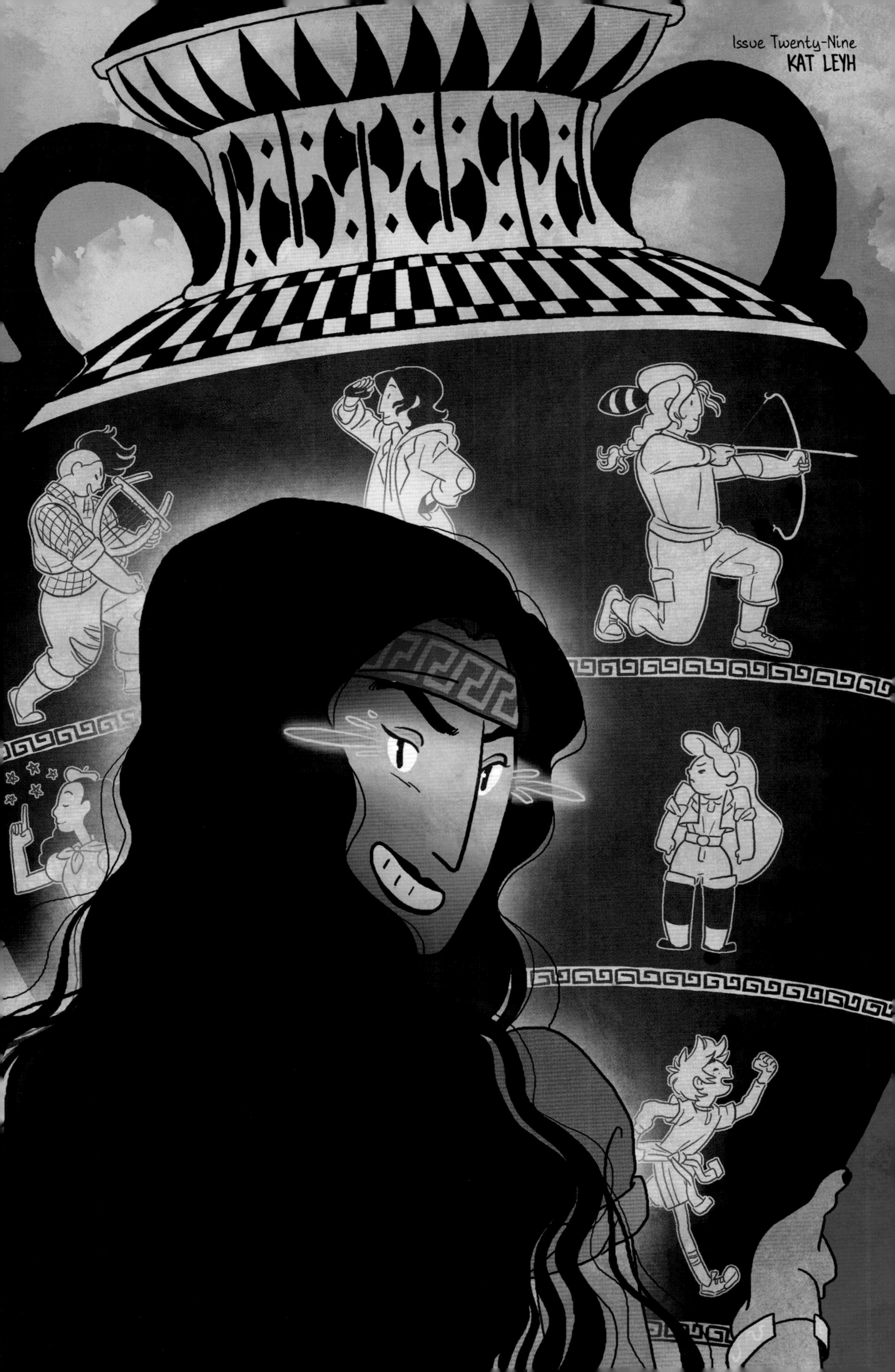
Issue Twenty-Nine
KAT LEYH

Issue Twenty Nine Variant
RACHAEL SMITH

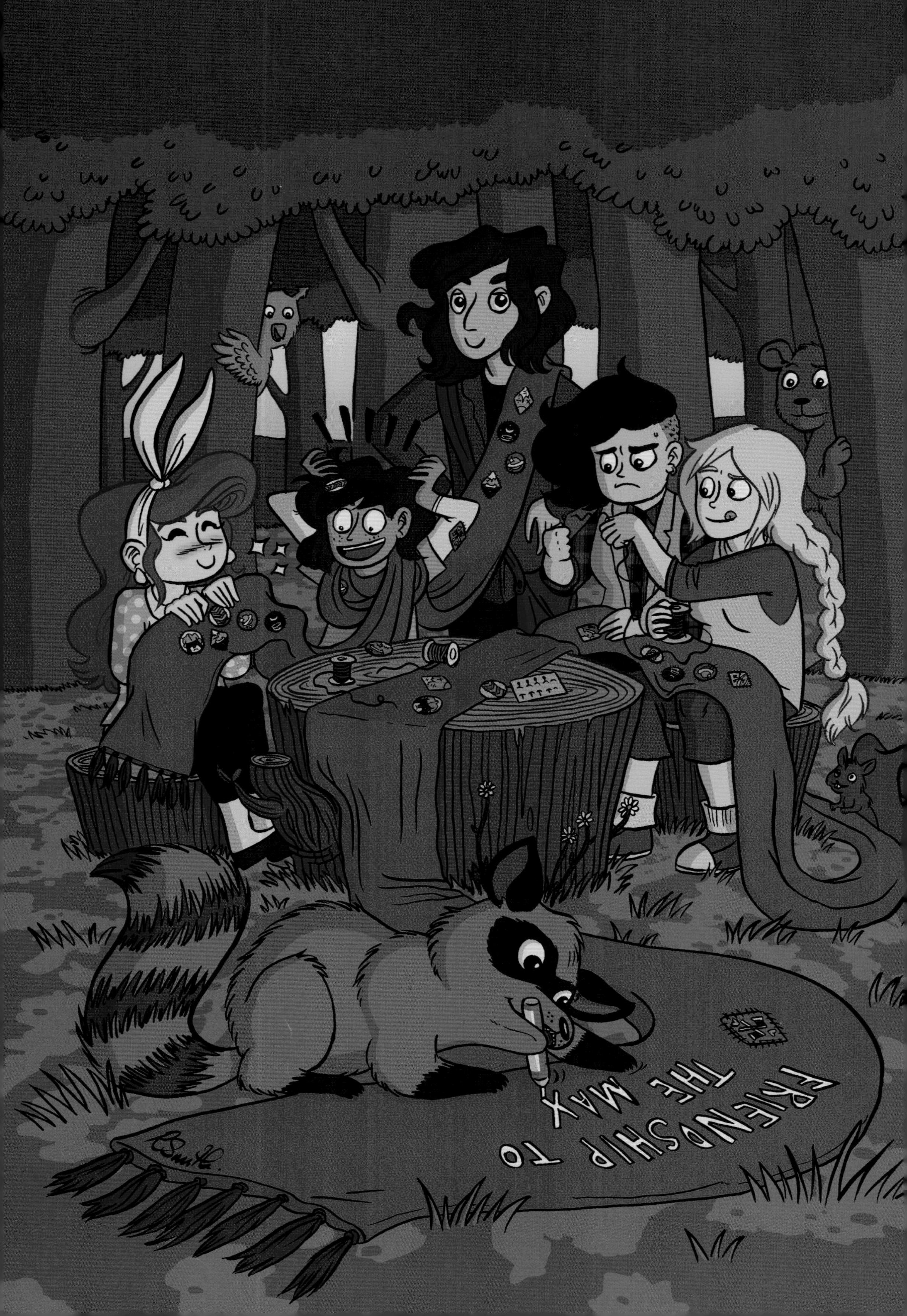
FRIENDSHIP TO
THE MAX

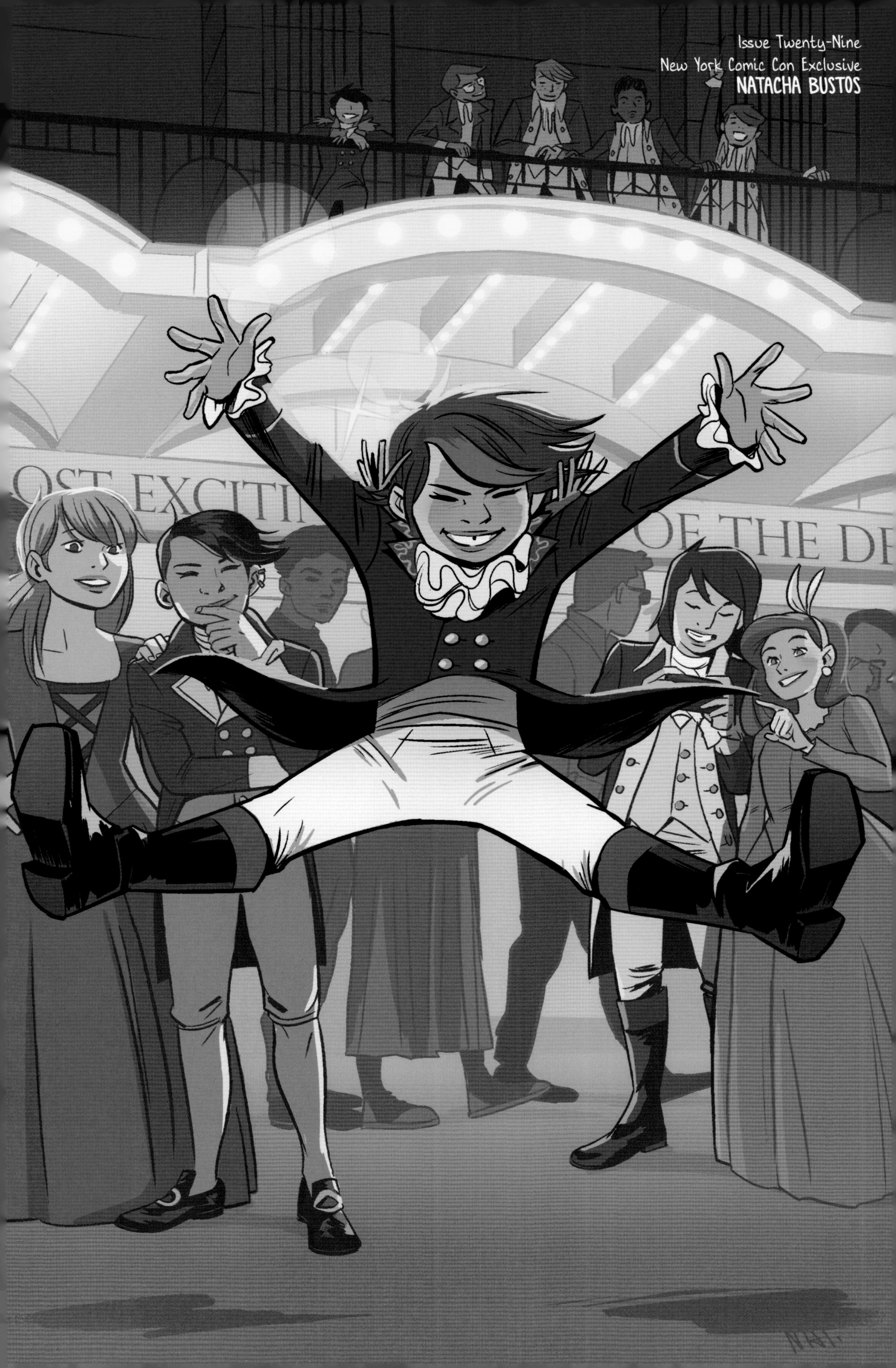

Issue Twenty-Nine
New York Comic Con Exclusive
NATACHA BUSTOS

Issue Thirty
KAT LEYH

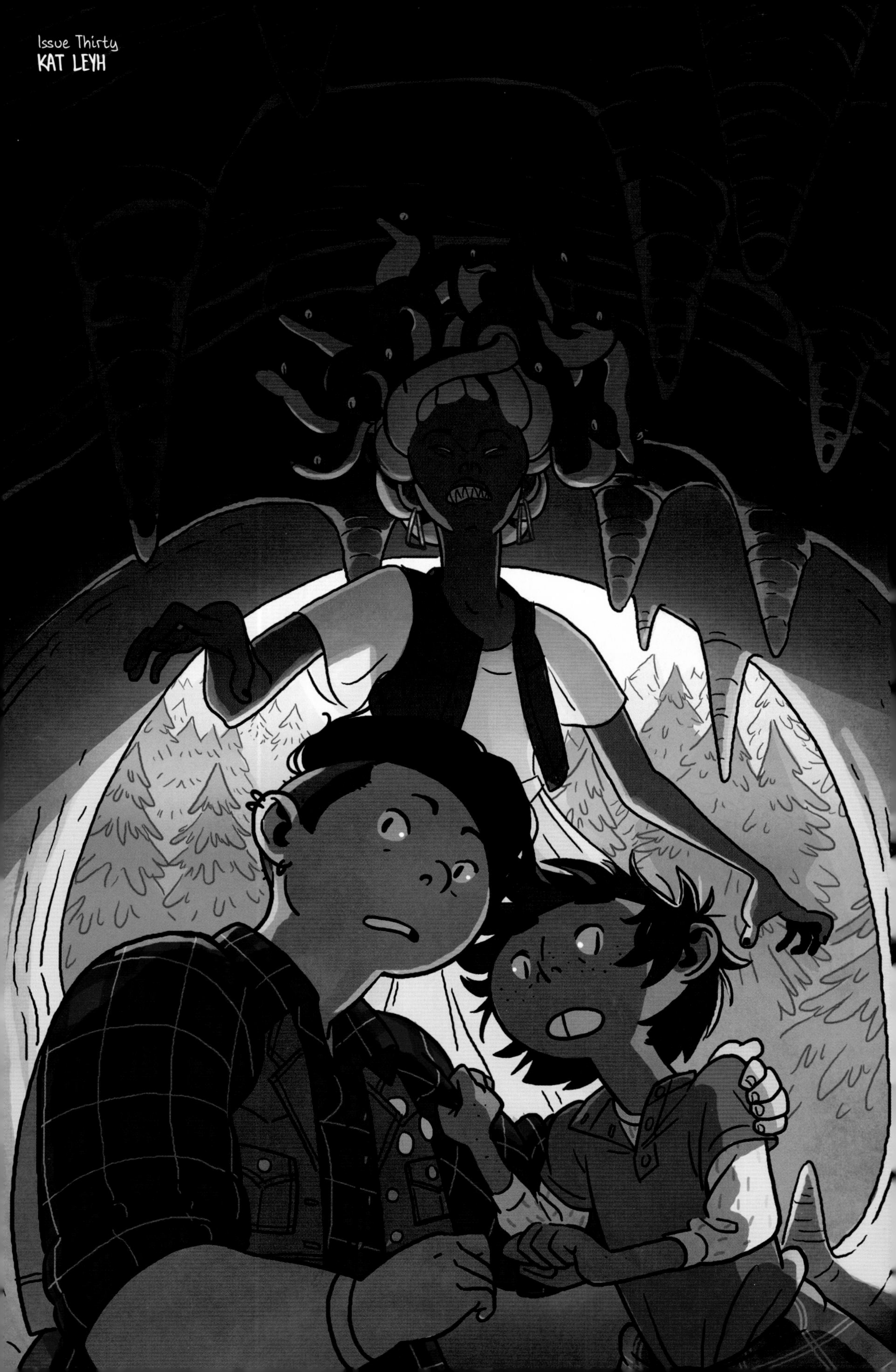

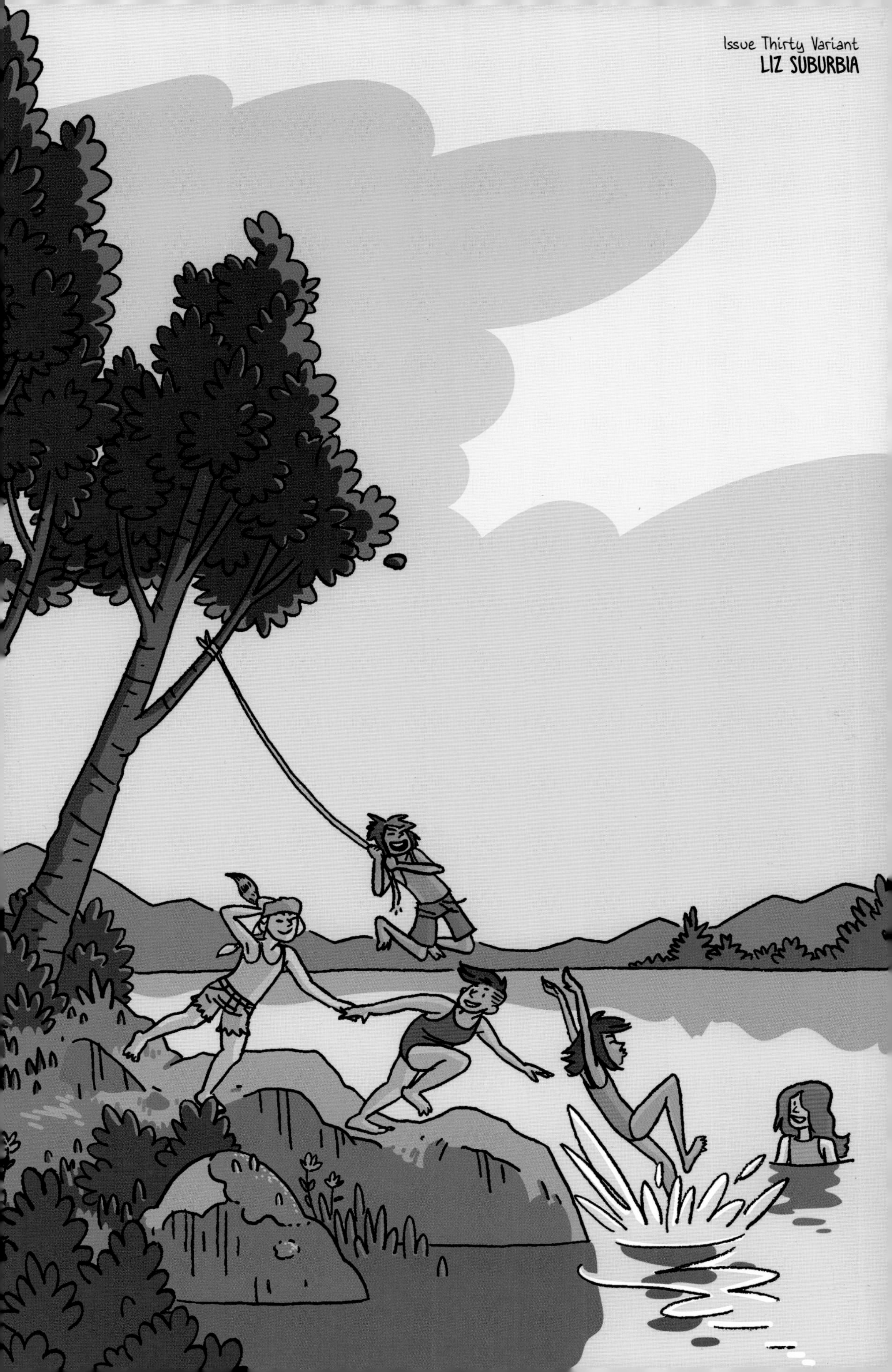

Issue Thirty Variant
LIZ SUBURBIA

Issue Thirty-One
KAT LEYH

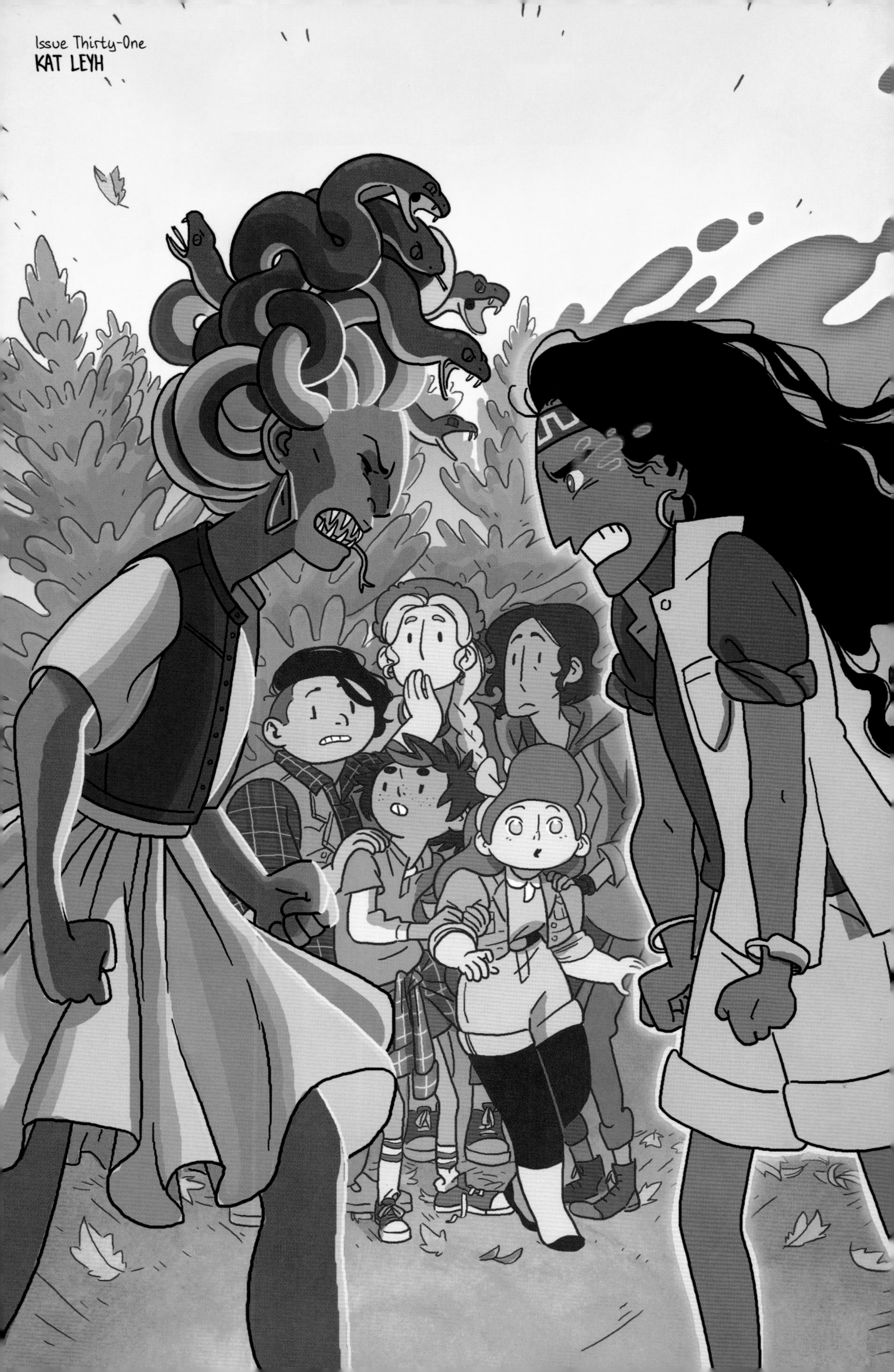

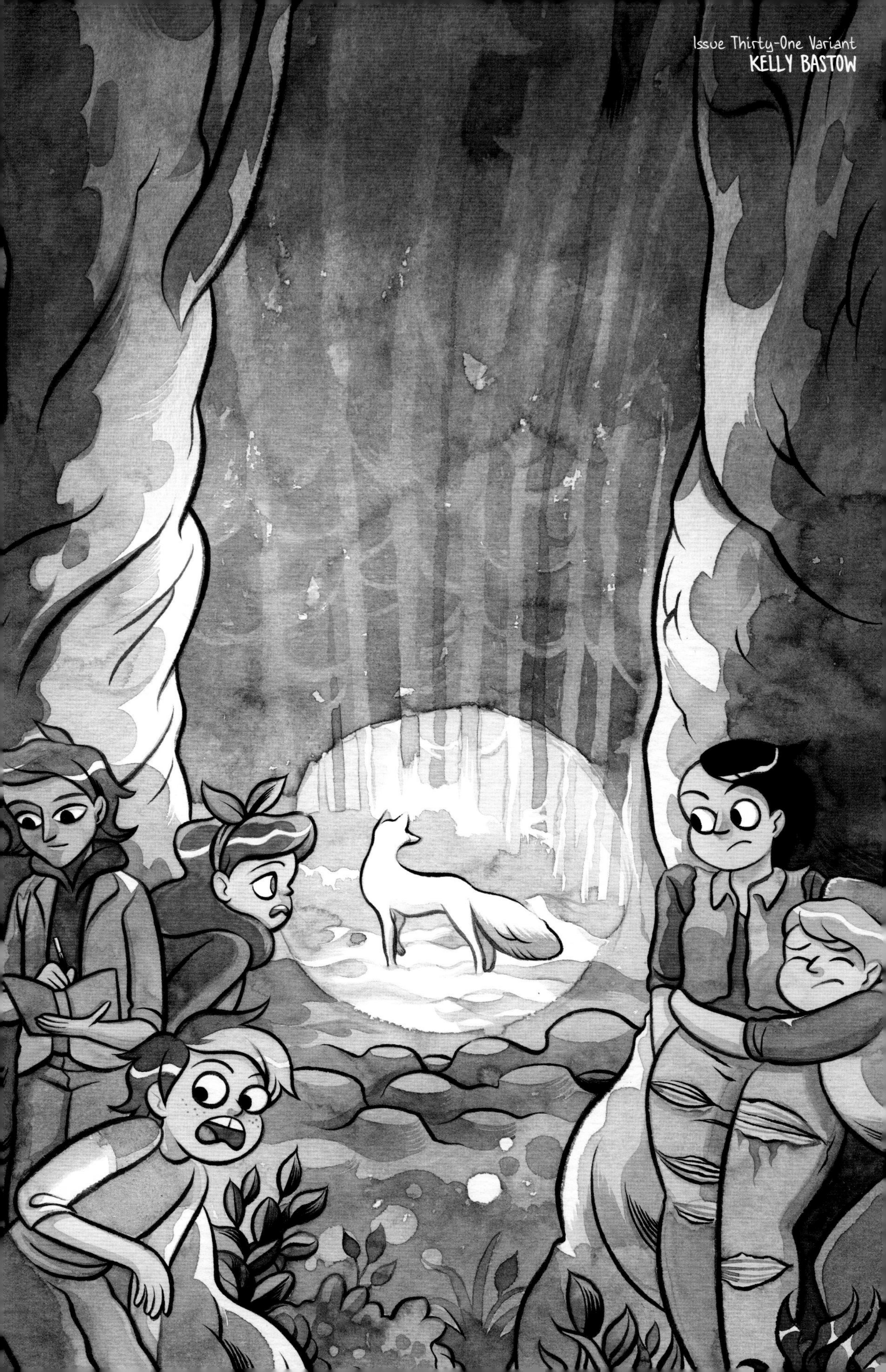
Issue Thirty-One Variant
KELLY BASTOW

Issue Thirty-Two
KAT LEYH

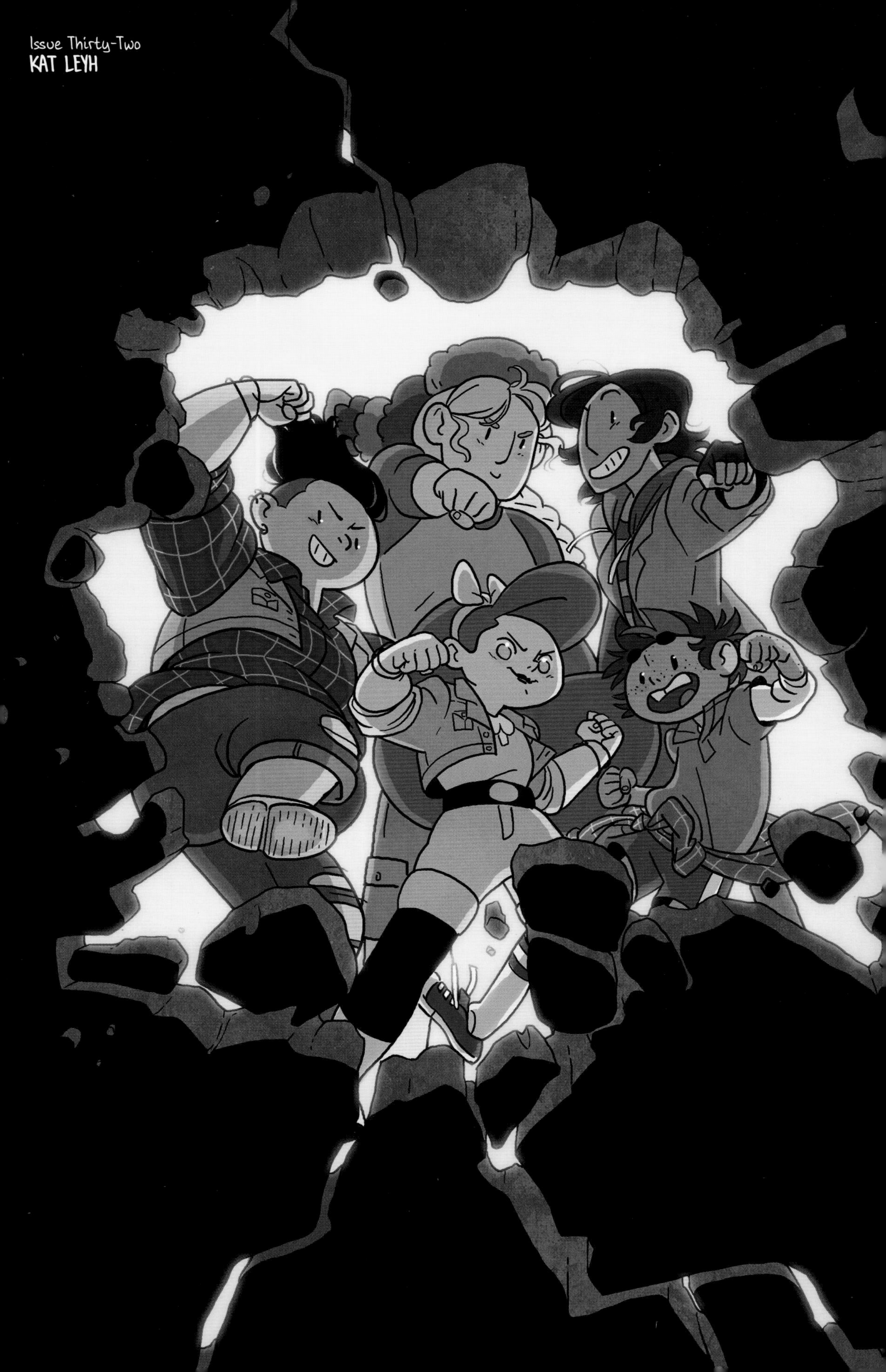

Issue Thirty-Two Variant
FEIFEI RUAN

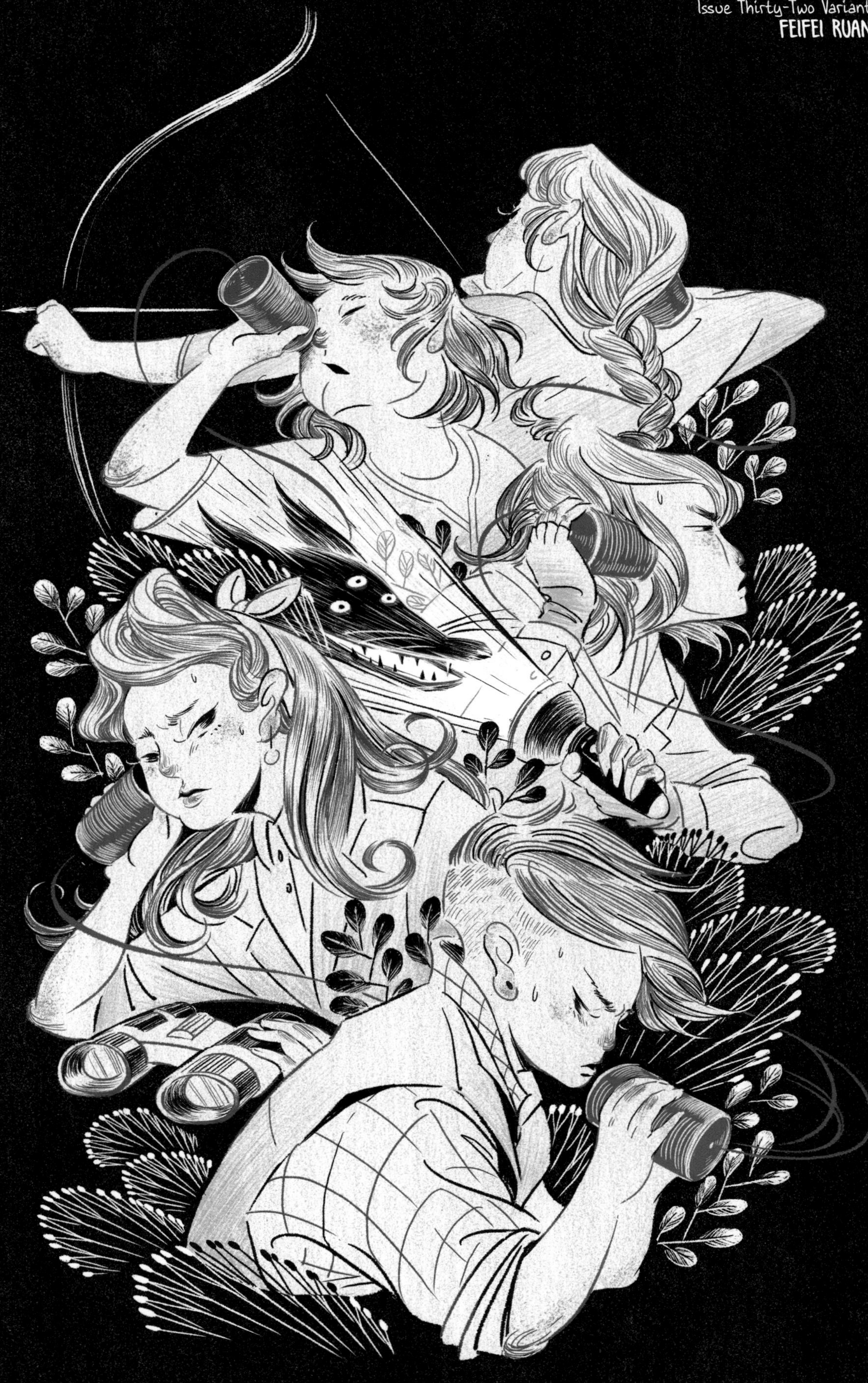

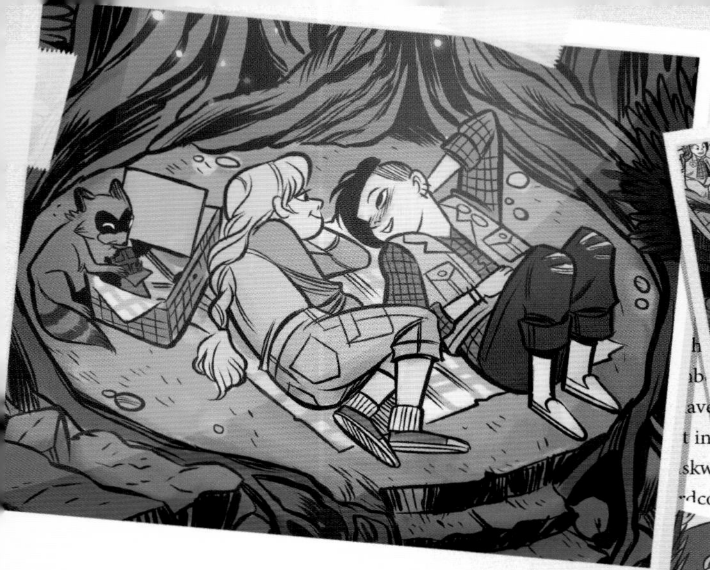

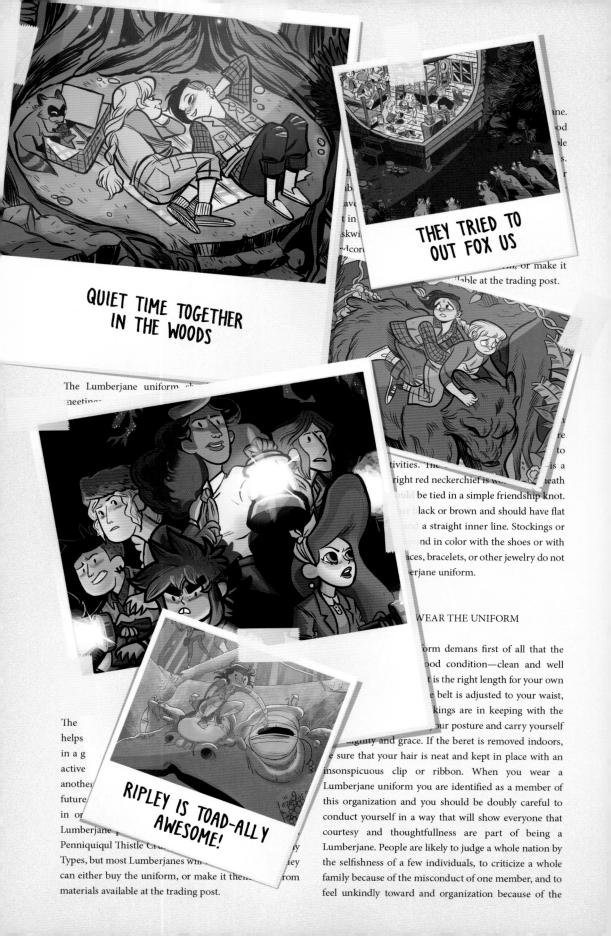

QUIET TIME TOGETHER IN THE WOODS

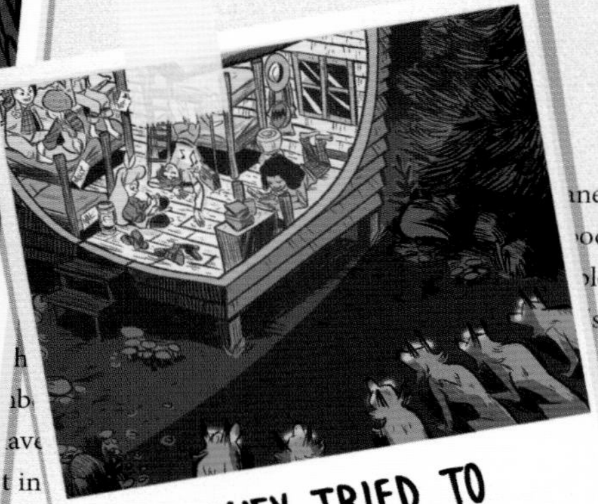

THEY TRIED TO OUT FOX US

ne.
od
le
s.
h r
ib
ave
t in
skwi
rdcor

n, or make it
ilable at the trading post.

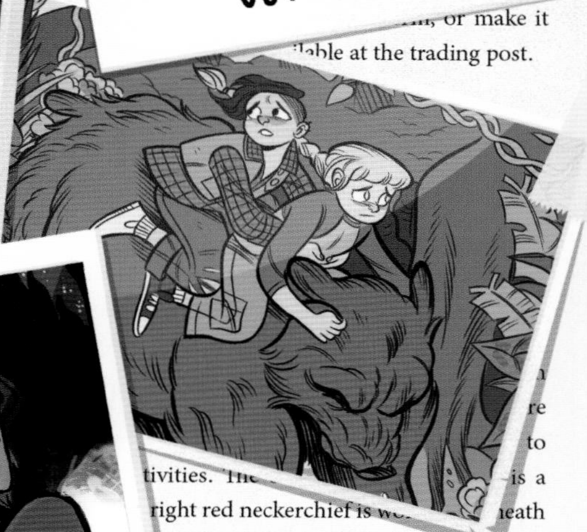

The Lumberjane uniform
meeting

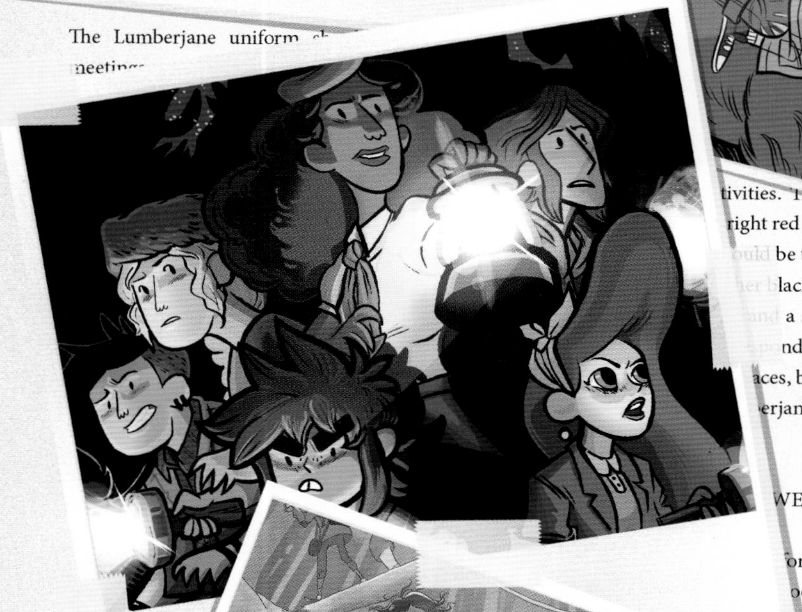

n
re
to
tivities. The is a
right red neckerchief is wo neath
ould be tied in a simple friendship knot.
her black or brown and should have flat
and a straight inner line. Stockings or
pond in color with the shoes or with
aces, bracelets, or other jewelry do not
erjane uniform.

WEAR THE UNIFORM

orm demans first of all that the ood condition—clean and well t is the right length for your own e belt is adjusted to your waist, kings are in keeping with the our posture and carry yourself dignity and grace. If the beret is removed indoors, e sure that your hair is neat and kept in place with an insonspicuous clip or ribbon. When you wear a Lumberjane uniform you are identified as a member of this organization and you should be doubly careful to conduct yourself in a way that will show everyone that courtesy and thoughtfullness are part of being a Lumberjane. People are likely to judge a whole nation by the selfishness of a few individuals, to criticize a whole family because of the misconduct of one member, and to feel unkindly toward and organization because of the

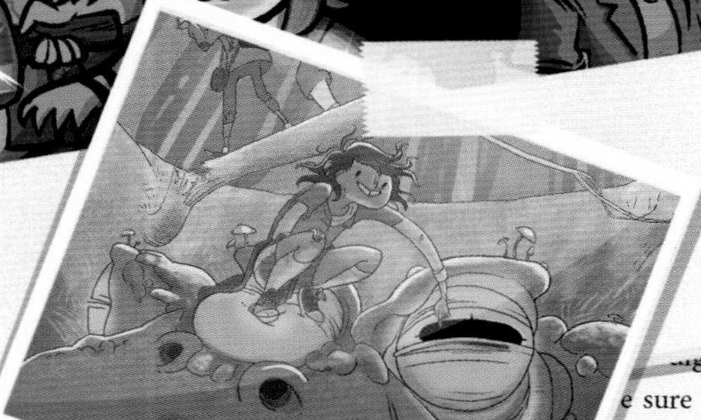

RIPLEY IS TOAD-ALLY AWESOME!

The
helps
in a g
active
another
future
in or
Lumberjane
Penniquiqul Thistle Cr y
Types, but most Lumberjanes wi ey
can either buy the uniform, or make it them rom
materials available at the trading post.

SKETCHBOOK

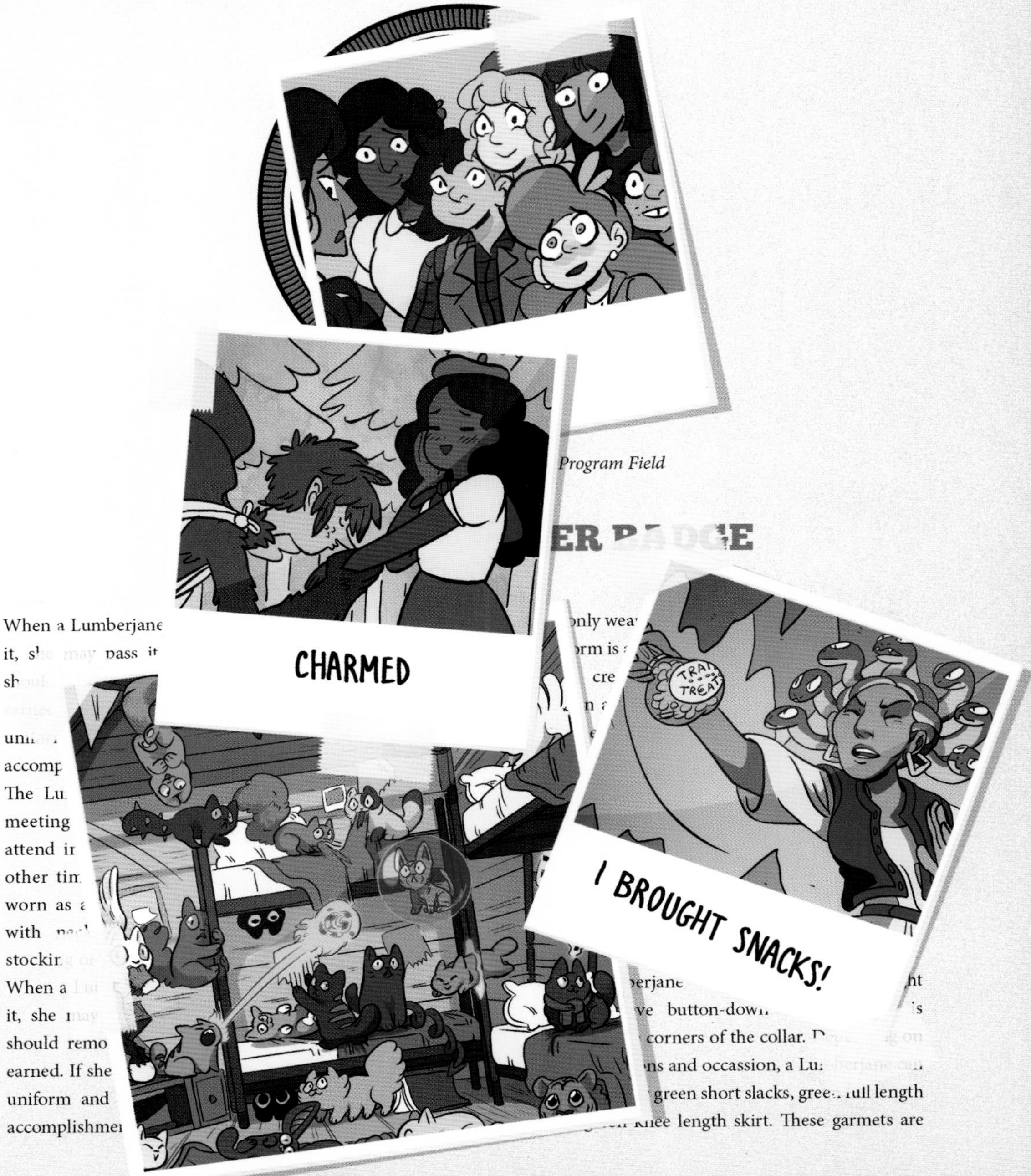
CHARMED
I BROUGHT SNACKS!

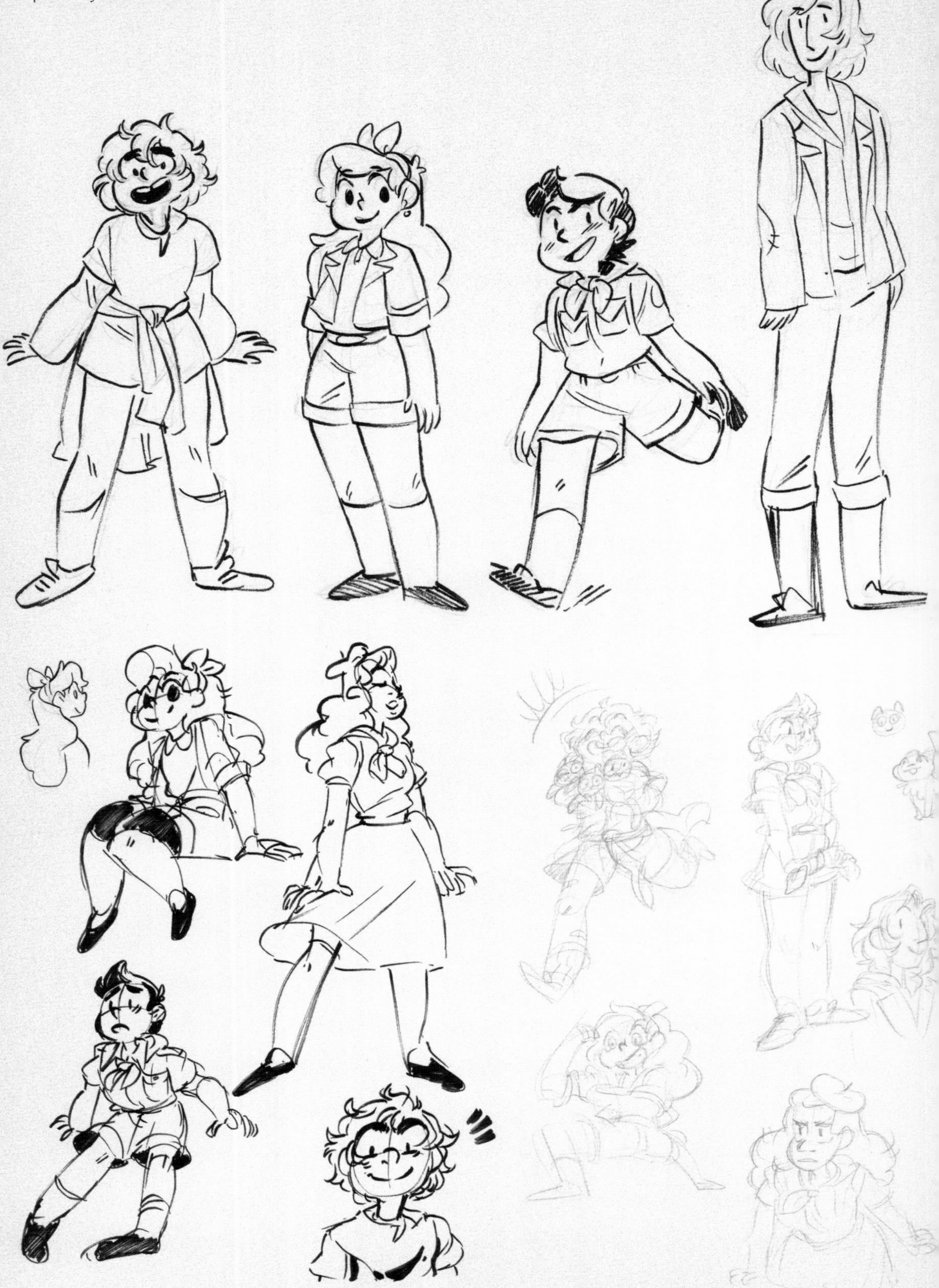

ILLUSTRATIONS BY AYME SOTUYO

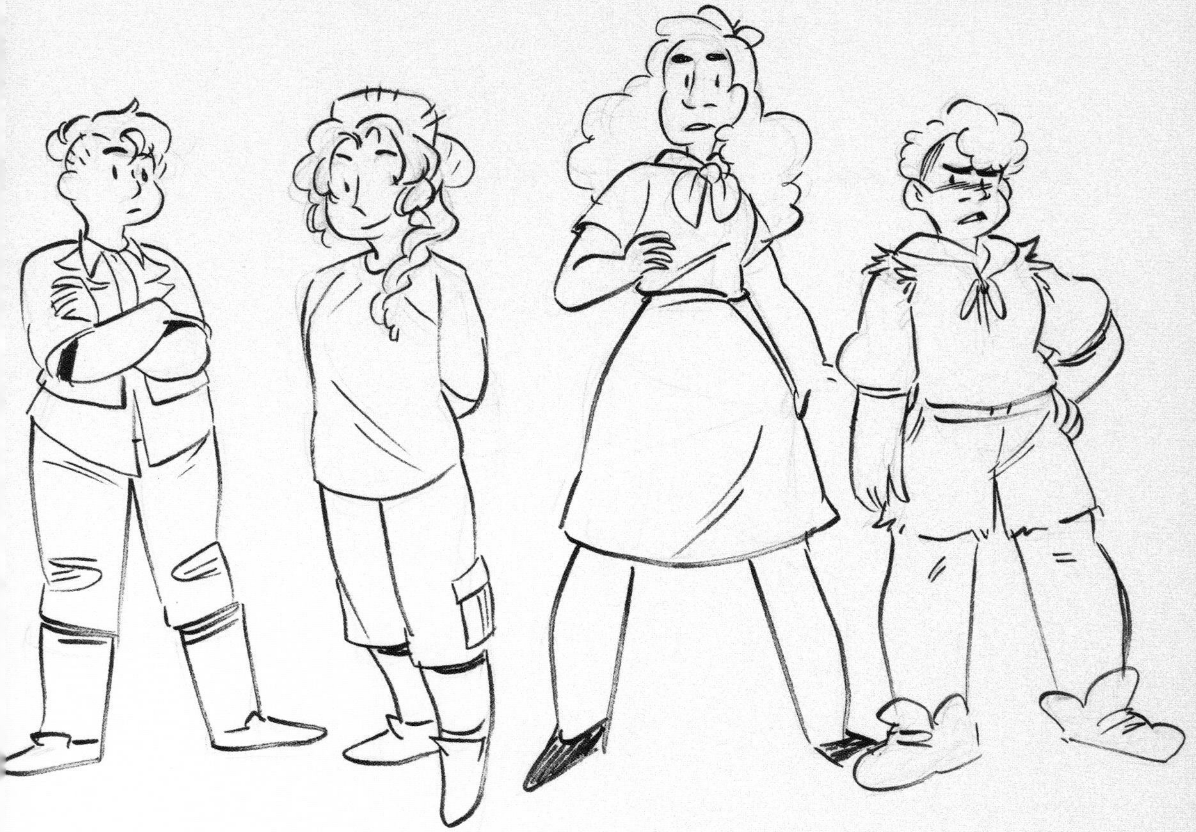

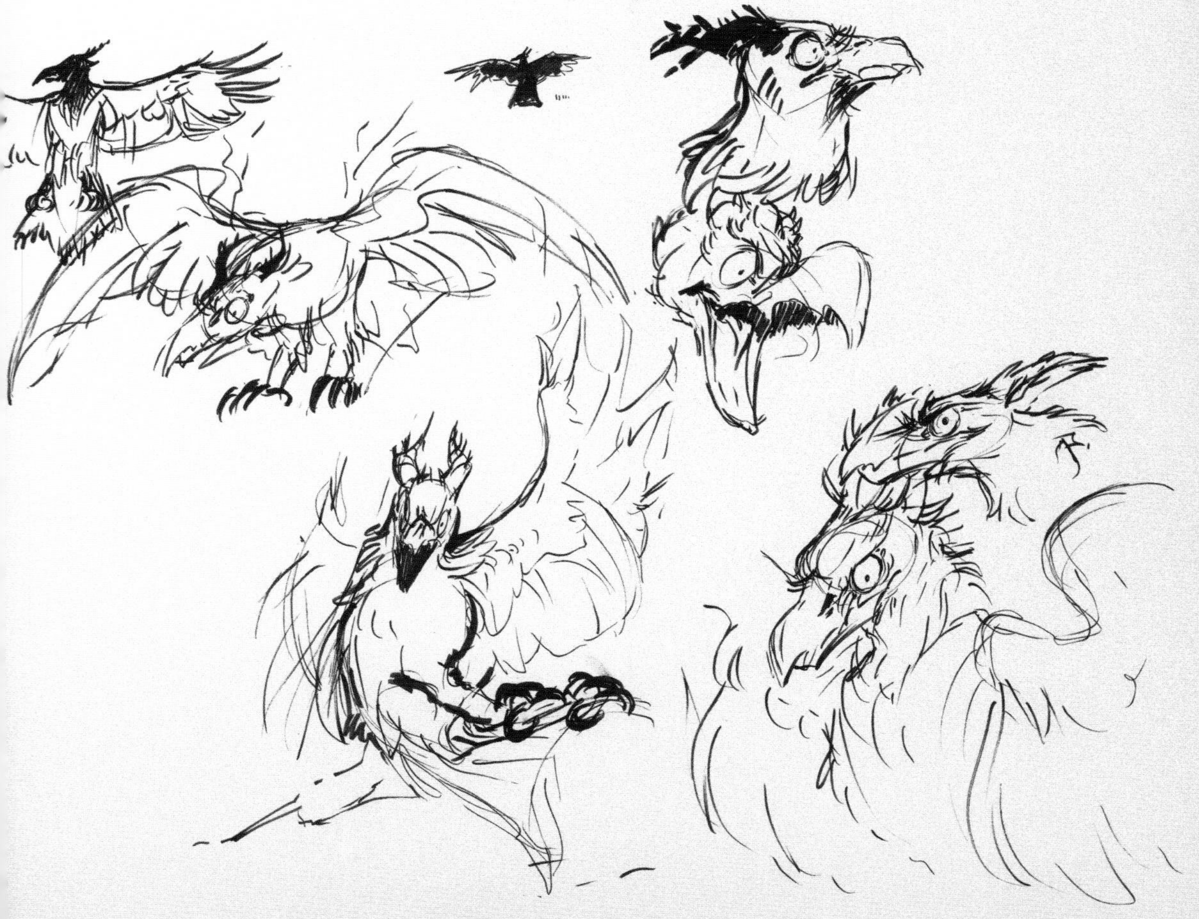

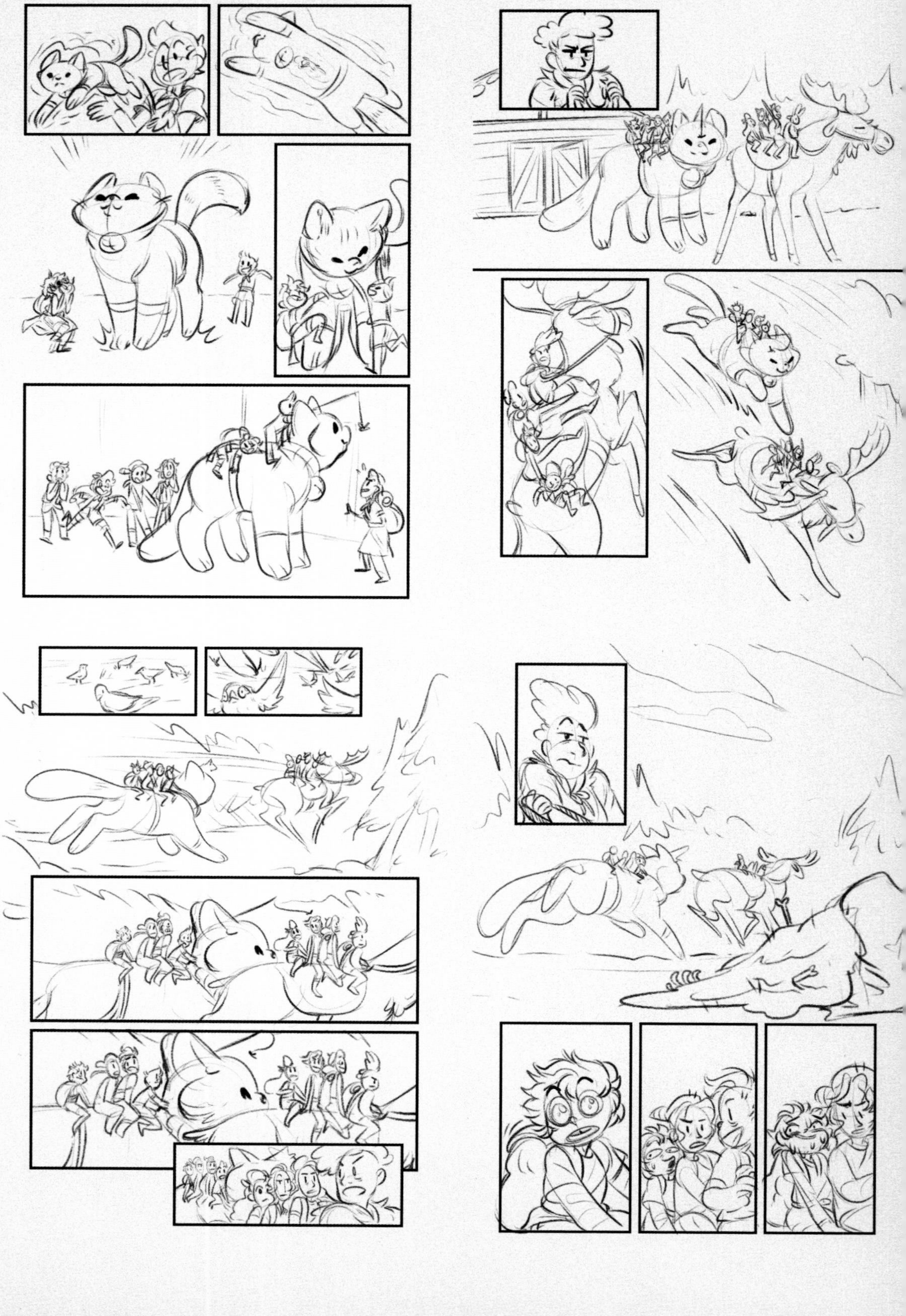

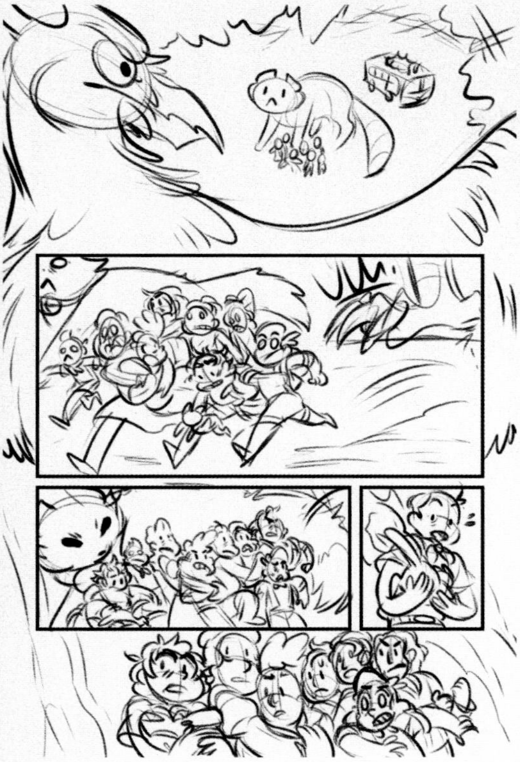

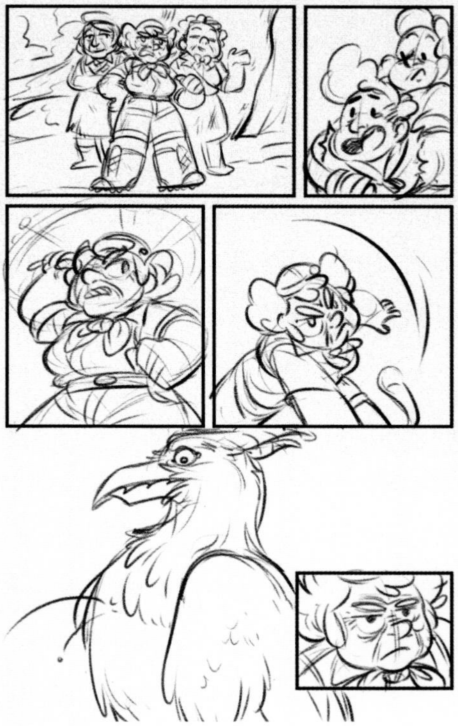

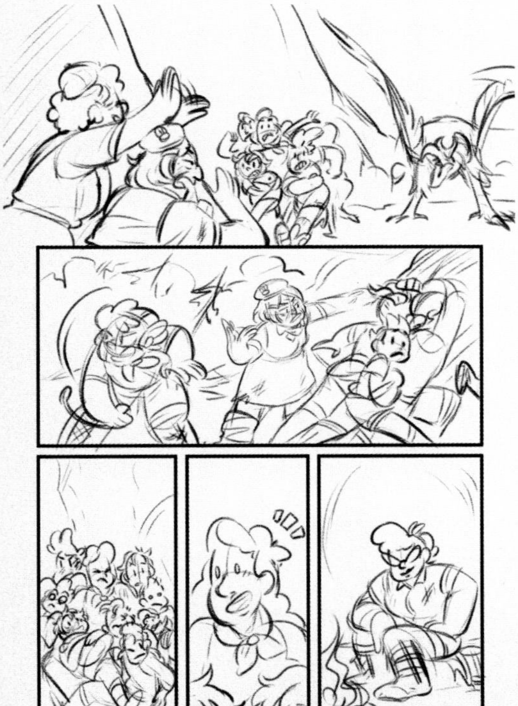

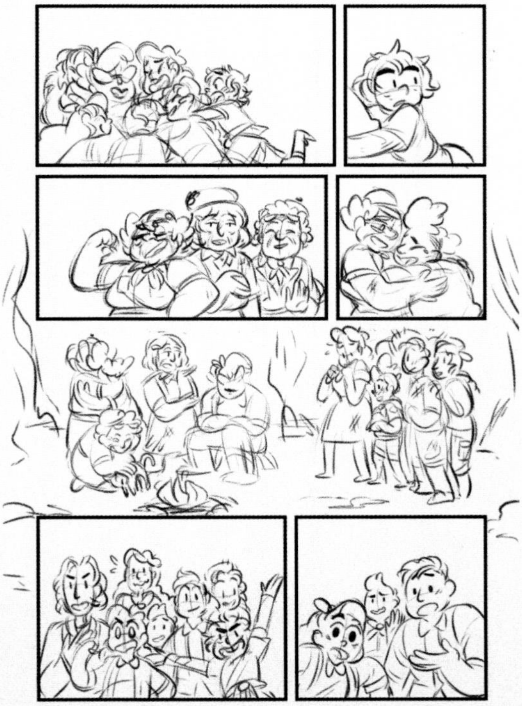

PENCILS BY **AYME SOTUYO**

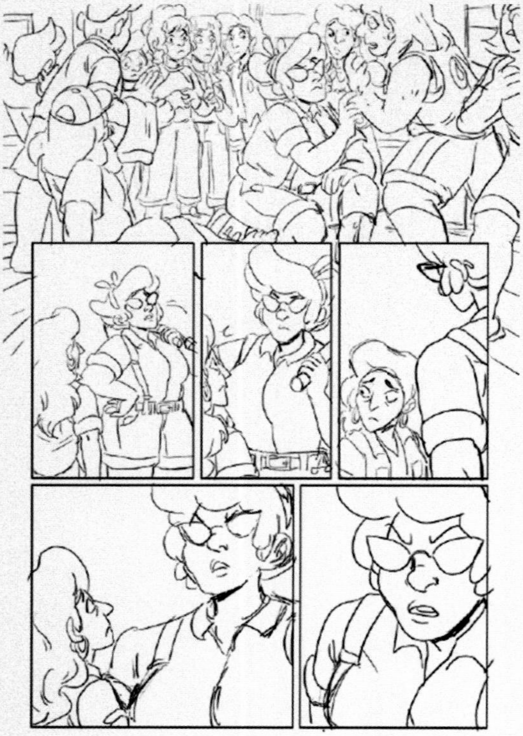

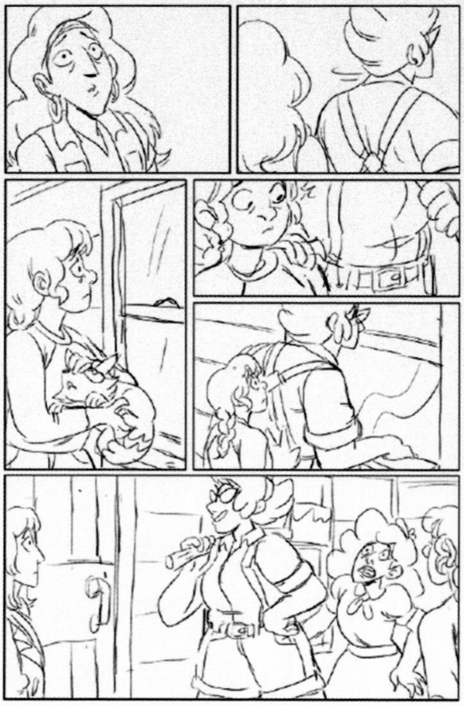

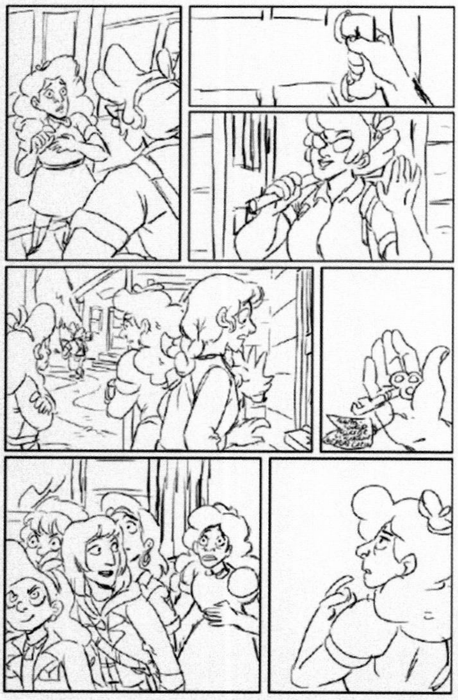

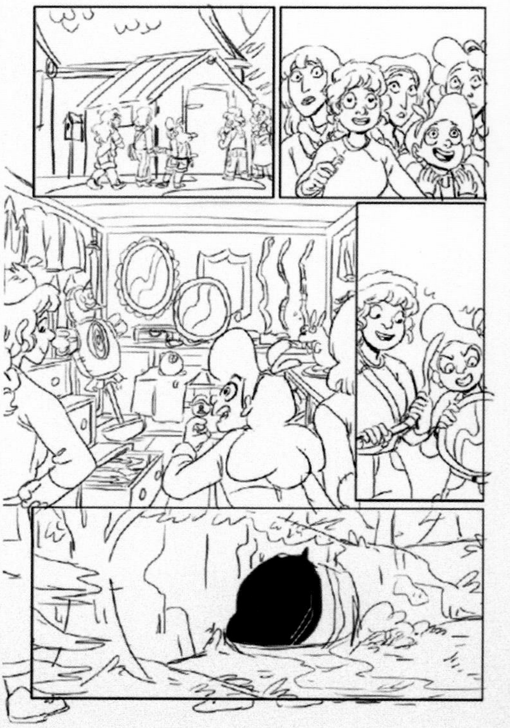

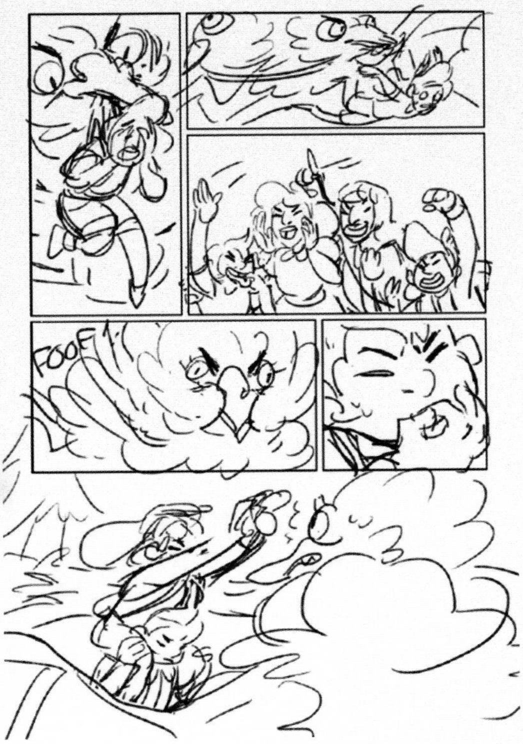
FOOF!

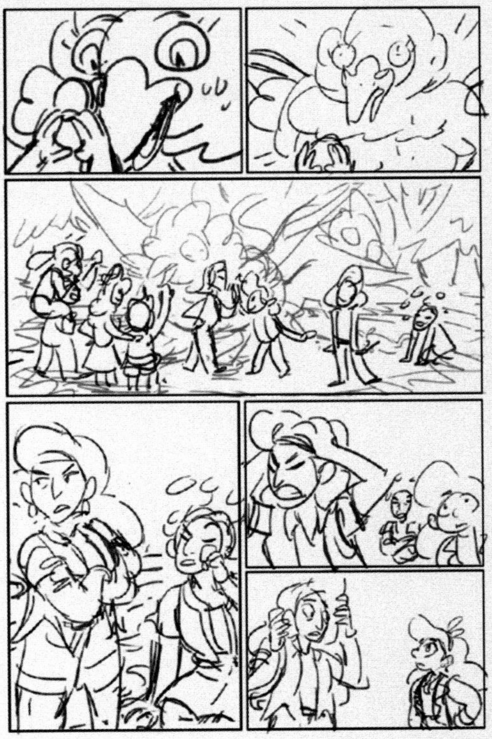

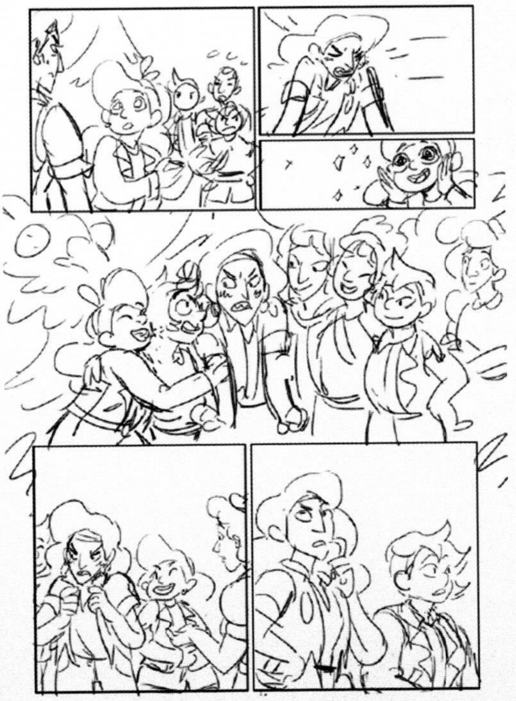

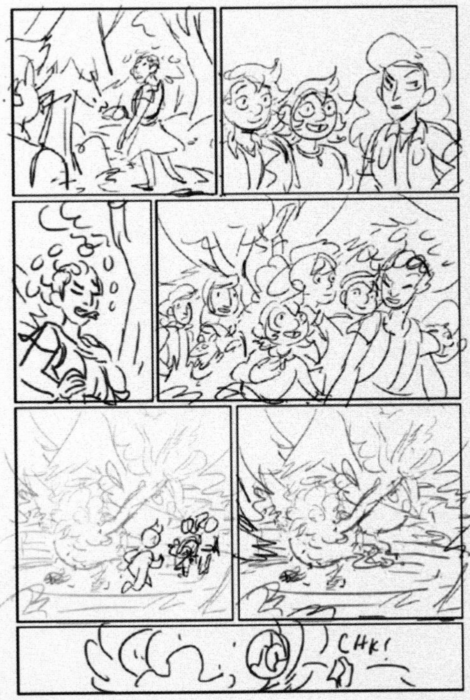
CHK!

PENCILS BY CAREY PIETSCH

Issue Twenty-Six, Page Nineteen

Panel 1: They're at the foot of the mountain, looking up. Jeremy is grazing near a tree.

    MOLLY: Wow.

Panel 2: High angle. Hes is rock climbing that mountain. The Lumberjanes are calling up from below.

    MOLLY: That is pretty hardcore.

    BARNEY: HES! WAIT UP!

    HES: grrr

Panel 3: Ripley is still on Marigold's back with the other kittens she has a bag of treats out and they're clamoring for them.

    HES: (off panel, from above) I have this under control!

    RIPLEY: Who wants a goodie?

Panel 4: Ripley is holding the baggie in front of April, who is realizing the plan.

    RIPLEY: April! Think you could throw this up the mountain?

    APRIL: Oh!

Panel 5: Low angle shot. April winds back for the pitch, aiming for the mountain top.

Panel 6: Back to Hes climbing the rock, she leans in close as a baggie goes rocketing past her.

Panel 7: Reaction shot of Plops Town. He's got big eyes.

    SFX: prow?

Issue Twenty-Seven, Page Ten

Panel 1: Huddle reformed! The Roanokes looks determined. Ripley's jazzed.

> JO: I think Ripley was right. They only way we're doing this is with those cats!

> MOLLY: Maybe the Grands don't have to know?

Panel 2: Ripley is in the foreground, covered in all kittens but Marigold. April is holding aloft her journal.

> SFX: Many purrs

> MAL: So what are we working with here?

> APRIL: I took notes back at camp!

Panel 3-4-5-6: Small panels for kitten roll call! (One of them should be licking its butt.) The last panel is empty.

> OFF PANEL: We've got Tater Tots! Easy. Fire breathing.

OFF PANEL: This one is…Scoots!

OFF PANEL: She can walk through walls!

OFF PANEL: Plops Town.

OFF PANEL: Telekinetics. So far he only uses it to knock things off tables though…

OFF PANEL: And…oh.

Panel 7: The 'janes are in the background, looking towards Barney in the foreground. Barney's face isn't in frame but they're patting Marigold who's curled up and purring in their lap.

APRIL: Nevermind…

Issue Twenty-Eight, Page Fifteen

Panel 1: The Roc postures, flapping its wings at Marigold

SFX: KRAK! KRAK!

Panel 2: Marigold puffs up, ears back and hissing.

MARIGOLD: HISSSSS

Panel 3: Shot of the van, only Marigold's paws are in frame, standing defensively over the van. Rosie is outside the van, pulling Jeremy closer to them.

ROSIE: C'mere Jeremy!

Panel 4: Wide shot. Marigold rears up, classic kitten intimidation technique. And it works! The bird shrinks back.

Panel 5: Close up of the Roc's eye as it looks towards the little jay who's flown over and is squawking at it.

     SFX: Jee! Jee!

Panel 6: The Roc turns around back towards the nest, following the retreating jay.

Issue Thirty, Page Nineteen

Panel 1: The girls are sprinting through the woods, eyes down.
    DIANE: WHAT HAPPENED TO "FORMATION?!"
    APRIL: LOOK THAT WAS A PLAN THAT REQUIRED STRUCTURE THIS IS A PLAN THAT REQUIRES STOUT LEG MUSCLES AND A HEALTHY HEARTRATE.

Panel 2: Cut to Jen and Diane. The Cockrice is hot on all of their tales.
    JEN: IT'S HUGE! ARE GORGONS USUALLY THAT BIG?!
    DIANE: IT'S NOT A GORGON! GORGONS ARE PERSON-SIZED AND HAVE A SNOTTY ATTITUDE LIKE MY SISTERS!

Panel 3: Molly, looking at her bow and arrow in her hands while she runs.
    DIANE (off): THIS IS AN ACTUAL MONSTER.
    JEN: GORGONS AREN'T ACTUAL MONSTERS???

Panel 4: Molly locks eyes with Bubbles.

Panel 5: Bubbles nods (Bubbles is a v. smart raccoon)

Issue Thirty-One, Page Two

Panel 1: Big panel. Ripley and Mal are barreling fully into the side of the monster, knocking it away from Molly. Their eyes are shut.

Panel 2: Mal, with her eyes clamped, is furiously waving her arms around. It is silly looking.

    MAL: MOLLY?! MOLLY, WHERE ARE YOU?!

Panel 3: Molly taking a flying leap into Mal's arms, smiling. (Molly note: She still has the bow and quiver.)

    MOLLY: MAL! You're ok!

Panel 4: Jo, April, and Jen are now similarly waving their arms around as they gingerly walk towards the voices. Jo and April are holding hands.

JO: MAL?
JEN: RIPLEY?
APRIL: Are you saving us!? Is that's what's happening!?

Panel 5: The girls are in the foreground, oblivious to the cockatrice in the background, moving towards them furiously. Ripley and Bubbles have joined the Mal and Molly hug.
JEN: Can we open our eyes now?

Panel 6: Jo, April, and Jen react to the new voice they're hearing.
LIGO: (off panel) NO! KEEP THEM SHUT!
JEN: Who is that?!

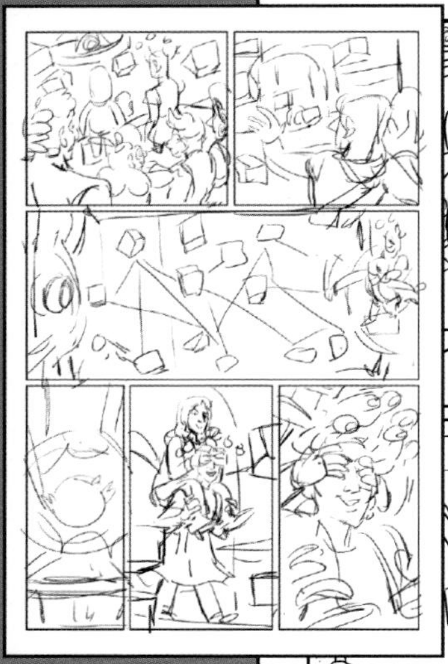

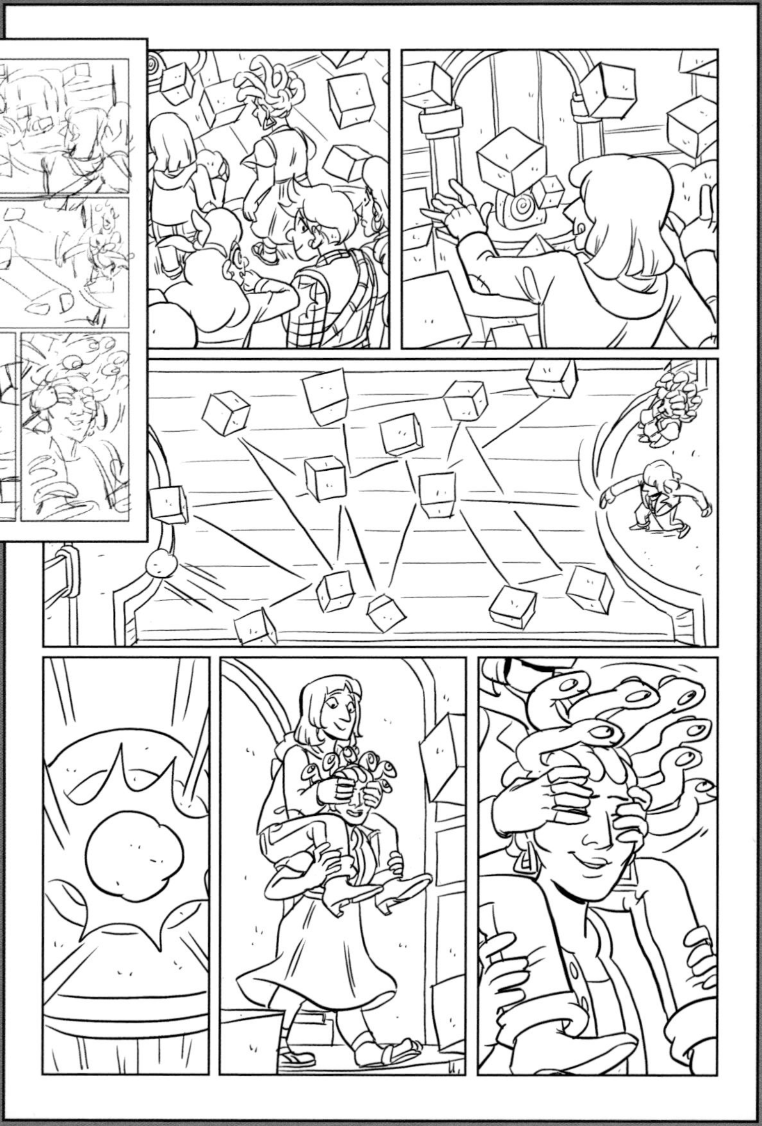

Issue Thirty-Two, Page Five

Panel 1: April and Diane stand with the other 'Janes. April's gently elbowing Mal. Jo and Ligo are stepping up to the squares, looking confident. Statue Guy is scratching his head.
STATUE: Hmmm, I really wasn't expecting more than one round.
APRIL: Watch this. Never play pool against Jo.

Panel 2: Over-the-shoulder shot. Jo rears back with the ball. She's calculating the angles and trajectories of all the floating blocks. You know, geometry.

Panel 3: Jo throws, the ball bounces perfectly against all the blocks.

Panel 4: The ball hits the target rock!
JO: (OFF PANEL) YES!

Panel 5: Ligo is comfortably carrying Jo piggyback, Jo has her hands over Ligo's eyes. They're both smiling.
LIGO: Oh no! However will I maneuver without being able to see?

Panel 6: Close on Ligo's snakes who are all pulling in one direction.

LUMBERJANES FIELD MANUAL
ABOUT THE AUTHORS

SHANNON
WATTERS

Shannon Watters is an editor lady by day
and the co-creator of *Lumberjanes*...also by
day. She helped guide KaBOOM!—BOOM!
Studios' all-ages imprint—to commercial
and critical success, and oversees BOOM!
Box, an experimental imprint created "for the
love of it." She has a great love for all things
indie and comics, which is something she's
been passionate about since growing up in
the wilds of Arizona. When she's not working
on comics she can be found watching classic
films and enjoying the local cuisine.

ART BY BROOKLYN ALLEN

GRACE ELLIS

Grace Ellis is a writer and co-creator of *Lumberjanes*. She is currently writing *Moonstruck*, a monthly comic about lesbian werewolf baristas, as well as scripts for the animated show *Bravest Warriors*. Grace lives in Columbus, Ohio, where she co-parents a preternaturally smart cat, even though she's usually more of a dog person.

NOELLE STEVENSON

Noelle Stevenson is the *New York Times* bestselling author of *Nimona*, has won two Eisner Awards for the series she co-created; *Lumberjanes*. She's been nominated for Harvey Awards, and was awarded the Slate Cartoonist Studio Prize for Best Web Comic in 2012 for *Nimona*. A graduate of the Maryland Institute College of Art, Noelle is a writer on Disney's *Wander Over Yonder*, she has written for Marvel and DC Comics. She lives in Los Angeles. In her spare time she can be found drawing superheroes and talking about bad TV.
www.gingerhaze.com

ART BY **BROOKLYN ALLEN**

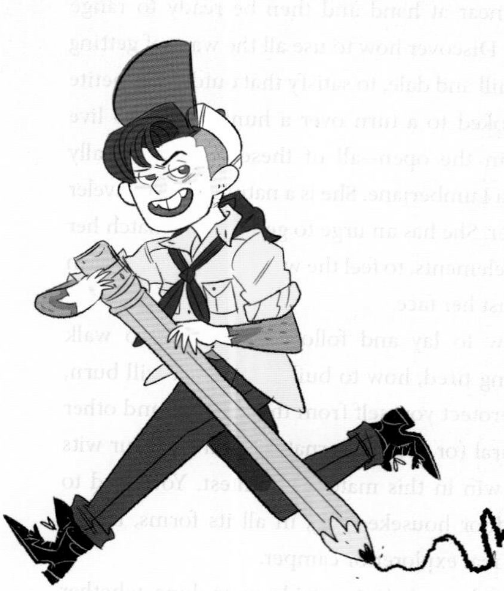

BROOKLYN ALLEN

Brooklyn Allen is the co-creator and the artist for *Lumberjanes* and when they are not drawing then they will most likely be found with a saw in their hand making something rad. Currently residing in the "for lovers" state of Virginia, they spend most of their time working on comics with their not-so-helpful assistant Linus...their dog.

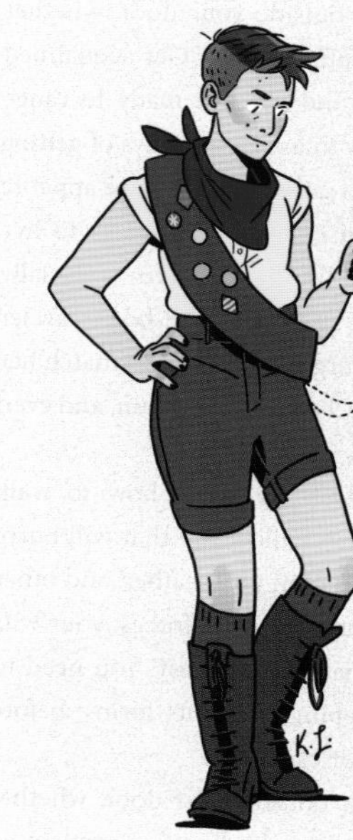

KAT LEYH

Kat Leyh has been co-writer of *Lumberjanes* since issue 18 and cover artist since issue 24. Growing up in the woods, attending 4-H camp in the summers, and creating comics about supernatural queer characters have all led to her feeling right at home with the Lumberjanes! She's done various short comics for series like *Adventure Time* and *Bravest Warriors*, and her own series, *Supercakes*; and upcoming graphic novel, *Roadkill Witch*. When not making comics, she loves to cook, travel and explore!

ART BY **BROOKLYN ALLEN** AND **KAT LEYH**

CAREY
PIETSCH

Carey Pietsch is a Brooklyn-based cartoonist.
She drew *Lumberjanes* #21-25, 29-32, the
Mages of Mystralia webcomic, and is currently
working on *The Adventure Zone: Here There
Be Gerblins*. Carey also makes original comics
about magic and empathy, plays too many
tabletop games and listens to a lot of good
podcasts about them. She's a for-real lifetime
Girl Scout!

AYME
SOTUYO

Ayme Sotuyo is a Cuban freelance comic artist
currently residing in the Pacific Northwest
and finally seeing snow for the first time.
She grew up in south Florida and attended
Savannah College of Art and Design. A
good chunk of her time is spent drawing her
webcomic *[un]Divine*, being yelled at by her
cat for attention, and watching old anime.

ART BY CAREY PIETSCH AND AYME SOTUYO

MAARTA LAIHO

Maarta Laiho spends her days and nights as a comic colorist, where her work includes BOOM! Studio's *Lumberjanes*, and *Adventure Time*; Oni Press's *The Mighty Zodiac*; and the graphic novel adaptation of the *Wings of Fire* series from Scholastic. When she's not doing that, she can be found hoarding houseplants and talking to her cat.
www.PencilCat.net

AUBREY AIESE

Aubrey Aiese is an illustrator and hand letterer from Brooklyn, New York currently living in Portland, Oregon. She loves eating ice cream, making comics, and playing with her super cute corgi pups, Ace and Penny. She's been nominated for a Harvey Award for her outstanding lettering on *Lumberjanes* and continues to find new ways to challenge herself in her field. She also puts an absurd amount of ketchup on her french fries.
www.lettersfromaubrey.com

ART BY **BROOKLYN ALLEN**

LJ

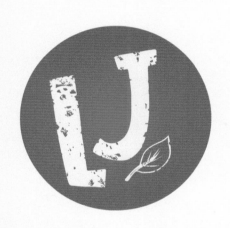

DISCOVER
ALL THE HITS

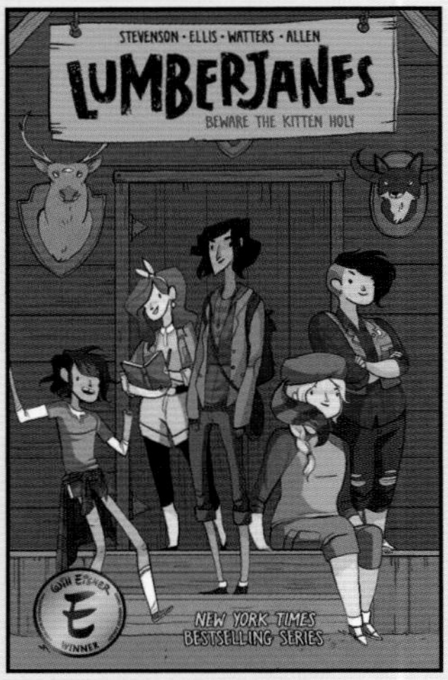
STEVENSON · ELLIS · WATTERS · ALLEN
LUMBERJANES
BEWARE THE KITTEN HOLY
NEW YORK TIMES BESTSELLING SERIES

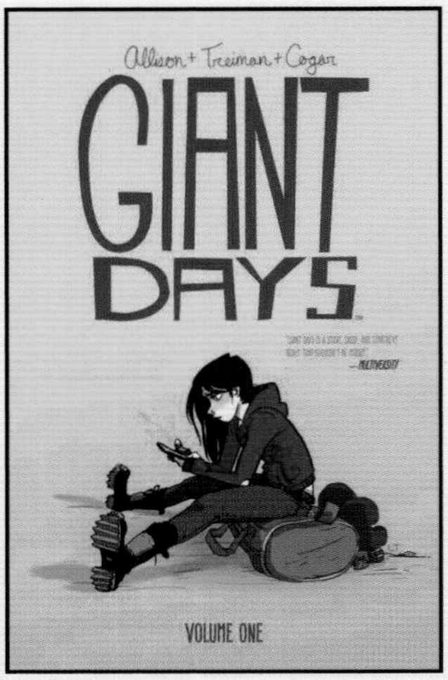
Allison + Treiman + Cogar
GIANT DAYS
VOLUME ONE

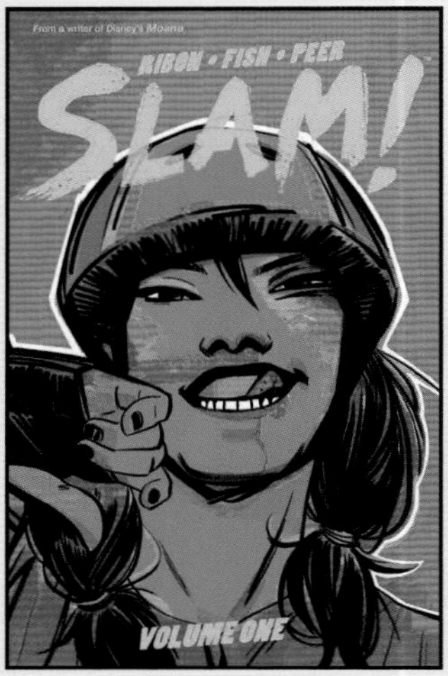
RIBON · FISH · PEER
SLAM!
VOLUME ONE

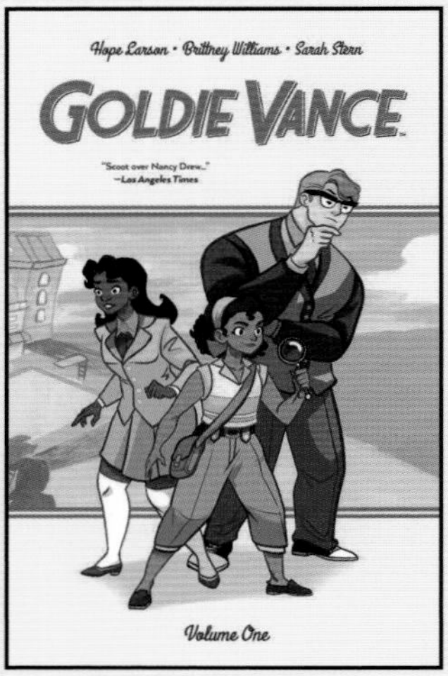
Hope Larson · Brittney Williams · Sarah Stern
GOLDIE VANCE
"Scoot over Nancy Drew..."
—Los Angeles Times
Volume One

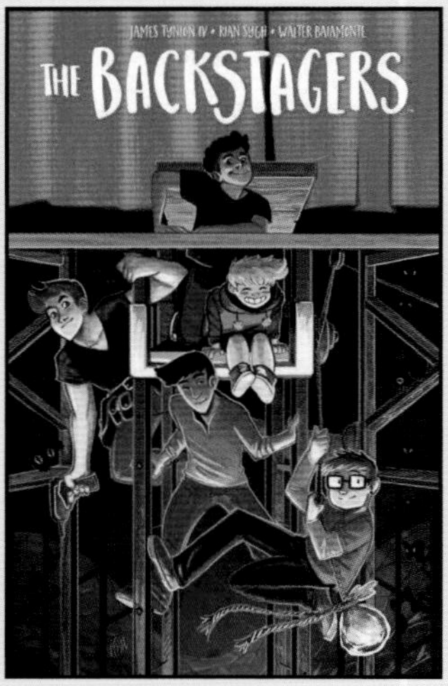
JAMES TYNION IV · RIAN SYGH · WALTER BAIAMONTE
THE BACKSTAGERS

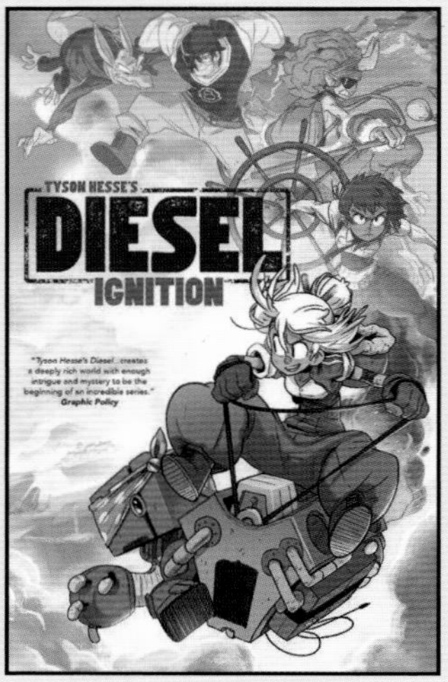
TYSON HESSE'S
DIESEL
IGNITION

BOOM! BOX™

AVAILABLE AT YOUR LOCAL COMICS SHOP AND BOOKSTORE

To find a comics shop in your area, call 1-888-266-4226

WWW.**BOOM-STUDIOS**.COM

Lumberjanes
Noelle Stevenson, Shannon Watters, Grace Ellis, Brooklyn Allen, and Others
Volume 1: Beware the Kitten Holy
ISBN: 978-1-60886-687-8 | $14.99 US
Volume 2: Friendship to the Max
ISBN: 978-1-60886-737-0 | $14.99 US
Volume 3: A Terrible Plan
ISBN: 978-1-60886-803-2 | $14.99 US
Volume 4: Out of Time
ISBN: 978-1-60886-860-5 | $14.99 US
Volume 5: Band Together
ISBN: 978-1-60886-919-0 | $14.99 US

Giant Days
John Allison, Lissa Treiman, Max Sarin
Volume 1
ISBN: 978-1-60886-789-9 | $9.99 US
Volume 2
ISBN: 978-1-60886-804-9 | $14.99 US
Volume 3
ISBN: 978-1-60886-851-3 | $14.99 US

Jonesy
Sam Humphries, Caitlin Rose Boyle
Volume 1
ISBN: 978-1-60886-883-4 | $9.99 US
Volume 2
ISBN: 978-1-60886-999-2 | $14.99 US

Slam!
Pamela Ribon, Veronica Fish, Brittany Peer
Volume 1
ISBN: 978-1-68415-004-5 | $14.99 US

Goldie Vance
Hope Larson, Brittney Williams
Volume 1
ISBN: 978-1-60886-898-8 | $9.99 US
Volume 2
ISBN: 978-1-60886-974-9 | $14.99 US

The Backstagers
James Tynion IV, Rian Sygh
Volume 1
ISBN: 978-1-60886-993-0 | $14.99 US

Tyson Hesse's Diesel: Ignition
Tyson Hesse
ISBN: 978-1-60886-907-7 | $14.99 US

Coady & The Creepies
Liz Prince, Amanda Kirk, Hannah Fisher
ISBN: 978-1-68415-029-8 | $14.99 US